Royal Blood

Royal Blood

Rhys Bowen

BERKLEY PRIME CRIME, NEW YORK

THE BERKLEY PUBLISHING GROUP
Published by the Penguin Group
Penguin Group (USA) Inc.
375 Hudson Street, New York, New York 10014, USA
Penguin Group (Canada), 90 Eglinton Avenue East, Suite 700, Toronto, Ontario M4P 2Y3, Canada
(a division of Pearson Penguin Canada Inc.)
Penguin Books Ltd., 80 Strand, London WC2R 0RL, England
Penguin Group Ireland, 25 St. Stephen's Green, Dublin 2, Ireland (a division of Penguin Books Ltd.)
Penguin Group (Australia), 250 Camberwell Road, Camberwell, Victoria 3124, Australia
(a division of Pearson Australia Group Pty. Ltd.)
Penguin Books India Pvt. Ltd., 11 Community Centre, Panchsheel Park, New Delhi—110 017, India
Penguin Group (NZ), 67 Apollo Drive, Rosedale, North Shore 0632, New Zealand
(a division of Pearson New Zealand Ltd.)
Penguin Books (South Africa) (Pty.) Ltd., 24 Sturdee Avenue, Rosebank, Johannesburg 2196,
South Africa

Penguin Books Ltd., Registered Offices: 80 Strand, London WC2R 0RL, England

This book is an original publication of The Berkley Publishing Group.

This is a work of fiction. Names, characters, places, and incidents either are the product of the author's imagination or are used fictitiously, and any resemblance to actual persons, living or dead, business establishments, events, or locales is entirely coincidental. The publisher does not have any control over and does not assume any responsibility for author or third-party websites or their content.

FIRST EDITION: September 2010

Library of Congress Cataloging-in-Publication Data

Bowen, Rhys.
  Royal blood / Rhys Bowen.—1st ed.
      p.   cm.
  ISBN 978-0-425-23446-4
  1. Vampires—Fiction. 2. Aristocracy (Social class)—Fiction. 3. Transylvania (Romania)—Fiction.
4. Weddings—Fiction. I. Title.
  PR6052.O848R679   2010
  823'.914—dc22   2010008216

PRINTED IN THE UNITED STATES OF AMERICA

10 9 8 7 6 5 4 3 2 1

This book is dedicated to my sister-in-law Mary Vyvan,
who always makes us so welcome in her lovely Cornish manor house
where Lady Georgiana would feel completely at home.

Acknowledgments

Thanks as always to my brilliant team at Berkley: my editor, Jackie Cantor, and publicist, Megan Swartz; to my agents Meg Ruley and Christina Hogrebe and to my at-home advisors and editors Clare, Jane and John.

Acknowledgments

Royal Blood

Chapter 1

Rannoch House
Belgrave Square
London W.1.
Tuesday, November 8, 1932
Fog for days. Trapped alone in London house. Shall go mad
soon.

November in London is utterly bloody. Yes, I know a lady is not supposed to use such language but I can think of no other way to describe the damp, bone-chilling pea-souper fog that had descended upon Belgrave Square for the past week. Our London home, Rannoch House, is not exactly warm and jolly at the best of times, but at least it's bearable when the family is in residence, servants abound, and fires are burning merrily in all the fireplaces. But with just me in the house and not a servant in sight, there was simply no way of keeping warm. I don't want you to think that I am a weak and delicate sort of person who usually feels the cold. In fact at home at Castle Rannoch in Scotland I'm as hearty as the best of them. I go out for long rides on frosty mornings; I am used to sleeping with the windows open at all times. But this London cold was different from anything I had experienced. It cut one to the very bone. I was tempted to stay in bed all day.

Not that there was much reason for me to get out of bed at the moment, and it was only Nanny's strict upbringing that did not allow bed rest for anything less than double pneumonia that made me get up in the mornings, put on three layers of jumpers and rush down to the comparative warmth of the kitchen.

This particular morning I was huddled in the kitchen, sipping a cup of tea, when I heard the sound of the morning post dropping onto the doormat in the upstairs hall. Since hardly anyone knew I was in London, this was a big event. I raced upstairs and retrieved not one but two letters from the front doormat. Two letters, how exciting, I thought, and then I recognized my sister-in-law's spidery handwriting on one of them. Oh, crikey, what on earth did she want? Fig wasn't the sort of person who wrote letters when not necessary. She begrudged wasting the postage stamp.

The second letter made my heart lurch even more. It bore the royal coat of arms and came from Buckingham Palace. I didn't even wait to reach the warmth of the kitchen. I tore it open instantly. It was from Her Majesty the queen's personal secretary.

Dear Lady Georgiana,

Her Majesty Queen Mary asks me to convey her warmest wishes and hopes you might be free to join her at the palace for luncheon on Thursday, November 8th. She requests that perhaps you could come a little early, say around eleven forty-five, as she has a matter of some importance she wishes to discuss with you.

"Oh, golly," I muttered. I'd have to get out of the habit of such girlish expletives. I might even have to acquire some four-letter words for strictly personal use. You'd think that an invitation to Buckingham Palace for luncheon with the queen would be an honor. Actually it happened all too frequently for my liking. You see, King George is my second cousin and since I'd been living in London Queen Mary had come up with a succession of little tasks for me. Well, not-so-little tasks, actually. Things like spying on the Prince of Wales's new American lady friend. And a few months ago she foisted a visiting German princess and her retinue on me—rather awkward when I had no servants and no money for food. But of course one does not say no to the queen.

You might also wonder why someone related to the royals came to be living alone with no servants and no money for food. The sad truth is that our branch of the family is quite penniless. My father gambled away most of his fortune and lost the rest in the great crash of '29. My brother, Binky, the current duke, lives on the family estate in Scotland. I suppose I could live with him, but his dear wife, Fig, had made it clear that I wasn't really wanted there.

I looked at Fig's letter and sighed. What on earth could she want? It was too cold to stand in the front hall any longer. I carried it down to the kitchen and took up my position near the stove before opening it.

Dear Georgiana,

I hope you are well and that the London weather is more clement than the current gales we are experiencing. This is to advise you of our plans. We have decided to come down to the London house for the winter this year. Binky is still weak after being confined to bed for so long after his accident, and Podge has had one nasty cold after another, so I think a little warmth and culture are in order. We plan to arrive at

Rannoch House within the next week or so. Binky has told me of your housekeeping prowess, so I see no need to pay for the additional expense of sending servants on ahead when I know you'll do a splendid job of getting the house ready for us. I can count on you, Georgiana, can't I? And when we arrive, Binky thinks we should hold a couple of parties for you, even though I did remind him that considerable amounts were already spent on your season. He is anxious to see you properly settled and I agree it would be one less worry for the whole family at this trying time. I hope you will do your part, Georgiana, and not snub the young men we produce for you as you did poor Prince Siegfried, who really seemed a most well-mannered young man and may even inherit a kingdom someday. May I remind you that you are not getting any younger. By the time a woman reaches twenty four, which you are approaching, she is considered to be on the shelf, remember. Her bloom has faded.

So please have the place ready for us when we arrive. We shall only be bringing the minimum number of servants with us as travel is so expensive these days. Your brother asks me to convey his warmest sentiments.

Your devoted sister-in-law, Hilda Rannoch

I was surprised she hadn't also put "(Duchess of)." Yes, Hilda was her given name, although everyone else called her Fig. Frankly if I'd been called Hilda I'd have thought that even Fig was preferable. The image of Fig arriving in the near future galvanized me into action. I had to find something to do with myself so that I would not be stuck in the house being lectured about what a burden I was to the family.

A job would be a terrific idea, but I had pretty much given

up all hope of that. Some of those unemployed men standing on street corners held all kinds of degrees and qualifications. My education at a frightfully posh finishing school in Switzerland had only equipped me to walk around with a book on my head, speak good French and know where to seat a bishop at a dinner party. I had been trained for marriage, nothing else. Besides, most forms of employment would be frowned upon for someone in my position. It would be letting down the family firm to be seen behind the counter in Woolworths or pulling a pint at a local pub.

An invitation to somewhere far away—that's what I needed. Preferably an invitation to Timbuktu or at least a villa on the Mediterranean. That would also get me out of any of the queen's little suggestions for me. "I'm so sorry, ma'am. I'd love to spy on Mrs. Simpson for you, but I'm expected in Monte Carlo at the end of the week."

There was only one person in London I could run to in such dire circumstances—my old school chum Belinda Warburton-Stoke. Belinda is one of those people who always manage to fall on their feet—or rather flat on her back, in her case. She was always being invited to house parties and to cruises on yachts—because she's awfully naughty and sexy, you see, unlike me, who hasn't had a chance to be either naughty or sexy.

I'd paid a visit to Belinda's little mews cottage in Knightsbridge when I returned to London from Castle Rannoch in Scotland a couple of weeks ago, only to find the place shut up and no sign of Belinda. I supposed that she had gone to Italy with her latest beau, a gorgeous Italian count, who was unfortunately engaged to someone else. There was a possibility that she had returned, and the situation was urgent enough to warrant my venturing out into the worst sort of fog. If anyone knew how to rescue me from an impending

Fig, it would be Belinda. So I wrapped myself in layers of scarves and stepped out into the pea-souper. Goodness but it was unearthly out there. All sounds were muffled and the air was permeated with the smoke of thousands of coal fires, leaving a disgusting metallic taste in my mouth. The houses around Belgrave Square had been swallowed up into the murk and I could just make out the railings around the gardens in the middle. Nobody else seemed to be out as I made my way carefully around the square.

I almost gave up several times, telling myself that bright young things like Belinda wouldn't possibly be in London in weather like this and I was wasting my time. But I kept going doggedly onward. We Rannochs are known for not giving up, whatever the odds. So I thought of Robert Bruce Rannoch, continuing to scale the Heights of Abraham in Quebec after being shot several times and arriving at the top with more holes in him than a colander, managing to kill five of the enemy before he died. Not a cheerful story, I suppose. Most stories of my gallant ancestors end with the ancestor in question expiring.

It took me a while to realize I was hopelessly lost. Belinda's mews was only a few streets away from me and I had been walking for ages. I knew I'd had to move cautiously, one small step at a time, with my hand touching the railings in front of houses for security, but I must have gone wrong somewhere.

Don't panic, I said to myself. Eventually I would come to a place I recognized and I'd be all right. The problem was that there was nobody else about and it was impossible to read the street signs. They too had vanished into the murk above my head. I had no choice but to keep going. Surely I'd eventually come to Knightsbridge and Harrods. I'd see lights in shop windows. Harrods wouldn't close for a little thing like fog. There would be enough people in London who had to have their foie gras and their truffles no matter what the weather. But Harrods never appeared. At last I came to what seemed to be some gardens. I couldn't decide what they would be. Surely I couldn't have crossed Knightsbridge and found myself beside Hyde Park?

I began to feel horribly uneasy. That's when I noticed the footsteps behind me—slow, steady footsteps, keeping exact pace with mine. I turned but couldn't see anyone. Don't be so silly, I said to myself. The footsteps could only be a strange echo produced by the fog. I started walking again, stopped suddenly and heard the footsteps continue another couple of beats before they too stopped. I started walking faster and faster, my mind conjuring the sort of things that happened in the fog in Sherlock Holmes stories. I stumbled down some kind of curb, kept going and suddenly felt a great yawning openness ahead of me before I bumped into some kind of hard barrier.

Where the devil was I? I felt the barrier again, trying to picture it. It was rough, cold stone. Was there a wall around the Serpentine in Hyde Park? I felt a cold dampness rising to meet me and smelled an unpleasant rotting vegetation sort of smell. And a lapping sound. I leaned forward trying to identify the sound I could hear below me, wondering if I should climb over the wall to escape from whomever was following me. Then suddenly I nearly jumped out of my skin as a hand grabbed my shoulder from behind.

Chapter 2

"I wouldn't do that, miss," a deep Cockney voice said.

"Do what?" I spun around and could just make out the shape of a policeman's helmet.

"I know what you was going to do," he said. "You were about to jump into the river, weren't you? I was following you. I saw you about to climb over the balustrade. You were going to end it all."

I was still digesting the information that I had somehow walked all the way to the Thames, in quite the wrong direction, and it took a minute for the penny to drop. "End it all? Absolutely not, Constable."

He put his hand on my shoulder again, gently this time. "Come on, love. You can tell me the truth. Why else would you be out on a day like this and trying to climb into the river? Don't feel so bad. I see it all the time these days, my dear. This depression has got everyone down, but I'm here to tell you that life is still worth living, no matter what.

Come back to the station with me and I'll make you a nice cup of tea."

I didn't know whether to laugh or be indignant. The latter won out. "Look here, Officer," I said, "I was only trying to make my way to my friend's house and I must have taken a wrong turn. I had no idea I was anywhere near the river."

"If you say so, miss," he said.

I was tempted to tell him that it was "my lady" and not "miss," but I was feeling so uncomfortable now that I just wanted to get away. "If you could just direct me back in the direction of Knightsbridge," I said. "Or Belgravia. I came from Belgrave Square."

"Blimey, then you are out of your way. You're by Chelsea Bridge." He took my arm and escorted me back across the Embankment, then up what he identified as Sloane Street to Sloane Square. I refused his renewed offer of a cup of tea at the police station and told him I'd be all right now I knew which street I was on.

"If I was you, I'd go straight home," he said. "This is no weather to be out in. Talk to your friend on the old blow piece."

Of course he was right, but I only used the telephone in emergencies, as Fig objected to paying the bill and I had no money to do so. I realized it would have been more sensible today, but actually it was human company I craved. It's awfully lonely camping out in a big house without even my maid to talk to and I'm the sort of person who likes company. So I set out from Sloane Square and eventually made my way to Belinda's mews without further incident, only to find it was as I suspected and she wasn't home.

I tried to retrace my steps to Belgrave Square, really wishing I'd taken the policeman's advice and gone straight home. Then through the fog I heard a noise I recognized—a train whistle. So some trains were still running in spite of the fog, and Victoria Station was straight ahead of me. If I found the station I'd be able to orient myself easily enough. Suddenly I came upon a line of people, mostly men, standing dejectedly, scarves over their mouths, hands thrust into their pockets. I couldn't imagine what they were doing until I smelled the boiled cabbage odor and realized that they were lining up for the soup kitchen at the station.

That was when I had a brilliant idea. I could volunteer to help out at the soup kitchen. If I volunteered there the family would approve, in fact the queen herself had suggested that I do some charity work, and at least I'd get one square meal a day until Binky and Fig arrived. I hadn't been able to afford decent food for ages. In fact there was a horrid empty sick feeling in my stomach at this moment. I started to walk past the line to try to find somebody in charge when a hand shot out and grabbed me.

"'Ere, where do you think you're going?" a big, burly man demanded. "Trying to cut in, weren't you? You go to the end and take your turn like the rest of us."

"But I was only going to speak to the people who run the kitchen," I said. "I was going to volunteer here."

"Garn—I've heard every excuse in the book. Go on, to the back of the queue."

I turned away, mortified, and was about to slink off home when the man behind him stepped out. "Look at her, Harry. She's all skin and bone and anyone can see she's a lady, fallen on hard times. You come in front of me, ducks. You look like you're about to pass out if you don't get a good meal soon."

I was about to decline this kind offer but I caught a whiff of that soup. You can tell how hungry I was when boiled cabbage actually smelled good to me. What harm could there be in sampling the wares before I offered my services?

I gave the man a grateful smile and slipped into the line. We inched closer and closer and finally into the station itself. It had an unnaturally deserted air, but I heard the hiss of escaping steam from an engine and a disembodied voice announced the departure of the boat train to Dover, awaking in me a wistful longing. To be on the boat train to Dover and the Continent. Wouldn't that be ripping?

But my journey terminated a few yards ahead at an oilcloth-covered table to one side of the platforms. I was handed a plate and a spoon. A hunk of bread was dumped onto the plate and then I moved on to one of the great pots full of stew. I could see pieces of meat and carrot floating in a rich brown gravy. I watched the ladle come up and over my plate, then it froze there, in midair.

I looked up in annoyance and found myself staring into Darcy O'Mara's alarming eyes. His dark, curly hair was even more unruly than usual and he was wearing a large royal blue fisherman's sweater that went perfectly with the blue of his eyes. In short he looked as gorgeous as ever. I started to smile.

"Georgie!" He could not have sounded more shocked if I'd been standing there with no clothes on. Actually, knowing Darcy, he might have enjoyed seeing me standing in Victoria Station naked.

I felt myself going beet red and tried to be breezy. "What-ho, Darcy. Long time no see."

"Georgie, what were you thinking of?" He snatched the plate away from me as if it were red-hot.

"It's not how it looks, Darcy." I attempted a laugh that didn't come off well. "I came down here to see if I could help out at the soup kitchen and one of the men in line thought I was coming for food and insisted I take his place. He was being so kind I didn't like to disillusion him."

While I was talking I was conscious of mutterings in the line behind me. Good smells were obviously reaching them too. "Get a move on, then," said an angry voice. Darcy took off the large blue apron he had been wearing. "Take over for me, Wilson, will you?" he called to a fellow helper. "I have to get this young lady out of here before she faints."

And he almost leaped over the table to grab me, taking my arm and firmly steering me away.

"What are you doing?" I demanded, conscious of all those eyes staring at me.

"Getting you out of here before someone recognizes you, of course," he hissed in my ear.

"I don't know what you're making such a big fuss about," I said. "If you hadn't reacted in that way nobody would have noticed me. And I really was coming to offer my services, you know."

"You may well have been, but it is not unknown for gentlemen of the press to prowl the big London stations in the hope of snapping a celebrity," he said in that gravelly voice with just the trace of an Irish brogue, while he still propelled me along at a rapid pace. "It's not hard to recognize you, my lady. I did so myself in a London tea shop, remember? And can you imagine what a field day they'd have with that? Member of the royal family among the down-and-outs? 'From Buckingham Palace to Beggar'? Think of the embarrassment it would cause your royal relatives."

"I don't see why I should worry about what they think," I said. "They don't pay to feed me."

We had emerged from the soot of the station through a side door. He let go of my arm and stared hard at me. "You really wanted that disgusting slop they call soup?"

"If you must know, yes, I really did. Since my last attempt at a career last summer—a career you cut short, by the way—I haven't earned any money and, the last time I heard, one needs money to buy food."

His expression changed and softened. "My poor, dear girl. Why didn't you let someone know? Why didn't you tell me?"

"Darcy, I never know where to find you. Besides, you seem to be broke yourself most of the time."

"But unlike you I know how to survive," he said. "I am currently minding a friend's house in Kensington. He has an exceptionally good wine cellar and has left half his staff in residence, so I don't do badly for myself. Are you still all alone at Rannoch House, then?"

"All alone," I said. Now that the shock of seeing him in such upsetting circumstances had worn off, and he was look-ing at me tenderly, I felt as if I might cry.

He steered me to the edge of the curb and found a taxi sitting there.

"Do you think you could manage to find Belgrave Square?" he asked.

"I could give it a ruddy good try, mate," the taxi driver replied, obviously only too glad to earn a fare. "At least we won't have to worry about traffic jams, will we?"

Darcy bundled me inside and we took off.

"Poor little Lady Georgie." He raised his hand to my cheek and stroked it gently, unnerving me even more. "You really aren't equipped to survive in the big world, are you?"

"I'm trying to," I said. "It's not easy."

"The last I heard of you, you were with your brother at Castle Rannoch," he said, "which I agree is not the jolliest place in the world but at least you get three square meals a day there. What in God's name made you leave and come down here at this time of year?"

"One word: Fig. She reverted to her usual nasty self and

kept dropping hints about too many mouths to feed and having to go without her Fortnum's jam."

"It's your ancestral home, not hers," he said. "Surely your brother is grateful for what you've done for them, isn't he? Their son would be dead and so might Binky be, had it not been for you."

"You know Binky. He's a likeable enough chap, but he's too easygoing. Fig walks all over him. And he's been laid up with that horrid infection in his ankle; it has left him really weak. So all in all it seemed more sensible to bolt. I hoped I'd be able to find some kind of work."

"There is no work to be had," he said. "Nobody is making money, apart from the bookies at the racecourses and the gambling clubs. Not that they make money out of me." He gave me a smug grin. "I won fifty quid at the steeplechases at Newmarket last week. I might not know much but I do know my horses. If my father hadn't sold the racing stable, I'd be home in Ireland running it right now. As it is, I'm a rolling stone like you."

"But you do work secretly, don't you, Darcy?" I said.

"Whatever gave you that idea?" He shot me a challenging smile.

"You disappear for weeks at a time and don't tell me where you're going."

"I might have a hot little piece on the side in Casablanca or Jamaica," he said.

"Darcy, you're incorrigible." I slapped his hand. He made a grab at mine and held it firmly.

"There are certain things one does not discuss in taxicabs," he said.

"I think this is Belgrave Square." The taxi driver pushed open the glass partition. "Which house?"

"In the middle on the far side," Darcy said.

We came to a halt outside Rannoch House. Darcy got out and came around to open the door for me. "Look, there's little point in going out anywhere tonight in this fog," he said. "It will be impossible to get a cab to drive us anywhere after dark. But it's supposed to ease up a little tomorrow. So I'll pick you up at seven."

"Where are we going?"

"To have a good meal, of course," he said. "Posh frock."

"We're not gate-crashing someone's wedding, are we?" I asked, because we had done that the first time we went anywhere together.

"Of course not." He held my hand as I started up the steps to the front door. "Society of Chartered Accountants dinner this time." Then he looked at my face and laughed. "Pulling your leg, old thing."

Chapter 3

Rannoch House
Wednesday, November 9
Fog has lifted. Dinner with Darcy tonight. Hooray.

I spent the day working on getting the house ready for impending doom. I took off dust sheets, swept carpets and made beds. I left laying the fires for another day. I didn't want my hair to be full of coal dust when I went out with Darcy. You see how frightfully domestic I had become. I kept darting over to the window to make sure the fog wasn't creeping in again, but a stiff breeze had sprung up and by the time I started to get ready for my date with Darcy, it had started to rain.

Having been home to Scotland, my posh frocks had been cleaned and pressed by my maid. I chose bottle green velvet and even attempted to tame my hair into sleek waves. Then I decided to go the whole hog and attacked my face with lipstick, rouge and mascara. I topped it with a beaver stole that was one of my mother's castoffs and was actually looking quite civilized by seven. Then of course I worried that Darcy wouldn't show up, but he was there on the dot, with a taxi waiting. We sped along Pall Mall, around Trafalgar Square and into the jumble of lanes behind Charing Cross Road.

"Where are we going?" I asked cautiously, as this part of the city seemed poorly lit and not too savory.

"My dear, I am taking you to my lair to have my way with you," Darcy said in a mock villain voice. "Actually we're going to Rules."

"Rules?"

"Surely you must have eaten at Rules—oldest restaurant in London. Good solid British food."

The taxi pulled up outside an unprepossessing leaded-glass window. We went inside and a delightful warmth met us. The walls were rich wooden paneling, the tablecloths starched and white, and the cutlery gleamed. A maitre d' in tails met us at the door.

"Mr. O'Mara, sir. How delightful to see you again," he said, whisking us through the restaurant to a table in a far corner. "And how is his lordship?"

"As well as can be expected, Banks," Darcy said. "You heard that we had to sell the house and the racing stable to Americans and my father now lives in the lodge."

"I did hear something of the kind, sir. These are hard times. Nothing makes sense anymore. Except Rules. Nothing changes here, sir. And I believe this must be the old Duke of Rannoch's daughter. It's an honor to have you here, my lady. Your late father was a frequent visitor. He is much missed."

He pulled out a chair for me while Darcy slid onto a red leather bench.

"Everyone who is part of London history has eaten here." Darcy indicated the walls, lined with caricatures, signatures, and theatrical programs. And indeed I could make out the names of Charles Dickens, Benjamin Disraeli, John Gals-worthy, even Nell Gwyn, I believe.

Darcy studied the menu while I was gazing around the walls, trying to see if my mother or father had made it into the array of signed photographs.

"I think tonight we start with a dozen Whitstable oysters each," he said. "Then for soup it has to be the potato leek. You do it so well. Then some smoked haddock and of course the pheasant."

"An admirable choice, sir," the waiter said, "and may I suggest a very fine claret to go with the pheasant? And per-haps a bottle of champagne to accompany the oysters?"

"Why not?" Darcy said. "Sounds perfect to me."

"Darcy," I hissed as he went away, "this is going to cost a fortune."

"I told you, I won fifty pounds on the gee-gees last week," he said.

"But you shouldn't spend it all at once."

"Why not?" He laughed. "What else is money for?"

"You should keep some for when you're hard up."

"Nonsense. Something always turns up. Carpe diem, young Georgie."

"I didn't study Latin," I said. "Only French and useless things like piano and etiquette."

"It means seize the day. Don't ever put off anything you want to do because you're worried about tomorrow. It's my motto. I live by it. You should too."

"I wish I could," I said. "You seem to fall on your feet, but it's not that easy for a girl like me who has no sensible education. I'm already considered a hopeless case—twenty-two and on the shelf."

I suppose I hoped he'd say something about marrying

him someday, but instead he said, "Oh, I expect a likely princeling will show up in good time."

"Darcy! I've already turned down Prince Siegfried, much to the annoyance of the family. They're all equally bad. And they are being assassinated with remarkable frequency."

"Well, wouldn't you want to assassinate Siegfried?" he asked with a laugh. "I know I would. My fingers are itching for his throat each time I see him. But some of the Bulgarians are okay. I was at school with Nicholas and he's the heir to the throne. He was a damned good scrum half on the rugby team."

"And to a man, that makes him good husband material?"

"Of course."

The champagne bottle opened with a satisfying pop and our glasses were filled. Darcy raised his to me. "Here's to life," he said. "May it be filled with fun and adventure."

My glass clinked against his. "To life," I whispered.

I am not a big drinker. After the third glass of champagne I was feeling decidedly carefree. The soup somehow came and went. So did the smoked haddock. A bottle of claret was opened to go with the pheasant, which appeared swimming in rich red-brown gravy with tiny pearl onions and mushrooms around it. I found myself deciding that I'd been stupid, trying to earn my own living. Life was for having fun and adventure. No more gloom and doom.

I finished every morsel on my plate, then worked my way through the bread and butter pudding and a glass of port. I was feeling content with the world as the taxi whisked us back to Rannoch House. Darcy escorted me up the steps and helped me put the key in the door when I was having trouble locating the lock. At the back of my brain a whisper was saying that I was probably just a little drunk while another whisper added that I probably shouldn't be letting Darcy come into the house late at night when I was all alone.

"Holy Mother of God, but it's cold and bleak in here," Darcy said as we closed the front door behind us. "Is there nowhere warm in this confounded place?"

"Only the bedroom," I said. "I try to keep a fire going in there."

"The bedroom. Good idea," he said and steered me toward the staircase. We ascended together, his arm around my waist. I wasn't conscious of taking the steps. I was half floating, intoxicated with the wine and his closeness.

The last embers of a fire still glowed in the bedroom fireplace and it felt comfortably warm after the frigidity of the rest of the house.

"Ah, that's better," Darcy said.

I saw the bed before me and flung myself down on it. "Ah, my bed. Bliss," I said.

Darcy stood looking down at me with amusement. "I must say, that wine certainly has done wonders for your inhibitions."

"As you very well knew it would," I said, wagging a finger at him. "I know your evil intentions, Mr. O'Mara. Don't think I can't see through them."

"And yet I haven't noticed your telling me to go."

"You just said that the purpose of life was to have fun and adventure," I said, kicking off one shoe so violently that it flew across the room. "And you're right. I've been miserable and boring for too long. Twenty-two years old and a boring virgin. What is the point of that?"

"No point at all," Darcy said softly, removing his overcoat and draping it over the back of a chair. His jacket followed and then he loosened his tie.

"Don't leave me all alone here, Darcy," I said in what I hoped was a seductive voice.

"I've never been known to turn down an invitation like that," Darcy said. He sat to take off his shoes, then he perched on the edge of the bed. "You'll make that lovely dress all rumpled. Let me help you off with it, my lady." He lifted me into a sitting position, which was no longer easy, as my limbs didn't seem to want to obey me and I have to confess that the room was swinging around just a little. I felt his hands down my back as he undid the hooks on my dress. I felt it swishing over my head and then the cold air on the silk of my underslip.

"I'm cold." I shivered. "Come and keep me warm."

"To hear is to obey," he said and took me into his arms. I turned my face toward him and his lips found mine. The kiss was so intense and demanding that I found it hard to breathe. His tongue was exploring my mouth and I was floating on a pink cloud of ecstasy.

This is bliss, I said to myself. This is what I've been waiting for.

I was off on that pink cloud, flying over fields with Darcy beside me until I realized that his lips were no longer on mine and I was feeling cold again. I opened my eyes. Darcy was sitting up on the side of the bed, putting on his shoes.

"What's the matter?" I asked blearily. "Don't you want me anymore, Darcy? You've been trying to get me into bed since we met and now here we are in a big empty house and you're going?"

"You fell asleep," he said. "And you're plastered."

"I confess to being just teeny bit tipsy, but wasn't that what you were planning?"

"That was my idea when I came up with the oysters and

the champagne, but I find I've got a moral streak I didn't know I had, when it comes to you." He laughed almost bitterly. "When I make love to you for the first time, my sweet Georgie, I want you to be awake and fully aware of what you're doing. I don't want you to fall asleep in the middle of things, and I don't want you to think that I took advantage of you."

"I wouldn't think that," I said. I sat up. "Why is everything going round and round suddenly?"

"Come on," he said. "Let me get you into bed. Alone, I mean. I'll stop by in the morning. You'll probably have a devil of a headache."

He helped me out of my slip. "My, but you've got a lovely body," he said. "I must want my head examined."

Suddenly he froze. "What was that?"

"What?"

"It sounded like the front door shutting. Nobody else is here at the moment, are they?"

"No, I'm all alone." I sat up, listening. I thought I could make out the sound of footsteps and voices down below.

"I'm going to see what's going on," Darcy said. He went out onto the landing, while I reached for my dressing gown on the hook behind the door. It wasn't easy to stand up at this stage and I had to hold on to the door to steady myself. Then I heard the words that sobered me up instantly.

"Binky, Fig, you're back."

Fig sighed and rolled her eyes. "Utterly hopeless," she uttered.

"Iniquity?" Darcy suggested. He seemed to be the only person not in the least put out by this. I was still making my way unsteadily down the stairs and didn't trust myself to let go of the banister. I didn't trust my voice, either.

"Precisely," Fig snapped. "A den of iniquity, Georgiana. Thank heavens we didn't bring little Podge with us to witness this. It might have scarred him for life."

"To know that normal people might want to have sex occasionally?" Darcy asked.

Fig put her hand to her throat at the mention of the word "sex." "Say, something, Binky," Fig said, pushing him forward. "Speak to your sister."

"What-ho, Georgie," he said. "Good to see you again."

"No, you idiot, I meant speak to her." Fig was almost dancing around in anger by now. "Tell her that her behavior is simply not on. It's not the way a Rannoch behaves. She's turning into her mother, after all we've done for her and all that money we've spent on her education."

"Now look here," Darcy said, but she leaped at him.

"You look here, Mr. O'Mara." Fig took a menacing step toward him, but Darcy stood his ground bravely. "I suppose you're to blame for this. Georgie has had a sheltered upbringing. She is inexperienced in the ways of the world and certainly lacking in judgment to allow you into the house when she is all alone. I think you had better leave us before I say any more, although I fear the damage is already done. Prince Siegfried would certainly not want her now."

For some reason I found this very funny. I sank onto the stair and started giggling uncontrollably.

"Don't worry, I'm going," Darcy said. "But I'd like to

Chapter 4

Rannoch House
November 9 and 10

I staggered out onto the landing, conscious that the floor kept rising up to meet me and that the stairs were floating out into infinity. I clutched the banister as I made my way down the first flight. In the hallway at the bottom of the second flight, standing on the checkered black-and-white marble, were two blobs in fur coats with pink things on top. Gradually they swam into focus as two horrified faces with mouths open.

"Good God, O'Mara, what are you doing here?" Binky demanded.

"I should think that even for someone with your limited imagination it's pretty clear what he was doing here," Fig said in an outraged voice as she stared up at me. "How dare you, Georgiana. You have betrayed our trust. We graciously offer the use of our house and you turn it into a den of—den of—what's it a den of, Binky?"

"Lions?" Binky said.

Chapter 4

I staggered out onto the landing, conscious that the floor kept rising up to meet me and that the stairs were floating out into infinity. I clutched the banister as I made my way down the first flight. In the hallway at the bottom of the second flight, standing on the checkered black-and-white marble, were two blobs in fur coats with pink things on top. Gradually they swam into focus as two horrified faces with mouths open.

"Good God, O'Mara, what are you doing here?" Binky demanded.

"I should think that even for someone with your limited imagination it's pretty clear what he was doing here," Fig said in an outraged voice as she stared up at me. "How dare you, Georgiana. You have betrayed our trust. We graciously offer the use of our house and you turn it into a den of—den of—what's it a den of, Binky?"

"Lions?" Binky said.

Fig sighed and rolled her eyes. "Utterly hopeless," she muttered.

"Iniquity?" Darcy suggested. He seemed to be the only person not in the least put out by this. I was still making my way unsteadily down the stairs and didn't trust myself to let go of the banister. I didn't trust my voice, either.

"Precisely," Fig snapped. "A den of iniquity, Georgiana. Thank heavens we didn't bring little Podge with us to witness this. It might have scarred him for life."

"To know that normal people might want to have sex occasionally?" Darcy asked.

Fig put her hand to her throat at the mention of the word "sex." "Say, something, Binky," Fig said, pushing him forward. "Speak to your sister."

"What-ho, Georgie," he said. "Good to see you again."

"No, you idiot, I meant speak to her." Fig was almost dancing around in anger by now. "Tell her that her behavior is simply not on. It's not the way a Rannoch behaves. She's turning into her mother, after all we've done for her and all that money we've spent on her education."

"Now look here," Darcy said, but she leaped at him.

"You look here, Mr. O'Mara." Fig took a menacing step toward him, but Darcy stood his ground bravely. "I suppose you're to blame for this. Georgie has had a sheltered upbringing. She is inexperienced in the ways of the world and certainly lacking in judgment to allow you into the house when she is all alone. I think you had better leave us before I say any more, although I fear the damage is already done. Prince Siegfried would certainly not want her now."

For some reason I found this very funny. I sank onto the stair and started giggling uncontrollably.

"Don't worry, I'm going," Darcy said. "But I'd like to

Chapter 4

I staggered out onto the landing, conscious that the floor kept rising up to meet me and that the stairs were floating out into infinity. I clutched the banister as I made my way down the first flight. In the hallway at the bottom of the second flight, standing on the checkered black-and-white marble, were two blobs in fur coats with pink things on top. Gradually they swam into focus as two horrified faces with mouths open.

"Good God, O'Mara, what are you doing here?" Binky demanded.

"I should think that even for someone with your limited imagination it's pretty clear what he was doing here," Fig said in an outraged voice as she stared up at me. "How dare you, Georgiana. You have betrayed our trust. We graciously offer the use of our house and you turn it into a den of—den of—what's it a den of, Binky?"

"Lions?" Binky said.

Fig sighed and rolled her eyes. "Utterly hopeless," she muttered.

"Iniquity?" Darcy suggested. He seemed to be the only person not in the least put out by this. I was still making my way unsteadily down the stairs and didn't trust myself to let go of the banister. I didn't trust my voice, either.

"Precisely," Fig snapped. "A den of iniquity, Georgiana. Thank heavens we didn't bring little Podge with us to witness this. It might have scarred him for life."

"To know that normal people might want to have sex occasionally?" Darcy asked.

Fig put her hand to her throat at the mention of the word "sex." "Say, something, Binky," Fig said, pushing him forward. "Speak to your sister."

"What-ho, Georgie," he said. "Good to see you again."

"No, you idiot, I meant speak to her." Fig was almost dancing around in anger by now. "Tell her that her behavior is simply not on. It's not the way a Rannoch behaves. She's turning into her mother, after all we've done for her and all that money we've spent on her education."

"Now look here," Darcy said, but she leaped at him.

"You look here, Mr. O'Mara." Fig took a menacing step toward him, but Darcy stood his ground bravely. "I suppose you're to blame for this. Georgie has had a sheltered upbringing. She is inexperienced in the ways of the world and certainly lacking in judgment to allow you into the house when she is all alone. I think you had better leave us before I say any more, although I fear the damage is already done. Prince Siegfried would certainly not want her now."

For some reason I found this very funny. I sank onto the stair and started giggling uncontrollably.

"Don't worry, I'm going," Darcy said. "But I'd like to

remind you that Georgie is over twenty-one and it's up to her what she does."

"Not in our house," Fig said.

"It's the home of the Rannochs, isn't it? And she's been a Rannoch a bally sight longer than you have."

"But it now belongs to the current duke and that is my husband," Fig said in her most frosty "I'm a duchess and you're not" voice. "Georgiana is living here on our grace and favor."

"With no heat and no servants. I don't consider that much of a favor, Your Grace," Darcy said. "Especially when your dear husband, the duke, might have been lying six feet under by now in the family plot, and your little son beside him, had it not been for Georgie. It seems to me you owe her more than a little thanks."

"Well, of course we're grateful for everything," Binky said. "Most grateful."

"Of course we are. It's her morals we're concerned about," Fig added quickly, "and the reputation of Rannoch House. Strange men going in and out at all hours will be noticed in Belgrave Square."

The choice of words made me start giggling again. Fig looked up the stairs and focused on me. I had just realized that my robe was not quite tied and I had nothing on underneath it. I tried to pull it around me to save what was left of my dignity.

"Georgiana, are you drunk?" Fig demanded.

"Just a little," I confessed and clamped my lips together so that I didn't giggle again.

"The champagne went to her head, I'm afraid," Darcy said, "which is why I brought her home and I thought it wise to put her to bed in case she fell and hurt herself, since she has no maid to help her. So if you want to know the sordid details of what happened, I put her to bed, she promptly fell asleep and I was just leaving."

"Oh," Fig said, the wind taken out of her sails. "I wish I could believe you, Mr. O'Mara."

"Believe what you like," Darcy said. He looked up at me. "So I bid you good night, Georgie," he said and blew me a kiss up the stairs. "See you soon. Take care and don't let her boss you around. Remember you have royal blood. She doesn't."

He gave me a wink, patted Binky on the shoulder and let himself out.

"Well, really," Fig said, breaking a long silence.

"It's bally cold in here," Binky said. "I don't suppose there's a fire ready for us in our bedroom, is there?"

"No, there isn't." I had rallied enough from my drunken stupor to be coherent, and more than a little angry. "You said you were planning to come in the next week or so, not the next day or so. And why is it that you are traveling without servants?"

"We're just on a flying visit this time, because Binky has secured an appointment with a Harley Street specialist for his ankle," Fig said, "and I also wish to consult with a London doctor, so we thought we could save the expense of bringing servants, since Binky told me what a whiz you had turned out to be around the house. Obviously he was exaggerating as usual."

I stood up, still a little uncertainly. My bare feet were freezing on the stairs. "I don't think that my father would expect me to act as a chambermaid in the family home," I said. "I'm going back to bed."

With that I turned and made my way back up the stairs. It would have been a grand exit had I not tripped over my dressing gown cord and gone sprawling across the first landing, revealing, I rather suspect, a hint of bare bottom to the world.

"Whoops," I said. I righted myself and hauled myself up the second flight. Then I climbed into bed and curled into a tight little ball. I had no hot water bottles to place around me but I wasn't going downstairs again for anything. And it did give me a certain sense of satisfaction knowing that Fig was about to climb into an equally icy bed.

∽

I opened my eyes to cold gray light, then promptly closed them again. Darcy was right. I did have a hangover. My head was throbbing like billy-o. I wondered what time it was. Half past ten, according to the little alarm clock on my chest of drawers. Then the full details of the previous night came back to me. Oh, Lord, that meant that Binky and Fig were in the house and by now they would have discovered that I had nothing to eat in the kitchen. I scrambled into a jumper and skirt and made my way downstairs, almost as shakily as the night before.

I was about to push open the baize door that led down to the kitchen and servants' quarters when I heard voices coming from my right. Binky and Fig were apparently in the morning room.

"It's all right for you," I heard Fig's voice with teeth chattering just a little. "You can go to your club where you'll be comfortable enough, but what about me? I can't stay here."

"It's only for two more nights, old thing," Binky said. "And it is important that you see that doctor, isn't it?"

"I suppose so, but being as cold as this isn't doing me any good. We'll just have to check into a hotel and never mind the expense. Surely we can still afford Claridge's for a couple of nights."

"You'll feel better after a spot of breakfast," Binky said. "It's about time Georgie woke up, isn't it?"

At that point I poked my head around the door. Both Binky and Fig looked haggard and grumpy, sitting wrapped in their fur coats. They also looked rather unkempt without a maid and a valet to dress them.

The atmosphere as Fig spotted me was frigid in more ways than one, but Binky managed a smile. "Ah, you're up at last, Georgie. I say, it's bally freezing in here, isn't it? I don't suppose there's any chance of a fire?"

"Later, maybe," I said. "It takes a lot of work to light a fire, you know. A lot of scrabbling in the coal hole. Perhaps you'd care to help me."

Fig shuddered as if I'd said a rude word, but Binky went on, "Then maybe you'd be good enough to cook us a spot of breakfast. That will warm us up nicely, won't it, Fig?"

"I was just about to make some tea and toast," I said.

"How about a couple of eggs?" Binky asked hopefully.

"No eggs, I'm afraid."

"Bacon? Sausage? Kidneys?"

"Toast," I said. "One cannot buy food without money, Binky."

"But, I mean to say . . . ," he sputtered. "Dash it all, Georgie, you haven't actually been reduced to living on tea and toast, have you?"

"Where do you think the money might have come from, dear brother? I have no job. I have no inheritance. I have no family support. When Fig says she has no money, she means she can no longer afford Fortnum's jam. I mean I can't afford any jam. That's the difference."

"Well, I'm blowed," Binky said. "Then why the deuce don't you come back and live at Castle Rannoch? At least we have enough to eat up there, don't we, Fig?"

"Your wife made it quite clear that I was one mouth too many," I said. "Besides, I don't want to be a burden. I want to make my own way in the world. I want a life of my own. It's just that it's so horribly hard at the moment."

"You should have married Prince Siegfried," Fig said. "That's what girls of your station are supposed to do. That is what your royal relatives wanted you to do. Most girls would have given their right arm to become a princess."

"Prince Siegfried is a loathsome toad," I said. "I intend to marry for love."

"Ridiculous notion," Fig snapped. "And if you're thinking of your Mr. O'Mara, then you can think again." Fig was now warming to her subject. "I happen to know that he doesn't have a penny. The family is destitute. Why, they've even had to sell the family seat. There's no way he's ever going to be able to support a wife—if he ever intends to settle down, that is. So you're wasting your time in that direction." When I didn't answer her she went on, "It's all about duty, Georgiana. One knows one's duty and one does it, isn't that right, Binky?"

"Quite right, old thing," Binky said distractedly.

Fig gave him such a frosty stare that it's a wonder he didn't turn into an instant icicle. "Although some of us are lucky enough to find love and happiness once we are married, isn't that so, Binky?"

Binky was staring out of the window at the fog creeping in again across Belgrave Square. "How about that cup of tea, Georgie?"

"You'd better come down to the kitchen to drink it," I said. "It's warmer down there."

They followed me like children behind the Pied Piper. I lit the gas stove and put the kettle on while they watched me as if I were a conjurer doing a spectacular magic trick.

Then I put the last of the bread onto the grill to make toast. Binky watched me and sighed. "For God's sake, Fig, call Fortnum's and ask them to deliver a hamper. Tell them it's an emergency."

"If you give me some money, I'll be happy to stock up the kitchen again for you—and more economically than a hamper from Fortnum's."

"Could you, Georgie? You're a lifesaver. An absolute bally lifesaver."

Fig glared. "I thought we agreed on a hotel, Binky."

"We'll dine out, my dear. How about that? I know that Georgie knows how to cook a splendid breakfast if we provide her with the ingredients to do so. The girl's a bally genius."

They sipped tea and ate toast in silence. I tried to get down my own tea and toast although every crunch of toast sounded like cymbals going off in my head. I was just wondering when Belinda might be home and how much better it would be to sleep on her uncomfortable modern sofa when the doorbell rang.

"Who can that be at this hour?" Fig said, staring at me as if she thought it was my next lover come to call. "Georgiana had better go. It wouldn't be seemly for you or I to be seen answering our own front door. Word does get around so quickly."

I went, as curious as she was to know who was at the door. I was half hoping it would be Darcy, coming to rescue me, although I suspected he wasn't the sort to be up and around before noon. Instead, the first thing I noticed was a Daimler motorcar parked outside and a young man in chauffeur's uniform standing outside the door.

"I have come for Lady Georgiana," he said, not guessing for a moment that I was anything other than a servant. "From the palace."

That's when I noticed the royal standard the Daimler was flying. Oh, golly. Thursday. Luncheon with the queen. With my brain pickled with alcohol I had completely forgotten.

"I'll inform her," I muttered. I closed the front door and was about to rush up the stairs in flat panic when Fig's head emerged from the top of the kitchen stairs.

"Who was it?" she asked.

"The queen's chauffeur," I said. "I'm supposed to go to the palace for luncheon today." I implied that luncheon with Her Majesty was a normal occurrence for me. It always annoyed the heck out of Fig that I was related to the royals and she was only a by-marriage. "I'd better go up and change, I suppose. I shouldn't keep her chauffeur waiting."

"Luncheon at the palace?" she demanded, scowling at me. "No wonder you don't bother to keep any food in the house if you are always dining in high places. Did you hear that, Binky?" Fig called down the stairs. "The queen has sent a car for her. She's going to lunch at the palace. She's going to get a decent lunch. You're the duke. Why aren't we invited?"

"Probably because the queen wants to talk to Georgiana," Binky said, "and besides, how would she know we are here?"

Fig was still glaring as if I'd arranged this little tête-à-tête just to spite her. I must say it gave me enormous pleasure.

Chapter 5

Buckingham Palace
Thursday, November 10

In spite of a head that felt as if it were splitting down the middle and eyes that didn't want to focus, I managed to bathe and make myself look respectable in fifteen minutes flat. Then I was sitting in the backseat of the royal Daimler being whisked toward the palace. It wasn't really a great distance from Belgrave Square down Constitution Hill and I had walked it on previous occasions. However, today I was most grateful for the car because the fog had turned again to a nasty November rain. One does not meet the queen looking like a drowned rat.

As I looked out through rain-streaked windows at the bleak world beyond I had time to wonder about the implications of this summons and I began to worry. The queen of England was a busy woman. She was always out opening hospitals, touring schools and entertaining visiting ambassadors. So if she made time to bring a young cousin to lunch, it had to be something important.

I don't know why I always expect a visit to Buckingham Palace to signal doom. Because it so often did, I suppose. I remembered the visiting princess foisted on me by my royal kin. I remembered the instruction to spy on the Prince of Wales's unsuitable woman, Mrs. Simpson. My heart was beating rather fast by the time the car drove between the wrought-iron gates of the palace, received a salute from the guards on duty and crossed the parade ground, under the arch to the inner courtyard.

A footman leaped out to open the car door for me.

"Good morning, my lady. This way, please," he said and led the way up the steps at a good pace. I followed, being extra careful as my legs have been known to disobey me in moments of extreme stress.

You'd have thought that someone who was second cousin to King George V would find a visit to Buckingham Palace to be old hat, but I have to admit that I was always overawed as I walked up those grand staircases and along the hallways lined with statues and mirrors. In truth I felt like a child who has stumbled into a fairy tale by mistake. I had been brought up in a castle myself, but Castle Rannoch could not have been more different. It was dour stone, spare and cold, its walls hung with shields and banners from past battles. This was royalty at its grandest, designed to impress foreigners and those of lesser rank.

I was taken up the grand staircase this time, not whisked along back corridors. We came out in the area between the music and throne rooms where receptions are held. I wondered if this was to be a formal occasion until the footman kept going all the way to the end of the hall. He opened a closed door for me, leading to the family's private apartments. I found I was holding my breath until I couldn't hold it any longer when finally a door was opened and I was shown into a pleasant, ordinary sitting room. This lacked the grandeur of the state rooms and was where the royal couple relaxed on the rare occasions they weren't working. At least it probably meant that I wasn't going to have to face strangers at luncheon, which was a relief.

"Lady Georgiana, ma'am," the footman said, then he bowed and backed out of the royal presence. I hadn't noticed the queen at first because she was standing at the window, gazing out at the gardens. She turned to me and extended a hand.

"Georgiana, my dear. How good of you to come at such short notice."

As if one refused a queen. They no longer chopped off heads but one obeyed nonetheless.

"It's very good to see you, ma'am," I said, crossing the room to take her hand, curtsy and kiss her cheek—a maneuver that required exquisite timing, which I hadn't yet mastered and always resulted in a bumped nose.

She looked back at the window. "The gardens look so bleak at this time of year, don't they? And what horrible weather we've been having. First fog and now rain. The king has been in a bad humor about being cooped up for so long. His doctor forbade him to go out during the fog, you know. With his delicate lungs he couldn't be exposed to the soot in the air."

"I quite agree, ma'am. I went out in the fog earlier this week and it was beastly. Nothing like the mist in the country. It was like breathing liquid soot."

She nodded and, still holding my hand, she led me across the room to a sofa. "Your brother—he has recovered from his accident?"

"Almost, ma'am. At least he's up and walking again but he has come to London to see a specialist."

"A disgusting thing to have happened," she said. "And the same person apparently shot at my granddaughter. It was your quick wits that saved her."

"And the princess's own cool head," I said. "She's a splendid little rider, isn't she?"

The queen beamed. Nothing pleased her more than talking about her granddaughters.

"I expect you wonder why I asked you to come to luncheon today, Georgiana," the queen said. I held my breath again. Doom will strike any moment, I thought. But she seemed jovial enough. "How about a glass of sherry?"

Usually I find sherry delightful, but the mere thought of alcohol made my stomach lurch. "Not for me, thank you, ma'am."

"Very wise in the middle of the day," the queen said. "I like to keep a clear head myself." Oh, Lord, if she knew how unclear my head felt at the moment.

"Why don't we go through and eat, then," she said. "It's so much easier to discuss things over food, don't you agree?"

Personally I thought it was absolutely the opposite. I have never found it easy to make conversation and eat at the same time. I always seem to have a mouthful at the wrong moment or drop my fork when under stress. The queen rang a little bell and a maid appeared from nowhere.

"Lady Georgiana and I are ready for our luncheon," the queen said. "Come along, my dear. We need good nourishing food in weather like this."

We went next door to a family dining room. No hundred-foot-long tables here, but a small table, set for two. I took my place as indicated, and the first course was brought in. It was my nemesis—half a grapefruit in a tall cut glass. I always seem to get the half in which the segments are imperfectly cut. I looked at it with horror, took a deep breath and picked up my spoon.

"Ah, grapefruit," the queen said, smiling at me. "So refreshing during the winter months, don't you think?" And she spooned out a perfectly cut segment. Hope arose that this time the kitchen staff had done their job. I dug into the grapefruit. It slipped sideways in the glass, almost shooting out onto the tablecloth. I retrieved it at the last moment and had to use a surreptitious finger to balance it as I dug again. The first piece came free without too much effort. No such luck with the second. I held on to that grapefruit, dug and tugged. This time two segments were joined together. I attempted to separate them and juice squirted straight up into my eye. It stung and I waited until the queen was busy before dabbing at my eye with my napkin. At least I hadn't squirted grapefruit juice at HM.

It was with incredible relief that I finished the grapefruit and the shell was whisked away. A thick brown soup followed, then the main course. It was steak and kidney pie, usually one of my favorites. With it was cauliflower in a white sauce and tiny roast potatoes. I could feel my mouth watering. Two good meals in two days. But the first mouthful revealed that this course was not going to be easy, either. I've always had a problem with chewing and swallowing large chunks of meat. It simply won't go down.

"Georgiana, I have a special favor to ask of you," the queen said, looking up from her own plate. "The king wanted this to be done formally, but I managed to persuade him that a private chat would be more appropriate. I did not want to put you in a spot, should you wish to say no."

Of course my mind was now racing. They'd found another prince for me. Or even worse, Siegfried had officially asked for my hand, one royal family to another, and turning him down would create an international incident. I sat frozen, my fork poised halfway between my plate and my mouth.

"There is to be a royal wedding later this month. You have no doubt got wind of it," the queen continued.

"No." It came out as a squeak.

"Princess Maria Theresa of Romania is to marry Prince Nicholas of Bulgaria. He is the heir to the throne, as I expect you know."

I gave a half nod as if the royal families of Europe always discussed their wedding plans with me. Thank God it was someone else's wedding we were talking about. I brought my fork to my mouth and started chewing.

"Naturally our family should be represented," the queen went on. "We are, after all, related to both sides. He is from the same Saxe-Coburg-Gotha line as your great-grandmother Queen Victoria, and she, of course, is one of the Hohenzollern-Sigmaringens. If it were in the summer, we should have been delighted to attend; however, there is no question of the king himself traveling abroad at this bitter time of year."

I nodded, having found a particularly chewy piece of meat in my mouth.

"So His Majesty and I have decided to ask you to represent us."

"Me?" I managed to squeak, my mouth still full of that large chunk of meat. I was now in a tricky situation in more ways than one. There was no way I could swallow it. There was no way I could spit it out. I tried a sip of water to wash it down but it wouldn't go. So I had to resort to the old school trick—a pretended cough, napkin to my mouth and the meat expelled into the napkin.

"I'm sorry," I said, collecting myself. "You want me to represent the family at a royal wedding? But I'm only a cousin's child. Won't the royal families in question see this as a slight that you only send someone like me? Surely one of your sons would be more appropriate, or your daughter, the Princess Royal."

"In other circumstances I would have agreed with you but it so happens that the Princess Maria Theresa has particularly requested that you be one of her bridal attendants."

I just stopped myself from squeaking "Me?" for a second time.

"I gather you two were such good chums at school."

At school? My brain was racing again. I once knew a Princess Maria Theresa at school? I was friendly with her? I went through a quick list of my friends. No princesses appeared on it.

But I could hardly call a foreign princess, apparently related to us, a liar. I smiled wanly. Then suddenly an image swam into focus—a large, chubby girl with a round moon face trailing after Belinda and me and Belinda saying, "Matty, stop following us around, do. Georgie and I want to be alone for once." Matty—it had to be she. I had never realized that it was short for Maria Theresa. Nor that she was a princess. She had been a rather pathetic, annoying little thing (well, not so little, but a year behind us).

"Ah, yes," I said, smiling now. "Dear Matty. How kind of her to invite me. This is indeed an honor, ma'am."

I was now feeling decidedly pleased with myself. I had been asked to attend a royal wedding—to be in a royal bridal party. Certainly a lot better than freezing and starving at Rannoch House. Then the ramifications hit me. The cost of the ticket. The clothing I would need . . . the queen never seemed to take money into consideration.

"I suppose I'll have to have a frock made for the wedding before I leave?" I asked.

"I believe not," the queen said. "The suggestion was that you travel to Romania ahead of time so that the dresses can all be fitted by the princess's personal dressmaker. I gather she has excellent taste and is bringing in a couturiere from Paris."

Had I got it wrong? Matty, who always looked like a sack of potatoes in her uniform, was bringing in a couturiere from Paris?

"I will have my secretary make all the travel arrangements for you and your maid," the queen continued. "You'll be traveling on official royal passports so there will be no unnecessary formalities. And I will also arrange for a chaperon. It would not do to have you making such a long journey alone."

Now I was digesting one word from that sentence. Maid. You and your maid, she had said. Ah, now that was going to be a slight problem. The queen had no idea that anyone of my status survived without a maid. I opened my mouth to say this, then found myself saying instead, "I'm afraid there might be a problem about finding a maid willing to travel with me. My Scottish maid won't even come to London."

The queen nodded. "Yes, I appreciate that could be a problem. English and Scottish girls are so insular, aren't they? Don't give her a choice, Georgiana. Never give servants a choice. It goes to their heads. If your current maid wishes to retain her position with you, she should be willing to follow you to the ends of the earth. I know that my maid would." She dug into the cauliflower. "Be firm. You'll need to learn how to deal with servants before you run a great household, you know. Give them an inch and they'll walk all over you. Now, come along. Eat up before it gets cold."

Chapter 6

Mainly at Belinda Warburton-Stoke's mews cottage
Thursday, November 10

The car was waiting in the courtyard to take me back me to Rannoch House. It would have been a triumphant return but for one small fact. In one week I had to come up with a maid who wouldn't mind a trip to Romania without being paid. I didn't think there would be many young women in London who would be lining up for that job.

Fig appeared in the front hall as I let myself in.

"You've been gone a long while," she said. "I hope Her Majesty gave you a good meal?"

"Yes, thank you." I chose not to mention the near disaster with the grapefruit and the steak. And the fact that blancmange had been served for pudding and another of my strange phobias is about swallowing blancmange, and jelly—in fact, anything squishy.

"A formal occasion, was it? Lots of people there?" she asked, trying to sound casual while dying of curiosity.

"No, just the queen and I in her private dining room."

Oh, I did enjoy saying that. I knew that Fig had never been invited to the private dining room and never had a tête-à-tête with the queen.

"Good gracious," she said. "What did she want?"

"Does a relative need something to invite one to a meal?" I asked. Then I added, "If you really must know, she wants me to represent the royal family at the wedding of Princess Maria Theresa in Romania."

Fig turned an interesting shade of puce. "You? She wants *you* to represent the royal family? At a royal wedding? What is she thinking of?"

"Why, don't you think I'll know how to behave? Do you think I'll drop my aitches or slurp my soup?"

"But you're not even part of the direct line," she blurted out.

"Actually I am. Albeit thirty-fourth," I said.

"And Binky is thirty-second and at least he's a duke."

"Ah, but Binky wouldn't look quite right in a bridesmaid's dress, holding a bouquet," I said. "You see, the princess particularly asked for me to be one of her bridal attendants."

Fig's eyes opened even wider. "You? Why on earth did she ask for you?"

"Because we were great friends at school," I said, not batting an eyelid as I said it. "You see, that horribly expensive education that you gripe about did have its advantages after all."

"Binky!" Fig shouted in a way no lady should. "Binky, Georgiana has been asked to represent the family at a royal wedding, in Romania."

Binky appeared from the library, still wearing his overcoat and muffler. "What's this?"

"She's been asked to represent the royal family, at a wedding," Fig repeated. "Did you ever hear of such a thing?"

"I expect they didn't want to send any of the direct heirs for fear of assassination," Binky said easily. "They're always assassinating each other in that part of the world."

It was clear that Fig liked this answer. I was being sent because I was expendable, not because I was worthy. It did put a different complexion on things. "And when is this wedding?" she asked.

"I'm to leave next week."

"Next week. That doesn't give you much time, does it? What about clothes? Are you expected to have some kind of dress made to be part of this bridal procession?"

"No. Luckily the princess is having us all dressed by her couturiere, from Paris. That's why I have to go early."

"What about your tiara? It's still in the vault in Scotland. Will we have to have it sent down to you?"

"I'm not sure whether tiaras will be worn. I'll have to ask the queen's secretary."

"And what about travel? Who is paying for all this?"

"The queen's secretary is taking care of everything. All I have to come up with is a maid."

Fig looked from me to Binky and back again. "How are you going to do that?"

"At this moment I have no idea. I don't suppose any of the servants at Castle Rannoch would like a jaunt to Romania?"

Fig laughed. "My dear girl, it's hard enough to persuade the servants at Castle Rannoch to come down to London, which they perceive as a dangerous and sinful place. If you remember, your maid Maggie wouldn't do so. Her mother wouldn't allow it."

I shrugged. "Then I'll just have to see if I can borrow a lady's maid from someone in London. Failing that, I'll have to hire one from an agency."

"How can you hire one? You have no money," she said.

"Precisely. But I have to come up with a maid somehow, don't I? I may have to sell some of the family jewels. Perhaps you can send down a diamond or two with the tiara." I was just joking but Fig shot me a daggers look.

"Don't be ridiculous. The family jewels have to stay in the family. You know that."

"Then what do you suggest?" I demanded. "I can't refuse to go. It would be an ultimate insult to Princess Maria Theresa and Her Majesty."

Fig looked at Binky again. "I can't think of anyone we know who might be willing to lend her a maid for such an exotic adventure, can you, Binky?"

"Don't know much about maids, old bean. Sorry," he said. "You women better sort it out. Georgie has to go, that's clear, so if necessary we'll have to come up with the money."

"You want us to come up with the money?" Fig demanded, her voice rising. "How are we going to do that? Sell the family jewels, as Georgiana suggests? Deny little Podge a tutor? It's too much, Binky. She's over twenty-one, isn't she? She's not our responsibility anymore."

Binky went over and put a hand on her shoulder. "Don't upset yourself, my dear. You know the doctor said you should try to remain calm and think peaceful thoughts."

"How can I think peaceful thoughts when we won't even have the money to pay doctors' bills or for the clinic?" Her voice was rising dangerously.

And without warning she did something I had never seen Fig, nor anyone in my immediate circle, do before. She burst into tears and rushed upstairs. Ladies are brought up never to show emotion, even in the direst of circumstances.

I stared after her openmouthed. I realized that a doctor's

visit for Fig had been mentioned, but it hadn't occurred to me until now that it might be a psychiatrist. Was her permanent bad temper due to something darker, like insanity in the family? How delicious. Too good to miss.

"She's a little upset today," Binky said in embarrassment. "Not at her best."

"Fig went to a doctor for her nerves?" I asked.

"Not exactly," he said.

He looked up the stairs after her, weighed up if the wrath of God might fall, then leaned confidentially close. "If you want to know, Georgie, Fig is expecting again. A second little Rannoch. Isn't that good news?"

It was amazing news. That they had done it successfully once, to produce an heir, was mind-boggling enough. That they had done it a second time took some getting used to. I tried to picture anybody actually making love to Fig from choice. But then I suppose it is cold in bed in Scotland. That had to be the explanation.

"Congratulations," I said. "You'll have the heir and the spare."

"That was one of the reasons for deciding to spend the winter in London this year," Binky said. "Fig hasn't been having an easy time of it and the doctor recommends feet up and nothing to upset her. And she's got a bit of a thing about our lack of money, I'm afraid. I feel like an awful failure, if you want to know the truth."

I felt sorry for Binky. "It's not your fault that Father shot himself and saddled you with crippling death duties on the estate."

"I know, but I should be able to do more. I'm not the brightest sort of chap and unfortunately I'm not equipped for any kind of work, apart from mooching around the estate and that sort of thing."

I put my hand on his arm. "Look, don't worry about the maid," I said. "I'll find one somehow. I'll go and see Belinda. She knows everybody. She travels to the Continent all the time. And you better go up to Fig."

He sighed and plodded up the stairs. I didn't like to go out again, in case Darcy telephoned or turned up in person only to be met by the hostility of my sister-in-law. But as I had no way of contacting him and I had learned from experience that Darcy was, to say the least, unpredictable, I decided I needed to get to work on the maid situation immediately. Perhaps Belinda had returned to London now that the fog had lifted. I decided it would probably not be wise to upset Fig even further by using her telephone so I walked through the rain to Belinda's mews cottage.

To my delight the door was opened immediately by Belinda's maid. "Oh, your ladyship," she said, "I'm awful sorry, but she's taking a rest. She's going out tonight and she said she wasn't to be disturbed."

I had trudged all this way in a bitter rain and wasn't about to go back empty-handed.

"Oh, what a pity," I said in ringing tones, projecting as we were taught to in elocution class. "She will be sorry that she missed me, especially when I came to tell her about the royal wedding I'm to attend."

I waited and sure enough there was the sound of shuffling upstairs and a bleary-eyed Belinda appeared, satin sleep mask pushed up on her forehead and wearing a feather-trimmed robe. She made her way gingerly down the stairs toward me.

"Georgie, how lovely to see you. I didn't realize you were back in London. Don't keep Lady Georgiana standing on the doorstep, Florrie," she said. "Ask her in and make us some tea."

She staggered down the last of the stairs and embraced me. "I'm so glad you're here," I said. "I came by a couple of days ago and the place was all shut up."

"That's because Florrie couldn't get here through the fog," she said, glaring after the departing servant. "Left me in the lurch. No sense of duty, these people, and no backbone. You and I would have made it, wouldn't we? Even if we had to walk from Hackney? I tried to survive without her, but in the end I had no choice, darling, but to check into the Dorchester until the fog lifted."

She led me into her delightfully warm sitting room and I peeled off outer garments. "I'm actually surprised to find you here. I should have thought Italy was so much nicer at this time of year."

A spasm of annoyance crossed her face. "Let's just say that the climate in Italy turned decidedly frosty all at once."

"Meaning what?"

"Paolo's horrid fiancée learned about me and put her foot down. She announced that she wants to get married right away. So Paolo's father told him to shape up and do his duty, or else. And since Pappa controls the purse strings it was *arrivederci* to poor little *moi*."

"You know, you're beginning to sound like my mother," I said. "I hope you're not turning into her."

"I think she's had a divine life," Belinda said, "all those playboys and racing car drivers and Texan oil millionaires."

"Yes, but in the end what does she have?"

"Some lovely jewels at the very least, and that little villa in the south of France."

"Yes, but in terms of family? Only Granddad and me and she ignores us both."

"Darling, your mother is a survivor like me," Belinda

said. "I was upset for a day or so when Paolo showed me the door, but then I decided there are plenty more fish in the sea. But enough about me, what's this I hear about a royal wedding?" She sank into the art nouveau armchair. I perched on the most uncomfortable modern sofa. "Don't tell me you've been forced to say yes to Fishface."

"Not if he was the last man on the planet," I said. "No, much more exciting than that. I've been asked to attend a royal wedding in Romania, as official representative of the family. And I'm to be in the bridal party."

"I say." Belinda looked suitably impressed. "What a coup! That's a step up in the world for you, isn't it? One day you're living on dry toast, the next you're representing our country at a royal wedding. How did this come about?"

"The bride specifically asked for me," I said. "Since we are old school friends."

"Old school friends? From Les Oiseaux?"

"It's the only school I ever went to. Until then it was all governesses."

Belinda frowned, trying to think. "An old school friend, in Romania? Who was that?"

"Princess Maria Theresa," I said.

"Maria Theresa—oh, God. Not Fatty Matty."

"I'd forgotten you used to call her that, Belinda. That wasn't very nice, was it?"

"Darling, one was only being honest. Besides, she wasn't a very nice person, was she?"

"Wasn't she? I know she was annoying, following us around and wanting to be included in everything. I used to call her Moony Matty, I remember, for the moon face and the way that she drifted around one step behind us all the time."

"And she was always pestering me to tell her about sex. Utterly clueless. Didn't even know where babies came from. But don't you remember, when we did include her, she betrayed our trust and ratted on me to Mademoiselle Amelie. Nearly got me expelled."

"She did?"

"Yes, that time I climbed out of the window to meet that ski instructor."

"That was Matty who told Mademoiselle?"

"We were never quite sure, but I always suspected. She had this smug look on her face when I was hauled into Mademoiselle's study," Belinda said.

"Well, let's hope she's improved by now. She's bringing in a couturiere from Paris to design our gowns."

"Oh, God. She'll look like a bally great meringue in a wedding dress," Belinda said. "Who is she marrying?"

"Prince Nicholas of Bulgaria, apparently."

"Poor Prince Nicholas. I'd forgotten she was a princess, but then I suppose a lot of our classmates were some kind of royalty, weren't they? I was one of the few commoners."

"You're an honorable. Hardly a commoner."

"But not in your league, darling. I say, what a scream—a bridal attendant to Fatty Matty. Let's hope the other attendants aren't her size or you'll be squished to death among them."

"Belinda, you are awful." I had to laugh. We broke off as tea was brought in. I watched Florrie serve it efficiently then depart.

"Your maid," I said, "she doesn't have a sister, does she?"

"Florrie? I've no idea, why?"

"Because I have been instructed by Her Majesty to take my maid with me to Romania. And since I don't have a maid to take with me, I'm going to have to beg, borrow or steal one from someone else, or hire one from an agency. I don't suppose you could do without Florrie for a week or so?"

"Absolutely not," Belinda said. "I nearly starved to death during that fog. If I hadn't been able to make a run on Harrods' food hall for pâté and fruit, it would have been the end of me. Besides, if Florrie wouldn't dare to cross London during a fog, I don't think she'd have the spunk to make it across the Channel, let alone to Romania."

"What about when you go abroad?"

"I leave her behind. I can't really afford a second ticket. There are usually enough servants to take care of me at the sort of villas I like to visit."

"Then do you have any suggestions as to where I might find a maid? Anybody you know who might be going on a cruise or to the south of France and leaving their maid behind?"

"People with money never leave their maids behind," Belinda said. "They take them along. You could probably pick up the right sort of girl in Paris, if you go a few days ahead."

"Belinda, I have no idea where one would find a maid in Paris. My mother took me there a couple of times when I was little and we went once with the school. Besides, I'd have to pay a French maid money that I don't have."

"That's true," Belinda agreed. "They are frightfully expensive. But worth it. If I wasn't living this miserable existence, I'd have a French maid like a shot. My dear stepmother has one, but then Daddy gives her everything she wants." She dropped a sugar cube into her teacup. "Speaking of mothers, why don't you ask yours to cough up the money for a French maid?"

"I never know where to find my mother," I said. "Besides,

I don't like asking her for things." A thought crossed my mind. "We could try asking Florrie if she knows any girls who are looking for work and want a taste of adventure."

"Anyone Florrie knows wouldn't want a taste of adventure," Belinda said. "She must be one of the most boring creatures on earth." But she rang the bell.

Florrie came rushing back into the room. "Did I forget something on the tea tray, miss?" she asked, anxiously clutching at her apron.

"No, Florrie. Lady Georgiana has a request of you. Go ahead, Georgie."

"Florrie," I said, "I am looking for a maid. You don't happen to know of any suitable girls who are out of work, do you?"

"I might, your ladyship."

"And would be up for a little adventure, traveling abroad?"

"Abroad? What, like France, you mean? They say it's terrible dangerous over there. Men pinch your bottom." Florrie's eyes opened wide.

"Farther away than France. And even more dangerous," Belinda said. "All the way across Europe on a train."

"Ooh, no, miss. I don't know no girls who'd want to do that. Sorry, your ladyship." She bobbed an awkward curtsy and fled.

"You needn't have played up the danger," I said. "We'll only be on a train and in a royal castle."

"You don't want one who's going to lose her nerve halfway across Europe and beg you in tears to be taken home," Belinda said. "Besides, what if the train is attacked by brigands—or wolves?"

"Belinda!" I laughed nervously. "Things like that don't happen anymore."

"In the Balkans they do—all the time. And what about that train buried in an avalanche? They didn't dig them out for days." She looked at me, then burst out laughing. "Why the somber face? You're going to have topping fun."

"When I'm not suffocating in an avalanche or being attacked by brigands or wolves."

"And Transylvania is part of Romania these days, isn't it?" Belinda was warming to her subject. "You might meet a vampire."

"Oh, come on, Belinda. There are no vampires."

"Think how intriguing that would be. I understand it is utter ecstasy to be bitten on the neck. Even more of a rush than sex. Of course, I believe one then becomes one of the undead, but it would be worth it just for the experience."

"I have no wish to become undead, thank you," I said, laughing uneasily.

"Come to think of it, I'm sure Matty told us that their ancestral home was actually in the mountains of Transylvania, so there you are. Vampires everywhere. How I envy you the experience. I do wish I were coming with you." Suddenly she sat up straight, nearly knocking over the little tea table. "I have a brilliant idea. Why don't I come along as your maid?"

I stared at her and started to laugh. "Belinda. Don't be absurd," I said. "Why on earth would you want to be my maid?"

"Because you're invited to a royal wedding in Transylvania and I'm not and I'm bored and it sounds as if it could be loads of laughs and I'm dying to meet a vampire."

"Some maid you'd be." I was still grinning. "You don't even know how to make tea."

"Ah, but I know how to press things, thanks to my clothes

design business. That's the important part, isn't it? I could press and dress you. And in case you have forgotten, I played the part of your maid once before and I did it jolly well," she said. "So why not? I'm itching for an adventure and you're providing one. You wouldn't even have to pay me."

I have to admit I was sorely tempted. It would be fun to be in a strange country with Belinda beside me.

"In other circumstances I'd take you up on your offer like a shot," I said, "and it would be a lot of fun, but you've overlooked one small detail—Matty would recognize you instantly."

"Nonsense," Belinda said. "Nobody looks twice at servants. I'd be in your room or in the servants' quarters. Her Highness and I would never have to meet. Come on. Do be a sport and say yes."

"I know you too well," I said. "You'd soon tire of being left out of the fun and festivities, wouldn't you? You'd only be there ten minutes and you'd find some good-looking foreign prince, reveal your true identity and leave me in the lurch."

"I am cut to the quick," she said. "Here am I, making you a generous and unselfish offer, and you keep finding reasons to turn me down. Wouldn't it be a lark to be there together?"

"A fabulous lark," I agreed, "and if I were going as an ordinary person, I'd take you along in an instant. But since I'm representing the royal family and my country, I have to observe protocol in every aspect. Surely you can see that?"

"You are becoming as stuffy as your brother," she said.

"Speaking of my brother, you'll never guess in a million years. Fig is in the family way again."

Belinda grinned. "I suppose in their case it's he who has to close his eyes and think of England when he does it. So you'll be bumped back to thirty-fifth in line to the throne. It doesn't look as if you'll ever make it to queen."

"You are silly." I laughed. "It will be good for Podge to have a brother or sister. I remember how lonely it was to be a child living at Castle Rannoch." I put down my teacup and got up. "Anyway, I must go on my quest for a maid. I've no idea where I'm going to find one."

"I've offered my services and been rejected," she said. "But the offer still stands if you can't come up with anyone better by the end of the week."

Chapter 7

A semidetached in Essex with gnomes in the garden
Still Thursday, November 10

This was turning into a tricky problem. There was nobody else in London I knew well enough to ask to borrow their personal maid. I realized when I reconsidered that it would be the most frightful cheek to turn up on somebody's doorstep and ask to borrow a maid, even if I did know them well. I wondered if I might get by with traveling alone and telling the dreaded chaperon that my maid had come down with mumps at the last moment. Surely they'd have enough servants at a royal castle to spare me an extra one. And I had become quite good at dressing myself. But probably not dressing myself in the sort of gown to be worn at weddings, with a thousand hooks or so down the back. There was nothing for it. I'd have to find an agency and hire a suitable girl, hoping that I could find some way to pay her at the end of the trip.

I was still dressed in my visiting-the-palace clothes so I set off again, scouring Mayfair for the right sort of domestic agency. I didn't dare return to the one that had supplied me with Mildred once before. The proprietress was so impossibly regal that she made the queen look positively middle class. I wandered along Piccadilly and up to Berkeley Square. Luckily the rain had slowed to a misty drizzle. I finally found what looked like a suitable agency on Bond Street. The woman behind the desk was another dragon— perhaps it was a requirement of the profession.

"Let me get this straight, my lady. You wish to employ a lady's maid to accompany you to Romania?"

"That's right."

"And when would this be?"

"Next week."

"Next week?" Her eyebrows shot upward. "I think it would be highly unlikely that I could find you the right sort of young woman to fill this position within one week. I can think of one or two who might be persuaded, but you'd have to pay her a premium."

"What sort of premium?"

Then she named an amount that I should have thought sufficient to run Castle Rannoch for a year. She must have seen me swallow hard, because she added, "We only handle the highest caliber of young women, you know."

I left in deep despondency. My brother could never find that sort of money, even if Fig would ever let him hand it over to me. It would have to be Belinda or nobody. As I walked through the growing twilight I pictured Belinda and all the sort of things that could go wrong with that arrangement. I was doomed whatever I did. Then I heard a newsboy calling out the headlines of the day in broad Cockney. That immediately made me think of the one person I had not yet turned to. My grandfather always had an answer for even the toughest problems. And even if he couldn't conjure a maid out of thin air, it was like a tonic just to see him. I almost ran to the Bond Street tube station and was soon speeding across London into darkest Essex.

I suppose I should explain that whereas my father was Queen Victoria's grandson, my mother had started life as the daughter of a Cockney policeman. She had become a famous actress and left her past behind when she married my father—only to bolt from him again when I was two.

The tube train was packed by the time it left central London and I emerged rather the worse for wear. It was raining hard again as I left the train. I was always glad to see my grandfather's little house, with its neat, pocket handkerchief–sized lawn and its cheerful garden gnomes, but never more so than that evening. A light shone out of the frosted glass panes on the front door as I trudged up the path. I knocked and waited. Eventually the door opened a crack, and a pair of bright boot-button eyes regarded me.

"Whatcher want?" a gravelly voice demanded.

"Granddad, it's me, Georgie."

The door was flung open wide and there was my grandfather's cheerful Cockney face beaming at me. "Well, I'm blowed. Talk about a sight for sore eyes. Come on in, ducks. Come in."

I stepped into his narrow front hall and he hugged me in spite of my wet overcoat.

"Blimey, you look like a drowned rat," he said, holding me at arm's length and grinning at me, his head to one side like a cheerful sparrow. "What on earth are you doing here, out on such a miserable night? 'Ere. You're not in some kind of trouble again, are you?"

"Not really in trouble," I said, "but I do need your help."

"Let me take your coat, love. Come into the kitchen and take a load off your plates of meat."

"My what?"

"Yer feet, love. Ain't I taught you no Cockney rhyming slang yet?"

He hung up my coat then ushered me down the hall to his tiny square of kitchen, which was already occupied by one person. "Look what the cat brought in, 'ettie," he said. It was his next-door neighbor, Mrs. Hettie Huggins, who had been setting her cap at him for ages and finally seemed to have succeeded.

"Pleased to see you again, yer ladyship," Mrs. Huggins said, dropping me a curtsy, although there wasn't really room for her ample hips to bend. "I've been taking care of your granddad, since he had a nasty bout of bronchitis."

"Oh, no. Are you all right now?" I turned to look at him.

"Me? Yeah. I'm right as rain, ducks. Couldn't be better, thanks to 'ettie 'ere. She fed me up like I was a prize chicken. In fact, we were just going to have some of her stew, weren't we, Hettie? Want to join us?"

"Her ladyship won't want stew, Albert. It ain't what posh people are used to."

"I'd love some, please," I said. Then added, "Just a little," in case they didn't have much. But Mrs. Huggins ladled out a big bowl with barley and beans and lamb shank and they nodded with satisfaction as I wolfed it down.

"Anyone would think you hadn't seen a decent meal in a month of Sundays," Granddad said. "You're not still growing, are you?"

"I hope not. I'm taller than some of my dancing partners," I said. "But I do love a good stew."

They exchanged a look of satisfaction.

"So what are things like up in the Smoke?" Granddad asked.

"Smoky. We've had horrible fogs. I've hardly been out."

"Same down here. That's what done in Albert's chest," Mrs. Huggins said.

"So what can we do for you, love?" Granddad asked, looking at me fondly.

I took a deep breath. "I'm looking for a maid, in rather a hurry, I'm afraid."

Granddad burst out laughing. "I didn't mind pretending to be yer butler, love, but I ain't wearing a cap and apron and being a maid for you."

I laughed. "I wasn't expecting you to. I was wondering if you knew anyone who had experience in service and who was out of work."

"I reckon we can come up with half a dozen girls who'd jump at the job, don't you, 'ettie?" Granddad turned to her and she nodded.

"A maid for you, yer ladyship? Your own personal maid, like?"

"Precisely."

"I shouldn't think the position would be hard to fill. You'd have girls lining up to work for a toff like you. Why don't you just put an advertisement in the newspapers?"

"There are some complications," I said, realizing as he said it that an advertisement might be a jolly good idea. Why hadn't I thought of it before? "Firstly, it's only a temporary position. I want a girl to accompany me to a royal wedding in Europe."

"In Europe?"

"Romania, to be exact."

"Blimey" was all Granddad could find to say to that.

"And I can't pay her much. I'm hoping I'll be able to pay her something when I return."

Granddad shook his head, making tut-tutting sounds.

"You are in a bit of a pickle, aren't you? What about your brother and his snooty wife, can't they spare you a servant?"

"Nobody at Castle Rannoch wants to travel to London, let alone abroad. I'm looking for an adventurous girl, but I can't afford to pay her much."

"Seems to me," Granddad said slowly, "that a girl might want to take up this position so that she could use you as a reference. Former maid to royalty. That might be worth a darned sight more than money."

"You know, you're right, Granddad. You're brilliant."

He beamed.

"My niece Doreen's girl is looking for work, as it happens," Mrs. Huggins said quickly. It was clear that her brain had been ticking as he made that suggestion. "Nice quiet little thing. Not the brightest, but it might help her land a good position if she had a reference from a toff like you. Why don't I speak to her about it and send her up to you if she's willing to give it a try."

"Brilliant," I said. "I knew I was doing the right thing coming to you two. You always have an answer for me."

"So you're going to a royal wedding, are you, your ladyship?" Mrs. Huggins asked.

"Yes. I'm going to be in the bridal party, but I have to leave next week, so that doesn't give me much time to hire a maid to travel with me. This girl you mentioned—she has had some domestic service training, has she?"

"Oh, yes. She's had several jobs. Not anything like as grand as your house, of course. This will be a step up in the world for her. But like I said, she's a quiet, willing little thing. And you wouldn't have to worry about her having an eye for the boys. She don't have an ounce of what they refer to these days as sex appeal. Face like the back end of a bus, poor little thing. But you'd find her keen enough to learn."

My grandfather chuckled. "If she was in the theater, I wouldn't hire you as her manager, 'ettie."

"Well, I have to tell it straight for her ladyship, don't I?"

"I won't be judging her on her looks, and at the moment I feel it really is a case of beggars not being choosers."

"So I'll tell her she can call on you at yer house, shall I?"

"By all means. I look forward to meeting her." I finished my stew and started to stand up. "I really should be getting back to London, although I can't say I'm looking forward to it. I have my brother and sister-in-law at the house."

"You're welcome to the spare bedroom," Granddad said. "It's a nasty night out there."

I was tempted. The safety and security of Granddad's little house versus the doubly frigid atmosphere of Rannoch House occupied by Fig. But I had a wedding to plan for, and I didn't want Fig suspecting that I'd spent the night with Darcy.

"No, I really should get back, I'm afraid," I said. "It was so good to see you."

"We'll want to hear all about it when you come back from wherever it was," Granddad said. "You take care of yourself, traveling in foreign parts."

"I wish I were a man, then I could take you as my valet," I said wistfully, thinking how much nicer it would be traveling across a continent with him at my side.

"You wouldn't catch me going to heathen parts like that," Granddad said. "I've been to Scotland now, and that was quite foreign enough to last my lifetime, thank you kindly."

I laughed as I walked up the front path.

Chapter 8

I arrived home, cold and wet, to be told by an almost gloating Fig that Mr. O'Mara had called and been told that Lady Georgiana would be attending a royal wedding in Europe, at the request of Their Majesties, and should be left in peace to make her preparations. She also hinted that she'd admonished him for preying on innocent girls and suggested that he should not stand in the way of my making a suitable match.

This made me furious, of course, but it was too late. The damage had been done. All I could do was console myself with the thought that Darcy would probably have found Fig's lecture highly amusing.

The next morning they left, abandoning me for the warmth and luxury of Claridge's for their last night in London. I breathed a long sigh of relief. Now all I had to do was to pack for my trip to Europe and hope that the promised maid materialized. A telephone call from the palace informed me that my chaperon had had to put forward her traveling date, so it was hoped that I could be ready by Tuesday next. Tickets and passports would be delivered to me and, yes, tiaras would be worn. I had to telephone Binky at Claridges and I imagined Fig was gnashing her teeth at the expense of sending a servant down from Scotland with my tiara. But one couldn't exactly have put it in the post, even if we had the time. Then I realized that I would now not have time to place an advertisement in the *Morning Post* or the *Times*. It would have to be Mrs. Huggins's relative or nothing.

For a while it looked as if it was going to be nothing and I was just about to rush to Belinda and confess that I had changed my mind when there was a timid tap at my tradesman's entrance. Luckily I was in the kitchen at the time or I would never have heard it. I opened the door and standing outside in the dim and damp November twilight was an apparition that looked like a giant Beatrix Potter hedgehog, but not as adorable. It then revealed itself to be wearing an old, moth-eaten and rather spiky fur coat, topped with a bright red pudding basin hat. Underneath was a round, red face with cheeks almost matching the color of the hat. When she saw me a big smile spread ear to ear.

"Whatcher, love. I'm 'ere to see the toff what lives here about the maid's position, so 'ere I am. So nip off and tell her, all right?"

I tried not to let her know that I found this amusing. I said in my most superior voice, "I happen to be the toff that lives here. I am Lady Georgiana Rannoch."

"Blimey, strike me down with a feather," she said. "Begging your pardon, then, but you don't expect to find a lady like you opening the back door, do you?"

"No, you don't," I agreed. "You'd better come in."

"Awful sorry, miss," she said. "No hard feelings, I hope? I don't want to start off on the wrong foot. My mum's aunt 'ettie knows your granddad and she told me you was looking for a personal maid and she said why didn't I give it a try."

"I am looking for a personal maid, that's correct," I said. "Why don't you take off your coat and I'll interview you here. It's the warmest place in the house at the moment."

"Right you are, miss," she said and took off the fur coat, which was now steaming and smelling rather like wet sheep. Underneath the coat she was wearing a rather too tight mustard yellow home-knitted jumper and a purple skirt. Color coordination was not her strong point, clearly. I indicated a chair at the kitchen table and she sat. She was a large, big-boned cart horse of a girl with a perpetually surprised and vacant expression. The thought passed through my mind that she'd be expensive to feed.

"Now, I've told you my name. What is yours?"

"It's Queenie, miss," she said. "Queenie 'epplewhite."

Why did the lower classes seem to have all these surnames starting with *H* when it was a letter they simply ignored or couldn't pronounce? And as for her Christian name . . .

"Queenie?" I said cautiously. "That's your Christian name? Not a nickname?"

"No, miss. It's the only name I got."

I could see that a maid called Queenie might present problems for one about to attend a royal wedding, where there would be several real queens, but I told myself that most of them wouldn't speak English and would probably never run into my maid.

"So tell me, Queenie," I said, taking a seat opposite her, "you have been in domestic service, I understand?"

"Oh, yes, miss. I've already been employed in three households so far, but nothing like as grand as this one, of course."

"And did you serve in the capacity of a lady's maid?"

"Not exactly, miss. Sort of general dogsbody, more like it."

"So how long were you with your former employers?"

"About three weeks," she said.

"Three weeks? Which employer were you only with for three weeks?"

"All of 'em, miss," she said.

"Why such a short time, may I ask?"

"Well, the last one was her at the butcher's, and she only wanted help during her confinement, so as soon as the baby came she told me to push off."

"And the other two?"

She chewed on her lip before saying, "Well, the first one got pretty upset when I knocked over her bottle of perfume when I was dusting. It went all over the mahogany dressing table and took the surface off, but that wasn't what really upset her. It was a really expensive bottle of perfume, apparently. She'd brought it back from Paris. Oh, miss, you should have heard the words she used. You don't hear words like that from a fishmonger down the Old Kent Road."

"And the third employer?" I hardly dared to ask.

"Well, I couldn't very well stay there," she said. "Not after I set her evening dress on fire."

"How did you do that?"

"I dropped a match on the skirt by accident when I was lighting the candles," she said. "It wouldn't have been too bad, but she was wearing it at the time. She made a terrible fuss too, although she was hardly burned at all."

I swallowed hard and wondered what to say next.

"Queenie, it appears that you are an absolute disaster," I said. "But it so happens that I'm desperate at the moment. I expect your aunt told you that I am due to go abroad to a very important wedding and I leave next Tuesday. It is essential that I take a maid with me to look after my clothes, help me dress and do my hair. Do you think you could do that?"

"I could give it a bloody good try, miss," she said.

"Then let us get a couple of things straight—one, there will be no swearing or any kind of bad language, and two, I am Lady Georgiana so you are expected to call me 'my lady' and not 'miss.' Do you understand?"

"Right you are, miss. I mean, my lady."

"And you do understand that this job means going abroad with me, to a foreign country?"

"Oh, yes, miss. I mean, my lady. I'm game for anything. It will be a bit of a lark, and wait till I see Nellie 'uxtable down the Three Bells, her what's always boasting that she took a day trip to Boulogne."

At least one had to admire her pluck, or maybe she was just completely clueless.

"And as to money—I do not intend to pay you any money at first. You will travel with me and receive your uniform and of course all your meals. If you prove satisfactory I will pay you what you are worth on our return and what's more I shall write you a letter of reference that will guarantee you a good job anywhere. So it's up to you, Queenie. This is your chance to make something of yourself. What do you say? Will you accept my terms?"

"Bob's yer uncle, miss," she said and thrust a big meaty hand in my direction.

I arranged for her to come to Rannoch House on Monday. She plonked the shapeless hat on her head and turned back to me at the door. "You won't regret this, miss," she said. "I'll be the best ruddy chambermaid you've ever had."

So I was due to undertake a journey fraught with avalanches, brigands and wolves with possibly the world's worst chambermaid who was likely to set fire to my dress. It would be interesting to see if I came out of it alive.

Chapter 9

Rannoch House
Monday, November 14
Due to leave for Continent tomorrow. Still no maid. Still
haven't heard from Darcy. Still raining.
How tiresome life can be.

By Monday morning I had still not heard from Darcy. Now I would be going abroad without letting him know. Really he was a most infuriating man. I simply didn't know what to make of him. Sometimes I thought he was really keen on me, and then other times he'd disappear for ages. Anyway, there was nothing I could do about him now. If he hadn't chosen to give me his address or even come to see that I had survived the visit from Binky and Fig, then too bad.

Queenie turned up a little after nine. It took some time rummaging through the housekeeper's closet to find a uniform that fitted and looked suitable, because she was a hefty girl, but eventually we poured her into a black dress, white cap and apron. She looked very pleased with herself as she stared in the mirror.

"Stone me. I look just like a real maid now, don't I, miss, I mean, me lady?"

"Let's hope you learn to act like one, Queenie," I said. "I

take it you have brought your case with you with the items you'll need to travel. You can now come up to my room and pack the clothes I shall need. Bring that tissue paper with you so that they don't become creased."

We spent a rather fraught morning as I stopped her from wrapping my boots with my velvet dinner gown, but eventually all was ready. Tickets, passports and letters of introduction were delivered from the palace. My tiara arrived by courier from Castle Rannoch and Binky had generously slipped a few sovereigns into the package with a note saying *I expect you'll need some expenses for the journey. Sorry it can't be more.*

He was a sweet man, useless but sweet.

The money at least allowed us to take a taxi to Victoria Station on the morning of Tuesday, November 15. As I followed a porter to the platform where the boat train departed, I felt a sudden surge of excitement. I was really going abroad. I was going to be part of a royal wedding, even if it was Moony Matty's. My compartment was found and the porter set off for the baggage car with my trunks, leaving me with my personal luggage. I knew that in normal circumstances I would have entrusted my jewel case to my maid but I thought that Queenie might try dressing up in my tiara or let the rubies slip down the sink in the lavatory.

"You should go and find your own seat now, Queenie," I said. "Here is your ticket."

"My own seat?" A look of panic crossed her face. "You mean I'm not traveling with you?"

"This is first class. Servants always travel third class," I said. "Don't worry. I'll meet you on the platform with our luggage when we reach Dover. And I expect my chaperon's maid will be sitting with you so you'll have someone to talk to. Oh, and Queenie, please don't let the other maids know

It was going to be a very long journey.

At Dover we alighted from the train and found Queenie and Chantal.

"Dear God in heaven, what is that?" Lady Middlesex demanded on seeing Queenie, who was wearing the spiky fur coat and red hat again.

"My maid," I said.

"You let her look like that?"

"It's all she has."

"Then you should have outfitted her suitably. My dear girl, if you let servants go around looking like oversized flowerpots you'll be a laughingstock. I only allow Chantal to wear black. Colors are reserved for people of our class. Come along now, Chantal." She turned to the maid. "My train cases. And I want you to stay with those porters every inch of the way until the trunks are safely on board the ship, is that clear?"

"You do the same, Queenie," I said.

"I ain't never been on a ship, miss," Queenie said, already looking green, "apart from the *Saucy Sally* around the pier at Clacton. What if I get seasick?"

"Nonsense," Lady Middlesex said. "You simply tell your-self that you are not going to be ill. Your mistress will not allow it. Now off you go and no dillydallying." She turned me. "That girl wants bringing in line rapidly."

Then she strode out ahead of me toward the gangplank. was a pleasant crossing with just enough swell to make realize one was on a ship. Lady Middlesex and I had h in the dining room (she had a hearty appetite and ured everything within sight) and emerged in time to he French coast ahead of us. We found Queenie, who linging to the railing as if it were her only hope of al.

that you've only been in my employ for a day or that you set fire to your last employer's dress."

"Right you are, miss," she said, then put her hand to her mouth, giggling. "I still can't get the hang of saying 'my lady.' I always was a bit thick. My old dad says I was dropped on my head as a baby."

Oh, brilliant. Now she told me. She probably had fainting spells or fits. I was beginning to wish I'd taken up Belinda's offer after all. I had gone to see her to tell her the funny story of my new maid, but neither Belinda nor her maid was at home. It had to mean that she had probably fled somewhere warm again. I couldn't blame her.

A very nervous Queenie made her way down the platform to find the third-class carriages. As I watched her go I pondered on the irony that my maid was wearing a fur coat, whereas I only had good Scottish Harris tweed. Some girls were given a fur coat for their twenty-first birthday. I had been tempted to buy one with the check from Sir Hubert, the one of Mother's many husbands and lovers of whom I had been the most fond, but luckily I had banked it instead. It kept me in funds for over a year but had finally run out. The thought of Sir Hubert sparked an exciting memory. He was still in Switzerland, recuperating from a horrible accident (or was it attempted murder?—now we'd never know). I could visit him on the way home. I'd jot him a line as soon as I reached my destination.

As I stood there alone in the carriage I realized two things. One was that my chaperon had not appeared and the other was that I had no idea of the actual destination to which we were going. If she didn't turn up I didn't even know at which station we were to alight. Oh, dear, more things to worry about.

The hour for departure neared and I paced nervously. I

was just double-checking that my jewel case was securely on the rack when the compartment door was flung open and a voice behind me said, "You, girl, what are you doing in here? Maids belong in third class. And where is your mistress?"

I turned to face a gaunt, horsey-looking woman wearing a long Persian lamb cape. Standing behind her was a most superior-looking creature in black, laden with various hatboxes and train cases. Both were staring at me as if I were something they had just discovered on the sole of their shoe.

"I think you've made a mistake. I am Lady Georgiana Rannoch, and this is my compartment," I said.

The horsey face turned decidedly paler. "Oh, most frightfully sorry. I only saw your back and you have to admit that that overcoat is not the smartest, so naturally I assumed . . ." She mustered a hearty smile and stuck out her hand. "Middlesex," she said.

"I beg your pardon?"

"That's the name. Lady Middlesex. Your companion for the journey. Didn't Her Majesty tell you?"

"She told me there would be a chaperon. She never gave me your name."

"Didn't she? Dashed inefficient of her. Not like her. She's usually a stickler for details. She's worried about the king, of course. Not at all well."

She pumped my hand energetically all the time she was speaking. Meanwhile the creature in black had slunk past us and was busy loading cases onto the rack.

"All is done, my lady," she said with a strong French accent. "I shall retire to my own quarters."

"Splendid. Thank you, Chantal." Lady Middlesex leaned closer to me. "An absolute treasure. Couldn't travel without her. Completely devoted, of course. Worships me. Doesn't

mind where we go or what hardships she has to endure. We're on our way to Baghdad now, y'know. Dashed awful place, baking in summer, freezing in winter, but m' husband has been posted there as British attaché. They always post him to a spot where they expect trouble. Damned strong man is Lord Middlesex. Doesn't allow the natives to get away with any kind of nonsense."

I wondered how Chantal and Queenie would get along. Our door was slammed shut and a whistle sounded.

"Ah, we're off. Right on time. Jolly good show. I do like punctuality. Absolutely insist upon it at home. We dine at eight on the dot. If ever a guest dares to show up late, he finds we have started without him."

I almost reminded her that she had nearly missed the train herself, but I consoled myself that she would not be coming to the wedding with me. I'd disembark and she would travel on to Baghdad where she would boss around the natives. started to move, first slowly past dingy gray buildings, over the Thames and picking up speed until the back became a blur and merged into bigger gardens and real countryside. It was a splendid autumn day, th day that made me think of hunting. Clouds raced clear blue sky. There were sheep in meadows. La up a nonstop commentary about the places to Middlesex had brought British law and order ar had taught the native women proper British h worshipped me, of course," she said. "But I h living abroad is a sacrifice I make for my h had a decent hunt in years. We rode with th hai, but it was only over the peasants' fi as jolly as good open countryside, is it? little people shouting at us and wavin ing the horses."

"It don't half go up and down, don't it, miss?" she said.

"Your mistress should be addressed as 'your ladyship,'" Lady Middlesex said in a horrified voice. "I can't think where she found such an unsuitable maid. Pull yourself together, girl, or you'll be on the next boat home."

Oh, dear. I'm sure that was exactly what Queenie wanted at this moment.

"Queenie is still learning," I said quickly. "I'm sure she'll soon be splendid."

Lady Middlesex sniffed. We sailed into Calais Harbor and then we sailed through the hassle of customs and immigration thanks to Lady M and the royal warrants, which allowed us to bypass the long lines and the customs shed. I had to admit she was marvelous—frightening, but worthy of admiration as she chivvied French dockworkers and porters until luggage was loaded and we were safely in our wagons-lits compartments of the Arlberg Orient Express.

"Run along now," Lady Middlesex said, waving Chantal away as if she were an annoying fly. "And take Lady Georgiana's maid with you."

I was relieved to find I had my own sleeping berth and didn't have to share with Lady Middlesex. I was about to come out into the corridor when I heard words I never would have expected to escape from Lady Middlesex's lips.

"Ah, there you are at last, dear heart."

I simply couldn't imagine Lady Middlesex calling anyone dear heart, and I knew her husband was already in Baghdad, so I was brimming with curiosity as I slid my door open. Coming up the corridor, clutching a bulky and battered suitcase, was a middle-aged and decidedly frumpy woman. She was wearing what was clearly a home-knitted beret and scarf over a shapeless overcoat and she looked hot and flustered.

"Oh, I've had the most awful time, Lady M. Most awful. There were two terrible men sitting across from me on the ship. I swear they were international criminals—so swarthy looking and they kept muttering to each other. Thank God it was not a night crossing or I'd have been murdered in my bunk."

"I hardly think so, dear heart," Lady Middlesex said. "You haven't anything worth stealing and they were not likely to be interested in your body."

"Oh, Lady M, really!" And the woman blushed.

"Well, you're here now and all is well," Lady Middlesex said. "Ah, Lady Georgiana, let me introduce you. This is my companion, Miss Deer-Harte."

"I am honored to meet you, Lady Georgiana." She bobbed an awkward curtsy, as she was still clutching the large suitcase. "I'm sure we'll have some jolly chats on the way across Europe. Let us just pray that there are no snowstorms this time and that none of those dreadful Balkan countries decides to make war with its neighbor."

"Always such gloom and doom, Deer-Harte," Lady Middlesex said. "Buck up. Best foot forward and all that. Your cabin is just down there. Why you had to struggle with that suitcase yourself instead of employing a porter is beyond me."

"But you know how hopeless I am with foreign money, Lady M. I'm always terrified of giving them a pound when I mean a shilling. And they always look so sinister with those black mustaches, I'm frightened they'll take off with my bags and I'll never see them again."

"I've told you before, nobody would want your bags," Lady Middlesex said. "Now, for heaven's sake go and get settled and then we'll find the dining car and see if they can produce a drinkable cup of tea."

As she finished speaking she looked down the corridor and opened her mouth in horror. "What in heaven's name?"

Queenie was rushing toward us, blindly pushing past people. She reached me and clutched at my sleeve like a drowning person. "Oh, me lady," she gasped, "can't I come in with you? I can't stay down there. It's all foreign people. Speaking foreign and acting foreign. I'm scared, me lady."

"You'll be fine, Queenie," I said. "You have Chantal, who has traveled on these trains many times and speaks the language too. Ask her if you need anything."

"What, 'er with the hatchet face?" Queenie demanded. "She gives me a look that would curdle milk. And she speaks foreign too. I had no idea it was going to be so— well, foreign."

Lady Middlesex faced the terrified girl. "Pull yourself together, girl. You are embarrassing your mistress by making a scene. There is no question of your remaining in first class with your betters. You will be perfectly safe with Chantal. She travels with me all over the world. Now go back to your own compartment and stay there until Chantal tells you to disembark. Do I make myself perfectly clear?"

Queenie let out a whimper but she nodded and scurried back down the corridor.

"Have to be firm with these girls," Lady Middlesex said. "No backbone, that's the problem. Disgrace to the English race. Now let's go and see if any of these French people can make a decent cup of tea."

And she strode out ahead of me down the corridor.

Chapter 10

On a train, crossing Europe
Tuesday and Wednesday, November 15 and 16
Thank God Lady Middlesex is traveling on to Baghdad. I
don't think I could stand her company for more than one
night. Reminds me of a brief and unhappy episode when I
tried to join the Girl Guides and failed my tenderfoot test.

Soon we were sitting in a lounge car drinking what passed
for tea—the light brown color of ditch water with a slice of
lemon floating in it.

"No idea at all," Lady Middlesex said. "I don't know how
the French exist without proper tea. No wonder they always
look so pasty faced. I've tried showing them the correct
way to make it, but they simply won't learn. Ah, well, one
must suffer if one has to travel abroad. Never mind, Deer-
Harte, you'll have decent tea once we reach the embassy in
Baghdad."

"And what exactly is your destination, Lady Georgiana?"
Miss Deer-Harte asked, taking what must have been her
fifth biscuit.

"Lady Georgiana is to represent Her Majesty at a royal
wedding in Romania."

"In Romania? Good heavens—such an outlandish place.
So dangerous."

"Nonsense," Lady Middlesex said. "I thought I mentioned it to you in my last letter."

"You might have done, but unfortunately my mother's naughty little doggie, Towser, found the post and chewed off one corner of your letter. He's such a scamp."

"No matter. We're all here now and we are going to accompany Lady Georgiana to her destination in the mountains of Transylvania."

"I'm sure there is no need for you to interrupt your journey," I said hastily. "I trust a car will be waiting for me at the station."

"Nonsense. The queen specifically asked me to deliver you safely to the castle and I am not one to shirk my duty."

"But Lady M, a castle in the mountains of Transylvania, at this time of year too," Miss Deer-Harte said, her voice quivering. "We shall be set upon by wolves, at the very least. And what about vampires?"

"What tosh you do talk, Deer-Harte," Lady Middlesex said. "Vampires. Whatever next."

"But Transylvania is an absolute hotbed of vampires. It's common knowledge."

"Only in children's fairy stories. There is no such thing as vampires in real life, Deer-Harte, unless you mean the bats in South America. And as for wolves, I hardly think they can bite their way through a solid motorcar on a well-traveled road."

Lady Middlesex drained her teacup and I stared out of the window at the twilight wintry scene. Rows of bare-branched poplar trees between bleak fields flashed past us. The lights were already shining from farmhouses. I felt a thrill of excitement that I was abroad again.

"What are you staring at, Deer-Harte?" Lady Middlesex asked in her booming voice.

"That couple across the aisle," she said in a stage whisper. "I am sure that young woman is not his wife. Look at the brazen way he's holding her hand across the table. Such goings-on the moment one is on the Continent. And that man in the corner with a beard. He is obviously an international assassin. I do hope our cabin doors can be locked from the inside or we'll be murdered in our beds."

"Do you have to see danger everywhere we go?" Lady Middlesex demanded irritably.

"There usually is danger everywhere we go."

"Fiddlesticks. Never been in real danger in my life," Lady Middlesex said.

"What about that time in East Africa?"

"Just a few Masai waving spears at us. Really, you do fuss about nothing. You're just a bundle of nerves, woman. Snap out of it."

I tried not to smile. It was such an improbable relationship—I wondered why on earth the overbearing and hearty Lady Middlesex had chosen such a simpering busybody as a companion, and why Miss Deer-Harte had accepted a position that took her from one uncomfortable place of danger to the next.

We approached Paris just as darkness fell. I peered out of the window, hoping to catch a glimpse of the Eiffel Tower or some familiar monument but all one saw through the darkness were little side streets with shutters already closed and the occasional *café-tabac* on a corner. If only I had money, I thought, I'd go and live in Paris for a while and pictured myself as a risqué bohemian.

The French failings at tea making were more than made up for with a superb dinner of coquilles St. Jacques and boeuf Bourguignon just after we left Paris. Lady M continued her monologue, interrupted only by Miss Deer-Harte spotting another international criminal and reiterating the fear that we should all be murdered in our beds. Toward the end of the meal, when we were savoring a spectacular bombe glacé, Miss Deer-Harte leaned toward us. "Someone is spying on us," she whispered. "I thought it earlier and now I am sure. Someone was watching us through the door to the dining car and when I tried to have a good look at him, he moved hastily away."

Lady Middlesex sighed. "For heaven's sake, Deer-Harte, don't be so silly. No doubt it was some poor fellow coming to see if anyone interesting was in the dining car, deciding he didn't want to dine with boring types like us and taking himself off to the bar for a while. Must you read drama into everything?"

"But our doors don't lock properly, Lady M. How do we prevent ourselves from being murdered in our beds? You hear what happens on these international trains, don't you? People vanishing in the night or found dead in the morning all the time. I think we should take turns in guarding Lady Georgiana. It may be an anarchist, you know."

"No anarchist would want to kill Lady Georgiana." Lady Middlesex gave a disparaging sniff. "She's not next in line to the throne, you know. I could understand your concern if it were one of the king's sons, but if someone is spying on us, he is probably a Frenchman with an eye for a pretty girl and wants a chance to meet our Lady Georgiana without two old fogies dogging her every step. I fear he will be unlucky because I have sworn to watch over her like a hawk."

I was grateful that Lady Middlesex suggested we retire to our sleeping berths early. As I came out of the bathroom at the end of the car I had the oddest sensation that I was being watched. I spun around, but the corridor was empty. It's that awful Deer-Harte woman, I thought. She is making me jumpy now. And I have to confess that I found myself wondering if there was any truth in what Lady Middlesex had said about a Frenchman wanting a chance to meet me away from the chaperons. That was an interesting thought. Belinda had always maintained that Frenchmen made the best lovers. Not that I intended to invite him in, but a harmless flirtation might be fun.

I lingered in my doorway but no Frenchman materialized, so I went to bed. Deer-Harte had been right, however. There was no way of locking the compartment. Then it occurred to me that maybe a Frenchman would be more interested in my jewel case than in me. Perhaps Queenie had confided to Chantal that I was carrying my tiara. Perhaps she had announced this loudly enough that everyone around them heard. This was a disturbing possibility. I put my jewel case at the back of my bunk, behind my head, and propped my pillow against it. Although the bed was comfortable enough, I couldn't sleep. As I lay there, being gently tossed by the rhythm of the train, I thought about Darcy and wondered where he was and why had hadn't contacted me since his encounter with Fig. Surely he wouldn't have been intimidated by her. Then I must have drifted off to sleep because I was standing in the fog with Darcy and he went to kiss me and then I found that he was biting my neck. "Didn't you know I was really a vampire?" he asked me.

I woke with a start as the train went over a set of points with great jolting and shrieking, and I lay there, thinking about vampires. Of course I didn't really believe in them, any more than I believed in the fairies and ghosts that the peasants in Scotland were convinced were real. Poor old Miss Deer-Harte was convinced they existed. Apart from reading *Dracula* long ago, which I'd found horribly creepy, I really knew very little about them. It might be rather exciting to meet one, although I wasn't sure I wanted my neck bitten and I certainly didn't want to become undead. I chuckled to myself, remembering that conversation with Belinda. Of course now I really wished that I had taken the risk and brought her along as my maid. We'd have had such a lark, and now I was stuck with a maid who was a walking disaster area and nobody to laugh with.

I was just drifting off again when I thought I heard someone at my door. We had been assured that the border agents would not disturb us during the night when we crossed from France into Switzerland and then into Austria. It could, of course, be Lady Middlesex, checking on me.

"Hello," I said. "Who's there?"

The door started to slide slowly open, and I was conscious of a tall, dark shape outside. Then I heard a stringent voice echoing down the corridor. "You there, what are you doing?"

Then a deep voice muttered, "Sorry. I must have mistaken my compartment."

Lady Middlesex's head appeared around my half-open door. "Some blighter was trying to enter your sleeping berth. The nerve of it. I shall have a word with the conductor and tell him that he should keep better watch on who comes into this car. Maybe I should keep you company, just in case he tries it again."

"Oh, no, I'm sure I'll be all right," I said, deciding that a night with Lady Middlesex would be worse than any international jewel thief or assassin.

"I won't sleep," she said with determination. "I shall sit up all night and keep watch."

In this knowledge I finally drifted off to sleep. In spite of Miss Deer-Harte's predictions that we'd be murdered in our beds, I awoke to a perfect Christmas card scene that was familiar to me from my days at finishing school. Adorable little chalets perched on snow-covered hillsides, their roofs hidden under a thick blanket of snow. As I watched, the sun peeked between mountains, making the snow sparkle like diamonds. I opened my window and stood on my bed, breathing in crisp cold mountain air. Then the train plunged into a tunnel and I hastily shut the window again.

We breakfasted somewhere just after Innsbruck and came back to find our beds stowed and normal seats in our compartments. Luckily the scenery was so breathtaking as we climbed through spectacular mountain passes that conversation was not necessary until we moved into the flat country before Vienna. Here there were only patches of snow and the countryside was bare and gray. We had luncheon between Vienna and Budapest and when we came back to our compartments after a long and heavy meal, we found Chantal and Queenie already packing up our things, ready to disembark.

"I ain't half glad to see you, miss," Queenie said, apparently forgetting already how to address me. "I've been that scared. I didn't sleep a wink among all them foreign types, and you should see what muck they eat—sausages so full of garlic that you could smell them a mile away. There was no decent food to be had."

"Well, I expect we'll have decent food at the castle," I said, "so cheer up. The journey's almost over and you've done very well."

"I wouldn't have come if I'd known," she muttered. "Give me a nice café in Barking any day."

"All ready?" Lady Middlesex's face appeared around my door. "Apparently the train is making a special stop for us. So they don't want to wait around too long. We must be ready to disembark the moment it comes to a halt."

I looked out of the window at the gray countryside. It had become mountainous again and flakes of snow were falling. There was no sign of a city.

"Aren't we going to the capital?" I asked.

"Not at all. The princess is being married at the royal ancestral castle in the mountains. That is why it is most important that I see you safely to your destination. I gather it is quite a long drive from the station."

As she spoke, the train began to slow. We could hear the squealing of brakes and then it jerked to a halt. A door was opened for us and we were escorted down onto the platform of a small station. Peasants wrapped up against the cold stared at us with interest, while our trunks were unloaded from the baggage car. Then a whistle blew and the express disappeared into the gloom.

"Where the devil is the person they've sent to meet us?" Lady Middlesex demanded. "You stay there with the bags and I'll go and find a porter."

A local train came in, people got off and on and the platform emptied out. Suddenly I felt the back of my neck prickle with the absolute certainty that I was being watched. I spun around to see a deserted platform with swirling snow. Of course someone is watching us, I told myself. We must be frightfully interesting to peasants who have never gone farther than the next town. But I still couldn't shake off the uneasiness.

"They can't know we're coming," Miss Deer-Harte said. "They've probably mixed up dates. We'll have to spend the night at a local inn and I can't even imagine how awful and dangerous that will be. Bedbugs and brigands, you mark my words."

At that moment Lady Middlesex reappeared with several porters. "The stupid man was waiting with his car, outside the station," she said. "I asked him how we were supposed to know he was there if he didn't present himself. Did he expect us to walk around looking for him? But he doesn't appear to speak English. You'd have thought the princess might have taken the trouble to send an English-speaking person to welcome us. A proper welcoming party would have been nice—with little peasant girls in costume and a choir maybe. That's how we would have done it in England, isn't it? Really these foreigners are hopeless." Suddenly she yelled, "Careful with that box, you idiot!" She leaped up and slapped the porter's hand. He said something in the local language to the others and they gave a sinister laugh and took off with our bags. Miss Deer-Harte's suspicions were beginning to rub off on me. I half expected the porters to have run off with our things, leaving us stranded, but we met up with them in a cobbled street outside the station.

Before us was a large square black vehicle with tinted windows. A chauffeur in black uniform stood beside it.

"My God," Miss Deer-Harte exclaimed in a horrified voice. "They've sent a hearse."

Chapter 11

Bran Castle
Somewhere in the hills of Romania
Wednesday, November 16
Cold, bleak, mountainous.

"Is this the only motorcar?" Lady Middlesex demanded, waving her arms in the way that English people do when speaking with foreigners who don't understand them. "Only one automobile? What about the servants? They can't ride with us. Simply not done. Is there a bus they can take? A train?"

None of her questions produced any response at all and in the end she had to concede that the maids would have to sit in the front with the chauffeur. He didn't seem to like the idea of this and yelled a lot, but it became clear that braver men than he had quailed before the force of Lady M's determination. Chantal and Queenie tried to squeeze into the other front seat, but there simply wasn't room. In spite of the spacious interior of the motorcar, there was only one seat and we three women fit rather snugly. In the end Chantal was given the front seat and poor Queenie had to sit on the floor with her back to the driver and the train cases and hatboxes piled beside her. The rest of the baggage was eventually loaded with some difficulty into the boot of the motorcar. It wouldn't close, of course, and string had to be found to tie it together. We looked anything but regal— more like a traveling circus—as we finally set off from the station.

It was now almost dark but from what I could see we were driving through a small medieval city with narrow cobbled streets, picturesque fountains and tall gabled houses. Lights shone out and the streets were almost deserted. Those few pedestrians we passed were bundled into shapeless forms against the cold. As we left the town behind, snow started to fall in earnest, blanketing the ground around us with a carpet of white. The driver mumbled something in whatever language he spoke, presumably Romanian. For a while we drove in silence. Then the road entered a dark pine forest and started to climb.

"I don't like the look of this at all," Miss Deer-Harte said. "What did I tell you about brigands and wolves?"

"Wolves?" Queenie wailed. "Don't tell me we're going to be eaten by wolves!"

The driver perked up at a word he understood. He turned to us, revealing a mouth of yellow pointed teeth. "*Ja—* wolffs," he said, and gave a sinister laugh.

Up and up we drove, the road twisting back and forth around hairpin bends with glimpses of a sickening drop on one side. Snow was falling so fast now that it was hard to see what was road and what might have been a ditch beside it. The driver sat up very straight, peering ahead through the windshield into murky darkness. There was not a light to be seen, only dark forest and rocky cliffs.

"If I had any idea it was this far, I would have arranged for a night in a hotel before we began the trip." For the first time Lady Middlesex's voice sounded tense and strained. "I do hope the man knows what he's doing. The weather is really awfully bad."

I was beginning to feel queasy from being in the middle and flung from side to side around those bends. Miss Deer-Harte's bony elbow dug into my side. Queenie tried to brace herself in a corner but had a handkerchief to her mouth.

"You are to tell us if you wish to vomit," Lady Middlesex said. "I shall make him stop for you. But you are to contain yourself until you can get out of the vehicle, is that clear?"

Queenie managed a watery smile.

"I'm sure it's not far now," Lady Middlesex said cheerfully. She leaned forward. "Driver, is it far now? *Est it beaucoup loin?*" she repeated in atrocious French.

He didn't answer. At last we came to the top of the pass. A small inn was beside the road and lights shone out from it. The driver stopped and went around to open the bonnet, presumably to let the motor cool down. Then he disappeared inside the inn, leaving us in the freezing car.

"What's that?" Miss Deer-Harte whispered, pointing into the darkness on the other side of the road. "Look, among the trees. It's a wolf."

"Only a large dog, I'm sure," Lady Middlesex said.

I said nothing. It looked like a wolf to me. But at that moment the inn door opened and several figures emerged.

"Brigands," Miss Deer-Harte whispered. "We'll all have our throats slit."

"Ordinary peasants," Lady Middlesex sniffed. "See, they even have children with them."

If they were peasants they certainly looked like a murderous bunch, the men with big black drooping mustaches, the women large and muscular. They poured out of the inn, a remarkably large number of them, peering into the motorcar with suspicious faces. One woman crossed herself and another held up crossed fingers, as if warding off evil. A third snatched a child who was venturing too close to us and held it protectively wrapped in her arms.

"What on earth is the matter with them?" Lady Middlesex demanded.

One old man dared to come closer than the rest. "Bad," he hissed, his face right at the window. "Not go. Beware." And he spat on the snow.

"Extraordinary," Lady Middlesex said.

The chauffeur returned, driving back the people, of whom there was now quite a crowd. He closed the bonnet, climbed into the driver's seat and started the engine again. Words were shouted at us and we took off to a scene of people gesticulating after us.

"What was that all about, driver?" Lady Middlesex asked, hoping that he miraculously now understood English, but the man stared straight ahead of him as the road dipped precariously downward.

I was now feeling rather uneasy about the whole thing. Had Lady Middlesex misunderstood and made us disembark from the train at the wrong station? Were we in fact in the wrong car? Surely no royal castle could be at such a godforsaken spot as this. Clearly Miss Deer-Harte was echoing my thoughts.

"Why on earth would they choose to hold a royal wedding at such an isolated place?" she said.

"Tradition, apparently." Lady Middlesex still attempted to sound confident but I could sense she was also having doubts. "The oldest daughter always has to be married at the ancestral home. It's been done for centuries. After the ceremony here the wedding party will travel to Bulgaria, where there will be a second ceremony at the cathedral and the bride will be presented to her new countrymen." She sighed. "Ah, well, if one will travel abroad, one is bound to encounter strange customs. So primitive compared with home."

We were slowing down. The driver grinned, showing his pointy teeth. "Bran," he said.

We had no idea what Bran was but we could see that there were lights shining from a rocky outcropping towering over the road. As we peered out of the window we could make out the shape of a massive castle, so old and formidable looking that it appeared to be part of the rock itself. The motorcar stopped outside a pair of massive wooden gates. These slowly rolled mysteriously open and we glided through into a courtyard. The gates shut behind us with loud finality. The motorcar came to a halt and the driver opened the doors for us.

Miss Deer-Harte was first to step out into the snow. She stood, peering up in horror at the towering stone battlements that seemed to stretch into the sky all around us. "My God," she said. "What have you brought us to, Lady M? This is a veritable house of horrors, I can sense it. I've always been able to smell death and I smell it here." She turned to Lady Middlesex, who had just emerged on the other side of the motorcar. "Oh, please let's leave straightaway. Can't we pay this man to drive us back to the train station? I'm sure there will be an inn in the town where we can spend the night. I really don't want to stay here."

"Fiddlesticks," Lady Middlesex said. "I'm sure it will be perfectly comfortable inside and of course we must do our duty to Lady Georgiana and present her properly to her royal hosts. We can't leave her in the lurch. It's simply not British. Now buck up, Deer-Harte. You'll feel better after a good meal."

I too was staring up at those massive walls. There seemed to be no windows below a second or third floor and the only chinks of light shone between closed shutters. I have to admit that I also swallowed hard and all the snippets of conversation came rushing back to me—Binky saying the king and queen didn't want to send their sons because it was too dangerous, and even Belinda making jokes about brigands and vampires. And why had those people at the top of the pass looked at us with fear and loathing and even crossed themselves? I echoed Lady Middlesex's words to myself. Buck up. This is the twentieth century. The place might look quaint and gothic but inside it will be normal and comfortable.

Queenie clambered out of the car and stood close to me, clutching at my sleeve. "Ain't this a god-awful-looking place, miss?" she whispered. "Gives you the willies. It makes the Tower of London look like a nice country cottage, don't it?"

I had to smile at this. "It certainly does, but you know I live in an old castle in Scotland and it's perfectly nice inside. I'm sure we'll have a grand time. Look, here comes somebody now."

A door had opened at the top of a flight of stone steps and a man in black and silver livery with a silver star-shaped decoration hanging at his neck was descending. He was silver haired and rather grand looking with high cheekbones and strange light eyes that glinted like a cat's.

"*Vous êtes Lady Georgiana of Glen Garry and Rannoch?*" he asked in French, which threw us all off balance. "*Bienvenue.* Welcome to Bran Castle."

I suppose I had forgotten that French tended to be the common language of the aristocracy of Europe.

"This is Lady Georgiana," Lady Middlesex said in the

atrociously English-sounding French of most of my country-men. She indicated me. "I am her traveling companion, Lady Middlesex, and this is my companion, Miss Deer-Harte."

"And for companion Miss Deer-Harte has somebody?" he inquired. "A little dog, maybe?"

I suspected he was attempting humor but Lady Middle-sex said coldly, "No animal of any kind."

"Allow me to present myself," the man said. "I am Count Dragomir, steward of this castle. I welcome you on behalf of Their Royal Highnesses. I hope you will have a pleasant stay here." He clicked his heels and gave a curt little bow, reminding me of Prince Siegfried, my would-be groom, who was also related to the royal house of Romania. Oh, Lord, of course he'd be here. That aspect hadn't struck me before. The moment I had this thought, another followed. This couldn't possibly be a trap, could it? Both my family and Prince Siegfried had been annoyed when I had turned down his marriage proposal. And Siegfried was the type who likes to get his own way. Had I been specially invited to this wedding so that I'd be trapped in a spooky old castle in the middle of the mountains of Romania with a convenient priest to perform a marriage ceremony?

I looked back longingly at the motorcar as Count Dragomir indicated we should follow him up the steps.

We entered the castle into a towering hall hung with banners and weapons. Archways around the walls led into dark passageways. The floor and walls were solid stone and it was almost as cold inside as it was out.

"You will rest after exhausting journey," Dragomir said. His breath hung visibly in the cold air. "I will have servants show you to your rooms. We dine at eight. Her Highness Princess Maria Theresa looks forward to renewing acquaintanceship with her old friend Lady Georgiana of Rannoch. Please do follow now."

He clapped his hands. A bevy of footmen leaped out of the shadows, snatched up our train cases and started up another flight of steep stone steps that ascended one of the walls with no railing. My feet felt as tired as if I'd been on a long hike and I realized it was a long way down if I were to stumble. At the top we came out to a hallway colder and draftier than anything at Castle Rannoch, then up a spiral staircase, round and round until I was feeling dizzy. The staircase ended in a broad corridor with a carved wooden ceiling. Again the floor was stone, and it was lined with ancestral portraits of people who looked fierce, half mad or both. Queenie had been following hard on my heels. Suddenly she gave a scream and leaped to grab me, nearly sending us both sprawling.

"There's someone standing behind the pillar," she gasped.

I turned to look. "It's only a suit of armor," I said.

"But I could swear it moved, miss. I saw it raise its arm."

The suit was indeed standing holding a pike with one arm raised. I opened the visor. "See. There's nobody inside. Come on, or we'll lose our guide."

Queenie followed, keeping so close that she kept bumping into me every time I slowed. A door was opened, curtains were held back and I stepped into an impressively large room.

Queenie was breathing down my neck. "Ooh, heck," she said. "It looks like something out of the pictures, don't it, miss? Boris Karloff and Frankenstein."

"Come," the footman now said to Queenie. "Mistress rest now. Come."

"Go with him, Queenie," I said. "He'll take you to your

room. Have a rest yourself but come back in time to dress me for dinner."

Queenie shot me a frightened glance and went after him reluctantly. The curtains fell into place and I was alone. The room smelled old and damp, in a way that was not unfamiliar to me from our castle at home. But whereas the rooms at Castle Rannoch were spartan in the extreme, this room was full of drapes, hangings and heavy furniture. In the middle was a four-poster bed hung with velvet curtains that would have been quite suitable for the Princess and the Pea. Similar heavy curtains covered one wall, with presumably a window behind them. More curtains concealed the door I had just come through. A fire was burning in an ornate marble fireplace but it hadn't succeeded in heating the room very well. There was a massive wardrobe, a dressing table, a bulky chest of drawers, a writing desk by the window and a huge painting on the wall of a pale, rather good-looking young man in a white shirt, reminding me of one of the Romantic poets—had Lord Byron visited these parts? But then Byron had been dark and this young man was blond. The lighting was extremely poor, dim and flickering, coming from a couple of sconces on the walls. I looked around, still feeling queasy from the ride and uneasy from the strange tension that had been building ever since that man had tried to enter my compartment. It wasn't the pleasantest feeling standing in a room with no obvious window or door and I decided to go and pull back the curtains on the far wall.

As I crossed the room I detected a movement and my heart lurched as I saw a white face looking at me. Then I realized it was only a pockmarked old looking glass on the wardrobe door. I pulled back the curtains enough to reveal the window, managed to open the shutters and stood looking out into the blackness of the night. Not a single light shone out from the dark forested hills. Snow was still falling softly and cold flakes landed on my cheeks. I looked down. My room must have been in the part of the castle built on the edge of the rock, because it seemed an awfully long way down into nothing. Far away I detected the sound of howling coming through the stillness. It didn't sound like any dog I had ever heard and the word "wolves" crept into my mind.

I was just about to close the window again when I stiffened, then peered intently into the darkness trying to make out what I was really seeing. Something or somebody was climbing up the castle wall.

Chapter 12

Bran Castle
Somewhere in the middle of Transylvania
Wednesday, November 16

I couldn't believe my eyes. All I could make out was a figure all in black with what looked like a cape blowing out behind it in the wind moving steadily up the apparently smooth stone wall of the castle. Then all at once it vanished. I stood there, staring for a while until the wind picked up, carrying with it the howling of wolves, and snow started to blow into the room. Then I closed the window again. I lay on the bed and tried to rest but I couldn't. Drat that Deer-Harte woman. If she hadn't brought up the subject of vampires, my thoughts wouldn't be running wild at this point. I lay looking around the room. The top of the wardrobe appeared to be carved with gargoyles at each corner. There were faces in the crown molding and—dear God, what was that? A piece of furniture I hadn't noticed, half hidden behind the door curtains. It looked like a large carved wood chest. A very large carved wood chest big enough to conceal a person. Or . . . it couldn't be a coffin, could it?

I got up and tiptoed across the room. I had to know what was inside that chest. The lid was infernally heavy. I was just struggling to get it open when I felt a draft behind me and a hand touched my back. I yelled and spun around. The lid crashed shut with a hollow thud and there was Queenie looking scared.

"Sorry, miss. I didn't mean to startle you. I came in real quiet-like, in case you were still sleeping."

"Sleeping? How can I sleep in a place like this?" I asked.

She looked around. "Blimey. I see what you mean. This is a spooky old place, ain't it? Gives me the willies. Reminds me of the Chamber of Horrors at Madame Tussauds. Except for the bloke on the wall. He's a bit of all right, ain't he?"

"I'm not sure I like him looking at me when I'm in bed," I said, and as I said it I realized that the portrait was directly above the chest/coffin. "What's your room like?"

"A bit like Holloway Prison, if you want my opinion. Plain and cold. And way up in one of the turrets. I don't see myself getting much sleep up there. And you have to go round and round this windy staircase to reach it. I got lost several times on the way down. I'd have ended up down in the dungeons by now, if it hadn't been for one of them blokes in the smashing uniform who rescued me and brought me here. I don't know how I'm ever going to find my way back." She stared at me. "Are you all right, miss? You look awful pale."

I was about to tell her about the thing climbing up the castle wall but then I realized that I couldn't. That Rannoch sense of duty kicked in and I was sure that Robert Bruce Rannoch or Murdoch McLachan Rannoch wouldn't have been frightened by a figure climbing up a wall. I had to appear to be calm and in control.

"I'm absolutely splendid, thank you, Queenie," I said. "Now, I wonder when my baggage will arrive."

Almost on cue there was a tap on my door and the bags were brought in by more tall, dark-haired footmen, all seeming to look identical.

"You might as well put away my clothes and then help me get dressed for dinner," I said. "I wonder where you're supposed to find water for me to wash."

We scouted out the hall and found a bathroom not too far away—a massive cavern of a room with great stone arches rising to a vaulted ceiling. The claw-footed tub in the middle was big enough to go swimming in. A geyser contraption over it presumably supplied hot water.

"I think I'll have a bath before dinner," I said. "Why don't you start running me a bath and then see if you can locate my robe."

I undressed while Queenie unpacked and hung up my things. That's when we discovered that she hadn't packed a robe for me. "Never mind," I said. "I'll have to walk down the hall in my nightdress. There doesn't seem to be anyone else around."

I scooted rapidly back to the bathroom, feeling rather self-conscious in my nightdress, and found the whole place full of steam and the bath temperature hot enough to boil a steamed pudding. What's more the window was jammed shut and it took ages for me to run out half the bathwater and fill it with cold. After that I had a lovely long soak, got out feeling refreshed and looked around for a towel. There wasn't one. Now I was in a pickle. The nightdress that I had worn had become so sodden with steam that it was almost as wet as I was. I had no way to dry off. I'd have to make a run for it.

I pulled my nightdress over my head with great difficulty. It clung to my wet body like a second skin. I opened
the bathroom door, looked up and down the hallway then
sprinted for my own bedroom. That was when I realized I
couldn't remember how many doors down the hallway was
mine. It was two, surely. Or was it three? I was conscious of
the trail of drips behind me, of the puddle forming around
me, and my feet freezing on the stone floor. I stood outside
the second door and tried to open it. It wouldn't open.

I tapped on it firmly. "Queenie, let me in, please."

No answer.

I rapped louder. "Queenie, for God's sake open the
door."

The door was flung open suddenly and I found myself
staring into the bleary-eyed face of Prince Siegfried. He
had obviously just woken from sleep. He looked me up and
down, his eyebrows raised in horror.

"I'm so sorry, I must have the wrong room," I mumbled.

"Lady Georgiana," he exclaimed. "*Mein Gott.* What is the
meaning of this? You are not wearing clothes. Most inap-
propriate. What has befallen you? You have had an accident
and fallen into water?"

"I am wearing something but it's rather wet. You see,
there were no towels in the bathroom and I forgot which
door was mine and . . ." I was babbling on until I heard
Queenie's voice hissing, "Psst. Down 'ere, miss."

"Sorry to trouble you," I said and fled.

Of course when I reached the safety of my room, I discovered that there were towels on the top shelf of the wardrobe.
I dried off still feeling utterly stupid and embarrassed. Of all
doors, I had to knock on Siegfried's. All in all it had been a
long and trying day.

It was lucky that I had had oodles of practice in dressing

myself, as Queenie was more hindrance than help. She got my dress stuck trying to put my head through one of the armholes. Then her idea of doing my hair made me look like I was housing a bird's nest. But eventually I looked presentable, wearing burgundy velvet and the family rubies, and I was ready by the time the first gong sounded.

"I'm going down to dinner now, Queenie," I said. "I'm not sure where you go for your supper, but one of the servants will show you."

Her eyes darted nervously and I felt sorry for her. "I can't be late on the first evening here," I said. "Honestly you'll be all right. Just go down to the kitchen."

I left her looking as if she wanted to follow me and made my own way, with some difficulty, to the predinner gathering in the long gallery. The gallery was hung with more banners, and adorned with the heads of various animals, ranging from wild boar to bears, but it looked bright and festive with hundreds of candles sparkling on crystal chandeliers. The assembled company was dripping with braid, medals and diamonds, reminding me of one of the more extravagant Viennese operettas. I felt the wave of nervousness that always comes over me on such occasions, tinged with the worry that I'll do something clumsy like trip over the carpet, knock over a statue or spill my drink. I am inclined to be clumsy when I'm nervous. I was wondering if I could join the company without being noticed, but at that moment I was announced and heads turned to appraise me. A young man detached himself from a group and came to greet me, his hand outstretched.

"Georgiana. How good of you to come. I don't know if you remember me but we met once when we were children. I am Nicholas, the bridegroom, and I believe we are second cousins or something like that."

His English was flawless, with a typical public school accent, and he was tall and good-looking, with the dark blond hair and blue eyes of many of the Saxe-Coburg clan. I felt an instant stab of sympathy that he was being landed with Moony Matty. He was actually a prince I wouldn't mind marrying myself—if one were absolutely forced into marrying a prince.

"How do you do, Your Highness," I said, bobbing a curtsy as we shook hands. "I'm afraid I don't remember meeting you."

"At a celebration for the end of the Great War. We spent it in England, you know. You were a skinny little thing at the time and we made short work of a box of Turkish delight under a table, if I remember correctly."

I laughed. "And felt horribly sick afterward. Oh, I do remember now. You were about to go off to school. I was envious because I was stuck at home with a governess." Then I remembered something else. "You were at school with Darcy O'Mara, weren't you? He mentioned that you were a good rugby player."

"So you know Darcy, do you? Damned good fullback himself. Plenty of speed. So how do you like the castle?" He grinned impishly. "Delightfully gothic, wouldn't you say? Maria insisted on having the wedding here."

"It's a family tradition, I suppose."

"Maybe for the original family—Vlad the Impaler, reputed to be Dracula, was one of them, I believe. But Maria's family hasn't been on the throne for that long. No, I think it has more to do with Maria's fond memories of summer holidays spent here as a child, and her romantic nature—wanting to be married in a fairy-tale castle." He leaned closer to me. "Frankly I would have preferred somewhere more comfortable and accessible."

"It does seem rather—gothic, as you say," I agreed.

We broke off as a large man barged up to us. "And who is this delightful creature? Introduce me please, Nicholas." He spoke with a heavy accent.

He was pale and light haired with the flat features of the Slav and his uniform was so covered in medals, sashes, orders and braid that he appeared almost a caricature of a general from Gilbert and Sullivan. And I noticed that he had called the prince Nicholas.

A slight spasm of annoyance crossed Nicholas's face. "Oh, Pirin. Of course; this is my dear relative from England. Lady Georgiana, may I present Field Marshal Pirin, head of the Bulgarian armed forces and personal adviser to my father, the king."

"Field Marshal. I'm pleased to meet you." I inclined my head graciously as we shook hands. His hand was meaty and sweaty and it held mine a little too long.

"So from England you come, Lady Georgiana. How is the dear old King George? Splendid old chap, isn't he, but rather boring. Hardly drinks at all."

"He was well when I last saw him, thank you," I said frostily, as I didn't like this supposed familiarity with the king, "although as you have probably heard, the king's health has not been the best recently."

"Yes, I hear this. And the Prince of Wales—is he ready to step into his father's shoes, do you think? Will he do a good job when the old man kicks the bucket, as you say in England, or will he still be the playboy?"

I really didn't want to discuss my family with a complete stranger and one not even royal. "I'm sure he'll be absolutely splendid when the time comes," I said.

The field marshal put a meaty hand on my bare arm and gave it a squeeze. "I like this girl. She has fire," he said to

Nicholas. "She shall sit beside me at dinner tonight and I will get to know her better." And he gave me what could only be described as a leer.

"I'm afraid that my bride has insisted that Georgiana sit close to her at dinner. They are dear friends, you know, and they will want time to chat. Have you met Maria Theresa yet, Georgiana? I know she is dying to see you again. Let us go and seek her out."

He took my arm and led me away. "Odious fellow," he whispered when we were out of earshot. "But we have to tread carefully in Bulgaria at the moment. He is from our southwestern province of Macedonia, and there is a strong separatist movement in that area, wanting to break away from us—and Yugoslavia would like to annex our part of Macedonia to its own. So you see, it's delicate. As long as Pirin holds power, he can keep them loyal. If he goes, they will try to break away. There will be civil war. Yugoslavia will undoubtedly take the side of the break-away province and before you know it another regional, if not world, war will be on our doorsteps. So we flatter and humor him. But he's a peasant. And a dangerous one."

"I see."

"That is why this alliance with Romania is so important. We need them on our side if there is any kind of Balkan conflict. But no talk of gloomy things tonight. Tonight we feast and celebrate my wedding. Ah, there is my lovely bride now. Maria, *Schatzlein*, look who I have found."

I turned to see where he was looking but there was nobody I recognized. Only a slim and elegant creature, obviously dressed from Paris, her dark hair sleekly styled and an ebony cigarette holder in one hand, was moving gracefully through the crowd. When she spotted me, her face lit up. "Georgie. You made it. How wonderful. I am so glad to see you."

And she came toward me arms open.

She was about to embrace me when she stopped and laughed. "Your face, darling. I keep forgetting that people who haven't seen me in a while don't recognize me. It's Matty, your old friend Matty."

"I can't believe it," I said. "Matty, you look stunning."

"Yes, I do, don't I?" she said with satisfaction. "All those months in the Black Forest certainly paid off, didn't they?"

"The Black Forest?"

"They sent me for a cure at a spa, darling. Three months of utter torture, drinking carrot juice, cold baths, long runs through the forest at dawn and calisthenics for hours. But this is the result. Thirty kilos miraculously vanished. And then I was a year in Paris to pick up sophistication and voila. A new me."

I still couldn't stop staring.

"She looks utterly beautiful, doesn't she?" Nicholas said. "I can't believe my luck."

Nicholas put his arm around her and I thought I detected a brief second of hesitation before she looked up at him and gave him a smile.

"You make a very handsome couple," I said. "I congratulate you both."

"And we will have such fun trying on our dresses, won't we?" Matty went on. "I have shipped in a wonderful little woman from Paris, you know. I do love exquisite clothes. Nicky has promised we can live part of the year in Paris, which will make me very happy. But do you remember that awful uniform we had to wear in school? It will be just like old times together with my dear school friends again."

"You have more friends from Les Oiseaux attending?"

"I do. You will never guess. Our old friend Belinda Warburton-Stoke is here."

"Belinda? Here? You invited her to your wedding?"

I was really angry. She had seen me only a week ago and said nothing.

"Not exactly," she said. "The most amazing thing happened. She was touring in this region and her car broke down right outside the castle. She had no idea who lived here or that I was celebrating my wedding. Wasn't it an incredible coincidence?"

"Incredible," I agreed dryly. "So you invited her to stay for the wedding?"

"My dear, I could hardly turn her away, could I? Besides, I knew you'd be thrilled to have her here with us. Belinda was always such fun, wasn't she, and most of the people here are so horribly stodgy and correct. Ah, there she is, over in that corner."

I followed Matty's gaze to the darkest corner of the room I could make out Belinda's back in the elegant peacock blue and emerald green dress she had designed herself. She had her head on one side, listening earnestly to another handsome and blond young man. He was smiling down at her with the rapt attention on his face that most men adopted when anywhere near Belinda.

"Who is that with her?" I asked.

"That's Anton, Nicky's younger brother. I'm afraid it's no good her setting her cap at him. He will have to marry royalty and keep the family firm going, like the rest of us." And she gave a brittle laugh.

The dinner gong sounded.

"You are sitting by me tonight," Matty said. "I want to hear all about what you've been doing since I last saw you. But you need an escort in to dinner. Anton looks as if he's otherwise occupied, so it had better be my brother."

She pushed her way through the crowd, dragging me by one hand.

"Siegfried, you know Georgiana, don't you?"

I knew that Siegfried was of the royal house of Romania but I hadn't realized that he was Matty's brother. How could I have been so stupid?

Siegfried eyed me warily. "Ah, Lady Georgiana. I am relieved to see you are fully clothed again."

"What's this, Georgie?" Matty asked, grinning in a way that reminded me of times at school when she overheard something she wasn't supposed to.

"I omitted to take a towel to the bathroom and I'm afraid Prince Siegfried saw me clad in only a wet nightgown," I said.

"Lucky Siegfried. Let's hope it gave him ideas," Matty said wickedly. "We can't seem to make him show any interest in girls. Papa despairs of him."

"I have told Papa I shall do my duty and marry," Siegfried said. "In fact, I tried to make a suitable match earlier this year. Now please let us drop this subject."

"Stop being such a stuffy old bore, Siegfried, and learn to have fun. Here, take Georgie in to dinner."

She forced my arm through his just as Count Dragomir approached us.

"Dinner is served, Your Royal Highnesses," he said. "May I suggest that you take your places to process in to the banqueting hall, naturally with you at the head, Prince Nicholas, since our own monarch and your father are not present. And may I also suggest that Lady Georgiana be escorted by His Highness Prince Anton?"

"I think Prince Anton is already taken," I said.

Count Dragomir looked horrified. "But she is a commoner. That can't be allowed. Your Highnesses should intervene right now."

"Oh, don't be so stuffy, Dragomir," Matty said. "Honestly. This is an informal occasion. My parents are not present. So stop fussing."

"As you wish, Your Highness." Dragomir bowed low and departed muttering.

"Such a bore," Matty said, shaking her head. As we made our way through to the banqueting hall another couple tried to cut in front of us. It was Prince Anton, with Belinda on his arm.

"Now here's a pretty problem," Anton said, grinning at Siegfried. "Who takes precedence here? Two princes, each of them only the spare, not the heir, and each with a pretty girl on his arm."

"Then I think I win this time," Siegfried said, "because my pretty girl is of royal blood and yours is decidedly not. And what's more, this is my family seat. But good manners demand that you please go ahead of me anyway."

Belinda put on an acting performance to rival my mother. "Georgie, it's you. What a lovely surprise," she cooed. "So you got here safely. I'm so glad. I had a beastly experience. Have you heard about it? If I hadn't come upon this castle, I'd have been done for."

"Poor Belinda's car broke an axle and she had to walk for miles in the snow," Anton said, gazing down at her adoringly. "Wasn't it lucky that we were in residence? Most of the year the castle is unoccupied."

"Belinda tends to be lucky," I said. I still found it hard to forgive her trickery, although I had to admire her gall.

We entered the banqueting room. It was impressively long and high ceilinged with arches along both walls and above them high leaded-pane windows. A white-clothed table extended for its entire length, big enough to accommodate a hundred diners, and footmen in black and silver livery stood at attention behind the gilt chairs. It was all very grand. Siegfried led me to the head of the table and I was seated across from Matty.

"Are your parents not here?" I asked Siegfried, realizing that we were being given places of honor and there was apparently not a king or queen in sight.

"My parents and the parents of Nicholas are supposed to arrive tomorrow," he said. "As will all the other royal guests. We are the advance party, so to speak, and thus we are rather informal." He looked across the table in distaste as Field Marshal Pirin was pushing his way into a seat close to us.

Nicholas saw that Pirin was aiming for me and forestalled him. "I suggest that my godfather sit next to you tonight, Georgiana. I am afraid his English is not brilliant but he tells me that he knows you." He turned to summon somebody. I wondered how many more surprises there would be tonight. Then I saw that the godfather in question was none other than Max von Strohheim, my mother's latest conquest.

"Georgiana, you remember Herr Von Strohheim, don't you?" Nicholas said easily. "And are you acquainted with his charming companion?"

I looked across the table into my mother's startling violet eyes.

"Yes, we are acquainted," I said.

Chapter 13

Later that night

It was not one of my favorite dinners. Max's English was severely limited. My mother was clearly miffed that I was there, a living proof to everyone that she was over thirty.

"You might have warned me that you were coming along for this beanfeast," she hissed at me.

"I didn't know until a week ago when the queen asked me to represent the family."

Those eyes that had wowed audiences on a thousand stages opened even wider. "Why on earth did the queen send you?"

"How about 'It's lovely to see you again, my darling?'" I said.

"Well, of course it is, although you really do need a good hairdresser. I must say I was stunned to find you were here. I would have thought the Princess Royal should have been part of the wedding party, and not you."

"The bride particularly requested me," I said. "We were school friends."

"Ah. Well at last something useful has come out of that school." She leaned across Max and lowered her voice. "You know, this might be a good opportunity for you. Lots of eligible princes and counts."

"Too many," I said, glancing at Siegfried, who was chatting away in German to Max.

"You have to do something with your life, darling. You desperately need a good wardrobe and the only way you're going to get it is to find yourself a rich man."

"Some mothers might actually pay for their daughter's clothes," I said dryly, "but failing that, I'd like to find a job. It's just that there don't seem to be any jobs going for someone like me."

"Girls of your station are not supposed to find jobs," she said with distaste, overlooking the first part of what I had just said.

"You had a job for years until you met Daddy," I reminded her.

"Ah, but I was an actress. I had talent. I see nothing wrong with making use of talents, if you had any."

I was glad when Matty demanded my attention and regaled those around us with tales of our school days, none of which were how I remembered them and all of which put Matty center stage in the escapades. But I smiled and nodded agreement, wishing that the dinner would hurry up and be over. Of course it went on for hours—course after course. The main dish was venison and I was given a leg shank, such a sweet delicate little thing that all I could think of was fawns leaping through the forest. It was cooked very rare and blood rushed onto my plate as I cut into it.

As I pushed it around my plate, pretending to eat it and wondering if I could drop it under the table, I remembered what I had pushed to the back of my mind until now—the figure who had climbed up the castle wall. I wanted to ask Matty about it, but one can hardly say at a royal banquet, "By the way, do you have creepy things that climb up your castle walls?"

Instead I said, "So I hear there are legends of vampires associated with this castle, Your Highness."

"Vampires?" And she gave a peal of laughter. "Oh, yes, absolutely true. Half our family are vampires, aren't they, Siegfried?"

Siegfried frowned. "Since our family originally comes from Germany, that would be hardly likely. However, there are many legends associated with this castle," he said in his prissy way of talking. "Of course the castle was built by Vlad the Impaler, whom the peasants regarded as being in league with the devil, and it is said that the Dracula tale began here. The local peasants are very superstitious. Ask them and they will all tell you of a relative who was bitten by a vampire or met a werewolf. They won't venture out at night, you know, and if anyone dares to venture forth after dark then it's said that person has to be in league with the undead."

"Ah, so that explains the way they crossed themselves when we stopped at the inn at the top of the pass," I said.

"So primitive and illiterate," Siegfried said. "I told Maria Theresa that she should set an example of modern behavior by having her wedding in the capital, but she wouldn't hear of it. She always was a hopeless romantic."

I personally wouldn't have called the castle a romantic spot but I dared to ask, "So do any of these undead creatures climb up castle walls?"

"Castle walls?" Matty asked sharply. "I hope not. I sleep with my window open."

Siegfried laughed mirthlessly. "I believe that vampires are reputed to climb down walls, headfirst. But do not worry, you will be quite safe—as safe as you are at your own castle in Scotland, which I understand has its share of ghosts and monsters."

He turned back to Max and I looked across at my mother. She was in a sulky mood because there was nobody near her to charm. But I saw her looking down the table on several occasions and decided that she was showing interest in Anton. That might prove interesting, watching Belinda and my mother compete for his attention. Of course Mummy was hampered by having Max in tow. Not that that ever slowed down Mrs. Simpson! Amusingly Field Marshal Pirin seemed to think that Mummy was making eye contact with him and he raised his glass to her, leering over it seductively. Mummy shuddered.

"Who is that awful man? He looks like the wicked baron from a pantomime."

"He's the head of the Bulgarian army," I said.

"How terribly democratic of them, inviting soldiers to the royal palace."

"I gather he wields a lot of power and has to be humored," I said.

"I don't intend to humor him," she said. "He keeps looking at me as if he's mentally undressing me."

"Who wishes to undress you?" Max demanded, suddenly showing interest.

"Nobody darling, except you," Mummy said quickly. She waited until Max had resumed his conversation. "His English has improved almost too well now. I liked it when he only understood what I wanted him to."

Field Marshal Pirin obviously had no sensibilities about eating venison. He too had a leg, which he now picked up in one hand while brandishing a wineglass in the other and taking alternate bites and swigs. I felt sorry for Nicholas and Anton if they were stuck with him as a frequent dinner guest at home.

Dinner finally came to an end and we ladies were led off to a salon while the men indulged in cigars and schnapps. Lady Middlesex intercepted me. She was dressed in a fearsome black gown, topped with a helmetlike affair that was no doubt intended to inspire awe among the inhabitants of the colonies. The effect was not unlike those suits of armor I had passed in the corridors.

"Ah, there you are. All settled in, then? Jolly good. Jolly good. We'll be off in the morning. The princess is kindly arranging for a car."

"Is Miss Deer-Harte not feeling well?" I asked, not seeing her among the ladies.

"She's right as rain, as far as I know, apart from being jumpy about staying in a place like this. I had a tray sent up to her room. She couldn't very well be allowed to join a glittering company like this for dinner, could she. She's only a companion."

"Here we are, then, isn't this jolly?" Matty came up to me, her arm linked with Belinda's. "I see you've made quite a conquest there, Belinda. Anton couldn't take his eyes off you all through dinner."

"Belinda's hobby is making conquests," I said. "She has left a long stream of broken hearts across Europe."

"I hope not," Matty said. "Fun is one thing, but broken hearts quite another. I hope I never have to break another heart as long as I live."

As we came into the room I saw a group of middle-aged women, dripping with jewels and furs, examining us critically—or rather it appeared as if they were examining me. They beckoned me over to them.

"You are the Lady Georgiana from England, correct?" one asked.

"Yes, I am."

"Relative of British king?"

"Yes, my father and he were cousins."

She looked at the other ladies and nodded. "Is good. English king has much power."

"So tell me. You know Prince of Wales?" one of them asked. She was dressed in the height of fashion with a sleek cap of Marcel waves and brilliant red lips.

"Yes, I see him often."

"One hears he has a new mistress?" she asked. "An American woman? A commoner?"

"I'm afraid so." There was little point in denying it if the rumor had already reached Romania.

"What she is like, this woman?" my inquisitor persisted. "She is beautiful?"

"Actually not. Rather boyish in features and figure."

"You see." The woman turned triumphantly to her friends. "What do I tell you? Secretly he prefers boys. He will never marry and make a good king, that one."

"Oh, I'm sure he'll do his duty, at the right time," I said.

"The right time? My dear, isn't he already forty? The right time was twenty years ago. It was suggested then that I might be a suitable match for him. But alas, he showed no inclination. Fortunately I married my husband, the count, instead and he still keeps me satisfied in bed, which I'm sure poor Prince Edward could never do."

Her friends laughed.

"They say English men are cold, no?" another of the women asked me. "They cannot feel passion because they are sent to the boarding school too early. You will do well to select a European husband, my dear. More fire and passion."

"Not all of them, remember, Sophia," the first woman said, giving her a warning glance that I couldn't understand. "Maybe the English lady does not want fire and passion. She may be content with good companionship."

They were laughing at a secret joke and I looked around uneasily. Suddenly I had the same feeling I had experienced on the station—someone was watching me. There were several archways along one side of the room and the passage beyond them was in darkness. I thought I could make out a dark figure standing just beyond the archway, but then it could have been the carved stone, or even a suit of armor.

At that moment the men came into the salon to join us. Nicholas came right over to Matty and me. Anton made a beeline for Belinda, and Field Marshal Pirin for my mother, which made Mummy decide that she was getting one of her headaches and excuse herself.

"Didn't you tell me there is an oubliette in this castle?" Anton said to Matty. "We should push Pirin down it. Really the fellow is too much. Did you see his behavior at dinner? Completely boorish."

"Much as I'd like to take up your suggestion, you know he has to be humored unless you want civil war or worse," Nicholas said. "And Father relies on him."

"Relies on him too much," Anton said. "He's getting too big for his boots. If you ask me the man is dangerous. He's using us for his own ends, Nicky. He sees himself as a future dictator, another Mussolini."

"You don't need to worry about it," Nicholas said. "You

can go back to your delightful existence in Paris. I might have to deal with him someday when I become king."

"That's me. The useless playboy," Anton said. "All I'm good for is providing escort to beautiful women." And he took Belinda's arm.

"I didn't ask to be born first," Nicholas said. "I don't particularly want the job, any more than our cousin Edward wants the job in England, I'd imagine." He looked at me for confirmation.

"I don't think most men would want to be king," I said.

"One hopes that Father lives for years, of course," Nicholas said.

We glanced up as Pirin laughed noisily. "That's a good one," he said, slapping his thigh. He was talking to the man who had welcomed us, Count Dragomir, who was not smiling. In fact he looked as if he were in pain.

"Well, I'm turning in," Lady Middlesex declared, appearing at my side. "We've had a long and strenuous day and tomorrow we have to face that pass again. Poor Deer-Harte is already a bundle of nerves." She looked at me critically. "And you look as if you could do with a good night's rest too. Come along." And she took hold of my arm in a firm manner.

Rather than make a fuss I bid my hostess good night and allowed myself to be led away. I entered my room, only to find someone sleeping in my bed. For an awful moment I thought I might have barged into Siegfried's room again. I tiptoed out again hastily and checked the hallway. I was sure this was my room this time. I went back in. The sleeper was none other than Queenie. I woke her up.

"Sorry, miss, I must have dozed off," she said. "It was that cold in here I got under the covers."

"Did you have your dinner?" I asked.

"I didn't like to leave the room, not quite knowing where I was going," she said.

"Oh, dear. Let's see if one of the servants can take you down to the kitchen and get you something now."

"It's all right, miss, thank you kindly," she said. "I think I'd rather just go to bed. I don't quite fancy foreign food at the moment. It's all been a bit much in one day."

I looked at her kindly, thinking how overwhelming it had been for me and then putting myself in her place, straight from a little London backstreet. "Good idea, Queenie. Just help me off with this dress first and hang it up and then you can go. You can find out in the morning where you go to bring up my tea tray."

She went and I was alone in the room. I climbed into bed and lingered for a while before I dared to turn off the bedside lamp. I had always thought of myself as the daring one in the family. I had allowed my brother and his school friends to lower me into the castle well at home. I had sat up all night on the battlements once to see if my grandfather's ghost really did play the bagpipes. But this was different. I felt a profound sense of unease. I wished I still had a nanny in the next room. Finally I curled up into a little ball and tried to go to sleep.

I was drifting off when I thought I heard the smallest of noises—a light click. My eyes shot open, instantly awake. Although the outer regions of my room were pitch-black I was somehow sure that someone was in the room with me. The curtains around the bed obscured my view. I leaned out a little, then drew my head back quickly. The fire had died down but from the glow I could make out a dark figure, moving closer and closer. At last he stood over the bed. I opened my mouth but I was too frightened to move or to scream.

The glow from the fire illuminated his face. It looked just like the young man from the portrait on the wall.

He leaned closer and closer to me and he murmured something in a language I didn't understand. He was smiling, his teeth reflected in the firelight. Everything Belinda had told me about vampires biting necks and the ecstasy of being bitten rushed back to me. In the safety of London and daylight I had laughed with her. But the face above me was all too real and it seemed as if those teeth were heading straight for my neck. However terrified I was, one thing was certain. I was definitely not about to be turned into an undead.

I sat up abruptly, making him leap backward.

"What do you think you're doing?" I demanded in a way that my great-grandmother Queen Victoria would have been proud of.

The young man gave an unearthly moan of horror. Then he turned and melted back into the shadows.

Chapter 14

A bedroom in Bran Castle. Darkness.
Wednesday, November 16

For a while I couldn't move. I sat up, my heart beating so rapidly that I could hardly breathe. Was the creature still in the room with me? How did one ward off vampires anyway? I tried to remember from reading *Dracula*. Some sort of herb or plant? Parsley? No, that wasn't it. I thought it might be garlic. Had I eaten enough of that on the venison to breathe on him? I wasn't about to try to find my way down to the kitchen to locate some. I also thought I remembered that crosses might work, but I didn't have one of those either. Stakes through the heart? I didn't think I could pull that one off even if I had a stake at my disposal.

Then I thought of something more solid, like maybe one of the large candlesticks on the mantelpiece. Surely even a vampire could be kept at bay with a whomp over the head with that. I slipped out of bed, made my way across the room and picked up the candlestick. Then I crossed the room cautiously until I reached the light switch. I turned it on and found nobody there. Of course then I had to lift the various curtains, one by one, experiencing at least one heart-stopping moment when a blast of cold air hit me in the face and I realized that one of the windows was open.

I tried to close it but it didn't latch properly. I told myself that Siegfried's room was next door, but I pictured myself standing at his door in a nightdress again, trying to explain that a vampire had just been trying to bite my neck. Somehow I didn't think he'd believe me. Then I noticed a large tapestry bellpull beside the bed and was half tempted to yank on it and see who it brought. But since they probably spoke no English and I would have felt equally foolish explaining a vampire attack to them, I left it and got into bed, still clutching the candlestick. At least I was relieved knowing that the bellpull was there and if he came back I could summon help before he could get his teeth into me.

The moment I was in bed I realized that I remembered the chest that I hadn't managed to open before. I could never sleep not knowing what was in there. I got up and crossed the room slowly while the portrait of the young man looked down with a mocking smile. I jumped again as I caught sight of my reflection in that wardrobe mirror and it did occur to me that I had never seen the young man's reflection as he came toward the bed. Wasn't that another thing about vampires—that one couldn't see their shadow or their reflection? I shuddered. The lid was too heavy to lift. I struggled and struggled until at last I had it open. To my intense relief it only contained clothing, including a black cape. The interesting thing was that there were some half-melted snowflakes on it, which made me suspect that my vampire visitor had climbed the wall into my room.

I stayed awake for most of the night but received no more unearthly visitors. Toward dawn I drifted off to sleep, then awoke to that strange lighting that indicates the presence of snow. I opened my window and looked out. It must have snowed hard all night, as the turrets and battlements each wore an impressive white hat. The road up the pass was untrammeled whiteness. It would have been pretty in Switzerland with the hillsides dotted with meadows and chalets. Here it just made the crags and the pine forest even more gloomy. And such a feeling of remoteness. I felt as if I were trapped in another time, another world far away from everything safe.

I looked at my watch and realized it was after eight. I would have welcomed my cup of tea but there was no sign of Queenie. In the end I got tired of waiting. I had to dress myself and found my way down to breakfast. The breakfast table was deserted save for Prince Siegfried. He rose to his feet and clicked his heels as I approached.

"Lady Georgiana. I trust you slept well."

"Not exactly," I said.

"I am sorry. Please let our people know if there is anything to do to make you more comfortable."

I could hardly request a guard against vampires, could I? I was glad I hadn't given in to panic and rushed to his room. I'd have to be really desperate before I knocked on Siegfried's door again.

"Today I take the men out shooting," Siegfried said. "Maybe we find a wild boar. But later I hope we have the chance to speak together again. There are matters I wish to discuss with you. Important matters." He got to his feet, gave that jerky little bow of his and departed. Oh, golly, he wasn't going to bring up the marriage thing again, was he? How did one find a polite way to say "Not if you were the last man on earth"?

The sound of voices coming down the hallway made me

look up. Lady Middlesex and Miss Deer-Harte came in, the latter waving her arms as she talked in animated fashion. Lady Middlesex cut her off when she saw me.

"Here's a how-de-doo," she said to me. "We've just heard that the wretched pass is closed. Avalanche or something. The car can't take us to the station. We have to stay here whether we like it or not."

"I really don't think I could face another night in this place," Miss Deer-Harte said. "Did you hear the wind moaning last night? At least I suppose it had to be the wind. It sounded like a soul in torment. And then someone was creeping down the hallway in the wee hours. I couldn't sleep and I was sure I heard footsteps, so I opened my door a crack and what do you think I saw? A dark figure creeping down the hall."

"It was only one of the servants, Deer-Harte. I've told you that already," Lady Middlesex said abruptly.

"Servants don't creep. This man was creeping—slinking as if he didn't want to be seen. Up to no good, I'm sure, if he wasn't a ghost or some other kind of creature."

"Really, Deer-Harte, your imagination," Lady Middlesex said. "It will get you into trouble one day."

"I know what I saw, Lady M. Of course in a castle this size I suppose all kinds of nighttime trysts and assignations occur. One hears about foreign appetites for bedroom activities."

"Don't be so disgusting, Deer-Harte. Ah, there's Her Highness now." She bobbed a curtsy as Matty came in. "So kind of you to allow us to stay on, Your Highness. Much appreciated." And she bobbed a jerky curtsy.

"We didn't have much choice as it happens," Matty said frankly. "There's nowhere else within miles. We're completely snowed in. But there's plenty of room and you are welcome to stay. I must say the snow has put a damper on the festivities. The parents and entourage were expected to arrive today, but it doesn't look as if they'll be able to get here for a while now. Not until the local people have managed to dig out the pass."

"Oh, dear. I do hope the wedding ceremonies can take place on time," Miss Deer-Harte said.

"The actual ceremony is not until next week, so let's hope all is back to normal by then."

"Presumably you'll have various royal representatives arriving," Miss Deer-Harte said.

"This will be a relatively small occasion, mostly relatives," Matty said. "After all, we are related to most of the royal houses of Europe. Horribly inbred, I'm afraid. No wonder we're all so batty." She laughed again and I got the impression that she was playing a part, forcing herself to be gay. "The big formal celebration will take place in Bulgaria when we return from our honeymoon. That's when there will be heads of state and an official blessing in the cathedral and I'm presented to the people as their own dear princess— all that sort of boring stuff."

"I expect you'll have to get used to the boring stuff, as you call it, when you are married to the heir to the throne," Lady Middlesex said. "I find some of my official duties as a high commissioner's wife quite taxing but one knows one's duty and does what is expected of one, doesn't one?"

"I suppose one does," Matty said, giving me a grin. "We're meeting with the couturiere from Paris this morning, Georgie. I'm looking forward to it. In the small salon. It's lined with mirrors so we can admire ourselves."

She paused and stared at the side table that was laden with cold meats, cheeses, fruits and breads, then she turned away. "Alas, just a cup of coffee for me if I'm to fit into that wedding dress."

"Fiddlesticks! One needs a good breakfast to start the day," Lady Middlesex said. "I don't hold with this ridiculous fad of dieting. A cup of coffee, indeed. That won't keep your strength up." As she said this she was piling cold meats onto her plate with abandon. "No egg and bacon, I notice," she added with a sigh. "Not a kidney in sight. Not even a kipper. One wonders how you folk on the Continent survive without a good hot breakfast."

I helped myself and sat down at the table. Matty poured herself a cup of black coffee then wandered off with it.

"I hear the men plan to go hunting," Lady Middlesex said. "How they expect to tramp through this snow, I have no idea. Insanity, if you ask me, but at least it keeps them out in the fresh air for the day. And hunting's a healthy pursuit for young men. Keeps their minds off sex. Maybe we should see if we can borrow snowshoes and go out for a walk ourselves, Deer-Harte."

I was glad she wasn't including me in this plan. I ate as quickly as possible, then excused myself, only to bump into Belinda in the doorway.

"Am I glad to see you," I said.

"That's quite a change from last night, I must say," she said with a frosty stare. "You looked daggers at me for some reason. I couldn't think what I might have done to upset you. It was almost as if you thought I'd spent the night with Darcy—which I haven't, by the way."

"I'm sorry," I said. "I was put out. At first I thought that you'd been invited to the wedding and hadn't told me, and then when I found out how you'd arrived here, I was annoyed by your utter subterfuge."

"Utter brilliance, darling, if you please. You do have to admit it was quite a coup. And you yourself said it would have been a lark if I could come to the wedding with you. So when you rejected my kind offer to become your maid, I decided that the wedding sounded like too much fun to be left out. So I packed my bags, caught the next train here, then I rented the oldest, most decrepit car and driver at the station, in the full knowledge that it would be likely to break down. Of course it did, at exactly the right spot, so I was able to present myself at the castle door and register surprise and delight when I found that Her Royal Highness the Princess Maria Theresa was in residence. 'But we were schoolmates,' I exclaimed and of course was received with open arms."

"You're as bad as my mother," I said.

"Not quite, but I'm working on it," Belinda said with a grin. "There was only one small glitch to my perfect scheme and that was when I didn't recognize Matty. My dear, can you believe the transformation? I suppose it is really she? Where did all those missing pounds go? And what about the moon face?"

"I know. I didn't recognize her either," I said. "She's quite lovely, isn't she? And her bridegroom isn't bad either."

"Neither is his brother." Belinda gave me her cat-with-the-cream smile. "Very satisfactory in all departments. Too bad he's a prince or I might snap him up for keeps. But he'll have to end up marrying someone like you. I know—you could marry him, I could remain his mistress in a delightful ménage à trois."

"Belinda!" I had to laugh. "I'd share a lot of things with you, but not my husband. Besides, Anton isn't the man I have in mind, although I have to admit that among available princes he's the best so far."

"Wouldn't suit you, darling. Too naughty. He told me some of his exploits last night and they made even me blush. Not an ounce of moral fiber in him. That's why we're perfect for each other."

"So I gather you didn't sleep in your own bed last night?"

"What a question to ask a lady! But darling, at beanfeasts like this who does sleep in their own bed? All you hear is curses and grunting as people bump into each other in the dark, tiptoeing between bedrooms. It's too, too funny for words. But I suppose you slept soundly and didn't hear a thing. I gather you've been given a room on the superior floor usually reserved for the family."

"Right next door to Siegfried, as it happens," I said, "but Belinda, that's what I wanted to talk to you about. Someone came into my room last night."

"Not Siegfried!" she exclaimed. "I thought his interests lay in quite another direction."

"Oh, God, no. But worse in a way. I think it was a vampire."

Belinda started laughing. "Georgie, you are too funny sometimes."

"No, seriously, Belinda. There is a spooky portrait hanging on the wall and this man looked just like him. I was half asleep and I woke to see him creeping toward me and then he stood over my bed, muttered something in a language I didn't understand then bent down toward me with this sort of unearthly smile, showing all his teeth."

"Darling! What did you do?" She yanked down my collar. "Did he actually bite you? What was it like?"

"He didn't get a chance. I sat up and demanded to know what he was doing. He gave this sort of unearthly moan and vanished."

"Vanished? As in just melted away, you mean?"

"No, merged back into the darkness, I suppose, but when I finally turned on the light he was no longer in the room. And what's more there's a large chest in the room and inside it was a cape still damp with snowflakes on it. Explain that."

"My dear, how frightfully thrilling," Belinda said. "If I didn't have other diversions to occupy me, I'd volunteer to sleep in your room tonight. I have always wanted to meet a vampire."

"So you believe me?"

"I'm more inclined to believe it was some young count or other, one of Nicky's groomsmen, who made a mistake and got the wrong room when he went to visit the lady of his choosing. It's easy to do in a place like this."

"I suppose you may be right," I said. "I'm going to watch when they set out hunting to see if I recognize him. Whoever it was certainly wasn't at dinner last night. And he didn't look—you know—earthly."

Belinda put her hand on my shoulder. "Georgie, I was only joking in London about vampires, you know. You don't really believe in them, do you?"

"Belinda, you know me."

"I do and that's what worries me. Until now I'd have said you were one of the most levelheaded people on earth."

"I know and I'd agree with you. But I know what I saw and I know the absolute terror that I felt."

"A nightmare, maybe? Understandable in a place like this. Darling, isn't it all too delightfully gothic?"

"But what about the wet cape in that chest? If you want gothic, you should see the chest in my room. Come up and I'll show you."

"If you insist," she said. "Very well. Lead on, Macduff!"

Chapter 15

I led her up the stairs and pushed aside the curtains. Belinda looked around the room and of course her gaze first alighted on the portrait on the wall.

"I say. He's not bad, is he? And look at that sexy open shirt. I wonder how long ago he lived."

"He still lives. That's the whole point, Belinda. I swear he was my vampire last night."

A wicked smile crossed her face. "In that case I may well volunteer to change rooms with you. I wouldn't mind being bitten by someone like him."

I looked at her and realized she was still joking. "You still don't believe me, do you?"

"I think the logical explanation is that you fell asleep with that portrait staring down at you and you had a little fantasy dream about him."

"All right, I'll prove it to you. Look, here's the chest." I stomped across the room to it. "And I bet the cape is still damp. See?"

I flung it open triumphantly, then stopped. The chest was completely empty.

"An invisible cape, how unique," Belinda said.

"It was here, I swear. And when I first came up here I saw someone crawling up the wall."

"Of this room?"

"No, the outside wall of the castle. Just over there."

"But that's impossible."

"That's what I thought. But this—whatever-it-was—climbed up the wall over there and then disappeared."

Belinda put a hand on my forehead. "No, you don't have a fever," she said, "but you must be hallucinating. This isn't like you, Georgie. After all, you grew up in a gloomy place like this."

"We had a couple of ghosts, but no vampires, at Castle Rannoch," I said. "I asked Siegfried and Matty about them. Siegfried made light of it but Matty was definitely cagey. You don't think she's been bitten and become undead, do you? And that's why she looks so gorgeous? She's sold her soul or something?"

Belinda gave that delightful tinkling laugh again. "I think it was more likely to be that expensive cure at a spa, and watching her weight. She has hardly eaten a thing since I've been here."

"Well, I think of myself as a sane, rational person but I've been uneasy since I got here. Before I got here, in fact. I think someone was following me on the train. And someone's been watching me from the shadows here."

"How deliciously dramatic, darling," Belinda said. "What a change from your boring existence in London. You wanted adventure and now you've got it. Who do you think could be following you?"

I shrugged. "I have no idea. I can't think why anybody would be interested in me. Unless vampires are particularly attracted to virgins. Dracula was, wasn't he?"

Belinda laughed again. "In that case my blood will be quite safe. You know, maybe someone is actually following that horrible woman who is chaperoning you. Perhaps her husband has paid to have her bumped off en route. I know I would."

"Belinda, you are so wicked." I had to laugh too now.

Belinda slipped her arm through mine. "Listen. It sounds as if the men are assembling for their hunt." The sound of barking dogs echoed up from down below, mingled with the shouts of men. "Let's go down and watch them and see if your handsome vampire really is still alive and among them. We'll see if you can pick him out in daylight, shall we? Of course, if he's going hunting then he's definitely not a vampire. They can't tolerate the sunlight, you know." She led me down the stairs to a gallery where we could overlook the front hall. A good-sized party of young men had assembled, the fur hats and traditional green jackets making it hard to tell the masters from their servants.

"There you are, plenty of counts and barons and whatnots, all single and all related to you, I suspect. Take your pick."

"I don't see my vampire," I said, studying the young men, some of whom were actually quite presentable as aristocrats go. "That proves it, doesn't it? He's not a normal young count staying at the castle. Now you have to believe me."

"I believe that the local red wine is stronger than you're used to and it gave you vivid dreams," Belinda said. "I say, they're not a bad-looking bunch on the whole, are they? Of course, Anton looks wonderful in his fur hat, doesn't he? So masculine and primitive. I wanted him to take me hunting with them, but I was told it was boys only. Spoilsports. I love shooting things, don't you?"

"Actually I don't. I don't mind grouse because they are so stupid, and I love hunting on horseback but I'm always relieved when the fox goes to earth."

"So what shall we do now?" Belinda looked around the deserted hallways.

"I've got to go and have a fitting for my dress," I said. "You can come and keep me company."

"I might," she said. "It's too bad I'm not still designing dresses or I could have picked up ideas."

"You're not? You've given up your dress design business?"

"Had to, darling." She frowned. "Couldn't afford to lose any more money. Nobody wanted to pay me, you see. They'd always say breezily 'Put it on my account' and when the time came to pay, they'd come up with every excuse in the book. One woman actually told me I should be grateful I was getting free advertising from her wearing my creation and I should be paying her. So I'm now unemployed like you. Maybe I'll be glad to be a maid, soon." She looked up at me with a grin. "So tell me, did you find a suitable maid and bring her with you?"

"I have a maid, but I can't say that she's suitable. Actually she's completely hopeless. She got my head stuck in the armhole of my dress last night, I found her sleeping in my bed when I came to my room and she forgot to come and wake me this morning."

"Where on earth did you find her?"

"She's a relative of my grandfather's neighbor Mrs. 'uggins."

"Well, then, serves you right," Belinda said.

"She means well," I said. "I'm actually quite fond of her in a way. She's been put in a situation quite remote from her normal life and she hasn't had a single bout of tears or panic. But I'll have to find out about that morning tea. I really do expect that much."

As we passed the stairs leading down to the kitchens we saw the young lady in question coming up, wiping the crumbs off her uniform.

"Oh, whatcher, miss," she said. "They don't half eat funny food here, don't they? Cold meat with garlic in it for breakfast. Whoever heard of such a thing? But the rolls were nice."

"Queenie, what happened to you?" I said coldly. "I was waiting for you to bring me my morning tea and to dress me."

"Oh, blimey, sorry, miss," she said. "I knew there was something I was supposed to be doing when I went down to the kitchen. But then I saw other servants having breakfast so I decided to tuck in too before it all went. I wasn't half hungry after missing me supper last night."

I felt rather guilty about this. I should really have made sure that she had had something to eat, but I remembered Lady Middlesex's admonitions about being firm with servants. "In future I expect my tea tray to be brought up to me at eight, is that clear?" I asked.

"Bob's yer uncle," Queenie said.

"And you are supposed to call me 'my lady,' remember?"

"Oh, yeah. I keep forgetting that one too, don't I? My old dad said I'd forget my head if it wasn't joined to my shoulders." She shook with laughter at that. "So what am I supposed to do now?"

"Go up to my room and see which of my clothes need

pressing. I'll want to wear a different dress for the banquet tonight."

"Righty-o," she said. "Where do I find an iron?"

"Ask the other servants," I said. "I have no idea where irons are kept."

I left her trudging up the stairs and rejoined Belinda, who had been watching from the shadows.

"Darling, utterly clueless," Belinda said. "If she were a horse, one would have to have her put down."

"You are wicked," I said.

"I know. It's such fun." She blew me a kiss. "Enjoy your clothes session. If the other bridesmaids are anything like Matty used to look, you'll be the star and all the men will notice you. Toodle-pip."

She blew me a kiss.

⌘

I found the small salon where a bevy of seamstresses were working away with a clatter of sewing machines while a formidable and unmistakably French little woman in black stalked up and down, waving her arms and yelling. A cluster of young girls stood and sat near the fire, some of them in their underslips, while the little woman took measurements. The other girls seemed to know each other and nodded politely to me. Matty came over, took my hand and introduced me in German, then in English.

"My dearest friend from school" she called me, although this was a slight exaggeration. But I didn't correct her and returned the smile she gave me. Why was I suddenly so popular when she hadn't contacted me once since we left Les Oiseaux?

The dresses turned out to be quite lovely and frightfully Parisian chic—a sort of creamy white, long, simple and elegant with a smaller version of the bride's train behind them. What's more, contrary to Belinda's prediction, the other bridal attendants were attractive girls, cousins from German royal houses. One of them was a tall, slim blond girl who looked at me with interest as if she knew me and came over to me.

"You are Georgiana, *ja*? I was supposed to go to England last summer but I became sick."

"You must be Hannelore," I said, light dawning. "You were supposed to stay with me."

"*Ja*. I heard about this. It must have been shocking for you. When we are alone you must tell me all."

I was glad to find that her English in no way sounded like an American gangster movie.

Matty came over to us, wearing her bridal gown, still pinned along the sides. "How do you like the dresses?"

"Lovely," I said, "and your bridal gown is absolutely gorgeous. You'll be the prettiest bride in Europe."

"One has to have some compensations for getting married, I suppose," she said.

"Don't you want to get married?"

"If I had my way I'd like to live the bohemian life of an artist in Paris," she said. "But princesses aren't allowed any say in the matter."

"But Prince Nicholas seems really nice, and he's good-looking too."

She nodded. "Nicky is all right, as princes go. He's kind and you're right. It could certainly have been worse. Think of some of the absolutely awful princes there are." Then she chuckled. "I gather my brother asked you to marry him."

"I turned him down, I'm afraid," I said.

"At least you had the option of saying no, which is of course what I would have done in your shoes. Who would possibly want to be married to Siegfried, unless they were desperate." She laughed again, and again I felt that she was forcing herself to be lighthearted. "So how is your room?"

I couldn't very well say gloomy and vampire ridden, could I? I was formulating a polite answer when she went on, "I gather they gave you the room next to Siegfried's. Maybe they were hoping some sparks would fly!" She chuckled again. "I always used to have that room when we came to the castle for the summer holidays. I love the view from that window, don't you?"

"It's rather snowy at the moment," I pointed out.

"In the summer it's lovely. Green woods and blue lakes and far away from the city and all the stuffiness of court life. I used to ride and swim with none of the rules of court life. It was blissful." And a dreamy expression came over her face.

"There's an interesting portrait on the wall of the room," I said. "A young man. Who is he?"

"One of the ancestors of the family that owned this castle, I suppose. I've never really thought about it," she said. "Castles are always full of old portraits." And she moved on to another subject.

I hadn't realized until the end of that day how much I missed the company of other young women and what fun we'd had at school. There was a lot of giggling and chatting in various languages, mostly German, of which I spoke little, but Matty was ready to translate for me. She looked the fairy-tale princess in her wedding dress with a train yards long, which we were to carry, and a veil falling around her, topped by a coronet.

By the time we had finished, the men came back from their hunt, exhilarated because they had shot a huge wild boar with fine tusks. I was ready for a cup of tea, but instead coffee and cake were offered. I'm sorry but if you're born Brit-

Chapter 16

Still Bran Castle
Thursday, November 17

I couldn't think what to say. My only thought was one of flight. I turned and went back up those stairs as quickly as possible. So it was true. She was one of them. Maybe half the castle was populated with vampires and that was why there was so much tiptoeing around at night. I was actually relieved to find my room still empty. I got into bed and pulled the covers around me. I didn't want to be here. I wanted to be safe and at home and among people I could trust. I'd even have settled for close proximity to Fig, which shows you how low I was feeling.

Tiredness overcame me and I drifted into a deep slumber, only to be shaken awake by Queenie.

"Miss, it's time to get ready for dinner," she said. "I've run you a bath and put a towel in there."

This was a great improvement. My little talk this morning had obviously worked wonders. I bathed, came back to my room and let Queenie help me into my green satin din-

ish there is no substitute for afternoon tea. It's in our gene:
The cake was rather rich and I began to feel sick. I suppos
it was tiredness as I hadn't really slept for two nights. I wer
up to my room, only to find no sign of Queenie. I was nov
becoming annoyed. It would soon be all over the castle if
had to go and look for her every time I wanted something
I was half tempted to yank on that bellpull and send who
ever came to seek out my maid, but I decided that she wa
probably in the servants' quarters wolfing down cake and
would be quicker to find her myself. So I went down stai
after winding stair and then that terrifying wall-huggin;
flight with no banister. I tried to remember exactly wher
I had bumped into Queenie this morning, ducked under a
arch and started down a straight flight of well-worn steps
As I turned into a dark hallway at the bottom I could hea
the clank of pots and pans and the murmur of voices. The
suddenly I started as I saw a figure crouched in a dark corne
The figure looked up at me and gasped

"Oh, Georgie. You startled me." She put her hand up t
her mouth and attempted to wipe it hastily. "Don't mentio
this to anyone, please. I can't help myself. I try, but it's n
good." It was Matty. Her mouth was bright red and stick
and she had blood running down her chin.

ner dress. I looked at myself in the mirror and somehow it hung wrongly. It had been a classic long evening gown before, smooth over the hips and flaring out to a gored skirt, but now it seemed to have a bump on one side, making my hip look as if it were deformed.

"Wait," I said. "There's something wrong with this skirt. It never bunched up like this before. And it seems awfully tight."

"Oh," she said. "Yes. Well . . ."

I looked up at her face. "Queenie, is there something you're not telling me?"

"I didn't think you'd notice," she said, toying with her apron. "I had to fiddle with the skirt because it got a bit scorched when I ironed it. I'm not used to ironing nice stuff like this and the iron must have been too hot." Then she demonstrated how she'd sewn the skirt together over a patch that had two big iron-shaped scorch marks on it. One scorch mark I could understand, but what had made her go back to repeat the mistake?

"Queenie, you are hopeless," I said.

"I know, miss. But I do try," she said.

"I'll have to wear the burgundy again," I said with a sigh, "unless Belinda's got something she can lend me. Run down to her room, tell her what you've done and ask her."

I waited impatiently, wondering how a dressmaker might be able to repair the damage in one of my few good dinner dresses. Almost immediately Queenie reappeared, her face scarlet.

"I knocked and went into her room, miss, and . . . and . . . she wasn't alone. A man was in bed with her, miss, and he was, and they were . . . you know."

"I can guess," I said with a sigh. "Rule number one. Always wait until someone says 'Come in' in the future."

"Yes, miss," she said.

So it was the burgundy velvet again. I did my own hair and went down to dinner. Tonight was to be a more formal occasion, as it was originally expected that various crowned heads would have arrived. Count Dragomir had had his way and insisted on the same degree of formality because there were place cards at the table and I was told I was to be escorted into the banqueting hall by Anton.

As I waited for him to join me, I was joined instead by Lady Middlesex and in her wake Miss Deer-Harte.

"Isn't this too exciting," the latter said. "So kind of Her Highness to insist that we join in the festivities. I've never been to an occasion like this. So glittering, isn't it? Like a storybook. You look very nice, my dear."

"Same dress as she wore last night, I notice," Lady Middlesex said bluntly.

"But very nice. Elegant," Miss Deer-Harte said, smiling kindly. She was wearing a simple flowery afternoon dress, quite wrong for the occasion.

"I hope I can sleep tonight," she whispered to me. "One can only go so long without sleep but the door to my room does not lock and with all that creeping around . . ."

The dinner gong sounded. Anton came to take my arm.

"What-ho, old thing," he said.

"Did you go to the same English public school as your brother?" I asked.

"Yes, only I was expelled," he said. "Or rather, politely asked to leave. Smoking in the bathrooms one time too many, I'm afraid. But I did pick up the lingo rather well." He grinned at me. "Your friend Belinda, she is a cracker, isn't she? A real live wire."

"So I've heard."

"Too bad she is not royal."

"Her father is a baronet," I said. "She is an honorable."

He sighed. "Probably not good enough, I'm afraid. Father is such a stickler for doing the right thing and family comes first and all that bosh. As if it matters who I marry. Nick will be king and produce sons and I'll never see the throne anyway."

"Would you want to?"

"I suppose I prefer my free and easy life, actually," he said. "I've been studying chemistry in Heidelberg. Good fun."

"You're lucky," I said. "I'd have loved to go to university."

"Why didn't you?"

"I'm a girl. I'm supposed to marry. Nobody was willing to pay for me."

"Too bad."

A trumpet sounded. The doors to the dining hall were opened by two of those servants in the splendid black and silver livery and we processed through. This time I was seated with Hannelore on one side of me and Anton on the other. Nicholas sat opposite with Matty on one side, and Field Marshal Pirin had again managed to position himself on the other. If anything, Pirin was wearing even more medals and orders this time. He looked first at me, then at Hannelore and his face lit up.

"This is good. Two pretty girls tonight for me to feast the eyes upon. Very nice. Feast for eyes and feast for stomach at same time." His smile was disconcerting. As my mother had said the night before, he was mentally undressing us.

"Beware that horrid man. He was pinching my bottom yesterday," Hannelore whispered to me.

"Don't worry. I've already encountered him and I'm avoiding him," I whispered back.

I noticed Anton looking around, obviously trying to locate Belinda, who was nowhere in sight, presumably sitting at a far end of the table with the lesser mortals. I couldn't help glancing at Matty and my gaze went straight to her mouth and neck. They looked perfectly normal but then she was wearing a high-necked dress. She caught my eye and then looked down uncomfortably. I found myself checking out the guests at the table to see if any of them showed obvious bite marks on their necks. One woman at the far end was wearing a lot of strands of pearls, but apart from that their necks seemed to be pristine. Maybe vampires bit each other. What did I know?

The meal began, course after course of rich food, culminating in a procession carrying a whole roast wild boar with an apple in its mouth.

"Not the one we shot today," Anton said. "Ours was much bigger."

"Who actually shot it?"

"I did"—Anton lowered his voice—"but we let Siegfried think that he did. He cares about these things, you know."

Throughout the meal Dragomir had been hovering in the background, directing servants like an orchestra conductor. As the main course came to an end he appeared at Nicholas's shoulder and banged on the table with a mallet.

"Highnesses, lords and ladies, please rise," he announced in French, then in German. "His Royal Highness Prince Nicholas wishes to drink a toast to the health of his bride and to her wonderful country."

Nicholas rose to his feet. "If the toasts are to begin, then more champagne, if you please," he said. "How can I toast my beautiful bride with anything less?"

"Forgive me. Of course. Champagne." Dragomir barked instructions and bottles were produced, opened with satisfying pops and poured. And so the toasts began. An endless stream of toasts. At home toasting at formal banquets is a stylized and decorous affair with the toastmaster drawling out, "Pray be upstanding for the loyal toast," and everyone murmuring, "The king, God bless him." Here it was what my mother would have called a beanfeast. Anybody who felt like it could leap up and toast whomever they pleased. So there was a great deal of scraping of chairs and shouted toasts up and down the table.

Dragomir, as toastmaster, tried to keep control of things, banging his mallet with a flourish before each speech. The toasts were conducted in a mixture of French, German and English as hardly any of the party spoke either Romanian or Bulgarian. If the two parties were close enough together they clashed glasses. If they were far apart they raised glasses and drank together, the rest of the diners often joining in with a swig of their own to show solidarity. One by one the men rose to make their speeches and toast their guests. Maria was the only woman who dared to rise and toasted her attendants, so I had to stand up and reach across the table to clink glasses with her. Then Nicholas rose to toast his groomsmen. "These men have watched me grow up from disreputable youth to serious manhood," Nicky said and various men at the table hooted and laughed. "And so I toast you now, you who know my darkest secrets. I drink to my dear brother, Anton, to Prince Siegfried, to Count Von Stashauer, to Baron . . ." Young men rose to their feet as he named them, twelve in all, reaching out to clink glasses with Nicholas. He was speaking in German and I couldn't take in all the names, until I was aware he had switched to English and was saying, " . . . and to my old friend who has valiantly arrived in spite of all obstacles in his path, the Honorable Darcy O'Mara from Ireland."

I looked down the table and there at the far end I saw

Darcy rise to his feet and raise a glass. If my heart had beaten fast at finding what seemed to be a vampire bending over me, it was positively racing now. As Darcy took a sip from his wine, he caught my eye and raised the glass again in a toast to me. I went crimson. I wish I could get over this girl-ish habit of blushing. It's so obvious with my light complex-ion. I was actually glad for once when Field Marshal Pirin rose unsteadily to his feet.

I had noticed that he'd been drinking more than his share of red wine all evening, holding up his glass to be refilled again and again. He had had a good swig at all the toasts whether they applied to him or not. Now he grabbed his glass and launched into a speech in what had to be Bulgar-ian. I don't think anyone else understood, but he went on and on, his speech slurred a little, his face beetroot red, then he thumped the table and finished with what was obviously a toast to Bulgaria and Romania. He drained his glass in one large glug. Then his eyes opened wide in surprise, he made a gagging noise in his throat and he fell forward into what remained of his plate of wild boar.

The company behaved exactly as one would have ex-pected of those who were brought up to be royal. A few eye-brows were raised and then guests went back to their meal and their conversation as if nothing had happened, while Dragomir fussed around, directing the servants to lift the unconscious man and carry him through to a couch in the anteroom. Nicholas had also risen to his feet.

"Please excuse me, I should see if there's anything I can do for him," he said quietly.

At the far end of the table Lady Middlesex had also risen. "I don't suppose there's a doctor in the house. Let me take a look at him. I was a nurse in the Great War, you know." And she strode down the room after them. I noticed that Miss Deer-Harte followed in her wake.

I could hear the murmurs of conversation.

"He was drinking far too much," Siegfried said. He had been sitting on the other side of Field Marshal Pirin. "Every time the servers came past he had them refill his wineglass."

"The man drinks like a fish," Anton agreed, "but I've never seen him pass out before."

"He was disgusting," Hannelore muttered to me. "The way he eats. No manners. And the wrong forks."

I noticed that Darcy had also excused himself from the table and was making his way toward the anteroom. Ice cream was served, then the cheese board was brought around and still neither Nicholas or Darcy reappeared.

When the meal was almost over, Nicholas came back to the table, leaned across and muttered something to Anton in German. I looked to Anton for a translation. He had a strange expression on his face. Before he could say anything Nicholas spoke in a loud, clear voice to the dinner guests.

"I regret to inform you that Field Marshal Pirin has been taken seriously ill," Nicholas said carefully. "May I suggest that, given the circumstances, we ask you all to leave the table and retire to the withdrawing room. I'm sure our hosts, Prince Siegfried and Princess Maria Theresa, will be good enough to arrange for coffee and drinks to be served there."

The only sound was that of the scraping of chairs as the dinner guests rose to their feet.

"Please follow me," Matty said with regal composure that I had to admire.

Anton pulled out my chair for me and I stood with the

rest, feeling rather sick and shaky that the event had taken place so close to me. Anton was staring into that anteroom with a strange expression on his face—a mixture of horror and delight.

"Was it his heart, did your brother say?" I asked.

He took my arm and drew me close to him. "Don't say anything to the others, but old Pirin has kicked the bucket," Anton muttered into my ear.

"He's dead, you mean?"

He nodded but put a warning finger up to his lips. "I can't say I'm exactly sorry. Couldn't stand the bastard, but Papa is not going to be thrilled. I suppose I should go in there and support my brother, although I can't stand the sight of dead bodies in general and I'm sure that Pirin's will be more revolting than most of them."

He held out his arm to me. "I should probably be gentlemanly and escort you to the safety of the drawing room first, in case you faint or something."

"Do I look as if I'm about to faint?" I asked.

"You look a little green," he said, "but I expect I do too. At least he had the courtesy to wait until the meal was over before he died. I'd have hated to miss that wild boar." And he gave me a grin that reminded me of a naughty schoolboy.

"I'm all right. I'll find my own way," I said. "I expect your brother would like to have you with him."

Everyone was behaving with the greatest decorum, leaving the table quietly, some of them glancing across at the archway to the anteroom where Pirin's feet could be seen sticking off the end of the couch. I heard my mother's clear voice over the discreet murmur. "The way that man wolfed down his food and drink he was a heart attack waiting to happen."

I wanted desperately to be with Darcy, but I couldn't

think of a good reason to intrude, as a mere guest at the castle. But I lingered as long as I dared until most of the company had passed through the big double doors and then slowly followed Anton toward the anteroom. As I neared the entrance of the anteroom I heard Lady Middlesex's strident voice saying, "Heart attack, my foot. It is quite clear that the man was poisoned."

Chapter 17

Bran Castle plus dead body
Still November 17

I needed no further reason to enter that room. After all, I had experienced more of my share of murder than most young women of my station in life. I was just about to follow Anton inside when Darcy came out, almost colliding with me.

"Hello," he said. "I was just coming to find you."

"Why didn't you tell me you were coming here?" I demanded.

"At the time of our last conversation I had no idea that you were planning to attend the wedding," he said. "And your terrifying sister-in-law made it quite clear I was never to communicate with you again."

"So when did you ever do what anyone told you?" I asked.

He smiled and I felt some of the tension of the past days melting away. Now that he was here I felt that I could tackle vampires, werewolves or brigands. I was brought back to frightening reality when Darcy pushed past me and grabbed the nearest footman who was starting to clear the table.

"No," he said. "Leave it. Leave everything." The servants looked up at him, confused and suspicious. Darcy poked his head back into the anteroom and beckoned to Dragomir. "I need your help right away," he said. "I don't speak Romanian or whatever they speak in these parts. Please tell the servants not to touch anything and to leave the table exactly as it is."

Dragomir stared at him suspiciously. Darcy repeated the command in remarkably good French.

"May I ask what authority you have here? You are from the police, monsieur?" Dragomir asked.

"Let's just say I have some experience in these matters and my one wish is that we handle this in a way that does not embarrass the royal houses of Romania or Bulgaria," Darcy said. "The servants should not be told the truth at this point. This is a most delicate matter and is not to be spoken about, is that clear?"

Dragomir looked long and hard at him, then nodded and barked a command at the servants. The men hastily put down the plates they were collecting and stepped back from the table.

"Tell them that nobody else is to come into the dining room, and tell them I would like to speak to them shortly so they should not go anywhere."

That command was also repeated, although in surly and unwilling fashion, and I saw inquiring glances directed at Darcy, who didn't appear to notice.

"We should go back in there." Darcy turned to me. "Nicholas will find himself in a pretty pickle, I'm afraid, if we don't do something quickly."

"Is it true, do you think?" I whispered to Darcy. "Was Field Marshal Pirin poisoned?"

"Absolutely," Darcy said in a low voice. "All the signs point to cyanide. Flushed face, staring eyes."

"He always had a flushed face," I said.

"And the unmistakable smell of bitter almonds," Darcy finished. "That's why it's important that nothing is touched on that table."

With that he stepped back into the anteroom with me at his heels. Field Marshal Pirin's body lay on the couch exactly as Darcy had described him, his face bright red and his eyes open and bulging horribly. He was a big man and the couch was delicate gilt and brocade so that his feet hung over the end and one arm was dangling to the floor. I shuddered and forced myself not to turn away. The other occupants of the room appeared to be frozen in a tableau around the body: Nicholas staring down at Pirin, Anton standing behind Nicholas while Lady Middlesex and Miss Deer-Harte hovered near Pirin's highly polished boots. Miss Deer-Harte looked as if she wanted to do nothing more than escape.

"You must telephone for the police at once," Lady Middlesex said. "There is a murderer in our midst."

"Impossible, madam," Dragomir said, reappearing behind us. "The telephone line has come down with all this snow. We are cut off from the outside world."

"And there is not a police station within reach to which you could send a man?"

"A man could probably go on skis over the pass," Dragomir said, "but I advise that we should not summon the police, even if we could, before Their Majesties have been told."

"But there has been a murder," Lady Middlesex said.

"We need someone who can find the culprit before he gets away."

"As to that, madam," Dragomir said, "anyone who tried to leave the castle would not get far in snow like this. Besides, there is only one way out of the castle and a guard is at the gate at all times."

"Then for heaven's sake make sure the guard knows that nobody is to leave," Lady Middlesex said angrily. "Really, you foreigners. Too slipshod in everything."

"Lady Middlesex, I'm sure Prince Nicholas would appreciate it if you didn't broadcast the facts all over the castle at the moment," Darcy said. "I assure you that we will do everything in our power to get to the bottom of this as soon as possible. And nobody is going to be slipshod."

"And you are . . . ?" she asked, turning to focus on him. If she'd had a lorgnette she would have stared at him through it. One almost expected her to utter the words "a handbag?"

"He is my groomsman and good friend Darcy O'Mara, Lord Kilhenny's son," Nicholas said shortly. "A good man to have around if you're in trouble. He was at school with me—the backbone of our rugby team."

"Oh, well, in that case." Lady Middlesex was quite happy now. Anyone who was the backbone of an English public school rugby team had to be all right. "So what do you want us to do?"

"I've told the servants not to touch the table," Darcy said. "One of the first things is to have the cause of death confirmed by a competent physician. I don't suppose there is one of those within reach, is there?" He repeated the question in French.

Dragomir shook his head.

"Then we must find out how the poison was administered. I don't suppose we have any scientific testing at our disposal?"

"I believe you need iron sulfate; that turns cyanide Prussian blue," Anton said, then again he gave that boyish smirk. "So you see, big brother, I did learn a thing or two at university. I'm not sure what iron sulfate is used for—something to do with woodworking or steelworking I believe. So possibly there may be some stored in the castle outbuildings or the forge or something. We could ask Siegfried and Maria."

"No," Nicholas said shortly. "I'd much rather they didn't know yet. Not until I've thought things through."

"Too bad they no longer have a royal food taster at your disposal," Darcy said, then he saw Miss Deer-Harte's shocked face and laughed. "It was an attempt at humor," he said.

"There may be some animals on which we could test various foods," Dragomir said. "I can send a servant to see if any stable cats have had a litter of kittens recently."

"Oh, no," I interrupted hastily, "you're not going to poison kittens. That's too horrible."

"You English with your sentimental attachment to animals," Dragomir said, then he appeared to be aware of me for the first time. "Lady Georgiana. It is not seemly that you should be here. Please return to the other ladies in the drawing room."

"I asked her to be here," Darcy said. "Believe it or not she has also had some experience with this kind of thing. And she's a good head on her shoulders."

Of course I blushed stupidly as they looked at me.

"First things first," Nicholas said. "You must understand that this is a very delicate situation for us and one that could have serious ramifications if the news leaked out. Pirin was a powerful man in my country. It was only his influence at court that kept a whole province from breaking away. If word gets out that he's been murdered—why, we could have a civil war on our hands by the end of the week, or, worse still, Yugoslavia could decide this would be an opportune moment to annex our Macedonian province. So I would prefer it that the true circumstances not be made known outside of this room."

"In that case we should let it be generally thought that he died of a heart attack," Darcy said. "We can't bring him back to life but I presume it was well known that he liked his food and drink, so his death will come as no great surprise."

"That was the general consensus of opinion as we were leaving the dining room anyway," I chimed in. "If nobody else overheard Lady Middlesex then I don't think you'll have much trouble with convincing everyone that he died of a heart attack."

"That's certainly helpful," Nicholas agreed.

Anton said nothing. He was still staring at the body in fascination and revulsion. Suddenly he looked up, his clear blue eyes fastening on his brother's. "I don't think anyone should be told that he's dead before Papa finds out," Anton said. "We should keep up the pretense that he's gravely ill until our parents get here."

Nicholas frowned. "I don't know if we can do that," he said. "I'm sure some of the servants overheard this lady's outburst."

"One assumes they don't speak English," Darcy said.

"Another thing you should consider," Anton said, still looking directly at his brother, "is that Papa may well want to call off the wedding."

"Call off the wedding, why?" Nicholas asked.

"Think about it, Nick. He will want to make a grand show of mourning for Pirin—to let our Macedonian brothers know how highly he regarded him. It would be most unseemly to have any kind of festivities during such a solemn time."

"Oh, damnation, you're right," Nicholas said. "That's exactly what he'll want to do. And Romania could take it as a slight if we postpone the wedding. And think of the expense—we've already invited all the crowned heads of Europe to the ceremony back home in Sofia. And poor Maria. She's so looking forward to her big day. What a horrible mess. Trust Pirin to get himself poisoned at the most inopportune moment."

"What we have to do is keep up the pretense," Anton said, warming to his subject now and strolling past the corpse. "We'll let Papa know that Pirin is ill, but he shouldn't find out that he's dead until we've had the wedding ceremony."

Nicholas gave a nervous laugh. "And exactly how are we going to do that? He'll want to visit the sickroom, I'm sure."

"Then Pirin will be sleeping. In a kind of coma maybe."

"He looks dead, Anton, and in case you haven't noticed, he's not breathing."

"We'll have to have someone hidden behind the curtains and snoring for him," Anton said. "We can do it, Nick. We can pull it off at least until Papa realizes it's too late to call off the wedding."

"You know how thorough Papa is. He'll want to summon his own doctor."

"It will take several days to get him from Sofia."

"He'll at least want to know that a doctor has been consulted," Nicolas insisted.

"Then one of us will have to play the part. Darcy, perhaps."

"He's met me before," Darcy said. "He could have just

missed the doctor who has been called out to a confinement in the mountains."

Nicholas laughed again. "You are turning this whole thing into a farce. It can't work. You know what court life is like. It will probably be all around the castle by morning that he's dead. Servants will come into his room—and who knows when Papa will get here? We can't leave a corpse lying around for days, you know. He'll begin to smell."

"How revolting," Lady Middlesex said.

Nicholas looked up at her, I think just realizing that strangers were present at what was a very private discussion. "We have no guarantee that the people in this room will not say the wrong thing."

"Unfortunately we all know the truth," Darcy said. "You can count on Georgie and me. That leaves Dragomir and the ladies. I'm sure Dragomir wants what is best for his princess and for Romania, but you may have to lock away the ladies until after the ceremony. There are plenty of dungeons here, aren't there?"

"Lock us away? Are you out of your mind, young man?" Lady Middlesex demanded, while Miss Deer-Harte whimpered the word "dungeons?"

"Then they must swear not to divulge anything they have overheard. I'm sure we can trust the word of the wife of a British high commissioner."

"You most certainly can," Lady Middlesex said.

"I must have the word of every one of you here that nothing that has been discussed in this room is ever repeated to anyone else," Nicholas said solemnly. "The future of my country is at stake. Can I trust you? Do I have your word?"

"I've already said you have mine," Darcy said. "I don't see how you're going to pull this off, but I'll do everything in my power to help you."

"Mine too," I said.

"Very well," Nicholas said. "And you, ladies?"

Lady Middlesex frowned. "I would normally not agree to go along with any kind of subterfuge or underhand behavior, but I can see the ramifications could be most difficult for your country, so yes, you have my word. Besides, Miss Deer-Harte and I shall be leaving as soon as transportation can be provided for us over the pass. I am expected by my husband in Baghdad."

"And I can be trusted to hold my tongue," Miss Deer-Harte said. "I have a long history of living in other people's houses and of hearing things not meant for my ears."

Nicholas looked at Count Dragomir. "And you, my lord steward. For the good of our two countries and the happiness of your princess?" Nicholas said to him, holding out his hand. Dragomir nodded and reached out his own hand. "I shall not let you down, Highness. However, I should like to choose a couple of my most trusted servants to be in the know and ready to assist us, should the need arise."

"That makes sense. Choose wisely and let us get to work." Nicholas sighed. "The first thing to do is to get Pirin up to his room. That in itself will not be an easy task. He was a big man when alive. Now he'll be a dead weight."

"I will call in those two servants I suggested," Dragomir said. "Both strong men and loyal to me and the crown. I will station one of them outside his door and I shall keep the key."

"Thank you, Dragomir. Much appreciated," Nicolas said.

"I don't know what you hope to achieve with this, Your Highness," Dragomir said. "It seems like a hopeless endeavor to me."

"Not so hopeless," Anton said. "I've been studying a bit

of chemistry at Heidelberg. The longer you leave it, the more chance cyanide has to dissipate from the system. A heart attack will be tragic but nobody can be blamed for it but the man himself. My father needs time to think out his strategy. We are giving him time."

I had been the silent onlooker until now but I took a deep breath. "It seems to me there is one thing you are all overlooking," I said. "And that's the murderer. Who wanted Pirin dead so strongly that he was prepared to take a risk and kill him in public?"

Chapter 18

Still Thursday, November 17
Still snowed in.

They all stared at me, as if I were putting a new thought into their heads.

Then Anton gave an uneasy chuckle. "As to that, the only two people who were glad to see the last of him were Nicholas and myself, and we are not stupid enough to risk our country's future by bumping him off."

"I can't think of anyone else here who actually knew the man, let alone would have had a motive to want him dead," Nicholas said.

"There are always ongoing feuds and hatreds seething in the Balkans," Darcy said. "Who is to say that one of the servants here does not come from an area where they have a longtime feud with Macedonia, or whose family has not suffered at the hands of Pirin?"

Dragomir shook his head. "That is most unlikely," he said. "These men belong to the castle, not the royal family.

Local men. They live and work here year-round. Our men are Transylvanian through and through."

"Money can always buy loyalty," Darcy said. "The people of this area live a harsh life. If an instigator or anarchist were to pay them enough money, which of them might not be tempted to slip a little pill into food or drink?"

"That, of course, is the big question, isn't it?" I said. "How was the poison administered? We were all sitting together at table. We all ate the same food and drink."

The others nodded thoughtfully.

There was a sound from outside the archway and a servant appeared saying something to Count Dragomir. Dragomir looked up. "This man says that Prince Siegfried sent him to see what was happening. The prince was about to come in himself. He was annoyed at being told to stay away."

Nicholas stepped forward to block the man's view of Pirin's body. "Please tell the prince that Field Marshal Pirin is being taken to his room," he said to Dragomir in French. "He appears to have suffered a heart attack and there is regrettably nothing that anyone can do, other than wait and see if he pulls through. Sleep and perfect quiet are what he needs."

Dragomir repeated this and the man withdrew. Dragomir turned back to us. "I have asked the two men in question to present themselves. They will carry the field marshal's body to his room."

"Excellent," Nicholas said.

"But what about the tables?" Dragomir asked, looking through at them. "Our men will become suspicious if they are left untouched. They will know that something is wrong."

"That's true," Darcy said. "Then we will rescue Pirin's plate and glasses while we can, and they can take the rest.

We have to assume that the poison was designed for one person and not randomly sprinkled on some part of the meal."

"The meal was at an end, anyway," Anton said. "Besides, I don't see how anyone could have poisoned the food. It was served to all of us from the same platters. The risk of setting aside one slice of poisoned meat or one poisoned potato to be put on a particular plate is too great."

"It is impossible," Dragomir said. "The platters come up from the kitchen in the dumbwaiter. They are handed to servers who whisk them to the table as rapidly as possible so that the food stays hot. There are too many links in this chain."

"I suppose it's possible that a particular server could put a cyanide capsule on one special morsel of food as he came through from the serving area," Darcy said thoughtfully, "but as you say, the risk of making a mistake is great." He broke off as two burly men appeared at the door. Dragomir intercepted them and spoke to them for a while in a low voice. They looked across at the body and nodded. Then they went over to him and lifted him between them. It was clearly heavy going.

"You and I had better help, or they'll never get him up the stairs," Nicholas said to his brother. "It may be easier if we seat him on a chair and carry him that way."

"Your Highness. That would be most unseemly," Dragomir said.

Nicholas laughed. "I'm afraid this is an occasion on which we put protocol aside, if we wish to succeed," he said. "Your job is to go ahead of us and make sure the coast is clear." He looked at the rest of us.

"And your job is to go back to the party and act normally. If asked about Pirin's health be vague. And remember the vow you made."

"But what about the investigation?" Lady Middlesex demanded. "And the plates that should be tested?"

"I'll retrieve them now and keep them safe," Darcy said. He went through to the dining room and wrapped Pirin's china and glasses inside a couple of napkins. "I moved the dishes around a bit to create some confusion," he said. "The removal of one place setting might make the servants suspicious. And if you don't mind, Count Dragomir and Prince Nicholas, I think I should have a word with the servers before they disperse and can gossip among themselves. I'll need you to translate for me, Dragomir."

"So your job is to keep the stiff upper lip, as they say in England, ladies," Nicholas said. "Go back to the party and be merry and gay."

"I think we should go straight to bed, Deer-Harte," Lady Middlesex said. "This has been most distressing for all of us. I sincerely hope that we can get away tomorrow and resume our journey back to normal life."

Miss Deer-Harte nodded. "Oh, I do hope so. I told you when we arrived that I sensed this was a place of death, didn't I? I am seldom wrong in my intuition."

And so they left. Darcy turned to me. "You should go back to the party. Above all keep talking to Maria and Siegfried so that they don't follow us. I'll come and join you when I can."

And so our group dispersed.

I tried to slip into the drawing room without being noticed but it seemed that everyone was on edge and Siegfried got to his feet as I came in.

"What news, Lady Georgiana?"

"I'm afraid I'm no medical expert," I said, "but everyone seems to think that the poor man suffered a heart attack. They have carried him to his room. There's not much more that can be done for him apart from letting him rest."

"I feel desolate that there is no doctor in our midst and no way of summoning one other than sending one of the cars back to Brasov. And given the condition of the pass, that could not be accomplished until morning."

The group was still sitting in subdued silence.

"Well, I'm not at all surprised he had a heart attack," my mother said, loudly and cheerfully. "That bloated red face is always a sign. And the way he ate and drank."

"He is a peasant. What can you expect," Siegfried said. "Nothing good ever comes of elevating these people to positions of power. It goes to their heads. Let those who are bred to rule do the ruling—that's how I was brought up."

"Siegfried, you are so stuffy," Matty said. Then she stood up. "I'm sorry the poor man has been taken ill, but enough gloom for one evening. It is my wedding celebration after all. Let's bring in some music and dance a little."

"Maria, do you think that's seemly?" Siegfried asked.

"Oh, come on, Siegfried, it's not as if there's been a death in the house. He may be right as rain by tomorrow and he won't be disturbed by us down here. These friends have come from all over Europe to celebrate with me and I want to dance."

She gave a command and the carpet was rolled back. A pianist and violinist appeared and soon a lively polka was played. I stood beside Siegfried as Matty dragged one of the young counts onto the dance floor. Siegfried always looked as if there were a bad smell under his nose. At this moment the expression was exaggerated. Then he turned to me and clicked his heels.

"I should see if the patient requires anything of me," he said. "After all, I am the host in my father's absence. It is not right that I neglect Prince Nicholas in his hour of need."

"Oh, I think that Dragomir has organized everything

beautifully," I said. "He's a good man. Everything runs like clockwork here."

"Yes, he is a good man," Siegfried said.

"Is the administration of this castle his only responsibility, or is he usually in Bucharest with the royal family?"

"No, his duties are confined to this place," Siegfried said. "He is not of Romanian birth, which would make him unpopular with the people."

"But you are not of Romanian birth either," I said, laughing. "None of the royal families in this region are natives of their countries."

"Ah, but we are of royal blood. That is what matters. People would rather be ruled by true royalty, wherever they come from, than by upstarts who would abuse their power."

"So where does Count Dragomir come from?"

Siegfried shrugged. "I can't quite remember. One of those border areas that has changed hands many times, I think. Just as Transylvania itself used to be part of the Hapsburg Empire."

"Interesting," I said. "The history of this whole area is fascinating, don't you think?"

"One long disaster," Siegfried said. "One long history of being overrun by barbarians from the East. Let us hope that Western European civility will finally bring peace and prosperity to these war-torn lands." He looked around again as he spoke. "I really feel that I should at least go up to the sick man's bedroom to make sure that he has all he needs."

He was about to leave. I did the unthinkable. "Oh, no, dance with me, please." And I took his hand and led him onto the floor.

"Lady Georgiana!" His pale face was flushed, apparently affronted by my boldness. "Very well, if you insist."

"Oh, I do. I do," I said with great enthusiasm.

He placed one hand upon my waist and took the other in his. His hand felt cold and damp, rather like clutching a fish. So my decision to dub him Fishface had been quite accurate. It wasn't just his face that was fishy. I forced my mouth into a bright smile as we glided around the floor.

"So," he said, "can one assume that you have finally come to your senses? You have seen the light, *ja?* Realized the truth about the situation?"

What situation was he talking about? Did he know something about Pirin's murder? Had he arranged for it? Or was he talking about vampires, by any chance? He wanted to know whether I had discovered the horrid truth about his family. I had to tread carefully. I was, after all, a guest in a snowed-in castle, with the telephone lines down and miles from any kind of help except for Darcy and Belinda.

"What situation is this, Highness?" I asked.

"You have realized that it is important for you to follow your family's wishes and make the correct match. You understand the importance of duty."

What exactly was he talking about? Then he went on and light dawned.

"Of course I realize that ours would be a marriage of convenience, like so many royal marriages, but you would find me a considerate husband. I would allow you much freedom, and I think you would have a pleasant life as my princess."

The words "not if you were the last man on earth" were screaming through my head, but I couldn't let him stomp off to find Pirin, could I?

"Highness, I am flattered that you even consider me as your bride when there are many ladies present of higher status than I. Surely Princess Hannelore would be a better match for you—a fellow German and a princess, not just a relative of the royal family."

"Ah," he said, his face clouding. "She would, of course, have been an excellent choice, but she has let it be known that she does not wish to settle down yet."

She's turned him down, I thought, trying not to smile. Good old Hannelore!

"She is very young," I said tactfully. "She may wish to experience life a little before she takes on the responsibilities of royalty."

Siegfried sniffed. "This I find ridiculous. Girls of her station marry at eighteen all the time. It is not good to let them have too much freedom and to become too worldly. Look at my sister. She was allowed to spend a year in Paris and now—" He broke off, checked himself then said, "At least she too has come to her senses. She realizes where her duty lies and has made an excellent match."

At the edge of the dance floor I saw Belinda's face light up and realized that Anton had rejoined the crowd. So had Nicholas. But there was no sign of Darcy. The music ended to polite applause. Siegfried clicked his heels to me. "I enjoyed our dance and our little talk, Lady Georgiana. Or now I shall call you simply by your first name, and you may call me Siegfried when we are in private. In public I still expect you to call me 'sir' or 'highness' of course."

"Of course, sir," I replied. "Oh, look, Prince Nicholas has returned. I wonder if he has news about the patient."

Luckily Siegfried took the hint and strode over to Prince Nicholas. I saw the latter gesturing and explaining, presumably preventing Siegfried from taking a look at the patient for himself. Belinda and Anton passed close to me.

"You and Siegfried looked awfully pally," she muttered.

"If you're trying to make Darcy jealous, it's not going to work. I gather he's sitting at Pirin's bedside all night."

"That's as pally as I ever plan to get with Siegfried," I said. "Let's just say that I did it for a good cause."

I looked around the room, my head suddenly spinning with the conversation and bright lights and the whole strain of the evening. If Darcy was spending the night playing guard to Pirin, then there was no point in my staying awake. Suddenly all I wanted was to be quiet and safe and away from danger. I slipped away unnoticed and made my way up to my bedroom. There was no sign of Queenie, which didn't surprise me. She was probably snoring by now. I checked the window to make sure the shutters were fastened securely from the inside. I even opened the wardrobe and, after several deep breaths, the chest, and, satisfied that I was the only person in the room, I pushed a heavy chair against the door and undressed. But I was loath to turn the light off. Did vampires come through walls, I wondered; or through locked shutters? Anything that could crawl up that castle wall could probably do a lot of improbable things. I climbed into bed and pulled the covers up around me. The fire still glowed in the fireplace but had done little to take the chill off the room. I couldn't close my eyes. I kept checking first one corner then the next, seeing those faces glaring down from the molding and the corners of the wardrobe, and then my gaze drifting to that chest.

"You are letting your imagination run away with you," I told myself. "There is a good explanation for all of this, I'm sure. It's an ordinary room and you are quite safe and—"

I broke off and sat up suddenly. There was now a completely different portrait hanging on the wall.

Chapter 19

Night in the chamber of horrors, Bran Castle
Thursday, November 17

Instead of the attractive and rakish young man there was now a different face staring down at me. This one looked as if it came from an earlier time, with a stylized royal sneer, not unlike Siegfried's, a high collar and a velvet hat like a powder puff perched on his head. I got out of bed to examine it more closely. The paint was cracked and lined like in so many old paintings. That's when I realized something about the other picture—the paint had been daubed on, in the manner of more recent art. And there was something about the freedom of the strokes that indicated French impressionists or later. It had been a relatively new painting.

I lay in bed, trying not to look at the supercilious stare of the man in the portrait, and tried to calm my racing thoughts. Too much had happened since I set out from London. There had been the man watching me on the train, the man who had tried to come into my compartment. Then that same feeling of being watched on the station platform.

Then the creature crawling up the wall, the young man from the portrait bending down over my bed, his teeth bared, Matty with blood running down her chin and now a dead field marshal. Miss Deer-Harte had called it a house of horrors and it seemed she wasn't wrong. But how did they link together? What possible reason could someone want for following me on a train? If the place was really populated with vampires, why kill someone with poison? Nothing made sense. I curled up into a little ball and wished I had never come. I also wished I knew which room was Field Marshal Pirin's because Darcy was there and all I wanted was his reassuring arms around me. It did cross my mind to wonder what he was doing here. Had Nicholas really invited him to be part of his wedding party or had he pulled off another spectacular wedding crash? After all, when I first met him he had dragged me to crash an important society wedding and he made it clear that he did this kind of thing on a regular basis. It was his way of ensuring that he had a good meal once a week, and, I suspect, he liked the thrill of it too.

At last exhaustion overcame me and I must have drifted off to sleep because I awoke to an almighty crash, and not of a wedding. I leaped out of bed so fast I almost levitated, instantly awake and regretting that I hadn't slept with the candlestick beside me this night. All I could make out from the glow of the fire was a large, bulky figure in white, standing just inside my door.

"Who's there?" I demanded, trying to sound fierce and confident and realizing that whoever it was stood between me and the light switch.

Then a voice said, "Sorry, miss."

"Queenie?" I said, anger taking over from fear. "What on earth are you doing? If you came to undress me, you're about two hours too late."

"I wouldn't have disturbed you, miss, and I didn't mean to knock anything over," she said, "but I had to come down to you. There's a man in my room."

"At any other time I would have said that was wishful thinking," I said.

"No, miss, honest truth. I woke up and he was just standing there, inside my door. I was that scared, miss, I didn't dare move."

"What did he do?" I asked, not wanting to hear the answer.

"Nothing. Just stood there, as if he was listening. Then I must have given a little gasp, because he turned and looked at me, then he opened the door and crept out, just like that. I came straight down to you, miss. I ain't going back in there for nothing." She had come over to the bed by now and was standing beside me, a rather terrifying figure in her own right in a voluminous flannel nightgown, her hair in curling papers. "You do believe me, don't you, miss?"

"As a matter of fact I do," I said. "I also had a man in my room last night." And a man had just been killed tonight, I didn't add. Was a stranger in the castle, attempting to hide out in the servants' quarters, or was it the resident vampire, who drifted around as he pleased?

Suddenly I decided that I was angry. I was not going to be a timid little mouse any longer. My Rannoch ancestors wouldn't have run away just because of a few vampires. They would have gone to find the nearest wooden stake, or at least a clove of garlic.

"Come on, Queenie," I said. "We're going back up to your room. We're going to get to the bottom of this right now."

With that I wrapped my fur stole around me and stepped out into the corridor.

"Lead on, Macduff," I said.

Queenie looked confused. "My name's 'eppelwhite, miss," she said.

"It's from the play we don't name," I said, quoting my mother, the actress. "Never mind. Come on. If we hurry we may catch him. Did you get a good look at him?"

"Sort of," she said. "The shutter doesn't close properly and the moon was actually shining in through my window. He was young, fair haired, thin." She paused. "That's about it, really. I couldn't see his face. But there's no point in going back up there now, is there? By the time I left my room he'd gone. And I didn't spot no one on the way down 'ere."

"We'll check it out, just in case," I said and strode down the hall so fast she had to run to keep up with me. Up a long and winding stair we went, round and round until we came out into what had to be one of the towers. Cold silvery moonlight filtered past the shutters, creating strange dark shadows. I have to confess that I was already feeling less brave than I had been in my room. When I saw the shadow of a man standing behind a pillar, my heart almost leaped into my mouth until Queenie said, "It's another of those suits of armor, miss. It nearly scared the pants off me the first time too."

"I was just being cautious," I said and tried to walk past it nonchalantly. It wasn't easy to do, with the empty eye slits in that visor staring at me. I could have sworn those eyes followed me. We reached Queenie's room, and I flung open the door and turned the light on. It was, as she had described it, spartan in the extreme. A narrow cotlike bed, two shelves, a hook on the wall and an old-fashioned washstand. Not even a jolly picture on the wall to cheer things up.

"Well, there's certainly nowhere to hide in here," I said.

"And I can't see any reason why anyone would want to come in here, either."

"Me neither, miss. Unless he was just ducking in here because he didn't want to be seen."

"Queenie, you're surprisingly bright sometimes," I said.

"Really, miss?" She sounded surprised. "My old dad says I must have been twins because one couldn't be so daft."

I went across to her window, opened the single shutter and looked out. Moonlight had turned the snow into a magical scene—deep and crisp and even sprang to mind. The only sound was the sigh of the wind around the turrets, then I thought I detected from far away a howl. It was answered by another howl, close by, this time. And I thought I saw a wolf slinking into the forest.

Of course my mind went straight to werewolves. If vampires appeared to really exist, then why not other creatures of the underworld? This was, after all, Transylvania. Was it in any way possible that the man Queenie had just encountered had now climbed down the castle wall and transformed himself into his wolf form? Or did that only happen at the full moon? The sensible part of me, that sound Scottish upbringing, was saying "rubbish" very loudly in my head, but on a night like this, in a place like this, I was prepared to believe anything.

As I leaned out farther and looked around I saw something snakelike and gleaming in the moonlight, dancing close to me with a life of its own. I leaped back until I realized that it was only a rope, hanging down the wall. If someone had climbed up here, he had been aided and abetted by a person already in the castle. And if someone had entered this way, he had gone again.

"You're right, Queenie. There is no sense in standing

around getting cold," I said. "I'm sure your mystery man is long gone. I'm going back to bed."

"Can't I come with you, miss?" She grabbed at my nightie sleeve. "I can't sleep up here, all alone, after what happened. I know I wouldn't sleep a wink. Honest."

"You want to come downstairs to my room, with me?"

"Yes, please, miss. I'll just sit on the rug by the fire if you like. I don't care. I just don't fancy being alone."

I was about to say that it simply wasn't done but she looked as white as a sheet, and I wasn't feeling too steady myself.

"Oh, very well," I said, not wanting to admit that I too was grateful for the company. "I suppose I can make an exception this once. Come on, then."

We retreated back to my room, encountering nobody along the way. Once in my room I got into bed. Queenie sat dutifully on the hearth rug, hugging her knees to her chest, giving a good imitation of Cinderella. My kind heart won out over every ounce of my upbringing. "Queenie, there is actually plenty of room in this bed. Come on, you'll freeze sitting there."

Gratefully she climbed into bed beside me. I found the warmth of another body beside me comforting and fell asleep.

Chapter 20

Bran Castle
Friday, November 18

I was awoken by the blaring of horns. It was the sort of sound I associated with an army going into battle or alerting a castle's occupants to the enemy's advance and it caused me to leap out of bed. I didn't think that conquering armies showed up unannounced these days in central Europe, but one never knew and I didn't want to be caught in my night attire. I fumbled with the shutters, which had iced up, and flung them open just in time to see a procession of big black motorcars flying royal standards crawling up the snowy ramp to the castle. Heralds were standing on the battlements blowing on long, straight horns. The pass must have opened and the kings and queens had arrived.

I closed the shutters hastily to keep out the bitter chill and decided that morning tea would be welcome before I had to be presented to visiting royalty. It was quite light and surely tea should have arrived by now. . . . That was when I remembered Queenie. I looked back at my bed where

Queenie still lay blissfully sleeping, mouth open. It was not a pretty sight.

"Queenie!" I yelled, standing over her.

She opened her eyes and gave me a vague smile. "Oh, 'ello, miss."

"The royal party has just arrived. I should be ready and dressed to be presented. Oh, and I'd like my morning tea. So up you get."

She sat up slowly, yawning her head off. "Right you are, miss," she said, not moving.

"Now, Queenie."

With that she staggered to her feet, then looked down at herself. "Lawks, miss, I can't go walking around in me nightie, can I? What would people say? I wouldn't half get an earful!"

"No, I don't suppose that would be an acceptable thing to do, but I don't have a robe I can lend you. Because you didn't pack me one." I opened my wardrobe. "Here, you'd better have my overcoat. Bring it back when you come up with my morning tea."

She paused at my doorway. "This tea bit. What am I supposed to do?"

"Go to the kitchen, tell them you've come for Lady Georgiana's tea tray and carry it up to my room. Now, is that too hard?"

She frowned. "Okay, bob's yer uncle, miss." And with that she sauntered out. That girl will have to go, I thought. Thank heavens I hadn't taken her on for the long term.

I decided not to count on help with my morning toilet, so I was washed and dressed by the time she reappeared, red faced and panting, carrying my tea tray. "There ain't half a lot of stairs in this place, miss," she said. "Oh, and there was a bloke asking after you."

"What kind of bloke?"

"Ever so handsome, miss. Dark hair and he spoke proper English too. Not like one of them wogs."

"And what did he say?"

"He said it was about time you roused yourself and he was waiting for you in the breakfast room."

"Oh," I said, feeling my cheeks going pink. "Then I'd better get straight down there, hadn't I?"

"'Ere, what about the tea what I just brought up for you?" Queenie demanded.

"You drink it," I said. "Oh, and my shoes need polishing."

With that I ran down the hallway. One of these days I'd better learn to be masterful with servants. Lady Middlesex was quite right. Not that I thought that Queenie would ever learn.

Darcy was alone, sitting with a cup of coffee in front of him as I came into the breakfast room. He rose to his feet as I entered.

"Well, if it isn't Sleeping Beauty," he said. "What sort of time do you call this?"

"I don't know. What time is it?"

"Almost ten."

"Oh, crikey," I exclaimed. "I had a disturbed night last night. I must have been making up for it."

"And what disturbed you?" He was looking at me in that special way, half laughing, that made my insides go weak.

"My maid woke me up to say there was a man in her room."

"Lucky maid. What did she want you to do about it? Give her your blessing or come and watch?"

"Darcy, it's not funny," I said. "She was terrified, poor thing. I went up to see, but of course he'd gone."

"Was it a hot-blooded Romanian who fancied a prim English miss?"

"I told you it wasn't funny, Darcy," I snapped. "I know exactly how she felt because the same thing happened to me the night before."

"Who was it? I'll see to him."

"Nobody I knew," I said, secretly delighted by this response. "In fact I think it might have been a vampire."

I saw the smile spread across his face.

"Don't you dare laugh," I said and hit him. He caught my hand in his and held me, looking down at me.

"Come on, Georgie. I know this is Transylvania, but you don't believe in vampires any more than I do."

"I didn't, until I came here," I said. "But there was definitely a strange young man bending over my bed, smiling at me and saying something in a strange language, and when I sat up, he just melted away into the shadows."

"Then I'd have to say that he was probably in the wrong room and got as big a shock as you did when you sat up. That sort of bed hopping goes on quite a lot in places like this, you know. Or perhaps you don't. You've led a sheltered life."

"But he looked just like the man in the portrait on my wall," I said. "Only last night the portrait had been changed, and someone was climbing up the castle wall. . . ."

"Up the wall? That's a pretty suicidal thing to do."

"Well, someone did it and there was a cloak in the chest in my room, with snowflakes still on it, and then it vanished."

"Dear me, it all sounds very dramatic," he said.

"Don't you believe me?"

"I'd suspect that the rich food has given you vivid dreams, my sweet."

"It wasn't dreams," I said. "I've felt a sense of danger

since I came here. Lady Middlesex's companion said that she sensed death as we arrived. And explain to me why all these other strange things have been happening."

"What strange things?" His tone was suddenly sharp and his grip tightened on my wrist.

"Well, to begin with there was someone spying on me on the train. He tried to come into my compartment and then at the station—" I broke off because he was grinning again. "What now? Don't you believe me?"

"Oh, absolutely. I have to confess something. The person on the train was I."

"You?"

"Yes, I got wind of which train you were traveling on and I thought it would be a good idea to keep an eye on you. I hadn't counted on the old battle-ax keeping me at bay."

"But wait a minute," I said. "If you were on the same train as us, how did you get here? An avalanche blocked the pass right after we came through."

"It certainly did," he said. "By the time I'd found a car willing to drive me to the castle, the wretched road was blocked."

"So how did you manage to make it here?"

"Used my initiative, my dear. Got a lift as far as I could, then bargained for some skis and skied over the pass. I must say it was a delightful run all the way down to the castle."

"You're pulling my leg."

"Absolutely not. Would I lie to you?"

"Sometimes, I'm afraid."

He was still holding my wrist and we stood there, staring at each other. "I don't ever remember lying to you," he said. "Omitting some of the truth, maybe, on occasions when I wasn't allowed to tell you everything."

"So tell me the truth now. Are you here because Nicholas

invited you to be his groomsman, or to keep an eye on me, or because you decided to crash another wedding?"

Darcy smiled. "What would you do if I said I couldn't tell you?"

"I'd say you've probably been sent here, by somebody you can't tell me about. Undercover, for some reason."

"Something like that. Let's just say that certain people felt it would be good to have some eyes and ears on the spot, in case of trouble."

"So you were expecting trouble?"

"Come for a walk with me," he said, taking my hand.

"Where?"

"In the castle grounds."

"There is deep snow, in case you've forgotten."

"Then go and put on your boots and coat. I'll meet you down here in five minutes."

"But I haven't had breakfast," I said, looking longingly at the spread on the sideboard.

"Breakfast can wait. We may not have another chance to be alone together. At this minute Their Royal Highnesses are greeting their respective parents and relatives, so we can slip away undetected."

"All right," I said. "Just let me pour myself a cup of coffee."

I gulped it down, then hurried up to my room, where, of course, I discovered that Queenie had forgotten to return my overcoat and thus had to wait while she went to her room to find it. Darcy was waiting impatiently at the foot of the stairs. The guards at the door saluted us as they opened it. Snow had been cleared from the courtyard, where the various motorcars now stood. We crossed it to the big outer gates. The gatekeeper looked at us with surprise when we indicated we wanted to go out. Much snow, he said in German. And nobody was to leave.

"We just go for a small walk. English people need fresh air," Darcy replied. So having decided we were mad English people, he opened a small door beside the big gates and we stepped through into the outside world. Pristine snow stretched before us. The boughs of the fir trees were bent heavy with snow and every now and then there was a soft whoosh and thud as snow slid off to the ground below. It was so bright that it was dazzling. Darcy took my hand and we crunched across the snow, keeping to the tracks the motorcars had made until we were among the trees at the base of the great crag on which the castle stood. An icy blast whistled down from the pass, freezing my nose and ears. The silence was absolute, except for the rattle of a dead branch in the wind.

"This is nice," I said, my breathing hanging like smoke in the chill air. "Nice but cold."

"I wanted to talk to you away from prying eyes and ears," Darcy said. "I wanted to sound you out on Pirin's death. Nicholas's parents arrived this morning. His father will want to know the truth sometime. Nicholas can't keep on pretending forever, and I'd like to have found out who might have killed Pirin before then, so that hopefully an international incident can be averted."

I nodded.

"You must have some ideas on the subject," he said.

"Actually I don't," I said. "I was sitting opposite him at dinner. And I don't see how he could have been poisoned. The only people who came anywhere near him were servers and Dragomir. The servers put food from the same platter on everyone's plate, and as for wine, well, the rate he was drinking it, his glass was being constantly refilled."

"You saw it being refilled, did you?"

"Yes, I did. From the same carafe as everyone else."

Darcy frowned. "Cyanide takes effect almost instantly," he said, "so it's unlikely to have been in the food because he'd cleaned his plate pretty well. Unfortunately he knocked over and spilled the remnants of his wine when he collapsed, but there doesn't seem to be any residue in his glass."

"Is it possible to put cyanide into some kind of capsule, so that it wouldn't work on the system until it was digested?"

Darcy nodded. "Possible, I suppose, but at the rate he was chomping and drinking, it seems likely he would have bitten through a capsule much earlier."

I nodded. "I suppose he would."

"Baffling," Darcy said. "Well, now that the pass is open I can send out the utensils to the nearest laboratory for testing and perhaps we'll know where the cyanide was hidden. But that still brings us to motive."

"Oh, I can think of a lot of people who'd want Pirin dead," I said.

"Can you?" He looked at me sharply.

"Well, he was an odious man, wasn't he?" I laughed uneasily. "He ogled women, he insulted men. He called Nicholas by his first name, you know. In public. Imagine an English general calling the Prince of Wales David. Only Mrs. Simpson dares to do that."

"I'm well aware that Nicholas and Anton disliked him," Darcy said, "but they are both intelligent young men. They realized his importance to the stability of the region. And if one of them wanted to kill him, there would have been better opportunities. They were out hunting, I gather. Why not mistake him for a wild boar? For that matter why not push him out of the train on the way here?"

"You're a bloodthirsty person at heart, aren't you?" I asked.

He grinned. "Oh, no, my dear, I'm a romantic. But I've seen plenty of hard reality in my life. So who else would have wanted him dead?"

"What about the servers?" I asked. "Did you have a chance to talk to them?"

"Only very briefly, but I have their names, and again, I can have someone look into their backgrounds further when we are back in communication with the outside world. But as far as I could gather they all seemed to be as that Dragomir chap described them: local men, long in the employ of this castle and thus with no reason to be concerned with what happened in Bulgaria."

"Which leaves Dragomir himself," I said. "He was standing behind the table. I wouldn't have noticed if he'd moved forward and dropped something onto Pirin's plate or into his glass. What do you know about him?"

"Dragomir? Very little."

"Do you know, for example, that he is not from Romania?"

"He's not?"

"Siegfried told me. He said that was why he hadn't risen higher in Romanian government. He comes from a border area that has changed hands several times. He could be in the pay of another government."

Darcy's eyes lit up. "He certainly could be. Good thinking, old bean."

I had to laugh.

"What?"

"I didn't know you thought of me as 'old bean.' I'd hoped for something a little more romantic."

He moved closer to me and slipped his arms around my

waist. "I'll reserve those words for the bedroom at some more opportune moment," he said and then he kissed me. "Mmm, what deliciously cold lips. They need warming up." The second kiss was not so gentle and left us both breathing hard. "I suppose I should be getting back to help Nick and Anton," Darcy said, releasing me with reluctance from the embrace. "Any minute now their father is going to want to visit the field marshal's bedside. I've no idea how we're going to pull this off, and I just wish that I had something concrete to tell them about Pirin's death. I can ask Siegfried about Dragomir, but again I can't find out much more about him until the telephone service is restored."

"And Siegfried will want to know why you are interested in Dragomir's past," I said. "He may be obnoxious but he's not stupid. He wanted to go up to the field marshal's room to check on him last night, and I had to dissuade him with my feminine wiles."

Darcy burst out laughing. "I don't think that feminine wiles work particularly well on Siegfried," he said.

We started to walk back up the slope to the castle.

"Siegfried talked about marriage again last night," I said.

I'd expected him to find this amusing. Instead he said, "Perhaps you should accept. You might not get a better offer. Princess Georgie, maybe Queen Georgie one day."

"Don't say that, even in jest," I said. "You wouldn't wish me married to Siegfried, would you?"

"I'm sure he'd let you keep a lover, since his own interests lie elsewhere."

"He actually said that. I suppose it's the way it's done in royal circles, but it's not for me."

I felt Darcy's grip tighten on my hand. "Georgie, you know I'm a rotten catch," he said. "I have nothing to offer a woman. I don't even have a nice little castle in Ireland any longer. I live by my wits and I can't see how I'm ever going to support a wife. So maybe you should think more sensibly and forget about me."

"I don't want to forget about you," I said shakily. "I don't need a castle."

"I can't see you being happy in a little flat in Putney," Darcy said. "And I don't think your family would be too happy either. But anyway, I'm not ready to think of settling down yet. I have to make my mark in the world first, and you have to experience more of life."

We walked the rest of the way in silence. Would I be happy in a little flat? I was thinking. Would I be able to fit into a world I didn't know, living a life only just getting by, with no luxuries, and with a husband who couldn't tell me about his career but who disappeared for long periods? I decided to put the future on hold for now.

Chapter 21

As we approached those formidable gates I looked up at the castle and a thought struck me. "Darcy, that man I saw climbing up the wall—the one who came into my bedroom. You don't think he had anything to do with Pirin's death, do you? You don't think he was sent here with that mission?"

Darcy frowned. "I don't see how any outsider could have administered the poison. As I said, death is usually almost instantaneous. And I discount your theory of vampires." He glanced at me and saw my mouth open, about to speak. "That man bending over you . . . who knows, maybe one of Nicholas's groomsmen took a fancy to you. Or more likely someone got the wrong room. It's easy to do in a place like this."

"I know," I said, remembering with embarrassment. "I went to Siegfried's door by mistake. His room is next to mine."

Darcy laughed. "Well, that explains everything, doesn't

it? I'll wager the young man was paying a nightly visit to Siegfried. No wonder he was shocked to see you instead."

I considered this as we went back up the steps. It did seem a likely explanation and one that I liked better than anything supernatural. It didn't get us any closer to solving who killed Field Marshal Pirin, but at least it made sense.

The door guards stepped forward smartly to open the castle doors for us. They saluted although their expressions betrayed that we were mad for trying to venture forth on a morning like this. In the entry hall we encountered Lady Middlesex and Miss Deer-Harte, dressed in their overcoats.

"Oh, there you are. We've been looking all over for you. Where have you two been?" Lady Middlesex demanded.

"Just for a quick hike over the pass," Darcy said.

"Rubbish," Lady Middlesex said. "Nobody could go far in this sort of snow."

"We went for a little walk," I corrected.

"Oh, so a walk is possible after all. These stupid people are telling us that the snow is too deep to go anywhere and they didn't seem to understand when we asked them for snowshoes," Lady Middlesex said. "Really these foreigners have no stamina at all."

"It is deep, actually," I agreed. "We only walked in the tracks the tires made."

"Dashed annoying," she muttered. "It seems that none of the drivers are prepared to drive us back over the pass yet. They say that it was bad on the way here and they're not going to risk it again yet, with the promise of more snow. So it looks as if we're still stuck. But at least we can be useful in your investigation into that man's death. When do we have our first council of war?"

"I'm going to find Prince Nicholas this very minute," Darcy said. "I'll let you know later." We left them and walked up the stairs to the main floor. "Those women are going to be trouble," Darcy muttered to me. "Poking their noses in and saying the wrong thing at the wrong minute. Can't you do something to distract them? Or better yet find a suitable dungeon and lock them in it?"

"Darcy." I laughed.

"I'm sure a castle like this must have an oubliette," he went on, chuckling now.

"You are terrible. And I don't see what I can do to distract them. I don't even know my own way around."

"They're going to ruin everything if they are left loose," Darcy said. "For God's sake try to keep an eye on them."

"I will," I said.

"Oh, and Georgie," he said, reaching out his hand to me as I turned away. "Take care of yourself. Someone in this castle has already been killed."

I considered that statement as I went slowly down the hall to my room. Someone in this castle was a ruthless killer. Not that the killing affected me in any way. It had to be of a political nature, carried out by someone who either wished to cause trouble between Balkan states or was a communist or anarchist. Maybe our own government suspected that trouble was likely and that was why they had sent Darcy— one never knew with him. But such a killer wouldn't pose any threat to someone like me, who was only thirty-fourth in line to a distant throne. But I had been threatened in a different way, hadn't I? The vampire bending over my bed. The strange man in Queenie's room. I didn't see how the two could be related. If vampires had wanted to kill Field Marshal Pirin, I imagined they would have done a far more impressive job of it—hurled him from the battlements or sent a great statue crashing onto his head, or even bitten his neck and turned him into one of them. Poisoning with cyanide was all too human a crime. . . .

I was startled from my thoughts by the figure with the raised arm until I realized it was just the suit of armor that had frightened Queenie. Really it was almost as if someone had arranged this castle to provide the maximum amount of shocks to visitors!

∽∾

In my room I found Queenie, sitting on my bed with a cup of tea in one hand and a biscuit in the other. She didn't even have the grace to jump up when I came in.

"Whatcher, miss," she said, attempting feebly to brush the crumbs from the front of her uniform.

"Queenie, you really will have to learn how to address your mistress properly," I said. "The correct thing to say is, 'Hello, my lady' or 'Welcome back, my lady.' Is that really too hard to learn?"

"I do try," she said, making me wonder whether she was a secret bolshie and doing this deliberately to let me know that she was my equal. This then started a whole train of thought in my mind. How much did one really know about servants? She had just shown up on my doorstep and I had no way of knowing who she really was. While I didn't think that anyone could pretend to be as stupid as she was, maybe the same circumstances were true for other servants in the castle. Maybe one of them had come here with the express purpose of killing Pirin.

"You can help me off with my coat and boots, Queenie," I said.

"Bob's yer—yes, me lady," she said. Maybe there was hope after all.

"Oh, by the way," she added as she took my coat, "there was a message came for you from the princess. She hoped you were feeling all right because she hadn't seen you this morning and to remind you that you were supposed to be meeting the other bridal attendants for a dress fitting at ten thirty."

I glanced at my watch. Ten forty-five. "Oh, golly," I said. "I'd better get going then. Oh, and give me that dress you scorched. Maybe one of the dressmakers can fix it for me if she has a moment."

I went back down the various staircases as fast as I dared because the steps were worn and smooth and the going was treacherous. In the great hallway at the bottom I encountered Lady Middlesex and Miss Deer-Harte, still wandering around in their coats.

"We thought we might follow your example and go for a little stroll," Lady Middlesex said. "Since the snow was apparently not too deep for you."

"It was lovely out there," I said, trying to convey enthusiasm. "A walk is a good idea. Good fresh mountain air." I didn't add the word "freezing" to that sentence. At least I'd done what Darcy had asked and sent them out of the way for a while. I didn't think even someone as hearty as Lady Middlesex could take that kind of cold for long, however.

At the doorway to the salon I heard the sound of girlish laughter and I paused, my mind racing back to that disconcerting moment when I had stumbled upon Matty the evening before. I had seen her with blood running down her chin and she had begged me not to tell anybody. She couldn't help it, she had confessed. Was it too improbable to believe that she had been bitten by a vampire and had become one of them? Darcy had been so amused by my stories of vampires that I hadn't even mentioned Matty to him. I suppose it did sound ridiculous to anyone who hadn't experienced it personally. I would have thought it ridiculous myself if it hadn't happened to me. My nightly visitation could be explained by a case of mixed-up rooms, but then a normal room-hopper would not need to climb up walls—let's face it, would not be able to climb up walls. And where could an outsider have come from with the pass closed and no habitation nearer than that inn, and snow too deep to walk through? I am normally a sensible person, I told myself, but the things I had witnessed defied rational explanation.

I took a deep breath, opened the door and went in. Matty rose from the sofa near the fire and came to meet me. "My dear Georgie," she said. "Are you well? I was worried when nobody had seen you this morning."

She looked and sounded completely normal, but she was wearing a scarf around her neck that would hide any bite marks.

"I'm quite well, thank you," I said. "Darcy O'Mara and I went for a little walk."

"Nicky's groomsman? Ah, so that's where your interests lie. Poor Siegfried, he'll be devastated."

That's when I remembered that I had actually not discouraged Siegfried the night before. Oh, no, Siegfried didn't really think I had changed my mind, did he?

"Of course, you're lucky," she said. "Nobody would mind whom you married. It wouldn't make any difference to world peace."

"My sister-in-law is keen for me to make the right match, and I think the queen expects me to cement ties with the right family," I said.

"It's such a bore being royal, isn't it?" She slipped her arm through mine and led me over to the other young women at the fire. "I'm really becoming convinced that communism is a good idea. Or maybe America has it right—choose a new leader every four years, from among the people."

"America maybe," I said, "but look at the mess in Russia. Communism doesn't seem to have made life for the ordinary people better there."

"Who cares, really." Matty gave one of her slightly fake laughs. "So no more talk of politics or any other boring subject. We are all going to be happy and enjoy my wedding. I could have killed that awful man for spoiling the evening last night."

"I don't think he intended to have a heart attack," I said cautiously.

"Maybe not, but I'm still angry with Nicky for inviting him. This morning Siegfried was muttering about trying to send one of the cars to Bucharest for the royal physician and Mama and Papa were distressed to hear that one of our guests had become sick."

"I don't think it was Prince Nicholas's choice to bring Pirin along with him," I said. "He's a powerful man in that country. I rather suspect he does what he wants."

"Well, I certainly didn't invite him to my wedding," she said. "He invited himself. I rather wish he'd hurry up and die and then we could all stop worrying about him. It's like a cloud of gloom hanging over us, knowing he's lying up there."

I didn't like to say that her wish had been granted. She turned to the other girls and obviously repeated what she had said in German, as it produced a titter of nervous laughter. I observed her critically. She was so different from the needy, unconfident girl I had known at school. I was almost prepared to believe she wasn't the same person. I'd already been fooled by one imposter this year, so surely two was a little much. And her parents obviously recognized her as their daughter, so she had to be Matty, but she had certainly grown up in a hurry. The couturiere approached, clapping her hands as if she were directing a flock of chickens.

"Highnesses, we have no time to waste. So much work to be done. Now, who is ready to volunteer to be first today?"

I was anxious to get out of there and find out what was happening with Nicholas and Darcy. I was also uneasy in Matty's presence. "I will, if you like," I said.

The dress was fitted with nods of satisfaction. "This young lady has no curves, like a boy," our couturiere said to her assistant in French. "On her the dress will look right." I wasn't so sure that having no curves and looking like a boy was a compliment but I took it for one, especially as she had very little to do in the way of pinning and altering. When I glanced at myself in those walls of mirrors a tall, elegant creation stared back at me. I noticed that the room was suddenly quiet and saw that the other girls had stopped talking and were now watching me.

"Georgie, I did not think that you would grow up to be so chic," Matty said. She came to stand beside me and put her arm around my waist as we stared at ourselves in the mirrors. "Wouldn't Mademoiselle Amelie and the other teachers be surprised if they saw us now. What a shame we are wasted in a remote castle in Romania. We should be on the French Riviera, or in Hollywood, flirting with all the men-about-town, don't you think?"

I laughed with her but my cheeks were very pink. It was the first time anyone had ever suggested that I might be elegant one day. Maybe there was some of my mother's blood in me after all.

I had just been unpinned from my dress and was retrieving my more practical jumper and skirt when there was a tap at the door. One of the seamstresses was directed to go and returned with a letter. Matty looked at it, then handed it to me. "From one of your admirers." She gave me a knowing look.

I glanced up at the door as I recognized Darcy's firm black scrawl. *I need to speak to you immediately,* it said.

"I'll be back," I said.

"A midmorning tryst. How romantic. Siegfried will be jealous." Matty wagged a finger and the other girls giggled as I went to the door. I hoped she was just joking. For a second I felt a stab of a different kind of fear—had I been brought here to be bride of this particular Frankenstein after all? Frankly if it was a choice between life with Siegfried and a bite from a vampire, I think I'd prefer to be undead. But I didn't have long to consider this as Darcy was waiting outside the door for me.

"Ah, there you are," he said, drawing me to one side. "Look, something has come up and I have to go."

"Go? Go where?"

"We've run into a complication," he whispered. "Nicholas's father demanded to be taken straight to see Pirin."

"Oh, Lord, so I suppose the game's up."

"Not yet. We kept the curtains drawn so that it was pretty dark. The firelight actually made his skin look reddish. I slipped into the room and hid under the bed, then I snored loudly to make it sound as if he was still breathing."

I started to laugh, it was so absurd.

Darcy smiled too. "It worked once, but the king is very concerned. He wanted to send one of the cars to bring his personal physician from Bulgaria immediately."

"How did you stop him from doing that?"

"Nick persuaded him that there was a good hospital with modern equipment in the nearest city and it would be better if Pirin were transported there immediately."

"Oh, no, what are you going to do?"

"I've volunteered to go to the hospital with him, since Nicholas can't leave his bride."

"But what good will that do? They'll pronounce him dead as soon as he arrives."

"If he arrives," Darcy said. "I'm also going to be driving and unfortunately the car is going to go off the road into a snowdrift somewhere up on the pass. By the time I've gone for help poor Field Marshal Pirin will have died, so there will be no point in summoning the personal physician. And the news of the tragic death won't reach the castle until after the wedding."

"So you're not going to be here for the wedding either?" The disappointment in my face must have shown.

"I have to do this, my love," he said. He raised his hand to my cheek. "I'm the only one who can do it, but I want you to help Nick and Anton in any way you can."

"Of course," I said. "Take care of yourself."

"You too." He leaned forward and kissed my forehead, then he went down the stairs without looking back.

Chapter 22

Still in Bran Castle

I returned to the salon.

"That was quick for a tryst," Matty said.

"He just had a message to give me," I said. "Your future father-in-law wants the field marshal to be taken to a hospital immediately and Darcy has volunteered to accompany him."

"Thank God he's going," Matty said. "Now we can return to enjoying ourselves."

I excused myself soon after, having decided not to ask one of the seamstresses to save my scorched dress. The way those sewing machines were clattering away indicated that they were busy enough already. Maybe when all the dresses were finished, I'd try again. I came into the hallway in time to run into Lady Middlesex and Miss Deer-Harte. "I don't know how you two managed to go for a walk in that snow," Lady Middlesex said accusingly. "We only ventured a few yards before Deer-Harte sank up to her middle. Had a dashed difficult time getting her out."

"I'm sorry," I said. "We walked in the tracks the cars had made."

"Better get you up to your room, Deer-Harte, before you catch your death of cold," Lady Middlesex said. "Saw them loading the field marshal's body into one of the hearses, by the way. And Mr. O'Mara went off with him. I hope they're taking him to a place where a proper autopsy can be performed."

I put my finger up to my lips. "Remember we're not supposed to be talking about this," I said. "Field Marshal Pirin has gone to hospital."

"Oh, yes. Right. Of course." She grinned like a naughty child. "Not that it matters. I'm sure none of the servants understand a word of what we're saying."

"I'm sure it's very easy to listen in on conversations in a castle like this," I said. "We have a laird's lug at Castle Rannoch—you know, a secret room where you can listen to conversations in the great hall. And sound carries through all the pipes in the bathrooms, so I'm sure it must be the same here."

"Well, I believe in calling a spade a spade," Lady Middlesex said, annoyed now that I'd caught her out. "I don't hold with trickery and deceit. Not the British way, you know. And if there is a murderer loose in this castle, then it's high time he was found."

I looked around to see who might be listening to this outburst. Luckily the hall appeared to be deserted, but at that moment I heard footsteps coming up the stairs. Prince Nicholas came toward us, taking the steps two at a time.

"Well, that's been accomplished, thank God," he said. "My father saw him off."

"How did you manage that?"

Nicholas grinned. "We carried him down to the car, wrapped head to toe in blankets against the cold. Father never had a chance to see any more of his face than a mustache peeping out. Good old Darcy. Splendid chap. Now we can hope that it takes a long time to mend the telephone wires."

"So when do we hold the council of war?" Lady Middlesex demanded.

Prince Nicholas looked wary. "War?"

"I mean when do we meet to plan strategy and work out how we are going to solve this?"

"Oh, right." Nicholas looked as if meeting with Lady Middlesex was not what he had in mind.

"We should pool our brains on this one, and our observations," she said. "Deer-Harte thought she noticed one of the servants acting shiftily."

"Very well. No time like the present, I suppose," Nicholas said. "Maria is still with her ladies and the dressmakers, I presume?" I nodded. "So I'll find Dragomir and my brother and we'll meet in the library in fifteen minutes. Agreed?"

"Just gives you time to get out of those freezing wet clothes, Deer-Harte," Lady Middlesex said.

I was making my way up to the floor that contained the library when I remembered that I hadn't had any breakfast and took a detour to the breakfast room in the hope that there was still a roll I could grab. The room was empty but for Belinda, sitting alone at the table with a coffee cup in front of her.

"Where have you been?" she asked. "I've been looking everywhere for you."

"I got up late and then went for a walk with Darcy," I said.

"How romantic. But where is everyone else? The place is like a morgue."

"Matty is having a dress fitting with her attendants and you know that the royal party arrived, don't you?"

Belinda frowned. "Oh, yes. Anton deserted me to rush to the side of his papa. And they all seemed to be heading for the sickroom of that awful man Pirin."

"Pirin's now on his way to hospital, thank goodness," I said, feeling strange about lying to my best friend.

"So why aren't you at the dress fitting?"

"I went first. And I have such a perfect lack of figure that not much alteration was involved."

"Good, then you and I can do something fun together. What shall it be?" She got up and slipped her arm through mine. "Not that this is the sort of place that I consider to be fun. No casino, no shops. Thank God for sex, or I'd be bored to tears."

"Belinda! You really shouldn't say things like that where they can be overheard."

She laughed. "There's nobody in the room but the two of us. Besides, it's the truth."

"You were the one who wanted to come here," I reminded her.

"Well, it did seem like a good lark at the time," she said. "And I have to admit that Anton is rather scrumptious. But now his parents are here, I'm afraid he'll have to behave like a good little boy. So what shall it be? Do you want to go and look for your vampires? We could find where their coffins are stored."

"Stop teasing. I know what I saw, why won't anyone else believe me?"

"But darling, of course I believe you, and I'm dying to meet a vampire." She attempted to drag me from the room.

"I'm sorry, but I can't come anywhere with you at the moment," I said. "I have to meet—" I stopped hastily. Of course I couldn't tell her that I had to meet the princes or she'd want to come along. "Lady Middlesex," I finished. "I have to meet Lady Middlesex and Miss Deer-Harte." I tried desperately to think of a reason for this meeting that would sound unappealing to Belinda. "She's writing a history of Sandringham House and she wants my insights."

Belinda wrinkled her nose. "I think I'll go and take a long bath so I can try out my new Parisian bath beads. The bathrooms seem to be unoccupied at this time of day. Toodle-pip."

I breathed a sigh of relief, put a slice of cheese onto a roll and fled. I arrived at the library to find that the others were already assembled, sitting around a big oval mahogany table in the center of an impressive if gloomy library. Shelves of leather-bound volumes rose into darkness, and a gallery circled the library at about twelve feet above our heads. High, narrow windows threw shafts of sunlight onto the floor, illuminating the dust motes. There was a pervading smell of must, dust and old books. I took the empty chair next to Lady Middlesex and opposite Nicholas and Dragomir.

"Sorry I'm late," I said. "I got held up by—" I broke off as I noticed that there was one person at the table I hadn't expected. Prince Siegfried was sitting beside Dragomir.

"Lady Georgiana." He nodded his head.

I looked at Nicholas. He raised his eyebrows. "Siegfried sensed that something was wrong and insisted on seeing Field Marshal Pirin, so naturally I had to tell him the truth and apologize for our secrecy in keeping this matter hushed up."

Siegfried pursed those cod lips. "This most serious matter was brought to my attention, and I now have to decide whether it should be brought out into the open, or kept from my parents."

I glanced at Dragomir. Had he been the one who had spilled the beans to Siegfried? And if he was the murderer, would that have been a wise thing to do?

"I have explained to His Highness the delicacy of the situation regarding the stability of my nation and the Balkans as a whole," Nicholas said in a clipped voice. It was clear there had been an argument about this already.

"And I have explained to His Highness that this is my country and I have to make sure that we behave as we would expect any citizen to behave—and that includes reporting a murder to the proper authorities."

"Obviously we may have to do that eventually," Anton said in a soothing manner, "but if we can solve it among ourselves here, then nobody else needs to know and the wedding can take place as planned. Surely that is what you wish, Siegfried?"

"Of course."

Dragomir cleared his throat. "But surely the simplest thing to do would be to claim that a communist or anarchist managed to climb into the castle, administer the poison and then make his getaway undetected."

"The simplest thing," Nicholas said, "would be to treat the death as a heart attack, which is what everyone else believes anyway. If they decide on an autopsy, it will be hard to trace the cyanide after that amount of time."

"If we are to believe your diagnosis that cyanide was administered," Siegfried said carefully, "then we must do our duty and find the person who committed this shocking act. Just because the occupants of this castle are royal does not put us above the justice system of our country."

"Well spoken, Your Highness," said a deep voice in guttural French, and a figure stepped from the darkness at the far end of the library. If I had been asked to describe Dracula, this man would have fit the bill perfectly. Tall, thin, hollow cheeked, hollow eyed and very pale, he was dressed head to toe in black, which accentuated the whiteness of his skin. For one ridiculous moment it crossed my mind to wonder whether Vlad the Impaler was still alive and still ruled this castle and the people in it. The man moved toward us with smooth, menacing steps. Then he looked around at us and smiled. "If the personages at this table were not of such exalted rank, I should think that I was witnessing a conspiracy and have you all arrested on the spot," he said. "However, as His Highness Prince Siegfried has just so wisely said, even royal personages are not above the law. If I understood correctly, and I admit that my English is not as fluent as it should be, you were planning to cover up a murder so that there would be no unpleasantness and the wedding could take place as planned. Am I right?"

"Who the devil are you?" Nicholas asked coldly.

"Allow me to introduce myself. I am Patrascue, head of the Romanian secret police." He pulled up a chair and squeezed himself in between Nicholas and Dragomir. "Given the importance of the occasion and the presence of foreign royalty, I elected to travel with Their Majesties to this royal wedding. How fortunate that I did, wasn't it? I had only just arrived when one of my men reported to me that he had overheard a conversation about a murder and a body being whisked away."

I looked across at Lady Middlesex, who had gone a little pink.

"So perhaps one of you would be good enough to tell me who died."

"Field Marshal Pirin," Siegfried said. "Head of the Bulgarian armed forces."

"Also senior adviser to my father and a powerful force in the politics of the region."

"Ah, so we are looking at a political murder, are we?" Patrascue licked his lips. "Very well. Understand this. I will be conducting the investigation and you will be answering my questions—royal or not. Do not think that your exalted rank puts you above the law in Romania. Dear me, no. Our country is a constitutional monarchy and you really have very little power."

"You have to understand," Anton said, "that we were not attempting to cover up a murder just so that a wedding can take place. This man's death could have significance for the future of my country and this entire region."

"And you are . . . ?" Patrascue asked insolently.

"I happen to be Prince Anton of Bulgaria," Anton said coldly. "In case you don't know, you are sitting next to Prince Nicholas, my older brother, heir to the throne and bridegroom."

"My felicitations." Patrascue nodded to Nicholas. "And these other people—your fellow conspirators. Why are they here?"

"I am Lady Georgiana, cousin to King George of England," I said, reverting to my imitation of my great-grandmother, as I always do when I feel threatened. "I am here representing Their Majesties at this wedding. These two ladies are my companions, sent to accompany me by Queen Mary."

"And the reason you sit here now? I did not think the power of the British Empire extended to central Europe." Patrascue eyed me insolently.

"Actually I'm here as a relative," I said. "As a descendant

of Queen Victoria I am related to the Bulgarian royal family and more remotely to the Romanian one. Also I was sitting opposite Field Marshal Pirin at the fateful dinner, and thus witnessed everything. My companion Lady Middlesex was the first to suspect that his death was not a heart attack."

"You say you witnessed everything," Patrascue went on. "What exactly did you see, *ma chérie?*"

I bristled at the words "my dear." I had come to believe that there is at least one obnoxious policeman in every country and he was facing me. "I saw Field Marshal Pirin give a long, rambling toast, take a swig of his wine and then seem to be choking and pitch face forward across the table."

"He seemed to be choking, you say. Was it possible that he was indeed choking and a simple slap on the back could have revived him?"

"He had finished eating at the time," I said. "There had been speeches and toasts for some minutes. Besides, he was dead almost immediately. Initially it was suspected that he had had a heart attack."

"But someone thought it might be murder?"

"I did," Lady Middlesex said. "I'm Lady Middlesex, the wife of the British high commissioner in Mesopotamia. My husband has represented the British Crown all over the world. I know poison when I see it."

"And what poison would that be?"

"Why, cyanide, of course. Red face, staring eyes and the odor of bitter almonds. A classic case. I saw it once before in the Argentine."

Patrascue turned back to me. "Did you see somebody administer this poison?"

"No. I saw nobody come near the table except the servers and Count Dragomir."

Dragomir made a coughing noise in his throat and said,

"I resent the implication that I was somehow involved in this farce. Why would I want to kill a man I had never met before? It is my duty to make sure all servers perform flawlessly. Naturally I was standing behind the table, in a position where I could watch them all."

"And yet you saw nothing amiss?" Patrascue asked.

"The men performed flawlessly as always."

"We have no idea how the poison was administered," Nicholas said. "I sat beside him. All food and drink was served from the same platters and carafes and with great speed. It would have been impossible to select a poisoned morsel for a particular person."

"Then I would suggest that it was placed in his glass before the meal," Patrascue said smugly.

"But we were told cyanide acted almost immediately," I said. "The field marshal had cleared his plate, had second helpings and had his wineglass filled countless times from the same carafe as everybody else."

"If the poison was indeed cyanide," Patrascue said. "I take it no doctor was present to make an accurate diagnosis. Amateurs are frequently wrong in my experience."

"There is no physician in the castle, unfortunately," Anton said. "But I have studied a bit of medicine at the University of Heidelberg and I can tell you that the telltale odor of bitter almonds was present and the face was flushed."

"Ah, a so-called expert," Patrascue said. "It is unfortunate that the body has already been transported away from the castle, or I myself could have determined what poison had been administered. I hope that somebody had the sense to put aside the utensils this person used at the dinner table. I shall send them off for testing and then we shall know."

"They did and they have been taken with the body to be examined by a competent laboratory," Nicholas said. I thought I detected a note of glee in his voice. "Naturally we didn't expect a trained policeman like yourself to arrive so soon, given the condition of the pass."

"Ah." Patrascue tried to come up with a response to something that might have been a compliment. "Then the next step is to interview those who served the meal. Count Dragomir, you are in charge of the running of this place, are you not?"

"You know very well that I am," Dragomir replied curtly. No love lost between those two, I thought.

"Then please be good enough to have those men who served at dinner brought to the library instantly for questioning."

"If we do that, then word will spread around the castle rather rapidly that the field marshal is dead, and probably murdered. That is the last thing we want at this moment," Nicholas said. "The men were questioned discreetly last night,"

"And it is as I told Their Highnesses," Dragomir said. "These are all local men, simple men who have been in the service of this castle for most of their lives. Why would any of them want to poison a foreign field marshal, even if they had the means to do so?"

"Money," Patrascue said. "Enough money can persuade a man to go against his conscience and to perform in a most ruthless manner. How many footmen were there serving at dinner last night?"

"There were twelve," Dragomir said. "But we would only be concerned with those who served the field marshal. Those who waited on the other side of the table would never have come near him."

"Ah, I see." Patrascue nodded jerkily. "And it would be impossible to lean across this table?"

"Any servant who leaned across a table would be instantly dismissed," Dragomir said. "Our standards of etiquette are of the very highest."

"I will speak with these men, one at a time," Patrascue said. "I will swear them to secrecy. They know enough of my reputation to realize what would happen to them if they were rash enough to lie to me or to break their vow. And if one of them has accepted money to commit this heinous act, then I shall make him confess, I promise you." He smiled unpleasantly. I noticed his teeth were unnaturally pointed.

"Of course we could have made a mistake all along," Anton said in a different, breezy voice. "As you say, we are only amateurs. Perhaps we were misinterpreting what was only a simple heart attack after all. It was this lady who suggested that she smelled the odor of bitter almonds, and we know that ladies are inclined to be hysterical in the presence of a body."

"I absolutely resent—" Lady Middlesex began. I kicked her hard, under the table. She looked at me in astonishment and shut up.

"As soon as the car bearing Field Marshal Pirin's body reaches civilization we shall know the truth," Anton went on smoothly. "Why don't we wait until a competent physician has given his assessment of the situation? It would be a tragedy if false rumors leaked out to my country and a regional war began for nothing. It wouldn't make you look good either, if you started a witch hunt for something that turned out to be a simple heart attack."

Patrascue stared at him, trying to assess the implications of what he was saying. There was a pitcher of water on the table. He reached forward, poured himself a glass and drank from it.

"There is something in what you are saying," he said.

"I have no wish to destabilize this region or cause any unpleasantness with our neighbors at this moment of joy and celebration. We will await the doctor's opinion. But in the meantime I will keep my eyes and ears open. Nobody will be above my scrutiny. Nobody!"

He put down his empty glass firmly on the table. The participants rose to their feet. Except for me. I was staring hard as if I were seeing a vision. I had just realized something that threw a whole new light onto this situation.

Chapter 23

I stood staring at the table until the others had left. In my mind's eye I could visualize Field Marshal Pirin giving his drunken, rambling toast. He had reached for a glass, and he was holding it in his left hand. Hannelore had mentioned that his table manners were abysmal and he never used the correct fork. Apparently he didn't use the correct glass either. It was not his glass at all he had grabbed for, but Prince Nicholas's.

It took me a moment to grasp the implication of this. The intended murder victim was not Pirin at all, but Nicholas. And the reason Nicholas hadn't drunk his own wine and died was that he had switched to champagne when the toasts started and had not touched his red wine after that. This would indicate that the glass had originally been free of cyanide during the main course when Nicky was drinking red wine with the wild boar. Somehow, someone had introduced the cyanide after that, unfortunately not realizing that Nicholas was going to call for champagne for his toasts. And if someone had introduced the cyanide, it had to be one of the servers or Dragomir.

Wait a minute, I thought. I was discounting the other diners at the table. Pirin obviously wouldn't have put cyanide into a glass he was going to drink himself. On Nicholas's other side was his bride and she was hardly likely to want to kill off her bridegroom. Opposite him was his brother, Anton, and as Dragomir had said, it was frightfully bad form to reach across the table. It would have been noticed instantly. And besides, the brothers seemed to be on good terms. Anton wouldn't have wanted his brother dead. I paused, considering this. Anton had made jokes about not being the heir and having no purpose in life. Did he secretly wish that he'd be king someday and not his brother? And of all the people around, he would have had a knowledge of poisons. After all, he had told me that he was studying chemistry in Heidelberg. And he was the one who had persuaded Patrascue to do nothing for now. Which would give him ample time to dispose of any traces of cyanide if he needed to.

"Lady Georgiana!" Lady Middlesex's strident voice cut through my thoughts. "Aren't you coming?"

"What? Oh—yes," I stammered. Now there was the question of whom to tell. I wished that Darcy hadn't gone away.

Lady Middlesex grabbed my arm with her bony fingers. "We must go somewhere to plan strategy."

"Strategy?"

She looked around. "Obviously we must make sure that everything is kept from that odious little policeman. We must work fast before he makes a complete mess of everything. Typical bungling foreigner. No clue how to run things properly. It is up to us now to unmask the murderer."

"I don't see how we're ever going to do that," I said. "I was there, facing Field Marshal Pirin all the time. If it was Dragomir or one of the footmen who slipped the cyanide into the glass, he was very slick and I don't see how we'd ever find out who did it."

"That's if it was Dragomir or one of the servants," Lady Middlesex said knowingly. She drew me closer. "Deer-Harte thinks she saw something. Of course, she is prone to flights of fancy, as we know."

"I am an excellent observer, Lady M," Miss Deer-Harte said, "and I know what I saw."

"What did you see, Miss Deer-Harte?" I asked.

Her face went pink. "As you recall on the first night here I was not invited to join the company for dinner. Lady M thought it wouldn't be right for a mere companion. I was told my supper would be sent up to my room. But after a while I thought that it wasn't fair to one of the servants to have to walk up all these stairs with my tray, so I decided to come down and fetch it myself. Well"—she paused and looked around again—"as I passed the banqueting hall I heard the sound of merry voices, so naturally I lingered and took a little peek inside."

"This was the first night," I interrupted. "The night before Pirin was murdered."

"It was, but what I saw could be significant. There was somebody watching from the shadows on the far side of the hall. He was dressed in black and he was standing half hidden behind one of the arches. He just stood there, not moving and watching. I thought it was odd at the time. I remember thinking, 'That young man is up to no good.'"

"You always think things like that, Deer-Harte," Lady Middlesex said. "You think that everyone is up to no good."

"But in this case I was proven right, wasn't I? And I'd like to wager that he was the same young man I saw creeping along the corridor in the middle of the night. I couldn't see his face clearly on either occasion, but the build and demeanor were the same. And the way he was slinking along, he was clearly up to no good."

"I am inclined to think she's been letting her imagination run away with her again," Lady Middlesex said, "but at the moment we are grasping at straws, aren't we?"

"I don't believe it was simply imagination," I said. "What color hair did he have?"

She frowned, thinking. "It looked light to me. Yes, definitely light. Why do you ask?"

"Because a strange man came into my room on the first night, and then my maid came to me in great distress the next night to report that a man was in her room."

"A young man with light hair?"

"Exactly. A good-looking young man with a Teutonic face."

"I didn't see his face, but I definitely saw the hair," Miss Deer-Harte said.

"He came into your room?" Lady Middlesex demanded. "With what intention? Burglary or designs on your person?"

"I didn't take the time to ask him. I rather fear the latter," I said. "He was bending over me with a smile on his face. But when I sat up he disappeared hastily."

"And your maid? Did he have designs on her person too? Clearly a man of great depravity."

The thought struck me that a man would indeed have to

be desperate to have designs on Queenie's person. I knew it was deadly serious but I had to stop myself from giggling. I suppose it was the tension. "He didn't touch her. He stood inside her door and when she gasped, he slipped out."

"And did you report these effronteries to anyone?"

"No, I didn't." I paused.

"I would have. If any man had dared to come into my room, I should have reported him immediately."

I hardly liked to say that nobody was likely to pay a nightly visit to Lady Middlesex. Nor did I want to bring up the possibility of vampires. Miss Deer-Harte, the one who had worried about vampires on the train, did not seem to connect her lurking young man with anything supernatural. And if the same man was our poisoner, then it was unlikely that he was anything more than a normal human. Vampires don't need to poison people. In fact they wouldn't want to taint their blood supply.

"One can only conclude," Lady Middlesex went on, "that he was casing the joint, as criminals would say. It is most probable that he is a trained assassin and has been hiding out, waiting for the right moment to kill."

I considered this too. It made sense that he was a trained assassin and that he was hiding out in the castle. But as Prince Nicholas had pointed out, there were surely easier ways to kill someone in a rambling old building like this than risk being detected at a very public banquet.

"And did you happen to see him at the banquet last night?" I asked Miss Deer-Harte.

"No, but then I was included in the party last night, not standing outside as an observer. One looks down to eat, so that one doesn't risk spilling food, doesn't one? One looks at the person to whom one is speaking. And I was naturally at the far end of the table, among the least important of the diners. But the interesting thing was I checked this morning that the spot where he had been standing was exactly behind Field Marshal Pirin's seat. If you want my opinion, he was planning a dummy run, plotting when he could dart out and put the poison in the glass."

"But I would have noticed any intruder, I'm sure," I said. "So would Prince Anton and Princess Hannelore, who were sitting on either side of me."

"Are you so sure?" Miss Deer-Harte said. "Supposing, for example, that you were in the middle of being served. Your server offers you the platter and says, 'Some cauliflower, my lady?' And you nod and say, 'Thank you,' and watch while it is put on your plate. For those moments you are not watching what is happening across the table, are you?"

"No, I suppose not," I said.

"And if someone were dressed in black, not unlike the footmen's uniform, or he had actually managed to procure himself a footman's jacket, then nobody would look twice if he passed the table with a carafe in his hands. Servants are always too busy making sure they do their job to perfection to notice other servants. And it has been my observation that people simply pay no attention to servants."

"Dragomir would have noticed," I said. "He was hovering behind Prince Nicholas, directing the proceedings. As he said, he would have noticed anything slightly wrong."

"Then let us consider that this Dragomir chappy is somehow involved," Lady Middlesex said.

I couldn't see why Dragomir would want to kill Prince Nicholas any more than he would want to kill Pirin. But if he were, in fact, from the Macedonian province that was now part of Yugoslavia it was just possible that he might want to cause civil war in Bulgaria as a way to reclaim its Macedonian lands. And what better way to do that than to assassinate its crown prince? Binky had said that they were always assassinating each other in this part of the world, hadn't he? I decided that I'd risk a little chat with Dragomir myself.

"We obviously can't snoop through every room in the castle," Lady Middlesex said, "particularly now that the royal party has arrived, but it seems to me that the first task is to find out how he came by the poison and where he's hiding the vial it came in."

"I presume that any assassin could have the poison in his pocket when he came into the castle and would leave again with the empty vial," I said.

"I don't know if you've noticed," Lady Middlesex said brusquely, "but there are no footprints leading from the castle, apart from yours and Mr. O'Mara's this morning. I checked particularly when we went on our little walk. He is still here, you mark my words." She looked down at Miss Deer-Harte and nodded.

"I shall be extra vigilant, Lady M," Miss Deer-Harte said. "If he is hiding somewhere he will have to come out eventually. He will need a bathroom and food and drink. I shall be watching for him."

"Well said, Deer-Harte. Splendid stuff. We'll show them how quickly and efficiently things are done when the flower of British womanhood takes over." She slapped Miss Deer-Harte on the back, almost knocking her over. "Onward and upward then."

And she marched down the hall like a general leading troops into battle.

Chapter 24

I was left alone in the cold, drafty hallway. I hadn't had time to consider what I should do about my big discovery. Whom should I tell that Prince Nicholas was the intended victim? Obviously not the two English ladies. They had caused enough trouble already. In fact, if Lady Middlesex hadn't spoken up, Pirin's death might well have been considered a heart attack and we wouldn't be in this uncomfortable situation with that horrid man Patrascue snooping on us. I couldn't tell Prince Anton because it was just possible that he was the murderer—although I found that hard to believe. But he did have knowledge of chemistry, he was agile and, as Belinda had said, he was reckless and loved danger. That left Siegfried or Matty and I rather suspected that Siegfried would report anything straight to Patrascue. Matty would probably think it was all a huge joke and not want to take it seriously. So the only person I could talk to was Nicholas himself. He had a right to know and he might have his own suspicions.

I was on my way to seek him out when a clear, melodious voice echoed down the hallway. "Yoohoo, darling!" and there was my mother, hurrying toward me, her long mink coat flying out around her. "There you are, my sweet," she said. "We've been in the same building for several days and hardly had a chance to say a word to each other."

She caught up with me and we kissed, several inches from each cheek, the way we always did. In spite of the way she showed copious affection to everything in trousers, my mother was not much of a hugger when it came to other women.

"That's because you don't like being seen with me," I said. "It reminds people you are old enough to have a daughter my age."

"What a wicked thing to say. I adore spending time with you, my sweet, or I would if you led a less boring life. We must do something to liven you up. That dress at dinner last night. So absolutely last year and it hides all the best bits of you. I know you don't have much bosom, but you should make the most of what you have. You really must let the men see the goods you are offering."

"Mummy!"

She laughed, that tinkling laugh that had captivated audiences everywhere, and slipped her arm through mine. "You really are so delightfully prudish, my sweet. I put it down to Scottish upbringing. So repressed. Let's go and have a girl talk somewhere, shall we?" She started to lead me down the hallway. "If I'd known I was going to be cooped up in this dreary place for days on end, I'd never have come. Of course Max had to be here, as Nicholas's godfather, but I could have popped to Paris on my own. I do adore it just before Christmas, don't you? So sparkly."

I didn't have a chance to protest. I was borne down the hallway and into a small sitting room where a fire was blazing in a hearth. It was actually quite warm and cozy compared to the rest of the building. Trust my mother to find the one comfortable spot. She draped herself into an armchair and patted the bearskin rug at her feet. "Come and talk to me. Tell me all."

"There's not much to tell," I said. "I've been at Rannoch House, but I'm hoping to go somewhere else for the winter because Binky and Fig are going to be in residence. Fig's expecting again."

"Good God. And they already have the heir. Binky really must be a saint, or blind or desperate. You don't suppose she could actually be good at it, do you? Secretly passionate when roused?"

I looked up at her. "Fig? Passionate?" I burst out laughing. Mummy laughed too.

"You must come and stay with us in Germany, darling," my mother said. "Max can introduce you to a nice German count. Come to think of it, why don't we set you up with one of Nicky's groomsmen? Young Heinrich of Schleswig-Holstein has oodles of money."

"I don't think I'd like to live in Germany, thank you," I said. "I'm amazed how you can do it and not think of the Great War."

"Darling, the people we mix with had nothing to do with it. It was those nasty militaristic Prussians. Your father's wretched cousin Kaiser Willie. No, you'd live well in Germany. Good food, if a little stodgy, and great wine, and Berlin is such a lively city. Or we could find you an Austrian and live in Vienna. Now there's a delightful city for you.

And the Austrians—all so fun loving and absolutely no in-terest in war or conquest."

"Isn't this new chap Hitler an Austrian?"

"Darling, we met him recently. Such a funny little man. I'm sure nobody will take him seriously. And there's also Nicky's brother, Anton. Now he would be quite a catch. I rather fancy him myself, but with Max as his brother's godfather—well, one has to draw the line somewhere."

"I'm surprised you're still with Max," I said. "He doesn't seem your type at all. He doesn't seem very lively. You're much more at home with people like Noel Coward—theater people."

"Of course I am, but so many of them are like dear sweet Noel—pansies, darling. And let me warn you that a cer-tain prince in this house is one of them too. Because I have heard rumors that you're being considered for the post of princess."

"Siegfried, you mean?" I laughed. "Yes, he's already pro-posed and let me know that I could take lovers after I pro-duced the heir."

"Aren't men funny?" Mother laughed again. "But I rather think your interests lie in another direction. A certain Mr. O'Mara?" She laughed at my red face. "Darling, you have bitten off more than you can chew there. He does have a reputation, you know. Wild Irish boy. I can't see him set-tling down and changing nappies, can you? And of course he has no money and money is rather important to happiness."

"Are you happy with Max?"

Those large china doll eyes opened wide. "What an inter-esting question. I get bored and think I'll leave and then the poor dear adores me so much that I simply can't do it. He wants to marry me, you know."

"Are you thinking of marrying him?"

"It has crossed my mind, but I don't think I'd like to be a Frau. I know he's nobility and a von and all that, but I'd still be Frau Von Strohheim and it simply isn't *moi*. Besides, I believe I'm still officially married to that frightfully boring Texan chappy, Homer Clegg. He doesn't believe in divorce. If I really felt strongly I could go to Reno or wherever it is that people go and pay for a quickie divorce there, but I simply can't be bothered. No, my advice to you, my darling, is that you marry well and keep someone like Mr. O'Mara on the side. Choose someone with dark hair and then the baby will match whoever the father is."

"Mummy, you say the most outlandish things. I can't believe how I came to be your daughter."

She stroked my cheek. "I abandoned you too young, I realize now. But I couldn't take another minute of that dreary castle. I never realized your father would want to spend half the year there and go tramping about the heather in a kilt. Simply not me, my sweet, although I have to confess that I enjoyed being a duchess. One got such good service at Harrods."

As she twittered on I sat there uneasily, aware of all the things I should be doing. My gaze drifted from the cracking fire to the portrait above the mantelpiece. Then I blinked and gave it another look. The man in the picture looked like Count Dragomir.

I got up and stood in front of the fire, staring up at it. The man in the portrait was younger than Dragomir but he had the same haughty face, the same high cheekbones and strangely cat-like eyes. But one hardly puts a portrait of a castle servant on the wall. Then I looked at the writing at the bottom. The painter had signed his picture and it looked as if the date was 1789.

"What are you looking at, darling?" my mother asked.

"This portrait on the wall. Doesn't it remind you of Count Dragomir?"

"They all look similar in this part of the world, don't they?" Mummy said in a bored voice. "It was those Huns. They were so good at raping and pillaging that everyone now looks like them."

I was still staring at the portrait. It reminded me of someone else I knew, but I couldn't quite put a finger on it. Something about the eyes . . .

"Darling, as I told you at dinner the other night, your hair is a disaster," Mummy said. "Who is your hairdresser in London these days? You should get a Marcel wave. Come up to my room and I'll have Adele do it for you. She is a whiz with problem hair."

"Later, Mummy," I said. "I really have things I should be doing now."

"More important things than keeping your poor lonely mother company?"

"Mummy, there are plenty of other women who would love to sit and gossip with you, I'm sure."

"They love to gossip in German and I never could get the hang of that language. And I'm not too hot at French either and I do so love to be the center of things, not a hanger-on."

"You could always find Belinda. She likes all the things you do."

"Your friend Belinda?" A frown crossed that flawless face. "Darling, one hears she is nothing more than a little tramp. Did you see how she was virtually throwing herself at Anton the other night? And I gather her bed wasn't slept in after that." She gave me a knowing wink.

I was amused at the pot calling the kettle black. Little tramp, indeed. So I suspected it was sour grapes, since

Mummy had confessed to being attracted to Anton. "Well, you'll have to find someone else to amuse you, because I'm supposed to be at the fitting for my bridal attendant's dress," I said. "You heard that I was one of Matty's attendants, didn't you?" I knew that a dress fitting would count as a good reason for my mother.

"Oh, well, then you should hurry off, darling," Mummy said. "I hear that the princess has brought in Madame Yvonne, of all people. She's a trifle passé, but she still makes some divine gowns. What's yours like?"

"Divine," I said. "You'll be pleased with me. I actually look elegant."

"Then we have hope of snaring a prince or a count for you yet," Mummy said. "Toddle along then. Don't keep Madame Yvonne waiting."

I took the opportunity and fled, leaving her sitting with her legs stretched out in front of the fire. When I came out to the vast entrance hall I paused. What should I be doing? Seeking out Nicholas; speaking with Count Dragomir? It all seemed so pointless. Would Nicholas want to know that someone had tried to kill him? And what about Dragomir? Obviously my mother was right and the resemblance to that portrait was purely a coincidence. He hadn't been alive since 1789—not unless he was one of the undead. That ridiculous thought flashed through my mind and I tried to stifle it. He had all the qualities one would expect of a vampire count—that pale skin, elegant demeanor, strangely staring light eyes, hollow cheeks. Rubbish, I said out loud, having picked up the word from Lady Middlesex. And as I had decided earlier, no undead person would need to administer poison. Poison at a dinner table bore the mark of a desperate, daring human being.

I wandered along hallways until I heard voices and came

upon a group assembled in the anteroom next to the banqueting hall. I spotted Prince Nicholas among them and
was making my way through the crowd toward him when
a voice said, in French, "Now, who is this charming young
person?" and of course I realized that I was among the royals who had arrived earlier. Then, of course, I felt highly
embarrassed, because I was dressed for warmth rather than
elegance. The embarrassment was doubled when Siegfried
stepped forward, took me by the elbow and said, also in
French, "Mama, may I present Georgiana, the cousin of
King George."

The elegant, perfectly coiffed, exquisitely dressed woman
beamed at me and extended an elegant hand. "So you are the
one," she said. "How delightful. You don't know how we
have longed to meet you."

I curtsied warily. "Your Majesty," I murmured.

"And you speak such fluent French too."

I hardly thought the word "majesty" comprised good
French and was seriously worried at the effuse greeting.
I had just been introduced to Siegfried's father, the king,
when the gong sounded and I was swept into luncheon
without having an opportunity to speak to Prince Nicholas. I was seated between a countess and an elderly baron,
both of whom spoke to me in stilted French, and then, when
they realized I knew nobody that they did, they spoke across
me: "So do tell me, what is Jean-Claude doing this winter?
Monte Carlo again? Too overrun with riffraff these days for
me. And what about Josephine? How are her rheumatics?
I heard she was in Budapest for the baths. I find them so
unhygienic, don't you?"

I managed to eat and answer when spoken to, while at
the same time watching what happened behind the table.
Servants came and went with such rapidity that I could see

there was a chance that an opportune assassin could have darted out from an archway, administered a dose of poison and vanished again without being noticed. Especially if someone were speaking at the time. I looked down the room. If someone at the far end of the table had been making a toast, all eyes would have been on him. The whole thing seemed impossible. I would have been happy to call it a heart attack and leave well enough alone, but for the fact that someone had tried to kill Prince Nicholas and that person was still among us.

I managed to eat my way through a rich and creamy soup, a sauerbraten with red cabbage and some delicious dumplings stuffed with prunes and dusted in sugar. Then, the moment luncheon was over, I tried to intercept Prince Nicholas as he left the room.

"Can we go somewhere to talk?" I said in a low voice. "There's something I need to tell you privately, about Field Marshal Pirin."

"Oh, right." He looked startled, then glanced around. "I'll get Anton."

"No!" The word came out louder than I meant it to, and several people around us looked up. "No," I repeated. "This is only for your ears. It's up to you whom you decide to share it with when I've told you."

"All right." He looked amused if anything. "Where shall we go for this secret meeting?"

"Anywhere that obnoxious man Patrascue isn't likely to overhear."

"Who knows where his men are lurking?" Nicholas said. "It's so easy to spy on people in a place like this. Oh, damn, speak of the devil—" Patrascue had come into the room and appeared to be making a beeline for us.

"You, lady from England," he said. "You will come with

me, please. I have something that I want you to explain to me immediately."

"Do you want me along too?" Nicholas asked.

"Just the young lady," Patrascue said.

I had no choice but to go with Patrascue, especially as he appeared to have two of his men in tow and I didn't want to cause a fuss.

"I'll see you later then," I called after Nicholas, then I turned to Patrascue, who was standing close beside me. "What's this about?" I asked.

"You will soon see," Patrascue said. He marched ahead of me with great purpose, up the stairs until we came out onto my hallway. Then he flung open my bedroom door. A frightened-looking Queenie was standing by the bed.

"You will please explain this," Patrascue said. He opened the chest and pointed at a small glass bottle lying there.

"I have no idea what it is or how it got there," I said.

"I, on the other hand, have a very good idea," he said. "I would like to deduce it was the receptacle that contained the poison." He stepped closer until he was leering down at me. "I have had my suspicions about you from the beginning," he said. "You were sitting opposite this field marshal. And why should the English king send you to the wedding? Why not send his own daughter, a princess, as would be more fitting?"

"Because Princess Maria Theresa personally asked for me to be part of her bridal procession, since we were old school friends. So the queen thought that it would kill two birds with one stone, so to speak."

"Do not worry, as soon as the telephone lines are restored I shall be calling the garden of Scotland to verify this."

The garden of Scotland? I grinned. He meant Scotland Yard.

"Please do. Are you suggesting that I came all the way from England to kill a field marshal I had never even heard of until this week?" I tried to give a carefree laugh that didn't quite come off. One heard rumors of the way justice was conducted in foreign countries, and I would certainly be an easy scapegoat for him. "What possible motive could I have? It is my first time in this part of the world. I never met any of these people before."

"As for motive, I could think of several. The young Bulgarian princes, they did not like this fellow, I have heard. You are their cousin, are you not? Perhaps you are in a conspiracy together to kill him for them."

"In that case," I said, "we could easily have labeled his death a heart attack and nobody would have challenged it. But why should I wish to get involved in Bulgarian politics, even if these are my cousins?"

"Money," he said with a horrible grin. "As I told you earlier, money can make anyone do evil acts. And you have none, so your mother's companion confided to me."

"I may not have been brought up with money, but certainly with plenty of integrity," I said haughtily. "If I were so desperate for money, I could have made a good marriage by now. Your heir to the throne here has already asked me."

"I know this," he said, waving a hand airily. "I make it my business to know everything."

"So if I married him, I'd hardly want to start off my marriage with a war between Balkan countries, would I?"

"But I heard you rejected him," Patrascue said. He turned to one of his men and said something under his breath in another language. The man took out a handkerchief, then leaned forward and removed the little bottle. He handed it, still in the handkerchief, to Patrascue.

"I assure you, you won't find my fingerprints on it," I

said. "And you'll probably discover that it is an ordinary medicine bottle containing someone's headache mixture."

Using the handkerchief, Patrascue removed the stopper, sniffed, then backed away hastily. "This did not contain a headache mixture," he said. "And I do not expect to find fingerprints on it. A clever killer will have wiped them away."

"Even a stupid killer would have hurled the bottle out of the window, where it would have sunk into snow that's not going to melt for ages," I said. "By which time the killer would be back in his or her own country."

Patrascue stared at the window, digesting this, the wheels in his brain working slowly.

"Isn't it obvious, even to you, that someone is trying to frame me?" I said. Actually I said "attach the blame to me" because the only French word I knew for "frame" was the one that held pictures on walls and I didn't think that would be right. "Why would the real killer not have disposed of the evidence? How easy that would be in a castle of this size, with so many nooks and crannies and gratings in walls and floors. Or why not keep it on his person?"

Patrascue said nothing for a while. "Because only a clever criminal would absolve herself from blame by making me think that she had been framed," he said at last. "I will tell you what I think, English lady. I think that this is a clever plot between you and your fellow Englishman, who conveniently drove away with the body before I could examine it or question him."

I grinned. "He's not English, actually. He's Irish."

He waved a hand in a bored manner. "English, Irish, what is the difference. I have heard of this Mr. O'Mara before. He was involved in a scandal at a casino, I believe. And he is interested in making money. But don't worry, I will send my men after him and he will be brought back here, and the truth will come out."

"Don't be so ridiculous," I said. "The queen of England would be horrified if she heard I had been treated this way when I have been sent to represent my country. Princess Maria Theresa, my dear school friend, will also be horrified, if I tell her."

He put his fingers under my chin and drew me closer to him. "I do not think you realize the spot you are in, young lady. I have the power to arrest you and lock you up, and I can assure you that our jails are not pleasant places—rats, disease, hardened criminals . . . and sometimes it takes months or years before a case comes to trial. But given that you are here for such a festive occasion, I will be gracious. I will merely inform you that you may not leave this castle without my permission."

His fingernails were digging into my chin, but I wasn't going to show him that I was scared. "Since I'm here for a wedding next week, I'm hardly likely to do that," I said. "Besides, I understand it may snow again, in which case no-body will be leaving for a while."

He leaned his face closer to mine. His breath was rank with garlic and worse. "Since you so emphatically insist on your innocence," he said, "you must have some thoughts on who committed this terrible crime. Who do you think it was? Dragomir, for example? You say you saw everything— did you perhaps observe Dragomir slipping something into a glass? Think hard, young lady, if you wish to go home after the wedding."

I saw then that he wasn't as stupid as I had thought. His plan had been to make me so fearful for my own safety that I would be willing to point the finger at Dragomir. He was about to discover that British girls are made of sterner stuff.

They do not collapse in sobs when a fierce policeman threatens them with prison. Even though I did have my suspicions about Dragomir, I certainly wasn't going to share them with this man.

"If you want my opinion," I said, "I think you should consider the possibility of vampires."

Chapter 25

"Ooh miss, I wasn't half scared," Queenie said as soon as the men had left. "Those horrid brutes, they barged in here and started going through your things. I didn't half give 'em an earful. 'Whatcher think you're doing?' I said. 'Them things belongs to a royal person and she won't want you mucking about with them and getting your dirty hands on them.' But it wasn't much good because they didn't speak English. What was that man saying to you?"

"He thought I'd poisoned the man who was taken ill at dinner last night," I said. "They found what looked like a vial of poison in that chest."

"I bet they planted it there themselves," Queenie said. "You can't trust them foreigners, can you? That's what my old dad says and he should know because he was in the trenches in the Great War."

"Your old dad may be right on this occasion," I said. Planting the evidence there themselves was definitely a possibility—but why choose me? Was it because I came from a faraway place and therefore would cause a local political problem if I was arrested? Or did he think that I looked vulnerable and would easily break down and confess or be willing to pin the blame on Dragomir? It was all too much like a gothic drama. I just hoped that his men didn't catch up with Darcy. I didn't think that was likely. The sky outside my window looked heavy with the promise of more snow. I glanced longingly at my bed. A quick nap sounded like a good idea, but I really couldn't put off having my chat with Nicholas. He may still have been in grave danger. Why, oh, why did Darcy have to choose this moment to leave? He could have kept an eye on Nicholas and prevented another murder.

I made my way downstairs again. The hallways seemed colder than ever, with banners actually wafting in the wind. As I looked around me I realized that servants were everywhere. Usually one does not even notice the presence of servants, but at this moment I was particularly aware of them. Which made me think—if an intruder was in the castle, someone else must know about him. It wouldn't be possible to sneak around without encountering a servant or two, so someone had to be feeding the intruder and keeping him safely hidden. That indicated that the assassin had to be from here, and not one of the guests from Bulgaria.

Of course then my thoughts turned again to Count Dragomir. I found that I was passing the door to the sitting room where I had spotted the portrait. I opened the door cautiously and found the room empty. I tiptoed over to the fireplace and stared up at the portrait. In the flickering light of the fire it looked almost alive.

"All alone, my lady?" said a deep voice behind me.

I gasped and spun around. Count Dragomir was standing

there, in the flesh. "Is there something I can get you?" he asked. "Some tea, maybe? You English like your tea at this hour, I believe."

"Er—no, thank you," I stammered.

"Then perhaps you came in here to be alone or to take an afternoon snooze," he said. "I leave you to sweet dreams."

He bowed and was about to retreat when I plucked up courage.

"Count Dragomir," I said, "I couldn't help noticing that there is a bad feeling between you and the policeman Patrascue."

"I'm sure the feeling is mutual," Dragomir said. "We were at the university together as young men. We took an instant disliking to each other. He was a sneaky, underhand sort of fellow even then." I felt that there was more but he was not going to tell me.

I took a deep breath and risked the second question. "That portrait on the wall. Have you noticed—the resemblance to you is striking. But I'm sure you weren't born in seventeen hundred and something." I gave a gay little laugh.

"You're right. The family resemblance is strong," he said, examining it. "One of my ancestors. We used to own this castle, you know. In fact, we used to be rulers of Transylvania when it was an autonomous state and not part of Romania."

"But I was told you came from Yugoslavia."

"One of my ancestors decided to risk battle against the occupying Turks," he said. "He was foolhardy and the Turks were all-powerful in those days. My ancestor counted on the help of his neighbors in what should have been a regionwide uprising, but I'm afraid my family had earned a reputation for brutality and ruthlessness. No help came. The castle was taken and my family had to flee into exile. So it is true I was raised in what is now part of Yugoslavia. I went to study in Vienna, where I met the present king of Romania, who was a fellow student. We struck up a friendship and later I was offered a government post when he came to the throne in his country. Times have been hard since the Great War and jobs not easy to come by, so I was glad to accept. Ironically I was put in charge of this castle, so I am now the glorified butler where my family once ruled. But that is life, is it not? Nothing is certain."

I nodded. "My family has also lost all its money. My brother is just scraping by at the family seat. Times are hard."

"I believe I would have risen higher in government circles had it not been for our friend Patrascue." He came closer to me. "Tell me—Patrascue has enlisted you to trap me, has he not? That is the way he works—he decides whom he would like to be guilty, arrests them and then invents the evidence to prove it."

"He did suggest to me that I might have seen you put the poison in a glass. I told him I saw no such thing."

"The English, they can always be counted upon to behave like gentlemen and like ladies." He smiled. "But do not underestimate this Patrascue. He wields considerable power in my country. There is a rumor that he is a puppet of Russia. They would like to extend their arm into this region, you know. I can understand why Prince Nicholas wanted to keep the death a natural one. The least little thing can spark off an international incident in these parts." He straightened a bowl of flowers on a small table, then looked up suddenly. "So I would stay out of any unauthorized investigation or amateur sleuthing, if I were you. You are playing with fire, my lady. Enjoy your role as bride's attendant and have a good time here. This is what young ladies should do, no?"

He nodded graciously and left. His tone had been pleasant enough but the threat had been real. Was he concerned for my safety or his own? So the castle was his ancestral home. And given his family history, he could well have an ax to grind with any of his Balkan neighbors. And a desire for revenge, going back generations. Maybe a little war between countries was just what he wanted.

I followed him out of the sitting room. If Dragomir were really the one who had administered the poison, why had he seemed so helpful when we met afterward? He had helped collect the utensils, handle the servants, get the body up to a bedroom and generally behaved the way a perfect butler would. Why? Was it that he wanted to appear above suspicion, or did he know that he had carried out a clever murder and would never be caught? Or was it that he felt guilty that the wrong man had died?

With these thoughts buzzing through my head I found myself in the long gallery, where afternoon coffee was being served. My mother had found the group of older countesses and was sitting eating torte with them. She waved as I approached.

"We're about to play bridge, darling. Care to join us?"

"No, thank you, I'm useless at bridge. Is the princess still in the fitting room?"

"Oh, no, darling. She appeared about half an hour ago, poured herself a black coffee and looked with longing at the cakes. That child is starving herself, if you ask me. Now she's definitely too thin. European men do like a woman to have a little meat on her bones."

"And Prince Nicholas, have you seen him recently?"

"I haven't seen him since lunch. I gather he and Anton went out to shoot, and I expect Max went with them. They're only happy when they're shooting something—apart from sex, of course."

"Mother!" I gave her a warning frown.

My mother glanced around at the other women, who were tucking into their torte with abandon. "They won't understand. Their English is hopeless, darling. Besides, it is about time you were acquainted with the facts of life. I've hopelessly neglected my duty in that area. Men only have two thoughts in their heads and those are killing or copulating."

"I'm sure there are plenty of men with finer feelings, who are interested in art and culture."

"Yes, darling, of course there are. They are called fairies. And they are quite adorable—so witty and fun to be with. But in my long and varied life I've found that the ones who are witty to be with are no use in bed, and vice versa."

She took a final bite of her cake, licked her fork—curling her tongue in what would have been a seductive gesture had any men been present—and went to join the other ladies, who were setting up a bridge table. I helped myself to coffee and cake and sat alone on a sofa, feeling uneasy. So Nicholas had gone out hunting again, had he? I had seen from experience how easy it was to shoot at the wrong target, and hadn't Darcy suggested exactly the same way to kill someone conveniently? But I could hardly go after Nicholas at this stage. I'd just have to wait until he returned. Dragomir had warned me against amateur sleuthing, but I was apparently the only one in the castle, apart from the killer, who knew the truth. I had to warn Nicholas as soon as he came back.

The cake looked absolutely delicious—layers of chocolate and cream and nuts. I took a slice but I found it hard to swallow. If I couldn't come up with a good answer for the first question—who wanted to kill Prince Nicholas?—then perhaps I should examine the next logical one: why? I understood that murder is committed for several reasons: fear, gain, revenge, with fear being the most compelling motive of the three. Who in this castle had something to fear from the prince, something so terrible that he had to be silenced forever? I couldn't answer that one. I knew so little about everyone here. So who had something to gain from his death? The obvious answer to that was Anton. He'd be next in line to the throne if his brother died. And he had the means—a knowledge of chemistry—and he had stood to clink glasses with his brother. No—that theory didn't work since the poison was put into the red wine when Nicholas had already switched to champagne and Anton would have observed that.

Of the other people within reach at the table, Matty wouldn't want to finish off her bridegroom right before the wedding. I was sitting opposite, so was Siegfried, and neither of us did it. So we were back to Dragomir or an unnamed server, bribed by a large sum of money to do the unthinkable. And if not these, a political assassination. That, I supposed, made the most sense, because an anarchist or communist wouldn't care about the murder taking place in such a public place—would actually prefer it to be visible and spectacular, like the assassination of the archduke in Sarajevo that had started the Great War.

This was out of my league. I had tangled once before with a team of highly trained communist infiltrators and had no wish to do so again. In fact I wanted to do as Dragomir suggested—have a good time with the other young women and enjoy the wedding celebrations. I just wished that Darcy wasn't counting on me.

$\mathcal{C}$hapter 26

The long gallery, Bran Castle
Still November 18

I was still toying with my cake when Matty came wandering in, looking distracted. "Isn't Nicholas back yet?" she asked. I noted that she pronounced his name in the French way, "Nicolah," and didn't call him Nicky or Nick as his brother did.

"I haven't seen him," I replied.

"Really, what a ridiculous thing to do, to go out shooting in weather like this. Aren't men silly—at least some men."

She perched on the sofa beside me, her eyes on my cake.

"My mother says that men are only interested in two things, killing things and sex," I said, trying to brighten her mood.

"Not all men," she said, looking away again. "In Paris I met artists, writers, men who had a romantic side and could express themselves."

"My mother claims they are all fairies."

"Not all," she said. She got up and went over to a tall,

arched window. Daylight was fading fast. "It's starting to snow again, you know. I hope they don't get lost. I suppose I'd better tell Dragomir and send servants out to find them."

And she left me. She had only been gone a few minutes when I heard raised voices and the clatter of boots on stairs, and Nicholas and Anton came into the room, snowflakes still dusting their hair and eyelashes. Their faces were alight and they were laughing.

"Your bride was worried about you," I said as Nicholas passed me.

"It was rather an absurd thing to do, I suppose," Nicholas said. "We got lost. Max fell into a snowdrift and had to be dug out."

"And after all that, we come home empty-handed," Anton added. "But it was great fun. And one hates being cooped up inside all day."

They made a beeline for the coffeepots and cakes, then came to sit beside me.

"What was it you wanted to tell me earlier," Nicholas asked, "when that brute Patrascue dragged you off? He wasn't arresting you for the murder or anything, was he?"

"Actually he was," I said. "He found a small glass bottle, containing what he believed was the poison, in a chest in my room."

"Good God," Nicholas said. "But surely even someone as thick as Patrascue didn't think that you'd hidden it there, did he?"

"I did point out that I could easily have thrown it out of the window into the snowy wilderness where it wouldn't have been found for months," I said.

"So the question is who planted it on you?" Anton asked.

"The assassin, I presume, as he had to make a quick getaway," Nicholas suggested.

"Or Patrascue himself, which I consider more likely," I said. "He wanted to scare me into implicating Dragomir."

"Oh, so he thinks Dragomir did it, does he? Interesting. I had the same suspicions myself," Nicholas said.

"In his case I don't think he cares whether Dragomir was guilty or not. He has a long-standing feud with the man—I couldn't exactly get to the bottom of it, but he'd love to frame Dragomir. I didn't play along and refused to be intimidated."

"Quite right," Anton said. "I love British girls, don't you, Nick? Such pillars of strength. Think of Boudicca." He reached across and gave my knee a squeeze.

"Behave yourself, Toni. You can't have more than one at a time, you know," Nick said, laughing.

"I don't see why not. The more the merrier, that's my motto. In fact I'm rather miffed that I wasn't born a Turk. I'd have enjoyed a harem. It would have been a challenge to see how many I could get through in one night."

"You are offending this young lady's sensibilities," Nicholas said.

"No, really," I said, laughing, but Anton stood up. "I shall go and find Belinda," he said. "She loves to hear of my exploits and she is quite willing to add to them."

"That young man will have to learn to take life seriously one day," Nicholas said as soon as Anton was out of hearing. "Father rather despairs of him. Too bad he was born a prince. He'd have done well as a film star in Hollywood, I feel—or better yet a stuntman."

I looked around. The ladies had begun their bridge game. An old man was holding forth to several of the young counts. I moved closer to Nicholas. "About what I wanted to tell you," I said.

"Oh, yes. You've discovered something important?"

"Very important, especially to you," I said and related exactly how I remembered the incident. "So it was your glass that he took," I concluded.

For a while Nicholas said nothing. Then he sighed. "It's rather sobering, isn't it? One lives with the threat of assassination, I suppose, but it's still a shock when it comes close to home. Then it's obviously some infernal anarchist. Probably did as Patrascue suggested and paid one of the servants to do his dirty work."

"You can't think of anyone else who might want you dead?" I asked. "Nobody here who bears you animosity?"

Nicholas gave a wry smile. "I've always thought of myself as a likeable sort of chap," he said. "Not the kind that makes enemies."

"But if it was a political assassination, why not aim for your father rather than you?"

"I can think of a couple of answers to that one: My father wasn't there on the night in question. His entourage had been held up by the avalanche on the pass, remember. If the whole thing had been planned for that night, maybe they decided I was the next best thing and went for it. And the second answer is that maybe it didn't matter which of us they got. Remember the archduke in Sarajevo? He was a minor player in the Hapsburg dynasty and yet the incident still started a world war."

I shuddered. "It's horrible. How can you live when you never feel safe?"

"I suppose one has no choice," he said. "One likes to think that we bring stability and culture to a region, but it's always been a hotbed of intrigue and violence. They've been killing each other around here since day one. And none more violent than the family that used to own this place. Vlad the Impaler and his descendants. I'm sure you've heard of him. What a bunch they were. Talk about cruel and ruthless. I've read some of the books in this library. Some of their vile deeds would turn your stomach. And of course the books and the local inhabitants claim that Vlad became Dracula and still lives on."

And he laughed.

"There you are at last, you wicked one." Matty came into the room and bent to kiss his forehead. "I was worried about you. And you still have snow on your head."

I decided to be tactful and leave them alone. I went back up to my room and looked out of the window. Snow was now falling fast—great fat flakes whirling and swirling around the turrets. And my thoughts went instantly to Darcy, somewhere up on that pass. I hoped he'd be sensible enough to take refuge at the inn up there. In fact I just wished this whole thing were over.

It did cross my mind to wonder where Queenie was. I presumed she was still in the kitchen, stuffing her face on cake. If she came back to London with me, she'd desert me as soon as she found out that I lived on baked beans and toast. I wondered whether to go and seek her out, but I couldn't get the disturbing image out of my mind of Matty with blood running down her chin. I didn't want to believe in vampires, but I know what I saw quite clearly. If she really was a vampire, then I had no intention of being next on her menu.

I paced the room. Soon I'd need to start dressing for dinner and it was almost impossible to get into an evening dress alone. I thought of going down to Mummy and seeing if her maid could do my hair for me, as promised. It would be interesting to see what I looked like, properly coiffured. Still no Queenie. I opened my wardrobe, cautiously, as I wasn't sure what might be lurking inside something of that girth, and took out my one presentable dinner dress. I couldn't wear it for a third night in a row, yet neither could I wear the one with the scorch marks. Too bad that my mother was such a tiny little person, I thought. I know she'd travel with oodles of delicious clothes. Suddenly I had a brain wave. Knowing Belinda, she would have come with a trunkful of fashionable dresses. Maybe she'd let me wear one of her dresses tonight.

I hurried down the first flight of stairs and along the hallway to where I thought Belinda's room was. As I passed a door I heard voices—a man's voice, low and calm, and a woman's voice raised in anger and shrill. "What were you thinking?" she demanded in French. "How could you? It will be the end of everything."

I didn't hear the man's reply. Interesting, I thought, and continued down the hall. At what I hoped was Belinda's door I knocked, never knowing what might be going on in Belinda's room. I waited, and I was about to go away when the door was opened by a bleary-eyed Belinda.

"Oh," she said, eyeing me with disappointment. "I thought you might be Anton. Sorry. I was taking a much-needed nap before dinner. Is it time to dress?"

"Almost," I said.

"Come on in, then," she said and led me into a small square room. She flung herself back on the bed and closed her eyes again. I looked around. It was plain and simple by castle standards. No terrifying wardrobe or chest for her.

"So who dresses you?" I asked. "I take it you didn't bring a spare maid along in your trunk, did you?"

"No, I left the faithful Florrie at home. She goes to pieces if I take her abroad. Luckily Matty is being sweet and sending her maid to take care of me when she's finished dressing her mistress. Her room is right next door. As you can see, I'm in what was probably a dressing room originally. Dashed inconvenient actually, as I suspect that the walls aren't exactly soundproof, and one does have the occasional nocturnal visitor."

I perched on her bed. "Belinda, the way you carry on, don't you ever worry about, you know, getting in the family way?"

Belinda chuckled. "You are so delightfully old-fashioned in your wording, my sweet. There are useful things called French letters and Dutch caps, you know. And if I were to get preggers, there is a wonderful little clinic on the coast near Bournemouth, and I'm sure the man in question would cough up the necessary funds to do the trick." The smile faded. "Don't look so horrified, darling. It's done all the time. Of course it's easier for married women—no need for clinics as long as the baby looks something like the official father. Accept the fact, Georgie—bed hopping is a major sport for our class. It whiles away the long hours between hunting, shooting and fishing." And she laughed again.

"Do you ever think you'll get married?" I asked.

"If I find someone rich and boring enough, and preferably old, and shortsighted." She reached up and put her hands on my cheeks. "I enjoy it, darling. I love the thrill of the chase. I can't picture myself ever tied down to one man."

"You and my mother must come from another planet," I said. "Settling down with one man sounds awfully nice to me."

"The problem is with whom, darling," Belinda said, dropping back to her pillows with a sigh. "Your beloved Darcy doesn't have the means nor the temperament for domestic bliss. In fact I see him turning into one of these enigmatic men who flit around the globe, living by their wits into old age."

I sighed. "You may be right. I wish I hadn't fallen for him, but I have. Everyone is pushing me to marry sensibly—I could probably even have someone like Anton if I wanted. But I don't want. And I certainly don't want to live in a part of the world where I could be assassinated any day."

"Don't be silly, darling. I'm sure Anton and his family are quite safe. Who'd want to kill them?"

I realized then that she didn't know anything. I got to my feet, before I spilled any beans. "Belinda, what I actually came for was to beg a favor. My maid Queenie has managed to put a huge scorch mark in my good evening dress. I can't keep wearing the same thing at dinner every night so I wondered if I could possibly wear one of yours."

"That maid of yours is a total disaster," Belinda said. "What will she do next? Give you third-degree burns when she spills your morning tea all over you? It's too bad we're snowed in or you could send her home on the next train."

"She'd never make it across Europe alone," I said, laughing in spite of everything. "She'd wind up in Constantinople and find herself in a harem. I gather big, chubby women are the thing over there."

Belinda got up and went across to a gilt-trimmed white wardrobe. "I suppose I can spare you a dress," she said and opened it. There must have been at least ten dresses hanging there.

"Belinda—how long did you expect to be here?" I asked in amazement.

"One never knows how long one will be abroad," she said. "One meets somebody and suddenly there's an invitation to the south of France or a château on the Loire, so it's always best to be prepared."

I examined the dresses one by one and chose what I thought was the least flamboyant—pale turquoise, straight and simple.

"Good choice," she said, smiling at me. "Not really my style at all, but I keep it in case I need to look virginal for somebody's parents."

"You must be a better actress than my mother," I quipped back.

"It's about time you tried it yourself and then you'd know what you were missing," she called after me as I carried the dress from her room. "And don't let your maid anywhere near it with an iron."

As I came out into the hallway there was no sound coming from behind the next door. I realized with a shock that this must be Matty's room. So who was in there with her? A man with whom she spoke French? And yet I knew she spoke German when she was with Nicholas. Her father maybe? Her mother was French, after all, so perhaps that was the language used at home, and yet Siegfried also preferred to speak German. I was tempted to go and peek through the keyhole. I crept toward the door, bent down and put my eye to it. But I could see nothing. Obviously the key was still in it.

Suddenly I heard the tap of brisk footsteps behind me. Two of the older countess chaperons were coming toward me. They looked at me with interest, on my knees in a strange hallway.

"I—uh—dropped my ring," I said. "It falls off sometimes when my hands get too cold."

"Then let us help you look for it," one of them said.

"Oh, no, thank you. I have already found it again," I said, scrambling hastily to my feet. "Most kind."

I heard a muttered exchange in German as I hurried on my way, my cheeks flaming.

I made it safely back to my room and shut the door with a sigh of relief. Still no sign of Queenie. Really this was now too much. Not that she was any use in dressing me, but one expected a maid to appear occasionally. I left the dress on my bed and made my way resolutely toward the kitchen. On my way down I passed one of the servants coming up. She curtsied.

"Is my maid down there?" I asked. Then I repeated in French, "I am looking for my maid."

"No, Highness," she answered in French. "Nobody is there."

Which probably meant that she was taking a long nap in her room. That girl could sleep more than anybody I had ever met. I chose what I hoped was the right tower and made my way up the spiral stair until I emerged to her cold and drafty corridor. If she'd snuggled under her blankets to keep warm, I couldn't blame her. As I stood there, trying to remember which door was hers, a door opened and a young woman, dressed elegantly in black, came out.

"What do you require, Your Highness?" she asked in French.

I told her I was looking for Queenie.

"She has the room next to mine. This one"—she pointed at a door—"but I do not think she is there. Excuse me. I must go to dress the princess for dinner."

I opened Queenie's door and fumbled for a light switch but couldn't find one. In the dim light from the hallway I could see that the room was unoccupied. The bed was made. Queenie was definitely not there.

Chapter 27

Still November 18
Have lost Queenie.

I retreated, puzzled and a little worried now. Where could she have gone? A secret tryst with a male servant? But I had little time to think about it. I'd have to hurry if I was to dress myself for dinner. I struggled into Belinda's dress, which fortunately had a zipper at the side and not hooks up the back, then I brushed my hair, powdered my nose and finished my toilette. Still Queenie didn't show up. I was alarmed and annoyed now. Where could she be?

I arrived in the gallery outside the banqueting hall to find it brimming with people and even more decorations and jewels than the night before. And tiaras. Oh, Lord, I should have worn my tiara. I was wondering whether I'd have time to sprint back upstairs to fetch it when I was grabbed by Prince Siegfried.

"You are looking enchanting, Lady Georgiana," he said. "A most suitable gown, if you permit me to say so."

"I didn't realize that tiaras were going to be worn," I said. "I left mine in my room."

"It does not matter. You look delightfully refreshing, the way you are."

Why was he being so charming? Did he think that I knew something about him that he would not wish to be repeated?

"Tonight you will allow me to escort you to dinner again?" he said and offered me his arm. I could hardly refuse and allowed myself to be led into the middle of the crowd. I was just wondering where his parents were when trumpets sounded. Dragomir, looking even more awe inspiring than ever, stepped forward. "The parents of the bride, Their Royal Majesties the king and queen of Romania, and the parents of the bridegroom, Their Royal Majesties the king and queen of Bulgaria," he announced. The crowd parted and the royal couples, the queens dripping jewels and suitably crowned, proceeded down the middle, while those they passed curtsied and bowed. As they passed me I curtsied. The king of Romania held out his hand to me and gave me a warm smile. "So charming," he said.

The rest of us lined up to follow the monarchs into dinner. I was seated opposite Siegfried, not far from his parents. The seat beside me was empty and I looked around, realizing I hadn't seen Matty. She came rushing in at the last minute, looking flustered.

"Sorry, Mama, sorry, Papa. I overslept and that stupid maid didn't wake me in time," she said.

Interesting, I thought. The maid had gone down in plenty of time. And the man I had heard her arguing with had not been her father. The meal started with a rich hunter's soup. Matty took a sip or two then toyed with it. I was now intrigued. Who had been in her bedroom before dinner? I looked up and down the table at the various young counts and barons, trying to put a name to each face. Nicholas had introduced them one by one as he toasted them last night, but it seemed to me that most of them spoke German, not French. The only other option was that Matty had been speaking to someone like Dragomir; but would protocol permit that she allow a retainer into her bedroom, especially as I now knew that her maid hadn't been present at that moment? Maybe Belinda had heard more and would be able to enlighten me, but my friend was now at the far end of the table, looking bored between two elderly gentlemen who were clearly both fascinated to be sitting next to her. Interestingly enough, my mother wore a similar expression at the other end of the table. Those two were so alike. It would have been much easier if Belinda had been her daughter instead of me.

Matty's unfinished soup was whisked away and a portion of trout was placed before us. The one good thing about this whole experience so far was that I had been eating good food again, but at this moment I was having as much trouble as Matty in eating anything much. Siegfried was saying something to me. I nodded and smiled, that knot of worry still in my stomach. Where the devil was Queenie? She couldn't have left the castle, which meant she was somewhere and presumably safe. Knowing her, maybe she'd found a warm corner to curl up in and would have awoken feeling guilty by now.

I glanced across at Matty, who was now trying to hide the trout under a lettuce leaf.

"Is something wrong?" I whispered to her.

"No, nothing at all. Why should anything be wrong?" she said. "But I just heard that the old man was poisoned. My maid told me."

"Your maid told you?" I asked with concern. "How did your maid find out?"

"She overheard Patrascue talking."

"I see." I wondered how many other people in the castle had overheard something and whether everyone now knew about the murder. So much for keeping it from Nicholas's father if even servants knew about it.

I observed her face. Just how much had her maid overheard? Did Matty really know that the poison was intended for Nicholas? She didn't seem to and she went on, "It's very upsetting. My whole wedding is turning into a nightmare. I don't know why I thought it was such a good idea to come to the castle in the first place. Stupid of me. Stupid, stupid, stupid. We could have been at the palace in Bucharest, going to theaters and enjoying ourselves."

She broke off as her father, the king, rose to his feet. Dragomir rapped on the table with his gavel. "Pray silence for His Majesty King Michael."

The king proceeded to welcome all his guests, especially the bridegroom and his parents, and raised his glass in a toast to friendship between the two nations forever. We drank—those of us who were in the know a little tentatively, our eyes watching everyone else. Nobody keeled over, however, and the king went on.

"As we share in the joy of our daughter's nuptials, I am delighted to announce that there will soon be a second celebration to follow this one. My son has informed me that he too will take a bride." Murmurs of approval from around the table. "And we shall be most delighted to welcome another descendant of our esteemed Queen Victoria into the family. Her father was my good friend, and I look forward to having her as my daughter."

I had been looking up and down the table to see who he was talking about.

He picked up his glass. "So I ask us all to be upstanding and raise our glasses in a toast to my son, Siegfried, and his bride-to-be, Lady Georgiana."

Everyone was on their feet. I felt as if I were falling down a deep well shaft. I wanted to scream "No-o-o-o!" but everyone was smiling and raising their glasses to me.

"You sly one. You didn't tell me." Matty embraced me and kissed me on both cheeks. "I can't say I'd want Siegfried, but I'm so glad you're going to be my sister."

What could I do? I had been brought up with etiquette rammed down my throat. A lady would never make a fuss at a banquet. A lady would never contradict a king. But this lady would never marry Prince Siegfried in a million years. Siegfried was raising his glass to me, pursing his cod lips in a kiss. Oh, God—please don't say I've got to kiss him. The company sat down again. I hastened to sit before any kiss might be required. I hadn't realized that the steward had pulled my chair out for me. One second I was standing, glass in hand; the next I was sitting on nothing and had disappeared under the table with a startled cry. Of course then all heads turned back to me again. I was hastily rescued from my undignified position, my face burning with embarrassment, and placed in my chair. Everyone around made a fuss of me, hoping that I wasn't injured and pressing glasses of champagne at me. I heard murmurs of "Too much champagne going to her head" and "Attack of nerves, poor little thing."

Believe me, if I could have crawled under the table and escaped at that moment, I would have done so. But there were too many legs around. I was profoundly grateful when the next course was brought in—a Hungarian delicacy of flaming meats on a sword. It was applauded with oohs and aahs. I watched it as if I were looking at a film of someone else's life. This couldn't really be happening to me. When had I ever given Siegfried any indication that I might marry him? I felt a cold sweat creeping over me. I had actually come close to flirting with him last night. I had begged him to dance with me to keep him from paying a visit to Field Marshal Pirin's room. And he'd taken that as a sign that I'd changed my mind. And this evening he had asked me something that I hadn't quite heard and I'd nodded and smiled. Oh, golly— had he asked me if I'd changed my mind then? I thought he was only talking about the food or the weather. Doomed, that's what I was. The words "producing an heir" echoed around my head. Followed by Belinda's laughing suggestion that I lie back, close my eyes and think of England.

That was never going to happen, if I had to throw myself off one of the turrets first. Well, maybe not quite as dramatic as that. Run away to Argentina, disguised as a peasant, perhaps, or even go and live with Granddad in Essex. I wasn't going to marry Siegfried, but I'd have to find a way out without anyone losing face. Maybe I could just happen to discover that he was more attracted to men than women and let his parents know that I could never condone such behavior. That ought to do it. Only not tonight. Not now. At this moment I had to be Siegfried's intended.

The meal finished with no more deaths, accidents or surprises and we ladies were escorted through to the withdrawing room for coffee and liquors. I was looking around to see if I could slip away unnoticed when the queen of Romania stood before me with open arms.

"My dear child," she said. "I can't tell you how happy this has made me. It was our dearest wish and that of your royal cousins too." And she embraced me.

Suddenly I saw clearly: this whole excursion had been a plot to get me to marry Siegfried. I was never Matty's dear friend at school. The queen could more properly have sent her own daughter to the wedding and not me. I was, as they say in American gangster films, set up. Framed. Duped. Ladies swarmed around me, patting me and offering congratulations. Even my mother came to peck me on the cheek. "Very sensible," she whispered in my ear. "You'll have a lovely dress allowance and he won't bother you. A little difficult about future babies that Darcy has dark hair, but so does Siegfried's mother, so that's all right."

I looked up to see Belinda looking at me with wonder and amusement on her face. As soon as she could she dragged me aside. "Have you lost your mind?" she demanded. "You can't be that desperate."

"I'm not and I haven't," I hissed back. "It's all a horrible misunderstanding. I never said that I would marry him, but I had to humor him last night and he took it the wrong way. What on earth am I going to do, Belinda?"

"Can I be a bridesmaid?" she asked, mirth bubbling up again.

"That is not funny," I snapped. "You've got to help me."

"You could let him know you're not a virgin," she said. "I gather that rather matters to people like Siegfried."

"But you know I am."

"Then remedy it rapidly."

"Thanks!" I laughed nervously. "And how am I supposed to do that? Darcy has gone away again, and I'm not desperate enough to want to remedy it with anybody else."

"I could lend you Anton, I suppose," she said as if we were talking about gloves.

"Belinda, you're not taking this seriously."

"You have to admit it is too, too delicious for words, darling. You becoming Mrs. Fishface. At least you'll be a princess and Fig will have to curtsy to you."

"I hardly think that makes up for being married to Fishface," I said. "This is turning into the worst day of my life. Speaking of which, you haven't seen my maid, have you?"

"Probably sneaking off again to get at the cakes," Belinda said.

"No, I asked and she wasn't below stairs. And she wasn't in her room, either. I'm worried about her, given everything that's happened."

"What do you mean?" she asked and I remembered that she wasn't in on Pirin's murder.

"The vampires and everything," I said, making her laugh again.

"Sweetie pie, you don't really still believe there are vampires in the castle, do you?"

"In a castle like this it's easy to believe in anything," I said.

"My lady, I believe congratulations are in order," said a deep voice right behind me. I spun around to see Count Dragomir standing there. He bowed low. "I look forward to serving you as my princess."

As he went to withdraw I remembered my worry. "Count Dragomir, if you have a moment."

"Of course, Your Highness." He put his hand to his breast and bowed. So I'd now been elevated to Highness in anticipation, had I?

I beckoned him to one side. "Count Dragomir, I am concerned because my maid seems to have disappeared. She didn't come to dress me for dinner and she is not in her room. I wondered if you could ask the other servants if they had seen her and perhaps even send out a search party to look for her for me. She may have taken a wrong turn and fallen down some dark staircase."

"You are right," he said, "there are plenty of dangerous spots in a castle like this for those who wander where they shouldn't. But do not concern yourself, my lady. I will set servants to the task immediately. We will find her for you." He was about to move off again when I spotted Lady Middlesex and Miss Deer-Harte, who had come into the room together. I decided to ask one more question.

"Count Dragomir. The English lady over there—she tells me that she observed a young man creeping about the hallways at night, and then the same young man hiding in one of the archways, watching the banquet on the first evening. I just wondered if you had any idea who that might be, or if it was possible that a stranger is hiding out in the castle."

"How can a stranger have come into the castle, my lady?" Dragomir asked. "You have seen for yourself—there is only one gate and it is guarded at all times. The only other way in would be to fly."

"Or climb up the wall?" I suggested.

He laughed. "You have been listening to the rumors of vampires, have you not? No man in his right mind would attempt to climb the castle wall."

"So none of the servants has reported seeing a strange young man—pale, with fair hair?"

"No, my lady. None of the servants has seen any kind of stranger in the castle. They would have reported to me instantly if they had. I'm afraid your English lady friend is letting her imagination run away with her. Remember how upset she was when she first arrived here. Of course His Highness, your betrothed, has light hair. Perhaps she saw him."

I wrestled with taking this one stage further and telling

him that I had seen the young man myself and his portrait had hung in my room until it was mysteriously changed for another one. But Dragomir decided this for me by saying, "Pardon me, Highness, but I am wanted elsewhere." And he backed away from me.

I was just considering how strange it would be if I really were a princess and people had to back away from my presence, when Lady Middlesex came over to me, with Miss Deer-Harte in tow.

"Well, there's a turnup for the books," she said. "I see you've made a good match for yourself. The queen will be pleased. My congratulations."

I managed a weak smile and nod. "I asked Dragomir if any of the servants had reported seeing Miss Deer-Harte's young man, but he dismissed the idea that there could be a stranger in the castle."

"I know what I saw," Miss Deer-Harte said emphatically. "And I'm going to prove to you all that I was right. He can't escape in this weather so I'll spot him eventually and I'm wearing my whistle. As soon as I see him I'll blow it to attract attention."

"Watch what you're saying, Deer-Harte—here comes that awful man." Lady Middlesex glanced over her shoulder. And sure enough, Patrascue, with a couple of his men in tow, had entered the drawing room. Although everyone else was dressed for the evening, he was still in a black street coat with the collar turned up. He stood in the doorway, looking around. It was as if an icy blast had entered the room. The women froze in midconversation. Patrascue waved his hand lazily. "Do not let me disturb you, Majesties. Pray continue."

He spotted me and women stepped aside for him as he made a beeline for me. "I hear that congratulations are in order. So you changed your mind and accepted his offer, did you, English Lady Georgiana? Soon you will be one of my people. I look forward to that day."

Again I felt the threat: soon I will have control over you. But I managed a gracious nod and words of thanks.

"The men have not yet left the dinner table, Mr. Patrascue," the queen said in her clear French voice. "I suggest you leave us ladies to finish our coffee and brandy in peace."

"Majesty." Patrascue managed a semipolite nod and retreated again. I heaved a sigh of relief.

"Don't let that man upset you, my dear," the queen said, extending her hand to me. "I can't think why he is so interested in you, but ignore him. We all do. Come and have a glass of cognac. You look quite pale." And she led me back into the fold.

Soon after, the men joined us. Siegfried and Nicholas came over to us. Siegfried took my hand and pressed his cold fish-lips against it. Uck. If it was that bad against my hand, I dared not think what it would feel like actually kissing him.

"You are a very wise girl," he said. "May I congratulate you on your good taste. You will lead a happy life."

I couldn't think of a thing to say back. I merely tried to force a smile and wished that the floor would open up and swallow me. Fortunately Matty didn't suggest dancing again so I wasn't forced to dance with Siegfried. Instead a roulette wheel was brought out and what seemed to me like large sums of money were soon being wagered.

"How old are you now, Georgiana?" Siegfried asked me.

I told him I was twenty-two. He placed a stack of chips on twenty-two. "In your honor," he said. "I feel sure you will bring me luck." And sure enough, the wretched wheel landed on the number the very next spin. Siegfried smiled and pushed a mound of chips over to me. I put random chips on the board, without the slightest idea what I was doing, and it seemed that I couldn't lose. I noticed that both Patrascue and Dragomir had entered the room and were standing watching in the shadows.

"I think I had better give you back your chips before my luck turns," I said when I could stand the tension no longer.

"Your luck will not turn while you are with me," he said, "and of course the winnings are yours to keep. You will need to start preparing your trousseau."

When I went to cash them in I was amazed and delighted to find that I had apparently won several hundred pounds. On any other occasion this unexpected windfall would have brought relief and jubilation. Tonight it was like a condemned man hearing that his horse came up on the Derby.

As soon as I was able I slipped away, up to my room. Still no sign of Queenie. I felt a growing knot of fear in my stomach. People didn't just disappear without reason. One person had been murdered already. Had Queenie stumbled upon the killer and been in the wrong place at the wrong time? If it was our light-haired young man, then she had seen him in her room and could identify him. Of course then so could I, which might mean I was also in danger. I went across and peered out into the night. It was snowing gently now and outside was the silence that only comes with snow.

"I wish you were here, Darcy," I said into the night. "I hope you're all right."

I latched my shutters, pulled the heavy drapes back into place and stood staring at the dying fire. My nerves were wound as taut as watch springs. In one day the head of a secret police had threatened me with jail, I had found that I was engaged to the repulsive Siegfried and my maid had vanished. Not to mention that there had been a murder in the castle. I certainly couldn't go to bed not knowing what had happened to Queenie. I lit a candle and made my way up to her room again. But it was untouched. The hallways and stairs were deserted. I really didn't know what else I could do. I stood peering down one dark passageway after another. Dragomir had promised to send servants to look for her and I didn't know my way around half of the castle. I had no choice but to go back to my room and get ready for bed.

I lay there for a long time, unable to sleep. I was just drifting off when I heard a scraping noise outside my window, then the rattle of my shutters. I sat up, awake and alert. I had latched the shutters from inside, hadn't I? I stared into the darkness, wishing the heavy drapes weren't covering the windows, every fiber of my being poised for flight. Nothing moved. There was no more sound. I relaxed. It must have been a sudden gust of wind that had rattled the shutters, nothing more, I told myself. But just to be on the safe side, I went to the mantelpiece and retrieved that candlestick again.

I lay there, gripping the candlestick, and began to feel rather silly. I was worrying too much, I told myself. Queenie had slipped and fallen down some disused stair. She'd probably twisted an ankle and would soon be found. And there was no such thing as vampires. Even as I had this thought I felt a waft of icy air strike my face and the curtains moved. Then, as I stared in horror, a white hand appeared between the curtains and a figure slipped noiselessly into my room.

Chapter 28

My bedroom in the middle of the night
Friday to Saturday, November 18 to 19

I sat up, gripping the candlestick. The dark figure came closer to my bed, moving with catlike grace. As he pulled aside the bed curtain and bent toward me I raised the candlestick to strike. Then I saw his silhouette against the fire. His head and neck were covered in fur. I must have gasped as I raised the candlestick because a hand grabbed my wrist as another hand came over my mouth.

"Don't make a sound," said a voice in my ear.

I stared up at him, trying to make out his features in the firelight glow. But I recognized the voice all right.

"Darcy? What on earth are you doing here?" I demanded, relief flooding over me. "You nearly scared the daylights out of me."

"I can see that." He took the candlestick from me. "Quite the little tiger, aren't we? If you hadn't taken a breath I'd have been lying here with my head bashed in. Rule one of the secrecy game—never breathe." And he smiled as he took off his coat and hat and perched on the bed beside me.

"I gasped because I caught sight of your head and I saw it was shaggy fur. I thought you were a werewolf."

"First vampires and now werewolves. What next—witches, fairies? Come to think of it there are some fairies in the castle already." He grinned. "For your information, it's only the sort of hat the local chaps wear to go hunting." He undid the strap under his chin. "See—it has earflaps. Wonderful for keeping out the cold."

"But what are you doing here?" I asked. "I thought you'd gone off with Pirin's body."

"I did," he said. "But I decided I didn't quite like what was going on at the castle so I thought I'd double back and keep an eye on things. Field Marshal Pirin won't mind. I left the car in a suitable snowdrift and skied back down again."

"Did you really just climb up the wall?"

"Not as impossible as it sounds," he said. "Someone had conveniently left a rope hanging down."

"What if it wasn't properly tied? You'd have fallen and been killed," I said.

"A fellow has to take the occasional risk in life, you know."

"Not this fellow," I said. "I don't want to find your broken body lying on rocks, is that clear?"

He looked at me tenderly and brushed back a strand of hair from my face. "Don't worry about me. I lead a charmed life. Luck of the Irish."

"Oh, Darcy, you are so infuriating I could kill you," I said and flung myself into his arms. My cheek nestled into the wet wool of his coat as he held me tightly. "You smell like wet sheep," I said, laughing.

"Stop your complaining, woman," he said. "I've plowed through a snowstorm and climbed a castle wall to see you. You should be grateful."

"I am. Very grateful. You don't know how happy I am to see you."

"So has anything significant happened since I went away?"

"Not much, apart from discovering for whom the poison was really intended, having evidence planted on me by the secret police, oh, and finding out that I'm engaged to Prince Siegfried."

"What?" He started to laugh. "You are joking, aren't you?"

"Deadly serious about all three things."

"You didn't really agree to marry Siegfried. Promise me you didn't."

"No, I didn't actually, but he thinks I did. His father announced the engagement at dinner tonight, so I could hardly leap to my feet and make a scene in front of all those people, could I?"

Darcy was scowling now. "What on earth gave Siegfried the idea that you were going to marry him?"

"I suppose I gave him too much encouragement last night."

"You encouraged him?"

"I had to find a way to keep him from going up to visit Marshal Pirin," I said. "So I begged him to dance with me. Then he said something to me this evening, but Matty was talking at the same time and I didn't quite hear what he said so I smiled and nodded." I looked up at him hopelessly. "What am I going to do, Darcy? I have to get out of it without causing an international incident."

"For now you'd better go along with it, I suppose," Darcy

said. "Don't worry. We'll sort it all out somehow. At least you don't have to worry about Siegfried trying to slink into your bedroom at night. So what about the other matters? You say you've found out that the poison wasn't intended for Pirin?"

I nodded and told him about the glass. His face was grave. "So it was intended for Nicholas. Have you mentioned this to anyone else?"

"To Nicholas himself. I thought he had a right to know and to be extra vigilant. I don't know if he's told anyone else. He might have told Matty for all I know."

"That would have been a mistake. It may be all around the castle by now."

"At least the poisoner is warned that we know the truth. He'll hardly dare try it twice."

"But he may try something else instead. It's all too easy to dispose of a person in a place like this."

"I know," I said. "My maid has disappeared too. I'm so worried about her. I can't think where she's gone."

"And you said the secret police attempted to plant evidence on you?"

"What appeared to be the vial of cyanide showed up in my trunk."

"That idiot Patrascue, I suppose." Darcy scowled again.

"You know about him?"

"Oh, yes. We've met before."

"He was so angry that you'd managed to escape with the body. He was rather horrible, Darcy. He threatened me with prison."

"What on earth would have made him suspect you? I know he's not very bright, but—"

"I think he was just trying to frighten me into implicating Dragomir," I said.

"That makes sense. It sounds like his modus operandi."

"But I didn't allow him to intimidate me. I think he was rather miffed."

Darcy was staring into the firelight. "I wonder if he has anything to do with the disappearance of your maid, then. He's taken her as a bargaining chip, maybe?"

"How horrible. I shall be furious if he's done that. She's a simple girl, Darcy. She'll be scared out of her wits."

Darcy's arm tightened around my waist. "Don't worry, I'm back now. We'll sort everything out tomorrow."

I nestled my head back against his chest and closed my eyes. "I hope so," I said. "I just wish someone would find the murderer and make everything right again."

"So you're no nearer to finding out the truth?" Darcy asked.

"If the poison was intended for Nicholas, then I suppose it's possible that we're dealing with a trained assassin, or even an anarchist who climbed in, using that rope you found, planted the poison and climbed down again. The only thing against that theory is that there don't appear to be any tracks leading away from the castle."

"You're overlooking something else," Darcy said. "Someone in the castle must have let down the rope for him. That means that he had inside help. More than one person is involved."

"We know that only Dragomir and the servants were anywhere near the table," I said, "but there is a mysterious Mr. X we have to factor in. Remember I told you a strange man came into my room and bent over my bed, and I thought he was a vampire?"

Darcy nodded. "And I told you it was a case of the wrong room."

"Well, I've looked all over the castle and I haven't seen

him anywhere again. Except that his portrait, or the portrait of someone very like him, was hanging on the wall when I first arrived and then someone changed it for the one you see now. Why would anyone do that?"

Darcy shook his head. "It doesn't make sense to me."

"If he wasn't a vampire, if he was a real person, then it is someone who knows the castle well. Perhaps the portrait was of one of his ancestors and he realized that it resembled him closely so he sneaked in and removed it." I sat up, suddenly realizing something. "Dragomir," I said. "He told me his family used to own this castle, and there is a portrait downstairs that looks just like him. What if this is another family member? Apparently they were driven from their castle by the Turks after a failed uprising. They expected their neighbors to help them, but nobody did. So what if this is a revenge killing?"

"Hardly," Darcy said. "That family was driven from the castle more than two hundred years ago. I know that vengeance is a strong force in this part of the world, but the current royal families of both Romania and Bulgaria only came to their thrones in the eighteen hundreds. They really have no ties to the Balkans. They were set in place by the European powers, and, as you know, Nicholas is from the Saxe-Coburg-Gotha line, like yourself. A Transylvanian dynasty could have no feud with them."

"Count Dragomir is bitter that he is now a glorified servant in a castle his ancestors used to own," I said.

"Then he'd want to strike at the Romanian royals, not a Bulgarian prince, wouldn't he?"

"Which brings us back to my mysterious Mr. X," I said. "Lady Middlesex's companion, Miss Deer-Harte—" I stopped as Darcy started laughing. "She can't help her name," I said. "Just stop it and listen. Miss Deer-Harte is a professional snooper. She claims she saw the same man creeping along one of the corridors at night and then she saw him lurking in an archway at dinner the first night. She says it was the archway immediately behind where Nicholas was sitting and she thinks he was casing the joint, as Lady Middlesex put it."

Darcy got up and walked over to the fire, taking off his wet coat and throwing it onto a chair. "Have you told anybody about this except me?" he asked.

"I didn't know who to tell," I said. "We've managed to keep it from the royals so far. Count Dragomir is the only one who could institute a thorough search of the place and he might well be involved."

"Don't tell anyone," Darcy said. He perched on the low chair by the fireplace and started to unlace his boots. "I may do some snooping of my own, but in the meantime don't let anyone know that I'm back. If you've no maid at the moment, all the better because I can hide out in here."

"You're not going to start snooping now, are you?" I asked.

"I have just made my way through a snowstorm and climbed a long way up a rope and I'm whacked out," he said. "Move over. I'm coming to bed."

He snuggled in beside me, wrapping me into his arms. "Now that you're betrothed to the heir to a throne I could probably face the guillotine for this," he whispered and kissed me. I tried to respond to his kiss, but the tension of everything that had happened kept intruding.

"I'm sorry. It's no use," I said. "I'm so upset by everything that I can't stop thinking and worrying."

"Don't worry about this leading to anything, because it's not going to," he said. "I'm so tired that I could fall asleep on the spot. In fact . . ."

And I saw his eyelids flutter shut. He looked adorable

with his eyes closed, almost like a child asleep, his eye-lashes unfairly long for a man's. I leaned over and kissed his cheek.

"Damn Siegfried," I muttered, even though a lady never swears.

My own eyes were drifting shut, lulled by Darcy's rhyth-mic breathing, when a terrible clattering sound, accompa-nied by an unearthly scream, jerked me awake. It sounded as if somebody had thrown every pot and pan in the castle down a flight of stairs. I leaped out of bed.

"What was that?" I asked.

Darcy opened his eyes lazily.

"Probably a servant dropped a tray of dishes. Go back to sleep."

"No, it was worse than that," I said. I grabbed the nearest cardigan, reached for my slippers and went out into the dark hallway. It seemed that the sound was loud enough to have woken other people. Siegfried was standing there, looking like a ghost in his long nightshirt. Oh, God, imagine facing that specter every night.

"Georgiana, *mein Schatz*, did you hear that noise?"

"I did."

"Do not worry. I shall protect you," he said, moving for-ward cautiously.

From below came shouts. Siegfried and I made our way to the nearest staircase.

A group had already gathered at the bottom of the spi-ral stair. They were bending over what looked like a suit of armor.

"Who can have knocked one of our suits of armor down the stairs?" Siegfried demanded. "What is happening here?"

The servants stood reverently at the sound of their mas-ter's voice.

"Highness, I heard the noise and came running," one of them said. "It appears that—"

He never finished the sentence, as a loud moan came from within the armor. Someone wrenched the visor open and a very human pair of eyes looked up at us. And the occupant groaned again.

"What is the meaning of this?" Siegfried demanded. "What foolery were you playing?"

"I was ordered to keep watch," the man said, his face twisted in pain. "Chief Patrascue set me on guard duty. He told me to disguise myself in this way."

"Ridiculous man," Siegfried snapped. "He had no right. These suits of armor are precious state heirlooms, not to be worn like carnival costumes."

"My leg," the man groaned. "Get me out of this contraption."

Just as they were extracting him with care a figure in black came flying toward us.

"What has just transpired?" the newcomer asked. He peered down at the suit of armor. "Cilic, is that you?"

"Yes, my chief, it is I," the man said.

"What are you doing down there?" Patrascue asked. I told you he wasn't very bright.

"I missed my footing and I fell," the man said, then groaned loudly again for maximum effect. "It is hard to see, wearing one of these visors."

"You had no right to instruct your man to wear our armor," Siegfried said. "What on earth were you thinking? Rather farcical, wouldn't you say?"

"I had my reasons," Patrascue said. "I placed my men invisibly on duty around the castle to protect your royal personages, but I didn't think this man would be foolish enough to attempt to move from his spot."

"I needed to find a bathroom," the man said, followed by an exceptionally loud groan as the armor was removed from his leg. "I didn't notice the top of the stairs."

"Get him to bed, and stop this nonsensical behavior at once," Siegfried said. "This is royal property and you have no authority here, Patrascue. Now go away and leave us in peace. You have upset my betrothed. Come, *mein Schatz*." And he extended his arm to me.

He escorted me to my door. "I am so sorry your sleep was disturbed by this idiot," he said. "Is there anything I can have brought to your room to help you sleep better? Some hot milk, maybe? Some more coal for the fire?"

"Oh, no, thank you, Your Highness," I stammered, conscious of Darcy presumably still lying in my bed. "I have everything I need."

"You need no longer address me as 'your highness,' *mein Schatz*," Siegfried said. "Now it is to be Siegfried and Georgiana."

"Thank you, Siegfried," I muttered.

He clicked his heels, something that had little effect in bare feet. "That is good then. Let us hope there are no more disturbances tonight." And he took my hand and put his fish lips on it again.

Chapter 29

My bedroom and not alone
Still the middle of the night

I let myself into my room with a sigh of relief. Even in the darkness I could see the bed turned back and no sign of Darcy.

"Darcy?" I whispered. He must have heard Siegfried's voice outside the door and decided to hide, just in case. I tiptoed around, lifting up drapes, peeping under the bed. "It's all right, you can come out now," I said. Still he didn't appear. I glanced over at that chest. I certainly wasn't about to open that. But I did open the wardrobe and peer inside. It was big enough to hide several men.

"Are you in there?" I asked.

"Who are you talking to?" A voice right behind me made me spin around, heart thumping.

Darcy was standing there.

"I was looking for you," I said. "Don't do that again. You're going to give me a heart attack."

"I heard the commotion and decided I better take a look

for myself," he said. "As usual that fool Patrascue was making a balls-up of things. Go back to bed, you're freezing."

I got into bed and he followed. I put my head on his shoulder. It felt wonderfully comforting and safe. This is what I want and need, I remember thinking. If only . . . I suppose I must have fallen asleep because the sound of screams at first seemed to be part of my dream. Only gradually I came to the surface and realized that they were part of the real world. Darcy was already standing up.

"What now?" he demanded. "Can't a fellow get a decent night's sleep in this place?"

"I'll go," I said. "It's probably another of Patrascue's men frightening the maids by walking around in a suit of armor."

Darcy laughed. "Quite possibly. I'll stay put for now. I really don't want anyone to know I'm here."

Siegfried was standing at his door again. "I must apologize, *mein Schatz*. Two ridiculous disturbances in one night is unforgivable. I will demand that this man Patrascue take his underlings and leave our castle immediately." He strode down the hallway with me in tow. This time we went down the first flight of stairs and met nobody. Other guests in night attire were standing at their doors along the second hallway as the screaming continued, coming up from down below.

"Some hysterical maid," my mother said as I passed her. "Probably had to fight off the footman. Happens all the time."

We came under a low archway and found ourselves at the top of that final flight of steps above the entrance hall—those alarming steps that hugged the wall with no kind of banister. A group was already assembled at the bottom. One of them was indeed a maid, now sobbing instead of screaming while other servants attempted to comfort her. Beside her was a spilled scuttle of coal. The rest of the group was standing around something on the floor.

"What is it?" Siegfried called, his voice echoing through the high-ceilinged hall. "Why are we being subjected to this noise?"

The group broke apart. A couple of maids curtsied. Dragomir stepped forward. "Highness, there has been a tragedy," he said. "The English lady. She must have fallen from a great height. There is nothing to be done."

And there at the bottom of the steps lay the body of Miss Deer-Harte, her head at an unnatural angle. I had seen death before but the heightened tension of the past few days brought bile up into my throat. My head started to sing and for a second I thought I was going to faint. I leaned against the cold stone of the wall and inched my way down the stairs before I could pass out and join Miss Deer-Harte on the flagstones below.

"Someone should let Lady Middlesex know," I said, trying to master myself. "This lady was her companion."

"Poor woman," Siegfried said, eyeing the body with distaste. "I wonder what she was doing wandering around down here in the middle of the night?"

"Maybe the commotion from Patrascue's men upset her and she was coming down for a hot drink or a cognac," Dragomir said. "Or maybe she was sleepwalking. Who knows. It is unfortunate that such a thing should happen."

There was a certain smoothness to his voice that made me look at him sharply. I knew very well why Miss Deer-Harte had been wandering around. Had she actually spotted the man she was seeking this time, and been foolish enough to follow him? And was it possible that Dragomir was somehow involved? I wanted to get back to my room to tell Darcy what had happened, but perhaps my first duty should be to break the news to Lady Middlesex.

We heard her long before we saw her. "What is this nonsense now? Why am I being dragged out of bed at this godforsaken hour?" Her voice echoed down the hallway. She came out to the top of the steps. "What do I care if some other stupid foreigner has fallen and—" She broke off, her face rigid with horror.

"Deer-Harte?" she gasped. "No. No, it can't be." And she pushed her way down to the bottom of the stairs until she was standing over the body. "Oh." She put her hand up to her mouth and a great gulping sob came out. I went over to her and put a tentative hand on her shoulder. She wasn't the sort of person one would think of embracing. She continued to stare down at her friend, her body heaving with convulsive sobs. I was as shocked as everyone else. It wasn't the reaction I had expected of her over someone I thought she considered a rather annoying companion.

"I'm really sorry," I said. "It's a horrible thing to have happened."

She nodded, fighting to compose herself. "Poor silly woman. Always imagining she saw danger and intrigue everywhere we went. She said she was going to keep her eyes and ears open."

"Yes, she must have been prowling around and fallen. Those stairs always struck me as awfully dangerous." I didn't say what I was thinking—that she hadn't fallen at all. She had been pushed.

"Come, my Lady Middlesex." Count Dragomir took over. "There is nothing you can do here. Let me escort you back to your room and have some cognac and hot milk sent up to you."

"It's all right. I'll take her," I said. "I know you have plenty to do down here."

I had to half drag Lady Middlesex back up those horrible

stairs. She staggered up like a person in a trance. But by the time we reached her room she had regained her stiff upper lip.

"So good of you," she muttered. "Bit of a shock, isn't it? Don't know what I'll do without her, actually. Grown used to having her around."

I assisted her into her room and over to her bed.

"I don't think I'll be able to sleep again," she said. "I must make arrangements somehow to have her body taken home. She wouldn't want to be buried on foreign soil. She hated it abroad, poor thing. She only came with me out of extreme devotion. I should never have expected it of her . . . it was wrong of me." And she rooted around for a handkerchief, which she pressed to her face.

"Do you want me to stay with you?" I asked.

"No, I'd rather be alone, thank you," she said stiffly.

"Send one of the servants for me if you need me, then," I said.

She nodded. As I reached the door she said in a flat voice, "She sensed it, didn't she? The moment we arrived she called it a house of death. But she never realized it was her own death that she was sensing."

I closed the door behind me and hurried back through the halls to my room. Again Darcy was nowhere to be seen. I slipped into the bed, still warm with his presence, and lay there, thinking how comfortable and secure it had felt to lie in his arms. Then an image swam into my mind of Siegfried lying in bed beside me. No! I wanted to yell. I just wanted to be away from this horrible place and to feel safe again. Because something had struck me on the way back through the hallways. If Miss Deer-Harte had been killed because she had spotted the murderer and could identify him, then I was also in similar danger.

I lay awake, staring at the dark canopy of the bed over me, trying to make sense of things.

Someone creeping into my room, bending over my bed. The portrait on the wall being changed. Matty with blood around her mouth. Pirin drinking from a glass intended for Nicholas. And now Miss Deer-Harte lying dead. What did they mean? What linked them together if I was trying to be rational and not believe that I was in a place inhabited by vampires? But I couldn't come up with a rational answer. In fact I didn't like the only answer that kept coming back to me—what if the young man we had seen was a vampire who haunted this castle and now Matty, Dragomir and God knows how many of the servants were under his spell. That would account for nobody else except for Miss Deer-Harte noticing him as he stood in the archway and watched the banquet. I knew this theory sounded ridiculous, but up in Scotland you'd meet plenty of people who swore that they had seen fairies, and we had a couple of ghosts at Castle Rannoch. So who was to say that vampires didn't exist?

Eventually I suppose I must have dozed, because when I opened my eyes slanted sunlight was shining on that hideous portrait on the far wall. I was lying alone in the enormous bed and there was still no sign of Darcy. I got up, washed and dressed, then went down to breakfast. The breakfast room was full of people, chatting amiably as they ate. Nobody seemed to know or care about last night's tragedy, but then to them she was only a companion who had lost her footing and fallen. Only Lady Middlesex was not present.

Nicholas smiled at me as I poured myself some coffee. "Lovely bright sunshine for a change. Good day for hunting, I think, if the snow is not too deep."

"My bridesmaids can't come, so don't try to entice them," Matty said. "It's our final dress fitting this morning."

"I wouldn't dream of luring young ladies away from their dress fitting," Nicholas said. "I want you all to look your beautiful and radiant best on the big day."

I happened to be looking at Matty's face. I saw the briefest flash of annoyance or panic before she smiled. "Of course we will all be radiant and beautiful, my dear Nicholas. We must look our best for the big day."

I continued to watch her as she took a nibble of toast. Something he had said had made her upset or angry. And now I studied her, I thought she looked terrible—white and drawn, with bags under her eyes. Not at all the radiant bride-to-be. She was now playing with the rest of her slice of toast, crumbling it into tiny pieces, before she pushed the plate away from her, got up and left. I got the sense that she was under a good deal of strain. So why would that be? I found an interesting train of thoughts creeping into my head. My grandfather, the former policeman, had always quoted his superior officer, an Inspector he greatly admired, as saying, "Go for the obvious and then work out from there. Nine times out of ten the answer is right under your nose."

So when it came to ease of putting poison into Nicholas's glass, then Matty and Dragomir would be the two people who could have done it most easily. Until now I had dismissed Matty as the bride. Why would she want to kill her future husband? But now, as I continued to observe her, I recalled that her gaiety had seemed forced at times. She had been playing the part of the happy bride-to-be and yet she had made remarks about Nicholas being a good choice, if one had to get married. She had talked about how she would rather have stayed on in Paris. What if she had decided to take the ultimate way out of this marriage by poisoning her bridegroom?

I decided that it was about time I tackled her and got

the truth out of her. I'd find an opportunity this morning during our dress fitting. After all, I'd be perfectly safe in a room full of young women and Darcy was somewhere in the castle. But just in case there was some truth to this vampire stuff, shouldn't I be prepared? I stood looking at the spread of breakfast dishes. Some of those cold meats had plenty of garlic in them, judging by the smell of them. Did that count as a defense against vampires, or did one need the actual cloves? I could hardly go down to the kitchen and ask for cloves of garlic, so I loaded up my plate with various slices of sausage. It wasn't exactly my choice of breakfast but I got through them. Afterward even I could smell the garlic on my breath—I only hoped any potential vampires could too. Now, if I could just find a small cross somewhere in the castle and slip it into my pocket . . .

As I got up to leave Nicholas was standing at the doorway, speaking with his father. His face was grim. There was a brief exchange and his father strode off down the hallway. Nicholas saw me and gave a grimace.

"The old man is making a fuss about Pirin," he said. "He wanted to know when the telephone wires will be repaired. He needs to know how Pirin is doing, whether he has reached the hospital safely and whether his physician is on his way from Sofia. He was demanding that a car be sent to find out. I kept telling him that it had snowed again and the pass would be closed, but he's not taking no for an answer. This could prove extremely tricky. I wonder where Darcy is."

I was tempted to tell him that Darcy was in the castle, but decided to leave that decision up to Darcy himself when he reappeared. I couldn't think what he might be doing, but I was sure it was important.

"Your bride is beginning to show the strain of the unfortunate events," I said.

"Yes, she's very sensitive," Nicholas said. "Another death last night. I wish to God I hadn't given in to Maria and agreed to hold the ceremony at this castle. It would have been so much more agreeable at the palace."

As I left him, I spotted Count Dragomir, hurrying ahead of me. I called his name and he turned, reluctantly.

"I was wondering if you had any news about my maid yet," I said. "I am extremely worried."

"I am sorry, Highness. I have had no news," he said. "But don't worry, my people will keep searching for her."

"She can't have disappeared," I said. "I want an out-and-out effort today to look for her, or I'll have to ask Mr. Patrascue to put his men on the job."

It was a good threat. I saw a look of alarm in his eyes. "Mr. Patrascue could not find his own nose if it were not attached to his body," he said. "I have promised we will find her and we will."

Then he hurried off, his cape flying out behind him. I wandered down the hallways, looking for a suitable cross, but could only come up with a six-foot-tall crucifix in a niche. I could hardly carry that around with me. I also spotted a cross around the neck of one of the servants, but she spoke no English and I couldn't make her understand that I only wanted to borrow it. So in the end I had no choice but to make my way to the small salon and our dress fitting. A small voice in my head whispered that I was being silly to be afraid of a school friend, but I didn't know what to believe anymore.

Some of the other bridal attendants were already in the small salon, talking together in German in a tight little group. They glanced up guiltily as I entered and I was sure they had been talking about me. Sure enough Hannelore called out to me, "We were talking of your betrothal to Prince

Siegfried. We are not very happy for you. We feel perhaps you may not know the truth about him. You should find out about this Siegfried before you agree to marry him."

"Thank you," I said. "I will take your advice."

She drew me closer to her. "We hear that his interest is not in women, you understand? He will not make you satisfied in the bed."

What should I say, that I had no intention of marrying him? Her concern was genuine and touching. "Thank you," I said. "I won't rush into anything, I promise."

"And if you think it is nice to be a princess," Hannelore continued, "it is not so much fun. Always duty, duty, duty."

The other girls who understood English nodded agreement. At that moment Matty came into the room.

"So are we ready to look divine?" she asked brightly. She had made up her face with bright circles on her cheeks and red lips. The fittings started. Our dresses were almost finished and it was only a case of a final nip and tuck to make sure they hung perfectly. To go over each dress was a floor-length white fur-lined cloak—one of the most heavenly things I had ever seen. When we tried them on we looked like snow queens. My own fitting was finished but I hung around by the fire, waiting for a moment to catch Matty alone. She was certainly acting in a bright and animated way, laughing and giggling with the other girls, making me wonder if perhaps it might be drugs and not being a vampire that accounted for her mood swings.

At last she came over to the fire and held out her hands to warm them.

"It's freezing in this place, isn't it?" she said. "Reminds me of school. Remember how cold it used to be in the dormitories?"

"That was usually because Belinda had left the window open to climb out at night and visit her ski instructor," I said, smiling at the memory. I came to stand beside her and decided to take the plunge. "Matty, you and I need to talk."

She reeled a little from the amount of garlic on my breath, but she didn't collapse, run off or melt away as any good vampire should have done in the presence of garlic. "What about? Something is wrong?" The smile faded from her face.

I looked around the salon. Everyone seemed to be occupied. "I know," I said in a low voice. "I know the truth."

She looked startled, then she shrugged. "Of course you do. He was silly enough to come into your room by mistake, and I was foolish enough to forget about his picture on your wall. He painted that picture for me, you know. He's a brilliant artist. He always had talent, even as a small boy."

As she talked she slipped her arm through mine and steered me away from the other girls and the clatter of sewing machines. At first I hadn't a clue what she was talking about, but gradually light began to dawn. She'd dropped enough hints that she didn't love Nicholas, that she'd wanted to stay in Paris. So she'd fallen in love with another man. But the phrase about the small boy was baffling.

"You knew him when he was a boy?"

"Of course," she said. "He grew up in this castle."

"In this castle?"

She nodded. "His father works for us. We played together when I came here in the summers. We were always such good friends as children. And then I was sent to Paris and I found he was there too, studying art. This time we fell in love—wonderful, passionate love. Then my father informed me that I must marry Nicholas. I begged him to change his mind, but he wouldn't listen. A princess always puts duty first, he said. I told him I loved someone else but he forbade me to see him again." She reached out and covered my hand with her cold one. "In the end one does one's duty. Just like you and Siegfried. I'm sure you don't love him. You can't love him. But you do what the family expects of you."

I nodded. "It must be really hard for you. I'm not sure I can actually marry a man I don't love."

"Vlad wanted me to run away with him," she whispered, glancing up to make sure that the other occupants of the salon were still far away and engaged in activity. "We'd live together in Paris and be happy. But I'd been brought up with duty rammed down my throat. I couldn't do it."

"So you asked to have the wedding here because of your happy memories?"

"Vlad suggested it so that we could be together one last time," she said. "He promised he'd find a way to come and see me. He knows this castle so well. You saw him climbing up the wall, didn't you? He always was one for taking horrible risks, but how else could he get in to see me without being seen himself?"

"You left a rope for him hanging down?"

"No, I had no idea he was going to try to scale the wall. We attached the rope afterward, from my maid's room, in case he had to make a hasty retreat."

"And I am sleeping in your old bedroom," I said, understanding now. "He was expecting to find you there. No wonder he looked so surprised."

"Yes, my parents announced at the last minute that I must sleep as far as possible from my future bridegroom and close to my chaperon, Countess Von Durnstein, until the wedding. My father is very much into old-fashioned protocol, you know."

"Is Vlad still here?" I asked.

"Oh, yes. There are fortunately several secret rooms in the castle. He's been hiding out and my maid, Estelle, is so wonderfully loyal. She brings him food. And speaking of food—you also saw my other guilty secret, did you not?"

"When was that?"

"In the hallway outside the kitchen," she whispered, glancing around again. "I couldn't resist, you know."

"What exactly were you doing?" I asked cautiously, not really wanting the answer.

She leaned closer. "Cook's cherry tarts. All that wonderful gooey cherry jam. I went down to the kitchen and she'd been baking them. I stole a couple. I've had to be on this strict diet, you see, so that I fit into the wedding dress, but I've always had trouble with my weight. I like to eat. That was another thing—Vlad didn't care when I had meat on my bones. He loved me just as I was." She chewed on her lip. "Now I'm afraid that Nicolas will not like me if I put back the weight and he sees me as I was when I was eating normally."

I looked at her with compassion. I could understand how awful it must be to give up one's true love and marry someone one doesn't love at all. And to condemn oneself to not eating. But I couldn't forget the big question that still remained unanswered. "Matty, about Pirin's death. Do you know who put the poison in that glass?"

"It had to be an outsider, an assassin," she said. "Who else could it be?"

"You don't think that your Vlad might have . . ."

"Killed a foreign field marshal? Why would he do that?" she demanded angrily.

"Matty, there's something you should know," I said, realizing I was taking a risk. "The glass of wine was intended for Nicholas."

"What?"

"Pirin was a peasant," I said. "He had never learned decent table manners. And he was very drunk. He grabbed the nearest full glass of wine when he made that toast and he grabbed it with his left hand. I was sitting opposite him. I saw. It was Nicholas's wineglass, only Nicholas had switched to drinking champagne when the toasts started, remember?"

"No," she said so loudly that the other women in the room looked over at us. Then she shook her head violently and lowered her voice again. "No, that's ridiculous. Unthinkable. Vlad would never. He's sweet. He's kind. You should see how he treated me in Paris. Like a princess should be treated." She took my hand. "I can trust you as my dear old friend. Come and meet him for yourself, come and ask him yourself, then you'll see. I've told him about you, and soon you are to be my dear sister."

"All right," I said.

She led me out of the salon, then opened a door in the paneled wall that led to a narrow side staircase. "My little shortcut to the secret room," she said. "This castle is full of them. We used to have such fun playing hide-and-seek when we were children. Except for Siegfried. He was stuffy even then. Watch your step, they are very narrow and it's dark in here."

She started up the steps ahead of me. I went to follow. One second I was standing on the stone floor; the next, the slab I was standing on tilted downward and I was plunging into darkness.

Chapter 30

In a dungeon. Not very nice.
Saturday, November 19

I was half sliding, half tumbling down a rough stone chute, unable to stop or slow my fall, waiting for the inevitable moment when I would crash onto a hard surface below. The ridiculous image of Alice in Wonderland, falling down the rabbit hole, flashed through my mind as I struck another stone panel that swung open. Then I tumbled into nothingness, had an odd sensation of arms reaching out to me, then landing on something softer than I'd expected, before I hit the stone floor and everything went black.

I came back to consciousness to some kind of awful noise—an unearthly wailing sound. I opened my eyes. I was lying on a cold stone floor in almost total darkness. A round white thing was hovering over me—a pale moon face, staring at me with its mouth open in some kind of horrible chant. Then I made out words in the wail.

"Oh, lawks, oh, blimey, oh, miss."

"Queenie?" I murmured. I tried to sit up and the world

swung around alarmingly while a pain shot through my head.

"Sorry, miss. I tried to catch you but you was coming too fast. At least I broke your fall a little."

"That was you I landed on?" I asked.

"That's right."

"Goodness. That was brave of you. Did I hurt you?"

"Not too bad. I'm well padded. But you come flying down at such a rate—"

"Well, you would too if the floor suddenly opened up beneath you," I said.

"I know. I did. Luckily I landed on me bum—pardon the expression, miss—and like I said, I'm well padded. But it weren't no worse than when my old dad used to take his belt to me when I was a kid." She helped me into a sitting position. "I ain't half glad I am to see you. You're a proper toff to come and rescue me. I knew you would, of course."

"I hate to disillusion you, Queenie," I said, "but I'm now a captive with you, not your rescuer."

"Where are we, miss? This ain't half a creepy old place."

I looked around. We were in a circular chamber. A glimmer of gray light came in through a small grille near the bottom of one wall. Apart from that, every surface was stone. There was no door of any kind.

"I rather fear we're in the oubliette we were joking about earlier."

"The oobly-what?"

"It's a place where you put unwanted guests," I said. "I've heard of them in old castles but I've never actually seen one before. You step on the wrong slab, it opens and you fall into a dungeon where nobody will ever find you again."

"Ooh, don't say that, miss." She grabbed at my sleeve. "Someone's going to find us, aren't they?"

"I hope so," I said. But even as the words came out I wondered who actually knew of the presence of this place. Matty had obviously been told about it because Vlad had grown up here and knew every nook and cranny. But did others know? Servants? Dragomir? I had a horrible vision of everyone hunting for me throughout the castle and not finding me, while Queenie and I starved to death. Not the ending I would have chosen; in fact, I think I'd actually have preferred to marry Prince Siegfried if I'd had an option—which shows you how desperate I was feeling. "Don't worry," I said. "We're going to get out somehow, I promise. How did you come to be in here, by the way?"

"I don't rightly know," she said. "I saw a man taking what looked as if it would be a shortcut to the kitchen. He opened a door in the paneling and he went through, and I saw he was going down a staircase so I thought I'd follow him. Next thing I knew, I was falling down a shaft and I landed up in here."

"This man—what did he look like?"

"I can't really tell you. He was dressed in black. One of the servants, I thought."

"Did he have light blond hair?"

"Now that you mention it, he did."

"Then he thought you were following him for a reason. That's why you landed up here."

"Who is he, miss? A criminal?"

"He's the young man you saw in your room that night, and he may well be a murderer," I said. "When we get out of this place, we'll have to go carefully."

"How are we going to get out?" she asked. "There's not even a door."

"Well, we got in," I said, trying to sound more cheerful than I felt. "So we can try getting out the same way. If you're strong enough to hold me on your shoulders, I can reach the ceiling. Perhaps I can push one of those slabs open."

She crouched down and let me climb onto her back, then we inched our way around until I was directly under the high point of the arched ceiling. I found the slab that had opened to admit me all right but it was positioned so exactly that there wasn't enough room to get a grip on it. I broke my fingernails trying to drag it down, but it was no use.

"That's not going to work," I said. "You'd better let me down."

I clambered off her back and we sat panting while I examined the room.

"There's that little grille in the wall down there," I said. "I'm quite skinny, maybe I would fit through it."

"Don't try it, miss. It's bound to be dangerous," she said.

"We're not just going to sit here and hope that someone finds us," I said. "I've already had people searching for you all over the castle. If they couldn't find you I don't think there is much hope that we'll be discovered." I lay on the floor and peered out. It wasn't encouraging. All I could see was another stone wall, about ten feet away. I tugged at the grille, I pushed it, but it wouldn't budge. Truthfully I didn't think it was likely to, having been in place for several hundred years, but I had to try.

"Help me pull this thing, Queenie," I said.

We pulled together but it was hard to get our fingers through the small holes of the grille. We turned around and tried kicking it. No use.

"We need some leverage," I said. "My petticoat is silk. Are you wearing a cotton one?"

"A cotton petticoat? Yes, miss."

"Then take it off."

She obeyed, eyeing me strangely as I attempted to tear it into strips. Eventually, using teeth and nails, Queenie's hairpins and my brooch, we did manage to rip it and ended up with a couple of long strips. We tied these to the grille.

"When I say pull, you brace your feet against the wall and pull with all your might," I said.

We pulled. Suddenly there was a cracking, crumbling sound as the grille came flying out. We looked at each other and nodded with satisfaction.

"But I don't see how you're going to get out of there, miss," Queenie said. "You'll get stuck, likely as not."

I had to say that I agreed with her. The opening couldn't have been much more than about fifteen inches high and two feet wide.

"Luckily I'm skinny and I have been told by milliners that I have a small head," I said.

"I'd go out for you if I could, miss," Queenie said, "but I don't think my big toe would fit through there, to say nothing of the rest of me."

I looked at her and smiled with real fondness. She might be the worst servant in the world, but she was trapped in a hopeless situation and she wasn't making a fuss.

"Well, here goes," I said and stuck my head out of the hole. What I saw wasn't encouraging. I was near the bottom of a long shaft of some sort. It might be a well, because there was ice below me, and there was another grille over the top, far above me. I couldn't even see any other openings in the side.

"Maybe if we shouted, someone would hear us," I said. "Try shouting 'help' with me, Queenie."

We shouted. I tried it in French. Nothing happened.

"There seem to be the remains of iron rungs on the far side," I said. "If the ice holds me, I could lower myself down and get across."

"What if it don't hold you, miss?"

"The worst that can happen is that I'll get really wet and cold," I said. "It's worth a try. I'm going out backward."

I lay on the floor and stuck my feet through the hole, then I inched myself backward until my feet were hanging down, then until I was bent at the waist and then until I was braced at my shoulders.

"Hold my hands and don't let go until I tell you," I said. Queenie took my hands in hers. I squeezed my shoulders together, then tilted my head to one side to take it through the hole. The ice was still about two feet below me.

"You can let go of my hands, Queenie," I said. "I'm going to try to climb down."

I hadn't bargained for the slippery rocks. I slithered down and landed hard on the ice, which groaned ominously. I immediately dropped to my knees then crawled forward. It bobbed as I moved but I reached the other wall. Then I found one of the old rungs and started to climb. They were broken and slippery and it was horrible going. One of them came out of the wall when I went to haul myself up on it and it landed on the ice with an echoing thunk.

"You can do this," I said to myself. "You've climbed mountains at home. It's no worse."

After what seemed an eternity I reached the top.

"I'm at the top, Queenie," I called back down. "I'm going to try to push up the grille."

As soon as I looked at it, I realized that this was going to be an impossible task. The grille was in the middle, a long stretch from where I was. I could just about reach the edge of it, but I couldn't push it with any strength at all, stretched out like that. I fought back tears of frustration. I cleared as much snow as I could from the grille and tried to look out. All I could see were blank stone walls. Not a friendly door or window in sight. Surely someone would come this way eventually. The question was how long I could hold on before my frozen hands stopped obeying me.

"Help!" I called again. "*Au secours!*" Drat. I wished I knew the word for help in German, as this area used to be part of the Hapsburg Empire and many of the peasants spoke that language.

Suddenly I heard heavy breathing above me and a face peered down at me. I looked up hopefully, only to find it was a long snout covered in gray fur. It was hard to tell, from this angle, whether it was a dog or a wolf.

"Good dog, good boy," I said.

The lip lifted in a snarl.

"That's right," I said, suddenly realizing, "go ahead and bark. Woof woof."

I flicked snow at it, making it step back. I even stuck my fingers through recklessly and waggled them. It cocked its head suspiciously but it didn't bark. Then in desperation I started to sing. I'm not the world's best singer and my singing once made the dogs at home start to howl. "Speed, bonny boat, like a bird on the wing," I sang. "The Skye Boat Song," one of my favorites.

"Are you all right, miss?" Queenie shouted.

"Just singing," I called back down. "Join in."

"I don't know it."

"Then sing something you know."

"At the same time as you?"

"It doesn't matter."

We sang. She, I believe, was singing "If you were the only girl in the world" while I continued with "The Skye Boat Song." It sounded terrible. At last the dog put his head back and howled. The song echoed up from the well and the howl echoed from those walls.

Then I heard a human voice, cursing the dog.

"Help!" I called. "Get me out."

A face appeared on the limits of my vision. The woman gasped, crossed herself and went to back away.

"Get help!" I shouted after her in English and French. "English princess."

She went. The dog went. I hung there, fighting back disappointment. She thought I was some kind of evil spirit or something. She had run away. They'd probably avoid this place for years after this. Then I heard the most blessed of sounds: several raised voices. And men stood over me, one of them carrying an ancient shotgun, the others with sticks, their faces taut with fear.

"Help me, please," I said. "Fetch Count Dragomir. I English princess." This was a slight exaggeration but I knew the word was the same in all the languages.

They were talking furiously among themselves, then suddenly one of them came back with a crowbar, the grille was pried open and hands pulled me free. At that moment Count Dragomir came striding into the courtyard. His face registered horror and shock as he recognized me.

"*Mon Dieu.* Lady Georgiana. What has happened to you?"

"I was tipped into your famous oubliette," I said. "My servant is still down there."

"But the oubliette, it was just a legend," he said. "Nobody ever discovered it."

"It exists, trust me. My servant is in it and the opening is too small to get her out. Send down some hot tea or soup or something to her and then we'll try to find the opening in the castle."

Dragomir was already barking commands.

"We'll soon get you out, Queenie," I shouted. "Help is on the way. Don't worry."

The sound echoed so strangely down the shaft that I wasn't quite sure she understood me. "My dear Lady Georgiana, come inside and let us warm you up," Dragomir said, opening a door into some kind of outbuilding. "Some hot coffee and blankets."

"We have to get my maid out first," I said. "Take me back to the castle immediately, please."

"Very well. As you wish." Dragomir escorted me across a couple of courtyards, through a door in a wall and up some steps and we were back in the castle proper.

"How did you happen to fall into this oubliette, Highness?" he asked.

"I was following Princess Maria Theresa," I said. "She went ahead of me and . . ." I couldn't bring myself to say to him that she had taken me that way deliberately so that I would step on the wrong slab and fall. I was now quite sure that she and Vlad had planned the murder of Prince Nicholas together. I didn't know which of them administered the poison, but one of them did. The problem was that we were all assembled for her wedding—two royal families, plenty of important personages and plenty of opportunities for a diplomatic incident. If only I could locate Darcy, he'd know what to do. But my first task was to rescue Queenie.

"I'll show you the oubliette," I said and led Dragomir through the halls until we reached the right spot. I was just searching for the door in the paneled wall when I heard the sound of feet behind me. I turned to see two of Patrascue's men bearing down on me.

"Please to come with us," one said in atrocious French. He grabbed my arm.

"Wait," I said trying to shake myself free. "Where are you taking me? We must save my friend first."

But another man grabbed my other arm and I was swept along the corridor at a great pace.

"Wait a minute. Slow down and listen to me," I shouted but to no avail. The third man went ahead and flung open a door. I was borne inside and came upon a tableau. The king of Romania and Siegfried were sitting in high-backed chairs on one side of the fireplace. The king of Bulgaria, Nicholas and Anton sat on the other. In front of them stood Darcy, his arms being held by two policemen. And beside him stood Patrascue.

Chapter 31

Bran Castle
Saturday, November 19

As I was thrust into the room, the tableau moved and they all turned to stare at me in horror.

"What is the meaning of this?" the king demanded, rising to his feet. "My dear, what has happened to you?"

"She was obviously attempting to flee and she was caught by my men," Patrascue said before I could answer. "Now we have apprehended both the suspects. The case is complete. You can proceed with your wedding with confidence and serenity."

"What are you talking about?" I demanded.

Darcy gave me a long look that warned me not to say too much. "This idiot has told Their Majesties that Pirin was poisoned, and what's more, he has got it into his head that you and I were paid to come and carry out the murder."

"It is too obvious for someone of my experience and talent," Patrascue said. "Mr. O'Mara thought he would cleverly pretend to drive away with the body before I had a chance to examine it. I expect he has tried to hide the evidence. And Lady Georgiana denies that she hid the vial of poison in the trunk in her room. But they cannot fool Patrascue. I ask myself, why are they really here? Why should she come to this wedding instead of a member of the British royal family?"

"I am a member," I said. "The king is my cousin."

"But why send a mere cousin to represent the English people, when the king could send one of his own children?"

"Because I asked my daughter to invite her," the king said in a voice taut with annoyance. "My son let it be known that he had selected her as his future bride and we wanted her to have a chance to know us better. So you will please treat her with the same respect you accord to us. Is that clear?"

Patrascue gave the merest hint of a bow. "Of course, Majesty. But if she is involved in the cold-blooded murder of an important man, surely your son would wish to know the truth about this before he entered into marriage with such a woman."

"Of course I'm not involved," I said.

Siegfried came over to me. "Georgiana, did these men hurt you? You look terrible. You are bleeding."

"Not these men," I said. "I fell into a dungeon. Count Dragomir did not believe me but there really is an oubliette in this castle. My maid is still down there."

"An oubliette in this castle? Surely it is just a legend."

"I assure you it's very real," I said.

"How did you come to stumble upon this oubliette?" the king asked.

I hesitated. I was in a foreign country about to implicate its princess. What if nobody believed me? It would be easy enough for the king to agree with Patrascue that Darcy and I were the guilty ones. But if I were her father, I'd want to know the truth, wouldn't I? Maybe I could make her confess somehow.

"Would you ask your daughter to join us, Your Majesty?" I said. "I believe she can help prove my innocence."

"Of course. Please tell the princess her presence is required in my private sitting room." One of Patrascue's men bowed and departed.

"Perhaps you are innocent, Lady Georgiana," Patrascue said. "Perhaps it is this Mr. O'Mara who hid the poison in your room to implicate you while he fled with the body. We have heard rumors about Mr. O'Mara. He is a ruthless man and very interested in making money, is this not correct? A certain scandal at a casino?"

Darcy actually laughed. "The scandal was that I was chucked out because I kept winning. They thought I was cheating. Actually I was just damned lucky. The luck of the Irish, don't you know? But let me assure you that I'm the son of a respected Irish lord. Killing people for money is not something I'd do. Killing people because they annoy me, on the other hand . . ." He stared hard at Patrascue. If the matter hadn't been so serious I would have laughed. Darcy didn't seem to be particularly worried.

"Then why are you here, Mr. O'Mara? I understand from interviewing the other young men that you are not a particular friend of Prince Nicholas."

"We were good friends at school," Nicholas said angrily. "The rest doesn't concern you."

Suddenly it struck me that Nicholas might have anticipated some kind of trouble at this wedding and Darcy had been invited to protect him.

"But understand that he is here at my invitation and I have absolute confidence that he has nothing to do with the death of Field Marshal Pirin. The whole suggestion is ludicrous. You should be looking for—"

He broke off as Matty came in, looking puzzled and concerned. When she saw me, a relieved smile crossed her face.

"There you are, Georgie," she said. "I wondered where you had disappeared to. We were all looking for you."

I smiled back. "Oh, I think you know very well where I went to, since you sent me there."

"What do you mean? One minute you were following me up the stairs, but when I reached the top, I turned around and you weren't there."

"Maybe that was because I was in the process of falling down the oubliette," I said.

She gave a tight, nervous laugh. "Oubliette? There's no such thing. Believe me, we hunted for it when we were children, didn't we, Siegfried?"

"Then allow me to show you," I said. "My maid is still trapped in the dungeon below and it's about time someone rescued her."

I marched them back through the halls until I recognized the place where the door had to be.

"Would you please show us the door in the paneling, Your Highness?" I asked Matty.

She shrugged, stepped forward and pushed open a section of the wall.

"You'll see a staircase leads up from here," I said, "and one of these flagstones tips an unsuspecting victim down into a dungeon. I'm not sure which."

"But I go up and down this way all the time," Matty said. "It is a shortcut from my room to the main floor."

"Then, Your Highness, would you like to try them out for us?" I asked.

"Of course." She walked confidently to the staircase and ascended the first couple of steps.

"You see?" She turned and smiled. "There is nothing here but an ordinary passageway."

"There must be a knob or a lever or something that triggers the mechanism," I said. "Look on the walls. Princess Maria was ahead of me, and—"

Matty looked up sharply. "One minute. You don't think that I sent you into this dungeon? That I brought you here to trick you?"

"I'm afraid that's exactly what I think," I said. "I'm sorry, Matty, but you didn't really want to introduce me to Vlad, did you? You wanted him to stay hidden."

"What?" Matty's father roared. "Vladimir? That boy is here, in the castle? When I forbade you to see him again?"

"No, Father. Of course not," Matty said. "Here's not here. I don't know what Georgiana is talking about."

"Come down here, young woman," the king commanded. "Come out into the light where I can see your face. I always know if you are lying to me."

"Father, please, not in front of these people." Matty came back down the stairs. Patrascue's men, who had crammed themselves into the narrow hallway, stepped aside for her. There was a lot of jostling and moving and as she stepped down from the bottom step the floor suddenly tilted beneath her. Matty screamed as she started to fall. Hands reached out to grab her and she was dragged back to safety. We stood staring at the black cavity below us.

"Now do you believe me?" I asked. "Queenie?" I shouted. "Can you hear me?"

"Is that you, miss?" a voice echoed up, sounding distant and hollow. "I'm still here."

"We'll have you out in a jiffy," I shouted back.

"Your Majesty, what is happening?" Count Dragomir appeared behind us. "Is there really an oubliette? After all these years! I thought it was just a legend."

"My maid is still down there," I said.

"I apologize, Lady Georgiana. We will have her brought out instantly."

The king turned to him. "And I ask you, Dragomir—did you know that Vlad was in the castle?"

"I did not, Majesty," Dragomir said angrily. "I made it clear to him that he should stay away."

"I want the castle searched in case he is hiding out," the king said. "You will set every available man to this task, is that clear?"

"Yes, Majesty," Dragomir said in a flat voice, "but Vlad gave me his word and—"

"He's not here, Father," Matty shouted.

"Every available man!" the king thundered. "And as for you, madam"—he turned to glare at his daughter—"I want to know the truth from you. Return to my study this instant. We can't have matters like this shouted up and down the halls for everyone to hear."

He marched his daughter back to the study. The rest of us followed. When the door was shut behind us the king spoke coldly.

"The truth, Maria. Is that boy in the castle? Have you dared to see him again?"

"No, Father," Matty said. "Georgiana misunderstood."

"I saw him," I said. "I'm sorry, Matty, if it weren't a question of murder I wouldn't have betrayed your secret, but it is. And your bridegroom has a right to know that you tried to kill him."

"What?" Matty shrieked. "No, that's quite wrong. I told you Vlad is sweet. He'd never kill anyone."

"And what about you?" I said. "You dropped enough hints that you didn't want to marry Nicholas, that you were being forced into it when you loved someone else."

"You think that I put poison in Nicholas's glass?"

"One moment, if you please." Patrascue stepped between us. "I do not understand. It was a Bulgarian field marshal who was poisoned. This I was told. Is it not true?"

"The poison was intended for me," Nicholas said. He was staring at Matty with horror and disbelief on his face. "Pirin was a peasant. He had no table manners. He grabbed the nearest full glass and it was mine." He shook his head. "I can't believe this of you, Maria. If the idea of marrying me was so abhorrent to you, why didn't you tell me? I would never have expected you to subject yourself to a life of unhappiness."

"No, Nicholas." She went over to him and put her hand gently on his arm. "You are not abhorrent to me. You are a kind, decent person and I should not object to spending my life with you. I just happened to fall in love with someone else. Someone beneath me whom I could not marry. But I swear that I didn't try to kill you. Neither did Vlad."

"Then you admit he was here?" Patrascue threw himself into the fray. It was almost like watching a play.

"All right. I admit it. But he just came to say good-bye to me, that's all."

"Where is he now?" Patrascue asked.

"Gone. Long gone."

"How could he leave the castle when we are snowed in?"

"He had skis with him," Matty said. "He left before that man was poisoned."

I didn't believe her for a minute and neither did Patrascue.

"You say that you saw him, Lady Georgiana?" he asked, spinning sharply to address me. "When was this?"

"On my first night here he came into my room by mistake. He thought that it was Princess Maria's room. And someone else spotted him, observing the banquet—Miss Deer-Harte, the English lady who is now also dead, whom we can conclude was pushed from a staircase as she was snooping at night."

"So, it is a question of two murders, not just one?" Patrascue asked.

"The English lady could have fallen," Siegfried pointed out.

"She would not have been going down those stairs if she had not been following somebody," I said. "She was determined to catch the man she had seen."

"I can prove to you that Vlad had nothing to do with this second death," Matty said. "All right, he is not long gone. He was with me all night. He didn't leave my side once." And she tossed her head defiantly.

"Maria!" The king opened his mouth in horror. "You do not announce this shameful conduct to the world. Do you think your bridegroom would want you now that you have told the world you are no longer a virgin?"

Matty looked across at Nicholas. "I'm sorry, Nicholas. I never wanted to embarrass you or put you in this awkward position, but I can't let the man I love be accused of a crime I know he didn't commit."

Nicholas nodded. "I applaud your bravery, Maria," he said.

"Then how do we know that the man this English lady saw was not Mr. O'Mara?" Patrascue asked. "I am still not satisfied that we have not all been barking up the wrong tree, since Lady Georgiana made these accusations against the princess. I think she was trying to throw us off the scent."

"As to that, I'm afraid I have the same alibi as Princess

Maria," Darcy said. "At the time the poor woman was being pushed down the stairs, I was in bed with Lady Georgiana."

Of course I turned scarlet as I felt all those eyes on me.

"Then this is true?" Siegfried asked me. "You do not deny it?"

"I'm afraid it is true," I said. "Darcy was with me when we heard the screams from down below."

"But if these people have an alibi for the second murder, what then?" Patrascue said. "I would like to discount one of these alibis but I see from the guilty looks on the faces of these young highnesses that their stories are true. Is the murderer someone quite different? Someone we haven't considered until now?"

Someone behind me cleared his throat and Dragomir stepped forward. I hadn't noticed him in the room until that moment. His cloak swirled rather impressively around him. "Your Majesty, this has gone on long enough. I do not wish to put your daughter through any more pain. I should like to plead guilty to the murders."

The king stepped toward him. "You, old friend? You tried to kill Prince Nicholas? But why? Why would you do this?"

"I have my reasons," Dragomir replied. "Let us just say that this is my ancestral home and I am avenging the ghosts of my ancestors for the wrongs done to them."

The door behind us was thrown open, letting in a great gust of cold wind. "Don't be ridiculous, Father," said a voice and the elusive Vlad stepped into the room. By daylight he was even more handsome than his portrait, but there was something wild about his eyes and in his right hand he held a gun.

"Father? He called you Father?" the king stammered.

"That's right," Dragomir said. "He is my son. I couldn't

marry his mother because of her lowly rank but I have done my duty by him. I paid for his schooling and sent him off to study in Paris. And I love him as any father loves his only child."

"And now he's trying to show his nobility and take the blame for something he didn't do," Vlad said. "I attempted to poison Prince Nicholas. I put a gelatin capsule containing cyanide into his red wine at the start of the meal. I planned to be well away by the time it acted. I was not about to let him have the woman I love. I am just angry that I failed. I shall not fail a second time."

"Vlad!" Matty ran toward him. "How could you? I trusted you. I loved you. I never thought for an instant . . ."

"For you, Maria," Vlad said. "I did it for you. I didn't want you to be condemned to marrying someone you didn't love, when you loved me."

"We went through that before," Matty said. "I told you that my duty to my family came first and always will come first. Now put that gun down. You're not going to shoot anyone."

"Stand aside, Maria." Vlad prodded her with the barrel of the pistol.

"You'll have to shoot me first," she said, eyeing him calmly and defiantly.

"Of course I don't want to shoot you." His voice had risen dangerously.

"I'm not going to let you shoot Nicholas," Matty said, "or anybody else."

"Why do you always have to be so bloody noble?" Vlad demanded.

"Because I was born to it," Matty said.

"Damn you," Vlad shouted. "Damn all of you to hell."

Without warning he grabbed Matty around the throat

and pulled her in front of him. "She's coming with me," he said. "Did you think I was going to give you up that easily?"

"You're mad. Let go of me," she gasped as the arm tightened around her throat.

Nicholas took a step toward them.

"Stay back," Vlad warned. "I won't hesitate to shoot her, you know. I have nothing to lose now. In fact, why not? Shoot her and then myself. At least we'll be together in death."

He was dragging her back to the door, which had now swung shut again. He was reaching behind him with the hand that held the gun when suddenly the door came flying open, catching him in the side of the head and knocking him off balance. As he staggered, Nicholas and Anton fell on him and overpowered him, while Patrascue dragged Matty clear. Vlad cried out in pain as he was pinned to the floor and Nicholas wrenched his arms up behind him.

In the doorway stood a grimy, disheveled and bewildered-looking Queenie.

"Sorry, miss, I didn't mean to hit nobody, but they said you was in here," she said. "He's going to be all right, ain't he?"

"Princess Maria is going to be all right, which is all that matters," I said.

Chapter 32

November 24
Finally going home. Can't wait.

After that only one strange thing happened, or possibly two. Vlad was locked in one of the old dungeons until the pass was cleared. When the snow melted sufficiently, two days later, the cell was found to be empty. Matty and Dragomir both swore that they had not helped him to escape, and indeed the only way out of that cell block was past a door that was guarded at all times. As far as I have heard he has never been found. And I was awoken one of those nights by what sounded like the flapping of large wings outside my window. By the time I got up and managed to open the shutters, there was nothing to be seen.

Lady Middlesex departed, accompanying Miss Deer-Harte's body home to England. She was a changed woman, subdued and grateful for any little kindness, the bullying and bluster gone out of her like a pricked balloon.

Matty and Nicholas were married as planned a few days later. Nicholas's father decided not to postpone the wedding, decreeing that the period of mourning for the field marshal would begin after his state funeral, which would be conducted with all the pomp and ceremony and, hopefully, appease the Macedonians. I thought Nicholas was being jolly understanding, considering everything, but he seemed to be genuinely fond of Matty and she of him. As we dressed for the wedding Matty drew me aside.

"We're friends again, I hope."

"Of course," I said.

"You don't still think that I sent you down that oubliette?"

"Since you almost fell down it yourself, I have to believe that you didn't," I said. "Vlad must have been hiding and pushed the button after you'd gone past."

"How awful if you hadn't managed to get out."

"It's all right. I'd have eaten Queenie," I said, laughing.

"Poor thing. She was frightfully brave, and she did save you, even if she didn't mean to."

We fell silent.

"I couldn't really vouch that Vlad was in bed with me all night," she said. "He could well have slipped out and pushed that English woman down the stairs."

"Or his father did it to protect him. I don't suppose we'll ever know now."

"I don't know what I was thinking," she said at last.

"I do," I said. "Vlad was awfully good-looking."

She smiled sadly. "Yes, he was, wasn't he? And I was alone in Paris and ripe for romance, and he appeared, my childhood playmate now turned into a gorgeous man. And what's more he was no longer a servant's son but a confident man-about-town. I was innocent and self-conscious and no man had ever looked at me that way before. It's no wonder I fell madly in love." She looked at me, pleading for understanding. I nodded. "But I should have seen," she said. "He took too many risks. He courted danger. He has the heritage of his terrible ancestor, after all."

"I think you'll find happiness with Nicholas," I said.

"He has been very understanding and kind," she said. "It could have been far worse. Speaking of which, I'm sorry that you are not going to be my sister-in-law."

I haven't yet mentioned that Siegfried and I had a little talk. He told me that after he heard about my wanton behavior with Darcy there was no way he could consider marrying me. I tried to keep a straight face when I said I quite understood and wished him well.

"You realize you have ruined my reputation forever, don't you?" I said to Darcy afterward.

Darcy grinned. "Which would you rather have—a sullied reputation or a lifetime of marriage to Siegfried?"

"So that's why you said it, wasn't it? You didn't really think either of us would be considered suspects in the murder of Miss Deer-Harte. You thought Siegfried would never marry me if he knew I'd spent the night with another man."

"Something like that," Darcy agreed. "My only regret is that we spent that night sleeping."

"I liked it," I said. "It felt so comforting having you beside me."

He slipped an arm around my waist. "I liked it too," he said. "But that doesn't mean I'm not open to other nocturnal pursuits with you, at a more suitable time and place."

"There will be other opportunities," I said.

And so the wedding took place with all the pomp and ceremony one expects at royal weddings. I wore my tiara and the smashing fur-lined cloak over my Parisian dress. I looked so good that even Mummy was impressed.

"If you weren't so tall you could go to Hollywood and try a career in films, darling," she said. "You have inherited my bone structure. The camera loves us."

Trumpeters heralded our procession down the aisle of the castle chapel. The organ thundered. A choir sang from the gallery and the congregation was resplendent with crowns and dashing uniforms. Nicholas and Matty made a handsome couple. There was only one small thing—she wore a thick collar of pearls, so I never did have a chance to see her neck up close. So I suppose I'll never really know, one hundred percent, whether Vlad really was a vampire or not. But I'll tell you one thing—I was really glad for once to be going home.

∽✦∾

Queenie echoed those sentiments as we stood on the deck of the Channel steamer as it docked in Dover. "I ain't half glad to see the coast of good old England again, ain't you, me lady?"

"Yes, I am, actually, Queenie."

Belinda had got wind of a house party at a villa in the south of France and was headed to Nice. She was going to try the car-breaking-down-outside-the-gates trick again and begged me to come with her. "Think of it: sun, good food, gorgeous men," she had said. It was tempting, but I had turned her down because I wasn't the party-crashing type; also I sensed that Queenie had had enough of being abroad, and I felt it was my duty to get her home safely. Besides, I too longed for the familiarity of life in London, even if it would include Binky and Fig at close quarters. At least I knew where I was with them. At least they didn't grow fangs in the middle of the night. And Darcy had promised he'd be back in London shortly, after a little matter he had to look into in Belgrade.

I glanced at Queenie's vacant moon face. I was actually coming home with a nice amount of money in my pocket, thanks to those roulette winnings. I could afford to pay a maid for a while, especially now that Binky and Fig would be buying the food. I took a deep breath, feeling that I might well regret what I was about to say.

"Queenie," I said, "I'm willing to keep you on as my maid, if you are prepared to learn how a lady's maid behaves properly."

"You are, miss?" She looked thrilled. "I did all right then, did I?"

"No, you were an utter disaster from start to finish, but you were brave and you didn't complain, and I've somehow grown fond of you. I can offer you fifty pounds a year, all found. I know it's not much, but . . ."

"I'll take it, miss," she said. "Me, going to be a toff's lady's maid. Just wait till I tell her down the Three Bells, what gives herself airs just because she went on that day trip to France and brought back a frilly garter."

"Queenie," I said. "It's not 'miss,' it's 'my lady.'"

"Bob's yer uncle, miss," she said.

THE CIVILIZATION OF THE AMERICAN INDIAN SERIES

The Kiowas

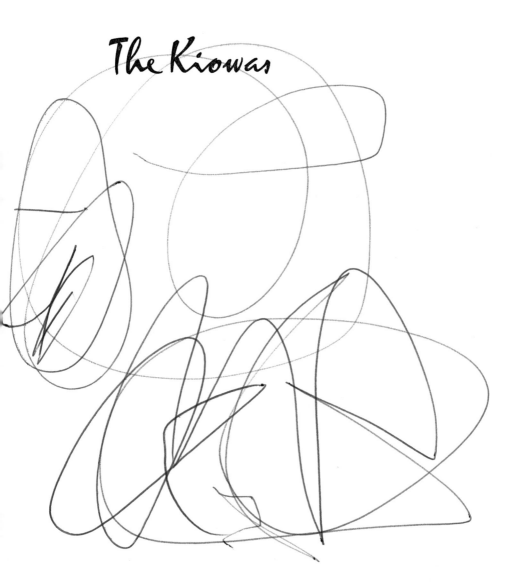

The Kiowas

BY MILDRED P. MAYHALL

UNIVERSITY OF OKLAHOMA PRESS NORMAN

Library of Congress Catalog Card Number: 62–16477

Copyright 1962 by the University of Oklahoma Press, Publishing Division of the University. Composed and printed at Norman, Oklahoma, U.S.A., by the University of Oklahoma Press. First edition.

To Temple, David, and Bill

❖ FOREWORD

T*HE* Plains homeland of the Kiowa Indians is a region of great beauty—beauty peculiarly its own. At times the Plains are still and quiet; at times, sudden, violent, ominous with weather and temperature changes. Almost always the wind blows. Suddenly a storm may appear out of nowhere, bringing thunder, lightning, rain, and perhaps sleet. Electrical storms and tornadoes breed over the Plains and sweep from mountain to prairie to plain. Fires, once started, burn the grasses, taking everything before them—animals and man—leaving behind them great swaths of destruction.

Dust storms and sandstorms find their homes here. Winds pick up sand and carry it in nervous, abrasive gusts, cutting, carving, and covering, according to their velocity. They rend their fury upon vegetation, animals, and man, so disturbing the air that breathing is difficult and the plant world recoils. Dust makes the sun a puny moon by day, but renders sunsets among the most beautiful phenomena in the world—warm, rich, and sensuous.

When the air is clear, distance cannot be measured accurately by the eye. The mountains, or any landmarks, for that matter, seem to march toward one. The Staked Plains, without a landmark, cup the traveler in a bowl. At night the stars dip down almost overhead.

In August the midday heat is almost unbearable; thermal waves and mirages shimmer before the eyes. Plants close their stomata to conserve moisture; native grasses become toast-brown and crack like salt underfoot. But in Nature's reversal, the breezes return at dusk and nights are cool and refreshing. By the end of summer the blue northers come, blowing cool winds from north to south, and temperatures may drop sharply within an hour. Devastating, too, are the snows and the blizzards of winter.

This land, in the old days, held no attraction for the farmer. It was the Great American Desert; something to get over, to pass through, to seek land and gold beyond.

There is a mysticism in the Plains and in the mountains and plateaus to the west. The Indians had it and still do, and it colored their religion, the worship of the Sun God. Old-timers, among the whites share the Plains spirit—a sort of fatalism characterized by a resignation to natural forces, coupled with a lively appreciation of sun and stars and vast distances.

The Plains are recent, both geologically and historically speaking. There are no great cities of old; no traditions of long generations of men building civilizations. It is an area abounding in myth and legend, and continues to be so as new people supplant the old.

The prehistoric tribes here were many in number, all awaiting a talisman—the acquisition of the white man's horse—to encompass the geographic area of the Plains. They were mountain-valley or edge-of-the-rivers people or refugees from the Great Lakes and the Mississippi Valley forced westward by white pressure until they found their talisman, an easy means of transportation allowing them to master the great arid distances of the Plains and to conquer the buffalo.

The Plains culture was the last American Indian culture to evolve, and it was contemporaneous with that being built anew by the white man to the south and to the east. For over a century—perhaps two centuries—the Indians held sway in the Plains, a barrier to white penetration; theirs was a dangerous and ferocious wall breached only here and there and always closed again. (The fur trader came first and, not averse to gaining the sharp dollar, undermined the wall and cracked the armor of the red man's sobriety with illicit alcohol.)

The history of the Plains for many years consisted largely of a series of crossings to better lands. Not until the railroads served to shrink the distances could towns and cities develop. There is still a rawness about the vast area that takes one back to the traders and trappers, to the mountain men, to the pioneers both good and bad, and to the Kiowas, who made their home there.

It is the story of these native people that I have to tell, and for the telling I must acknowledge the good fortune which, during my nineteen years as an instructor in anthropology at the University of Texas, put me in touch with their life and vicissitudes. Ethnohistory is its own justification, but in our time it may serve also as a corrective of the distortions resulting from the efforts of many media other than ethnology and history to popularize the life of the Plains Indians. The Kiowas deserve our best efforts, for, as a leading tribe of the Plains, their courage, strength, and resolute will held back the encroachments of white settlement of their area for a long period of time. Their story is not closed. They continue to have a life of their own and to make their way in the midst of the surrounding white culture which has overtaken Oklahoma.

I am grateful to H. Bailey Carroll, professor of history in the University of Texas, for his interest in my work, for his reading of this manuscript, and for his helpful criticism of it. Mrs. Pearl Nesmith read the manuscript before its final completion and added comments that were appreciated. Miss Frances Nesmith also gave encouragement and useful criticism. For their kindness in supplying me with information, thanks are due to Mr. Philemon Berry and Mr. Adolph Goombi of Fort Cobb and Mountain View, Oklahoma. Mrs. Alice Driscoll also read the manuscript and helped with criticism.

I also wish to thank the staff of the University of Texas Library for their many courtesies. Especially helpful were the reference librarians, Miss Kathleen Blow, Mr. Frank Shmaus, and Mr. Charles Dwyer. By their efforts, books were obtained from the Library of Congress, the library of Louisiana State University, and the library of the University of Oklahoma, through the inter-library loan service. Miss Lorena Baker and Miss Llerena Friend were helpful in securing needed books.

The archivists of the University of Texas Library were most kind and considerate—Miss Winnie Allen and Mr. Dorman Winfrey, former archivists, and Mr. Chester Kielman, present archivist.

For their aid and assistance and their many courtesies, I wish to thank the staff of the National Archives, Washington, D. C.; Mr. Arrell M. Gibson, head of the Division of Manuscripts, and Mr. Jack D. Haley, assistant archivist, of the University of Okla-homa Library; Mr. Norman Feder of the Denver Art Museum; Mr. Gillett Griswold, director of the Fort Sill Museum; Mrs. Joan B. Johnston, Fort Sill Museum; and Mr. E. M. Davis of the Anthropology Museum, University of Texas.

The drawings of the Kiowa encampment and of "Kaskaia, Shi-enne Chief, and Arrappaho" are from the Yale University Library. The George Catlin sketch of an Indian riding feat is from his *North American Indians*. Millie Durgan Goombi's photograph is part of the collection of the U. S. Army Artillery and Missile Cen-ter Museum, Fort Sill, Oklahoma. The photograph of Big Tree belongs to the Stephenson Collection in the University of Texas Library. The Denver Public Library Western Collection kindly granted permission to reproduce the photographs of Satank and of Sun Boy. The detail from the Sett'an and Anko annual calen-dars was adapted by Temple B. Mayhall from James Mooney's "Calendar History." The picture of Kiowa and Apache Indians gambling under a brush arbor is courtesy of the Division of Manu-scripts, Library, University of Oklahoma. All other illustrations were loaned by the Smithsonian Institution, Bureau of American Ethnology. For permission to reproduce all of these illustrations, I am most grateful.

Time is a precious commodity for a busy teacher and housewife.

For the gift of time to write, I especially want to thank my family
—Temple, David, and Bill.

MILDRED P. MAYHALL

Austin, Texas
September 26, 1962

❖ CONTENTS

❖ ILLUSTRATIONS

between pa...

xvii

The Kiowas

CHAPTER ONE

❖ IN THE BEGINNING

THE Kiowas were the proud possessors of the southern Great Plains. With the Comanches and the Kiowa-Apaches, these predators of the Southwest were great horsemen, horse thieves, horse breeders, and horse traders. For over a century and a half they disputed passage of the white man moving westward. Even the reservation system settled them only temporarily until their horses were taken from them and the buffalo disappeared.

The Kiowa Indians were known to the white people, Spanish, Mexican, and Anglo-American, as inhabitants of the southern Plains area in present western Oklahoma and the Panhandle of north Texas and west into a part of New Mexico. Early moving eastward from the fastnesses of the Rocky Mountains in the region of the present Yellowstone National Park, the Kiowas emerged upon the northern Plains. This was the beginning of a long trek southward—recorded in documents of various travelers and, in part, in their own calendars—which would ultimately place them in the area of the Red and Canadian rivers and their tributary creeks. They would go across the Republican and Smoky Hill rivers, southward to the Arkansas, and finally to the headwaters of the Cimarron. There they would live and control the area from the Arkansas to the headwaters of the Red River.

The earliest inhabitants of the Great Plains area were Athapascan-speaking peoples—Apaches. Archaeological investigations
confirm that they ranged from present west Texas up the Plains,
at least as far north as the Platte, and probably into Canada. According to Waldo R. Wedel:

> West of the regions in Kansas for which Caddoan and Siouan
> occupations can be historically demonstrated was formerly the
> habitat of various wandering people of alien affiliations, notably the
> Apache and Comanche. The former, of Athapascan linguistic affini
> ties, were clearly the earlier inhabitants. Their representatives were
> met by the first Spanish expeditions eastward from the upper Rio
> Grande; they were present in numbers throughout the 17th century,
> and evidently dominated much of the western Plains from the upper
> Rio Grande northward at least to the upper Platte valley until well
> into the 18th century. The Shoshonean-speaking Comanche first
> appear on the pages of history about the year 1700. Adapting them
> selves readily from a mountain-based to a nomadic Plains life and
> taking over the horse, they steadily expanded their range at the
> expense of the Apache. By the middle of the 18th century, they had
> swept the latter from the Plains north of the Canadian. The Co
> manche likewise drifted steadily southward through the High Plains,
> so that by 1800 or soon after, they were sharing the upper Arkansas
> valley and territory to the north with the Kiowa, Arapaho, and
> Cheyenne, and still later with Dakota Siouan and other tribes.[1]

East of the Spaniards in New Mexico were the Plains Apaches.
First allusions to them are found in the descriptions of the Coronado Expedition of 1540–42. Fourteen days east of the Pecos, near
the Canadian River, the Spanish expedition met with encampments
of roaming, hunting people, called "Querechos." Eyewitnesses described a pre-horse Indian economy in the southern Plains. The

---

[1] *An Introduction to Kansas Archeology*, 68–69; *Environment and Native Subsistence Economies in the Central Great Plains*, 8–10, 17–21; and *Culture Sequence
in the Central Great Plains*, 291–352. See also George E. Hyde, *Indians of the High
Plains*, 3–27, 28–51.

For a brief résumé of the archaeology of the Plains, see the Appendix of this
volume.

4

Querechos, and the Teyas met with later, did not sow or reap corn, but sustained themselves entirely upon the buffalo. They traded dressed hides for maize and other provisions with the settled Indian towns, some parties going to Cicuyé [Pecos], some toward Quivira[2] (in the Great Bend region of the Arkansas River in present Kansas), and others to settlements farther eastward.

The Plains Apaches, also called "Apache Vaqueros" or "Eastern" Apaches, moved over an area of several hundred miles east and north of Spanish New Mexico. They are known, archaeologically, to have occupied the western third or more of present Kansas from earliest white contact until the first quarter of the eighteenth century, and seem to be the Padoucas described by the French.[3] As Apachería gave way to Comanchería, the Comanches were known as "Padoucas."

Wedel says that the evidence

> . . . long ago assembled by Grinnell should have made clear . . . the most reasonable interpretation . . . seems to be that the name [Padouca] under which the Plains Apache were known to the French and their Indian allies before circa 1750 was transferred after that time to the people who displaced the Apache, namely, the Comanche.[4]

The Comanches began to trouble the Spaniards around the middle of the eighteenth century in Texas. It has been said that they

[2] Wedel, *An Introduction to Kansas Archeology*, 61; and *Archaeological Remains in Central Kansas*. Quivira was thought to be an early Wichita village. Spanish chain-mail armor has been found in Kansas archaeological sites; see *ibid.*, 320. See also Jack D. Forbes, *Apache, Navaho, and Spaniard*, 75n.

[3] Wedel, *An Introduction to Kansas Archeology*, 69–74. Some confusion attends the use of the word "Padouca." Up to 1750 it applied to Plains Apaches; later, to the Comanches. The same is true for "Jumane," which generally meant to the Spanish any tattooed people and was often associated with the Wichitas or Pani Piqués of the French. The early Jumanos of west Texas were Apaches, a partly agricultural, partly hunting tribe, Athapascan in language. See Forbes, *Apache, Navaho, and Spaniard*, xxiii, 196–99, 283.

[4] Wedel, *An Introduction to Kansas Archeology*, 78. See also George Bird Grinnell, "Who Were the Padouca?" *American Anthropologist* (hereinafter cited as *A.A.*), Vol. XXII, No. 3 (1920), 249–60.

5

first showed up in Texas in 1746, but they—especially the Pena-tekas—may have been in northwest Texas as early as 1700.

Juan de Oñate's expedition of 1598 had opened New Mexico to Spanish settlement and control; Albuquerque and Santa Fe were settled by the Spanish early in the seventeenth century. The Mexicans claimed the southern Great Plains area as their Spanish heritage after they threw off the burdensome yoke of the mother country in 1821. It was also demanded after 1803 and up to 1819 by the United States, after the purchase of the Louisiana Territory from the French. Texas, after winning the Battle of San Jacinto in 1836, claimed it and much more: the Río Grande as a boundary to its headwaters and up to the forty-second parallel, including a strip of territory that went northward into present Wyoming. Even though this land had never been occupied by Texans, they sought to bring it under the control of the Republic.

The Kiowas, Kiowa-Apaches, and Comanches had actually taken over west Texas from its aboriginal inhabitants, the various Apache tribes, before the Spanish, French, Mexicans, or Texans had ever settled upon it. The taking was done, however, after the Europeans had claimed it by right of discovery and exploration. Spanish missionary work and attempted settlements failed, but Spanish claims were valid, despite the fact that the Kiowas and Comanches held the land by force and by their adaptation of life to its peculiar environment.

The eastern part of New Mexico was later part of the homeland of the Kiowas, along the Cimarron and Canadian headwaters. East of this region and over into present Oklahoma, the Kiowas lived for well over a century and a half. They were finally settled by expediency and military force on reservations in the eastern sector of their former extensive area, in and around present Fort Sill, Anadarko, and Apache, Oklahoma.

According to Kiowa myths and legends, their first ancestors were called into the world, one at a time, from a hollow cottonwood log, by a supernatural being. As he tapped on the log, they emerged until one pregnant woman got stuck and no others could get out.

Their creator gave them the sun, made day and night, taught them hunting and various arts, and then went up among the stars. All of their traditions refer to hunting; they had no agriculture. The Cheyennes and Arapahoes who lived near the Kiowas for many years remembered having lived east of the Missouri and cultivating corn; but not so the Kiowas.

A supernatural boy Hero, child of the Sun by an earthly mother, did many wonderful things for them. He transformed himself in two and gave himself to them in a eucharistic form. This was the tribal medicine which they still retained in 1896,[5] in the form of the Ten Grandmother bundles.

These marvelous stories of their creation, lightened by the magic and mischief of Coyote, were often heard by the Kiowa children of a later day as they sat about the lodges watching the old men make arrow shafts and fashion their weapons. Many times after the dances of the Rabbits (little boys' society), replete with food and fellowship, the old men told them these tales. Grandmothers, too, told their granddaughters of the past as they did the chores of the household and fashioned and embellished skins for clothing.

The Kiowas, in 1896, could remember when their grandparents had lived in the north near the Crows and Arikaras. One of their legends concerned the origin of the Black Hills; another had to do with Bear Lodge or Devil's Tower, near present Sun Dance, Wyoming. They remembered many northern tribes. Beyond the Yellowstone had lived the Blackfeet and Arapaho Gros Ventres. They had also known the Shoshonis, who had formerly lived in houses of woven rushes, as also the Kiowas may have done in their early days. (The author has a picture of a grass house in a collection of Kiowa prints, but whether it is something of their ancestral traits, or something copied after the Wichita houses of later date, is not known.)

They also remembered the northern Arapahoes and Dakotas. The Sarsis, who had visited and intermarried with the Kiowas in

[5] James Mooney, "Calendar History of the Kiowa Indians," B.A.E., *Seventeenth Annual Report*, Pt. 1, 153. (Hereinafter cited as Mooney, "Calendar History.")

their early days, had lived at the source of the northern Saskatchewan in Canada. They lived with the Blackfeet and spoke a language resembling that of the Apaches. Some important persons of the Kiowas were of Sarsi descent, namely Ga'apiatan and Patadal. Chief Set-angia or Satank, killed at Fort Sill in 1871, was also of Sarsi descent. His Sarsi maternal grandmother had married a Kiowa during one of the friendly visits of the tribe. These men, by reason of their Athapascan or Sarsi blood, considered themselves relatives of the Kiowa-Apaches.

The historic traditions of the Kiowas locate them at this time on the sources of the Yellowstone and Missouri rivers in what is now western Montana. It was a region of great cold and deep snows. They had the Flatheads as neighbors. They called the mountains "Gai K'op," Kiowa Mountains. On the other side of the mountains was a great river flowing westward, probably a branch of the Columbia.

When they lived in the mountains, the Kiowas were a hunting people though there were traditions of wars, dependent on the bow and arrow, and had only the dog as a domesticated animal. The travois, drawn poles attached to a harness, was used with the dog, and probably the sled or sledge was used also. They hunted small game and apparently knew nothing of the buffalo, which leads to the belief that the buffalo did not winter in the Yellowstone region at that time. There are some links with people to the north and west of this area, such as the use of decorated cradleboards, which would cause head-flattening,[6] as well as their associations with the Sarsis. There are also tales of the use of shell necklaces, which probably came from an area far to the west, over to the Pacific.[7]

---

[6] *Ibid.*, 155. Mooney mentioned an old cradleboard that was different from later Kiowa cradles. It was a solid board, carved and painted in the style of the Northwest Coast, with a buckskin covering. It would definitely produce a flattened skull. An old woman said that it was the kind the Kiowas used to make a "long time ago." It indicated Kiowa associations to the west. It is now in the National Museum in Washington. The Kiowas may have flattened their heads in the past, but never in historic time.

[7] M. [François Marie] Perrin du Lac, *Travels through the Two Louisianas*, in *A Collection of Modern and Contemporary Voyages and Travels*, VI, 3–106. The Eng-

According to legend and tradition, the Kiowas moved out of the region about the headwaters of the Yellowstone River because of a tribal fuss, a trivial but meaningful quarrel growing out of the division of spoils of hunting: who should have the udders of an antelope. Two rival chiefs' desire for possession of the prize developed into a quarrel which split the tribe into dual factions. Accompanied by the chief who lost the prize, the unsuccessful group moved northwestward and was never heard of again. The victorious hunters, who were to become the Kiowas of later history, moved southeastward, crossed the Yellowstone, met and were friendly with the Crow Indians, and came to live east of them in the Black Hills. (Even today the Kiowas insist that the Black Hills belong to them and have sued for the return of this land.)

The Kiowas were apt pupils in learning the ways of the Plains from the Crows. They made a permanent alliance with them about 1700, after the Crows had separated from the Hidatsas and long before the Dakotas came into the Black Hills (about 1775). The Crows seem to have given the Kiowas many cultural elements and intermarried with them. About 1765 the Kiowas got the "Tai-me," a fetish representing the Sun Dance medicine. They became typical Plains tribes, using the horse and buffalo-skin tipi; having the Tai-me and medicine lodge or annual summer Sun Dance, individual medicine bundles, and soldier societies such as the Koitsenko; and subsisting mainly on buffalo which they hunted with the bow, arrow, and lance. A special sacred arrow lance (in Tanguadal's family) came from the Crows. Even after they had moved away, they would make visits back to the Crows and leave their children to visit for two or three years to keep up their old friendship. One of the Kiowas' later leading chiefs, Kicking Bird, was part Crow (his grandfather was a Crow Indian).

Living with them in the Black Hills was the tribe that they had

lish translation is a shortened version of the original French. Another partial, but imperfectly translated, version is in Father José Antonio Pichardo, _Pichardo's Treatise on the Limits of Louisiana and Texas_, edited by Charles W. Hackett, I and II. The original French edition is _Voyage dans les deux Louisianes et chez les nations sauvages du Missouri_.

9

brought with them from their former home in the mountains, the small tribe of Athapascans called the "Kiowa-Apaches." They had always been in association; the Kiowa-Apaches formed a component part of the Kiowa tribal council. They were not a detached band of the Apache tribes of Arizona, but moved from the far north onto the Plains with the Kiowas and thence south. Their movements were east of the Rocky Mountains, whereas the other Athapascans moved down west of the mountains. They called themselves "Nadi isha Dena," meaning "Principal People." Though speaking distinct languages, the Kiowas and Kiowa-Apaches were one politically, socially, and culturally.

Horses had been unknown to the Kiowas before they came out of the mountains and settled near the Crows. Up to that time, as has been mentioned, they had used the dog and the travois. Once they had the horse, the Kiowas became able horsemen, traded in horses, and began to raid the Spanish frontiers. La Salle, in 1682, said that the "Gattackas" (Kiowa-Apaches) and "Manrhoats" (probably the Kiowas) had "plenty of horses, probably stolen from Mexico."[8] The Kiowas were mentioned in Spanish documents in 1732 and 1735[9] as a hostile tribe. In 1748, Villa-Señor said that their warriors had horses.[10] By the beginning of the nineteenth century, the Kiowas had large herds of horses and traded them with the Arikaras and Mandans for European goods which they received from trading posts on the Missouri. In 1868, Ten Bears, a Comanche chief, took to task the Kiowas at a council at Fort Cobb for their raids into Mexico and Texas. He said:

[8] La Salle said that there were many horses among the "Pana, Pancassa, Manrhout, Gataea, Panimaha et Pasos." Pierre Margry, *Découvertes et établissements des français dans l'ouest et dans le sud de l'Amérique Septentrionale (1614–1754)*, II, 168. Mooney believed the "Manrhoats" of La Salle (*ibid.*, II, 201) to be the Kiowas. (Mooney, "Calendar History," 161.)

[9] Mooney, "Calendar History," 156. Mooney says that they were mentioned as "Cargua" for Caigua in 1732 and as "Caigua" in 1735. In 1748 the Spanish historian José Antonio Villa-Señor y Sanchez mentioned the "Cayguas" in connection with the Comanches, Apaches, Navahos, and Utes as enemies of New Mexico.

[10] *Ibid.*, 161.

When we first knew you, you had nothing but dogs and sleds. Now you have plenty of horses, and where did you get them if they were not stolen from Mexico?[11]

This was a case of the pot calling the kettle black. Each tribe was noted for its raids for horses and captives, since both were tradable.

The possession of the horse brought about a revolution in transportation in the life of the Indian of the Plains. It was also an evolution of culture, with emphasis upon a set of psychic values attached to the "horse culture." The Kiowas and Comanches would come to exploit this predatory way of life to the fullest; it would not have been possible without the horse, nor could they have adapted themselves to the complete area of the southern Plains without the horse. Mooney said:

> Without it he was a half-starved skulker in the timber, creeping upon foot toward the unwary deer or building a brush corral with infinite labor to surround a herd of antelope, and seldom venturing more than a few days' journey from home. With the horse he was transformed into the daring buffalo hunter, able to procure in a single day enough food to supply his family for a year, leaving him free then to sweep the plains with his war parties along a range of a thousand miles.[12]

On the Grand River (or Ree River) of present South Dakota lived the Arikaras, with whom the Kiowas developed a great friendship. There were three tribes in this confederacy: the Arikaras, a branch of the Pawnees; the Hidatsas, formerly part of the Crows; and the Mandans, distinct from though remotely related to the Hidatsas. They were sedentary, agricultural, and lived in earth-covered round log houses, "bee-hive" in shape, with top openings for smoke exits from the interior cooking fires. They spoke different languages. They traded corn and tobacco from their

[11] *Ibid.*, 161.

[12] *Ibid.*, 161. See also Clark Wissler, "The Influence of the Horse in the Development of Plains Culture," *A.A.*, Vol. XVI, No. 1 (1914), 1–25.

fields, entirely owned and cultivated by the women, with the Kiowas. These people were also buffalo hunters, but retained pottery-making and agriculture from their former way of life. In 1832, George Catlin visited for some time among them, painted pictures of them, and described many phases of their life, particularly the Sun Dance with its terrible tortures among the Mandans.[13]

The Kata or Arikara band of Kiowas took its name from a trading intimacy with the Rees. Dohasan, great chief of the Kiowas, and several other chiefs belonged to this band. The Kiowas called the Mandans a "tattooed people" in the sign language, and many Kiowa women who had small tattooed circles on their foreheads probably picked up the practice from the Mandans.[14] The Hidatsas were called "Water People" and used round, tub-shaped boats or bullboats which the Kiowas remembered.[15]

While the Kiowas lived in the Black Hills, the Comanches, a part of the Shoshonis of Wyoming, lived south of them. Having horses at an early date, the Comanches ranged from the Platte River far south to Mexico. The Kiowas called them "Gyai'-ko," "Enemies." The Osages, Dakotas, and other tribes called them "Padoucas." They were mentioned by Bourgmont in 1724 as living between the headwaters of the Platte and Kansas rivers.[16]

In the Black Hills, too, the Kiowas had come to know the Arapahoes, Cheyennes, and later the Dakotas. Then they moved south from their great friends, the Crows, and came to the south fork of the Platte.

About 1775, the Dakotas drove the Kiowas and their southern neighbors, the Comanches, still farther southward. The Dakotas

---

[13] George Catlin, *North American Indians*, I, 175–208. See his description of the Mandans, I, 91–175.

[14] As late as 1864, Kiowa captives were marked with blue tattooed circles on their foreheads. Lottie Durgan, a ransomed captive, was thus marked. (Sallie Reynolds Matthews, *Interwoven*, 49.)

[15] Catlin, *North American Indians*, II, 297. Bullboats were made of a willow framework, covered with buffalo hide, and shaped nearly round.

[16] Mooney, "Calendar History," 162. Bourgmont's "Padouca" may have been Apache tribes.

exterminated an entire band, the Kuato, of the Kiowas, whose chief had urged them to stand and fight. According to Te'bodal, oldest man of the tribe in 1896, this massacre took place when his grandfather was a young man. One woman who had fled survived, and Te'bodal remembered seeing her. This band was said to have spoken a peculiar dialect of their language, and was noted for doing foolish and ridiculous things.[17]

After their dispute with the Dakotas, the Kiowas and Comanches moved southward and inhabited the area of the upper Arkansas. One division of the Comanche tribe, the Penateka, had separated and moved south into Texas long before. In striking relief, the Kiowas began to stand out and pushed the Comanches south of the Arkansas.

A peace between the two tribes was finally effected in a New Mexican home by a Mexican who was friendly to both sides. A Kiowa chief, Gui-k'ati, Wolf-Lying-Down, next in authority to the principal chief, agreed to accompany the Comanche leader, Paréiya, Afraid-of-Water, back to his camp to discuss peace. A Mexican captive and a few Mexicans went with them. They visited the Comanche encampment on Ganta P'a, Double Mountain Fork of the Brazos in Texas. The rest of the Kiowas returned to their own people. They had been instructed to return when the leaves were yellow (early fall in New Mexico), and if he, Gui-k'ati, was not found, to avenge his death. Gui-k'ati remained with the Comanches all summer and was well treated and well entertained.

The Comanches and Kiowas then met and made peace and an alliance for concerted action. Though different in language and temperament, they became confederates. The date was probably about 1790.[18]

---

[17] *Ibid.*, 158.

[18] *Ibid.*, 164. The date does not appear in their calendars but can be established by the memories of various informants and the tally date of 1833, "when the stars fell," a period of meteoric displays. Informants whose ages could be ascertained in 1833 were checked as knowing people who had lived at the time of the treaty. Te'bodal, about eighty years old in 1896, remembered the Comanche chief, Paréiya, when Paréiya was an old man. Paréiya was later killed by the Cheyennes.

The principal leader of the Kiowas at the time of the treaty was Políakya, Hare-Lip. He was followed by Tsónbohón, Feathercap, who was succeeded by A'date, Islandman, who was deposed in 1833, after the Kiowas were massacred by the Osages, in favor of Dohasan. He ruled the whole tribe until he died in 1866.

The Comanche-Kiowa peace was permanent. The two tribes, along with the Kiowa-Apaches, now lived, hunted, and raided together, save for the Penateka Comanches in Texas, who had little to do with the northern bands. They now held the territory of the southern Great Plains in common, although the Comanches kept to the Staked Plains and the Texas frontier while the Kiowas moved south and along the Arkansas River. The entire confederation, as a sort of southward-projecting wedge, drove the indigenous and aboriginal Mescalero and Lipan Apaches westward and southwestward from the Colorado River (Texas) drainage area into New Mexico and Old Mexico and into a war of proposed extinction at the hands of the Spanish, later Mexican, settlements. To the northeast, they thrust back the Wichita confederation of Plains-adapted former agricultural tribes of Caddoan ancestry, moving them back east along the route they had followed west, the Red River. In the eastern central area of Texas they pushed the Tonkawa confederation, a former southward-moving Plains group who had adapted to some horticulture, almost entirely off the southern edge of the Plains and central prairies, cramping and compressing them and taking from them and the Wichitas their great joint hunting grounds.

Meanwhile, raiding and trading became profitable businesses. The Kiowas raided far south and southwestward, to Matagorda Bay in Texas, south of Durango and through Sonora and Sinaloa in Mexico to the Gulf of California, and at one time into the canyon of the Colorado with a raid and massacre of the Havasupais. Plunder, scalps, horses, and captives were the objects of these parties, which sometimes lasted two years. Fear and dread struck the settlements of northern Mexico and the settled area of Texas. The Texans mobilized militia and later developed the Texas Rangers to guard their frontiers. The Kiowas, with the Comanches farther south, were the masters of the south Plains, and a harsh hand fell upon all who might dispute their sway.

An uneasy peace was made with the Mescalero Apaches, but the Mescaleros continued to fear the Kiowas. To the east, the Kiowas had got on friendly terms with the Wichita confederation—Wichitas, Taovayas, Tawakonis, Wacos, and their allies in Texas, among whom were the Kichais. Other tribes friendly with the Kiowas were the Crows, Arapahoes, Arikaras, Hidatsas, Mandans, Shoshonis, and Flatheads. Enemies of the Kiowas were the Caddos and Tonkawas in Texas, and to the west the Navahos, Utes, and Jicarilla Apaches. The Kiowas were frequently at war with the Cheyennes and continually at war with the Dakota and Pawnee tribes. With the Pueblos, the Kiowas carried on friendly trading relations, and they scarcely ever came in contact with the Apaches of Arizona. They were at war with the Osages to the east until 1834 and mentioned these conflicts in their calendars. Most of their enemies made a grudging peace after 1834, and the confederated Kiowas, Kiowa-Apaches, and Comanches ruled the territory they had pre-empted. In 1840 they struck against the Texans at Victoria and Indianola, to the waters of the Gulf of Mexico, far south of their usual range.

In 1896, James Mooney described the calendars of the Kiowas and gave a history of the tribe to that date.[19] There were three Kiowa calendars: the Sett'an yearly calendar, beginning in 1833, covering a period of sixty years; the Anko yearly calendar, beginning in 1864, covering twenty-nine years; and the Anko monthly calendar, covering thirty-seven months.[20] All were obtained in 1892 and brought up to the date of 1896.

A fourth Kiowa calendar was obtained on the Kiowa reservation in 1892 by Captain Hugh L. Scott of the Seventh Cavalry, who was stationed at Fort Sill, Oklahoma; it was placed at Mooney's disposal, together with Scott's notes. This was the calendar of

[19] *Ibid.*, 129–468. The only Plains Indians known to have kept calendars were the Kiowas and the Dakotas. The calendars were original documents, pictographs on skins. Mooney's study is the main source of all later writings on the Kiowas and the Kiowa-Apaches. The report includes primary sources and many secondary sources.

[20] *Ibid.*, 143. See the review of Kiowa calendars in Chapter IV of this volume.

Dohasan, or Little Bluff, nephew of the celebrated Dohasan. The nephew, who was head chief of the Kiowas for more than thirty years and who died at an advanced age in 1893, told Scott that it was originally drawn on hides, renewed as they wore out. When the calendar was delivered to Scott, it was on heavy manila paper, drawn with colored pencils. This was also true of Mooney's Sett'an calendar, which begins in the lower right-hand corner and is arranged in a continuous spiral, ending near the center. Winter is shown by an upright black bar; summer is portrayed by a figure of the medicine lodge, marking the annual religious ceremony or Sun Dance.

The Anko calendar was originally drawn with black pencil in a small notebook and later redrawn at Mooney's direction in colored inks on buckskin. In artistic execution, the Sett'an calendar ranks first. Another calendar, that of Polanyi-katón or Rabbit Shoulder, is supposed to have been buried with him a few years before 1896. Probably others were disposed of in this manner, but their means of burial would not preserve them. The first calendar was probably kept by the old chief Dohasan, whose hereditary tipi occupied the first place in the camp circle. In his family, priestly functions of the medicine dance had been handed down in regular succession. After his death in 1866, the calendar was continued by his nephew and namesake.

The Sett'an calendar was probably reproduced as an inspiration from the Dohasan calendar, largely from memory; but it is better executed. The making of the calendars was probably the work of many a winter's evening, from gatherings of "come and smoke" invitations, shouted by a host in front of his tipi.[21] The pipe was filled and smoked as it was passed around, while men recounted myths and deeds of valor that would in time be history. Sett'an, or Little Bear, cousin of the old war chief, voluntarily gave his calendar to Mooney for the museum collection; wanting no money for it, he desired only that the young men should remember their history and that the white people should learn what the Kiowas had done.

[21] *Ibid.*, 145.

From a modern point of view, the events are trivial. They did not record what modern historians might consider important. For example, they did not record the Custer campaign of 1868, which resulted in the Battle of the Washita and forced the southern tribes to go on the reservation. The outbreak of 1874 is barely mentioned; yet it meant their final subjugation. The death of one individual might be remembered, or the initiation of a man into the Koitsenko or Soldier Society; or they might show, and usually did show, epidemics like those of smallpox, cholera, and measles. These calendars are now in the museum collections of the Bureau of American Ethnology.

Names for the Kiowas were many and given in various languages. "Gâ-i-gwŭ" is the proper name of the tribe and also the name of one of the tribal divisions. The name may indicate two halves of the body or of the face painted in different colors. From this name came the many forms of "Caygua" and "Kiowa." The oldest name is "Kwŭ'da," or "going out," by which the Kiowa designate themselves; and also "Tépdá," meaning "coming out." These refer to their mystic origin of entering the world from a hollow log. The Dakotas called them "Wi'tapähä'tu."

The tribal sign for them was a movement of the right hand, held close to the right cheek, back down, fingers touching and slightly curved, moving in a rotary motion from the wrist. This probably came from the cutting of the hair on the right side of the head to display ear pendants; the hair on the left side was not cut. They wore their hair long, braided, and wrapped with otter skins. In addition they wore the usual small scalp lock hanging to the side.

CHAPTER TWO

❖ DESCRIPTIONS OF
THE KIOWAS

*A*MERICAN travelers, following the French explorers, missionaries, and fur traders, began to move into the West around 1805.
As early as 1682, La Salle, moving down the Mississippi River in
his explorations south from Canada, heard about the Kiowas from
the Indians at Fort St. Louis.[1] On January 3, 1682, he made caches
at the juncture of the Missouri and Mississippi, then awaited the
arrival of his companion, Tonti, at St. Louis. Much of his information of tribes to the west, "four hundred leagues" up the Missouri,
came from a Pani boy, a captive. Since his is the first mention of
the Kiowas, La Salle's description is of interest:

> Les eaux estant toujours escouleés le mois de Mars, il seroit
> plus aisé de faire les transports du fort Saint Louis au lac par terre,
> en se servant de chevaux qu'il est aisé d'y avoir, y en ayant beau-
> coup chez les Sauvages appelez Pana, Pancassa, Manrhout, Gataea,
> Panimaha et Pasos, un peu eloignez, a la vérité, vers le couchant,
> mais avec qui on peut avoir une communication trés-facíle tant par
> la rívière des Missourites, qui tombe dans le fleuve Colbert [Missis-
> sippi], si ce n' en est pas la principale branche, toujours navigable
> l'espace de plus de quatre cents lieues vers l'Ouest, au par terre

[1] Margry, *Découvertes*, II, 201–202.

tant le pays qui est entre ces peuples et le fleuve Colbert [Mississippi] estant des couvert et comme une vaste campagne par òu on aisement les emmener par terre.[2]

He continued:

Il en a desjà qui parlent Français, et qui sont des nations plus esloignées. Ils seront bien propres à y servir d'interprètes et à y faire la paix. J'en ay un de la nation des Pana, qui demeurent a plus de cents lieues a l'Ouest, sur une des branches du Mississippi, et y habitent deux villàges l'un pres de l'autre. Ils sont voisins et alliez des Gattacka et Manrhoat, qui sont au sud de leur villages, et qui vendent des chevaux qu'ils, dérobent apparemment aux Espagnols du Nouveau-Mexique. Ces Chevaux, comme j'espère nous seront d'un grand usage. Ces Sauvages s'en servent à la guerre, à la chasse et au transport de toutes choses, n'ont point l'usage de les fermer, les laissent coucher dehors, mesme à la neige, et ne leur donner point d'autres nourritures que de les laisser pasturer. Ces sortes de chevaux doivent estre d'une grand fatigue et bien forts, parcequ'on dit qu'ils porte la viande de deux boeufs, qui pèse pres de mil livres les deux. Ce qui me fait croire qu'ils ont ces chevaux des Espagnols, c'est que, quoyqu'ils soient tout nuds, ils se servent, quand ils vont à cheval, d'un chapeau de cuir tanné qu'ils font eux-mesmes.[3]

According to this description, the Kiowas ("Manrhoats") and Kiowa-Apaches ("Gattackas") lived south of the Panas, one of the Pawnee tribes, and possessed great numbers of horses, which they used in war, in hunting, and for transportation. The horses were extremely hardy, even subsisting in winter on natural pasturage. The Indians traded in horses. The numbers of the tribes are not given, but an estimate made by D'Iberville on June 20, 1702, said that the "Sioux had 4,000 families, Maha—1,200 families, Totata and Ayaoués [Otos and Iowas]—300 families, Cansés [Kansas]—1,500 families, Acansa [Quapaws], Aesetooue, and

[2] *Ibid.*, II, 168.

[3] *Ibid.*, II, 201–202. La Salle, describing "Rívières et peuplades," no date.

Tongenga—200 families, and the Pani [Pawnees] near the Acan-
sas—2,000 families."[4]

The French explorers did not penetrate the Plains area, up the
Missouri, very far until about 1719–20. Bénard de la Harpe, in
1719, wrote of his visit to the tribes north and west of Red River.[5]
He met the Osages, Arkansas, Tonicas, Illinois, and several other
wandering nations on the border of the Red River. These nations
were at war with the "Cannecy" (Apaches) of New Mexico, where
the Spanish had settlements. On the Arkansas River he mentioned
the Canicons. He said that Du Rivage had come back from a voyage, with two Indians of the Quidehais (Kichais), from the west
and had encountered some roaming nations, including the Quidehais, Naouydiches, Joyvans, Huanchanés and Huanés (both Waco
tribes), and Tancaoyes (Tonkawas). They came from a battle
with a party of the Cancy (Apaches).[6] He described them as following the buffalo for food, clothing, and robes. Among themselves
the nations numbered 2,500 men, and they usually dispersed by
bands to find subsistence more easily. The principal nation was the
Touacara (Tawakoni). These nations were allied with those of the
Quichuans (Kiowas).[7] He said that the Cancys had an advantage
over their enemies because they had good horses. The other nations
had skin tents and dogs which carried their goods on marches. An
advantage of making peace with these Indians would be that the
French could penetrate into New Mexico and among the nations
of the Padoucas (Comanches).[8] La Harpe also met the Anahous
or Osages as well as the Touacaras.

[4] *Ibid.*, IV, 601–602.

[5] *Ibid.*, VI, 241, 261–62. "Bénard de la Harpe, envoyé pour établir le poste des
Cadodaquious."

[6] *Ibid.*, VI, 277. A note by Beaurain said that these nations sought to destroy a
party of the Cancy (Apache) nation of eleven villages established toward the source
of the Red River, in the neighborhood of the Spaniards. The tribes given above were
Wichita tribes along the Red River and some allies below the Red River, including
the Tonkawas and Yoguanes, who lived below them in central Texas.

[7] *Ibid.*, VI, 278. A note by Beaurain calls them "Quihohuans." These were the
Kiowas. (Frederick W. Hodge, ed., *Handbook of American Indians North of Mexico*,
B.A.E., *Bulletin 30*, II, 701 [hereinafter cited as Hodge, *Handbook*].)

[8] *Ibid.*, VI, 279. Beaurain said that one of the principal villages of the Cancys

In September, 1719, on the Washita and Canadian rivers south-west of the Arkansas, La Harpe met the chief of the Touacara nation and six chiefs of other nations on fine horses with Spanish-type saddles and bridles. They were leading a group of nations which included the Touacaras, Toayas, (Taovayas), Caumuches (Comanches), Aderos, Ousitas (Wichitas), Ascanis (Yscanis), Quataquois (Kiowa-Apaches), Quicasquiris (Wichitas), and Honechas (Wacos). They comprised about six thousand persons of both sexes.[9] According to La Harpe, the Touacara was the most responsible of all these nations. They had good horses. La Harpe visited with them, smoked the peace pipe (the Touacaras grew tobacco), and gave them gifts. He found them friendly and hospitable.[10]

From Bénard de la Harpe's account, the Kiowa-Apaches (Quataquois) seem to have been pretty far south at this time—probably on a raid. The Wichita tribes also seem to have been unusually far north of the Red River; the Naouydiches (probably the Nabedaches of the Hasinais) and the Tonkawas, too, were far north, but were probably on long buffalo hunts. All of the names are not identifiable with later tribes, but enough are familiar to show that some interesting contacts were being made.

(Apaches) was that of the Quirireches, who had "very good horses." This is interesting because of the "Querechos" that Coronado met in 1541. "Padouca" here means Comanches, and not Apaches, since "Cancys" or "Canecys" is used for Apaches.

[9] *Ibid.*, VI, 288–89. In note 2, Le Chevalier de Beaurien [*sic*] added: "These nations are the Toucara, Toayas, Caunouche, Ardeco, Ousita, Ascanis, Quataquon, Quirasquiris, Houechas. One believes that they are the Mento." Although spellings differ slightly, one may recognize the Quataquois as Cattakas or Kiowa-Apaches, and the Quirasquiris as Wichitas. The Quichuans of La Harpe or Quihohuans of Beaurain were Kiowas. (See note 7 above.) He said that all together they composed five thousand persons. (La Harpe said six thousand.) He noted that they were allied with the Panioussas (Wichitas) to the north and were at peace with the Osages to the northeast. They were also allied with wandering nations on the headwaters of Red River but had a cruel war against the Canecys (Apaches), the Padoucas (Comanches), and some of the Pani (Pawnee) villages. They were known to the Aricaras, established beside the Canses (Kansas) on the Missouri.

[10] *Ibid.*, VI, 290–93, 294. Anthropophagy or cannibalism was mentioned among them.

The next mention of the Kiowas is from Perrin du Lac, who left Bordeaux, France, on August 14, 1801, to visit America and the territory of Louisiana, which was then held by the Spanish but was shortly to return to France.[11] He visited New York, Philadelphia, and other cities, and then journeyed to St. Louis. On May 18, 1802, he outfitted an expedition to go up the Missouri to trade with the Indians for furs. He took along as guide an old trader who, he said, had ascended the river farther than anyone else in the country and had formerly been employed by a fur company of upper Missouri.[12]

Perrin du Lac stated that the Canadian or English merchants met the Sioux Indians every year at a rendezvous on the Dog Field, five hundred miles from St. Louis, and on St. Peter's River, three hundred miles farther, to trade. Skins were traded for guns, gunpowder, lead, vermilion, and trinkets.

With ten men accompanying him, Perrin du Lac set out with blue and scarlet cloth, woolen clothing, copper cauldrons, knives, wines, and silver trinkets, in addition to the customary trade

[11] See note 5 above. (Pichardo, *Treatise*, II, 30 *et seq.*)

[12] The *"ancien traiteur"* of Perrin du Lac may have been Jean Baptiste Trudeau or Pierre-Antoine Tabeau. See *Tabeau's Narrative of Loisel's Expedition to the Upper Missouri*, ed. by Annie Heloise Abel, trans. by Rose Abel Wright; and Jean Baptiste Trudeau, "Journal of Jean Baptiste Trudeau among the Arikara Indians in 1795," trans. by Mrs. H. T. Beauregard, Missouri Historical Society *Collections*, Vol. IV (1912–13), 9–48. Abel says that Jean Baptiste Trudeau was sent up the Missouri in 1794. Others followed, including Victor Collot in 1796. Régis Loisel, accompanied by Pierre-Antoine Tabeau, went up the Missouri in 1802. Loisel made one earlier trip and built a fort on the Isle of Cedars. Loisel died in 1805; Tabeau lived until 1820. Loisel had been commissioned in April, 1803, to undertake an examination of English intrusions and report on aboriginal inhabitants, then of political importance. He probably entrusted the writing of this to Tabeau, who lived among the Arikaras and met Lewis and Clark. *Tabeau's Narrative* shows that he deleted Loisel's importance. In 1805 he had had about eight months' experience in dealing with the Arikaras. Abel says that "Trudeau's Description of the Upper Missouri" (*The Mississippi Valley Historical Review*, Vol. VIII, Nos. 1 and 2 [1921], 149–79) is much like Victor Collot's *A Journey in North America*. It was probably used by Collot in 1806, which gives an approximate date for Trudeau. Perrin du Lac probably used Trudeau's information in 1802. Trudeau may have been Perrin du Lac's *"ancien traiteur . . .* unless indeed Pierre-Antoine Tabeau was." *Tabeau's Narrative*, 15n.

goods.[13] He met and traded with the Osages, Kansas, Otatates, Great Panis (and mentioned the Loups or Wolf Pawnees near them but did not trade or visit with them), Mahas, Poncas, Cheyennes, Arikaras, and others. The Mahas were 735 miles up from the mouth of the Missouri on the Mahas (Big Sioux) River and had suffered exceedingly in 1801 from smallpox. He went to the second Sioux River (probably the Vermilion), to the Ponca village on the Rapid (James) River, and then on to the White River and the Cheyenne River, the terminus of his voyage. There he met some of the Cheyenne Indians, a party of 120 men hunting buffalo; most of these Indians, he said, had never seen white men before.[14] They gave Perrin du Lac some three hundreds pounds of meat, and he gave them gunpowder which they did not know how to use. They made it into flares, which they liked to ignite on the ground to admire the sparks and the running flame. He also gave them vermilion, mirrors, and silver pins. Of the Cheyennes (whom he called "Chaguyennes"), he said:

> The Chaguyenes, although they *travel by water* [wander] during most of the year, nevertheless sow maize and tobacco near their rancheria, and reap the harvest at the beginning of autumn. They are generally good hunters, and kill many beaver, with which they carry on trade with the Sioux. Many wandering peoples, but who are allied with the Chaguyennes, hunt in the same country. These people are the Cayoavvas, the Tocaninambiches, the Tokiouakas, and the Pitapahatos.[15]

[13] Perrin du Lac, *Travels*, 49–50.

[14] Jacques d'Église claimed to have discovered the Mandans and Cheyennes in 1791. The Mandans were then in communication with the British. He reported his journey to Zenon Trudeau in St. Louis in 1792. In 1793 he set out again with Joseph Garreau to open trade with the Mandans. The expedition was not successful. See Abraham P. Nasatir, "Jacques d'Église on the Upper Missouri, 1791–1795," *The Mississippi Valley Historical Review*, Vol. XIV (June, 1927–March, 1928), 47–56, 57–71.

[15] Pichardo, *Treatise*, II, 36. The italics are mine. The first sentence of this quotation was incorrectly translated; the French original says "wander." "Cayoavvas"

He continued:

Concerning them [the Cheyennes] it has been learned that some years ago a large band for war and for hunting was formed, and, in the region to the west, they had crossed some very rugged mountains, at whose foot there flows a beautiful river, in the same direction. Having descended it for many days, they encountered seven families, whom they attacked and put to flight without difficulty. Having entered their huts, they discovered nothing that could cause them to think that they might have had the slightest contact with the whites. Their clothing, their footgear, the trappings of their horses, were of skins of beaver, of otters, of foxes, of wolves, or hares, or of other animals in which the country abounds. Their tents were made of rush mats, for the lack of buffalo hides, of which they appeared to be deprived. A small sack of maize, which they found in the baggage, led them to ask some of the women prisoners if their nation cultivated it. They replied that they did not, but that down the river was a large rancheria where it was harvested in abundance.

Having seen various small shells, pierced and strung on small cords of rawhide, around the necks and in the ears of these women, they desired to know where they had got them. They replied that at the mouth of the river there was a great quantity of water, which extended so far that it was impossible to see its opposite shore; that this water rose and fell alternately at a certain time of the day and

---

refers to the Kiowas, and "Pitapahatos" was one band of the Kiowas or another name applied to them, or a misspelling of "Wetapahatoes," the Dakota name for them. Later Lewis and Clark would incorrectly describe the Wetapahatoes as a separate tribe, rather than as a division of the Kiowas. "Tokiouakas" probably refers to Gattackas or Kiowa-Apaches. Mooney said that the Tokiouakas may have been the To-che-wah-coo or the Fox Indians who traded with the Arikaras. (James Mooney, "The Cheyenne Indians," American Anthropological Association, *Memoirs*, Vol. I, No. 6 [1905–1907], 357–478.) The "Tocaninambiches" were the Arapahoes. See "Arapaho" by James Mooney in Hodge, *Handbook*, I, 72–74.

The Cheyennes were a former sedentary and agricultural people, using pottery, who moved west from Minnesota and lost their sedentary arts as they adapted to buffalo-hunting. As late as 1850, some of them did a little planting. See "Cheyenne" by James Mooney in Hodge, *Handbook*, I, 250–57; and Mooney, "The Cheyenne Indians," *loc. cit.*, 357–478.

24

of the night; that the neighboring peoples fastened large pieces of meat to the ends of cords, which they threw out when the waters were high, and drew in when they were low, and that the shells with which they adorned themselves were found in great numbers adhering to the meat, from which they took them.

The great nation of the Padaws [Comanches], which extends [to] the Rio Plate is not separated from that of the Ricaras more than about ten days journey for a hunter, who is able to [travel] regularly about twenty-five miles each day. The Halisanes, or Bald-Heads, are wanderers and hunt on the other side of the Rio Plate, as far as the borders of the Arcanzas, and go out to the foot of the mountains of New Mexico, in a region abounding in all kinds of animals.[16]

Perrin du Lac also described the Sioux, "four wandering bands . . . warlike and fierce," who preyed upon "the Ricaras, Chaguyenes, and occasionally, the Mandannes." Descriptions were given of the "Mandannes, Gruesos Ventres and Asseniboynes." Of the Crows, early teachers of the Kiowas, he said:

At 160 miles to the west of the Missouri, above the nation of the Gruesos Ventres, there is found the mouth of a large river, named Roca Amarilla [Yellowstone]. Its banks abound in buffaloes, and in all sorts of wild animals, and it is inhabited by the Cuervo [Crow] nation, numerous, but as yet little known.

The savages who inhabit the western bank of the Missouri are tractable and kindly toward the whites, for whom they have a great veneration, and they call them without distinction by the name of spirits. Trade is carried on with them in security and peace. *It may be regarded as an inviolable maxim that the less communication the*

16 Pichardo, *Treatise*, II, 36–37. Here are described the neighbors of the early Kiowas. "Padaws" refers here to the Comanches. Tabeau used "Padaux" in his *Narrative* and "Padaucas" in the Montreal version of his *Narrative*. Mooney said that the Comanches were known by the name "Paducas" to the Osages, Dakotas, and related tribes. (Mooney, "Calendar History," 161–62.) Abel says "Paducas" refers to the Comanches. (*Tabeau's Narrative*, 137n.) The "Canninanbiches" were the Arapahoes, also called thus by Trudeau earlier (in his "Journal," *loc. cit.*, 31). Trudeau, in addition, called them "Tocaninanbiches" (in his "Description," *loc cit.*, 167).

Indians have had with the civilized peoples, the more fair, generous, and kindly they will be toward them. It is probable that a bad choice of the men who are sent to trade with them soon causes them to lose their exalted opinion, which it would have been well to preserve, by virtue of which they regarded them as privileged children of him whom they call the Great Spirit.[17]

Perrin du Lac left on August 26, 1802, to return to St. Louis, having been on the trip up the Missouri three months. He went down to the Arkansas, where he had left a cache of furs, and was shot at by the Sioux, this being the only hostility of the trip. He had to embark hurriedly, leaving some of the furs. He reached St. Louis on September 20, then went down the Mississippi to visit New Orleans. While there, he deplored the Spanish control of Louisiana, remarking upon its privilege and corruption and evils. Later he returned to France. Whether his visit was prompted by any political significance, or commercial interest in the fur trade, he does not say. By the time he reached France, Louisiana was sold to the United States.

He compiled some statistics on population and on the fur trade. The population of the tribes given was: Osages, 1,200 men (bearers of arms); Kansas, 450 men; Republicans, 300 men; Otatoes, 350 men; Great Panis, 500 men; Loups (Wolf Pawnees), 200 men; Mahas, 600 men; Poncas, 300 men; and Arikaras, 1,000 men. He said that the Mandans, Cheyennes, and Minatares did very little trade, but that other nations bought their furs and then sold them to the whites. He also noted that the Padoucas (Comanches) supplied some furs. All of these nations together had some 5,000 hunters. The Osages could supply 800 bundles of squirrel skins and 150 bundles of fine skins; the Kansas could supply 200 bundles of

---

[17] Pichardo, *Treatise*, II, 37. Italics are those of Perrin du Lac; but had he not italicized, I would have. How true his words were, thirty years hence, after the fur trade spread havoc among the Indians! In 1832, Catlin remarked this friendship, sincerity, and exalting of the whites where the Indians had not been corrupted from contacts with trading, alcohol, and bad treatment. (Spanish names were used in Pichardo's *Treatise*, translated from French to Spanish by Pichardo, then into English by Hackett.)

squirrel skins and 40 bundles of fine skins.[18] Estimates were given for annual supplies of furs for a number of tribes. He said that the commerce with the tribes of the Missouri amounted to 20,000 French livres annually.[19] He also noted the abundant wildlife, and of the bison, he said:

> The wild bulls or buffaloes were formerly so numerous in Upper Louisiana, that hunters were contented to cut out their tongues, and to leave the carcases for carnivorous animals or birds.[20]

Some points relating to the tribes and their culture were given in detail. He said that the Arikaras formerly had thirty-two villages but then had only one tribe, mostly destroyed by the Sioux or by smallpox. Two leagues from their village was the Cheyenne River, where the Cheyennes lived. They consisted of "three hordes," Cheyennes, Ouisys, and Chousas. They continually wandered on both banks of the river in pursuit of the buffalo and hunted on the savannahs near the Platte River. Beyond it were great lakes where they believed the "Father of the Beavers" lived. Although wanderers, the Cheyennes planted maize and tobacco, which they came to "reap at the beginning of autumn."[21]

From the White River, 240 miles lower than the Cheyenne, as far as another river whose name was unknown, probably the Platte, lived the Sioux "all along the eastern bank." They plundered the Arikaras and Cheyennes of their clothes and horses and plundered the Mandans of tobacco and maize. The Mandans, formerly numerous, had only three villages and three hundred warriors then. The Assiniboines, a wandering nation to the north, supplied the Mandans with guns in exchange for horses, maize, and tobacco. About 150 miles west of the Missouri was the Yellowstone River, where buffalo and deer abounded.[22]

[18] Perrin du Lac, *Travels*, 56. A bundle was one hundred pounds. "Plus," later called and spelled "plew," meant fine skins—beaver, otter, and mink.

[19] *Ibid.*, 56.

[20] *Ibid.*, 61.

[21] *Ibid.*, 63.

[22] *Ibid.*, 63.

PERRIN DU LAC: EARLIEST DESCRIPTION OF PLAINS CULTURE

Since Perrin du Lac's is the first description of the culture of the northern Plains people, including the Kiowas, it is of great interest for comparison with later accounts. Later, in 1804–1805, Lewis and Clark would pass through this same area. Thus, Perrin du Lac antedated them by three years.

These tribes had a Lodge of the Old Men and reverence for the sun; they venerated cedar and planted a cedar tree before the Lodge of the Old Men. Members of the tribe would often go off to a hill for several days of fasting. For gifts of courage from the Great Spirit, they would make offerings of their fingers.

> Others bore holes in their arms and shoulders, into which they pass wooden pegs, and to them attach long cords, from which their military weapons, and many heads of oxen, are suspended. In this state they make the circuit of the village, and having repeated the ceremony for five successive days, they depart for the war.[23]

All believed in a future life, a village where every want would be supplied. Some paid scant attention to the dead. "The Sioux, the Tocaninambiches [Arapahoes] and the Cheyennes" were inconsolable for the loss of their dead. They bewailed them for a whole year. They interred the bodies with weapons and gifts of food.

The old men would exhort the youths of the tribe to bravery and generosity. There were no laws but rules of conduct governed. The old men deliberated, and if the village approved their decisions, their wishes must be executed. Each village had a great chief. On the buffalo hunt, the old men selected the bravest warriors to mark out the distance of the hunt. If anyone went beyond it, he was beaten and his horses and dogs were killed. The warriors were accorded as much respect as the chief.[24]

[23] *Ibid.*, 64–65. Compare Catlin's description of the Mandan ceremony in 1832 (Catlin, *North American Indians*, I, 176–208). The Lodge of the Old Men was a council house or men's club, not to be confused with the Sun Dance, described later. Lonely fasting in the hills was the vision quest of the later Plains culture.

[24] *Ibid.*, 67. This might be a description of much later time; it is remarkably true. The warriors were later known as the "dog soldiers" who served as police in the

28

Children were kindly treated. They were never beaten. Great deeds were related to them, and they were exhorted to be brave. The women occupied an inferior position, doing the work of carrying water and preparing food. The savages were "tall and swift walkers." War they held in the "greatest respect" and indulged in it for glory and for a love of revenge. Anyone might form a war party. Small raiding parties went after horses. Chiefs of the first class determined on the wars or might decide after young men, "out for fame," solicited them. They had to confer over a pipe. If a man accepted the smoking of the pipe, he assented to go with the war party. If the chiefs accepted, they chose a day and had a feast of dog's flesh prepared, and then took many days to get the followers ready. Wars were conducted by surprising the enemy. The victims usually fled, some were killed, and some prisoners were taken, usually women.[25] A returning war party lighted fires, if successful. The women sang and the old men carried scalps on sticks painted red. Scalps were put in the Lodge of the Old Men. On the following day, they held a scalp dance. They danced in a circle where meat, ox tongue, and a dried human heart were placed.[26]

Treaties were sometimes made with other tribes, usually after a great amount of warfare had gone on. These treaties were usually for hunting privileges. In determining on a peace treaty, they would smoke the calumet while a servant[27] served meat at a feast.

hunt and at the Sun Dance. In the late history of the Plains, the soldier societies came to have more power than the chief, specifically among the Cheyennes, because of their horsemanship and prestige in raiding for horses.

[25] *Ibid.*, 67–70.

[26] *Ibid.*, 71.

[27] *Ibid.*, 73–74. A note on page 74 says it was a male servant or "berdache." This refers to a eunuch or homosexual, also mentioned among the Mandans in 1832 by Catlin. Cabeza de Vaca described the berdache among the Karankawas in Texas in 1528. The berdache was also known among the Cheyennes and other Plains tribes. The berdaches or transvestites were called "hemanch" (half-men–half-women) by the Cheyennes. They were male homosexuals who often served as second wives in a married man's household. They took charge of Scalp Dances and were often respected as medicine men and intermediaries in marriage proposals. They accompanied war parties also. See E. Adamson Hoebel, *The Cheyennes*, 77.

The calumet dance was performed after a peace was made, and horses for the dancers were presented to them by the chief.[28]

The Sun Dance was not practiced by all; it belonged "exclusively to the Sioux of the savannahs, to the Cheyennes, Tocaninambiches [Arapahoes], and other neighboring nations."[29] (The Kiowas and Kiowa-Apaches were neighboring nations.) For the Sun Dance a large cabin was erected in the middle of a meadow. Old men sat in the most distinguished places, and women and girls with their faces painted sat near by. The bravest warriors were distinguished by special ornaments—for example, only those who had killed a white bear could wear a necklace of its claws. This was a particular mark of distinction, for a bear would attack a man before it was wounded. Sometimes bears entered lodges and destroyed their inhabitants.

A fire and boiling cauldrons of meat were part of the ceremony. Presents were offered to the sun, and these offerings had to be made before sunrise. Singing of songs and smoking of the calumet began the dance. Youths of both sexes danced, and twelve naked boys danced in the open all day and fasted. Those inside the lodge took some refreshment. The ceremonies of the Sun Dance lasted ten successive days. After the dance ended, presents were divided among the warriors. The dance was held to ensure courage, health, and an abundant supply of buffalo.[30]

Other dances included a buffalo dance, wherein the dancers mimicked the actions of the buffalo while the singers beat a drum. The Indians generally enjoyed good health. Old men often committed suicide. The dwellings of the villagers were skin tents, as they were nomadic. Their tents were drawn by dogs.[31]

[28] Perrin du Lac, *Travels*, 74–75. This probably refers to gifts given a visiting tribe. In later days, the Kiowas gave visitors horses.

[29] *Ibid.*, 76.

[30] *Ibid.*, 76–77. In all essential points, this description parallels the dance of later times. It seems to have been an outgrowth of associative magic.

[31] *Ibid.*, 77. The English translation says "on four wheels," which is a mistake. The original says "chariot . . . rudely constructed." This may be translated as a drawn conveyance, even a cradle. Hence Perrin du Lac is not discredited. The Indians had no wheels. This refers to the travois or drag, tent poles harnessed to the dogs, with the poles dragging on the ground.

Marriage customs were simple. A relative of the man would go to the father of the intended bride and entreat him to give the girl in marriage. The father would consult all of her relations. If he was found satisfactory, the man made gifts to the father and took the girl as a bride. Polygamy was common. A young man would live with the wife's family until they had a child; then he would have a lodge of his own. The "Sioux, Cheyennes, and Tocaninambiches [Arapahoes]" were extremely jealous of their wives; the Mandans, Arikaras, and others held conjugal felicity in no estimation.[32]

In conclusion, Perrin du Lac said: "These people may be conquered, but no power on earth can make them laborious cultivators or artizans."[33]

It is remarkably true that Perrin du Lac's cultural descriptions of the early Kiowas and their neighbors would fit a later time. It is the pattern of a culture that would spread the length and breadth of the Plains, to be diffused by mobile and daring horsemen. Only a few of these Indians knew the French fur traders, and some had never seen a white man before 1802. At this time the Louisiana Territory was under the Spanish government. In 1803 it passed to the United States after France reclaimed and sold it. The Spanish paid little attention to the fur trade; articles of trade were coming in to the Indians largely from the English in Canada, the trade moving across to the Sioux. Some bands of traders, largely Frenchmen, at or near St. Louis and Ste Geneviève, below St. Louis, were moving farther up the Missouri than before, but trade had fallen off under Spanish control. This account antedates that of Lewis and Clark.

In 1804, Pierre-Antoine Tabeau was living and trading among the Arikaras and their neighbors. He met Lewis and Clark when they were on their way westward. *Tabeau's Narrative* covers from June 22, 1803, to May 20, 1805. (Jean Baptiste Trudeau was sent up the Missouri River in 1794 by the Missouri Company, but he

[32] *Ibid.*, 80.
[33] *Ibid.*, 82.

did not write his "Description of the Upper Missouri" until about 1806.

Tabeau lived under the patronage of Kakawita, an Arikara chief. He mentioned that the Arikaras were hard to please and that he, Tabeau, came to dislike them. In 1804 there were many dissensions, and the Arikaras became angry with the traders who were getting enormous profits. Tabeau and another Frenchman in whose lodge Tabeau lived were threatened with injury. Finally Kakawita grudgingly offered some protection and called off the threateners. There was a general uprising, but the "presence of more than fifteen hundred men—Sioux, Chayennes, Padaux, Can-ninanbiches, etc., restrained the Ricaras and I hastened to do some good trading."[34]

Tabeau said:

> The Ricaras, before this year [1804], carried to the foot of the Black Hills, tobacco and maize. They accompanied the Chayennes and found at the meeting place, eight other friendly nations—the Caninanbiches, the Squihitanes, the Nimoussines, the Padaucas, the Catarkas, the Datamis, the Tchiwak and the Cayowa. The first two speak the same language, but all others speak a different one.[35]

The need for communication, said Tabeau, among these tribes gave rise to the sign language. Tabeau said that no one could understand a word of Tchiwak. The nations roamed over territory between the River Platte and the Yellowstone River, whose sources were quite close together. These nations lived in perfect harmony and formed a league against the Mandans, Gros Ventres, and all the other northern nations above.

[34] *Tabeau's Narrative*, 137.

[35] *Ibid.*, 154–55. The first two, Caninanbiches and Squihitanes, were Arapahoes "who speak the same language." Abel says that the Datamis and Cayowas were the modern Kiowas. The Nimoussines, Catarkas, and Padaucas were the modern Comanches. (I would identify the Catarkas as the Gattackas or the later Kiowa-Apaches. The Tchiwaks may have been Chauis, a tribe of the Pawnee Confederacy. But I believe that the Tchiwaks were probably Cheyennes.) All lived on the headwaters of two branches of the Cheyenne River.

Tabeau mentioned that the Cheyennes gave up agriculture. They were established for a few years on the Missouri but were so vexed by the Sioux that they had to resort to open war. They then abandoned agriculture and their hearths and became a nomadic people.

The Cheyennes settled near the Arikaras on the banks of the river. The Cheyennes opposed the Sioux, who crossed the river and bothered the Arikaras, stealing and plundering. Finally a temporary truce was made by the Sioux and the Arikaras. The Cheyennes ceased to till the soil and roamed over the prairies west of the Missouri "on this side [east] of the Black Hills, from which they come regularly at the beginning of August to visit their old and faithful allies, the Ricaras."[36]

For the Cheyennes, this was a quick change to nomadism, within one year.[37] Ten years earlier (1794), Trudeau noted their settled villages and their cultivation of maize and tobacco.[38]

The first official American notice of the Kiowas was that of Lewis and Clark. They ascended the Missouri in 1804 and wintered among the Mandans before going on to the west. Toussaint Charbonneau and his Shoshoni wives, Sacagawea and Otter Woman, were to lead them. Sacagawea gave birth to a son and carried him on her back while leading the way to her people. (She had been captured at an early age by the Hidatsas.) Otter Woman, being pregnant, was left with the Mandans. Lewis and Clark did not see the Kiowas, but they heard about them. Captain Meriwether Lewis said that the Wetapahatoes or We-te-pâ-hâ-to, including the Kiowas, had seventy tents or lodgings, with two hundred warriors, the probable "number of souls" being seven hundred. They lived on the Paduca Fork of the Platte River and had no trader. But Lewis thought that a principal establishment to supply these Indians could be made at or near the Cheyenne

[36] *Ibid.*, 154.

[37] Wedel, *Culture Sequence in the Central Great Plains*. Wedel says that the archaeological evidence of Cheyenne sites shows that they changed from sedentary villages to nomadism within fifty years.

[38] *Tabeau's Narrative*, 154, citing "Trudeau's Description" (*loc. cit.*, 165–66).

River. They carried on a defensive war against the Sioux and had friendly alliances with wandering neighbors to the west. They exchanged horses and mules with the Arikaras, Mandans, Minnetarees, and others. They were a wandering nation living in the open country. They raised great numbers of horses and traded them for articles of European manufacture. They also bartered articles that they obtained to the Dotames and Castapanas. They were a "well disposed people."[39]

Lewis and Clark gave the Wetapahatoes incorrectly as a separate tribe. Mooney believed that they were a part of, or, the Kiowas, and that the numbers given for them and the Kiowas were much too low."[40]

Lewis wrote that the Kiowas had the same number as given for the Wetapahatoes; in fact, information applicable to the Wetapahatoes was in all respects applicable to the Kiowas. They had no trader; they had a defensive war with the Sioux. Neither these people nor the Cheyennes had an idea of exclusive right to the soil.[41]

The Kaniná'vish[42] or Kun-na-nar-wesh Indians, called by the

---

[39] Meriwether Lewis and William Clark, *Travels in the Interior Parts of America,* reprinted from Thomas Jefferson, *Message from the President of the United States, Communicating Discoveries Made in Exploring the Missouri, Red River and Washita, by Captains Lewis and Clark, Doctor Sibley and Mr [William] Dunbar,* in *A Collection of Modern and Contemporary Voyages and Travels,* VI, 20–21. Hereafter cited as Lewis and Clark, *Travels.*

[40] "Calendar History," 166. Perrin du Lac called them "Pitapahatos." The Dakota name for the Kiowas was "Wi'tapähä'tu," people of the "island butte." "Witapä'hat" and "Witapä'tu" were Cheyenne forms, probably derived from the ancient name Tépdá, for the Kiowas. "Vi'täpätu'i" was a name used by the Sutaya division of the Cheyennes for the Kiowas. (*Ibid.,* 149f.)

[41] Lewis and Clark, *Travels,* 21.

[42] *Ibid.,* 22. These are the Arapahoes, according to Mooney. They called themselves "Inûna-ina," equivalent to "Our People." There were five main divisions of the Arapahoes, one of which was the Aä'ninéna, Atsina, or Gros Ventre of the Prairie. (Perrin du Lac's Tocaninambiches was the same, joining "Aä'ninena" and "Vach." Mooney said that they were once a sedentary agricultural people in the Red River Valley of northern Minnesota; they moved down about the same time the Cheyennes moved down from Minnesota, and they formed a permanent alliance with the Cheyennes. The Aä'ninenas or Atsinas, after associated with the Siksikas, separated and moved off to the north after their emergence on the Plains. See Mooney, "Arapaho," *loc. cit.,* 72–74.

traders "Gens des Vaches" ("Buffalo People"), had 1,500 souls, 150 lodges, and 400 warriors. They lived at the head of the Paducas Fork of the River Platte, and south of the Cheyenne River. They also had a defensive war against the Sioux, and the same was "applicable to these people as to the Wetapahatoes and Kiowas."

The Staitans, called "Kites" by the Canadian traders, had 40 lodges or tents, 100 warriors, and 400 souls. They lived on the headwaters of the Cheyenne and frequently lived with the Kaniná'-vishes. They, too, had a defensive war against the Sioux, and "what had been said of the Wetapahatoes and Kiowas" applies to them.[43]

The Gáta'kas, or Cá'takâs, had 25 lodges or tents, 75 warriors, and 500 souls. They lived between the north and south forks of the Cheyenne River. "What has been said of the Wetapahatoes and Kiowas, applies here, too."[44]

All of these people were friendly with and visited the Arikaras. Others nearby were the Nemousins and Dotames on the head of the Cheyenne River and the north fork of the Cheyenne, but they had wars against the Arikaras and Sioux. In all other respects, they were the same as the Wetapahatoes and Kiowas. Further descriptions were given for the Castahanas, Crows, Sioux, Pawnees, and Aliatans or Snakes (three large tribes of these). In regard to the Paducas (Comanches), Lewis and Clark said:

[43] Lewis and Clark, *Travels*, 22. The name "Staitan" is known only from the Lewis and Clark description. They were known as Kites because they were always "flying," that is, always on horseback. They were friends of the Cheyennes and Kaniná'vishes or Arapahoes. They may have been the Sutaio Indians, later incorporated with the Cheyennes. See James Mooney, "Staitan," in Hodge, *Handbook*, I, 254–55; II, 632. See also Mooney, "The Cheyenne Indians," *loc. cit.*, 369–70. Staitan was probably Sútai'-itä'n, or "Sutai man." The Sutaio or Sutai Indians spoke the Cheyenne language, crossed to the Missouri with the Cheyennes, and were absorbed by the Cheyennes. From the Sutaioes the Cheyennes got the Sun Dance and the "buffalo cap medicine" later preserved in the Sutai band of the Cheyennes.

[44] Lewis and Clark, *Travels*, 22. These are the Kiowa-Apaches, always a part of the Kiowas. In 1719, La Harpe called them "Quataquois," and Beaurain called them "Quataquon." Perrin du Lac called them "Tokiouakos." Arapaho names for them were "Tha'ká-hine'na" and "Tha'káitän," derived from "Gáta'ka" and "hiné na," meaning "people," and "itan," meaning "tribe." See Mooney, "Calendar History," 245; also Mooney, "Kiowa-Apache," in Hodge, *Handbook*, I, 700–703. "Gáta'ka" was the Pawnee name for them.

35

This once powerful nation has, apparently, disappeared; every inquiry I have made after them has proved ineffectual. In the year 1724, they resided in several villages on the heads of the Kansas river, and could, at that time, bring upwards of two thousand men into the field (see Mons. Dupratz history of Louisiana, page 71, and the map attached to that work). The information that I received is, that being oppressed by the nations residing on the Missouri, they removed to the upper part of the river Platte . . . [and] divided into small wandering bands, which assumed the names of the sub-divisions of the Paducas nation, and are known to us at present under the appellation of Wetepahatoes, Kiawas, Kanenavish, Katteka, Dotame, etc. who still inhabit the country to which the Paducas are said to have removed.[45]

Although Lewis and Clark could not find the Paducas, they described the "la Playes" division of the Aliatans or Snake Indians, who were the Comanches, according to Mooney, and were then inhabiting the headwaters of the Arkansas. They possessed no guns but were brave and warlike and owned a number of horses.[46]

A few years later, Zebulon M. Pike stated in his book describing his travels that he estimated the Kiowas to number one thousand men and that, in 1803, they had been driven by the Dakotas to the headwaters of the Platte and Arkansas and were north of the Comanches. They owned immense herds of horses, were armed with bows, arrows, and lances, and hunted the buffalo. They were then at war with the Dakotas, Pawnees, and Utes. In another place he

[45] Lewis and Clark, *Travels*, 38–39. Lewis and Clark did not visit these tribes, but only heard about them; their ideas about the Paducas were erroneous. The citation refers to Antoine M. le Page du Pratz, *The History of Louisiana*. The Paducas visited by Bourgmont in 1724 may have been Apaches rather than Comanches. (See notes 3 and 4, Chapter I, in this volume.) Lewis and Clark use "Kattaka" for "Cataka." The Dotames and Castapanas or Castahanas, living back of the Kiowas on the headwaters of the North Platte and the Yellowstone, may have been bands of the Shoshonis. (Mooney, "Calendar History," 166.) Hodge identified the Dotames as Kiowas and the Castapanas as Arapahoes. The Dotames spoke Comanche, a Shoshoni language, but Hodge called them Kiowas. The Castapanas were mentioned as Snakes (Shoshonis) and also as speaking the Minnetaree (Atsina) language by Lewis and Clark. See Hodge, *Handbook*, I, 212, 399.

[46] Lewis and Clark, *Travels*, 23; Mooney, "Calendar History," 166.

mentioned that the Utes and Kiowas were living in the mountainous regions of northern New Mexico. He said that they fought a battle in September, 1806, near the village of Taos. The Kiowas and Tetans (Comanches) fought the Utes, but the battle was stopped by the Spanish authorities. In 1807, Pike met a party of Kiowas and Comanches returning from a trading expedition to the Mandans.[47]

The Kiowas were for some time at war with the Dakotas. According to the Dakota calendar, the Dakotas sent a delegation to visit the Kiowas, then on the junction of Kiowa and Horse creeks, headwaters of the Platte, to make peace, but it was defeated by a quarrel.[48] In 1816 a smallpox epidemic ravaged the tribes from the Red to the Río Grande rivers. The Kiowas and the Comanches lost great numbers. This was the first smallpox epidemic within the memory of the tribes, although Mooney stated that there had been one in 1801, which a Pawnee war party had brought back from northern Mexico, and which had spread from Missouri to the coasts of Texas. In 1801 the prairie tribes were said to have lost half their numbers, and the Wichitas and others in the south suffered as severely. Perrin du Lac also wrote of its terrible effects among the Mandans, Arikaras, and others on the upper Missouri.

MAJOR STEPHEN LONG'S EXPEDITION

In 1820, Edwin James, with Major Long's expedition up the Arkansas, spoke of the Kiowas as wandering with the Arapahoes and others over the region of the Arkansas and Red rivers, having great numbers of horses, and trading them to the Cheyennes and others.[49] He mentioned that a great gathering of tribes had taken

[47] *The Expeditions of Zebulon Montgomery Pike*, ed. by Elliott Coues, II, 743–46.
[48] Mooney, "Calendar History," 168.
[49] Edwin James (ed.), *Account of an Expedition from Pittsburgh to the Rocky Mountains, Performed in the Years, 1819, 1820, under the Command of Major S. H. Long* (hereinafter cited as James, *Long Expedition*). The object of this expedition was to explore the Mississippi and Missouri and navigable tributaries for the Secretary of War. Major S. H. Long was pessimistic about the country, called it the "Great American Desert," and believed it unsuitable for the agricultural interests of the colonists then moving west of the Mississippi. In 1821, Austin's colony began in

place in present Colorado. The Cheyennes had come down with goods from the traders of the Missouri to trade for horses with the Kiowas, Arapahoes, and Kaskaias or "Bad Hearts" (Kiowa-Apaches), and with a party of traders from St. Louis.[50]

A romantic interlude occurred when an Indian and a woman of the Kaskaias met the Long party. They were fleeing from below the Arkansas River north to the mountains near the sources of the Platte. The Indians were friendly and advised Long's party that six nations were encamped nineteen days' journey below. The nations were the Kaskaias, Arapahoes, Kiowas, Bald Heads (Comanches), Cheyennes, and a few Shoshonis or Snakes. They had been engaged in warfare against the Spanish, probably the Spanish of Old Mexico. The fugitive Indians also gave an account of a battle

---

Mexican Texas, and Anglo-Americans would shortly move into parts of the Great American Desert.

There are two accounts of the Long Expedition: James's and John R. Bell's. For many years it was thought that James's account was the only one, even though the Reverend Jedidiah Morse wrote an account taken in part from Bell's notes (Jedidiah Morse, *Indian Affairs* [New Haven, 1822]). In 1932 the John R. Bell account was found in California, and it was published in 1957. This was the official journal, but it never reached the Secretary of War and may have been lost by Morse. The journal was given by the Arthur B. Saunders family to the Department of History, Stanford University. Its value was discovered by Harlin M. Fuller.

John R. Bell went to Florida, after 1820, then to Savannah Harbor, Georgia, and in 1824 to Fort Moultrie, South Carolina. In poor health, he visited friends in New York and died in Henrietta, New York, on April 11, 1825. The Saunders family brought the journal from New York to California, but the family knew no particulars of its acquisition. See John R. Bell, *The Journal Of Captain John R. Bell*, ed. by Harlin M. Fuller and LeRoy R. Hafen (Vol. VI, *The Far West and the Rockies Historical Series, 1820–1875*). (Hereinafter cited as Bell, *Journal*.)

[50] Mooney, "Calendar History," 168. This is the first mention of the Kiowas on Red River, which was, says Mooney, probably the Canadian, as they called the Canadian "Guadal pia," or "Red River." (There is also a Red River in northern New Mexico that flows into the Río Grande. The Continental Divide separates this Red River of the Red River Valley and the headwaters of the Cimarron Creek in northern New Mexico. The Red River is north of Taos and Cuesta and west of the present town of Cimarron.) Cimarron Creek, joined by Ponil and Rayado, flows into the Canadian. The Cimarron River and the Canadian, both flowing east, take their beginnings in the north and east of New Mexico. The Red River of Texas begins in the Cap Rock drainage at the edge of the Great Plains. The Cimarron River is a tributary of the Arkansas River.

between the "Tabby-boos" (Anglo-Americans—from "tabe-bone," Shoshoni for "white man") and the Spanish, in which great guns were used. (The battle is unidentified but may have been a part of the Mexican Revolution which was successfully completed in 1821.)

The Indian man carried a gun in a case of leather. The two Indians camped near the whites and gave them directions in regard to the country. They gave the whites some of their jerked meat and in return received some tobacco and mirrors. They sold their third horse to the Long party. The fugitives were very much in love and were eloping, as was ascertained later. In fact, the man was running away with another man's wife; hence their great hurry.[51]

BELL'S ACCOUNT

Captain Bell's *Journal* adds more details. On July 21, 1820, they met the two Kaskaias. The interpreter, Bijeau, managed to talk with the Kaskaias in Crow. It was learned that fifteen days earlier, the Indians had encamped on the Arkansas with the Arapahoes, Kiowas, Bad Hearts (Kiowa-Apaches), Cheyennes, La Plays (Comanches), and a few Shoshonis from Columbia River of the Snake nation who spoke the Crow language. A fight with the Spaniards had occurred on "Red River," and the Spaniards had suffered many killed and a loss of property. The Indians had taken many horses down to the settlers on Red River and sold them to American traders. The informant agreed to accompany the Long party.

The Indian (Kiowa-Apache), whose name was Buffalo Calf, was in mourning for his brother killed in the Spanish engagement and was "divested of all ornaments." Bell said:

> His squaw is most superbly dressed & ornamented, her dress consists of a curious fashioned loose gown of dressed deer skins, it fits close about the neck, extend[s] down below the knees, has large sleeves that reach below the elbow, moccasins, & legings that come above the knees, wears a belt around her waist, the whole dress ornamented with beads of different colours, a heavy flaunce around

[51] James, *Long Expedition*, II, 247–49.

39

the bottom of beads and an abundance of tin trinkets of tubular form, that make a jingling noise, not in the least disagreeable— several rings on her fingers—her hair parted on the forehead but hanging loose on neck & shoulders. When riding she puts it from before her face, placing it behind her ears, and brings the ends up and holds them in the corner of her mouth—she has an agreeable countenance, rather high cheek bones and person short & thick. She carries, in addition to all their baggage & travelling utenticils—his war implements, of a gun, lance, shield, powder-horn & bullet pouch, he only carrying his bow & arrows and riding whip. They are both mounted on tolerable good horses & saddles of the Indian fashion. The Squaw leads a beautiful bay horse, which he says he caught but three days ago. . . . I traded with the Indian and his squaw for the bay horse, by giving a mule, some Indian trinkets and an old dragoon jacket.[52]

Beatte (a guide) retained the mule and gave his horse instead, intending to take the mule, called "Jenny," to one of the chiefs at the Pawnee village who had admired it.

There was, said Bell, "something mysterious" about the Indian's conduct—"why he should be travelling alone with his squaw to join a nation of which he is not a member." The Indian and woman proceeded on their journey to the nation of the Crows, somewhere in the mountains. It was later discovered that they were eloping.

The Long expedition then (July 24, 1820) split into two parties —one with James to follow the Red River, one with Bell to travel down the Arkansas to Belle Point. With Captain Bell's division were Dr. T. Say, Lieutenant Swift, Samuel Seymour, as an artist, and Stephen Julian (or Julien), Joseph Bijeau (or Bissonet; he was called Joseph Bijeau from his mother's second marriage name) and Abraam Ladeau, as interpreters and guides. A detachment of the Rifle Corps accompanied them.

The Bell division of Long's Expedition met some Kiowa Indians near the Purgatoire. Indian lodges stretched along the river, and one of the chiefs rode out to meet the interpreter. They had to use signs. They were Kiowas and had that day arrived at their present

[52] Bell, *Journal*, 181f.

camp. The chief invited the whites to occupy lodges in his camp, but the soldiers declined and moved four hundred yards away, pitched tents, and staked their horses in a semicircle of tents. A number of Indians visited the soldiers' camp, including three inferior chiefs—"a Kiawa, a Chayenne, and a Kaskaya." They were somewhat inquisitive and were made to understand that a council would be held the next day. They all smoked the pipe, and a "Kiowa Chief made me a present of a horse," said Bell, and examined the equipment and shoes on Bell's horse. The

> . . . men, women & children would take up his fore feet to examine of what they were made & how fastened on. They all conducted with great civility & propriety, and about sun-set retired to their respective camps, leaving one or two of their soldiers as a guard, whose duty it was, to see that their people conducted properly when at our camp—as well as to watch us I presume.[53]

The guards, with three other Indians who had seen Bijeau in his hunting tours,

> . . . set up around our fire talking to him of their wars and feats of heroism performed by some of their braves & soldiers, in two recent engagements with the Pawnee Loups and the Spaniards.[54]

By signs and a few words of the Crow tongue, Bijeau was able to understand the Indians. He learned that a strong war party was then out against the Pawnees and that Bear's Tooth, the grand chief of the Arapahoes, whose influence extended over all the tribes, was encamped on a fork of the river below and would arrive in a few days.[55]

On July 27, a council was held. Buffalo robes were spread in front of Bell's tents, and the chiefs sat on them; opposite on bearskins sat the officers and scientific gentlemen of Bell's party. The Indians would not sit on bearskins—these were "medicine" to

[53] *Ibid.*, 192. It will be noted that Bell gave excellent descriptions of the Indians.
[54] *Ibid.*, 192. Dr. Say took down the vocabularies of all the Indians the party met.
[55] Bear's Tooth was not met by either the Bell or James division. See below.

41

them. Of the seated chiefs, two were Kiowas, one Cheyenne, one Kiowa-Apache, and one Arapaho; one Indian who had been a prisoner among the Pawnees served as an interpreter. One of Bell's interpreters, Ladeau, spoke Pawnee. In order to converse, Bell spoke in English to Julian, who spoke in French to Ladeau, who spoke in Pawnee to the Kiowa (former Pawnee prisoner), who translated the conversation into the different languages of the chiefs: Kiowa, Kiowa-Apache, Cheyenne, and Arapaho.

> The Indian soldiers or rather a sort of constables with sticks kept back the crowd, who from curiosity to witness the ceremony and to hear what was said pressed close around us.[56]

First the pipe was smoked for fifteen minutes. Then Bell told them that his party was made up of Americans and had been traveling "18 moons." The "Great Father," president of the United States, had not authorized him to hold councils, or he would have furnished them many presents; but he was sent to explore the country, collect insects, animals, and plants, and report on the conditions of the Indians. The party had been on the Platte, had seen many Indians such as the Pawnees who had traders among them, and all were friendly. He wished to return and toll the Great Father that all had treated them well.

The Indians replied that they were happy to see the Americans, "that we were the first party they had ever seen," and that they would treat well traders sent among them. They were pleased with the talk, and their war parties would be instructed to shake hands and be friends with the Americans. The first chief of the Kiowas presented Bell with a valuable mare, which he brought from camp on the opposite side of the river, as a testimony of friendship.[57]

Bell gave to each chief tobacco, a knife, looking glasses, a comb, and fire steel. These the chiefs distributed to the men standing about them.

[56] Bell, *Journal*, 193.

[57] The name of the chief was not given; it was probably A'date. A picture of the Kiowa encampment was sketched by Dr. Samuel Seymour in *ibid.*, 195.

42

Bell then asked the chief if the party might purchase meat. The word was passed to the women, who forded the river, waist-deep, and assembled, bringing meat and other articles. Bijeau made the trades—"such crowding & pushing, scolding & talking among the squaws I never witnessed"; all wanted to trade first lest someone might get left out. For a parcel of "jerked buffalo" of six or eight pounds, the Indians received an awl, a comb, a small looking glass, or "as much vermillion as would lay on the point of a knife," and the party was soon supplied.[58]

The Indians then retired, and two of their soldiers remained at the white camp to see that nothing was stolen and to keep order. Their discipline was rigid—"When rabble and boys did not instantly obey," they "did not hesitate to apply the rod," which they carried, "and not a murmur or complaint did I hear," said Bell. Lieutenant Swift exchanged a mule for two Kiowa horses and purchased another for tobacco. They offered a good horse for a camp kettle. The interpreters bartered with them for two or three horses, even trading buttons and a few trifles.

By eight o'clock in the morning, the lodges were all down, and by ten o'clock Bell's party was marching up the river. Some of the chiefs embraced Bell; others were dissatisfied with the paucity of presents. Bell said that he learned then that during the night the Cheyennes stole and ran off seven horses belonging to the Arapahoes.

One Kaskaia (Kiowa-Apache) told the interpreter that Bell's Indian horse was his, that he had stolen it two years earlier from the Caddoes, that after he had lost it on a buffalo hunt, it had joined some wild horses. The interpreter told the man that Bell had purchased it from the Pawnees and would not part with it. The Indian then offered to buy the horse, but Bell would not sell. The Indian desired the animal because he "said he was the greatest racer among all Indian horses."[59]

Friendly gifts of women's company, and prostitution, were noted:

[58] *Ibid.*, 192–97.
[59] *Ibid.*, 197–98.

The first evening of our arrival among them, the Chiefs politely offered me the use of one of their wives, during the time we should remain among them—which I as politely declined, they said we had no squaws with us and must necessarily want them and it was with some difficulty I could object to their solicitations without offending them—during each night we remained with them several of the Indians brought their wives into camp & remained all night, the husband going around to the members of our party soliciting as a favor, connection with his wife, for a small pile of tobacco or a little vermillion—during the time, the wife would be laying on a buffalo robe covered with another, they were not generally their youngest or handsomest wives, before daylight in the morning they would retire . . . to their respective camps.[60]

Bell saw but few of the females whose

. . . countenances and persons were not disagreeable, generally high cheek bones, low stature, and fat, hair hanging loose on their shoulders, and filthy. They would eat the lice from each other & from their children. Their dress consists of a short sort of petticoat and a buffalo robe—some kind of loose gown fitted close about the neck fastened about the waist & came down below the calves of the legs.[61]

The Cheyenne chief reported that one young man hunting buffalo had been taken by four Spaniards to the Spanish camp on the fork of the Arkansas. They released the Indian with word that they would descend the Arkansas to meet the Indians. When Bell registered no objection to meeting the Spaniards, the chief said that he thought the Americans did not like the Spaniards and were fearful of them. Bell replied that the Americans did not fear the Spaniards, but that if they were ill-treated, the Americans would fight.

Between sunset and dark, the first chief of the Kiowas came to Bell's camp and asked for tobacco. Bell gave him some; then he asked for a knife. Bell told him that they were packed up but that

[60] *Ibid.*, 199.
[61] *Ibid.*, 199.

he would give him one the next day. Displeased, he left. During the night two Arapahoes arrived from Bear's Tooth's camp.

On July 28 the Bell party bought some salt from an Arapaho woman who had arrived in the night and learned that the Indians would strike their lodges and move off; also that Bear's Tooth would not come that way. Dr. Say was busy collecting vocabularies. The Kiowa who spoke Pawnee was not assisting him, as the Indians were getting ready to move. One old Indian asked to see the skin of Bell's arm. He looked at face, hands, and the natural color of skin on his arm and at Bell's whiskers and was amazed.

Bell surmised that "these nations" came from "the once powerful nations of the Paducas,"[62] but he was puzzled over their origin because all spoke different languages and had different general appearances and dispositions. He characterized them as follows: The Arapahoes were

> . . . generally well formed men, tall slim good features and well disposed, they wear the hair long, which is collected on the forehead and so fixed as to form a large kind of roll, many of them mat it with a kind of clay—in this way it serves to shade the sun from their eyes.

The Kiowas

> . . . wear their hair long in three plaits, one hanging down the back, the others from behind each ear & hanging front all ornamented with buttons, beads, etc.

The Kaskaias or Bad Hearts (Kiowa-Apaches)

> . . . part across the head from ear to ear, that in front is parted in two parts and brought a little back of the eyes and is tied & ornamented—and cut off about even with the nose—the part behind, is cut off to 8 or 10 inches in length & tied with a piece of skin— feathers or some other ornamental fixture.

[62] "Paducas" refers to Comanches here. See note 3, in Chapter I of this volume, in regard to usage. Victor Tixier, in 1840, said that the Osages called the Comanches "Patokas." (John Francis McDermott [ed.], *Tixier's Travels on the Osage Prairies*, 125, 150, 154, 265–71.)

They all wear a piece of leather or cloth about a foot wide & 2½ long, between their legs, one end brought up before the other behind and secured by a strap around the middle & moccosins, bodies & legs entirely naked, except covered with a buffalo robe, which they generally wear thrown over the shoulders . . . some had rich blue & scarlet robes richly ornamented with beads . . . from the Spaniards.[63]

The interpreter said that the Crows divided into wandering bands and that the Cheyennes resided on Cheyenne River—this band had left their nation and attached themselves to the Arapahoes. The Cheyennes "appear to be of bad disposition, faithless, fond of plunder—they wear the hair tied behind." The "La Playes and Shoshones" were a band of Snakes who attached themselves to "the Great Bears Tooth." The number of persons in the bands seen by Bell's group "did not exceed 500," but the combined bands under Bear's Tooth "numbered 500 warriors" and they had recently declared war against the nation of Cheyennes,[64] an Arapaho having been killed by them. The Cheyennes were at war with "Pawnees, Kawas [Kaws or Kansas], Ottos & Osages," but were then at peace with the "Pawnee Piques [Wichitas]."

Bell said that the bands remained in a place a few days following buffalo, which appeared to be their only subsistence. They hunted buffalo on horseback and killed them with the bow and arrow. They jerked meat in the sun or over a slow fire, and, when pounded, it was "quite a delicious food." Their lodges were made by erecting six or eight poles, ten to twelve feet long, and covering them with skins; a lodge contained twelve to fifteen persons. On the march the poles and skins were carried by horseback with all their luggage; the "business of this devolves on the squaws [and] the whole, children & all are on horseback."[65]

They traded with the Crows, who in turn bartered with the

---

63 Bell, *Journal*, 202.

64 *Ibid.*, 203. This was the beginning of the removal south of part of the Cheyennes. Grinnell places the permanent movement south, dividing the Cheyennes, around 1826. Samuel Seymour sketched three of the Indians: "Kaskya-Chayenne-Arrapaho," (see *ibid.*, p. 205).

65 *Ibid.*, 203.

Mandans and other nations supplied by resident traders. Bell saw but few firearms, and those were not highly valued by the Indians. Their weapons were the bow and arrow, a lance about eight feet long, and a war club. The warriors carried a "shield about 2 feet diameter." They were fond of smoking tobacco, and Bell believed they were ignorant of spirituous liquors. They had many opportunities to steal, but not a single article was taken.

The Indians then marched off, and Bell's party resumed its journey.[66]

On July 30 the expedition met nine Arapaho men and one woman and invited them to the camp. They were a war party that had gone against the Pawnees, but finding them too numerous to attack or to steal horses from, they had returned. They had left Chief Bear's Tooth early in the morning. Bell asked one to take some tobacco to Bear's Tooth and invite him to Bell's camp. Bell gave them tobacco and fresh antelope meat. After feasting and smoking, they declined to return to the chief, saying that Bear's Tooth was with a party that had moved off.

Dr. Say tried to obtain a vocabulary of their language during the afternoon. One Indian attempted to mount Bell's Indian horse, and a guard had to be posted by the horse. The Indian succeeded in getting the horse and led him to the tents. Bell caught hold of the line; the Indian dismounted but held on. He said that he had lost the horse two years before on a buffalo hunt. Bell told him that he had heard the same story "from doz Indians of the Bad Hearts." Then he ordered his guard to drive a stake in the ground, and Bijeau fastened the horse. Bell took his pistols from their holsters and told the Indian that if he removed the horse he would be shot. He let go but said that Bell's "little guns would not injure him, that he wore a charm about him which would protect him from the effects of the balls."[67] Seeing that Bell was determined to keep the horse, the Indian walked about and examined the saddle and equipment. Bell learned that he was "a Kiawa" and that the war party did not support his attempts to take the horse. Bell then

[66] *Ibid.*, 204.
[67] *Ibid.*, 209.

47

ordered him off. He rode away. His "medicine" consisted of "1/2 a dozen leaden balls on a string suspended from his neck." The Arapahoes said that they had advised him to go, that the chief was angry with him for his conduct, and that they would remain with Bell's camp; they promised that they would be civil "and not an article [would be] molested."

One of them requested Bell, if he met Chief Bear's Tooth, to tell him that he had seen their party and that they had acted properly. They had some dried buffalo and little cakes made of mashed wild cherries, stones and all, mixed with buffalo fat, dried and delicious. Bell's party purchased two of their medicine bags. Bell watched his horse all night and until the Indian party left.

Later in the day a Cheyenne war party came up at full speed; there were forty men and four or five women. They had been against the Pawnees and four days before had taken a woman's scalp. They were on their way to join the Arapahoes.

Some of them were painted black[68] & had a most horrid frightful appearance—the whole well equiped with their war implements & decorated with feathers and ornaments.[69]

They smoked the peace pipe with the Indians, but kept armed men around the horses. The Indians let their horses loose but kept bows in their hands. Still another claimed Bell's horse, but he refused to listen. The "Partizan or Chief" said that Bell's men would be well treated and that "their nation was in want of traders among them"; they did not know why white people had failed to visit them for some years past. Bell replied that traders would come if they were treated as friends. They had a Crow prisoner who interpreted for them, speaking Crow with Bijeau. Tobacco and knives were given to the "Partizan," who distributed them. Dr. Say added more to his vocabulary, but the war party left, fearful that the Pawnees might pursue them. The chief embraced Bell and requested his handkerchief, which he received. Bell said that

68 This was a sign of success of the war party.
69 Bell, *Journal*, 211.

his party rode off congratulating themselves on the happy issue because a Cheyenne war party was "the most to be dreaded & feared of all other nations." Bell was told that the Ietans had returned—so they had "no more war parties" to meet.[70]

The Bell expedition proceeded east down the Arkansas, at times hunting buffalo and "jerking" it. Dr. Say questioned Bijeau about Chouteau's trading excursions with the "Indians of the Rock Mountains." On August 7, Bijeau and Ladeau left the party to return to their trade with the Pawnees upon the Kansas River; they had been faithful and of great service. "Bijeau was all important, from having spent the greater part of his life with Indians."[71]

On August 8 the expedition came to "Dumun's Creek" and on to the place where Chouteau's party was attacked by Pawnees in 1817, suffering the loss of one man. Four Indians were killed and they retreated. The creek is Big Coon Creek today.

On August 12 another party of Indians, "Ietans or Comanch" was met. The chief embraced Bell. They said that two nights before, while they were asleep, they had been attacked and defeated by "Ottoes," losing three killed and having six wounded, and losing fifty-six horses and their robes and moccasins and clothing. The party consisted of thirty men and five women, most walking and without robes, leggings, or moccasins. The wounded and women were on horses. The wounded were supported by some walking on each side of them. The wounds were all of gunshot. Many relatives of those killed had scarified themselves, and blood which had dried on them gave them a "distressing appearance." The "Partizan" asked that Bell encamp with them to give them security. Bell consented to stop an hour and smoke the peace pipe. Then they moved

[70] *Ibid.*, 211–12.

[71] *Ibid.*, 213–17, 219. Joseph Bijeau (or Bissonet), according to James, had been a member of the Chouteau–De Mun trading company to the Rockies in 1815–17 and had been taken prisoner by the Spaniards in New Mexico. He knew the Crow language, extensively understood by the western tribes, and also the sign language. He may be the same Joseph Bissonet who had a trading post near Fort Laramie in the 1840's.

Ladeaux (or Abraham Ledoux) was the Pawnee interpreter. He gave Dr. Say a vocabulary and notes on customs of the Indians (*ibid.*, 122–23; and Reuben Gold Thwaites, *Early Western Travels*, XVI, 225–27, cited by Hafen in Bell, *Journal*, 217).

49

to the river. The Indians waded in and drank and borrowed a cup from one of Bell's men to take water to their wounded, assisted by the women.

They begged for blankets, robes, and everything Bell had, but it was "denyed" them. Noting their restless disposition, Bell pushed the peace pipe briskly—at one time the chief concealed the pipe under his leg. One of the Comanches wanted to look at a soldier's rifle, but the soldier refused. An Indian tried to take Bell's horse and Bell rose on his knees, having been seated to smoke in front of the chief, and spoke to the man and made him leave the horse and take a seat. Bell gave the chief his own blanket, a dozen knives, and five "plugs of tobacco." Julian, the guide, gave them a skin for moccasins, and Bell resumed the march. Julian was the last to mount. He was seized by three or four Indians who tried to take his horse and equipment while another ran among the pack animals and caught a horse. Lieutenant Swift ordered him to let go, which he did. Then, noting Julian's difficulty, Bell turned back and saw two soldiers aiming a rifle at the Indians detaining Julian while the Indian party stood "in a kind of semi-circle with their arrows out ready for action." The "Partizan" then ordered his men in and motioned for Bell's party to proceed, which they did "without further molestation."

They pushed on seven miles until dark. Bell said that the well-known disposition of the Ietans (Comanches) and the wretched condition of the defeated party made them fear that their horses might be stolen in the night; thus, they did not pitch tents or build fires but kept their arms near and ready for action. However, the Indians did not attempt it.[72]

The party moved on, through heat, and lacking provisions. One of their dogs died, and the other was carried before a man on horse-back. They passed several abandoned Indian villages where they saw ripe "watermellons, pumpkins & corn," some of which they ate. They hoped to reach the Osages. Occasionally they ate turkey or got a fawn from the kill of the wolves; they even had to eat a

[72] Bell, *Journal*, 224–30.

skunk. On August 31 three soldiers deserted, taking the best horses, clothing, rifles, and the valuable manuscripts of Dr. Say. On September 1 the worn party reached the Osages under Chief Clermont; there they feasted on meat, corn, and pumpkins. Clermont's son and his wife accompanied them to Belle Point, passing Hugh Glenn's trading house.[73] On September 9, at Fort Smith, they were hospitably received by Captain James H. Ballard, officer of the post, and there they met Hugh Glenn, also. Major Long, James, and the rest of the party, following down the Canadian instead of the Red River, arrived at Fort Smith on September 13. The expedition broke up, with Long and Bell going to Cape Girardeau. Then Long went to St. Louis and Bell traveled on, still riding his Indian horse, to Washington, D. C.

JAMES'S ACCOUNT

Shortly after meeting the two Kaskaia Indians, the Long expedition, on July 24, 1820, divided into two parties: Bell to follow the Arkansas and James and Long to explore the Red River. However, Major Long missed the Red River and followed the Canadian. On July 21, the Long expedition stopped to hunt a few days; then both divisions moved out on July 24. Shortly thereafter, James and Long met a large party of Indians, all on horseback, with many horses dragging their lodgepoles. The Indian outriders (soldier-society police) came up to shake hands, and the rest of the party hurried on to cross the river. Many small children were lashed to the saddles to keep them secure. At the river the women stopped to fill vessels with water. The chief crossed last and stopped to shake hands with the Americans. They were Kaskaias (Kiowa-Apaches), coming from a hunting expedition to the sources of the Brazos and Colorado rivers in Texas, and were on their way to meet Spanish traders on "Red River," probably the Canadian. They told the whites that ten days' journey or one hun-

[73] *Ibid.*, 265–67. Glenn and Jacob Fowler would set out on an expedition to the Rocky Mountains in 1821.

51

dred miles away was the village of the "Pawnee Piques" (Wichitas), and that a large body of "Cumancias" (Comanches) was two or three days below.[74]

They were three days' ride from Santa Fe. The party of Indians was under Chief Red Mouse, a man of large stature, and they were called "Kaskaias" (Kiowa-Apaches). Since Long's party wanted to buy some horses from them, the chief "insolently" invited them to camp close by. Suddenly a village was set up and arose "like an exhalation," with lodges provided for the whites. Each lodge had six to eight lodgepoles, twenty to thirty feet in length. Bijeau told James (in earlier conversations, before Bijeau left with the Bell party) that the Kaskaias purchased the poles from Indians of the Missouri region—five poles in trade for one horse.

Before trading for horses, the Indians insisted that all of the soldiers' packs be opened. The soldiers refused, a scuffle resulted, and some of the women, frightened, ran off. The soldiers stopped trading and indicated their need for food. Finally Red Mouse's wife brought them some half-boiled bison. They asked for more and got some jerked meat, given with ill grace. Water was brought in containers made of the bladders of bison. These vessels were unwieldy, and the women suspended them on tripods of sticks. Red Mouse's wife asked for presents in exchange for the food, but the soldiers treated her demands much as she had done theirs. A number of small articles were pilfered until the soldiers got out their guns; then the Indians behaved with less rudeness. They had 32 lodges, 250 people, and 500 horses. The Indians stationed 22 armed men constantly about the soldiers; these were probably the outriders mentioned, or the dog-soldiers.

The next day the soldiers missed some horses, as well as kettles and other things. The chief was told but insisted that the horses had strayed off. Major Long ordered the horses seized, and this produced the desired effect. The lost property was restored, and they "parted as friends." These Indians, said James, had aquiline noses, good features, large regular teeth, complexions darker than many of the eastern Indians, and were inferior in stature and form

[74] James, *Long Expedition*, II, 290–92.

to the Otos, Pawnees, and most of the Missouri Indians. The men wore their hair long, to the ground, eked out with horses' tails. They wore some images and amulets portraying alligators. Their range extended to alligator areas, for they moved from the Platte and Arkansas to the Río del Norte and the upper Brazos and below.[75] They had a captive child who spoke Spanish. They were the most inhospitable Indians met with. There were some diseased Indians among them, and they had lice and vermin. The Long journal stated that they were the "most degraded" and "uncivilized Indians on this side of the Rocky Mountains."

The Long party met no more Indians on its way to Fort Smith. However, James included in his journal some of the observations written down by Dr. T. Say (six chapters of James's account) about the Indians encountered by the Bell party on the Arkansas River. Dr. Say noted that they met an encampment of Kiowas, Kaskaias, Cheyennes, and Arapahoes. They smoked the pipe and were happy to see the white men. Presents were exchanged. The Indians traded jerked meat, skins, and hair ropes for some small articles of the white men. One woman got a small wooden comb and used it immediately to rid her hair of lice. Crowds hovered about and would not disperse. Then an electrical storm came up and the crowd left. These Indians were of average stature. They had Roman noses, according to Dr. Say, but they were less predominant than those of tribes of the Missouri region; cheekbones, lips, teeth, chins, and retreating foreheads were similar to those of the tribes of the Missouri. They kept the hair plucked from their faces. The men wore long hair; the women had hair shoulder-length. Red clay was rubbed into the hair parts. Shells were in slits of the ears; the shells were from the Northwest Coast.[76]

The Grand Chief was Bear's Tooth of the Arapahoes. He was supposedly encamped several days' journey below the river and was said to admire the "Tabby-boos," or Americans. The Indians told Dr. Say that they had met some American traders a year

[75] *Ibid.*, II, 299–301. They knew the rivers of the Gulf Coast of Texas where alligators were found.

[76] *Ibid.*, III, 46–47.

earlier and had traded with them. A brother of Bear's Tooth offered the soldiers gifts of the women's company for the night, but the soldiers ordered him and some others away.[77] When they left, a Kiowa chief called to make a parting visit.

Dr. Say related that they also met some "Ietans or Comanchees," back from a war against the Osages. They had a few wounded. These people were indistinguishable from the Kiowas, Kaskaias, and Arapahoes. There was some trouble with them—a scuffle over guns—but finally the pipe was smoked. Then there was danger again over the loss of one soldier's bridle. The expedition feared that the Indians might try to steal their horses in the night, but they managed to protect them against theft.[78] Later Dr. Say with Bell's party met the Osages, who were enemies of the Kiowas and others, on the way to the Hot Springs of the Washita.

The James party followed the Canadian instead of the Red River and returned to the Arkansas. Their journal stated that the "Arapahos, Kaskaias, Kioways, Ietans and Shiennes" traded "last year [1819]" with the whites on Red River. (Who were the whites? Whether they were citizens of the United States or freebooters of Barataria has never been ascertained.) Bear's Tooth of the Arapahoes was the head chief of all of the groups they met; the Cheyennes with them were a "small band of seceders," and all were skilled horsemen.[79]

At Fort Smith the Long expedition broke up, after reuniting with Captain Bell. Major Stephen Long said that the country he had seen was "almost wholly unfit for cultivation, and uninhabitable by a people depending upon agriculture for their subsistence."[80] Dr. James concurred in this, and both hoped it might

[77] *Ibid.*, III, 50–52. This was a common custom and a friendly courtesy. The Tonkawas furnished forty girls to their Comanche guests during a visit of Mokochocope's band at the time the Indians were gathering with Major R. S. Neighbors to go on the reservations in north central Texas. (W. B. Parker, *Notes Taken during the Expedition Commanded by Captain R. B. Marcy, U. S. A., through Unexplored Texas, in the Summer and Fall of 1854*, 237.)

[78] James, *Long Expedition*, III, 72. The Comanches were probably the same party that Bell had met.

[79] *Ibid.*, III, 244–47.

[80] *Ibid.*, III, 281–82.

"forever remain the unmolested haunt of the native hunter, the bison and the jackall."[81]

In short, it was the Great American Desert.

THE GLENN AND FOWLER EXPEDITION, 1821–22

Jacob Fowler wrote a journal of a trading trip to the Rocky Mountains made in 1821–22, when he met the Kiowas and other Indians friendly with them. The party included Fowler and twenty men, commanded by Colonel Hugh Glenn, and was inspired by the Long Expedition.

The Glenn and Fowler party crossed the Plains and reached what is now Pueblo County, Colorado. There they found an Indian camp on the north side of the Arkansas. Fowler says:

> ... amongst party Was the principle Cheif of the Kiaways for these Ware of that nation—the Cheif with the others stayed With us all night the others Returned to their camp about Sundown.[82]

The Indians were friendly and helped Fowler's party cross the Arkansas. They carried the white men across the frozen river behind them on their horses because the horses of the white men were loaded and the whites were afoot. The chief gave the whites one of his lodges to store their goods in and cared for their horses. More Indians arrived, said Fowler, "so that by night We Ware a large town Containing upWards two Honderd Houses."[83] The "Houses" were filled with men, women, and children, and dogs and horses. This was new to a party which had seen no persons but themselves on their long journey from Fort Smith, Arkansas, over to the mountains.

The Indians took the white men into the lodges of their great men and gave them meat to eat, and sometimes also boiled corn, beans, or mush procured from the Spaniards. On November 21, 1821, they "lay in camp," smoking with the Indians. The next day

[81] *Ibid.*
[82] *The Journal Of Jacob Fowler*, ed. by Elliott Coues, 50.
[83] *Ibid.*, 51.

they did the same, as well as a little trading with the Indians. The snow was ten inches deep, but it did not deter the Indian children, naked, from playing on the ice of the frozen Arkansas River.

Then arrived "the Highatans [Ietans or Comanches] amounting to about 350 lodges [to camp]. We are now incresed to a Cettey."

The next day a council was held with the chiefs of both nations and with Colonel Glenn and his interpreter. The Comanche chief said that the Indians were ready to receive the goods Colonel Glenn had, that they had been promised goods from his "father," the President. When told there were no such goods, the Comanche chief flew into a passion and said that Glenn had stolen goods sent to the Indians and that they would take his goods and kill the party.

The council went on all day. It was an unpleasant situation; "the Kiaways Ware our frends But the others Ware the most numerous." The young warriors crowded around so the whites could hardly stir; then at sundown a tall Indian ran into camp calling out, "Me arapaho Cheif White Mans mine and Shaking Hands with us." Upon being shown to Colonel Glenn's lodge, he thumped his breast with his fist, saying, "White Man mine arapaho Plenty," and pointing the way he came to show that his whole nation was at hand and that the whites need have no fear of the Comanches. Fowler said that the whites now had "two out of three nations" in their favor.[84]

On November 24, 1821, the camp had about 350 lodges. When the whites first arrived, there were about 40 lodges of "Kiowas and Padducas [Kiowa-Apaches]."[85] The Indians continued to increase:

Counting them over find now four Hundred of the following nations—Ietans—Arrapahoes—Kiawa [and] Padduce—Cheans—Snakes—the Ietan the most numerous and the most Disperete [desperate] the Arrapohoes the Best and most Sivvel to the White men Habits.

[84] *Ibid.*, 53.

[85] *Ibid.*, 54. "Padducas" or "Padduce" as given by Fowler means "Kiowa-Apaches," and he mentioned them with the Kiowas before the Comanches came in. He called the Comanches "Highatans [Ietans]."

There were difficulties. There was no interpreter save "Mr. Roy," and "he Spoke Some Pane [Pawnee] and [in] that language our Councils Ware Held." Fowler said the Indians had less capacity "to larn" than any Indians he had ever seen, that they had many wants but no means of supplying them—they had nothing to trade save horses. They had only about twenty beaver skins and did not hunt them, only hunting "the Buffelow."[86]

The whites purchased a Spanish prisoner for $150 in goods, but he had only one night of freedom. The goods were returned, and his owner took him back. He was from San Antonio, Texas, "with which the Indians are at War—tho at peace With new maxeco and the Spanish in Habetance there."[87]

Taos was "six days" travel from the Indian camp and the Indians said that there were some white men near the (Pike's) Peak, and some three days' travel to the River Platte.

Fowler remarked the Indian children playing on the ice—"over a thousand children" and "all naked." The little ones too young to walk were set down on a piece of skin on the ice and kicked their legs and they "Hollow[ed] and laff[ed]" at the play. He noted that a white child probably would not live half an hour under such cold conditions.

On the twenty-third, four Ietans brought news that a peace was being made with the Osages. Five days before Fowler's party arrived, the Crows had battled the Osages, the Crows losing fifteen men and the Arapahoes with them losing nine.

The Kiowa chief reported that he had been in council all day with the Comanches. The Comanches wanted the Kiowas to join in a war against the Osages and the white men, but the Kiowas disagreed. The Ietans, said Fowler, were very disagreeable to his party. The principal chiefs told them that Major Long (in 1820) had promised that the President would send them plenty of goods; the Ietans said that Fowler's party had those goods and had no right to trade them—they *belonged* to the Indians. When the Co-

---

[86] *Ibid.*, 55. Cheans were Cheyennes; Snakes were Shoshonis. See the interpreter's remarks in regard to the Cheyennes (note 64 above).

[87] *Ibid.*, 56.

manche chief discovered that his demands would not be complied with, he changed his disposition and got friendly and "this night offered Conl Glann and Mr. Roy Each one of His Wifes—the greates token of friendship those Indeans Can offer—but the offer Was deClined telling Him that it Was not the White mans Habits."[88]

Although threatened by the "Ietan and the Kiowa and Padduce Indians," the white men moved to another camp, with "the old Kiowa Chief Who moved along With us," followed by the Arapahoes, and by night they had two or three hundred lodges around them again. The Ietan chief came to visit, pretending to know nothing of the difficulty.

Fowler said:

> We Have Heare now about seven Hunderd lodges of the nations mentioned on the 25th With the addicion of the Cheans—about two Hunderd lodges. We Sopose those Lodges to Contain from twelve to twenty pursons of all Sises—Some Horses have been Stollen Every night Since We arived amongst them Seven of our own are amongst the mising a party of one Hunderd and fifty men Went In pursute of the theefs . . .[89]

but could not find them. Another party of two hundred set out to recover the stolen horses but was unsuccessful. Fowler said that "between 4 and 500 Horses" were stolen from them since they arrived, mostly from pens in the center of the village surrounded by seven hundred lodges "of Wachfull Indeans."

One of the Indians picked up Fowler's spectacles that had one glass broken and came back, laughing, having put them on a one-eyed Indian, saying they would suit him better. Then the joke ended, and he returned "the Specks in much good Humor."

After a time, they moved up the river to the timber near the present Huerfano River. It was cold and wood was needed.

During their stay, the whites met the Spaniards who came to trade. The Kiowas and Arapahoes both wanted the whites to stay

[88] *Ibid.*, 58.
[89] *Ibid.*, 59.

with them, which led to some jealousy. The Kiowas would not sell them horses because they did not want them to leave. Of the Kiowas, Fowler said: "More Sevelity Exsists amongst those Indeans than anny I have Ever knone," but they were difficult to camp with because the young men and "old begers" continually crowded them. Fowler noted that "there is about 20,000 [horses] in our inCampment and the [Indians are] distetute of Every thing," but still they could not trade for horses. Needing ten more horses, they sought them from the Arapahoes, but they had few since they had already traded with the Cheyennes of the Missouri.[90] "The Ietan and Kiawa Have great nombers of very fine Horses—and Equal to any I have Ever knone."[91]

On December 18, the Kiowas paid a visit and invited the whites to a feast, and all were friendly again. On December 20, Fowler saw an Indian fight. One Indian pursued another and struck his victim with his "tamehak," felling him with a blow on the back of the neck. The women interfered and carried off the supposedly dead man. They saved his life. He was the son of the Kiowa chief and "first frend amongst the Indians." His "murdorer" was the brother of the "great Arrapoho chief" and the friend and protector of Fowler's party. The party was now fearful that there might be a fatal war.

The next day the wounded man was better. The fight was brought on by the Kiowa's stealing of a medicine bag of the other, who was a chief. The difficulty was settled by the return of the bag and its acceptance. Fowler's party finally succeeded in purchasing enough horses on that day.

The white party then decided to move to the mountains, and the Arapahoes said that they would move with them. Colonel Glenn gave a medal to the Kiowa chief and paid him for the use of his lodge. He also gave a medal and shirt and presents to the Ietan chief, and the Ietans promised to treat the whites kindly. According to Fowler: "It is but Justice to Say We find the Ki-

[90] *Ibid.*, 65. Northern Cheyennes; presumably these "Cheans" were the southern ones. See notes 64 and 86 above.

[91] *Ibid.*, 65.

awa the best Indeans possing [possessing] more firmness and manly deportment than the Arrapoho and less arogance and Hatey [haughty] Pride than the Ietan.[92]

Colonel Glenn gave the Arapaho chief a medal and remarked: "I never parted with a man who showed as much sorrow as the chief of the arapaho." The whites were invited to eat with one of the Arapaho chiefs. They ate heartily of a fat meat, and then were asked if they knew what the meat was. "He then Said it Wa[s] a dog telling us it [was] a great feest With the Indeans." The party moved up the river, accompanied by the Arapahoes, fortunate, said Fowler, to part with the rest of their neighbors without difficulty. Then the group parted with the Arapahoes, who showed much "sorrow"; they wanted the whites to stay "one moon longer" and warned of the danger of their horses' being stolen.[93]

The Fowler party, a couple of days later, was invited to return and meet the Spanish traders, a party of sixty, at the Indian camp. Roy and Fowler returned and were received with much joy, as though they had been gone a year. The Spaniards arrived in a charge, dismounted, and embraced the Indians. They were "Creoles," said Fowler, perhaps meaning "half-bloods." They were well disposed but poorer than the Indians. Their trading equipment would "not sell for fifty dollars" in the United States. The Indian chief asked the white men if the Spanish captain could sleep with them, to which they agreed. The Indians then directed the Spaniards to pray, so that the whites might see "their fashion." This they did, reciting their Catholic prayers, and afterward "prayed fervently" for the whites. Fowler noted that during the prayer the Spanish captain caught a louse on his shirt and ate it. The Spaniards were ordered about by the Indians "much as negroes are commanded."

On the day they traded, the Spaniards painted themselves like the Indians. The Spaniards then moved up to the camp of the whites to sell them some corn. Corn cost $10 per bushel, a mule

92 *Ibid.*, 68.
93 *Ibid.*, 68.

cost $30, and the price was $100 apiece for their best running horses. Colonel Glenn accompanied the Spaniards to Santa Fe, and Fowler remained in charge of the camp, building a house or fort and a wooden pen for the horses. Men sent to hunt buffalo were captured by a party of thirteen Crows, who later released them, giving them nine horses for the powder, ball, and blankets they had taken. The Crows said that they were friendly with the whites and had met whites on the Platte. There was also a skirmish between the Arapahoes and the Crows, and the white men escaped. This road, said Fowler, was the "great war road" of many nations, the road to the Spanish settlements.

The Arapahoes continued their visits to Fowler. They brought in one lost mule and received presents. One Arapaho found his lost horse in the white pen, and this caused some difficulty. But it was finally settled and they smoked over it. A party of Crows visited them, and after eating and smoking, "the[y] Sung a long Song and all lay down and Slept." When they left, many things were stolen. After a fight with the Arapahoes, the Crows returned. The whites kept their guns ready to keep the Crows from the horse pen. The chief said that he was the white man's friend, but when they went away again, they stole more things.

Fowler's party trapped and hunted. Colonel Glenn sent word for them to join him in Taos, which they did on January 31, 1822, after having gone down the San Luis Valley. The Mexicans were by this time free of Spanish control, and anxious to trade. The whites explored and trapped for beaver, moving up the Conejos and into the mountains, where they met some of the Utes.

In May, 1822, the party started home. They returned across the Plains to Missouri (Jacob Fowler, to his home in Covington, Kentucky), after having been gone eleven months and eleven days.

THE DRAGOON EXPEDITION OF 1834

The period of the Kiowa Calendars began in 1833. In the early spring of that year, the Osages massacred a large number of Ki-

61

owas. This led to the dragoon expedition of 1833–34,[94] the first treaty of the prairie tribes with the United States government in 1835, and the 1837 treaty with the Kiowas.

George Catlin, whose self-appointed mission it was to draw pictures of and record notes on all the American Indians, accompanied the dragoon expedition to meet with the Plains tribes and invite them to Fort Gibson for peacemaking. Through his eyes, one sees them clearly in 1834. Catlin said that the Kiowas were undoubtedly one of the most interesting groups that had ever visited the frontier. Catlin went from New Orleans to Fort Gibson, seven hundred miles up the Arkansas. The steamer *Arkansas* took him to within two hundred miles of the fort, where Colonel Henry Leavenworth was in charge. In 1833, Fort Gibson was the "extreme southwestern outpost on the United States frontier." Catlin had seen and pictured many of the Indians up the Missouri River in 1832 and wanted to see some of the Indians of the Southwest. He had permission from the Secretary of War to accompany Colonel Henry Dodge[95] and the United States Dragoons on their summer campaign. For two months, Catlin awaited the arrival of the troops, who were on their way to Fort Gibson from Jefferson Barracks. The object of the campaign was to meet with the Wichitas, Comanches, and others, and to endeavour to get acquainted with them,

[94] The United States was also aware of the imminence of war between Texas and Mexico. There were three accounts of the expedition: Colonel Henry Dodge's letters to the Secretary of War, accompanied by Lieutenant T. B. Wheeloch's official report, "Journal of Colonel Dodge's Expedition from Fort Gibson to the Pawnee Pict Village," *American State Papers*, Military Affairs, V (1934), 373–82; Hugh Evans, "The Journal of Hugh Evans, Covering the First and Second Campaigns of the United States Dragoon Regiment in 1834 and 1835," ed. by Fred S. Perrine and Grant Foreman, *Chronicles of Oklahoma*, Vol. III, No. 3 (1925), 175–215 (covers 1834 campaign only); and Catlin, *North American Indians*, II, 44–95. A fourth account of the dragoon expedition is that of James Hildreth, *Dragoon Campaigns to the Rocky Mountains*. Hildreth was a soldier in the expedition, but his account of the Indians is copied from Wheeloch's and Catlin's writings.

[95] Henry Dodge was captain, major, and lieutenant colonel in the Missouri Volunteers, 1812 to 1815; colonel in the Michigan Mounted Rangers, June 21, 1832; colonel in the First Dragoons, March 4, 1833. He resigned on July 4, 1836; died, June 19, 1867. (Francis B. Heitman, *Historical Register and Dictionary of the United States Army*, I, 376.)

A Kiowa encampment
as sketched by Samuel Seymour
during the Long Expedition, 1820–21

"Kaskaia, Shienne Chief, and Arrappaho"
depicted by Seymour, 1820–21

DOHASAN
prominent chief of the Kiowas
portrayed by George Catlin, in 1834

CATLIN SHOWS A KIOWA RIDING FEAT—A STRATAGEM OF WAR
by which the Indian is able to throw himself down
by the side of his horse and thereby screen himself from his enemies

MILLIE DURGAN GOOMBI
white captive of the Kiowas

BIG TREE
a Kiowa chief, about 1870, as photographed by W. S. Soule

SET-ANGIA or SATANK (SITTING BEAR)
posed for this photograph by W. S. Soule about 1870

SUN BOY

TENÉ-ANGÓPTE (KICKING BIRD)
in photographs by W. S. Soule

as they were "endangering trade and travel of our citizens across the plains."[96]

Two regiments of 400 dragoons finally set out from Fort Gibson on June 21, 1834. Catlin said that they started too late for the season. Runners were sent out to get the Indians to come in and confer with the expedition. The command purchased from the Osages several prisoners who might be of service in bringing about a friendly interview. General Leavenworth accompanied the expedition for two hundred miles to the mouth of the False Washita River. There it stopped, because half of the men were sick with a "bilious fever," and half of the horses were down also. Colonel Dodge with 250 men went on; Colonel Leavenworth was to meet them later at the Cross Timbers.[97]

The expedition met a large group of Comanches under a flag of truce. One Comanche warrior (a Spanish captive) could speak Spanish. They had a talk, and Colonel Dodge explained the object of the trip. The Comanches were friendly and entertained them at their "Great Camanchee Village" which held two hundred tipis. From there Colonel Dodge went on to meet the Pawnees (Wichitas) in their village to the west, but some who were sick, including Catlin, remained at the Comanche village. After fifteen days, Dodge's party returned in a fatigued and destitute condition. The trip to the Wichita village was pictured by Catlin's friend Joe Chadwick, who had taken along Catlin's sketchbook.

The expedition had reached the Pawnee or Wichita village after four days' travel. Back of the village was a range of reddish granite mountains. It was on the bank of the Red River, about ninety miles from the Comanche town.[98] It was at the junction of Elk Creek and the North Fork of Red River. The village contained

[96] Catlin, *North American Indians*, II, 44–45. The command was in charge of Colonel Henry Dodge, aided by Lieutenant Colonel Stephen Watts Kearny. Indian guides of Osage, Cherokee, Delaware, and Seneca tribes accompanied the troops. One of these was Beatte, a Frenchman who lived among the Osages. He guided Washington Irving in 1832 (see *A Tour on the Prairies*, 369–527.) See also Wheeloch, "Journal of Colonel Dodge's Expedition," 373; Bell, *Journal*, 181ff.

[97] Catlin, *North American Indians*, II, 53–56.

[98] The Pawnee-Pict or Towiash village of the Wichita confederacy.

five or six hundred lodges, "all made of long prairie grass, thatched over poles which are fastened in the ground and bent in at the top; giving to them, in distance, the appearance of straw beehives."[99]

The people cultivated extensive fields of corn, pumpkins, watermelons, beans, and squash, and with "abundant . . . buffalo meat" lived very well. The dragoons camped for three days, a half-mile out of the village. Colonel Dodge held a council with the chiefs in the chief's lodge, explaining that the government wanted to establish a lasting peace with them. The chiefs and warriors assured Dodge of their friendship.

Then the Colonel got down to brass tacks and demanded that they return the Martin child, whom the Comanches had told him they held. Judge Martin and his family of Pecan Bayou had been murdered, and one child taken captive. Catlin said that the Wichitas denied this until a Negro man living with them confirmed that the boy was a prisoner.[100] Excitement, then gloomy silence, followed. Colonel Dodge promised them two Wichita girls and one Kiowa girl, captured by the Osages. The Colonel demanded also the restoration of a United States ranger, by the name of George Abby, captured the summer before. They told him the man had been seized but had been taken by a party of Comanches, over whom they had no control, into Texas and there killed. After long consultation, they brought the boy in from his hiding place in a cornfield, and received their girls affectionately. The old chief embraced Colonel Dodge and, tears streaming down his face, placed his left cheek on the Colonel's cheek. Each officer was embraced in

---

[99] Catlin, *North American Indians*, II, 79. also fig. 173 facing p. 178.

[100] Wheeloch said that "We-ter-ra-shar-ro" (not the principal chief who had gone on an expedition to the Pani-Mahas) readily admitted that they had the boy, and also a Negro (brought in by the Comanches). In response to Dodge's questions, he stated that the Mounted Ranger Abby had been killed by the Texas Comanches, the Oways, who were nomadic but had a village across Red River; he also observed that the Indians had traded with the Spaniards who were with them not long since and "went west," and that a roving band of bad Indians, Wakinas (Arikaras), had killed the Santa Fe traders that Dodge asked about. (Wheeloch, "Journal of Colonel Dodge's Expedition," 377–78.) See especially Catlin's pictures of Wichitas—fig. 174, "We-ta-ra-sha-ro," ninety years old; "Sky-se-ro-ka," fig. 175; and two girls, figs. 175 and 177, in his *North American Indians*, II, facing p. 82.

turn, and the council became a joyous meeting. Hugh Evans said that the father of the returned Kiowa girl made a speech; then the Kiowa chief, presumably Dohasan, made a speech:

> White men & brethren this day is the most interesting period of our existance. The Great Spirit has caused a light to shine all around us so that we can see each other. The Great Spirit has sent to see us these white men & brothers Kiowas, take them by the hand and use them well they are your friends; they have brought home your lost relation. When you meet a white man take him to your lodge give him Buffaloe meat & corn and then he will always be your friend.[101]

The chief ordered the women to supply the dragoons with food. Their rations had all been eaten twelve hours before, and they were delighted to see the women bring in "back-loads" of dried buffalo meat and green corn, which they threw down amongst them.

For several days the council proceeded pleasantly, while warriors of "Kioways and Wicos, two adjoining and friendly tribes living further to the west, were arriving." There also came other bands of Comanches, until "two thousand or more of these wild and fearless looking fellows were assembled, and all, from their horses' backs, with weapons in hand, were looking into our pitiful little encampment, of two hundred men, all in a state of dependence and almost literal starvation."[102] T. B. Wheeloch said that another

---

[101] "Journal," *loc. cit.*, 205.

[102] Catlin, *North American Indians*, II, 82. Mooney described the Osage massacre of the Kiowa village in 1833; mostly women and children were killed, as the men were off on a hunt. This was the "Cutthroat Massacre" at the head of the west branch of Otter Creek, near what is known as Cutthroat Gap in present Oklahoma. The children who Dodge returned were those captured by the Osages in the massacre, and one Wichita girl captured earlier by the Osages. See Wilbur Sturtevant Nye, *Carbine and Lance*, 3–7.

Wheeloch, "Journal of Colonel Dodge's Expedition," p. 378, said that the Comanche "principal chief" arrived on July 23. This was Chief Ta-we-que-nah. He wanted peace and said that there were many bands of Comanches, and he would "visit them all this year" and tell them what Dodge said. He was "an old man now" but had never killed an American. The Chief Ta-we-que-nah was the same mentioned by Josiah Gregg as "Big Eagle" or "Tábba-quenas." Gregg met him in 1839 with a

band of about sixty Kiowas rode up, led by a principal man, handsomely dressed:

> He wore a Spanish red cloth mantle, prodigious feathers, and leggins that followed his heels like an ancient train. Another of the chiefs of the new band was very showily arrayed; he wore a perfectly white dressed deer-skin hunting shirt, trimmed profusely with fringe of the same material, and beautifully bound with blue beads, over which was thrown a cloth mantle of blue and crimson, with leggings and moccasins entirely of beads.[103]

The Kiowa chief, Titche-toche-cha (Dohasan), and his men shook hands and seated themselves with grace and dignity. Colonel Dodge continued his talk and urged them to go with him to Fort Gibson. Titche-toche-cha said that he would go:

> The American captain has spoken well today; the white men have shown themselves our friends. If a white man ever comes to my country, he shall be kindly treated; if he wants a horse, or anything that I have, he shall not pay for it; I will give him what he wants.[104]

Wheeloch said that the Comanche women were "very trouble-

---

party of Comanches and a few Kiowas near Chouteau's Fort, north of the Canadian River, looking for Chouteau. The Indians traded some mules to Gregg. Tábba-quenas could speak Spanish and was a friend of the whites. Gregg told him of Chouteau's death. (Josiah Gregg, *Commerce of the Prairies,* in *Early Western Travels, 1748–1846,* ed. by Reuben Gold Thwaites, XIX, 155–349; XX, 111.)

Paréiya was the head chief of the Comanches when the Kiowas made their treaty with the Comanches in 1790. From 1830 to 1850, Shaved Head, or Wulea-boo, was the head of the Comanches. Bull Hump, or Buffalo Hump (Poche-ha-que Heip). was a leading chief from 1830 to 1850, and helped to make the peace with the Cheyennes in 1840. He was a Penateka Comanche as was Pa-ha-yu-ca, head chief of the Penatekas during the 1840's in Texas. Both are also mentioned as chiefs of the Noconis. Buffalo Hump was a resident on the Comanche Reservation in Texas in 1857. Another Buffalo Hump, third chief of the Penatekas, almost certainly a son or nephew of the older one, signed the Treaty of 1865 as "Pocha-naw-quoip." Mooney mentioned that some of the names given by Catlin were not decipherable. The same is true for other writers.

103 "Journal of Colonel Dodge's Expedition," 380.

104 *Ibid.,* 380. The Wichitas demurred about accompanying Colonel Dodge, and the Comanches were "cautious and suspicious," but the Kiowas were ready to go.

some . . . they steal everything they can secrete." The Toyash (Wichita) women were "infinitely respectable." The differences between the tribes were "somewhat thus":

> The Comanche is an arrogant, jealous, savage don the Toyash, a savage farmer; whilst the Kiowa, more chivalric, impulsive, and daring than either, reminds one of the bold clannish Highlander, whose very crimes are made by the poet captivating. This tribe has roamed more towards the Rocky Mountains until within a few years past.[105]

As the party, with the boy, Matthew Wright Martin, and the Negro, started for Fort Gibson, accompanied by Dohasan, We-ter-ra-shar-ro, two Toyash warriors, a Waco chief, and some Comanches, the Pani-Maha guide left them; "but he was no loss," and a Toyash guided them to the northeast. In conversation with Wheeloch, "Ski-sa-ro-ka," an "intelligent Toyash," said that his nation formerly lived in the south, that their oldest men were born there, and that they and the Comanches had long been in friendly intercourse. But the Comanches were:

> . . . not much liked by the Toyash; they cheat them and ride away. The Kiowas, a newer acquaintance, more honest and gentle. The Comanches of Texas [were] a much more powerful tribe than those on this side of the Red river; they are called the Ho-ishe Comanche.[106]

The Comanche delegation "left us today . . . on account of sickness of the squaw." On July 29 the expedition reached the sick camp and stopped to hunt buffalo. On July 31 it moved on to the Canadian River and again hunted buffalo; "one of the Kiowas killed three buffaloes with *three arrows*."[107]

It was decided to move to the head of the Canadian, a hundred

---

[105] *Ibid.*, 380.

[106] *Ibid.*, 381. Ski-sa-ro-ka was sketched by Catlin. See his *North American Indians*, II, 82, fig. 175.

[107] Wheeloch, "Journal of Colonel Dodge's Expedition," 381. The italics are Wheeloch's; he was amazed at such skill.

or more miles north, to better conditions and food supply, where the Indians said that there were immense herds of buffalo. Days elapsed and during this time "continual parties of the Pawnee Picts and Kioways," as well as Comanches, came in and offered to go with the dragoons to the frontier; meanwhile, Catlin did their portraits.

The Pawnee Picts, in their own language "Tow-ee-ahge [Tawe-hash]," had a powerful tribe and occupied the country on the head-waters of the Red River with the Kiowas and Wicos (Wacos). The old chief, We-ter-ra-shar-ro, said he had "altogether three thousand warriors," which would make a total of about twelve thousand people; or, said Catlin, even if boasting, it would be about "eight to ten thousand."[108]

Catlin described the Kiowas thus:

> The Kioways are a much finer looking race of man than either the Camanchees or Pawnees—are tall and erect, with an easy and graceful gait—with long hair, cultivated oftentimes so as to reach nearly to the ground. They have generally the fine and Roman outline of head, that is so frequently found at the North—and decidedly distinct from that of the Camanchees and Pawnee Picts. These men speak a language distinct from both of the others . . . . The head-chief of the Kioways, whose name is Teh-toat-sah [Doha-san], we found to be a very gentlemanly and high-minded man, who treated the dragoons and officers with great kindness while in his country. His long hair, which was put up in several large clubs, and ornamented with a great many silver broaches, extended quite down to his knees. This distinguished man, as well as several others of his tribe, have agreed to join us on the march to Fort Gibson . . . . Bon-son-gee (the new fire) is another chief of this tribe, and called a very good man; the principal ornaments which he carried on his person were a boar's tusk and his war-whistle, which were hanging on his breast.

[108] Catlin, *North American Indians*, II, 82. Catlin's numbers of Indian population are usually too large, but this comprises three tribes—the Kiowas, Wichitas, and Wacos. In the early days of the Wichita confederacy, the Wichitas and Tawehashes or Taovayas were separate tribes; but they were later synonymous. See "Tawehash" by Herbert Eugene Bolton in Hodge, *Handbook*, II, 705–707.

Quay-ham-kay (the stone shell) is another fair specimen of the warriors of this tribe; and, if I mistake not, somewhat allied to the mysteries and arcana of the healing art, from the close company he keeps with my friend Dr. Findley, who is surgeon to the regiment, and by whom I have been employed to make a copy of my portrait of this distinguished personage.

Wun-oan-to-mee (the white weasel), a girl, and Tunk-aht-oh-ye (the thunderer), a boy; who are brother and sister are two Kioways who were purchased from the Osages, to be taken to their tribe by the dragoons. The girl was taken . . . and the fine little boy was killed . . . near Fort Gibson, the day after I painted his portrait . . . . He was a beautiful boy of nine or ten years of age, and was killed by a ram, which struck him in the abdomen, and knocking him against a fence, killed him instantly.

Kots-a-to-ah (the smoked shield), is another of the extraordinary men of this tribe, near seven feet in stature, and distinguished, not only as one of the greatest warriors, but the swiftest on foot, in the nation. This man, it is said, runs down a buffalo on foot, and slays it with his knife or his lance, as he runs by its side![109]

After seven days the party, accompanied by the Indians, reached the Canadian, where it stopped to hunt buffalo and dry meat, and tend their sick, many of whom were carried on litters. They had difficulty getting water; much of it was salt, and pools were "dirty lavers, from which we drove the herds of wallowing buffaloes, and into which our poor and almost dying horses . . . ran and plunged their noses, sucking up the dirty and poisonous draft . . . the men also . . . drank to almost fatal excess."[110]

Men and horses were, he said, dying of the same disease, "a slow and distressing bilious fever" which seemed to affect the liver. An express arrived on August 5, telling of the death of General Henry Leavenworth and of ten or fifteen of the men left at the mouth of the False Washita. On August 10 the party reached Camp Holmes (then under construction) and received rations. After leaving the

[109] *Ibid.*, II, 84–85. For pictures or portraits of the Kiowas, see figs. 178 (Dohasan), 179 (Bon-son-gee), 180 (Quay-ham-kay), and 182 (captive girl and boy).
[110] *Ibid.*, II, 86–87.

camp, the dragoons reached Fort Gibson in fifteen days—many had been left behind with attendants; others were buried. Still more died after reaching Fort Gibson. Out of 450 dragoons, about 150 perished. Catlin believed that they should not have been sent into the southern climate in the hottest months of the year, July and August, and wearing heavy clothing.

After their return, they had a "bustling" time with the Indians. The Negro was returned to his master, and Matthew Wright Martin to his mother. Contiguous tribes were invited to the council. Seven or eight tribes (including the Cherokees, Creeks, Osages, and Choctaws) came in and met their untamed brethren of the west. They embraced each other, smoked the calumet together, and pledged lasting peace.

At the council on September 2, Evans described the manner in which the Kiowa embraced: the Kiowa "hugged the chiefs of the different tribes by placing his hands alternately on the left then on the right shoulder of his more corpulent and civilized Brethren then placed his hand on his own bosom then the bosom of his friend also each others forehead in like manner."[111] Evans also noted that "the Kiowa Chief took his seat and it was some time before he would assent to shake hands with the Osages. At last he arose and huged [sic] the Osage chief as he had the others."[112] The council was presided over by Colonel Henry Dodge, Major William Armstrong, superintendent of Indian affairs, and General Montfort Stokes, Indian commissioner. After the council adjourned and the Indians were given presents, they started for their own country with an escort of dragoons. Taking part in this council were "three of the principal chiefs of the Pawnees, fifteen Kioways, one Camanchee, and one Wico chief," all of whom had their portraits painted by Catlin, as did seven Comanche chiefs who had turned back before reaching Fort Gibson. After the council Colonel Dodge's expedition returned to Fort Leavenworth.

Eighty men were fitted out to follow the Indians home, and to start a trading house among them. Catlin advised that the govern-

111 Evans, "Journal," *loc. cit.*, 213.
112 *Ibid.*, 213.

70

ment should prohibit such establishments and instead invite the Indians to trade at frontier posts, where they would meet honorable competition and a good market; then they would not have to judge all whites by "the sellers of whiskey." He added that although it was worth while to have brought these people to a peace, the achievement had been costly in lives and money to the United States.[113]

As a result of the friendly relations established by the dragoon expedition, a treaty was made on August 24, 1835, at Camp Holmes, near the site of present Purcell, Oklahoma. The United States commissioners were General Montfort Stokes and Brigadier General Matthew Arbuckle. Major William Armstrong had been appointed also, but he died and the government was deprived of his services; however, the other commissioners succeeded.[114] The chiefs of the Comanches and Wichitas agreed to peace with each other and with the United States and with the Creeks, Cherokees, Muskogees, Osages, and other immigrant tribes. Because of delays, the Kiowas became impatient and returned home, so they were not parties to the original treaty. On May 26, 1837, the Kiowa delegation came to Fort Gibson and made its first treaty with the government and with the Muskogees and Osages. The tribes were the "Kioway, Ka-ta-ka, and Ta-wa-karo nations."[115]

Peace and friendship were the main objects of the treaty. All were to have equal hunting rights on the southern prairies as far west as governmental jurisdiction extended. United States citizens were to have the right to travel across the Indian hunting areas to and from Mexico and Texas. The Kiowas and their allies were to

113 Catlin, *North American Indians*, II, 94–95.

114 "Indian Treaties and Councils Affecting Kansas," The Kansas State Historical Society, *Collections*, Vol. XVI (1923–25), 746–72. Annual Report of the Secretary of War [Lewis Cass], November 30, 1835, accompanying Annual Message of the President, December 8, 1835, 24 Cong., 1 sess., *House Exec. Doc. No. 2*, Vol. II, No. 2 (1835); also in *American State Papers*, Military Affairs, Vol. V, No. 613 (1935), 631–32.

115 Mooney, "Calendar History," 169. These were the Kiowas, Kiowa-Apaches, and Tawakonis, one tribe of the Wichitas, who were largely in Texas, and still a separate tribe of the Wichita confederacy at that time. See also "Indian Treaties and Councils Affecting Kansas," *loc. cit.*, 746–57.

71

be at peace with Mexico and Texas. The peace with the Osages and Creeks was never broken. That with the United States was kept for a while; but a peace with Mexico and Texas, the Indians ignored. They regarded Texas as distinct from the United States. The Texans continued to drive the Indians from their best hunting grounds, in violation of treaties and without compensation. To the Kiowas and Comanches, the "Tejannas" were enemies. There was never peace in this quarter until reservation days.

At the 1837 meeting, General Montfort Stokes and Colonel A. P. Chouteau were treaty commissioners. Witnesses were comprised of officers at Fort Gibson: Colonel William Whistler, Captain Benjamin Louis Eulalie de Bonneville, and Colonel R. L. Dodge.[116] The treaty was signed by ten Kiowa chiefs and warriors, three Kiowa-Apaches, and four Tawakonis. The Kiowa signers were Ta-ka-ta-couche (Blackbird), Cha-hon-de-ton (Flying Squirrel), Ta-ne-congais (Sea Gull or Blackbird), Bon-congais (Black Cap), To-ho-sa or Dohasan (Top of the Mountain or Little Bluff), Sen-son-da-cat (White Bird), Con-a-hen-ka (Horned Frog), He-pan-ni-gais (Night), Ka-him-hi (Prairie Dog), and Pa-con-ta (My Young Brother). Signers for the Kiowa-Apaches were Hen-ton-te (Iron Shoe), A-ei-kenda (One Who Is Surrendered), and Cet-ma-ni-ta (Walking Bear). The Kiowas and Kiowa-Apaches were living on the headwaters of the Arkansas, Canadian, and Red rivers in 1835. They were friends of the Comanches and Wichitas who lived south

---

[116] Hiram Martin Chittenden, *American Fur Trade of the Far West*, I, 99, 382; II, 497, 545–46. Auguste Pierre Chouteau, born May 9, 1786, and died, 1838 (Fowler, *Journal*, 32), was the eldest son of Jean Pierre Chouteau. (Chittenden, *American Fur Trade of the Far West*, I, 396–433.)

Mooney, in his "Calendar History," says that "Colonel R. L. Dodge" led the dragoon expedition of 1834 on page 170, and calls him "Colonel Henry Dodge" on page 264 (the latter name is correct). Lieutenant Colonel William Whistler of the Seventh Infantry was stationed at Fort Gibson. Captain B. L. E. Bonneville had overstayed his leave in the West, was dropped from the army in 1834, then reinstated by President Andrew Jackson in 1836 and sent to Fort Gibson. He was noted for his exceptional humaneness in dealing with the Indians. See the *Dictionary of American Biography*, II, 438. Washington Irving glorified Bonneville. See *The Adventures of Captain Bonneville*, XI in *The Works of Washington Irving*.

and east of them. This area they continued to occupy until reservation days.[117]

The Kiowas in the north had no communication with traders by 1802 when Perrin du Lac wrote about them, or by 1805 when Lewis and Clark heard about them. Zebulon Pike noted that James "Pursley [Purcell]," first American to penetrate into their region, spent a trading season (1802 to 1803) with the Kiowas and Comanches, operating for a French trader out from the Mandans. Purcell stayed with the Kiowas through the next spring, until the Dakotas drove them from the Plains to the mountainous country at the heads of the Platte and Arkansas.[118] Then Purcell lived in Santa Fe with Spanish permission. Edwin James, with Major Long's expedition of 1820, noted that the Kiowas had traded with some Americans from St. Louis in 1815. The Kiowas were then farther south than the North Platte River, where they were noted by Lewis and Clark in 1805; and traders from St. Louis went up the Arkansas River to trade with the Kiowas, Cheyennes, and others. The Indians also traded some with the Spaniards of New Mexico. It was in 1834 that the first regular American trading expedition entered the Plains, when the eighty men accompanied the visiting chiefs back from Fort Gibson.[119]

Colonel A. P. Chouteau built in 1835 a trading house on the same site as Camp Holmes, about five miles northeast of present

[117] Mooney, "Calendar History," 170–71.

[118] *Ibid.*, 171. Pike, *Expeditions*, II, 757–58. Chittenden, *American Fur Trade*, II, 486n., 492–93.

[119] The fur trade of the first few decades of the nineteenth century was a cutthroat competition and left a vicious imprint on many tribes that had been friendly at first. The government prohibited the use of intoxicants for the Indians, but they were smuggled by the traders. McKenzie, of the American Fur Company, used a still for a while at Fort Union, until required to desist by the government. See Chittenden, *American Fur Trade*, I, 22–31, 327–62. See also Rev. Pierre-Jean de Smet, *Life, Letters and Travels Of Father Pierre-Jean De Smet, S. J., 1801–1873.* One reference will suffice: "Liquor is rolled out to the Indians by whole barrels; sold . . . by white men even in the presence of the agent. Wagon loads of the abominable stuff arrive daily from the settlements, and along with it the very dregs of our white neighbors . . . drunkards, gamblers, etc. (*Ibid.*, I, 175–76.)

Purcell, Oklahoma, at a spring on a small creek near the Canadian River.[120] This was an Indian camping ground and the site of a Kichai village in 1850. Trade was carried on with the Kiowas, Comanches, Wichitas, and other tribes until Chouteau's death in 1838, when the place was abandoned. Chouteau was called "Soto" and was affectionately remembered by the Kiowas. The first trading post in Kiowa rather than in Comanche territory was on Cache Creek three miles below present Fort Sill, Oklahoma. It was established by Chouteau; the trader in charge was named Thomas, called by the Indians "Tométe." It did not last long. In 1869, William Madison, or "Terrible Beard," opened a store in the same area, after the tribes were on the reservation. William Bent put up some trading posts along the South Canadian in 1844, in the Texas Panhandle, near the trails of the Kiowas. The Kiowas also traded at various points on the Arkansas.[121]

In the summer of 1835, Colonel Henry Dodge and approximately 125 dragoons, with about 12 officers and Major Dougherty, Indian agent, and Captain John Gant, Indian trader, as guides, undertook another trip to make peace treaties with the Indians of the Plains.[122] They visited the Otos, Omahas, Grand Pawnees, Republican Pawnees, Loup Pawnees and Tapage Pawnees, Arikaras,

[120] Chittenden, *American Fur Trade*, II, 879–80. Fort Kiowa, though named for the Kiowas, traded with other Indians; see *ibid.*, II, 880.

[121] Mooney, "Calendar History," 171–72. See also David Lavender, *Bent's Fort*; George Bird Grinnell, *Beyond the Old Frontier: Adventures of Indian Fighters, Hunters, and Fur-Traders*, 128–29, 138 (Bent's Fort, Fort St. Vrain, and Fort Adobe on Canadian), 140, 158, 162–70. (Description of Bent's Fort on the Arkansas [in 1939]). "At one time no less than three hundred and fifty lodges of Kiowa Apaches were camping near the fort"—*ibid.*, 188. When the Kiowas and Apaches were camped there the number was "very large," and "six or seven thousand Cheyennes were camped there at one time"—*ibid.*, 188. In 1840 the Kiowas and Comanches had a great celebration of their peace treaty with the Cheyennes. There was feasting, singing, dancing, and drumming. Two great camps moved up to Bent's Fort—the Kiowas, Comanches, and Kiowa-Apaches on the south side of the river, the Cheyennes and Arapahoes on the north. Colonel Bent warned against any liquor's getting to the Indians, fearful that it might break up their peace, 188.

[122] Colonel Henry Dodge, "Journal of a March of a Detachment of Dragoons, under the Command of Colonel Dodge, during the Summer of 1835," 24 Cong., 1 sess., *House Doc. No. 181*, 2–36.

Arapahoes, a party of Cheyennes, and two villages of Cheyennes at Bent's Fort. While at Bent's Fort, Colonel Dodge met William Bent, who had just returned from a trading trip to the Comanches on Red River; he had seen "upwards of 2,000 Comanche," and they "expressed a desire to be included in the peace" made with the Comanches the year before.[123] At Bent's Fort a council was called for the Arapahoes, Cheyennes, and a few Gros Ventres (Atsinas) and Blackfeet. The Cheyennes were in disorganization, were separated into three villages, had killed their principal chief, and were at war with the Comanches, Kiowas, Pawnees, and Arikaras. A large war party was sent out against the Comanches. The Osages had made a peace with the Cheyennes and Arapahoes early in the summer. Dodge said that the Cheyennes left the north shortly after 1825. They had "now [1835] 220 lodges, 660 men or 2,640 souls in all." The Arapahoes had 360 lodges, 1,080 men, "3,600 souls in all." About 350 Gros Ventres lived with the Arapahoes, whose principal chiefs were Nash-hine-e-Thaw (Elk Tongue) and Ka-ow-che (Bear's Tooth). The Cheyennes told Dodge that they would agree to a peace with the Pawnees. Dodge also appointed three chiefs selected by Little Moon to receive medals. They were White Cow, The Flying Arrow, and Walking Whirlwind.[124]

Dodge did not meet the Kiowas in 1835, but he remarked:

> A band of Kiowas, called the Upper band, consisting of one thousand eight hundred or two thousand, and another who are called Appaches of the plains [Kiowa-Apaches], consisting of about twelve hundred, also frequent this portion of the country. All of these Indians frequent the Arkansas and the Platte near the mountains, for the purpose of killing buffalo, upon which they subsist, and make their clothes of skin. They all have large numbers of horses, upon which they hunt buffalo and pack their baggage. The women do all the work, and wait upon the men, who do nothing but kill the game.[125]

[123] *Ibid.*, 34–35.
[124] *Ibid.*, 24–27.
[125] *Ibid.*, 25.

Dodge also noted that Spaniards from Taos were camped at the Cheyenne village near Bent's Fort, selling the Cheyennes whisky, and that the Indians would give "everything they possess" for it. They had few guns.

On the march back to Fort Leavenworth, Colonel Dodge met a war party of the Cheyennes and gave another medal to "White Man's Chief." The expedition was considered of great importance and encouraged hopes for peace, according to General Edmund P. Gaines, in reporting to the Adjutant General, February 23, 1836— especially in view of events in Texas. By this time the Texas Revolution was on.

Grinnell said that the Adobe Fort on the South Canadian was built prior to 1840.[126] The chiefs desiring the post for trade were Dohasan and Eagle Tail Feathers of the Kiowas, Shaved Head of the Comanches, and Poor Bear of the Kiowa-Apaches. All were chiefs of importance. Shaved Head was a friend of the whites and a man of influence on other tribes. He signed the Treaty of Fort Atkinson, 1853, as head chief of the Comanches. His name on the treaty is "Wulea-boo." He probably died before 1865, as he did not sign the treaty made in 1865 or that in 1867. William Bent traded with the Kiowas and Comanches before a fort or post was built at Adobe Walls. As noted earlier, William Bent was trading with the Comanches on Red River in 1835; after the peace of 1840 with the Cheyennes, the Kiowas and Comanches freely visited Bent's Fort.

In 1839, Gregg met a party of Comanches and some Kiowas near Chouteau's Fort north of the Canadian River, led by Tábba-quenas (Big Eagle). It "consisted of about sixty persons, including several squaws and papooses, with a few Kiowa chiefs and warriors, who, although of a tribe so entirely distinct, are frequently found domiciled among the Comanches."[127] The chief could speak

126 George Bird Grinnell, "Bent's Old Fort and Its Builders," *The Kansas State Historical Quarterly*, Vol. XV (1919–22), 28–91.

127 Gregg, *Commerce of the Prairies*, 109. The Comanches were inclined to be larger than the Kiowas. Gregg had one Comanche guide, "Manuel el Comanche," married to a Mexican girl, a sober, civilized citizen and an excellent buffalo hunter.

Spanish and boasted of his friendship for the Americans. They wanted "mulas para swap," so some trading in mules was done, and the Indians departed. They were looking for their friend Chouteau, and Gregg had to tell them of the trader's death at Fort Gibson the previous winter.[128]

Gregg states further that he met a number of Comanches, one band numbering three hundred persons, and that another band of three hundred Comanches raided Parral in Chihuahua in 1835. Trading in mules was carried on with the Comanches, and one Mexican boy of fifteen years was bought for the price of one mule and sent to his family in Chihuahua. (A mule was worth between $10 and $20 in trading goods.) Blankets, looking glasses, awls, flint, tobacco, beads, and vermilion were the principal goods traded for mules. Several Mexican women, wives of Comanches, tattooed like the Indians, had no desire to return to the Mexicans.[129]

The modern history of the Kiowas began with the Treaty of 1837 and the penetration of traders among them. Colonel A. P. Chouteau made arrangements to have some of the Kiowas, Comanches, and others visit Washington. A party of chiefs visited Fort Gibson in the summer of 1839, only to learn that the proposed trip had been abandoned since Chouteau's death. They were given gifts and returned home.

In 1839–40, a smallpox epidemic swept the Plains. It almost wiped out the Mandans before it swept down to the Gulf of Mexico. The Kiowas, at this time, made a peace with the Cheyennes and Arapahoes that continued into reservation days. They were then at peace with all the Plains tribes save the Pawnees and the Tonkawas.

THE KIOWA-COMANCHE PEACE WITH THE
CHEYENNES AND ARAPAHOES, 1840

The Cheyennes crowded the Kiowas and Comanches southward. The Kiowas were found by the Cheyennes to be living in the Black

This Comanche, he said, was among the largest of his tribe, bony and muscular and weighing two hundred pounds. (*Ibid.*, 207.)

[128] *Ibid.*, 111.

[129] *Ibid.*, 125–30.

Hills and along the Little Missouri, Powder and Tongue rivers.[130] The Little Missouri was called "Antelope Pit River" by the Kiowas; it was there that the Kiowas used to trap great numbers of antelope in pits, and that the Cheyennes learned to do so in the same manner.

Early meetings of the Cheyennes with the Kiowas and Comanches were friendly, but later fighting took place. The result was that the Kiowas and Comanches were pushed down to the North Platte River, and from there they moved farther south, largely to obtain horses.

Around 1835 the Arkansas River divided the range of the two groups: the Cheyennes and Arapahoes, and the Kiowas, Comanches, and Kiowa-Apaches allied. Between 1826 and 1840 bitter warfare occurred between the two factions. In 1840 the Kiowas, Kiowa-Apaches, and Comanches made a peace with the Cheyennes and Arapahoes.

Paving the way for the peace had been the efforts of William Bent of Bent's Fort and the dragoon expedition of Colonel Henry Dodge across the Plains in 1835. Some of the overtures leading to the 1840 peace were conducted by the Arapahoes and the Kiowa-Apaches. A kinsman of Little Raven, an Arapaho, had married a Kiowa-Apache woman. On one occasion some Kiowa-Apaches visited the Arapaho camp and told them that the Kiowas and Comanches wanted a peace with them. The visiting Kiowa-Apaches were guests in the lodge of Bull, a noted Arapaho chief.

A war party of eight Cheyennes, led by Seven Bulls, visited the Arapaho camp while on their way to steal horses from the Kiowas. The Cheyennes were invited to meet the Kiowa-Apaches. In Bull's lodge the pipe was offered to the Cheyennes, but Seven Bulls refused to smoke, saying that they were not chiefs and could not smoke or make peace, but that they would carry home a message. Bull told the Cheyennes that if a peace was made, the Kiowas

---

[130] George Bird Grinnell, *The Fighting Cheyennes*, 36. Grinnell said the Cheyennes—not the Dakotas (Sioux), as Mooney believed—pushed the Kiowas out of the Black Hills. Grinnell gives the details of the peace on pages 38–67. According to Mooney, the Cheyennes had sought the peace. See Mooney, "Calendar History," 276.

78

would return the scalps of the Bow String soldiers (Cheyennes killed in a battle with the Kiowas in 1837), and that the Kiowas and Comanches would give the Cheyennes many horses.

Seven Bulls carried back the proposition to the Cheyennes, then on Shawnee Creek, a tributary of the Republican. Little Old Man and White Antelope of the Dog Soldiers were called to the council by the chiefs and briefed on the question by High-Backed Wolf; they were instructed to call the Dog Soldiers together for a decision.

It was decided that a peace should be made. High-Backed Wolf rode about the camp and announced it to the people. Runners were sent to Bull's camp to tell him of the peace plans, and the visiting Kiowa-Apaches rode south to notify the Kiowas, Comanches, and Kiowa-Apaches.

At Two Butte Creek the Cheyennes met with their former enemies. Dohasan (Little Bluff) led the Kiowa contingent, along with Satank, Yellow Hair, and Eagle Feather. Bull Hump and Shavehead represented the Comanches; and Leading Bear, the Kiowa-Apaches. In the group was a boy, Yellow Boy, son of Yellow Hair. They were welcomed, and after all were seated, Yellow Hair stood up and lighted the pipe. Each smoked, thus sealing the peace.

The Kiowas had a bundle with them. Eagle Feather told the Cheyennes that they had brought the scalps of the Bow String soldiers. High-Backed Wolf then said they did not want them—it would "only make bad feeling" and disturb the new peace. Then he called his people to present gifts. Dohasan stood and said:

> We all of us have many horses; as many as we need; we do not wish to accept any horses as presents but we shall be glad to receive any other gifts. We, the Kiowas, Comanches, and Apaches have made a road to give many horses to you when we all come here.[131]

Many gifts were given to the delegation; Yellow Boy was almost covered, as the blankets piled up about him. Then the guests were taken to a lodge and served a feast. Dohasan told the Cheyenne chiefs to choose a place for a meeting of their tribes—a wide place because there would be many horses.

[131] Grinnell, *The Fighting Cheyennes*, 66.

The Cheyennes chose a place below Bent's Fort, and Dohasan agreed and said: "There we will make a strong friendship which will last forever. We will give you horses, and you shall give us presents."[132]

The promise was fulfilled. The Kiowas came to the appointed place and camped up the river—not in a circle, which they did only for the Sun Dance. High-Backed Wolf crossed the river and invited the Kiowa and Comanche chiefs to his camp to feast. After the feast Dohasan said:

> Now, my friends, tomorrow I want you all, even the women and children to cross over to our camp and sit in a long row. Let all come on foot; for they will return on horseback.[133]

The next day all waded the river and sat in rows—men in front, women and children behind them. Satank, with a big bundle of sticks, started down the row and gave a stick to each one. Dohasan told them to keep the sticks and they would get horses for them. All the Kiowas gave horses. Satank was said to have given 250 horses himself. The chiefs received the most, but even the unimportant men and women got four, five, or six horses. The Cheyennes did not have rope enough to lead the horses; they had to drive them off in bunches.

High-Backed Wolf then invited the Kiowas, Comanches, and Kiowa-Apaches to visit the Cheyennes and Arapahoes the next day and to bring their horses to carry back the things that would be afforded them. The visit was made, food was served, and they were given guns, blankets, calico, beads, kettles, and many presents. The visitors enjoyed the meal, which included such civilized foods as rice, dried apples, corn meal, and New Orleans molasses. The guns given were fired into the air; this was customary, perhaps to show that they were good guns. For a while it sounded like a battle, with guns popping off. After the peace was made, the people were told they could trade together.

132 *Ibid.*, 67.
133 *Ibid.*, 67.

The peace was never broken. It was a historic one. It joined five nations; and these nations acting together formed a barrier to the westward-pushing eastern or prairie Indians (Indians well armed with the white man's guns), and a barrier to the northern Indians (who could not break through to get to the Spanish settlements for horses), as well as a barrier to the encroaching whites (especially the northward and westward moving Texans).

Before the peace, the Kiowas had wanted to trade at Bent's Fort, but were kept away by the Cheyennes. William Bent wanted to trade with all the Indians, although he favored the Cheyennes. For some time the Comanches did not desire to trade. In 1838 they told Albert Sidney Johnston in Texas, who was trying to negotiate a peace treaty with them, that they did not want trading posts in their country. The usual white trading goods did not interest them. Their trading needs were met by the Wichita tribes on the Red River, by the Comancheros out of New Mexico, and also by the plunder secured in Old Mexico.

But they did need guns and ammunition, especially against the Texans, who were free of Mexico in 1836 and pushing a war of extermination or removal of the Indians from Texas territory, particularly against the Comanches. In the spring of 1840 the Comanches suffered losses at the Council House Fight at San Antonio and along the edges of the white settlements from the military campaigns of Texas Rangers. The Comanches sought aid from the Kiowas to fight the Texans.[134] They needed men as well as guns. In 1840 allies were probably of more importance than trade to the Comanches. Whether for trade, guns, or solidarity against their white and Indian enemies, the Comanches, Kiowas, and Kiowa-Apaches did join with the Cheyennes and Arapahoes in peace. It was a formidable union.

[134] In the summer of 1840, Comanches and Kiowas raided to the Texas Coast, Victoria and Linnville; and the battle of Plum Creek made the Indians flee northward, followed in the fall by another battle against the Comanches on the Colorado River in west Texas. See Joseph Jablow, *The Cheyenne in Plains Indian Trade Relations, 1795–1840*, American Ethnological Society (hereinafter cited as A. E. S.) *Monograph No. 19* (1950). Jablow stresses the need for trade with the whites and the Cheyenne need for horses.

In 1841 the Texas expedition to Santa Fe—Texas claimed New Mexico—came in contact with the Kiowas.[135] Kendall described them as occupying the headwaters of the Colorado, Brazos, Wichita and Red rivers. He said that they were a powerful people, not so well known to the Texans as the Comanches farther south. Horses were stolen, probably by the Kiowas, as the expedition left the Wichita River and neared the Red River. Then more horses were stolen. One of the expedition's hunting parties reported a large body of Indians, believed to be the Kiowas. The Indians, dressed in buckskin and carrying lances, bows, and arrows, were mounted on fine horses. The expedition came on a camp that the Indians had deserted quickly and ate the food that the Indians had left.

Kendall wrote of their extraordinary horsemanship and their ability to throw themselves on the side of their horses, concealing their bodies while discharging arrows under their horses' necks. The Texans had a disastrous encounter with this tribe: five men were killed, stripped, scalped, and mutilated by the Kiowas.[136] The Indians carried off their own dead, but they moved fast and could not be overtaken. Later the party (before meeting its tragic failure in New Mexico) met a group of Comancheros who traded with the Kiowas and Comanches during a two-month trip.

THE ABERT EXPEDITION OF 1845

Lieutenant J. W. Abert, under orders of Captain John C. Frémont, was instructed in 1845 to make a reconnaissance of the southwestern area, then imperfectly known, from Bent's Fort on the Arkansas through eastern New Mexico, down the Canadian River, across the Texas Panhandle and through the present state of Oklahoma, thence back to St. Louis. Abert said that he was to "survey . . . Purgatory Creek, the waters of the Canadian and False Washita."[137]

[135] George Wilkins Kendall, *Narrative of the Texan Santa Fe Expedition.*
[136] *Ibid.*, I, 198–214, 262–63.
[137] Lieutenant J. W. Abert, in H. Bailey Carroll (ed.), *Guadal P'a, the Journal*

At Bent's Fort a Kiowa Indian, Tah-kai-buhl, who knew the country, was made tempting offers to accompany the party, but he refused. However, Thomas Fitzpatrick accompanied the party as far as Bent's trading houses on the Canadian. He was an old hand on the Plains, having been trader, trapper, and guide for many expeditions, including those of Captain Frémont.[138] Mr. Hatcher, "who had great influence with the Kioways" and was a guide employed by Bent, also went along.[139]

They met with a band of "Buffalo Eaters" (Comanches), gave them tobacco, and talked with them. They learned that most of their braves were off with the Kiowas to overrun Chihuahua, Mexico; also, that the Comanches and Pawnees, long enemies, had concluded a peace. Abert's party noticed that one Spaniard among the Indians, who was one of their warriors, was well treated and shared in their tobacco.[140]

Later, they were startled one night by a band of Indians who rode up outside their camp. At daylight they saw the Indians and invited them in. They proved to be Kiowas and "Up-sah-rokees," or Crows. At first having believed Abert's group to be the hated Texans, the Indians had crept up on them at night and watched them until daylight. Although they could have wiped out the whole party during the night, at some point the Indians had decided that their prey might actually be Americans, with whom they were friendly. During the morning visit, they recognized Hatcher, who

of Lieutenant J. W. Abert, from Bent's Fort to St. Louis in 1845. (Hereinafter cited as Carroll, *Abert's Journal*.)

[138] *Ibid.*, 11, 16–17. See also Chittenden, *American Fur Trade*, I, 259–260, for a description of Fitzpatrick. Fitzpatrick and Hatcher were traders for William Bent of Bent's Fort, along with Kit Carson, Lucien Maxwell, and others. Fitzpatrick was known to the Indians as "Broken Hand" and "Three Fingers," because of an accident suffered from the bursting of a rifle. He was also called "White Hair," from a terrible experience with the Gros Ventres that turned his hair white. A noted trapper and guide, he became, in 1846, Indian agent of the Upper Platte and Arkansas, serving the Cheyennes, Arapahoes, and certain bands of Sioux. In 1851 he made a peace with the Plains tribes north of the Arkansas, and in 1853 at second Fort Atkinson (near present Dodge City, Kansas) signed a treaty with the Comanches, Kiowas, and Kiowa-Apaches. See *Dictionary of American Biography*, VI, 442–43.

[139] Carroll, *Abert's Journal*, 17–18.

[140] *Ibid.*, 63.

was known to them as a trader; he made them "cigaritos," which they enjoyed.

The Indians mounted their horses and accompanied the party. They told the members of the expedition that some of the Comanches with them had become frightened and fled, urging the Kiowas to do the same, and had left their "mules and furniture" scattered. Abert wrote:

> The Kioways are a people excelling the Comanches in every respect, and though far inferior to them in number, not counting more than 200 lodges in all, yet exercise almost absolute control over them.[141]

The Kiowas were quite friendly. They told of their origins in the north and of their smoking the peace pipe with the Comanches, with whom they had "remained in close friendship ever since." The Kiowas spoke an entirely different language from the Comanches, "being much more deep and guttural, striking upon the ear like the sound of falling water." The two tribes were bound together to mutual advantage:

> The Kioways sustain a character for bravery, energy, and honesty, while the Camanchees are directly opposite, being cowardly, indolent, and treacherous. The Kioways are particularly noted for their honesty; and, while we remained with them, nothing was stolen— an occurrence sufficiently uncommon to merit special notice.[142]

Abert's party visited the Indians' village and camped near them. The Indian horses had eaten the grass "very short." The soldiers

---

[141] *Ibid.*, 66. This interesting observation is borne out by later writers. Battey noticed it during the 1870's in his dealings with the Kiowas. They were an independent, "think-for-themselves" people. When I talked with some Kiowas in Anadarko, Oklahoma, on July 17, 1957, at the Kiowa Agency, they touched on the subject of independence. One said the Kiowas were still independent. He said that the Comanches would have been wiped out, had not the Kiowas sought them and advised them to go on the reservation.

[142] *Ibid.*, 66. Carroll points out that this was a significant appraisal, contrary to much that had been written about them.

were importuned to trade but, shortsightedly, had brought no trading articles with them. They did manage to give the Indians some tobacco. The squaws and children brought ropes of plaited thongs, moccasins, and skins to trade. Abert said:

> We were much struck by the noble bearing and fine athletic figures of these people, which we partly attributed to their being constantly on horseback, which not only gives them palpable evidence of their superiority over the animals they bestride, but makes them conscious of their elevation over all the lower orders of creation, which is communicated to their whole character.[143]

Abert noted also that they rode beautifully and managed their horses with astonishing skill. They mounted by wrapping a blanket several times around their own body and legs, then throwing themselves lengthwise on the horse, and rising up in the seat; the blanket, binding their limbs, assisted them in clinging to the animals.

They were gay, cheerful, and "fond of frolic," constantly chatting and joking. Abert's soldiers organized shooting matches with the Indian boys, and they showed remarkable skill, shooting at a button from fifteen to twenty paces. The soldiers noticed some

> . . . whose features and hair betokened Spanish blood; they had been taken prisoners, and, being well treated, were perfectly content . . . in fact, better situated than in their own country . . . . In dress, the Kioways resemble the roving tribes of the great desert, being habited in buckskin. Their moccasins are furnished with a fringed appendage, 8 or 10 inches in length, which is attached to the heel, which could not be conveniently worn by other than mounted Indians, and is said to be peculiar to their tribe.[144]

All had blankets or buffalo robes. They wore long hair, "braided so as to form a queue, sometimes lengthened by means of horsehair until it reaches the ground." The queue was often ornamented with convex silver plates obtained from the Spanish. The dress of

[143] *Ibid.*, 66–67.
[144] *Ibid.*, 67.

the women was like that of the northern tribes, the "same leathern cape, tunic, leggins and beaded moccasins." Abert was particularly struck with the profusion of trappings with which the men ornamented themselves and their horses. Both trappings and horses were procured by robbery or barter from the Spaniards, "with whom they had considerable intercourse."

Abert's party desired the Kiowas to travel with them at least as far as Bent's houses. One young man of "frank and generous demeanor [who] elicited the sympathies and procured the friendship of all of us" wished to do so, but had first to consult the chiefs. One old woman showed affection at again meeting Hatcher. "She wept for joy" and insisted on giving him a "bale of tongues and some 'pinole' " made from mesquite beans, and called him "son," having "adopted him ever since his first trading with her nation."

Two braves and one woman joined the camp later. They had waited "to paint themselves." Two Comanches who had come up from below brought information that Texans were coming to fight them. The chiefs persuaded their men to act as guides and to help Abert's party, as they were having great difficulty with the heavy wagons drawn by mules.

The guides were received cordially by the soldiers. The young man the soldiers had wanted, Tiah-na-zi, was one; the other was Cassalan and the woman was Up-sah-ro-kee, his wife. Tiah-na-zi professed a warm friendship for the whites; with his blanket about him, he climbed a prominent hill and made a long harangue to warn all Indians to keep away and "not attempt to steal our horses or do us any mischief," or they would be shot—"that we were Americans and not Texans, and that he, Tiah-na-zi, was our brother."[145]

The Indians were much amused at the soldiers' mosquito nets. They recognized some sketches that Abert had made of the Indians at Bent's Fort, and were especially delighted with the portrait of Tah-kai-buhl, the one who had been sought as a guide. "Tia" sprang around constructing his shelter for the night, repeating the words: "How d'ye do" and "yes" in playful mimicry of the whites.

[145] Ibid., 67–69.

These were the only English words he knew, save a few profane oaths.

The next day the party crossed the Canadian River near the site of present Borger, Texas. The Indians had to paint themselves; the toilet was a complicated job. They made themselves presentable with comb, looking glass, and vermilion. "Tia" served well as a scout. Once Abert's party met a Comanchero party. The Comancheros wore sombreros, and "long bag breeches" to the knee, with long stockings. They were shabbily dressed and badly armed.

Another group of Kiowas came to visit. One of the Indians recognized the Abert party from having met them at Bent's Fort, and had there been told by Abert to advise his tribe that the party was on its way and would visit them. They informed Abert that their best warriors had gone to fight the Mexicans. The Kiowas were to leave the next morning, as was Hatcher, who was to go to Bent's trading house. Meanwhile, Abert's men exchanged gifts with the Indians, giving a few pieces of tent cloth, tobacco, powder, and lead; some of the soldiers even gave up a few of their own knives, and a few needles and thread. The needles and thread delighted the Indians, as they were accustomed to use awls and leather cord or sinew for sewing skins. The sinew came from the "fleece" of the buffalo, in a broad sheet along the back muscles, divided to form a thread. The Indians, pleased, said "they were now rich." Abert added:

> The Indian, with his blanket, awl, knife, bow and arrow, can house, clothe, feed and defend himself. In going to war, or in long excursions, they generally carry several pairs of moccasins, finding convenient storage for them between the skins which form their snow-white shields.[146]

"Tia" was a devoted friend and gained the hearts of all. When it was time for him to return to his tribe, he signified his deep attachment by a gesture peculiar to Indians. The last night, Abert

[146] *Ibid.*, 72.

heard him groaning and found him in a nightmare. "Tia" awoke and appreciated Abert's concern over him. He said that he was talking with the Great Spirit. "Tia" later warned the party not to separate, as Red Jacket, one of the Comanche chiefs was near by and "enraged against Texans," and some Comanches were scattered to hunt buffalo. The Comanches had been known to charge and lance stragglers; hence the importance of keeping the party together.

The expedition then crossed the Llano Estacado, or the Staked Plain. They saw a few Indians on bluffs farther on, hovering about. Later a flag was displayed. There were Indians all around, but they proved to be Kiowas who had been trying to decide if Abert's group was American or Texan. They came up and shook hands cordially, and wanted to warm themselves at the fire, after the shivering cold of the night. The Kiowas were given tobacco, and they offered to guide the party as far as their village. Abert was then told he had the honor to be entertaining "To-hah-sun" (Dohasan), or "Little Mountain" or "Overhanging Bluff," head chief of the nation.

> He was a man of middling stature, quite fat, with a very wide mouth, upon which there played a constant smile, and his whole face showed an intriguing character.[147]

Dohasan was intelligent and appreciated the difficulties that the soldiers were having with their heavy wagons and their mules. He told them that they were on Buffalo Creek (the true Washita), and made inquiries about their adventures. They told him of meeting Tah-kai-buhl, well known to the Indians, at Bent's Fort. Dohasan asked about Hatcher, and he drew his eye down with his finger, pulling the lower lid, in mimicry of Hatcher. When the Indians

[147] *Ibid.*, 78. Dohasan was a small man in comparison with some of the leading Kiowa war chiefs. The Kiowas were often described as tall and thin by contrast with the Comanches, who were shorter in stature and corpulent. The average Kiowa stature was about five feet, eight inches, although some individuals were over six feet tall. Wissler states that the average stature for the Kiowas was 67.2 inches, and for the Comanches 66.06 inches—the shortest of all the Plains Indians; the Sioux were the tallest. See Clark Wissler, *North American Indians of the Plains*, 49. The Kiowas were brachycephalic or roundheaded, averaging 82 in the cephalic index.

were getting too good a bargain in trading, that was an action used by Hatcher. Dohasan said that he wanted to see him, as he "loved him" very much. Hatcher was a universal favorite with all of the Indians.

When they reached Dohasan's village, they camped near it. They received visits of old men, women, and children, all eager to trade. Again the soldiers had little to trade. Some of the Indians were dissatisfied; they wanted memorials of the coming of the Americans, "even if they paid double" to get something to show in the village when the gossip commenced.

Abert showed the Kiowas a map and asked if Buffalo Creek ran into the Red River or the Canadian. The old men pondered. There was great discrepancy of opinion, and they finally compromised by showing all rivers as running parallel. Tah-kai-buhl's map was then corrected, and, said Abert, the relative positions of various topographic features were preserved in a surprisingly exact manner.

An old man, father of Dohasan, was:

> . . . wrinkled and thin, bearing evident marks of extreme old age. He wore on his head a seal-skin cap, a very unusual circumstance, as they seldom cover the head. On his shoulder hung a tattered uniform coat of a Mexican soldier, triumphant memorial of the daring prowess of his son, to whom he was also indebted for his handsome little Spanish wife. She told us that she had been their prisoner four years, and that the Kioways and Comanches had a number of Texas prisoners.[148]

The old man was garrulous and constantly importuned the soldiers for gifts. He asked the Americans about their nation and their object in venturing upon the prairies.

Mr. Simpson, one of Abert's party, told Abert that a young chief, "The Bear" (probably Satanta), was then a rival of Dohasan in his authority over the tribe. If successful, "The Bear" would exercise despotic sway. Simpson mentioned instances in which "The Bear" caught his lance and rushed at one of his men for a

[148] Carroll, *Abert's Journal*, 79.

trifling disobedience, saying that he was chief and should be respected as such. He always moved about in great state, being constantly attended by a young man as aide-de-camp, whose duties consisted of such things as spreading his buffalo robe for him to sit on, lighting his pipe, and doing other chores.

Abert noticed that:

> . . . many of the women had their hair cut close to the head, and their faces deeply gashed and covered with clotted blood, in mourning for some departed relatives. They presented a revolting sight, not being allowed to wash the face until the time of sorrowing had elapsed.[149]

The Indians told them that some Comanches near by had decamped, fearing Abert's party; they had fled in a great state of alarm and in considerable numbers. Some of their trails were visible. Fitzpatrick told Abert about some of the linguistic divisions of the Indians. He said that the Kiowa language was distinct. He also said that cannibalism was not a custom of the northern or western tribes; although they had some ceremonies where human sacrifices had occurred, these had gradually ceased. He knew of only one such ceremonial sacrifice in the whole of his experiences. He said it was once a custom of many tribes for the medicine men and braves of distinction to eat of the victim's flesh as the perfecting of the ceremony but not for relish of human flesh.[150]

As they went on their way, the party met some Quapaws and Kickapoos near their villages. They were then approaching white settlements. They met some Creeks, and Negroes among the Creeks. Fitzpatrick went on to Fort Gibson near present Muskogee, Oklahoma, and Abert moved on to fix the junction of the Canadian with the Arkansas. They met a few Cherokees. Abert then returned to Fort Gibson and back to St. Louis. One observation is interesting. Abert said that from Fort Gibson on, the prairies were "literally lined with wagons of emigrants to Texas," and on

---

[149] *Ibid.*, 79.
[150] *Ibid.*, 80, 82–83, 85.

the way to St. Louis they continued "daily to see hundreds of them."[151]

In D. W. C. Baker's *Texas Scrap Book*, there is a description and an appraisal of the Kiowas in the 1860's, showing the general Texan view of them:

> The Kiowas are a numerous, warlike, and treacherous tribe. They are not perhaps, strictly speaking, Texas Indians. Inhabiting a portion of country frequented by the Comanches, and partaking of their habits and customs, they are sometimes confounded with them. They are nevertheless a distinct tribe, and differ widely from the Comanches. The latter are usually of a stouter build, lower stature, and more agreeable appearance. The Kiowas are sullen, dogged, and reserved. They roam from the upper waters of the Arkansas River to the Red River, and down that stream to the Cross Timbers, and when on the war-path, far into Texas. Their home is properly the territory between New Mexico and Kansas. They have always been at war with our people. They have never kept their treaties with the whites.
>
> The wild tribes of Indians still continue their depredations upon the frontiers of Texas. From official sources it appears that since May, 1865, and August, 1867, no less than 162 persons were murdered, 24 wounded, and 43 carried into captivity from Texas by the Indians. Many thousand dollar's worth of property was also stolen or destroyed.
>
> These outrages still continue . . . .
>
> The Comanches, Kiowas, and Lipans could probably put into the field 5,000 warriors.[152]

[151] *Ibid.*, 113.

[152] "Texas Indians," in *Texas Almanac, 1869*, reprinted in *Texas Scrap Book*, 134–35.

CHAPTER THREE

❖ THE EVOLUTION
OF A CIVILIZATION

THE culture-area concept is a neat way of cataloguing and dividing Indian material for museum display, conceived by Clark Wissler.[1] As such, it has served admirably. Not so neat is the actual geographic division, or a sequential basis upon archaeology. Some culture areas typify the concept nicely—for example, the Southeast. The Plains culture, of historic growth and development, the last culture to evolve in North America, cannot show a definite archaeological sequence. It was a complex of many tribes of varied ancestry, language, and culture. In fact, there was no such thing as a Plains culture or Plains Indians, aboriginally. It developed within the period of white penetration into the Americas.

One might call it a "margin of the Plains" culture, to begin with. The marginal areas differed in many cultural traits. Much of its material came from the Northeast woodland Indians, Algonquians and others, who moved westward because of white pressure, always along the waterways, with emphasis upon water as a necessity, and

[1] Faye-Cooper Cole told me that he was with Clark Wissler when he hit on the idea of labeling clothing and materials by area for museum display. Thus was born the culture area. (Conversations with author, University of Chicago, Summer Session, 1933).

then up the rivers bordering and crossing the area of the Plains.[2] The real area of the Plains was not habitable and serviceable in its length and breadth until the use of the horse opened it up and characterized it, and became its *modus vivendi*.

Horse culture in the Plains is probably over three hundred years old. First to receive horses were the tribes or nations bordering Spanish movements north of old Mexico, into Texas, and into New Mexico and California. Beginning about 1630, the Plains Indians began to acquire horses.

The Jumanos and other Apaches, the Caddoes, Tonkawas, Bidais, and various Texas tribes definitely had horses by 1690. The Comanches pushed south to get horses, and the Kiowas followed them south for the same reason.

The Apaches seem to have made more use of the Plains in the early days than other Indians. Athapascan languages spread from Canada to Texas and into northern Mexico. The Apaches were the oldest inhabitants of the Plains, living in small villages, cultivating corn and a few vegetables along the fertile silt overflows of the rivers, and then venturing out (by foot and with dog travois), "following the cows," as the Spanish said, upon the Plains to hunt the bison.

These people, the Apaches (probably called "Paducas" up to 1750), were scattered helter-skelter when the Plains horsemen hit their stride.

In Texas the Lipan Apaches stretched from the Colorado River westward to and across the Río Grande. To the north of the Lipans were their friends and relatives, the Mescaleros, and along the Río Grande were the partly agricultural, partly buffalo- and deer-hunting Jumanos and "Cibolos." From the Colorado east to the

[2] The Pawnees moved far northward and westward (from their original Caddoan origin in the southeast) along the banks of the Platte. The Wichita confederacy likewise moved north and west up the rivers from a Caddoan origin in the south to adapt themselves to a partly Plains, partly agricultural, way of life. The Cheyennes, Arapahoes, and Sioux moved west from the Mississippi Valley, and others like the Kiowas and the Comanches moved east out of the mountains to debouch upon the Plains.

Brazos (and up it) were the Tonkawas, traditional enemies of the Apaches. The Tonkawas, like the Wichitas, had associations with the Plains, although both peoples had some agriculture. The Tonkawas probably moved south into Texas from an earlier passage down the Plains (along the east), giving the Apaches a wide berth to the west; the Wichitas, like the Pawnees and Arikaras, moved north and west from the Southeast.

The Plains Indians came from diverse origins; a culture trait was borrowed here, another there, if it suited life on back of a horse, and a culture was made. Its pattern was quickly diffused, and eleven of its thirty-one tribes became "typical," twenty tribes still remaining partly Plains Indians. It was a meteoric rise—of great glamour and pageantry. To almost all Ameicans the Plains Warrior symbolized the American Indian.

But it did not last long—about a century, from 1775 to 1875. Within it were the seeds of its own deterioration: its predatory characteristics were antisocial and vicious—against other Indians as well as against the whites. Not all the Plains tribes were settled by 1875, but this was the last of the free life. And the culture ended as it had begun—with the dependence on the horse. Their horses were taken away from the Plains Indians—the buffalo was practically gone by 1875—and their spirit was stifled. On foot, the "centaur personality" was gone.

The Plains culture was essentially and fundamentally a horse culture, after it became a type culture, and it was historic. Some of the marginal cultures remained marginal; that is to say, they stuck to river valleys, lived in villages, and kept up their horticulture and sedentary arts—though adding the use of the horse. Others completely adapted themselves to the horse, and these form the type. The horse came from the white man's culture, from the Spaniards of Mexico and the Southwest. Accouterments, saddles, bridles, and other gear used with the horse were of Spanish origin. So were the names. The Indians generally mounted their horses from the right, not from the left as the white man did. They had meat—and lots of it, by hunting the buffalo—and they could go places. Then, and then only, could the Plains be completely traversed. Before there had been only the dog to carry burdens, save for the backs of their women, and there could be only short sorties of a few days' duration on the Plains to get a food supply—mainly, to hunt the buffalo. With the horse there was not only a revolution but an evolution. It was more than just using another animal instead of (or with) the dog and a faster means of travel; it meant the evolution of a whole new complex of ideas centering about the horse. First and mainly, the Indians became riders of the animal— *horsemen,* whereas they had been pedestrians before. Secondly, ideas regarding the horse pervaded their culture. The author believes the riding of the horse (and the "horse complex")—those ideas associated with the horse as wealth, or as a medium of exchange or money in trade; values of life which depended on the horse as a basis of war and depredation, as well as of the hunt; the addition of the horse as sacred in religion, with the sacrifice of horses to the Sun God; and scientific knowledge of horse-breeding, -gelding, and care—must be regarded as a completely new cultural trait, material and psychical. The significance of the horse in the culture of the Plains needs re-evaluation. The horse was not just a "big dog," and a faster one; it was the hub of the wheel of a new life—the historic Plains culture.

Everything now had to be accommodated to travel—quite lengthy travel. Changes came about: there were tipis rather than lodges, vessels that could be carried, and clothing and weapons to suit the new nomadism. Agriculture underwent change, and the bow and lance were shortened. Everything gave way to mobility.

Wissler says that the horse only augmented the culture of the Plains—that it added movement, or was a sort of catalyst.[3] It is true that there was a cluster of material and nonmaterial traits present, but there was no *typical* culture until the horse made it so.

Who were the typical Plains Indians? The Plains area contained thirty-one tribal groups. Of these, eleven were typical. These were

[3] "The Influence of the Horse in the Development of Plains Culture," *loc cit.*, 1–25.

95

the Assiniboins, Arapahoes, Blackfeet, Cheyennes, Comanches, Crows, Gros Ventres, Kiowas, Kiowa-Apaches, Sarsis, and Teton-Dakotas.[4]

Their chief traits were dependence on the buffalo, limited use of roots and berries, absence of fishing, lack of agriculture, the movable tipi, transportation by land only, use of the dog and travois (later the horse), no basketry or pottery, no true weaving, clothing of buffalo and deerskins, a special beading technique, high development of work in skins, special rawhide work (parfleches, cylindrical bags, etc.), circular shields, and weak development of work in wood, stone, and bone. Their art was strongly geometric and not symbolic. Their social organization was the simple band; they had a camp-circle organization, societies for men, Sun Dance ceremony, sweat house, and scalp dance.[5]

The horse made the Plains Indians independent. In the winning of the Plains, horseflesh was as important as human flesh—at times the latter, in fact, depended on the former. With horses, the Indians conquered the land, their enemies, and starvation. One day's good hunt could bring in enough food to last a year, or at least a season. Some earlier hunting techniques, such as the communal hunt, in which animals had been driven into corrals and over bluffs, were made obsolete. The horse split the large tribe into small bands, to subsist with their large per capita number of horses, although the tribe still came together for religious ceremonies and social gatherings, usually associated with the Sun Dance. The horse did more than augment their culture. Augmentation alone might apply to the marginal tribes such as the Mandan, who did not change their agriculture or pottery-making, or earth lodge or permanent village life, but used the horse, sparingly, for the hunt.

The eleven tribes of the Plains became horsemen. The horse made the Plains Indian a new man, psychically as well as phys-

---

[4] Clark Wissler, *The American Indian*, 218.

[5] *Ibid.*, 220. Fourteen tribes to the east were marginal: the Arikaras, Hidatsas, Iowas, Kansas, Mandans, Missouris, Omahas, Osages, Otos, Pawnees, Poncas, Santee-Dakotas, Yankton-Dakotas, and Wichitas. On the west were the Wind River Shoshonis, Uintahs, and Uncompahgre Utes; and on the northeastern border, the Plains-Ojibways, Plains-Crees, and Canadian Assiniboins. (*Ibid.*, 220–22.)

ically. It gave him wealth and prestige. It made him not just a hunter but a warrior, not just a warrior but a dangerous predator. It increased the power of the soldier societies even to conflict with that of the chiefs. The Indian closely paralleled the Mongol and the Arab in his way of life. Except for confederates and friendly tribes, he was antisocial. His predatory activities were mainly manifested against the Spanish, Mexican, and Texan peoples. In the later days of his cultural history, he had every reason to be antisocial. No Indians fought harder to keep their territory than did the Plains Indians. The war pony was the epitome of this predatory development. There were Indians who loved and cherished their war horses above every other thing. Such a horse even accompanied his owner to the grave and supposedly carried him into paradise. A war horse would not be used to fetch in bloody buffalo meat; a war horse had medicine made over him before going to war. Such a horse could mean life or death to his owner.

To sum up, the horse helped evolve the Plains culture, the elements of which it rapidly diffused from north to south. The horse not only augmented, conditioned, and modified a cluster of traits already in use but added a new trait, riding, that had far-reaching nonmaterial or mental associations. These associations developed the war complex and led the Indians to unify themselves into confederacies for waging war. The dog was not merely replaced as a burden bearer and drawer of the travois. The horse pulled a travois better, but dogs continued to be used as such. The horse was ridden; the dog had never carried a passenger. The whole area of the Plains was now opened up to "the man on horseback."

The horse raised men above the ground—when their feet were literally removed from the clay, psychologically they lost "feet of clay." This elevation placed the rider's sight upon far distant horizons, expanded his vision and quickened his ambition. With the leisure afforded by riding, his mentality leaped to new intrests, including war and wealth, trade, magic, and religion. In personality there arose the attitude of the "centaur," combining values of human and horse, and the man now dominated an environment

97

that had frustrated him as a walker over dangerous distances of
the Plains. He was master of his environment, no longer a slave
to it.

Love of a horse could even take an Indian into battle. Sanchez,
a White Mountain Apache chief, had a fine pony. The hostiles at
San Carlos, Arizona, "made the mistake of stealing a pony that
was the apple of Sanchez' eye." He went on "the warpath himself
with a dozen braves" and "threw in with the troops at San Carlos."
They aided Captain Adna Chaffee in the battle at Chevelon's Fork
(even saving Chaffee's life), and the fight was successful. The
ponies taken by the hostiles were recovered. Presumably Sanchez
got his horse back.[6]

Of the horse Indians, the Kiowas had the most horses per person
and were foremost in possessing the character traits associated
with the horse—bravery, predatism, and audacity. Notable also
was the specialization in the use of horses—reserving certain fleet
and picked horses for war and buffalo-hunting, never using them
as burden bearers or draggers of travois. This specialty belonged
to those of rank and wealth.

Had the Plains Indians not used the horse, they might have been
quietly pacified, perhaps destroyed, by the encroaching white man.
But with the horse and the development of the soldier societies and
the war complex, they were able to hold out and protect their land
in a striking manner until the Wars of the Plains in 1874 and 1875,
and the last aftermath at Wounded Knee in 1890.[7]

Perhaps all of the thirty-one tribes might have evolved into the
"type" in time, had no social forces disrupted their culture. They
tended to this in the warfare of the last Plains tribes in the north

[6] Britton Davis, *The Truth about Geronimo*, 10, 16–28.

[7] Since writing the above, I have read and found corroboration for these views,
especially in regard to the social and psychic values attached to the horse, in John C.
Ewers, *The Horse in Blackfoot Indian Culture*, B. A. E., *Bulletin 159*. See also Bernard Mishkin, *Rank and Warfare among the Plains Indians*, A. E. S., *Monograph
No. 3* (1940).

Frank Gilbert Roe, *The Indian and the Horse*, gives an exhaustive study of the
horse but prefers to follow Clark Wissler's idea that the horse merely added mobility to the Plains culture.

against the United States Army. The great pressure of the westward movement of white civilization ruined their native culture: there came diseases to which they had no immunity, alcohol that debauched them, trade that despoiled and corrupted them, and the loss of their land—and with it, food—to the gold seeker and the settler. But in order for the white man to accomplish this, the Indian had to be de-horsed.

THE GOLDEN AGE

From about 1740 to 1835, the Kiowas lived their Golden Age. After 1837, the time of their first treaty with the government, demands were made upon them, and those demands were increased by the treaty of 1867. Social forces began to change their culture.

The fur trade had brought the whites into the north; it also brought them south. After the Lewis and Clark expedition, the movement to Oregon, though hard, was feasible. Trails westward were easier through the southwest, except for the Indian menace, mainly the Kiowas. The crossing of the southern Plains was feeble at first, but it began to assume greater proportions with the profits to be made at Santa Fe. Expeditions to Santa Fe had to move in strength in order to contest their passing with the Kiowas and the Comanches. Wealth and adventure lured the settlers on, but the fear of the Indians held them back. The Santa Fe Trail, the gold rush to California in 1849, the Colorado gold rush in 1859—which was more pressing on the Indians of the southern Great Plains than the California rush—and the westward movement of the settlers, all contested their mastery of the area. The need of the government to protect its citizens from depredation and slaughter grew stronger and forced its army into action. The Kiowas and their allies never ceased to fight all forces that sought to cross and take their homeland.

After 1836 the Republic of Texas mushroomed, as did the states west of the Mississippi. For a while, the Americans could be distinguished from the Texans, whom the Comanches and Kiowas always considered their own fair game. After the Civil War, when

99

the United States had to force upon them the recognition of Texas as a part of the Union, they professed to accede but still hated and pillaged the Texans.

The beginning of the end of the Indians' native culture came when the loss of the buffalo, mainstay of their food supply, forced them onto the reservations; there, though they ate of rationed food, they made little attempt to change their way of life. The horses, the grass, hunting—their nomadic habits drew them off the reservations. So did the wagon trains crossing the Plains, which offered opportunity for plunder. Rewards and triumphs still awaited the young; the older men had had theirs and could foresee changes, but the pattern and traditions of the past still demanded the warrior training of youth.

Hounded by the military, forced to accede to their promises for peace, life became dull and the reservation an imprisonment for the Kiowas. Finally their cherished ways were forbidden, notable among them the Sun Dance and the medicine lodge. Robbed of their festivals, their religion was confused and their "medicine" was gone as a tribal force, even though individuals of "great medicine" arose among them. This was the real end of Kiowa prestige; their spirit was broken. It is true that they looked to the Ghost Dance Revival (1890) of the northern Plains Indians as a way of bringing back the golden past, but they partook of little of it. In part they turned to the Peyote Cult, and in part to the teachings of the missionaries working among them. From then on, down to the present, the "white man's road" was rocky and uphill.

CULTURE OF THE KIOWAS

The Kiowa was a typical tribe of the Plains, exhibiting the complex of cultural traits characteristic of the area. In general, these traits included nomadic movement, the skin tipi, household furniture and vessels of skin, paunches, horn, and some articles of wood, including tent poles. Bundles or envelopes of skin (parfleches) and small leather trunks made of stiffened rawhide carried clothing, objects, and provisions. They moved by the travois, while cradleboards on mothers' backs took care of the infants. Small children rode in saddles, sometimes lashed on, or on the travois, often with the puppies.

MATERIAL CULTURE

Buffalo furnished the main food and was the source of clothing, tipi covering, robes for cold-weather wear (coats or blankets), bedding, and products for household utility—paunches for water, leather bundles, sinew for thread, tough neck leather for shields, horns for cups or spoons, and various other uses, including brains for tanning skins, and hooves for glue. Other animals such as deer, antelope, and goats were also used for food and clothing. Women's dresses were often made of deerskin, decorated and embroidered. Moccasins were made of skins and embellished. The Kiowas, at least for some time, used long flaps on their moccasins; these were cumbersome in walking, and marked their distinctive riding habits. Narrow strips of tin were wound around the fringe of moccasins, and made "a tinkling sound as they walked." Fresh meats were roasted, broiled, or boiled; but most were sun dried in strips, pounded into a powder, mixed with oil, sometimes with flavorings of plants and berries, and made into pemmican, to be used in the winter. Battey said that the Kiowas and Comanches would eat all kinds of meat unless the "medicine tabus [taboos] it." They did not eat fish or birds. The Kiowas did not eat bear because it was taboo. The only use of the turkey was for feathers to wing arrows.[8] The preparation of food and the tanning, dressing, and sewing of clothing was woman's work.[9] Care of children was also women's work, but the men helped in baby-sitting and devoted much time to training the boys.

Use of Plants—Some vegetable food and products, such as fruits and nuts and leaves, were gathered in season; some, such as

[8] Thomas C. Battey, *The Life and Adventures of a Quaker among the Indians*, 323.

[9] Mooney, "Calendar History," 227ff.; Hodge, *Handbook*, I, 699–701; Battey, *Life and Adventures*; Gregg, *Commerce of the Prairies*, 331–32, 341.

tobacco, corn, beans, and melons from the Wichitas and Caddoes, were bartered with other tribes. Commonly used on the Plains was Tipsin or *Psorolea esculenta,* a root of a species of the bean family called *"pomme blanche."* Another plant used was the ground bean, *Falcata comosa,* stored in their nests by the meadow mice. The Indians robbed the nests but always left some for the mice, to show their "good heart."

Tobacco was usually mixed with sumac and other dried leaves to form kinnikinnick. The calumet pipe was used for social and religious smoking; it was meaningful: a man who smoked the pipe agreed, pledged his word, or made peace thereby. Small rolled cigaritos after the Mexican and Mescalero Apache fashion were often used for private smoking; the large calumet was used for gatherings and ritually smoked.

Battey mentioned the use of the starchy mesquite bean. It could be fermented into a drink, or its fermented meal made into dried cakes with a wine flavor.[10]

As a nomadic warring group with an economy based on the buffalo and dependent on the horse, one might think that plants were of little importance to the Kiowas. But, surprisingly, they used a number of plant foods in addition to the prevailing diet of buffalo meat. Some were used for food; some were used with tobacco for smoking; and some were curative, medicinal, and religious.[11]

Despite wide wandering, the Kiowas used many plants, some of which were ancient, and occurred in Montana and in the foothill regions of northern Wyoming. The majority of plants used were known during the period of the tribe's prominence. The exception is peyote, which belongs to the reservation days. Their basic foods, medicines, and symbolic plants extend to the tradi-

[10] Battey, *Life and Adventures,* 283.

[11] For detailed economic use of plants, see Paul A. Vestal and Richard Evans Schultes, *The Economic Botany of the Kiowa Indians as it Relates to the History of the Tribe.* See also Melvin Randolph Gilmore, "Uses of Plants by the Indians of the Missouri River Region," B. A. E., *Thirty-third Annual Report* (1919), 43–154.

tional home of the Kiowas in the north.[12] This ramifies Mooney's theory of a northern origin for the Kiowas. Because of a linguistic association of Kiowas and Tanoans, some ethnologists postulated a southern origin for the Kiowas before they moved north into the mountains. But it could mean that the Tanoans originated in the north. However, there is some doubt of a close association of Kiowas and Tanoans, according to B. L. Whorf and G. L. Trager.[13]

Tools—Tools were used for working skins and in household routine. Knives and arrow points were fashioned of chipped flint, and there were also tools of polished bone, buffalo horn, and deer antlers. Steel or iron for arrow points and skin scrapers later supplanted chipped flint. The women used a blade of flint, later of iron, attached to a curved handle of bone or antlers for defleshing and working skins. The hair was removed by sharp stones. Chipped flint was used for straightening arrow shafts. Knives and awls (for needles and punching) were also of chipped flint; some awls were of bone. Brushes for painting skins were made of light bone feathered on the edges. Paints were of colored earth, usually iron oxide, or of vegetable dyes before trading introduced prepared paints. Spoons, cups, and pounders for pemmican, mesquite beans, and seeds were made of wood or horn. Tweezers were used for removing hair.

Skins—Skins were used for containers, sacks or bags, parfleches, buffalo robes, clothing, and tipi coverings. Strips of rawhide (or horsehair) were used for ropes and thongs. Many skin or fur bags, tobacco pouches, quivers for arrows, and saddle bags, were employed. Rawhide made moccasin soles, shoes for horses, and small trunks for storage, especially of pemmican. Paunch vessels were

---

[12] Vestal and Schultes, *Economic Botany*, 83–84. Some of these are the purple coneflower (*Brauneria angustifolia*), used as a cough medicine, and not reported for other tribes; poison ivy (*Rhus radicans*), used in treatment of boils and sores, and not reported for other tribes; and dwarf plantain (*Plantago virginica*), used as one of the ancient symbols of the Kiowas for health, which no other tribes are known to have used.

[13] See "The Relationship of Uto-Aztecan and Tanoan," *A.A.*, Vol. XXXIX, No. 4, Pt. 1 (1937), 609–24.

water jars; leather or rawhide was also used for boiling. Most cooking was done by roasting over an open fire or baking in coals or ashes.

Clothing—Children wore little or no clothing. Men wore buck-skin shirts, long sleeved, with fringe of human hair in the side seams; leggings; breechcloths; soft- or hard-soled moccasins with long flaps that trailed the ground, all the flaps beaded and orna-mented with tinkling metal bits; war bonnets of eagle feathers; some fur caps; and furry buffalo robes, painted inside. Male ornaments were breastplates of pipestone, pendants on leather thongs, earrings, feathers in scalplocks, fur wrappings on hair braids, necklaces of shells and beads, sometimes a bear's tooth as fetish or amulet, and often silver disks attached to hair braids. Women wore wrap-around skirts, knee-length boots, and poncho-like upper shirts or full-length dress-and-belt skin robes. Their clothing was decorated with beads, elk teeth, and quills. Some tattooing was used. Feminine ornaments were earrings, pendants, pipestone necklaces, or necklaces of shells and beads. Women also used combs and mirrors obtained in trade, and painted their faces and hair-parts with vermilion.

Wood—Wood was used for lodgepoles, back rests (willow rods), arrow and lance shafts, cradles, coup sticks, and gift sticks (which were given to guests and were redeemable for one horse per stick). Cradles were early made of skins or fur bags; later they had frame-works of flat wood, with pointed projections at the tops (upright shaped), and hooded pockets of leather or skins, laced, and often elaborately beaded—apparently there was at this time no head-flattening.

Housing—Skin-covered tipis, with twenty or more supporting wooden poles, were painted according to heraldic or personal wishes of the owner. (Satanta had a red painted tipi). Large tipis more than twenty feet in diameter took thirty skins cut and fitted and sewn together. Inside the tipi was an inner band or wall of skins often elaborately painted to show personal exploits of the warrior. Tipis were placed in a formal circle only for the Sun Dance gathering in the summer. The Indians also had sweat lodges of wood and brush arbors of wood covered with tree branches to form outdoor living rooms.

Weapons—Bow and arrow, lance or spear (the length of the bow and lance was shortened for use on horseback), club or tomahawk were the common weapons. A self-bow and sinew-backed bow was often made of *bois d'arc,* and sometimes of bone; arrow shafts were usually of willow or dogwood. Circular shields of rawhide which came from the necks of buffalo were dried and hardened in fire, painted with heraldic or individual totemic designs, and kept in skin covers. Guns were obtained from the Spaniards and Anglo-Americans.

Hunting—There were drives into enclosures, and stampedes, through fire and trickery, over cliffs; there was also hunting in disguise, alone, or in small groups. Later hunters set out under the leadership of soldier police, all on fleet and trained hunting horses, rushed buffalo and shot them with arrows or lanced them with spears. With the gun they could kill great numbers of animals. The women followed the hunt and brought back meat on their own horses. Hunting and war horses were not used for meat-packing. The women used pinto or paint horses; men preferred solid-colored horses, especially those with black ears.

Transportation—All the Kiowas rode horses; the travois or drag was drawn by dogs or horses.

Saddles—Saddles were of wood, covered with rawhide and leather. Women's saddles had high pommels and cantles. Saddlebags were of leather; saddle blankets of leather or skins. Bridles of leather or hair were often single ropes attached to the horse's lower jaw. Lariats and girths were made of leather or hair. Hobbles and temporary horseshoes were rawhide. Quirts were plaited leather in the Spanish fashion. Decorations and paint were used on war horses.

Pottery—At first there was none. Later copper pots were obtained in trade.

Games—Hoop-and-pole, races, especially horse races with wagers, handball, and some other hand games were played by men and boys only. Dice (like ball games) were played by both men and women but in separate groups. Both men and women were given to gambling on the throw of the dice. Painted leather cards, in imitation of the white man's cards, were later used.

Pipes—Catlinite was fashioned into the large calumets or ceremonial pipes; smaller pipes were of stone, and later of corncobs for personal use; cigarettes were used after the Mexican fashion. Tobacco or kinnikinnick (sumac and other leaves) were chopped and mixed on flat boards.

Whistles—Whistles were made of bone.

Musical instruments—Drums, flutes, notched sticks, and sticks beat on rawhide comprised the Indians' musical instruments.

SOCIAL CULTURE: MAGIC AND RELIGION

The keepers of the medicine bundles or Ten Grandmother bundles were highly respected for their medicine. They were sought for cures of illness and for vision quests. Young men sought their personal medicine, totem, and name in the solitary vision quest, characteristic of the Plains. The sacred tipi holding the bundles offered sanctuary to anyone in need.

Taboos among the Kiowas concerned some distinctive foods and objects. They did not eat birds, but a bird such as the owl, turkey, and others might be a personal totem, talisman, or protective spirit. Turkeys existed in great flocks along the rivers of Texas, but they were not eaten by the Kiowas. Nor did they eat fish or bears. The bear was feared and venerated among most of the Plains tribes. The fact that the Comanches hunted and ate bears was believed to have caused Heap-of-Bears' death on a joint raiding party of Kiowas and Comanches against the Utes. Many Kiowa names were derived from dreams of the bear. Alligators and turtles, known to them from movements to the Texas Gulf Coast in their long range, also served as symbols for amulets and fetishes and designs. Their sacred shields, with special symbols and medicine, had their own special taboos.

Thomas Battey mentioned in 1873 that medicine was used on him to make him safe from some of the Comanches and Kiowas who did not approve of his being in the camp, who looked upon him as a spy and were disposed "if they meet me out anywhere, to put me out of the way." Sun Boy took Battey into a wood, where his medicine shield was placed on poles after the fashion of a painter's easel. He told Battey to remove the coverings and handle the shield, decorated with a representation of the sun, raven feathers, and with an attached bone whistle, made of the principal bone of an eagle's wing. Battey was then led back to Kicking Bird and Stumbling Bear.

> Kicking Bird explained the object of the adventure, which was to render me safe from the bullets or arrows of the Comanches and Cheyennes. I had looked the shield in the face, had handled the sacred ornaments, and the spirit residing in it had not been angry, and would now watch over and protect me.[14]

One day while Battey was a guest in the lodge of Stumbling Bear, Sun Boy and others came in. Ko-yone-mo (Stumbling Bear's daughter) brought her infant in its cradle on her back, seated herself by Sun Boy, and laid the cradle behind her. The side opposite Sun Boy was occupied by hooks with kettles of food which completely obstructed passage. Battey's name was called, and in moving to the entrance he had to cross in front of or behind Sun Boy. A part of Sun Boy's medicine prohibited anyone's passing between him and the fire. Battey passed behind Sun Boy and stepped over the baby's cradle.

> A smothered groan was uttered by every woman in the lodge, with the hand laid upon the mouth in token of bad medicine . . . . I had stepped over a living child as over a grave; that child would surely die; and unhappily, in less than three weeks its grave could be walked over . . . . I was awakened in the night by the death-wail in the lodge . . . . The child had been sick for nearly two weeks, and its death expected for some days . . . . I heard the passionate cries of the mother, whose face and arms were smeared in blood from gashes of her own inflicting . . . . [and] the wailing of family and near relatives,

[14] Battey, *Life and Adventures*, 208–209.

as they left the lodge for the burial, burst upon the ear in a prolonged dismal cry . . . . I heard also the groanings, singing, and unearthly noises made by the medicine-man in his attempts to drive away the evil spirits which were the cause of the child's sickness and death.[15]

Battey mentioned the personal taboo of a guest among the Kiowas. After returning from a visit to the Kickapoo camp with Kicking Bird, Battey found White Wolf, a Comanche chief, and his wife occupying the tipi where Battey had made his home. Dangerous Eagle and his brother Big Tree and their people arrived for a "big smoke." Battey was then asked if he had a looking glass in his trunk. He said he did and was asked to remove it from the lodge as it was not good medicine for White Wolf.[16]

The mother-in-law taboo was the most common one in social life. A man did not speak to his mother-in-law and practiced avoidance of her. A daughter-in-law did not speak to her father-in-law and avoided his presence. These customs were part of a taboo against incest. Some specific taboos were common and tribal; some were personal.[17]

The Kiowas interred dead bodies in the ground, or buried the bones of warriors retrieved from battle. All or most of a deceased person's property, including weapons, his cherished war pony, and offerings of food, was either burned or consigned to his grave. The scalp lock was buried with the dead. After death, a "give-away" might be held to distribute some gifts. The name of a dead person was not mentioned again, unless that name had been given by its owner to another and thus was no longer personal property. Mothers often visited the graves of their children for months and years. Wailing and cutting off of hair accompanied the sorrow of the loss (the only time either men or women ever cut their hair, except as a punishment for women, or when men cut off some locks over the right ear, an early tribal convention); cutting and slashing of face and body and cutting off of a finger memorialized the

[15] *Ibid.*, 242, 244–45. The Indians did not blame Battey, but accepted the death as fate.

[16] *Ibid.*, 237.

[17] *Ibid.*, 184, 211, 230, 244, 323.

dead. The period of mourning usually lasted until the hair grew out again. The women were especially horrible in appearance during their grieving period.[18]

Abandonment—The Kiowas abandoned their old people, even though they mourned for them. They were "thrown away" because it was feared that the evil spirits took possession of the aged. Battey said that there were several instances of abandonment among the Comanches and Wichitas, "but not among the Kiowas or Apaches";[19] other writers have mentioned it, however.

Often characterized as cruel by the whites, abandonment involved no malice or passion. It was rather the recognition of a reality and in the best interests of the larger group. Grief over the individual was shown, but it was an acceptance of fate. Those who were on the way to death were given up as dead, en route to the Spirit World. They were made as comfortable as possible and left to die. This was often voluntary on the part of the aged, the wounded, or the ill, and accepted with a religious submission. Rescues effected by whites often found the recipient ungrateful and emotionally disturbed.

Battey said that Dangerous Eagle (brother of Big Tree), whose wife had lost a child and had been very sick, had to remain behind when the camp moved. Later he arrived with his wife carried on a litter dragged by a mule. Shortly thereafter, Dangerous Eagle was again delayed by his wife's illness, which continued several days before she expired. Battey said:

> Before leaving, I saw women engaged in digging her grave. This led me to fear that the patience of her husband was so nearly exhausted by his repeated detentions, that violent means would be resorted to if she did not soon die. I have known instances among these people—though not among the Kiowas—of men becoming discouraged, and killing their wives with their own hands, when they have been for some time sick, and their medicine (jugglery) failing to effect a cure. Indeed, I know a Comanche chief who cut the throat

---

[18] *Ibid.*, 57, 91–92, 244–45, 325; Gregg, *Commerce of the Prairies*, 351.
[19] *Life and Adventures*, 91.

of his wife for that reason. She was sick a long time, and their medicine did not cure her; so, to avoid the inconvenience of caring for a sick wife, who was not able to care for herself, after making "medicine of preparation," to fit her for a happy reception in the unknown land of spirits, he took her life, though mourning her untimely death. Such deeds are rare among them, but are still sometimes practiced, they setting but small value upon human life, and sick or very aged people are a great hinderance [*sic*] to their wild, roving, unsettled way of life.[20]

An instance of abandonment was found among the Comanches, some of whom had joined the Kiowas under Kicking Bird in a settlement near the agency in 1873. Ten Bears, head chief of the Yamparika Comanches, was left with the whites by his people, "thrown away" during a long illness by all save his son who arrived two hours after his death. Battey said that some old people even took their own lives when abandoned.[21]

THE HORSE AS A FACTOR IN SOCIAL CHANGE

The use of the horse particularly marks the Kiowas, as it did the Comanches. The Kiowas had the greatest number of horses per person of all tribes on the Plains. The horse was the medium of exchange and the gift of generosity and of peace. Horses served for buying a wife or indemnifying injured parties. Great numbers were kept as wealth, and in hard times the animal might serve as food.[22] The attitudes of the Spanish and later Mexican "man on horseback" or "*haciendado*," marking superior status, also characterized the Kiowas. At religious festivals, horses were sacrificed to the Sun. Special horse medicine came to be used by some Plains

---

[20] *Ibid.*, 143–44.

[21] *Ibid.*, 90–92.

[22] *Ibid.*, 133 *et seq.* Battey said he saw a "young colt dressed" for food when the Indians' rations gave out, and, having lost his appetite, decided to accompany Kicking Bird into the agency.

The horse was both a material trait and a basis of a complex—a psychical trait. In economic life, its role cannot be exaggerated; it also was interwoven in rank and warfare.

tribes, and the Blackfeet developed a horse-medicine society.

The use of the horse made the procuring of food, meat and fat, easy and abundant. It made the use of buffalo meat a specialization—the chief food in their diet. It gave leisure for other activities. The horse was the foundation for what came to be the major business of the Kiowas—raiding, stealing horses and mules, taking captive slaves and hostages. The south drew the Kiowas as a magnet, for in Mexico there were the wealth, the fine horses, and the people for slaves and wives—which were the same thing. Captive children, who were valorous enough, were adopted and trained as their own, and actually replaced their own losses. These people certainly believed in the efficacy of education, in environment rather than heredity, for once trained, the captives became a part of the tribe.

As the Indians were given more and more to raiding, scalps, formerly a matter of bravery and valor, could be had by stealth rather than by hand-to-hand battle. Annual raids, sometimes lasting two years, were made into northern Mexico. There could be had silver; clothing; various ornaments; woven blankets of bright colors; the fleetest horses—many of Arabian blood; and women of beauty—pure white, mestizo, or pure Indian. The young Mexican women were especially attractive in their youth, though inclining to loss of figure and increase in obesity with age. They were generally docile and easily incorporated into the tribe, although captives out of Texas were not so tractable. In Mexico the people gathered in numbers about their towns for protection, leaving the exposed haciendas and rancherias to those brave enough to stay. The Mexican police were few, relatively inefficient, and no match for a large Indian band. The frontier receded before the dreaded onslaughts of the Kiowas and their allies. Guns and ammunition came into usage by the Indians, and with this added increment to their culture, they became formidable opponents and could fight the white man with his own weapons. They were always behind the evolution of the gun used against them, but they procured new types constantly.

Great herds of horses necessitated grass for forage. Everything led the Kiowas and Comanches south in the spring—the buffalo, the grazing, the opportunities for their peculiar way of life. For some time they were undisputed in their field of activities and in their range. Other Indians, loath to admit them into their hunting grounds, feared, fought, and were vanquished by them—the Mescaleros and Lipan Apaches moved back and actually out of their old indigenous area.

Social Organization of the Kiowas

PHRATRY

Ruth Murray Underhill states that the Kiowas had phratries and a mother clan that was endogamous.[23] Mooney, who knew the people better than any investigator, claimed that the "clan system does not exist among the Kiowa, and there is no evidence that they ever had it," and that it did not exist among the majority of the Plains tribes. Neither, according to Mooney, did the Kiowa-Apaches have any phratries or clans. He stated that the Kiowas, before being confined to reservation life, were grouped into two general divisions known as "T'o-k'inahyup" ("cold men" or men of the north) and "Gwá-halego" (from the Comanche name "Kwáhadi"). These names, however, were geographic and equivalent to "northern" and "southern," the former ranging along the Arkansas River and the latter associated with the Kwahadi Comanches. They were "merely temporary local designations and not proper band or gentile names," and ceased to be of any practical importance after they reached the reservations.[24]

KINSHIP SYSTEM AND BEHAVIOR

The Cheyennes and Arapahoes represent a simple and basic type of kinship—the generation type, or classification type, where col-

[23] *Red Man's America*, 155, Table 5.
[24] Mooney, "Calendar History," 227.

lateral and lineal relatives are classed together.[25] The Kiowas and Kiowa-Apaches seem to vary only slightly from this type.[26]

In this system the father's brother is classed with the father, and the mother's sister with the mother. Separate terms are used for mother's brother and father's sister. Grandparents are distinguished according to sex, and grandparental terms are extended to their siblings and spouses. In ego's generation older brothers and older sisters are distinguished, while younger siblings are classed together. These terms are extended to both parallel and cross-cousins. The children of brothers are sons and daughters on the male side, or nephews and nieces on the female side. The children of sisters are the reverse. All children of sons, daughters, nephews, and nieces are called grandchildren.

In regard to affinal relations, the Cheyennes classify the father-in-law with the grandfather, the mother-in-law with the grandmother, and the children-in-law with the grandchildren.

In ego's generation, a man's wife's siblings are classed with his sibling's spouses as brothers-in-law or sisters-in-law; and a wife's brother's wife are called brother and sister respectively, and their children classed accordingly. A woman classifies her husband's relatives in the same way.

The Comanche kinship system is quite different from the general Plains pattern and in keeping with Plateau affiliation. The Southern Athapascans, Lipans, Kiowa-Apaches, and Jicarilla Apaches, vary toward a type represented by the Chiricahua Apaches and Mescalero Apaches.[27]

Behavior patterns of the Kiowas were interesting. A mother held an intimate relationship with her son, but a father trained and pushed his son to prominence, and later gave feasts and paved his way to the future. Sons respected their fathers and the older men. Boys were not punished corporally but could be shamed and ridiculed by the older men. The attentions of the whole family attached

---

[25] *Ibid.*, 227.

[26] See "Cheyenne and Arapaho Kinship," in Fred Eggan (ed.), *Social Anthropology of North American Tribes* (1937), 42.

[27] *Ibid.*, 89–91.

to a boy, and he received more notice than a girl, particularly if he was a favorite son.

Grandparents and grandchildren were on intimate terms. Grandparents were teachers as well as companions—"they got along." They could even use obscene language, play jokes, and indulge each other. The association with grandparents was the first schooling of a child, and most unfortunate was the child who did not have grandparents.

Avoidance of affinal relatives was a strict and formal behavior pattern. A man could tease and joke with his wife's sister, because he stood in relationship to her as a future husband. He could even speak vulgarly to her with social sanction. Marriage of sisters was the most common type of polygyny, and worked out well because sisters got along with each other and had little jealousy.

The basic social and economic group was made up of brothers and their wives and children, and sisters and their families.[28] Friends or blood brothers also joined the group. (Young men became blood brothers and carried the relationship through life, calling each other "brother" and treating their children as sons.) This basic group was related affinally to other families and kept up close associations by visiting with them, especially during the Sun Dance.

KIOWA-APACHE KINSHIP AND BEHAVIOR

The Kiowa-Apaches have a classificatory system, since lineal and collateral kin are merged.[29] The Kiowa-Apaches were and are actually a large endogamous band, related to each other by blood or marriage. They were closely associated with the Kiowas, and had some, though limited, intermarriage with them. Some of the Kiowas said that the Kiowa-Apaches had a much larger admixture of Mexican blood than the Kiowas did. At present the tribe proper has about 150 members. There are many more that are not pure-

28 *Ibid.*, 90.
29 See "Kiowa-Apache Social Organization" in *ibid.*, 103–108.

bloods. There are admixtures with whites and with other Indians such as Cheyennes, Arapahoes, and Comanches.

In kinship pattern they are close to the Kiowas. There are four categories of kin: father and anyone he calls brother; mother and anyone she calls sister; anyone father calls sister; and anyone mother calls brother. All relatives in the second ascending generation are grandparents. In the third ascending generation, the men are called older brothers and the women are called older sisters.

In ego's own generation, distinctions are made between older and younger brother and older and younger sister. This applies to both parallel and cross-cousins. One's own children and those of a sibling of the same sex are classified similarly and distinguished from the children of a sibling of the opposite sex.

A man calls his own son and his brother's son *"jaan;"* his own daughter and his brother's daughter, *"tceyan."* His sister's children are grouped together and called by a single term, *"dayan."* Similarly, a woman calls her own and her sister's son *"jaan,"* and her own and her sister's daughter, *"tceyan."* Her brother's children she distinguishes from her own also by sex, calling her brother's son *"cindjaan,"* and her brother's daughter, *"tetcaan."*

When ego is male, there are three primary categories in the first descending generation; there are four when ego is female. In the second descending generation, all relatives are "grandchild," the same term for "grandparent"—*"soyan."* In the third descending generation, great-grandson becomes "younger brother" and great-granddaughter becomes "younger sister," as far as they go, but the Kiowa-Apaches say that "old people never live that long."

Affinal relatives were of three categories: *"tcetcaan,"* wife, or *"denan,"* husband; *"tcana,"* in-law; and *"zedan,"* spouse not one's own. Other affinal relatives were classed with blood relations. Sibling terms were not used for friends, but sibling behavior patterns obtained, and their children were considered as siblings both in terminology and behavior.

With changing social conditions, older behavior patterns are being discarded. But pronounced patterns such as mother-in-law and father-in-law avoidance have not lost their importance. The uncle-nephew (mother's brother) relation is an intimate one. The uncle is indulgent to his nephew. The grandparent-grandchild relationship is also intimate. Jokes and obscenities are permissible to grandchildren of both sexes. The training of a son is by the father and the older male relatives, and in this respectful relationship there is no teasing or joking.

A close association of brothers, or friends treated as brothers, is of long usage. Brother and sister patterns of close association are found, but after adolescence there comes avoidance and formality. Even so, brother looks after his sister's interests, and his consent is necessary for both marriage and divorce.

THE CAMP CIRCLE

The Kiowas had six subtribes or bands. The extinct Kuato probably made a seventh. These divisions were political; they were not clans or gentes based on marriage relations. Each band had its own chief, subject to leadership of the tribal head chief. Some bands had their own "medicine" or religious ceremonies. The bands may have represented distinct, though related, tribes in the early days. The Kiowa-Apache tribe was distinct but had been confederated with the Kiowas from their earliest days.

For all tribal gatherings the bands or subtribes followed a recognized plan for camping in a circle:[30]

The divisions, in order of their seating, were:

1. *Kata, or Biters and Arikaras.* This was the largest division. It occupied the first place in the camp circle, south of the door or entrance. Dohasan, the great chief of the Kiowas for over thirty years, belonged to this group. His family held the hereditary duty of furnishing the buffalo for the Sun Dance. The Kata represented the aristocracy of the tribe. The name came from a close trading association with the Arikaras or "Rees," not from Arikara admix-

[30] Mooney, "Calendar History," 227.

116

ture. Mooney believed that the word might have been a substitute for a discarded name, since many Kiowa names were not used after an individual's death.[31]

2. Kogui, or Elks. This division was noted for its leadership in war ceremonies. Adate, whose camp was destroyed by the Osage

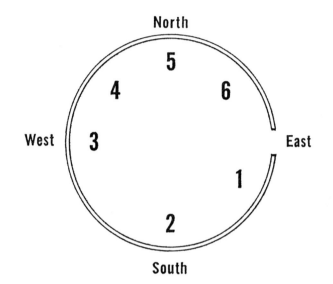

massacre in 1833, was its chief, and to it also belonged Satanta and Big Bow of later years.

3. Kaigwu, or Kiowas proper. This was probably the original Kiowa group. It commanded respect as the keeper of the sacred Taime and the K'adô Dô, the priestly tipi at the Sun Dance. Because of its small numbers, individuals of other bands sometimes camped with this division.

4. Kingep, or Big Shields. This division owned a sacred image used in the Sun Dance, but it was later lost.

5. Semat, Thieves or Kiowa-Apaches. This division was a distinct tribe that had been part of the tribal circle since earliest memories.

[31] *Ibid.*, 228.

6. *Kongtalyui, Black Boys or Síndiyúis.* This band was called the children of Sindi, the great mythical hero of the Kiowas.

7. *Kuato, or Pulling Up.* This division was exterminated by the Dakotas about 1780. Its members spoke a peculiar dialect, and their place in the tribal camp circle is not known.

RANK AND WARFARE

The Kiowas had distinct social classes based upon rank. Rank was obtained largely through military exploits, religious power, and wealth. Wealth alone was not sufficient to place one in first rank, but associated with war or religion, it had its effect upon the great as well as the common people. There was some mobility in social class.

Onde (Ondeido), or first rank, represented the aristocracy. The men of this rank were great warriors, important *topadok'is,* the owners of the ten medicine bundles, and the wealthy, if they also possessed fine military records. To be *onde*-born was a birthright. Women were also *onde. Ondes* were generous, courteous, and considerate. If cruel or mean, they lost rank. Perhaps about 10 per cent of the tribe belonged to this rank.

Ondegup'a, or second rank, represented a much larger group, consisting of about 40 per cent of the tribe. These were the small *topadok'is,* those second in war honors, though perhaps wealthy, warriors struggling up the ladder of success, and some captives, medicine men, and persons of limited property.

Kaan (koon), or third rank, were the poor people who comprised about half of the total population.

Dapom were few. They were the no-accounts or misfits. Some were bad characters. Some were lazy and lacking in ambition, sometimes considered to be crazy.

The classes were not static. Vertical mobility was constant, and men could rise to high rank by important deeds and public acclaim. Class could also be lost by misdeeds—by lying, stealing, killing a fellow tribesman, or by moral weakness.

Attainment of high rank became a prerogative of the superior class. The wealthy could afford it. As the warrior gained honor, he also gained wealth by horses. Perpetuation of rank helped to create an aristocratic caste. Women were *onde* mainly by being born into it, or by marriage to an *onde* man. Women also achieved rank by proficiency in crafts, possession of good looks, and by becoming famous in women's sports. Social, economic, and religious characteristics attached to the *onde*, and it tended to become a powerful hereditary elite. Punishment was lopsided—the *onde* did not lose caste for many offenses. Having one's horses stolen could lead to penury, but not to loss of *onde*.

Bernard Mishkin says that the horse, rank, and warfare were inextricably interwoven in Plains society.[32] Horse ownership led to acquiring more horses, i.e., wealth and opportunities in war. In the climb to fame as a warrior greatest credit came from counting first coup (the Kiowas allowed four counts on the body of an enemy), charging the enemy while one's party was in retreat, rescuing a comrade while one's party was retreating before the charging enemy, and charging a leading man of the enemy alone (comparable to suicide).

Lesser credit came from killing an enemy, counting second coup, getting wounded during battle in hand-to-hand combat, fighting on foot, counting third and fourth coups, serving as a *topadok'i,* and stealing horses.

Warfare was the most honorable profession for men. War raids were of two kinds: small raids for horses and wealth, and larger raids for revenge or obtaining scalps, customarily tribal in personnel. These usually set out after vows made at the Sun Dance. A travel song, or *gua-dagya*, helped enlist recruits to smoke the pipe. A large party usually had four captains. The most common raids came to be the small ones for horses.

Raiding for horses and war honors by unusual bravery were the activities that led to tribal success. Deeds on the field of battle gained a man the title of *kietai* or *kataiki,* warrior. Performing four deeds out of a list of twelve or more gave one the right to *kietai*. Great bravery elevated one to *kietaisopan,* or great warrior. He

[32] *Rank and Warfare among the Plains Indians*, 63.

was then eligible for the Koitsenko honorific society. Recitations of deeds were made and checked upon by eyewitnesses or other warriors, and vouched for by swearing on the pipe.

War parties were family, *topadoga,* or tribal, with the war leader, or *topadok'i,* in absolute control and exercising a military discipline. Positions of authority were for the full-bloods. Captives, half-bloods, and quarter-bloods might become notable warriors, or be adopted by prominent families, but did not become *topadok'is.* Rank and honors usually fell to the sons of prominent men, whose elders and kindred helped them by giving away gifts and feasts and opening opportunities for success and the achieving of high status—making them "friends of the people." The war record was the one most important criterion of status. Favorite sons, *ades,* were loaded with wealth and special indulgences. A family often spent its wealth unduly on such sons, bringing to mind Thorstein Veblen's "conspicuous waste" to be found in modern society.

MILITARY ORGANIZATION

The Kiowas possessed an elaborate military or warrior organization known as *Y'apahe* (warriors). Among the Plains tribes, similar groups were commonly called the dog-soldier societies, from an early association of dogs in visions or dreams. There were six divisions of soldier societies, the first, Polanyup, or Rabbits, including all the younger boys.[33] One might belong to it indefinitely, or go into one of the other societies: Adaltoyuo, Young Sheep; Tsentanmo, Horse Headdresses; Tonkonko, Black Legs; Taupeko, Skunkberry People or Crazy Horses; Ka-itsenko (or Koitsenko), Real or Principal Dogs, or probably horses.

The Kiowa societies were roughly graded according to age and

[33] Mooney, "Calendar History," 229; Battey, *Life and Adventures,* 14. There were no girls in the society, as claimed by Andele, or Andres Martinez, in Rev. J. J. Methvin, *Andele, or the Mexican Kiowa Captive.* In the above book Martinez said that the Kiowa-Apache Rabbits included all children, boys and girls. Kiowas and Kiowa-Apaches differed slightly. See also Robert H. Lowie, "Societies of the Kiowa," American Museum of Natural History, *Anthropological Papers* (hereinafter cited as A. M. N. H., *A.P.*), Vol. XI, Pt. 11 (1916), 837–51.

achievement. Men of ordinary families usually entered the Adal-toyuo society first. Some favored sons of prominent families joined an older men's group immediately, and the family gave gifts to the membership for that privilege.

The Koitsenko honorific society included the greatest warriors of the tribe and was limited to ten members. According to Captain William P. Clark, the Kiowa-Apaches had three bands, Big Horse, Raven, and Swift Fox.[34] The dog soldiers were leaders at tribal ceremonies and served as camp police, *akacitas*. They also served as guards on the hunt and as courageous warriors.

Battey described the work of the soldier-police while he was living with the Kiowas in 1873:

> After the close of the medicine dance, I continued in the Kiowa camp some three weeks, during which time the men were busy in killing buffalo, and the women in curing the meat and preparing skins for making lodges.
>
> Being determined that none of their thoughtless young men should go raiding in Texas, and thereby bring trouble upon the tribe, the Kiowas, immediately after the whole tribe got together on Pecan Creek, organized a military system, under the control of the war chiefs, which was put immediately into operation. By this a strong guard of soldiers were continually watching, day and night, while in camp, to prevent any such enterprise from being undertaken. In moving from place to place, these soldiers marched on each side of the main body, while a front guard went before, and a rear guard behind, thus preventing any from straggling.
>
> Their buffalo hunts were conducted in the same military order. The soldiers, going out first, surrounded a tract of country in which were a large herd of buffalo; and no one might chase a buffalo past this ring guard on pain of having his horse shot by the soldiers.
>
> Within the ring, hundreds of men on horseback were chasing and shooting those huge creatures, with revolvers, or bows and arrows,

[34] Mooney, "Calendar History," 230, cited by Captain William P. Clark, *The Indian Sign Language*. Methvin, from Andele's information, wrote about the Rabbits, and said that there were five orders of dog soldiers—probably in addition to the Rabbits. (Methvin, *Andele*, 143–72.)

until each had killed as many as his female attendants could skin and take care of; when the day's sport is ended.

Not so the work of the women. When her lord has killed a buffalo, the woman's work begins. She has to skin it, the meat to secure, and all to pack upon ponies or mules, and carry to camp, where the meat must be cured.[35]

HERALDIC SYSTEM

Heraldry had its place in the ornamentation of shields and tipis. Special taboos and regulations belonged to the heraldic tipis. At one time, there were some fifty shield patterns used in the Kiowa and Kiowa-Apache tribes.

PERSONAL NAMES

There were no clan names. Personal names were given to children soon after birth, usually by the grandparents or relatives. The name might commemorate some event of prowess or might be hereditary, actually given away by its owner. Names could be changed and often were. Dream names were secured in the vision quest common to the Plains Indians. A warrior might give away his name as an honor to the recipient. Unless given to another, a name died with its owner, and dropped out of the language.[36]

MARRIAGE CUSTOMS AND DIVORCE

Marriage was simple. Usually gifts of horses were made to the parents of the intended bride by the prospective groom's friends. Relatives and the girl's brother helped the bride's parents reach a decision. Simple contract, or occasionally elopement, was the usual form of gaining a wife. Girls usually married at the age of fourteen; boys, at sixteen. The husband generally went to live among the wife's people, but occasionally the new couple might

[35] *Life and Adventures*, 185–86.
[36] Mooney, "Calendar History," 231.

live near the groom's parents. Residence with the wife's family did not result in matrilineal clans, however. The father exercised more control over his children than among tribes having the clan system and mother right. There was no fixed rule of inheritance, but band name, shield, and tipi usually were patrilineal. Polygyny was usual for the chiefs and warriors, and had utility where male mortality was high in hunting and in warfare. The father of Te'bodal was famous for having had ten wives. In the old days, two wives was the usual number. Monogamy was common, also, for it was the most economical type of marriage. The sororate and levirate obtained; that is, it was common for a man to marry his deceased wife's sister, and for a widow to marry her deceased husband's brother.

Divorce was easy but not common. If a wife wished to leave her husband, her brother usually had to give his consent. Adultery was punished by taking property or horses from the guilty man or by destroying his property. An aggrieved husband could kill the offending woman or cut off her nose. More drastic punishment than nose-cutting, such as the casting of "a woman on the prairie," where the members of a soldier society raped the victim, probably did not often obtain among the Kiowas.[37] This practice meant that

[37] See Hoebel, *The Cheyennes*, 95–96. This was also a type of sacrifice to the gods, as when Long Knives, who encountered bad luck in putting on the Holy Hat to wear in battle, pledged himself to "give a woman to be passed on the prairie." See Grinnell, *The Fighting Cheyennes*, 88. The same association adhered to the treatment of captive white women by Kiowas and Comanches. Kiowas returning to the reservation from raids in Texas boasted of ravishing women "all they wished" and then "throwing them away" on the prairie.

An outraged husband invited all the unmarried members of his military society, except his wife's relatives, to a feast on the prairie. "There the woman is raped by each in turn. Big Footed Woman was forced into intercourse with forty or more of her husband's confreres when a young wife. She survived it and lived to be a hundred, but no one ever married her afterwards. Tassel Woman was nearly dead when she was rescued by Blue Wing and his wife." At times, relatives fought the soldier bands to protect a woman, and "Little Sea Shell fled to the wife of the Keeper of the Holy Hat, for the band was on the march and the Hat Keeper's wife had the Buffalo Hat Bundle on her back at the time," and found sanctuary. Hoebel said that the deed ran counter to public opinion. Men who participated in a gang rape were taunted by the women in the camps and hung their heads in shame. The right of the husband to do this to his wife was probably very old and had sacred significance.

the woman was "any man's wife." It was tantamount to death, although some women did survive it.

The Kiowas had a head chief, chiefs of the subtribes or bands, and war chiefs or military officers. In early days the head chief was feared and respected and exercised almost despotic power.

The chief or band leader was called *topadok'i*. The band or group he led was the *topadoga,* the primary political and economic unit in the tribe. A head chief or civil chief was a leading *topadok'i* chosen by all the *topadok'is* from their councils. In the population of some 1,600 to 1,800 people there were ten to twenty bands. The band might have only ten tipis or fifty or more tipis, depending on the strength and sagacity of its leader. The band was largely a group of close relations. Distant kindred tended to join the most illustrious leader of their family. The group was fluid because of the death of a leader or loss of influence of a leader (that is, if the followers elected to follow another leader). Nonrelative members were usually those lacking kindred or the poor, who were welcome as a labor group. The band leader's responsibilities were economic and governmental; he maintained law and order, and gave protection from enemies. Advisory men and police helped at certain times, particularly during the hunt and the Sun Dance.

Band groupings developed with nomadic life on the Plains, and were economic as well as political. These kindred groups, voluntarily joined, would spread out after the annual Sun Dance and community hunts, and earn their own subsistence. Geographic environment seems to have been the causative factor in the development of the band.

The war chiefs could rise to prominence by bravery and sagacity in leading exploits. War chiefs were not despots; they had to have the confidence of their followers and were chosen in a democratic process. The last great head chief was Dohasan, or "Little Bluff," who died in 1866. From then on, there was no complete allegiance given to one chief because the tribe was divided over which policy to pursue toward the whites. Lone Wolf led the war group, and Kicking Bird led the peace party until his death in 1875. In 1879, Lone Wolf, who was then head chief, gave his name to a younger man, his nephew, and the younger Lone Wolf was still recognized as chief in 1896.[38]

CARE OF CHILDREN AND EDUCATION

Children were appreciated and well cared for. But the hard life of the Plains took its toll in infant life, and children were not numerous in the early days. There were many childless couples who adopted captives and reared them as their own. Many writers have remarked on the love and affection heaped upon Indian children. They were taught and rewarded rather than punished and corrected. They were regarded as individual personalities in the best traditions of modern progressive education. There was no slapping or switching of children, so commonly found in whites and abhorred by the Indians. Crying was not tolerated, and a baby soon learned not to cry. If he did so, the cradleboard was placed in the woods, and the baby squalled unheeded. A crying child could be dangerous to the safety of a camp.

History, religion, and tribal lore came to the children daily. They were also taught good manners and respect for their elders. Children learned to ride almost as soon as they learned to walk. Their education was a direct process. Little girls helped their mothers in gathering wood, water, and performing household duties. Little boys learned to care for horses, use weapons and lariats, and imitate the warriors. Their play activities imitated the life of their elders. They were given public recognition and rewards— usually ponies. As boys grew up, their fathers trained them. At the age of twelve or thirteen, boys were old enough to join the hunting and war parties, in order to learn from the older men.

Battey said that boys had more attention given to them than

[38] Mooney, "Calendar History," 233.

girls. Boys were seldom chided, but if one became unbearably insolent, cutting sarcasm used by older men caused him "to conduct
himself with more becoming dignity and decorum."[39]

The Cheyenne chiefs and men told John H. Seger, superintendent
of the Indian school, that men did not have time to manage children. That was done by the medicine man. They said:

> The children obey them and we do not have to bother with them.
> We are chiefs and have charge of the soldiers and the management
> of tribal affairs. We cannot bother ourselves with the discipline of
> children. You better get a medicine man to run your school.[40]

CHARACTER

The Kiowas, Mooney said—perhaps regretfully, for Mooney
liked the Kiowas—were "below the standard," or deficient in many
qualities. But Kicking Bird was an exception. He was honorable,
friendly, and sought to bring his people to conformity with the
wishes of the agency control. Battey formed a deep friendship
with him and commended him highly.

Mooney said:

> Tribal traits are strongly marked among Indians. The Sioux are
> direct and manly, the Cheyenne high-spirited and keenly sensitive,
> the Arapaho generous and accommodating, the Comanche practical
> and business-like, but the Kiowa, with some honorable exceptions,
> were deficient in all these qualities. They have the savage virtue of
> bravery, as they have abundantly proven, but as a people they have
> less of honor, gratitude and general reliability than perhaps any
> other tribe on the plains. The large infusion of captive blood, chiefly
> Mexican, may have influenced them either for good or for evil.[41]

Certain writers who met the Kiowas liked them. Catlin and
Abert found them friendly. Abert was particularly drawn to them.

[39] Battey, *Life and Adventures*, 330.
[40] John H. Seger, *Early Days among the Cheyenne and Arapahoe Indians*, 63.
[41] "Calendar History," 234.

Mooney says that others have described them in unfavorable terms. Gregg, in 1844, described them as one of the most savage tribes of the western prairies. General John Pope, in 1870, called them the most faithless, cruel, and unreliable Indians of the Plains, the worst Indians that the government had had to deal with in the previous twenty-five years. General Philip Sheridan particularly disliked Satanta and Lone Wolf and felt that they should have been hanged after Custer's Washita campaign. General George Armstrong Custer did not like Satanta and some of his group. Tatum, as Indian agent, fully realized their deficiencies. Battey, as minister and teacher, though friendly and anxious to win the Kiowas to a new way of life, knew that they were guilty of crimes and that all of the tribe were involved. Kicking Bird prepared the way for Battey to live with the tribe, to teach and counsel them. Battey gained the respect of the Kiowas, but the war party was always against the general agency and the reservation system. Some of the hostile Kiowas planned to hold Battey as a hostage, and there were plots to take his life. Kicking Bird and Battey became staunch friends, even though Kicking Bird insisted that Battey go back to the agency until conditions became more peaceful within the tribe.[42]

In 1873, Battey described the notorious Kiowa raiders who had refused to settle on the reservation—Big Bow and White Horse. Battey said that, while camping with the Kiowas on North Fork of Red River:

> . . . an indian rode up to me, asking me if I knew him. I at once recognized in him the notorious Kiowa raider Big Bow, who has, probably, killed and scalped more white people than any other living Kiowa; and who, with his brother raider, White Horse, has been for years the terror of the frontiers, not only of Texas, but of Kansas, Colorado, and New Mexico. These two men, with small companies of their braves, have been continually going up and down, not as roaring lions, but prowling about in secret, seeking whom they might destroy; and woe to the white man, woman, or child, who fell in their way.

[42] *Ibid.*, 235; Battey, *Life and Adventures*, 16.

Big Bow and White Horse were responsible for the raid on the Lee family of Texas (four killed, three captured), the captives from which were purchased by Kicking Bird and delivered to the Wichita Agency; and, said Battey:

> Big Bow has a more treacherous and ferocious countenance than when I last saw him,—quite the reverse of his brother raider, White Horse, who wears an open smiling face, and is a much more powerful man physically, as well as many years his junior. Neither of them are likely to atone for the evil they have done . . . . [White Horse], though terrible as an enemy, I think is capable of warm friendship.[43]

HOSPITALITY

The Kiowas were a kind and hospitable people to their guests. One even cooked bread for Battey on sticks, so that it would not be soiled by the ashes of the fire.

In 1873, Battey related an instance of hospitality which occurred among some Comanches then camped near the Kiowas. Battey was forced to stop overnight at a camp on his way to Kicking Bird's camp. Imagine his consternation when he found it was the camp of White Wolf, one of the most determined and unfriendly of the Comanche chiefs.

> Yet now I was wholly in their power,—had as it were, voluntarily placed myself in their hands. In answer to their direct questions, I told them I was alone, and was unarmed. After a few moments' consultation, White Wolf said to me, "The sun will soon go away; will you sit down by me, and sleep?" I answered, "My mules are tired, and I came to your camp for that purpose." He replied, "That is good; when the sun comes back, you may go on your road."

The mules were taken care of by White Wolf's wife, supper was served, and:

> I partook of the rude cheer of a hostile chief, rendered propitious by his ideas of the sacred rights of hospitality . . . . After breakfast in

[43] Battey, *Life and Adventures*, 140–51.

White Wolf's lodge, I was soon *en route* for the camp of my destination, accompanied by the wife and little daughter of "mine host," who went with me several miles, in order to answer the challenges of the several Comanche pony herders whom I would have to pass. Afterwards they pointed out Kicking Bird's camp to me, and left me to pursue my journey alone.

What a lesson is here for civilized man! A rude chief of an unfriendly tribe of savages, whose hand is skilled in the shedding of blood, manifesting such a sense of the sacredness of the rights of hospitality, as not only to receive and entertain one whom he regarded as an enemy, but, after having done this, set him on his right road in peace.[44]

RELIGION

The Kiowas were polytheistic and animistic. There was a general belief in supernatural agencies. Their great tribal ceremony was the worship of the sun, or, more properly, the obtaining of power from the sun in the K'ado or Sun Dance. The sun was not thought of as an anthropomorphic deity leading a hierarchy of lesser deities. The sun was one of many powerful spirit forces. Objects of religious veneration were:

1. Adalbeahya, the worship of Sun Boy, and medicine in ten portions kept by the priests, often called the Ten Grandmothers or religious bundles. Sun Boy was their supernatural hero, and many stories and legends detailed his exploits and adventures.

2. Tai-me, or sacred images, fetishes, or dolls. There were three of these originally, later only one. The Tai-me was the central figure of the K'ado.

3. Gadombitsouhi, "Old Woman under the Ground." This belonged to the Kingep band of the Kiowas. It was an image about a foot high, with flowing hair. It was stolen and later lost.

4. Seni, or peyote. This was the worship of the cactus plant, *Lophophora williamsii.* It involved a system of myth and ritual, of recent use among them, probably coming from the Mescalero

[44] *Ibid.,* 275–77.

Apaches. It became more important during the reservation period and after.[45]

The Sun Dance was an annual ceremony, in spring or early summer, that brought the whole tribe together. It included the worship of the sun and regeneration of the sacred buffalo. Many sacred objects were housed inside the specially constructed Sun Dance Lodge where dances and ceremonies were carried out. At this time, law and order reached maximum proportions, the military societies serving as police with special powers to enforce the regulations. In addition, the Sun Dance strengthened the tribal bonds and served as a social get-together and as a time of courtship for boys and girls. At the end of the period, vows to the sun were carried out in the gatherings of the war parties.

Mooney says that the Kiowa Sun Dance differed from that of the Cheyennes, Dakotas, and others in the "entire absence of those voluntary self-tortures which have made the sun dance among other tribes a synonym for savage horrors."[46] This is not borne out by other writers, although the Kiowas certainly never reached those depths of self-torture and cruelty that the Mandans and some others exhibited.[47] Even in late days, strips of flesh were torn from thighs and legs in some of their religious ceremonies.[48] The Sun Dance, which lasted about ten days from construction of the sacred lodge to completion of the ceremonies, culminated in the campaigns of the young warriors for warfare and raids. Complete accounts of the ceremonies were given by some early visitors.[49] The last Kiowa

[45] Mooney, "Calendar History," 237–41. See also J. S. Slotkin, *The Peyote Religion*, 41–47, for a description of the peyote religion and the native American church.

[46] Mooney, "Calendar History," 242.

[47] Catlin, *North American Indians*, I, 175–208.

[48] Nye, *Carbine and Lance*, 337–39. Perrin du Lac described these ceremonies after his visit up the Missouri in 1802. (Perrin du Lac, *Travels*, 64–65.)

[49] Battey, *Life and Adventures*, 173–84; Methvin, *Andele*, 58, 63–67; Hugh Lenox Scott, "Notes on the Kado, or Sun Dance of the Kiowa," *A.A.*, Vol. XIII, No. 3 (July-September, 1911), 343–79; Mooney, "Calendar History," 439–45; Leslie Spier, "Notes on the Kiowa Sun Dance," in Clark Wissler (ed.), *Sun Dance of the Plains Indians*, A.M.N.H., *A.P.*, No. XVI, Pt. 6 (1921), 433–50. See also Leslie Spier, "The Sun Dance of the Plains Indians: Its Development and Diffusion," in Wissler (ed.), *Sun Dance of the Plains Indians*, A.M.N.H., *A.P.*, Vol. XVI, Pt. 7 (1921), 451–527.

Sun Dance was held in 1887. The Comanches had no Sun Dance, but sometimes visited the Kiowa Sun Dance.

THE SUN DANCE

The dance was held primarily from a dream vision. The Tai-me keeper made the announcement of the dance by riding out with the Tai-me, a small image representing a human figure, in a robe of white feathers and a headdress of a single feather. It had pendants of ermine skin and blue beads around its neck. It was painted with designs of the sun and of the moon. Mooney said that there were three of these stone fetishes at one time, but two were lost. It was never exposed save at the K'ado Dance; then it was wrapped in a bundle of skins and kept in a parfleche.

When the tribe assembled, the keeper circled the camp, riding about with the doll on his back. Next a sacred tree had to be procured. Two young men from one of the military societies, after purification in the sweat lodge, sought out the tree. The tree was cut and put up, following a ritual of halting four times and smoking. A buffalo bull was killed by a man and his wife, who fasted while on the hunt. The tree or center pole was chopped down by a captive woman. The soldier societies took a prominent part in the setting up of the pole in a hole dug in the ground. The center pole was not painted. Buffalo hide was fastened across its forks; various offerings were tied to it, including the Tai-me doll; and on it the buffalo head faced east. Then the building of the lodge was finished with rafters. The lodge was forty-two to sixty feet in diameter. The entrance was to the east, and there a flat stone was put on the ground. Cottonwood and cedar branches were used to cover the lodge, and incense smudges were made.

Next the old women held a dance, and the pipe circulated. When the lodge was completed, the soldier societies held a frolic. Musicians, drummers, and dancers took part in the ritual, and the ornamental shields were hung up with the sacred medicine. A "buffalo" dance took place and the "buffalo" were driven into the sacred lodge. Hugh Lenox Scott says that the preparations took six days, and mentions that free sex license was permitted at the beginning of the lodge construction. This period of sex license was probably of ancient sanction, allowing for procreation and renewal of the tribe. Other tribes, such as the Dakotas, practiced it, also.

Then began the dance proper, which would last four nights and four days. The dancers were mainly young men, but women could dance also. The Tai-me owner was the director and principal performer; he was painted red and yellow. The four main dancers, assistants to the Tai-me keeper, knew the songs and ritual. They were also painted and danced the whole four-day period without food or water. They appeared in successive Sun Dances for four years, and then chose their successors (if chosen, one could not refuse), who paid them for this privilege in horses or buffalo robes. All carried eagle-bone whistles. The Tai-me shield keepers had to observe many taboos, and common dancers also took part.

Andele or Andres Martinez once saw a horse tied to the center pole as a sacrifice to the Sun, and it stayed there until it starved to death. Horses were painted and placed on high hills as sacrifices. The Kiowas sacrificed their flesh and finger joints to the Sun,[50] but never suspended the dancers by cords through the flesh of the shoulder blades and other parts of the body as other tribes did. The sun and moon were painted on the chest and on the back of the dancer; then the skin was cut away as a sacrifice and to make the designs permanent after his first Sun Dance.

Smoking and Sun adoration were part of the ritual. Visions were sought and promises made to the sun. "Feather killing," running after the dancers with feathers, occurred, and scalps were displayed. Some of the dancers would become unconscious. In the dance of the last night, everyone joined in the hilarious time. At the close of the dance, the dancers ended their abstinence and drank a prepared drink of roots. After the festival terminated, the camp broke up and the people moved off.

[50] Scott, "Notes on the Kado or Sun Dance of the Kiowa," *loc. cit.*, 345. Scott said that there was "no cutting of flesh or shedding of blood," but Scott's information was fairly late. In the spring of 1890 he was with the command ordered from Fort Sill to Anadarko at the request of Agent W. D. Meyers to stop the dance. See *ibid.*, 369n.

The purpose of the Sun Dance was to cure illness and to secure material benefits from the Tai-me or medicine doll, and from the sun. It was a regeneration of the buffalo and of life, associated with the spring or early summer. In addition, it was a powerful bond for cementing the union of the tribe, displaying loyalty and patriotism.

In regard to the Sun Dance, Battey said:

> One circumstance I must not fail to mention, as corroborating their superstitious ideas. The leaves forming the shady roof of the medicine house wilted. The heat of the sun preyed upon the naked dancers. To-haint (no-shoes), the great medicine chief, made medicine for clouds and rain. The rain came, with a tempest of wind and the most vivid lightning. Peal after peal of thunder shook the air. The ground was literally flooded. Two Cheyenne women were killed by the lightning. The next morning To-haint apologized for the storm. He was a young man, and had no idea of making such strong medicine. He hoped the tribe would pass by his indiscreetness. He trusted that, as he grew older, he would grow wiser. The Cheyenne women were dead, not because of his medicine, but because of their wearing red blankets. All Indians know they should not wear red during the great medicine dance of the Kiowas.
>
> The apology was accepted.[51]

THE SCALP DANCE

Triumphant warriors were honored by the scalp dance, often called a victory dance. The scalp dance was called A-dalde-guan or "hair-kill dance." Mooney said of it:

> Should one of the war party have been killed, all the others go into mourning (doat) and do not rejoice or paint themselves as they return even though bringing back a scalp. In this case they hold no dance, but sacrifice the scalp to the sun by "throwing it away" on some hillside. If, on the contrary, they have taken one or more scalps without the loss of one of their own party, they return to camp in full war dress, including their war bonnets, and with faces painted

[51] *Life and Adventures*, 183–84.

black, to show that they have killed an enemy. They enter the camp running, to imitate a charge, firing their guns and discharging arrows, to show how they had met and struck the foe; if they approached in silence, they might be mistaken for enemies. Their friends run out to meet them, shouting "Imkagyá gya!" ("They are coming in triumph!")[52]

Then preparations were made for the dance. The warriors lifted the women up behind them on their horses and rode around in a circle singing, while the scalps were carried on long poles. Men engaged in the war party and all the women took part in the dance at night around a fire in the center of a circle. The scalps were stretched over hoops and painted red inside. They were carried by women in the dance. The interpreter told Mooney, "Everybody very happy time like picnic."

The dance might last for days, every afternoon and night, or for a month, after which the scalp was usually thrown away as an offering to the sun. Battey remarked that some scalps were kept as trophies, and hung within the lodges of their owners.

POSITION OF WOMEN

Women were drudges and menials in Kiowa society. They took no part in tribal government and were always subsidiary to the men. Theirs were the duties of caring for the tipis—setting up, packing, and moving them and the household articles. They harnessed and packed the dogs and horses. They prepared food, cared for the children, and cut and packed home the meat and hides obtained from the buffalo hunt. They tanned the hides and robes, made clothing, and in general cared for the household.

They also served as herders for the horses, unless children, usually boys or slaves, took over this duty under their supervision. The captives served the women, fetching firewood and water. In the absence of slaves, the women did all of this. The wife took care

52 "Calendar History," 291.

of her husband's war medicine, shields, weapons, and war ponies. A wife often accompanied her husband on a raid to take care of the "medicine" and the extra horses, although young boys sometimes served in this capacity.

While occupying a low social status, a woman did have some rights. If mistreated, she could leave her husband and return to her family. In such a case, the husband had horses or other gifts returned to him, and a divorce would be effected. Favorite children, called *"ade,"* both boys and girls, often a chief's children, were given special consideration and held a high status. Kicking Bird's daughter, Topen-toneonino, was a favorite child. After her father's death, her uncles, jealous of her status, refused to give her a part of her father's property and horses. This may have been due to her having accepted Christianity and having been "thrown away." Satank's second son was a favored child, and his death almost provoked Satank to suicide.

There was only one group lower in status than the women; that was the slave or captive group. This group held an impermanent status, for captives, showing fortitude and bravery, could be accepted into the tribe, usually by adoption into a family. For a girl, also, marriage with an important man might change captive status. Many captives did not desire to return to their own people.[53]

PURIFICATION RITES AND THE SWEAT LODGE

The sweat bath was a means of purification before religious ceremonies, as well as a curative for disease and for exorcism of evil spirits. It was performed in a small lodge with a fire in the center. Rocks were heated, and a vessel of water was brought in by women and sprinkled over the hot rocks. Steam vapors caused profuse

[53] Gregg, *Commerce of the Prairies*, 125–30. John Sibley mentions a woman from Chihuahua, tattooed in Indian fashion, and married, who did not wish to return to Mexico. John Sibley, "Historical Sketches of the Several Indian Tribes in Louisiana" in *American State Papers*, Indian Affairs, IV, 721–25. Andres Martinez was taken from New Mexico (Methvin, *Andele*); see also the adoption of Millie Durgan in the Elm Creek Raid of 1864, in Chapter V of this volume.

sweating. After several hours the person, naked save for a buffalo robe, rushed out and plunged into cool water in a near-by creek or river.[54]

THE CALENDAR

The Kiowas counted twelve moons or months to the year, although theirs was not an exact calendar system. Of great interest in the recording of events were the calendar histories kept by some individuals which give the title to the study of the Kiowas made by James Mooney.[55]

LANGUAGE

The Kiowa language was long considered to be distinct and unrelated to any other American language. Later, with more study, it was believed to have some affinity with the Tanoan language and was classified as Kiowa-Tanoan by Harrington.[56] Harrington obtained material from Kiowa informants near Anadarko, Oklahoma, and Tanoan etymologies from the Tewa dialect at San Juan Pueblo near Santa Fe. Such studies would seem to relate the Taos and Jemez Indians to the Kiowas, linguistically. However, B. L. Whorf and G. L. Trager would question this.[57] They do not agree with Harrington in saying that Kiowas and Tanoans have a close relationship. For a long time, it was thought that the Uto-Aztecan and the Tanoan linguistic families were related. Edward Sapir includes

[54] Gregg, *Commerce of the Prairies*, 334; Methvin, *Andele*, 59–61; Battey, *Life and Adventures*, 148–49.

[55] "Calendar History," 367–69. Mooney gives detailed descriptions of the specific events recorded in the calendars. Chapter IV of this book summarizes the records as given by Mooney.

[56] *Ibid.*, 389–439; Mooney, "Kiowa," in Hodge, *Handbook*, I, 700. See also John P. Harrington, *Vocabulary of the Kiowa Language*, B. A. E., *Bulletin 84*; and his "On Phonetic and Lexic Resemblances between Kiowan and Tanoan," *A.A.*, Vol. XII (1910), 119–23. And see Parker McKenzie and John P. Harrington, *Popular Account of the Kiowa Indian Language, Monographs* of the School of American Research (1948).

[57] "The Relationship of Uto-Aztecan and Tanoan," *loc. cit.*, 609–24.

the two families in Azteco-Tanoan, in which Tanoan is coupled with Kiowa, and Zuñi is given (with a query) as a third component.[58]

Trager made a study of the Taos Indians, and Harrington made a study of the Tewas. Whorf and Trager prefer to include the two families in Azteco-Tanoan. They say:

> As for Kiowa, Harrington has stated that the relationship is close, but on examination of the "Tewa etymologies" he cites, and a comparison of that material and of the whole Kiowa vocabulary with Trager's Taos . . . [they] indicate only a small number of very striking resemblances, more to Taos than to Tewa, and a larger list of more distant resemblances . . . [and] we prefer to leave the question of the inclusion of Kiowa in the Azteco-Tanoan stock till another occasion.[59]

Kiowa, then, may be considered as a unique language until the linguists come to more definite conclusions. Paul A. Vestal and Richard Evans Schultes note this in their study of the economic plants of the Kiowas, and they utilize ethnobotany to place the Kiowas in the Montana and Yellowstone area at the beginning of the historic period, in agreement with Mooney.[60]

The Kiowa language has only one dialect and no dialect variations. It has the same genetic background as Aztec. Aztec and Tanoan relationships have been proved. Some features of the Kiowa language are six short buccal vowels, each having a nasalized counterpoint, long vowels, and with accentuation seventy-two distinctive vowels in the language. There are three diphthongs and twenty-three consonants. There are also aspirations and clicks. There are several allants and two pitches, acute and grave, and two loudnesses. There is no *r* in Kiowa. Mooney said that the language was full of nasal and choking sounds which were not rhythmic.

The Kiowa verb has three tenses—past, present, and future—and all are used in both the positive and negative. There are seven

[58] *Ibid.*, 609.
[59] *Ibid.*, 609–10.
[60] *Economic Botany of the Kiowa Indians.*

gender-number classes of nouns. In the personal pronoun, singular is made to serve also as plural, and there is no third person. The Kiowa count is decimal, based on ten fingers and ten toes. Other features of the language are described by Parker McKenzie and John P. Harrington, but will be of more interest to the linguist than the general reader.

The possible association with the Pueblo tribes such as those of Taos and Jemez (Tanoan languages) is interesting, and since there was no historic association, postulates a migration from north to south on different sides of the mountains, as well as a different culture pattern.[61]

ART

All of the Plains Indians had decorative or applied art. The objects upon which it was displayed were functional. In a buffalo-hunting culture, the buffalo skin was the most readily available material for decoration. Painting and porcupine-quill embroidery were used in hide decoration before glass beads became common in the historic period after trade with the white man developed. In trade, painted robes were doubly valuable—one painted robe was equal to two unpainted. Painting was used more than embroidery with dyed porcupine quills. Stone pipes, rattles, and wooden objects were also painted and decorated with quills, feathers, and beads.

Buffalo robes, clothing, tipi covers, tipi linings, parfleches, drums, shields, saddlebags, and many small skin containers for medicine, tobacco, and other objects were painted and embroidered. Robes with the hair left on were used as winter coats or blankets, worn with the hair side in. In mild weather they were worn with the skin side in. Skins with the hair scraped off were worn as cloaks or mantles in milder weather. The head of the animal was worn

[61] McKenzie and Harrington, *Popular Account of the Kiowa Indian Language*, 1–2, 12–15. Harrington, *Vocabulary*, and "On Phonetic and Lexic Resemblances between Kiowan and Tanoan," *loc. cit.*, 1–2, 11. Harrington includes a detailed alphabetic vocabulary in his *Vocabulary*.

to the left, and the longer dimension of the hide around the body. Some of the hides were cut in halves and sewn together with sinew.

The colors for painting included brown, red, yellow, black, blue, green, and white. Charcoal served for black, and iron oxides and colored clays furnished much of the pigment.

Melvin R. Gilmore stated that various clays were baked to powder over a fire, then ground in small wooden or stone mortars, mixed with tallow, and packed in buckskin.[62] White was from selenite stone, heated and formed into a fine white powder. This was used with water for whitening buckskin and skin tipis. Some powdered paints—one a dark brownish red—were used as a remedy for eczema and eruptions of the skin and for protection of the skin in frosty weather.

Some dyes were obtained from vegetable juices and roots. Vermilion was one of the main trade articles early obtained from the whites.

Brushes were made of chewed cottonwood or willow sticks or of horn or bone. Preferred brushes were made from the porous part of a buffalo leg bone. Thin, sharp bones were used for outlining; then color was applied by a brush and a sizing or mordant was put over the paint to set it. The sizing was made of thin glue made from skin scrapings boiled in water or from the juice of crushed prickly pear leaves. The hides, usually scraped and treated with brains until they were smooth and soft, were white, and the application of the transparent mordant allowed the white to show through.

The Indian men painted naturalistic figures of men, horses, buffalo, and other animals. The figures were shown in profile and without background. Women painted geometric designs and figures. Sometimes a man would add geometric designs on the same robe with naturalistic figures.

The most frequently depicted figures were those of horses, showing the concern of the Plains Indians with the horse, its capture, and its use. Men and their weapons were the next most frequently depicted figures. Men painted the history of their great war ex-

[62] *Prairie Smoke*, 61–62. Also conversations of author with Mr. Gilmore, 1936–37, in Austin, Texas.

ploits, or made records of their personal lives.

Composition involved small scenes. Perspective was lacking. A more distant figure was placed partly behind or above a closer one without a reduction in size. A group of horses might be shown by several figures in back of or higher than the main one.

Parfleches were decorated with geometric patterns. Tipi covers had geometric borders at top and bottom, and in between were naturalistic pictures showing the exploits of the owner. Chief Satanta had an entirely red tipi with red streamers at the end of poles atop it. The heraldic tipi, hereditary in the family of Chief Dohasan, was known as the Do-gíagya-gúat ("Tipi with Battle Pictures"). The north side of it was ornamented with battle pictures, and the southern side had alternating horizontal stripes of black and yellow.[63]

Shields often had both geometric and naturalistic figures, usually of the owner's guardian spirit or fetish obtained from the vision quest. Sun Boy's shield was painted with a picture of the sun, his particular medicine. Religious symbols were painted on men's shirts and on the heads of skin drums, and upon the body of a warrior when he entered battle. Heap-of-Bears was said to have painted the Taime symbols on his body when he carried one of the Taime dolls (his friend carried another) into battle with the Utes. (He lost it, and there followed his death and the flight of the Kiowas and Comanches.)

Porcupine quills were softened in water, flattened, and dyed in various colors. Sewn onto hide, they presented a smooth, strawlike surface. Quills were well suited to geometric designs. After the Indians came in contact with the whites, some floral and naturalistic designs developed. Beadwork became more important and elaborate after the Indians were settled on the reservations.

Naming of the designs used and color symbolism differed from tribe to tribe. Black signified victory for some tribes, and red usually signified blood or man.

The dominant geometric patterns of the Plains Indians were

[63] Mooney, "Calendar History," 336, and Plate LXXIX, following p. 336.

the border and box, border and hourglass, feathered circle, and horizontally stripped and bilaterally symmetrical designs.[64]

Hide paintings with naturalistic pictures were of three kinds: time-counts or calendars, personal records or biographies, and imaginative records of visions.

The Kiowas were noted for their calendars, and so were the Sioux (Dakotas). The Kiowas also recorded their personal history on hides and drew some religious images and elements of the Sun Dance.

Buffalo were rarely shown on hides. The main figures are those of horses and armed men. The deeds shown are deeds of war, especially the stealing of horses and touching of an enemy with a coup stick. Other animals, such as the bear, deer, or antelope, are few in Plains Indian painting, and dogs are not seen at all. Red, yellow, and blue were preferred colors. Blue and yellow were sacred colors of the Sun Dance for the Kiowas. The drawing of horses by the Kiowas followed a realistic portrayal, often showing colored ears, manes, and tails, and realistic hoofs. Sometimes the hoof was shown by a hook, and the horse was shown with a projecting phallus. The running horse was shown with forelegs extended forward and hindlegs extended backward, which was unnatural but aesthetically pleasing. Little care was given to over-all effect, as forms were scattered over the hide.

Painting on hides reached an epitome among the Plains Indians, although Indians in other areas of North America practiced the art. Of the Plains Indians, the Sioux generally excelled in their artistic efforts.

POPULATION

The early accounts of numbers are probably greatly exaggerated. Mooney said that the Kiowas and Kiowa-Apaches probably never numbered more than 1,600 to 1,800 persons. In 1865, Agent Leav-

---

[64] John C. Ewers, *Plains Indian Painting*, 8–15. The border and hourglass design was especially predominant on Comanche robes. It was also used by the Kiowas. Kiowa paintings on robes are pictured in Plate 14, following p. 14, *ibid.*

enworth gave 1,800 for the Kiowas alone.[65] In 1873, Battey counted 1,600 to 1,650, probably including the Kiowa-Apaches. In 1892, Mooney stated that the Kiowas numbered 1,014 and the Kiowa-Apaches, 241; in 1896 the Kiowas numbered 1,065 and the Kiowa-Apaches, 208. In 1905 the Kiowas numbered 1,165 and the Kiowa-Aapches, 155.[66]

In 1961, the number is higher; however, these numbers are not for purebloods but for all those called by the tribal name, which includes a great admixture. Recent estimates were given as around 3,500 for the Kiowas and 1,000 for the Kiowa-Apaches.[67] Estimates of pure-blooded Kiowas might be about 1,000, and of Kiowa-Apaches, about 100 or 150.

PERSONALITY AND CULTURE

Ruth Fulton Benedict characterized the Plains personality or "ethos" as Dionysian, given to extreme indulgence in violence, grief, trance, and other emotional states.[68]

In brief, these are some of the pertinent points: Plains Indian mothers nursed their children for years and treated them with tenderness. The child was closely attached to the mother, and the father was away a large part of the time. The concept of the "manly-hearted woman" reflects the role many women played. The child developed more hostility to the mother than to the father. Hostility was projected to the wife and to other women. The boy tended to congeniality with the father and was honored

[65] Mooney, "Calendar History," 235–36, citing Jesse Leavenworth, Report on Condition of Indian Tribes, 1867, 37. DeB. Randolph Keim gave the number for the hostile Indians of 1868 as the following: Kiowas—1,085, Kiowa-Apaches—281, of all ages and sexes. (DeB. Randolph Keim, *Sheridan's Troopers on the Borders*, 26.)

[66] Mooney, "Calendar History," 235; Hodge, *Handbook*, I, 700, 702.

[67] Conversations of author with Philemon Berry and Adolph Goombi at the Kiowa Agency, Anadarko, Oklahoma, July 17, 1957.

[68] "Configurations of Culture in North America," *A.A.*, Vol. XXXIV (1932), 1–27; and Ruth Fulton Benedict, *Patterns of Culture*. Controversy occurred over the characterization of the Pueblos as Apollonian (modest, gentle, co-operative) and of the Northwest Coast Indians as Dionysian, with egocentrism pointed at paranoia. Later writers have enlarged and revised the early personality studies.

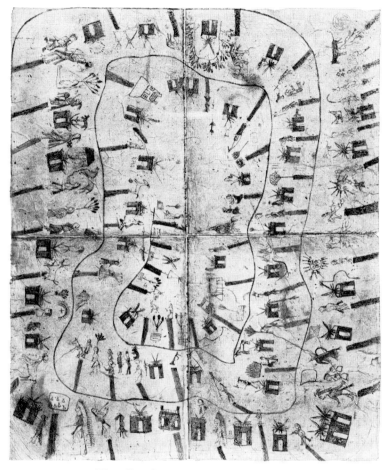

The Sett'an annual calendar

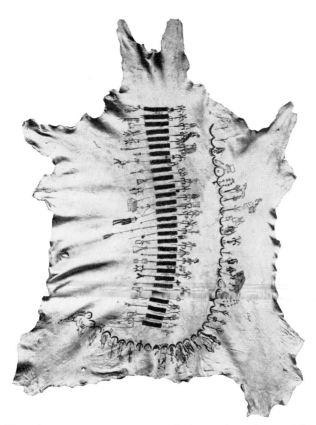

THE ANKO CALENDAR—annual (center) and monthly
(at side, with crescents for moons under each picture)

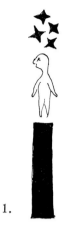

1.   WINTER 1833-34
2.   SUMMER 1844
3.   SUMMER 1854
4.   SUMMER 1861
5.   WINTER 1861-62
6.   SUMMER 1892

1.

2.

5.

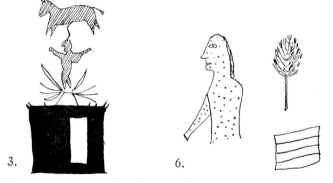

3.

6.

DETAIL FROM THE SETT'AN AND ANKO ANNUAL CALENDARS

A KIOWA WARRIOR LANCING AN OSAGE
From a drawing made by Hogoon (Silver Horn)
a Kiowa, at Fort Sill, about 1887

PACER

former head chief of the Kiowa-Apaches, when he was a delegate
to Washington, 1872, from a photograph by Alexander Gardner

GÚIPÄ'GO (LONE WOLF)
once head chief and leader of the Kiowas
Photograph by Alexander Gardner, Washington, D. C., 1872

SET-TAINTE OR SATANTA (WHITE BEAR)
onetime principal war chief of the Kiowas

WHITE HORSE
a noted chief and raider. Photograph by Lanney, 1892

by the father with feasts and rewards for prowess. Spirit helpers were also usually male.

George Devereux stressed the "antisexual orientation" of Plains Indians, pointing out the long periods between births as the mother's disinterest in renewing sexual relations during lactation.[69] Chastity was highly valued by the Plains Indians, but it was not expected of all women. Ritual continence was common. Certain men's sodalities practiced a legitimized stealing of other men's wives for a few days.

Conflicts arose over these adventures for men while the women were kept chaste (chastity belts were commonly worn after the first menstruation). Men had to protect the females of their own families and yet sought to dishonor other females. Relations with women were symbols of prestige. Ambivalence toward sex resulted in infliction of severe penalties, even death, on adulterous women.[70]

Certainly men held dominance over women in the Plains area, probably more so than in any other area north of Mexico except the Northwest Coast. There were some women who differed from the usual type. "Manly-hearted" women were the defiant type. They broke away from restrictions; they owned property, were ambitious, handsome women, and held high position, even showing independence in sex, differing from passive women. They were favored wives, often the chief or "sit-by" wife.

Men had more outlets than had women. Prestige was achieved in religion, in tribal generosity such as giving horses to visitors, "give-aways," and in war, tribally sanctioned. Men who were not masculine—had no interest in becoming warriors—escaped into the practice of "medicine" or the priesthood (keepers of the medi-

[69] *Reality and Dream, Psychotherapy of a Plains Indian.* See pages 62–74 for a résumé of Plains Indian personality. This study concerns the treatment of a schizophrenic Plains Indian, given in detail. See also Oscar Lewis, "Manly-Hearted Women among the North Piegan," *A.A.*, Vol. XLIII (1941), 173–87, and *The Effect of White Contact upon Blackfoot Culture*, A. E. S., *Monograph No. 6* (1942); and Esther S. Goldfrank, "Historic Change and Social Character, a Study of the Teton Dakota," *A.A.*, Vol. XLV, No. 1 (1943), 67–83, and *Changing Configurations in the Social Organization of a Blackfoot Tribe during the Reserve Period*, A. E. S., *Monograph No. 8* (1945).

[70] Devereux, *Reality and Dream*, 62–74.

cine bundles) or into the *berdache* and wore women's clothing, lived homosexually with other men, and performed some accepted roles in scalp dances. Men also related their exploits publicly in recounting coup. All of these activitities served the male ego.

The search for prophecies and a return to the old ways was accepted by the Plains tribes in several revivals, notably the Ghost Dance religion of 1890. The Kiowas and Comanches paid little attention to this revival, however. Its spread was largely in the north.

On the Plains generosity was regarded as a virtue, but there was nothing like the potlatch of the Northwest Coast. The Kiowas were famous for their generosity in giving horses to visitors and to friends. For a so-called primitive people we see a remarkable similarity in modern society. Their generosity in giving feasts and gifts to others was a social norm that accords well with ideas of social prestige and class mobility in our own society. The miser was not able to win friends. Undue giving was a prerogative of the powerful. For those who wished to climb the ladder of success, certain social amenities were important.

The Kiowas do not fit neatly into the pattern described by Ruth Fulton Benedict for the Plains personality; neither do the Kiowa-Apaches nor the Comanches, who were less given to tribal religious worship—they had no Sun Dance. (The Comanches have even been called sacrilegious.) In many ways, the Kiowas showed strong wills, independence of thought, even factionalism within the tribe. They seemed to have cast off or modified some of the customs of the northern Plains tribes. On the whole, the Kiowa-Apaches seemed a quieter and less ambitious group than the Kiowas.

CULTURE OF THE KIOWA-APACHES

The culture of the Kiowa-Apaches was in most respects identical to that of the Kiowas.[71] Even though the two tribes lived together, there was not much intermarriage between them. In

[71] Mooney, "Calendar History," 245–53; Mooney, "Kiowa-Apache," in Hodge, *Handbook*, I, 701–702. See also J. Gilbert McAllister, "Kiowa-Apache Social Organization," in Eggan (ed.), *Social Anthropology*, 99–169.

customs, dress, and general character, the Kiowa-Apaches resembled the Kiowas, although the former were more agreeable and reliable.

Pacer was chief of the Kiowa-Apaches for many years. He had considerable ability, was intelligent, and was a consistent advocate of peace. He desired and approved the establishment of a school among his people in 1874, established by A. J. Standing, a Quaker. Pacer died in 1875 and was given a civilized burial by request of and with consent of his people. (The same had been done for Kicking Bird of the Kiowas.)

In 1894, Apache John (Gonkon, "Stays-in-Tipi") was a conscientious leader. In 1901, their chief was Tsáyadíte-ti ("White Man").

Marriage was of two kinds: by formal arrangement or by elopement. Matrilocal residence was more common that patrilocal residence, but there were no rules in regard to the matter. Divorce was simple but not of common occurrence. Families with children were stable, and the marital partners seldom separated. Children were cherished and formed a bond between the parents.

The levirate and sororate were found. There were no clans and no clearly defined descent group.

There were dancing groups. The Rabbits included all the children, both boys and girls. For the adults there were two dancing groups: the *Manatidie* and the *Klintidae*. The *Klintidae* ranked higher for it contained the bravest warriors. The dances were long and tedious, and the members were called on for police and community work. The women had a dancing society known as *Izuwe*. This was a religious and secret society and was given to owl worship.

Death was awesome, and names of the deceased were avoided and dropped from use. The Kiowa-Apaches, like the Kiowas, believed in the passage of the spirit into another world.

Today the Kiowa-Apaches live near Apache, Oklahoma, and in and around Fort Cobb, Caddo County, Oklahoma, while the Kiowas are around Anadarko, Fort Cobb, Mountain View, and Carnegie, Oklahoma.

CHAPTER FOUR

❖ THE KIOWA CALENDARS

*TH*E Sett'an calendar was a semiannual notation of some striking events that stirred the tribe. The winter notation or pictograph was indicated by an upright black bar below the principal figure; the summer notation was often designated by a picture showing a medicine lodge for the annual Sun Dance.

The annual calendars were correlated by Alice Marriott with the more recent calendars of George Poolaw, George Hunt, and Mary Buffalo. The Sett'an calendar ended in 1892, and the Anko monthly calendar ran from August, 1889, to July, 1892. The Anko yearly calendar ran from 1864 to 1892. Both of Anko's calendars were redrawn on the same skin. The calendars given by Miss Marriott run through 1901.[1]

The Sett'an and Anko annual calendars give the following events:

Winter, 1832–33—Some money was captured from American traders near the South Canadian River. In the fight Guikongya ("Black Wolf") was killed. The pictograph shows a man's head

[1] Mooney, "Calendar History," 254–379, and Plate LXXV, following p. 254. For a comparative table of the calendars of Sett'an, George Poolaw, George Hunt, and Mary Buffalo, see Alice Marriott, *The Ten Grandmothers*, 292–305.

146

with the figure of a black wolf attached to it by a line—a sort of "name-scroll" in the same way that the Maya pictures used a line issuing from the mouth to show a "speech-scroll." A sketch of a silver dollar with an eagle on it indicates the money. Twelve traders left Santa Fe with ten thousand dollars in specie packed on mules. Two men were killed in the fighting. The remaining ten men separated into parties of five. Seven of the ten finally reached the Creek Indians on the Arkansas and were saved. Until they were told by the Comanches, the Kiowas did not know the value of the silver discs; thus, they used them as decorations in their hair.[2]

Summer, 1833—"Summer that they cut off their heads." This picture commemorates a massacre by the Osages, who cut off the heads of the Kiowa victims and left them in their own copper cooking kettles. Most of the Kiowa warriors were absent, and the village was surprised. A'date, the head chief who had allowed his village to be attacked, was deposed and Dohasan became head chief.

Winter, 1833–34—On November 13, 1833, there occurred a meteoric display observed all over North America. Sett'an was born the preceding summer, and the figure of a child over the winter bar indicates his first winter; the stars above represent the meteors. The Kiowas, then camped on a tributary of Elm Fork of the Red River, were awakened by a bright light, and rushed out into a night as bright as day with meteors darting about. They awakened their children, saying, "Get up, get up, there is something awful going on!"[3]

Summer, 1834—The Dragoon expedition met the Comanches, Wichitas, and Kiowas and returned a captive girl, Gunpa-ndama ("Medicine-Tied-to-Tipi-Pole"), taken by the Osages when they

[2] Mooney, "Calendar History," 254–57.

[3] *Ibid.*, 260–61. Marriott adds (in the Poolaw calendar) that the Taime god was stolen, along with several Kiowa women, by the Osages. One of the women returned with the Taime in March. (Marriott, *The Ten Grandmothers*, 292.)

had massacred the Kiowa village in 1833. The pictograph shows a tipi attached by a line to the figure of a girl. This meeting with the Americans opened up trade with the allied tribes, and arrangements were made at a meeting at Fort Gibson for the subsequent treaties of 1835 and 1837.

Winter, 1834–35—The winter that Bull-Tail was killed by the Mexicans from Chihuahua while the Kiowas camped on the southern edge of the Staked Plains. The pictograph shows only Bull-Tail, although several others were killed too.

Summer, 1835—Cat-tail rush Sun Dance. After the recovery of the Tai-me, a Sun Dance was held on the south bank of North Canadian River, where many rushes (*Equisetum arvense*) grew. The pictograph shows a sketch of the medicine lodge, and a box above it represents the Tai-me in the rawhide box. Immediately after the Sun Dance a party of Kiowas made a raid far down on the Texas coast and captured Boin-edal ("Big Blond"), a German who was still living with the Kiowas in 1892.

Winter, 1835–36—To-edalte ("Big Face," or "Wolf Hair") was shot and killed by Mexicans while on a raid in Mexico.

Summer, 1836—The Wolf Creek Sun Dance is shown by the sketch of a wolf attached by a line to the medicine lodge. After the dance the Kiowas moved north of the Arkansas. A portion of the Kiowas were attacked by Cheyennes, but they threw up breastworks and defended themselves successfully. The Kingeps went to visit the Crows.

Winter, 1836–37—K'íñähíate was killed in an expedition against the Timber Mexicans or Mexicans of Tamaulipas and the lower Río Grande. The wide range of the Kiowas is shown here—one band raiding in Mexico, another band visiting the Crows on the upper Missouri.

Summer, 1837—"Summer that the Cheyennes were massacred." The battle is shown by the conventional Indian symbol: the party attacked defend themselves behind breastworks while the arrows fly toward them; below is the figure of a man wearing a war bonnet. The Cheyennes came on the Kiowas while they were preparing to hold a Sun Dance on a tributary of Scott Creek, a branch of the North Fork of Red River, near later Fort Elliott in the Texas Panhandle. All forty-eight of the Cheyennes were killed, and six Kiowas lost their lives.

Winter, 1837–38—"Winter that they dragged the head." The head of an Arapaho was dragged behind a horseman. The German captive Boin-edal, then a little boy who had been with the Indians about two years and who witnessed the barbarous spectacle, told Mooney in 1892 that he could still remember the thrill of horror that passed through him.

Summer, 1838—The Cheyennes and Arapahoes organized a war party and attacked the Kiowas, Comanches, and Apaches on Wolf Creek, a short distance above where that stream joins Beaver Creek and forms the North Canadian River. A circular breastwork was dug and the camp was saved although the Kiowas lost several warriors. The picture shows arrows and bullets, indicating that the Cheyennes had some guns. Black dots with wavy lines indicated the bullets.

Winter, 1838–39—A battle with the Arapahoes occurred, and all the Arapahoes were killed.

Summer, 1839—The Peninsula Sun Dance was held. The peninsula was on the south side of the Washita a short distance below Walnut Creek. An expedition of about twenty Kiowas under Guadalonte against the Mexicans of El Paso took place. At Hueco Tanks the Kiowas were attacked by Mexicans and some Mescalero Apaches. The horses were killed, and the Kiowas were penned up to starve. But they climbed out of the cave, having to abandon one wounded man, Dagoi, who accepted his fate as a warrior. Although fired on by the Mexicans and having another man, Konate, wounded, they managed to escape. Konate was abandoned by a spring under an arbor of branches, and Dohasan (the elder) and others returned to their homes. On their way they met six Comanches en route to Mexico and asked them to bury Konate. The Comanches found Konate alive, helped him on a horse, and gave up their proposed raid to bring him safely home, where he recovered. Konate assumed a new name, Patadal, Lean Bull, which he later bestowed on another man, known to the whites as Poor Buffalo. He said that a wolf had come to him in his anguish, licked his wounds, and slept beside him. Then a rain came and washed his wounds, and a spirit told him that help would come.

Winter, 1839–40—"Smallpox Winter." The Kiowas were ravaged by the disease. The pictograph shows a man with spots all over his body. The disease began on the upper Missouri among passengers on a steamer in the summer of 1839. It was communicated to the Mandans and swept the Plains, destroying perhaps more than a third of the natives. It reached the Kiowas by way of some visiting Osages. The Kiowas and Kiowa-Apaches fled to the Staked Plains in an effort to escape it. The terrific toll of the Plains Indians appeared later in official reports: from 1,600 to 3,100 persons for the Mandans; from 2,000 to about 4,000 for the Arikaras and Minnetarees; and the Blackfeet, Crows, and Assiniboins were estimated to have lost from 6,000 to 8,000. How many persons the Kiowas lost is not known.

Summer, 1840—Red-Bluff Sun Dance—on the north side of the South Canadian, about the mouth of Mustang Creek in the Texas Panhandle. The prominent event of the summer was the peace made by the Arapahoes and Cheyennes with the Kiowas, Comanches, and Kiowa-Apaches. No mention was made of one of their raids, however. In the summer of 1840 the Comanches and Kiowas made a raid to the coast of Texas. They were followed and intercepted at the Battle of Plum Creek, where a number of Indians were killed.

Winter, 1840–41—Hide quiver war expedition. The figure of a quiver is shown above the black winter bar. A war expedition was made by the old men into Mexico. They carried old bows and quivers of buffalo skin, as all the younger warriors had already set out for Mexico carrying the better weapons and ornate quivers of panther skin or Mexican leather.

Summer, 1841—Friends of the Kiowas, the Arapahoes, attacked a party of Pawnees at White Bluff on the upper South Canadian and killed all of them. The Kiowas were not present but met and joined the Arapahoes after the battle. The Pawnees are shown in the pictograph before a white bluff—the tribe indicated by the peculiar Pawnee scalp lock and headdress.

On "American Horse" River south of Red River (probably a branch of the Pease River), where the whole Kiowa camp was located, some Texas soldiers advanced and the Kiowas killed five army scouts, took their large American horses, and fled. They returned a few days later, found the soldiers still there, and killed another.

This was the fight with the Texan-Santa Fe expedition, August 30, 1841. The Texans heard from Mexican traders that the Kiowas had lost ten of their warriors and a principal chief.

Mooney remarked that the Indian account, corresponding remarkably with George Wilkins Kendall's account of the Santa Fe expedition, was handed down orally for over fifty years without any knowledge of the printed statement by either Mooney or his informants.[4]

Winter, 1841–42—Â'dalhabä'k'ia was killed. The pictograph shows the man with a bird on top of his head to show the ornament of red woodpecker feathers he always wore on the left side of his head.

[4] Mooney, "Calendar History," 277–79.

Summer, 1842—Two Sun Dances were held on Sun Dance Creek or Kiowa Medicine Lodge Creek, which enters the North Canadian near the one-hundredth parallel. Two dreamers had been instructed to hold dances and made their requests to the Tai-me keeper almost simultaneously.

Winter, 1842–43—There is a picture of a man with a crow in front of his neck. This was the winter that Crow-Neck died in Wind Canyon at "Trading River," an upper branch of Double Mountain Fork of the Brazos. He was the adopted father of the German captive, Boin-edal.

Summer, 1843—The Nest-Building Sun Dance was held on Sun Dance Creek, a favorite place for the dance. It was called "Nest-Building Sun Dance" because a crow built her nest and laid her eggs upon the center pole after the dance was over.

Kicking Bird led a raid into Texas, captured some horses, and later returned them to a party carrying an American flag. They afterward learned the party was Texan, and had deceived them. The Texans had two captives, a Comanche and a Mexican. The Kiowas rescued the Comanche but left the Mexican since no one wanted him.

Winter, 1843–44—A woman was wounded in the breast after the Nest-Building Sun Dance. Dohasan had invited the woman to ride behind him, as was customary, while the freshly cut trees were dragged to the lodge. Her husband was enraged and he stabbed her. She recovered and the Chief Dohasan rebuked her husband by saying that he ought to have better sense, that he, Dohasan, was an old man—too old to be running after girls.

A raiding party went into Tamaulipas and killed a number of people, but was attacked while recrossing the Río Grande and three Kiowas were killed.

In the following winter, 1844, a clerk of Bent's Fort, called Wrinkled Neck, built a log trading house a few miles above Adobe Walls in the Texas Panhandle. It was also stated that the same man later built another trading post at a spring above the first one at Gúadal Dóha on the same (north) side of the river.

Summer, 1844—Dakota Sun Dance. A number of the Dakotas visited the Kiowas to dance and receive presents of ponies at the Sun Dance held again at Kiowa Medicine Lodge Creek. The pictograph shows a medicine lodge with the figure of a Dakota wearing a k'ódalpa or necklace breastplate of shell or bone tubes, known among traders as Iroquois beads. The Kiowas called the Dakotas, who were of long-standing friendship with them, and the original wearers of such necklaces, the "Necklace People," K'odalpä-K'iñago. Mooney says that this explanation appears to be a myth founded on a misconception of the tribal sign for Dakota, a sweeping pass of the hand across the throat commonly translated as "beheader."

Winter, 1844–45—Ä'taha'ik'i ("War-Bonnet-Man") was killed. A raid was made by Big Bow to avenge the death of his brother in Tamaulipas. After "giving the pipe" at the last Sun Dance, over two hundred Kiowas, Comanches, and Kiowa-Apaches joined the party which crossed the Río Grande and reached the Salado. Here some Mexicans took refuge in a fort, where the party charged them. Ä'taha'ik'i was killed. The fort was fired and its defenders were killed. The party then went farther into Mexico and had another fight in which Big Bow (grandfather of the later Big Bow) was killed.

Summer, 1845—The Stone-Necklace Sun Dance was held at Kiowa Medicine Lodge Creek and named after a girl called Tso-k'odalte ("Stone Necklace") who died and was mourned during the ceremony.

Winter, 1845–46—A sketch of a house shows the trading post built by William Bent (called "Mantahakia" or "Hook-Nose Man") in the Texas Panhandle, just above Bosque Grande Creek. In 1844, Bent had built a trading post higher up on the South

Canadian River. Both posts were in charge of a clerk called "K'odal-aka-i" ("Wrinkled Neck"). The removal of Bent's operations from the Arkansas to the Canadian seems to have marked the southward movement of the tribes.

Summer, 1846—Sun Dance when Hornless-Bull was made a Kâ'itsénk'ia. The figure shown is that of a man with a feather headdress and paint of the Koitsenko warrior society, a part of the Yápahe or military organization. Ten brave men formed the Koitsenko. During raids their leader carried a sacred arrow, with which he anchored himself to the ground by means of a black sash of elk skin and pledged himself not to retreat. If the party was not victorious, he had to remain and die unless his comrades pulled up the arrow. Three of the members' sashes were made of red cloth, and six were made of elk skin dyed red. If a member became too old to go to war, he gave his sash to a worthy younger man and received blankets or gifts for it.

Winter, 1846–47—The winter when they shot the mustache. Mustaches, said Mooney, were not infrequent among the Kiowas. Set-angia ("Sitting Bear") had almost a full beard. In a fight with the Pawnees Set-angia slipped in the snow, and a Pawnee shot him in the upper lip or mustache with an arrow.

Summer, 1847—There was no Sun Dance, but the summer was remembered because of the death of the Comanche chief, Red Sleeve, in an attack on a party of Santa Fe traders at Pawnee Fork on the Santa Fe Trail. Set-angia advised against the attack, and Red Sleeve taunted him with cowardice. The Kiowas drew off, and Red Sleeve and his Comanches attacked the train. Red Sleeve was shot through the leg by a bullet that entered the spine of his horse and caused the animal to fall and pin Red Sleeve beneath him. He called on Set-angia for help, but the Kiowa refused because of the taunt, and the white men came up and shot Red Sleeve.

Winter, 1847–48—The pictograph shows a camp of tipis with a brush windbreak about it. All winter the Kiowas camped on T'ain P'a, White River, an upper branch of the South Canadian.

Summer, 1848—A Koitsenko initiation Sun Dance was held on the Arkansas River near Bent's Fort. The figure represents an initiate with his red body paint and sash.

Winter, 1848–49—While camped near Bent's Fort, the Kiowas made antelope medicine for a great antelope drive. A sketch of an antelope marks the winter. Antelope drives, which were unusual, were made when buffalo meat was insufficient, and could be made only in winter when the animals gathered in herds. The drive was led by the "antelope medicine man," and the whole tribe, mounted and on foot, took part. The animals were encircled and seized by hand or by lassos. No shooting was allowed in the circle, but an animal that broke away was pursued and shot outside the circle.

Summer, 1849—This was the Cramp or Cholera Sun Dance. In the spring and summer, cholera swept the Plains; it came from the East with the emigrants to California and Oregon. The Kiowa Sun Dance was held on Mule Creek between Medicine Lodge Creek and the Salt Fork of the Arkansas. Cholera was brought by visiting Osages who came to the dance. The disease appeared immediately after the dance. The Kiowas said that half their number perished; whole families and camps were exterminated, and many committed suicide. The survivors scattered in different directions until the disease spent itself.

Winter, 1849–50—This winter was remembered because of fighting with the Pawnees, securing some Pawnee scalps, and holding a scalp dance.

Summer, 1850—A sketch of a chinaberry tree over a medicine lodge marked the Sun Dance which was held near a thicket of chinaberry trees on Beaver Creek or upper North Canadian River near present Fort Supply, Oklahoma.

155

Winter, 1850–51—The pictograph shows a sketch of a deer with antlers and a line attached to a human head. It marked the winter that Tañgíapa (whose name signified a male deer) died. He was killed in a raid into Tamaulipas.

Summer, 1851—Dusty Sun Dance was held on the north bank of the North Canadian, just below the junction of Wolf Creek. Strong winds prevailed and kept the air dusty. The summer was remembered for a fight with a band of Pawnees, ostensibly friends, who acted treacherously and were attacked and defeated. The Kiowas lost two prominent warriors.

Winter, 1851–52—A figure of a woman over the winter bar recalls the "winter the woman was frozen." Chief Big Bow, then a young man, stole a woman, a pretty one, whose husband was away on the warpath. He took her to his home camp and left her in the woods while he went into his father's tipi to obtain food. His father knew what he had done and held him. Exposed to the cold, the waiting woman had her feet frozen. "Stealing" a woman was contrary to tribal *mores*.

Summer, 1852—There was no sun dance. The pictograph for the summer notation is that of a man wearing a cuirass, probably obtained from Mexico. The Cheyenne chief, A'patate or "Iron-Shirt-Man," was killed by the Pawnees in Kansas or Nebraska. The Kiowas and Kiowa-Apaches joined the Cheyennes, Arapahoes, and some Dakotas in the fight against the Pawnees but were defeated by the larger Pawnee force.

Winter, 1852–53—A picture of a horse (with hooked feet which portrayed hoofs) held by a rope in the hand of a man portrays the loss of Set-angia's two horses, including the finest one in the tribe, a bay race horse known as "Red-Pet." The figure is that of the Pawnee boy who stole the horse. The fact that this theft was the most significant event of the winter marks the importance of the horse to the equestrian Kiowas.

Summer, 1853—Showery Sun Dance was the name given the Sun Dance celebration because of constant rain. A black cloud, with rain descending, and red flashes of lightning are shown over the medicine lodge.

A deliberate violation of the Tai-me rules distinguished this Sun Dance. Ten-piak'ia, father of the historian Sett'an, broke the rules by riding inside the camp circle with a small mirror. He afterward tried to poison Anso'te, the Tai-me keeper, with mercury scraped from the back of the mirror and placed in tobacco, which he gave the priest to smoke. Anso'te took one puff and put the pipe away, refusing to smoke. Shortly thereafter, Ten-piak'ia was thrown from his horse and killed; this was believed to be punishment of sacrilege. It is interesting to note that there were occasional, though rare, instances of deliberate nonconformity among some bold spirits in the tribe.

Winter, 1853–54—After the Sun Dance of the summer, a raid was made into Chihuahua where a mule train was attacked. As Pa'ngyagiate was striking the mules with his bow (counting coup and sealing ownership), he was shot and killed. The pictograph shows a Koitsenko warrior with his red sash and shield, denoting the warrior killed.

Summer, 1854—The Sun Dance was held at Timber Mountain Creek, where the Medicine Lodge Treaty would be signed in 1867. The pictograph portrays a black horse joined by a line to a human figure above the Sun Dance lodge, thus noting the death of Tsen-konkya ("Black-Horse"), a war chief.

Stumbling Bear's brother had been killed by the Pawnees, and at the Sun Dance, Stumbling Bear sent the pipe around to recruit a revenge expedition. A large war party consisting of several hundred warriors from seven tribes—Kiowas, Kiowa-Apaches, Comanches, Cheyennes, Arapahoes, Osages, and Crows—crossed the Arkansas and on the Smoky Hill met about eighty Sac and Fox Indians and a few Potawatomis, recently removed from beyond the Mississippi to Kansas. A fight disastrous to the Kiowas and their allies took place. The Sac and Foxes, armed with rifles, killed about twenty of their enemies, twelve of them being Kiowas. The Kiowas were impressed with the rifles and said that "they hit every time."

Some of the Kiowas stated that the expedition was directed against the new immigrant tribes, in an attempt to exterminate them. The report for 1854 by the Commissioner of Indian Affairs stated that the enemies of the one hundred Sac and Foxes in the fight had numbered fifteen hundred. The Osages had a few guns, but the other attackers had used bows and arrows. Six of the Sac and Foxes were killed from rifle shots.[5] Whirlwind, a famous war chief of the Southern Cheyennes, had every feather shot out of his war bonnet. He said it was the hardest fight he had ever been in, but he believed the medicine hawk on his war bonnet had saved him.

Winter, 1854–55—Another Koitsenko warrior, Gyai'koaóñte ("Likes-Enemies"), was killed by the Osages, or Quapaws, on a horse-stealing raid.

Summer, 1855—The pictograph shows a seated man. It was a hot summer with no Sun Dance and no grass. The horses were too weak to travel, and the Kiowas "sat down."

Winter, 1855–56—The brother of Gyai'koaóñte, A'dalton-edal ("Big-Head"), is pictured killing an Osage to avenge his brother's death. During the winter a large number of horses were taken in Chihuahua, and only one man, Going-on-the-Road, was lost.

Summer, 1856—Near Bent's Fort in Colorado the Prickly-Pear Sun Dance was held, late in the fall, when the prickly pears ripened.

[5] *Ibid.*, 298, citing the Report of the Commissioner of Indian Affairs, 1854. Old traders estimated the number assembled on the Arkansas at twelve to fifteen hundred lodges, even including the Texas or "Woods Comanches," and the number of horses and mules at from forty to fifty thousand. This assemblage, intended to wipe out the immigrants, was doomed to failure.

The fruit was generally eaten raw, and the fleshy leaves were used in painting on buckskin.

Winter, 1856–57—Two tipis sketched above the winter bar mark the winter that the tipis were left behind. After the summer Sun Dance, while camped near Bent's Fort, a war party led by Big Bow and Stumbling-Bear proceeded against the Navahos. Lone Wolf led the rest of the Kiowas after buffalo. Their tents were rolled up and left in care of William Bent. On returning, they found the Cheyennes had their tipis. When they complained to Bent, he said, "I have given them to my people." Bent's people were the Cheyennes, as Bent had married a Cheyenne woman. A quarrel took place, in which Lone Wolf's horse was shot and one Kiowa was wounded. The Kiowas were driven off, and the Cheyennes kept the property.

Summer, 1857—A Sun Dance was held on Salt Fork of the Arkansas at Elm Creek. A Kiowa, K'aya'nte, owned a sacred medicine forked stick of chinaberry, about four feet long, and placed it as a sacrifice inside the medicine lodge. Next year someone found that it had reversed and sprouted. This confirmed the mysterious power ascribed to the medicine. The stick had been trimmed of its bark. Ten years later the chinaberry was still growing.

Two war parties went out that summer—one against the Mexicans of El Paso and another, with the Comanches, against the Sac and Foxes. An engagement occurred near the location of the former battle with these people, and several Sacs were killed.

Winter, 1857–58—The Kiowas camped near Bent's Fort in Colorado. The Pawnees stole six bunches of horses. The Kiowas pursued them and intended to strike, but a snowstorm stopped them when only one Pawnee had been killed. The figure above the winter mark represents the stolen horses.

Summer, 1858—The Sun Dance was held on Mule Creek where it entered the Salt Fork of the Arkansas. The calendar depicts a natural circular opening in the timber, showing trees surrounding the medicine lodge.

Winter, 1858–59—After the Sun Dance, the Kiowas made a raid into Chihuahua and captured many horses. The Mexicans followed and attacked the Kiowas after they had recrossed the Río Grande. All fled save Gui-k'ati ("Wolf-Lying-Down"), who rode a mare which was delayed by a colt. He was shot and killed. Satanta and Set-imkia made a raid against the Utes on the upper South Canadian and killed one man.

Summer, 1859—The Cedar Bluff Sun Dance was held on the northern side of Smoky Hill River; the Kiowas were drawn far north by the abundance of buffalo.

Winter, 1859–60—Giaka'ite ("Back-Hide") died, and a cross was erected over his bones. The pictograph shows a man with a cross over his head. His name—Back-Hide—is the word for a piece of rawhide worn over the shoulders by women to protect the back when carrying wood or other burdens.

Giaka'ite was an old man and was abandoned on the Staked Plain of Texas. Returning to the spot afterward, a war party noted that someone had placed a cross over his skeleton. (The year before his death, while the Kiowas were moving, Adalpepte and his wife had met the old man on a feeble animal far behind the main party. It was cold, and Adalpepte had given the old man his buffalo robe to keep him warm. A year later, he was abandoned.)

Summer, 1860—There was no Sun Dance. Some of the Kiowas went south of the Arkansas, and some went north with the Kwahadi Comanches under the chiefs Tabananica ("Hears-the-Sunrise") and Isa-ha-bit ("Wolf-Lying-Down"). The latter group were attacked by white soldiers with allies of the Caddoes, Wichitas, Tonkawas, and Penateka Comanches. A Comanche named Tin Knife and a Kiowa, T'ene-badai ("Bird-Appearing"), were killed. The Commissioner of Indian Affairs reported in 1860 that the Kiowas and Comanches were hostile and that the army had been ordered to chastise them because many citizens were being murdered on the Santa Fe Trail. The Penateka Comanches, who had settled on a Texas reservation (Clear Fork or Upper Reservation), and the Caddoes and others from the Brazos reservation often aided the whites. All of these Indians were moved in 1859 to Indian Territory.

Winter, 1860–61—While the Kiowas were camped on the south side of the Arkansas, Gaabohonte ("Crow-Bonnet") raised a party to avenge the death of his brother who had been killed by a Caddo in the preceding summer's engagement. They went to the Caddo camp in the present Wichita reservation and there killed and scalped a Caddo. A scalp dance was held on the south side of Bear Creek or "Antelope-Corral River." From this rejoicing, the place got the name of Foolish or Crazy Bluff. A war party entered Texas about the same time but lost three men.

Summer, 1861—The pictograph shows a pinto horse tied to the medicine lodge. It was the Sun Dance "when they left the spotted horse tied." On the Arkansas River near the Great Bend in Kansas the dance was held. One man performed crazy and sacrilegious acts. After he came to his senses, he gave the horse to atone for his acts. This tying of a horse inside the medicine lodge was never known before, but horses were sometimes sacrificed to the sun by being tied to a tree out upon the hills. Ga'apiatan twice sacrificed a horse in this manner—once during the cholera of 1849 and again in the smallpox epidemic of 1861–62. These were propitiatory offerings with a prayer to save himself, his parents, and his children. His faith was rewarded; none of his relatives died. One of the horses offered was called "t'a-kon" ("black-eared"), considered by the Kiowas as the finest of all horses.

A war party of seven, including one woman, went into Mexico. It never returned. In 1894, Big Bow visited the Utes and found the woman married to a Ute and the mother of his three children. Big Bow learned that the others of the party had been killed. He tried to get the woman to return to the Kiowas, but she would not leave her family.

Winter, 1861–62—The pictograph shows a spotted man. This was "Smallpox Winter," when the Kiowas were in southwestern Kansas. A party on its way into New Mexico to trade stopped in a small town in the mountains at the head of the South Canadian. There they were warned of the disease. They left, but one Kiowa had bought a blanket and insisted on bringing it back even though he was warned not to do so. After they returned to their home camp, this man died and the epidemic broke out. They scattered to escape the disease.

For some years the Kiowas had been drifting eastward from their former camping grounds on the upper Arkansas. With the large influx of whites into Colorado following the discovery of gold at Pike's Peak in 1858, there was a great displacement of the buffalo as well as of Indians.

Summer, 1862—There was no event of importance, but a Sun Dance was held near the junction of Medicine Lodge Creek with the Salt Fork of the Arkansas after the smallpox epidemic.

Winter, 1862–63—The Kiowas camped on Upper Walnut Creek, which enters the Arkansas at the Great Bend in Kansas. Deep snow on the ground kept the horses from getting grass, and they tried to eat the ashes thrown out from the campfires. This was the "winter when horses ate ashes."

A war party went into the Texas Panhandle, crossing the Canadian near Kiowa Creek and passing on by Fort Elliott. They sang the "travel song" on Wolf Creek, and the treetops returned their echo. It may have been due to a bluff just south of the camp, but the Indians ascribed it to spirits. The pictograph shows a tree with a wavy line around its top. The travel song or *gua-dagya* was a part of the recruiting of a war party. The recruits and women beat on rawhide with sticks and sang the song. It was sung at intervals after the party set out.

Summer, 1863—The picture shows a one-armed white man over the medicine lodge. The Sun Dance was held on No-Arm's River or Upper Walnut Creek in Kansas. It was named after the trader, William Allison, who kept a store at the mouth of the river. Allison had lost his right arm. In 1864, Fort Zarah was built near Allison's trading post.

Winter, 1863–64—This was the winter that Big Head died. He was the uncle of the later chief Go-ma-te who took the same name, Adalton-edal. In this winter Anko began an annual calendar of events.

Summer, 1864—This was the summer of the Ragweed Sun Dance, called thus because many weeds grew at the junction of Medicine Lodge Creek and the Salt Fork of the Arkansas. The ragweed is pictured over the medicine lodge. The Kiowas had an encounter with United States troops, but it was apparently unintentional.

The Kiowas later camped near Fort Larned, Kansas. There they held a scalp dance. Set-angia and his cousin approached the fort and were warned away by a sentry. Not understanding, they advanced and the soldier threatened to shoot. Thereupon Set-angia shot two arrows at the soldier, shooting him through the body, and another Kiowa fired at him with a pistol. Panic ensued, the soldiers' horses were stampeded by the Indians, and the Indians abandoned their camp. They did not attack the fort, but the soldiers could not follow without mounts. The summer was full of depredations executed by several different tribes.

Winter, 1864–65—This was called the "Muddy-Traveling Winter" because of mud and heavy snows. The Kiowas and some Comanches camped on Red Bluff on the north side of the South Canadian between Adobe Walls and Mustang Creek. Early in the winter they were attacked by Kit Carson with troops and Ute and Jicarilla Apache allies. The picture shows tipis with arrows and wavy lines for bullets, symbolic of an attack. Five persons of the

Kiowas and their allies were killed, two of them women. The enemy burned their camp, and the Kiowas had to abandon it. A Kiowa-Apache was shot from his horse, and a Ute warrior got his war bonnet. One old Kiowa-Apache, who was left in his tipi in the hurry of flight, was killed.

According to the Indians, most of their warriors were off on the warpath. Their families were in the camp in charge of the old Chief Dohasan. Some of the men went out to bring in their horses one morning and saw the enemy creeping up to surround them. They ran back to give the alarm, and the women and children fled while the men mounted their horses to repel the enemy. Stumbling Bear was one of the leading warriors in the camp, and he distinguished himself by killing one soldier and a Ute, then causing another soldier to fall from his horse. Set-tadal ("Lean Bear") was another warrior who fought nobly, singing the war song of his order, the Tonkonko, which forbade him to save himself until he had killed an enemy. The Kiowas escaped but the camp was destroyed. The enemy was repelled. An army officer later wrote of the engagement:

> I understand Kit Carson last winter destroyed an Indian Village. He had about four hundred men with him, but the Indians attacked him as bravely as any men in the world, charging up to his lines, and he withdrew his command. They had a regular bugler, who sounded the calls as well as they are sounded for troops. Carson said if it had not been for his howitzers few would have been left to tell the tale.[6]

Carson's forces lost two soldiers killed and twenty-one wounded, several mortally. There was one Ute killed and four wounded.

Summer, 1865—The Peninsula Sun Dance was held—so called from the bend of the Washita, a short distance below the mouth of Walnut Creek.

[6] *Ibid.*, 315.

Winter, 1865–66—Ta'n-konkya, or "Black-Warbonnet-Top," died on the upper South Canadian. The Anko calendar also related the death of Chief Dohasan. The event is indicated by the figure of a wagon; Dohasan was the only Kiowa who owned a wagon (destroyed in Kit Carson's attack).

The winter is also notable for a large trading party from Kansas led by John Smith, called "Poomuts" or "Saddle-Blanket" from the articles of his trading stock. Various things were traded for buffalo hides. Smith also traded with and served as a government interpreter for the Cheyennes, especially at the Medicine Lodge Treaty of 1867.

Summer, 1866—The Flat Metal (or German Silver) Sun Dance was held on Medicine Lodge Creek near its mouth in Oklahoma. A trader brought the Kiowas a large amount of flat sheets of German silver which they hammered into belts and ornaments. The pictograph shows a medicine lodge and a strip of hide covered with silver disks finished with a tuft of horsehair. Such pendants were attached to the scalp lock. They obtained some genuine silver disks in the old days from Mexican silversmiths near present Silver City, New Mexico, and also used silver dollars. Charles W. Whitacre brought the German silver to the Kiowas. He was known as "Tsoli" (Charley). For years he had a trading store near the present agency at Anadarko, until he died accidentally in 1882.

Winter, 1866–67—This was the winter that Ape-mä'dlte was killed. The name signifies "Struck-His-Head-Against-a-Tree." He was a Mexican captive and was killed on the California Road in southwestern Texas by troops or Texans. As a member of Big Bow's raiding party, he was trying to stampede some horses of the Texans.

Another captive, later famous, was obtained by purchase from the Mescalero Apaches, who had stolen him near Las Vegas, New Mexico. This was Andres Martinez who was then seven years old and taken on a raid into Mexico. He was adopted by Set-dayá-ite,

("Many Bears" or "Heap-of-Bears"), who was killed in a raid against the Utes in 1868.

Summer, 1867—The Sun Dance was held on the Washita near the western line of Oklahoma. The Cheyennes attended the dance. The Navahos stole a whole herd of ponies, including a highly prized white race horse with black ears. The three tribes, finding their horses stolen, set out against the Navahos, then placed on the Mescalero reservation in eastern New Mexico, and recaptured their horses. The pictograph shows a white horse with black ears and a black spot on his rump, over a sketch of a medicine lodge.

At the Sun Dance there was an initiation of members of the Koitsenko. Some who had been cowardly were degraded and had their sashes taken from them.

Winter, 1867–68—This "Timber-Hill Winter" received its name from the treaty of Medicine Lodge Creek, called "Timber Hill River." The pictograph is quite clear. It shows a seated white soldier and a seated Indian shaking hands beneath a hill with trees on it. The Anko calendar records the killing of a Navaho by a Kiowa party under White Horse on the upper South Canadian. The Navaho man had no ears. A large party of Kiowas and Comanches fought the Navahos on the Pecos and defeated them, then returned in time for the treaty.

The Kiowas received notice to come in and camp near Fort Larned from General Winfield S. Hancock, then in command in that section. They called him "Old-Man-of-the-Thunder" because he wore epaulets showing the eagle or thunderbird. They were given rations, then returned to Medicine Lodge Creek to prepare a council house, some twelve miles above their camp (near present Medicine Lodge, Kansas).

Philip McCusker interpreted the terms of the treaty for the three confederated tribes. McCusker spoke only Comanche; translation into Kiowa was done by Ba'o ("Cat"), alias Gunsadalte ("Having-Horns"). The Kiowas said that the commissioners promised them "a place to go," schools, and food for thirty years, in the hope that they would then learn how to care for themselves. Only a few of the Comanches were present; most of the Kwahadi band were then on an expedition against the Navahos.

At the peace treaty there were about 5,000 persons (850 tipis) of the Cheyenne, Arapaho, Kiowa, Kiowa-Apache, and Comanche tribes, and some 600 whites, including commissioners, aides, a part of the Seventh infantry, and various interested groups—probably the largest Indian encampment ever held on the Plains.

Summer, 1868—The Sun Dance was held near where the treaty was made. The Cheyennes and Arapahoes frequently held their Sun Dance there separately from the Kiowas but also attended the Kiowa dance, as did many of the Comanches, who only once had a dance of their own.

The summer was noted for a disastrous battle with the Utes, when the Utes captured forever the Kiowas' sacred palladium. Some two hundred warriors smoked the pipe and, led by Patadal ("Poor-Buffalo" or "Lean Bull"), moved against the Navahos to revenge the Ute's killing of Lean Bull's stepson. Many Bears took with him two small Tai-me images. As the party moved out, the omens were unpropitious. Taboo to the Tai-me were bears, skunks, rabbits, and looking glasses. First a skunk crossed their path; then it was discovered that the Comanches were wearing their looking glasses or mirrors. They refused to give them up, but they did conceal them at a camping place. One night the Kiowas smelled bear cooking. The sacrilegious Comanches were broiling bear over a fire. This was bad. Some of the warriors turned back. Many Bears trusted to his powerful medicine and went on.

They met the Utes under the leadership of Kaneatche, head chief of the Utes and Jicarilla Apaches (after his death Ouray succeeded him). The Utes killed seven, including Many Bears and his adopted son. (Many Bears had ridden a balky horse and had dismounted. When his son returned to save him, both were slain.) His friend Pa-gunhente was also killed. The sacred images were taken by the Utes, who later suffered such bad luck that they gave the images to the trader Lucien Maxwell, who kept them in his store. The Utes said that the Kiowas were afraid to go there and that they were later lost. A brother of George Bent, of the noted Bent family, saw the "medicine." They were two small carved stones, one having the shape of a man's head and bust, decorated and painted, and one having the shape of a bear's kidney.

The Kiowas mourned their loss. They moved down to the Washita and camped near Black Kettle of the Cheyennes, whose village would soon be destroyed by Custer. Steps were then being taken to confine the Indians on the reservation.

Winter, 1868–69—A small raiding party descended upon the Texans, and Tanguadal was killed by a white man. The pictograph shows a man carrying a medicine lance or *zebat*. The dead warrior had been the hereditary owner of a medicine lance or arrow lance. Satanta then claimed the hereditary right to the lance through marriage into the family of one of Tanguadal's relatives. Satanta did not get the lance so he made one for himself, similar to Tanguadal's but with two arrow points—an ornamented wooden point (ceremonial) and a steel point (for actual use).

Stumbling Bear led a group to the Canadian to bury the bones of those killed with Many Bears by the Utes.

Summer, 1869—This was the summer of the War Bonnet Sun Dance. Although the Kiowas resided on the reservation, they moved away from it to hunt and dance. This Sun Dance was held on Sweetwater Creek near the western line of Oklahoma. Big Bow returned with a party that had gone on a revenge raid against the Utes; he brought back the war bonnet of a Ute whom he had killed.

Winter, 1869–70—A bugle is pictured over the winter sign. The Kiowas were camped on Beaver Creek near Fort Supply, Oklahoma. It was a winter of chronic alarm. The Cheyennes were on the warpath and were hard pressed by Custer. During this time a party of young men or probably Satanta blew a bugle on returning to camp, and the Kiowas, fearing soldiers, fled.

Summer, 1870—The Sun Dance was held on the North Fork of Red River in present Greer County, Oklahoma. Seeds of corn and watermelon brought by the traders had been thrown down, and had sprouted in the fall. This gave the name "Plant-Growing Sun Dance" to the dance.

Winter, 1870–71—The bones of young Set-angia were brought home, and the picture shows a sitting bear over a man's skeleton. In the spring of 1870, Set-angia, second son of Chief Set-angia, was shot and killed in Texas. The father, almost crazed, went to Texas, found the bones, put them in fine blankets, bundled them on the back of a red horse, and brought them home. On the return journey he killed and scalped a white man.

Set-angia placed the bones in a special tipi and gave a great feast in the name of his son. Until his death, Set-angia venerated the bones and carried them about on horseback. After Set-angia was killed at Fort Sill, his son's bones were buried. The young Set-angia was a favored child, *ade*, and held the office of *tonhyopde*, the pipe bearer or leader who went in front of the young warriors on a war expedition.

Another event of the winter, recorded by the Anko calendar, was the killing of four Negroes in Texas by a party led by Mama'nte ("Walking-Above"). Britt Johnson, the Negro who had traded for the return of the Fitzpatrick and Durgan captives (and of Johnson's own family as well) in 1864, was one of those killed.

Anso'te ("Long-Foot") also died in this winter. He had been the Taime keeper for forty years. There was no Sun Dance for two years until his successor was elected.

Summer, 1871—The Anko calendar notes the death of Konpa'te ("Blackens-Himself"), who was shot in a skirmish with soldiers. The Sett'an calendar records the arrest of the chiefs Satanta, Set-angia, and A'do-ette ("Big Tree"), who had not ceased their raids into Texas. On May 17, 1871, a party of one hundred warriors attacked Warren's wagon train in Texas and killed seven men and captured forty-one mules. Lawrie Tatum, agent, called on the commander at Fort Sill to arrest Satanta, Big Tree, Big Bow, Eagle Heart, and Fast Bear. Only three were arrested and imprisoned. By order of General Sherman, they were sent to Texas to stand trial. On the way Set-angia attacked the guard and was himself killed. Satanta and Big Tree were later confined in the penitentiary at Huntsville, Texas.

Winter, 1871–72—Some of the Kiowas camped on a branch of Elk Creek of upper Red River. Others camped near Rainy Mountain on the Washita. A large Pawnee party visited for peacemaking and were given horses by the Kiowas. The pictograph shows three Pawnee heads above the winter bar. (The Pawnees also visited the Washita in 1873 and determined to move to Indian Territory, which they did in 1875.) There was a mistake in the date by the calendar maker. Notices by Battey and others gave the date as 1872–73. Battey was with Kicking Bird, camped on Cache Creek, when forty-five Pawnees came to visit in March, 1873; he described the gift-giving, the peace, and the dance that followed.

Summer, 1872—There was no Sun Dance. The Anko calendar records a drunken fight between Sun Boy and T'ene-zepte (Bird-Bow), in which Sun Boy shot his opponent with an arrow. A large raid into Kansas took place, and the Kiowas captured a large number of mules. A Mexican captive, Biako (Viejo), was shot but later recovered. The Kiowa chiefs were trying to stop the raids at this time in order to conform to the demands of the government, but the tribe was split into factions.

Winter, 1872–73—The Sett'an calendar records a visit of the Pueblo Indians, who came to trade *biscocho*, or bread, and eagle feathers for horses and buffalo robes. The pictograph shows a Pueblo Indian, with his hair tied into a bunch behind, driving a burro with a pack on its back. (The Pawnees visited in the fall, and the Pueblos came in the winter.)

The Anko calendar records the burning of the heraldic tipi,

hereditary in the family of Dohasan, known as the "Tipi with Battle Pictures," which had occupied second place in the ceremonial camp circle.[7]

Summer, 1873—The Sun Dance, held on Sweetwater Creek, was described in detail by Thomas Battey who visited it. The Indians were much concerned over the promised release of Satanta and Big Tree. Battey had to tell them that the Modoc war (in California) had affected the release and cautioned them to wait peaceably. Some of the Kiowas, along with some of the Comanches, were hostile to the government. While the dance was under way, Pa-konkya ("Black Buffalo") "stole" the wife of Guibadai ("Appearing Wolf"), who in retaliation killed seven of Pa-konkya's horses and took a number of others according to tribal *mores*. A threat to kill the seducer brought the Tonkonko dog soldiers to interfere. Both the Sett'an and Anko calendars recorded the event. Pictured by the side of the medicine lodge, the horse bleeds from an arrow.

Winter, 1873–74—This was the winter of Satanta's return (October 8, 1873). The pictograph shows the red tipi and the figure of Satanta, distinguished by a red headdress. The Anko calendar records the killing in Mexico of two sons (i.e., one son and one nephew) of Lone Wolf. Lone Wolf went to bury his son, and from then on, was hostile to the whites.

Summer, 1874—The Sun Dance was "at the end of the bluff," near Elm Creek in Greer County, Oklahoma. Satanta gave his medicine or arrow lance to Áto-t'ain ("White Cowbird"). There were only two lances of this kind; one belonged to Satanta, the other belonged in the family of the deceased Tanguadal.

Winter, 1874–75—This was the winter "that Big-Meat was killed." The southern Plains tribes, including a large party of the Kiowas, went together on the warpath, in what became known as

[7] *Ibid.*, 336, and Plate LXXXIX.

the Outbreak of 1874. After the fight at the Wichita Agency at Anadarko in August, 1871, the Comanches fled to the Staked Plain and the Kiowas, to the head of the Red River, whence they were pursued by troops. A horse-stealing raid into New Mexico occurred also. On its return, it was suddenly attacked by soldiers. Gi-edal and one other were killed. At the close of the campaign, when the fugitives were returned to Fort Sill, a number of the hostiles were sent to Fort Marion, Florida.

Summer, 1875—The Sun Dance was held near Mount Walsh in Greer County, Oklahoma. It was called the "Love-Making Sun Dance" because some young men "stole" two girls. Troops accompanied the Kiowas because conditions were still unsettled since the outbreak.

Winter, 1875–76—In this winter 3,500 goats and sheep were issued to the Kiowas. The calendar shows a goat over the winter bar. These animals (and cattle) were bought by selling the Kiowa ponies—the idea was to make the hunting Kiowas into pastoral herders. About 600 cattle were distributed. The allied tribes had 16,000 horses and mules, reported officially, in 1874. After the outbreak, they had only 6,000 left; they were literally "unhorsed" and reduced to foot. The sheep and goat experiment was a failure, but some success was made with the cattle.

Summer, 1876—The Sun Dance was held on Sweetwater Creek. While it was going on, Mexicans stole all of Sun Boy's horses. The Kiowas pursued the culprits, but their mounts gave out and they failed to get the stolen horses back. The calendars record the summer with a picture of the medicine lodge and horse tracks. The Tai-me priest Dohente ("No-Moccasins") died and was succeeded by Set-dayá-ite ("Many Bears"), who had charge of this dance. (He was the uncle of Many Bears, killed by the Utes.) Later his cousin (called brother) Taimete had charge of the Tai-me.

Winter, 1876–77—This season was remembered by the killing

of the woman A'gábai ("On-Top-of-the-Hill"), by her husband Iapa ("Baby"). It had occurred sometime after the summer Sun Dance. The woman was ill. She promised Iapa, a medicine doctor, that she would marry him if he cured her. He did cure her and she married him, but she soon left him and for this he stabbed her. Agent Haworth asked the chiefs to arrest the man. (They said they would kill him if the agent wanted them to do so.) Dangerous Eagle and Big Tree made the arrest. The man was confined with a ball and chain for several months, and worked around the guardhouse. The chiefs requested that his life be spared, as "he was young and foolish and did not know the white man's laws or road."

Anko's calendar records the enlisting of twenty Kiowa scouts at Fort Sill; Anko was one of them. The first scouts were organized in 1875.

Summer, 1877—The troops accompanied the Kiowas to their Sun Dance encampment on Salt Fork of the Red River. It was called the "Star-Girl-Tree River Sun Dance," named for a sapling used in a sacrifice to the star girls or Pleiades. The summer was noted for an outbreak of measles which killed more Kiowa children than would the measles epidemic of 1892. The government school was turned into a hospital when its seventy-four children became sick, but not one child died there.

Winter, 1877–78—A party of the tribe camped near Mount Scott, and the remainder camped at Signal Mountain, which was named for a stone lookout station built in 1874. The pictograph shows a house on a mountain. The Anko calendar noted that buffalo were hunted at Elk Creek, called "Pecan River."

The winter was noted for an epidemic of fever. In the fall of 1877 the government built six-hundred-dollar houses for ten prominent chiefs of the three tribes, including Stumbling Bear, Ga'apiatan, Gunsadalte ("Cat"), and Sun Boy of the Kiowas, and White man and Taha of the Kiowa-Apaches.

Summer, 1878—The picture shows two medicine lodges, for the

173

Sun Dance was repeated. The dances were held on the North Fork of Red River. Part of the Kiowas had gone to the Plains in the western part of the reservation to hunt buffalo, while the rest had stayed at home. Since each group had pledged a Sun Dance, two were held. Troops again escorted the buffalo hunters to the dance.

Winter, 1878–79—Both calendars record the killing of Áto-t'ain ("White Cowbird"), to whom Satanta had given his medicine lance. Satanta committed suicide in Huntsville penitentiary at about the same time.

Áto-t'ain was the brother of Chief Sun Boy, also known as Arrowman. Áto-t'ain was killed by Texans while with a party that had gone to hunt buffalo, which were becoming scarce, in what is present Greer County, Oklahoma. The Indians had permission of the agent for this unusual winter hunt, and were accompanied by troops. When nothing was done about the murder, some Indians slipped into Texas and killed a white man named Earle for revenge.

Summer, 1879—This was the year of the Horse-Eating Sun Dance. A horse's head appears above the medicine lodge in the Sett'an calendar. The dance was held on Elm Fork of Red River. The buffalo were so few that the Indians were obliged to kill and eat their ponies during the summer to keep from starving. This was the date of disappearance of the buffalo from the Kiowa country. The official report stated that "the Indian must go to work and help himself or remain hungry on rations furnished," since buffalo meat could no longer support them.

Winter, 1879–80—This was the Eye-Triumph Winter. Káasa'-nte ("Little Robe") and several other persons went to the North Fork of Red River to look for antelope and probably for their old enemies the Navahos, who had removed to a reservation in New Mexico but still penetrated the Plains. One of the party, Pododal, believed that an owl (believed by the Kiowas to be an embodied spirit) had warned him that the Navahos would steal their ponies.

That night Pododal fired at something. In the morning they followed a bloody trail but turned back. Again came word from the owl that they would find a dead Navaho. In the morning they found an eye of a dead Navaho. With this, they returned to have an "eye" (attached to a pole like a scalp) dance.

Summer, 1880—There was no Sun Dance; a buffalo could not be found. The Anko calendar recorded the death of a large, tall chief named Pabóte (American Horse). He was buried in a coffin by the whites. Anko would not mention the name of American Horse, according to Kiowa custom. Three years later he consented to do so. Other names used in the calendars were similarly not mentioned for years.

Winter, 1880–81—A house was shown over the winter mark. It was probably the house of Paul Zontam, who returned from the East as an ordained Episcopal minister. There was also a visit from the Pueblo Indians of New Mexico.

Summer, 1881—The Hot Sun Dance was held in August on North Fork of Red River. A solitary buffalo was found. The Sett'an calendar also recorded that a young man, Masate ("Six"), had a hemorrhage. "Six" referred to the man's twelve fingers and twelve toes; his brother, Bohe, also had six fingers on each hand. These malformations were rare among the Indians.

Winter, 1881–82—This was the "winter when they played the *do-a* medicine game." Pa-tepte, or Datekan, and his rival, the Kiowa-Apache chief and medicine man Daveko, sought honors for the most powerful medicine. The Kiowa won. It was said that Pa-tepte tried to revive the old customs and amusements. The *do-a* or tipi game was played inside the tipi. It was the "hunt the button" game—a guessing game. The button was a small, fur-covered stick. One group played against another. The game was played by both sexes but never together. It was accompanied by one of the peculiar

175

do-a songs, in which members of the group joined. Points were scored by tally sticks, and wagers were made. The games often lasted far into the night.

Summer, 1882—There was no Sun Dance. Dohasan (nephew of the former chief), whose hereditary duty it was to procure a buffalo, could not get one. The Anko calendar noted the death of a beautiful girl, Patso-gáte ("Looking-Alike"), a daughter of Stumbling Bear.

The Sett'an calendar noted the attempts of Datekan or Pa-tepte ("Buffalo-Coming-Out") to bring back the buffalo. The Indians were much excited. They could not accept the fact that the buffalo were gone, but believed that they had gone underground. Originally, according to Indian mythology, the buffalo lived underground and were released by the hero god Sindi. Datekan sought to release them again. Many people believed him, brought him gifts, and obeyed him implicitly. Big Tree and other skeptics refused to take part. Finally, he said his medicine had been ruined by violations of taboos and that they must wait five years longer for the buffalo's return.[8]

Winter, 1882–83—The Sett'an calendar recorded the death of a woman, Bot-edalte ("Big Stomach"). The Anko calendar recorded that the Indian police camped this winter on Elk Creek of North Fork of Red River. There the Texas cattle trail crossed, and the police were on hand to keep cattle off the reservation. Quanah Parker, chief of the Comanches, persuaded the allied tribes to lease their grasslands to the cattlemen.

Summer, 1883—The Nez Percé Sun Dance was held, so called because the Nez Percés came to visit the Kiowas. The Nez Percés, intercepted in Montana by General Nelson Miles, were sent to Fort Leavenworth, then assigned to a reservation in Indian Territory. In 1885, after much unhappiness and illness, they were returned to reservations in Washington and Idaho. The Nez Percés

8 Marriott, *The Ten Grandmothers*, 142–54.

danced with the Kiowas at "Apache Creek" (Upper Cache Creek).

Set-dayá-ite ("Many Bears"), keeper of the Taime medicine, died, and the office was taken by Taimete ("Taime-man").

Winter, 1883–84—The Sett'an calendar had a picture of a canvas house with smoke issuing from it. It was said to be the house of Gakinate ("Ten"), the brother of Lone Wolf. A large number of children went this winter to the Chilocco Indian School, near Arkansas City, Kansas. A party of Dakotas also paid the Kiowas a visit to dance with them.

Summer, 1884—No Sun Dance was held. The agent said that he hoped "we have heard the last of the dance." The Anko calendar noted the hauling of government freight by the Kiowas, under a policy of hiring the Kiowas to get them to adopt the white man's industries. Most of the freight came from the railroad at Caldwell, Kansas, a distance of 150 miles. The Indians received nearly $8,000 during the year for this work, which they performed well.

Winter, 1884–85—The Sett'an calendar shows a house over the winter mark, indicating that the Kiowas were beginning to build houses for themselves. In 1886 it was officially stated that only nine families lived in houses, while all the rest lived in tipis. The Anko calendar recorded the "stealing" of another man's wife by Ton-ak'a ("Water-Turtle"), a medicine man. The injured husband whipped his wife and killed a number of Ton-ak'a's horses.

Summer, 1885—The Little Peninsula Sun Dance was held in a bend of the Washita about twenty miles above the agency. Dohasan went to the Staked Plain to get a buffalo. The Anko calendar noted that the Comanches received their first grass-lease money. The Kiowas did not make leases until a year later.

Winter, 1885–86—The outstanding event mentioned in both calendars was a prairie fire that destroyed much of the property of Te'bodal's and Á dal-pepte's camps, northwest of Mount Scott.

It occurred while most of the tribe had gone to the agency for rations.

Summer, 1886—There was no dance; no buffalo could be found. The Anko calendar records that Anko enlisted in the agency police force and that the Kiowas received their first money for grass leases.

Winter, 1886–87—The suicide of Peyi ("Son-of-the-Sand"), nephew of Sun Boy, was noted in both calendars. He took a horse without permission and was reproved for it. He was hurt and said, "I have no father, mother, or brother, and no one cares for me." He killed himself with a revolver. The Indians were very sensitive to reproof or derision, a most effective means of social control in primitive societies, and often took their own lives when they suffered sharp ridicule.

Summer, 1887—The Oak Creek Sun Dance was held, and the agent said that it was held with his permission but with the understanding that it was to be the last and it was not to be "of a barbarous nature." It was held on a tributary of the Washita above Rainy Mountain Creek. The buffalo for the dance was bought from Charles Goodnight, who kept a small herd of domesticated buffalo on his ranch in the Palo Duro Canyon area. Another payment of grass money was received by the Kiowas.

Winter, 1887–88—This winter, in addition to a money payment, the Indians received a large number of cattle in part payment of their grass money. The calendars show a cow's head over the winter mark.

Summer, 1888—No Sun Dance was held. The agent was instructed to prevent the dance, and even to call on the military, if necessary. The Anko calendar noted the preaching of the prophet Pá-ingya, who claimed to be invulnerable to bullets. He advocated

178

the destruction of the whites and caused great excitement. The agent said that the Kiowas were troublesome and followed the bad advice of Pá-ingya and Lone Wolf, refused to plant their seed, and took their children out of school. The prophet predicted that wind and fire would clear the white man off the land; then he would restore the buffalo and the old way of life. Sacred new fires were made, and the people were gathered in the western part of the reservation near Lone Wolf's camp. Sun Boy and Stumbling Bear were skeptical and refused to follow Pá-ingya. The prophecies failed and the Kiowas lost hope. Nothing was done to punish the prophet.

Winter, 1888–89—The Sett'an calendar recorded that during the winter the Kiowas camped on the Washita. The Anko calendar noted the death of Chief Pai-talyi ("Sun Boy").

Summer, 1889—There was no Sun Dance, and everyone remained at home on his farm. Grass money was received, and a son of Stumbling Bear died.

Winter, 1889–90—The Kiowas spent the winter in their camp on the Washita. Another grass payment was received. The Comanches visited the Kiowas to perform the *iam* dance. The dance had as a main feature the formal adoption of a child of the other tribe by the visitors. Two men danced while the rest sat around. There was an exchange of horses by the visited tribe for presents placed on the ground by the visitors. At the end of the ceremony the adopted boy was returned to his tribe. The same dance was known among the Wichitas and Pawnees.

Summer, 1890—A Sun Dance was started but was stopped by the military forces. The tribal circle had been formed and the center pole placed when the dance was stopped. A buffalo could not be had, so an old buffalo robe was put over the pole. Quanah Parker sent word to Stumbling Bear to advise the Kiowas to stop the dance or the soldiers would kill them and their horses. Stumbling Bear sent two young men to the encampment to tell them. After much discussion, they dispersed.

Winter, 1890–91—This was the winter that Sitting Bull, the Arapaho prophet of the Ghost Dance, came. The human figure above the winter mark signified Sitting Bull. Almost the whole tribe attended the first dance on the Washita at the mouth of Rainy Mountain Creek. Ápiatan ("Wooden Lance") went to visit the prophet Wovoka, to investigate the truth of the reports about the Ghost Dance religion. He returned in February, 1891. The Kiowas were convinced of the falsity of the doctrine of the return of the buffalo and the revival of the dead.

The Anko calendar recorded the death of three schoolboys who fled the government school. One had been whipped. They were frozen during a terrible blizzard. An outbreak was feared, but Captain H. L. Scott was sent to investigate and the Indians were quieted.

Summer, 1891—There was no Sun Dance. The event of the summer was the killing of P'odala-nte, or P'ola'nte ("Coming Snake") in Greer County, Oklahoma. He was shot by a white man in self-defense.

The Kiowas visited the Cheyennes during the summer.

Winter, 1891–92—The Sett'an calendar records the enlistment of the Indians, chiefly Kiowas, at Fort Sill. They became Troop L of the Seventh Cavalry under the command of Lieutenant (later Captain) H. L. Scott.

Summer, 1892—The summer was noted for a measles epidemic. Both calendars show a human figure covered with red spots. The children were sent home from the government school where the disease started. This spread the infection, and the Indians made the mistake of trying to wash off the spots in cold water. Mooney said that when he returned to the Kiowa reservation in the early summer of 1892, deaths were still occurring, and nearly every woman in the tribe had her hair cut off in mourning and her face and arms gashed by knives. Some had even chopped off a finger in grief. The men also had their hair cut in mourning and cuts on their bodies. Wagons, houses, tipis, and property were burned, and horses and dogs were shot over the graves to accompany their owners to the next world. During 1892, 221 Kiowas and Kiowa-Apaches died because of this epidemic. Dr. J. D. Glennan, attending surgeon to the Indian Troop at Fort Sill, distinguished himself in treating the stricken Indians. The Kiowa soldiers got together a sum of money to give him a horse, the favored gift of the Kiowas, but since he already had a horse, a gift of silver was given him.

Grass money was received during this summer. Noting the value of the money, the Indians sent a group to Washington to negotiate leases for the whole reservation. Quanah, Lone Wolf, and White Man were chosen to represent the Comanches, Kiowas, and Kiowa-Apaches, respectively. Permission was granted and leases were made, producing for the three tribes about $100,000 a year. Under the new and old leases, $70,000 (already due them) was paid, marking an era in their history. Some of the money was invested in building homes. About sixty homes were built within the year. The agent was encouraged to say that "in the future" the tipis would be banished and replaced by "comfortable houses."

The yearly calendars ended here. Later calendars of George Poolaw, George Hunt, and Mary Buffalo continued some of the important events.[9]

Some of the incidents of later years are unexplained by the drawings. In 1892–93, Big Bow visited the Pueblos. In 1893, Behodtle won the Fourth of July beauty contest in Anadarko. The winter of 1894–95 was when "they took the horses away from us." A big camp meeting was held in 1895, and 1895–96 was noted for the issuance of cattle. In 1897, Black Beaver and Crow died. During the winter of 1897–98, "they made the trip to Washington." In 1899 came the smallpox summer, and in the summer of 1900

9 *Ibid.*, 304–305.

the men surveyed for allotments and the Ghost Dance was ordered stopped. In 1900–1901 there was another smallpox epidemic. An annuity payment was made in 1905. In 1905–1906 was recorded the last event—Red Buffalo's wife died.

The Kiowa calendars were an unusual record of a people—a history of exploits, and of tribal and personal deeds, events, and tragedies for future generations—each with pictographs to serve as mnemonic devices.

CHAPTER FIVE

❖ CONTEST OF CIVILIZATIONS

*I*N 1845 the frontier of northern Mexico, receding for a century under the menace of the Comanches, Kiowas, and displaced Apaches, Lipans, Mescaleros, and others, continued to recede. Great areas had been depopulated, and their inhabitants gathered into towns and villages that had military protection. Texas joined the United States in 1845 and turned its "Indian problem" over to the United States—or so it thought. The war with Mexico, 1846–48, which brought United States troops into Texas, New Mexico, and California, to some extent quieted the Indians. After the Treaty of Guadalupe Hidalgo in 1848, the United States agreed to guard the boundaries of the Mexican cession, which stretched from the Río Grande and Gila to the Pacific. Texas still claimed New Mexico east of the headwaters of the Río Grande with territory to the forty-second parallel, into the present state of Wyoming, but never actually took control of it. The United States Congress finally bought the land north of Texas' present boundaries for $10,000,000 and made New Mexico a territory. It was then necessary to control passage across the Plains.

Gold was discovered in California in 1849. The Americans moved west in numbers far greater than the total of those who had essayed the Santa Fe Trail. The principal routes to California were north of the Kiowa range, although the Kiowas still moved as far north as present southern Colorado. Some caravans had military protection in crossing the Plains. Captain Randolph B. Marcy led one party west along the Canadian River and over to Santa Fe, from whence it went on to California. In 1849 a cholera epidemic, resulting from the gold rush, spread across the Plains from the east. It was worse than the smallpox epidemic of nine years before. Hundred of the Indians, as well as the emigrants, died, and some committed suicide in despair. More than half of the Kiowas perished in 1849. The trails were thick with travelers, and white contacts were increasing. The Kiowas turned their fury on those who tried to cross the southern Plains, and earned the reputation of being "the most predatory and bloodthirsty" of all the prairie tribes. It was said that they had killed more white men in proportion to their numbers than any other tribe.

In the 1850's, in response to complaints of Texas settlers over Indian murders and pillaging, and to keep the Indians from crossing into Mexico, a series of military forts was established along the western line of the Texas frontier. The Comanches had appropriated almost all of west Texas and shared north Texas with the Kiowas and Kiowa-Apaches. To the northeast, in Indian Territory, beyond these two dominant tribes were the Wichita tribes, who became more friendly with them. The Wichita confederacy was hemmed in by the Osages, Chickasaws, and Choctaws, and by great numbers of other Indians such as the Cherokees and Shawnees, who had been removed westward by government treaties into Indian Territory. Ever since the destruction of San Sabá Mission in 1757, the Wichitas had joined with the Comanches and their allies. The Wichita tribes, mainly the Taovayas, had long served as an agency for the trading of horses and mules stolen by the western Comanches and Kiowas, to the French as early as the 1750's, to the Spanish in Louisiana, and later to the Americans. In addition to livestock, the slaves, furs, and hides made up a lucrative trade. The Wichitas, from 1790 on, as the Spanish control over them weakened, joined the Kiowas in the raiding in west Texas and in the north along the Red River, moving back and forth from Texas to Oklahoma. In 1834 the Wichitas, Kiowas, and Wacos counted their warriors in a group. The old Chief We-ta-ra-sha-ro of the Wichitas told Catlin that they had three thousand warriors, making a total estimated population of twelve thousand for the three tribes. Catlin said that they occupied the whole country on the headwaters of the Red River into and through the southern part of the Rocky Mountains.[1]

The line of forts did not stop Indian raiding. The forts were fairly far apart, and the Indians slipped between them with ease. Fort Graham, 130 miles from Austin, was one of the early forts and was followed by Fort Worth, Fort Croghan, Fort Belknap, and others. Near the present site of Davis, Oklahoma, Fort Arbuckle was built in 1851, and the Fort Arbuckle Road was begun. It later ran to Fort Belknap on the Brazos, a mile south of present Newcastle, Texas.[2]

In 1852, Captain Marcy and Captain George B. McClellan (later of Civil War fame and Marcy's son-in-law) explored the country north of Red River. Marcy named Mount Scott, the highest peak of the Wichita Mountains. The site of the old Wichita village at Medicine Creek was recommended for a military post. No action was taken then, but it later became Fort Sill. Marcy's exploration had begun at Fort Belknap and ended at Fort Arbuckle.[3]

PEACE AND RAIDS

The Fort Atkinson Treaty was effected in 1853, in Kansas. Agent Thomas Fitzpatrick executed the treaty on July 27 with the Kiowas, Kiowa-Apaches, and Comanches. This treaty had as its purpose the protection of persons moving onto the Plains and of the growing traffic over the Santa Fe Trail, which was bringing

[1] *North American Indians*, I, 82.

[2] The remains of Fort Belknap are two miles from Newcastle, Texas.

[3] Nye, *Carbine and Lance*, 21–22; Colonel Randolph B. Marcy, *Thirty Years of Army Life on the Border* and *Border Reminiscenses*. See also Grant Foreman, *Marcy and the Gold Seekers*, and W. Eugene Hollon, *Beyond the Cross Timbers*.

in wealth of $2,000,000 a year. The tribes agreed to peace with the United States and Mexico and to the building of roads and military posts in their territory. For this they were to receive an annuity of $18,000 for a term of ten years, which might be further extended for five years. The treaty was not noted in the Kiowa calendars.[4]

The main difficulty in executing the treaty was the unwillingness of the Kiowas to cease raiding in Mexico and to give up their Mexican captives. Kiowa wealth came out of Mexico; the name of the tribe struck terror to the Mexicans. Agent Fitzpatrick said that adopted captives had become part of the tribe and that few would leave the tribe. How could the Kiowas give up their wives and children, or the husbands of their daughters? This was incomprehensible to them. All the treaty could accomplish was a provision for the future. Signing the treaty for the Kiowas was Satank ("Sitting Bear" or Set-angia, for the Kiowa-Apaches, Si-tah-le ("Poor Wolf"), and for the Comanches, Wulea-Boo ("Shaved Head").[5]

Percival G. Lowe, an enlisted soldier of the dragoons present at the treaty, said that Major R. H. Chilton had many talks with leading men of the Kiowas and Comanches. Lowe, who witnessed some of these talks, described "Satanta," but his description fits Satank ("Sitting Bear") better. He said that Satanta (more likely Satank)

> . . . the war chief of the Kiowas, always came rather neatly dressed in fine buckskin, and wore a handsome cavalry saber and belt. He was a man about five feet ten, sparely made, muscular, cat-like in his movements—more Spanish than Indian in his appearance—sharp features, thin lips, keen restless eyes, thin mustache and scattering chin whiskers that seemed to have stopped growing when one to three inches long . . . about thirty-five years old. He invariably came with one servant, a Mexican Indian, to the line of sentinels, dismounted, leaving his handsome horse and Spanish equipment with the servant.[6]

[4] Mooney, "Calendar History," 173.
[5] "Indian Treaties and Councils Affecting Kansas," *loc. cit.*, 763.
[6] Percival G. Lowe, *Five Years a Dragoon*, 131.

At one time the Major felt that his interpreter, who talked to Satank by signs, was not interpreting correctly. The Major described what he would do if certain trains on the road were bothered. Satank was mild and unconcerned. Major Chilton called his guard, and "Pyle (the interpreter) found himself tied to the wheel of a cannon . . . and there he remained until dark, when he was confined in the guard house . . . until he could tell the truth."

Satank was made to understand the threat and why the man was tied. He did not come again until Major Fitzpatrick came to make the "big talk." Lowe said there were thirty thousand Indians present. A big ox-train brought in the presents. Feasting and sham battles took place. Fitzpatrick had the confidence of all the Indians. The Indians then went south, and the troops remained until October, when they left "the dismantled fort" of Atkinson and returned to Fort Leavenworth.[7]

In 1854, as the buffalo began to decrease on their hunting grounds, the Kiowas, Comanches, Arapahoes, and Cheyennes organized a war party against the immigrant tribes in eastern Kansas, in an attempt to cut off their competition. The largest war party of the southern Plains—some 1,500 warriors—set out against the Sac and Foxes. It was a disastrous defeat for the Kiowas and their allies. The enemy numbered only 100, but they were equipped with American long-range rifles, strikingly effective against bows and arrows. The Kiowas regained some prestige, shortly afterward, by slaughtering a party of 113 Pawnees. In the next few years the Kiowas became increasingly warlike, even moving westward into New Mexico and Colorado to fight the Navajos and Utes. Although turned back by the military authorities, they raided the countryside. They continued to grow "more insolent and unmanageable."[8]

The Indian Agent, Robert S. Neighbors, tried to keep the northern Comanches and Kiowas from visiting the Penatekas on the Indian reserve in Texas, fearing that the peaceful Comanches might be led astray. While about half of the southern Comanches

[7] *Ibid.*, 134–35.
[8] Mooney, "Calendar History," 175.

were settled on the Clear Fork Reservation, five miles from Camp Cooper, they often watched the horse races of the officers at Camp Cooper. Captain Nathan Evans, Captain Newton Curd Givens, and other officers owned some Kentucky thoroughbreds.[9] These were fast and beautiful horses. The northern Comanches and the Kiowas came down to visit the chiefs Sanaco and Ketumsee on the reservation and watch the horse-racing—drawn as by a magnet to fast horseflesh. Needless to say, the officers kept careful watch over their horses.

On July 19, 1857, Agent Robert Miller met the Kiowas and Comanches at Pawnee Fork on the Arkansas. The Comanches were unwilling to treat with the United States and threatened to annul the Fort Atkinson Treaty of 1853. The Kiowas and Comanches were arrogant and confident of their superiority over United States forces. Miller reported to the Commissioner of Indian Affairs: "Nothing short of a thorough chastisement, which they so richly deserve, will bring these people to their proper senses."[10]

In the summer of 1858, Colonel E. V. Sumner, en route from Fort Kearney to the Arkansas, met Dohasan and the Kiowas and conferred with them. The Kiowa chiefs wanted peace but had difficulty in restraining their young men. They pledged that they would try to keep their young men off the warpath.[11]

In 1858, during the distribution of annuity goods on the Arkansas, fifteen hundred lodges of Cheyennes, Arapahoes, Comanches, Kiowas, and Kiowa-Apaches were set up in the encampment. The agent warned the Kiowas that if they did not cease their depreda-

[9] Captain Givens was stationed at Fort Belknap for a number of years and later (in 1858) at Camp Cooper. He built a hunting lodge called the "Old Stone Ranch-house" in 1853, near the site of Camp Cooper on the Clear Fork near the Comanche Reservation. It is today a part of the Matthews ranch near Albany, Texas. Givens introduced some fine cattle and sheep, all of which were either stolen or destroyed by the Indians. See Don H. Biggers, *Shackelford County Sketches.*

[10] Report of the Secretary of the Interior, 36 Cong., 1 sess., *Sen. Exec. Doc. No. 2,* Vol. I, Pt. 1 (1859–60), 448–52.

[11] Report of the Secretary of War, 35 Cong., 2 sess., *House Exec. Doc. No. 2*, Vol. II, Pt. 2 (1858–59), 425.

tions, the government would withhold their presents and would send troops to punish them. Dohasan sprang to his feet and said:

> The white chief is a fool. He is a coward. His heart is small—not larger than a pebble stone. His men are not strong—too few to contend against my warriors. They are women. There are three chiefs— the white chief, the Spanish chief, and myself. The Spanish chief and myself are men. We do bad toward each other sometimes, stealing horses and taking scalps, but we do not get mad and act the fool. The white chief is a child, and like a child gets mad quick. When my young men, to keep their women and children from starving, take from the white men passing through our country, killing and driving away our buffalo, a cup of sugar or coffee, the white chief is angry and threatens to send his soldiers. I have looked for them a long time, but they have not come. His heart is a woman's. I have spoken. Tell the great white chief what I have said.[12]

The raids into Texas were worsening, and Texas was bitter over the defense problem on its northern frontier. In 1858 the Secretary of War decided on punitive measures against the Indians. Captain Earl Van Dorn organized a punitive force at Fort Belknap consisting of several companies of the Second Cavalry. Lawrence Sullivan ("Sul") Ross marched with them, leading a force of 135 friendly Indians. These included Wacos under Nasthoe and Tawakoni Jim, with some Caddoes and Tonkawas from the reservation at Fort Belknap.[13] While they were starting out, Captain William E. Prince of Fort Arbuckle was making a treaty with the Comanches, not aware of the punitive plans. After concluding the

[12] Mooney, "Calendar History," 176, citing Annual Report of the Commissioner of Indian Affairs, Agent Miller, 1858.

[13] The Texas legislature authorized the establishment of two temporary reservations on February 6, 1854. Four leagues were set aside on the Clear Fork of the Brazos, and eight leagues on the Brazos. In 1855 the majority of the Tawakonis and Wacos, with the Caddoes and Tonkawas, were gathered in and placed on the eastern reservation below Fort Belknap. The Comanches under Chiefs Sanaco and Ketumsee were placed on the western reservation. Because of continued friction, theft, murder, and reprisal, the reservations were abandoned in 1858, and the Indians were removed to a temporary settlement on Washita River in present Oklahoma. See Mildred P. Mayhall, "The Taovaya Villages."

peace, the Comanches under Buffalo Hump (Pochanaw-quoip), Quo-ho-ah-te-me ("Hair Bobbed on One Side"), and Ho-to-yo-ko-wat ("Over the Butte") visited with the Wichitas living at Rush Springs.[14] Nasthoe and his son-in-law Wau-see-sic, scouting ahead, met the Wichitas and warned their chiefs, How-its-cahde and Esa-dowa, of the impending war against the Comanches. The Comanches first thought of flight, then determined to rely on the treaty just made or to fight.

After marching all night, Captain Earl Van Dorn fell on them in the early dawn of October 1 at Rush Creek, five miles southeast of Rush Springs. This was the Battle of the Wichita Village.[15] After about five hours of hard fighting, the Comanches fled, having lost several of their bravest warriors. About seventy Comanches and some of the Wichitas were killed. Captain Charles Whiting took command after Captain Van Dorn was badly wounded. Cornelius Van Camp was killed when an arrow pierced his heart; two others were killed and several, including Sul Ross and a medical officer were dangerously wounded. Help was received from Fort Ar-buckle. Captain Van Dorn later recovered. Meanwhile, the Co-manches joined the Kiowas on the Arkansas River and the Wichitas fled their village and sought sanctuary at Fort Arbuckle. While with the Kiowas, the Comanches sold them a Mexican boy, by the name of Esteban, captured in Arikarosap's raid into Chihua-hua. In later years he became Quitan, warrior and medicine man of the Kiowas.

Captain Van Dorn's company settled at Camp Radziminski for the winter. The punitive expedition had not settled the Indian troubles. The Texas reservations for the Penateka Comanches on the Clear Fork of the Brazos, and for the Wacos, Tawakonis, Caddoes, and Tonkawas on the Brazos below Fort Belknap, were

[14] Hodge, *Handbook*, II, 949; Nye, *Carbine and Lance*, 24–25. Buffalo Hump's name could not be politely translated, having to do with priapism.

[15] Report of the Secretary of War, including Captain Earl Van Dorn to George W. Thomas, October 15, 1858, reporting fight against Comanches; D. E. Twiggs to Lieutenant Colonel Thomas, November 1, 1858; Jno. Withers, Orders No. 25, October 19, 1858; all in 35 Cong., 2 sess., *Sen. Exec. Doc. No. 1*, Vol. II, Pt. 2 (1858–59), 272–78.

having trouble with the near-by settlers. The Indians were accused of stealing horses, raiding, and murdering, although most of the stealing was coming from north of the Red River. Some settlers fell upon the Indians camping below the reservation near Belknap and destroyed them. Finally it was decided to move the Indians north to Indian Territory, for their own good.[16]

Fort Cobb, which was in Kiowa territory, was to be the reservation area. The removal began on August 1, 1859.[17] Major Robert S. Neighbors, the Indian agent, was in charge, accompanied by Agents Samuel A. Blain, Shapley P. Ross, and Matthew Leeper. Soldiers accompanied them under Major George H. Thomas. Horace P. Jones and Philip McCusker were the interpreters for the agency. McCusker married a Comanche woman and was the only white man allowed in the Comanche villages. When the Indians reached the site west of the present Anadarko, they came on great numbers of buffalo, and were eager to hunt. The Indians were allowed to go buffalo hunting while the soldiers rested about the valley and watched them. Blain became the agent for the Wichitas, Caddoes, Tonkawas, and Penateka Comanches at the agency four miles northeast of present Fort Cobb. Following the settlement of the Indians, Neighbors, Leeper, and Ross returned to Texas.[18]

On September 16, 1859, Agent William Bent met the Kiowas and Comanches at the mouth of Walnut Creek on the Arkansas. They numbered 2,500 warriors. They appeared peaceable in the presence of federal troops but assumed a threatening attitude after the troops left. Bent believed that they had a passion for revenge and thought that military forces should be constantly present. White settlement pressure was disturbing them, and he foresaw a

[16] Nye, *Carbine and Lance*, 33. See also note 13 above. See Carl Coke Rister, *Fort Griffin on the Texas Frontier*; Rupert N. Richardson, *The Comanche Barrier to South Plains Settlement*; Walter Prescott Webb, *The Texas Rangers*, 171 (on the removal of Indians from Texas); and Kenneth Franklin Neighbors, "Robert S. Neighbors in Texas, 1836–1859."

[17] A number of settlers signed petitions asking for the removal of the Indians. One of these was sent to Captain Newton Curd Givens at Camp Cooper in 1858.

[18] Nye, *Carbine and Lance*, 33–34. Major Neighbors was killed in a quarrel at Fort Belknap, by Ed Cornell, who hated him for his concern for the Indians.

war of extermination unless the nomads could be settled into a pastoral or agricultural way of life.[19]

The military post of Fort Cobb was established on October 1, 1859. Texas Rangers later camped at Camp Radziminski for a year, patrolling the border. In 1860 the Rangers, with Tonkawas, Caddoes, and Wichitas, attacked a camp of Kiowas and Comanches near the head of the Canadian in the Oklahoma Panhandle. The Comanches were led by Tabananica ("Hears the Sunrise") and Isa-ha-bit ("Wolf Lying Down"). A number of Comanches were killed, and a prominent Kiowa, Bird Appearing, was killed by the Caddoes. The Tonkawas indulged in eating the slain. This infuriated the Kiowas and Comanches, who sought revenge against these Indians for many years.[20] During the Civil War, the federal troops moved into Kansas, but the agency continued under the Confederate government. On October 23, 1862, the Comanches and Kiowas (along with the Delawares, Shawnees, and Caddoes) revenged themselves on the Tonkawas with a massacre. Those left fled to Fort Arbuckle and later, in 1863, back to Texas. After the Civil War, when Fort Griffin was established, they congregated at the Tonkawa village at Fort Griffin, serving as scouts for the army.

In 1860 military forces moved across the Plains. A few skirmishes with Indians took place. One detachment went to the North Fork of the Canadian (June 15, 1860) and prepared to meet the Kiowas but found only a herd of mustangs.[21] In July, near Bent's new Fort, Lieutenant J. E. B. Stuart and twenty men pursued a small body of Kiowas and, combined with the forces of Captain William Steele, killed two warriors and captured sixteen women and children. In the same campaign Captain S. D. Sturgis encountered some Kiowas and Comanches on the Republican Fork

[19] Report of the Secretary of the Interior, 36 Cong., 1 sess., *Sen. Exec. Doc. No. 2, Vol. I, Pt. 1* (1859–60), 506–507.

[20] Nye, *Carbine and Lance*, 36. See also Rupert N. Richardson, *The Comanche Barrier*, and Webb, *The Texas Rangers*, 151–72.

[21] Lieutenant J. E. B. Stuart, "The Kiowa and Comanche Campaign of 1860 as Recorded in the Personal Diary of Lt. J. E. B. Stuart," ed. by W. Stitt Robinson, *The Kansas Historical Quarterly*, Vol. XXIII (1957), 382–400.

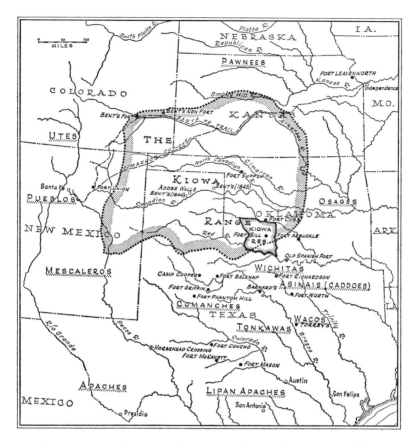

on August 6 and reported twenty-nine Indians killed.[22] After marching 1,404 miles, Major John Sedgwick's column completed the campaign. These operations of 1860 gave an appearance of force to the government. In November, 1861, Indian Commissioner William P. Dole reported that the Indians had manifested a disposition to resume friendly relations with the government and to be restored to its confidence. The Indians were then going into winter quarters, and tensions were lessened.[23]

[22] Report of the Secretary of War, 36 Cong., 2 sess., *Sen. Exec. Doc. No. 1*, Vol. II, Pt. 2 (1860–61), 18, 19–22.

[23] Report of the Secretary of the Interior, 37 Cong., 2 sess., *Sen. Exec. Doc. No. 1*, Vol. I, Pt. 1 (1861–62), 634.

After leaving the dragoons, Percival G. Lowe became first a wagon master for the government and later a private contractor. During the Civil War he returned to government work. In September, 1862, he was assigned the job of taking 600 horses and a wagon train of 120 six-mule wagons with supplies across the Plains to Fort Union, New Mexico. The train left Fort Riley and had to pass through the "whole Kiowa and Comanche nations" camped along the Arkansas near present Dodge City, "and the sight of 600 fine horses passing close would be a great temptation to them."[24]

For miles along both sides of the Arkansas, Lowe saw Indian tipis. At one time a hundred Indians came to visit the camp of the wagon train, but only two were allowed to cross the guard line— Satanta and Lone Wolf. They dined with Lowe and the officers of the small army escort. "Joe" Armijo, Lowe's interpreter, gave the Indians to understand that they had more soldiers than could be seen—that soldiers were asleep in the wagons. Each teamster had his musket sticking out of the wagon covers. The Indians were told not to get too near the wagons, and the chiefs promised. The Indians observed their chiefs' commands. "For more than ten miles these people [the Kiowas] trudged on foot, or cavorted about on ponies on either side of the train, never approaching nearer than 200 yards," and the two chiefs "came to shake hands and say goodbye [and Lowe] gave them a barrel of hard bread and small sack of sugar."[25]

The wagon train went on to Fort Lyon, commanded by Colonel Jesse Leavenworth, took the Raton route, and arrived safely at Fort Union. Leavenworth had warned them of guerrillas, but none were met. On the trip only three horses and four mules were lost.[26]

Smallpox again spread across the Plains during the winter of

[24] Lowe, *Five Years a Dragoon*, 382.

[25] *Ibid.*, 385.

[26] *Ibid.*, 385–86. Lowe later served as a contractor for supplying cattle to the Sioux agencies, and in 1876 he served as guide for the army troops who chained the Santa Fe Trail from Fort Leavenworth via the Raton route. It measured 752 miles to Fort Union. (*Ibid.*, 407.)

1861–62. It was brought back from northern Mexico by some of the Kiowas returning from a trading trip. Following the epidemic, the government determined to vaccinate the Indians against this disease. In the summer of 1863, a delegation of Kiowas visited Washington and while there gave permission for the establishment of mail stations in their country.

War on the Plains broke out in the summer of 1863. The Kiowas, Kiowa-Apaches, Comanches, Cheyennes, and some of the Arapahoes were actually the masters of the Plains and arbiters of the right to cross the Plains. The Civil War had drawn off most of the soldiers, and the Indians feared no military action. The Kiowas desired revenge against the Caddoes. Crow Bonnet, brother of the killed Bird Appearing, led a Kiowa war party south from the Arkansas to the Caddo camp (north of the site of Anadarko) and killed and scalped a Caddo. A war party under Tone-tsain was not so fortunate; few survivors returned. Another revenge party against the Caddoes lost four dead.[27]

The West was in a ferment. There were rumors that a general Indian war was planned against the whites for the spring of 1864. The gold fields of Colorado had been discovered in 1858, and the rush to the gold and silver mines about Pike's Peak in present Colorado had led great numbers of whites across the Plains in 1859 and thereafter. The Indians were alarmed over this and desired to re-establish their superiority and authority. During the period of the Civil War, as homesteaders (and deserters) moved west, there was constant fear of an Indian war. Indian Agent S. G. Colley, at Fort Lyon, Colorado, who had charge of the Cheyennes, Arapahoes, Kiowas, and Comanches, said that all the Plains Indians were to blame for murders and depredations and "needed a sound threshing." The Commissioner of Indian Affairs, William P. Dole, included in his annual report of 1864 a letter from George K. Otis, superintendent of the Overland Mail Line, stating that the

---

[27] Mooney, "Calendar History," 176; Nye, *Carbine and Lance*, 41–42, 44. Tone-tsain had violated the Sun Dance taboos. No warrior was supposed to leave during the Sun Dance, as Tone-tsain had done; hence his lack of success, according to general belief.

Indians intended to regain and hold their country, even if they had "to destroy every white man, woman and child."[28]

While the Civil War raged on, the Indians had a carnival of raids —in Kansas, Colorado, New Mexico, and as usual, Texas. The frontier receded before the might and viciousness which they visited upon the captives and the dead. Numerous attacks occurred along the Santa Fe Trail. The Kiowas attacked United States volunteer troops at Fort Larned, Kansas, which was then the government distribution point for the Kiowas and Comanches. While encamped near Fort Larned, the Kiowas held a scalp dance, honoring a raid made by Satanta near Menard, Texas. Several whites had been killed, and Mrs. Dorothy Field had been captured. After the dance, the Indians tried to go to the sutler's store, but were warned by the sentry to stop. Satank shot two arrows into the sentry, and the Indians fled. When the soldiers turned out to defend the post, the Indians raced away. Later, Satanta sent word back to the quartermaster that he should provide better horses, for those taken were poor.[29]

Despite hostilities, the Indians frequently visited the military posts in Kansas. The Kiowas and Comanches loved horse racing and bet heavily on their races—ponies, robes, and doeskins against the silver dollars of the soldiers. In 1863 they brought to Fort Larned, Kansas, a black Texas stallion considered to be the best racer on the Plains. People came from three hundred miles away to watch the race. The black stallion won and the Indians received three hundred dollars. In their joy over the victory, they spent their money on a feast for the spectators; they bought candy and canned goods from the sutler and had a big "give-away." The soldiers from Fort Riley were so impressed that they purchased the black stallion from the Indians.[30]

[28] Mooney, "Calendar History," 177. See 38 Cong., 2 sess., *House Exec. Doc. No. 1*, Vol. V (1864–65). Report of the Secretary of the Interior, including Annual Report of the Commissioner of Indian Affairs, pp. 147–91. Letters 95 and 109, pp. 388, 397–99.

[29] *Ibid.*, 176–77; Nye, *Carbine and Lance*, 44–45. It was never learned what became of Dorothy Field. She was still inquired after at Fort Sill in 1872. From 1872–78, the agent was James Haworth, whose efforts to rescue prisoners were inadequate.

It was believed that the Indians would not begin any war until the grass was high in the spring of 1864; their horses had to fatten up before they could move out. In April, 1864, a government physician was sent to vaccinate the Plains Indians against smallpox. He found the Indians friendly. He spent two weeks among the Kiowas on the Arkansas River and four days in Satanta's village. He believed Satanta to be their principal chief and said: "He is a fine-looking Indian, very energetic and as sharp as a brier." Satanta was friendly, and the doctor ate three meals a day with him in his lodge. Satanta put on "a good deal of style," had a carpet for his guests to sit on, and painted fireboards, twenty inches wide by three feet long, ornamented with bright brass tacks all around the edges, to use for tables. He had a "brass French horn" which he blew when meals were ready. The doctor said that he slept with Yellow Buffalo, one of the chiefs who had visited in Washington. The Indians then had many horses from Texas and planned another raid into Texas in "about five or six weeks." The doctor surmised that success in the raids would encourage them to try farther north. By this time, the doctor had vaccinated nearly all of the Indians on the Upper Arkansas.[31]

In June, 1864, messages were sent to all friendly Indians to report to the military posts, with the warning that all who were not there were to be considered hostile. The Indians in eastern Kansas were prohibited from going on their usual buffalo hunt on the Plains. The official reports were full of stories of murder, pillage, and slaughter of the settlers. The overland mail abandoned all stations for a distance of four hundred miles. Frontier ranches were deserted. The Kiowas and their allies reasserted their right to rule their homeland.

ELM CREEK RAID OF 1864

The Kiowas moved south to the Staked Plain. At Red Bluff, on

[30] William E. Unrau, "The Story of Fort Larned," *The Kansas Historical Quarterly*, Vol. XXIII (1957), 257–80, 375.

[31] Mooney, "Calendar History," 177, citing the Annual Report of the Commissioner of Indian Affairs, Letter of Dr. H. T. Ketcham (1864), 258.

the Canadian, they formed a large war party with the Comanches under Little Buffalo. In October, 1864, Little Buffalo led them to Young County, Texas. Sixty miles south of present Wichita Falls, they attacked Fort Murphy, a Confederate outpost near Fort Belknap, killing five soldiers. Then they ravaged the area of Elm Creek, sixteen miles west of Fort Belknap. During these exploits, the party killed eleven Americans and captured seven women and children—more captives than they usually took, and kept, alive.

A number of homes were attacked on October 13, 1864. These included the Elizabeth Fitzpatrick home, the Tom Hamby and Thomas Wilson homes, the George Bragg and several other homes. The Indians charged the Fitzpatrick home, killed several people, and took some captives, including a small child, Millie Durgan. Mokeen saw Aperian Crow (Au-soant-sai-mah) rescue the child from under a bed. Aperian Crow said, "Ah, I find a child," and he took her back home for his wife, Ah-mate ("Medicine Hunt Girl").

The Bragg family later moved to Fort Griffin (established after the Civil War) from Elm Creek. Mrs. Bragg told the story of the Elm Creek Raid to her neighbor, Mrs. B. W. Reynolds. She said that they were cut off from the house where the women and children were gathered, so they ran down the creek and hid in a sort of cave. They were afraid that their dog would bark and betray them, but the dog lay quietly. They were under the rock all day, "with the Indians some of the time walking over their hiding place so close that they could hear the tinkle of their moccasins. The Indians would wind very narrow strips of tin around the fringe of their moccasins and these made a tinkling sound as they walked."[32]

After dark the family crept out and went home, to find everything sacked. Feather beds had been ripped open and the ticking taken, and their clothing was gone. Fortunately the house was not burned.

Britt Johnson, a Negro orderly at Fort Belknap whose wife and children were among the captives, bravely set out to follow and ransom them. He secured the assistance of Asa-Havey ("Milky

[32] Matthews, *Interwoven*, 48.

Way") at the Penateka camp on the Washita and traded horses for the captives. All who were still alive were ransomed, save one child of eighteen months, Millie Durgan, who they said was dead.[33] Millie (Sain-toh-oodie) grew up a Kiowa, married a chief, Goombi, had children, and only learned late in life of her true origin. Then she returned to identify and visit her relatives in Texas. She toured a number of schools and told her story to the school children. She visited the state capitol and sat in Governor Dan Moody's chair. When Moody's secretary (Governor Moody was out of town) asked her what the state of Texas could do for her, she said that all she wanted was to go back to Oklahoma.[34]

Sallie Neighbors Matthews went to school with Millie's older sister, Lottie Durgan, ransomed from the Kiowas. Lottie was "a rosy-faced, black-eyed girl, pretty in spite of a mark that had been put on her forehead by the Indians, a tattooed ring the size of a dime or a little larger."[35]

Because of Indian depredations, settlers moved down below Fort Belknap and established a temporary, fortified village known as Fort Davis, which was to be abandoned after the Civil War.

CHEYENNE MASSACRE AT SAND CREEK

In the autumn of 1864, Colonel J. M. Chivington and the Colorado Volunteers fell upon a Cheyenne village (which had made a peace), surprising and wiping out a large part of the population. This was much deplored by friends of the Indians and was known as the "Sand Creek Massacre." It aroused indignation across the

[33] Nye, *Carbine and Lance*, 45–46. The story of Millie Durgan is as interesting as that of Cynthia Ann Parker, but it differs in having a happy ending. Millie was adopted by Au-soant-sai-mah, a warrior and member of the Koitsenko soldier society, and hence of high status. Millie was loved by her Kiowa parents. A picture of her is shown in Nye, *ibid.*, 286. See also George Hunt, "Millie Durgan," *Chronicles of Oklahoma*, XV, No. 4 (1937), 480–82.

[34] Adolph Goombi, grandson of Millie Durgan Goombi, in conversation with author, July 17, 1957, at the Kiowa Indian Agency, Anadarko, Oklahoma. A clipping from the Gainesville *Register* (August 22, 1932), tells of Millie Durgan's visit to Texas. In "Indian Captives Scrapbook," Archives, University of Texas Library.

[35] Matthews, *Interwoven*, 49.

country. Black Kettle had brought his Cheyennes to Fort Lyon, Colorado, for roll call. He camped near the fort at Sand Creek and flew an American flag. In the surprise attack, sixty-nine Indians— men, women, and children—were cruelly killed. Scalpings and mutilations were resorted to, and the details horrified the nation. This massacre increased Indian hostility.[36] Wynkoop said that "since this horrible murder" the country was desolated, and that "already over 100 whites have fallen as victims to the fearful vengeance of these betrayed Indians. All this country is ruined."[37]

KIT CARSON AND THE BATTLE OF ADOBE WALLS IN 1864

In the summer of 1864, Kiowas, Comanches, Cheyennes and other Indians "held high carnival" on the western Plains. The army issued orders to attack them. In New Mexico, General James H. Carleton sent Colonel Christoper ("Kit") Carson against the Kiowas and Comanches in their winter quarters on the Canadian. Carson had 14 officers, 321 cavalrymen, 72 Utes and Jicarilla Apaches, and 2 Ute women (women often accompanied the warriors and had the right to dance the victory dance when they returned). The forces left Cimarron, New Mexico, on a snowy November 3, 1864, after being outfitted at Lucien Maxwell's Indian Agency. Carson's forces followed the valley of the Canadian and came upon the Kiowas and Comanches near Bent's old trading post of Adobe Walls in the Texas Panhandle. Carson fell on the

[36] See Hodge, *Handbook*, I, 253; George Bird Grinnell, "Black Kettle," in *ibid.*, I, 152–53; and "Nov. 29, 1864. Engagement with Indians on Sand Creek, Colo. Ter.," *The War of the Rebellion*, Ser. 1, Vol. XLI (1902), 948–72, including the reports of Colonel John M. Chivington, of Major Scott J. Anthony, of Major Edward W. Wynkoop on his investigation of Indian affairs in the vicinity of Fort Lyon, and of John Smith (United States Indian interpreter) and others. Chivington said that he fought nine hundred to one thousand Indians and left five to six hundred dead on the field. Smith, visiting the Indians as a trader, was in the village when it was attacked, and his own half-blood son was killed. Smith said that there were only five hundred Indians in the village and that sixty to seventy of those, mostly women and children, were killed. Others told of the scalpings and the terrible mutilations done to the Indians.

[37] Report of Major Edward W. Wynkoop, in *ibid.*, 961.

village in early morning. The Indians fled the village, and Carson's forces overtook them and a brisk fight ensued. Dohasan rushed downstream to warn the next settlement, a Comanche village, but had his horse shot from under him. The women and children fled as the warriors rushed to the fight. As more and more warriors arrived from the line of camps, Carson was forced to abandon the fight. Two twelve-pounder howitzers were used to hold back the furious charges of the Indians. Lieutenant George H. Pettis, in command of the howitzers, brought his guns up to the line of skirmishers, and Colonel Carson said, "Pettis, throw a few shells into that crowd over thar." Pettis later recalled of the fight:

> Our Indians, mounted and covered with war paint and feathers, were charging backwards and forwards and shouting their war cry, and in their front were about two hundred Comanches and Kiowas, equipped as they themselves were, charging in the same manner, with their bodies thrown over the sides of their horses, at a full run, and shooting occasionally under their horses' necks, while the main body of the enemy, numbering twelve or fourteen hundred, with a dozen or more chiefs riding up and down their line haranguing them, seemed to be preparing for a desperate charge on our forces.[38]

During the morning and afternoon fighting, an Indian bugler who knew the army calls blew the opposite calls to those blown by Carson's bugler. So well was this executed that Carson believed he was a white man.[39] It may have been Satanta, who often blew a bugle. During the retreat, a Mexican secured a Comanche scalp, which delighted the Utes; over it they held a scalp dance every night.

As they returned to the first village, they found the Indians there, who had gone around the hills and were trying to retrieve their possessions. The howitzers were used again to drive them out, and the Kiowa village was burned—176 lodges and all their winter

[38] *Personal Narratives of the Battles of the Rebellion*, No. 5, "Kit Carson's Fight with the Comanche and Kiowa Indians, at the Adobe Walls on the Canadian River, November 25th, 1864," 23–24.

[39] *Ibid.*, 28–29.

provisions. About 60 Indians were killed in the battle, and about 150 were wounded.

The Indians had some traders visiting them; these were held captive at the second village during the battle. Later the traders told Carson that there were also some white captives there, and the Indians said that if the whites had not had "the guns that shot twice" (the howitzers), they would never have allowed a single white man to escape.[40]

The Indian scouts, estimating the numbers of the Indians against them, warned Carson to retire before dark as more and more Indians came up the Canadian to fight. The howitzers held off the Indians while the troops retired. Even though the Indians followed them and set fire to the dry grass, the troops managed to retire in good order. This was called a victory in army reports, but Carson himself called it a defeat. In Carson's official report, he said:

> About 150 lodges of the best manufacture, a large amount of dried meat, berries, buffalo robes, powder, cooking utensils, etc., also a buggy and spring wagon, the property of Sierrito or Little Mountain, the Kiowa chief of the Indians which I engaged [were destroyed]. The principal number were Kiowas with a small number of Comanches, Apaches, and Arapahoes, all of which were armed with rifles, and I must say that they acted with more daring and bravery than I have ever witnessed.[41]

Carson lost two soldiers killed and ten wounded; one Ute Indian was killed and five wounded. Carson added:

> I flatter myself that I have taught these Indians a severe lesson, and hereafter they will be more cautious about how they engage a force of civilized troops.[42]

[40] *Ibid.*, 43–44. Little Millie Durgan was hidden in the hills by her adopted Kiowa mother, and retrieved after the battle was over.

[41] "Nov. 25, 1864, Engagement with Indians at Adobe Fort," in *The War of the Rebellion, loc. cit.*, 939–44.

[42] *Ibid.*, 942.

He also suggested another campaign (at least one thousand soldiers strong) against them during the winter because the Indians were congregated in great numbers, hunting "immense quantities of buffalo in two days travel of the point of the fight," and could then be brought to terms.[43]

In the battle a young Kiowa warrior wearing a Spanish coat of mail was killed. Irving Wallace, in *The Fabulous Showman, The Life and Times of P. T. Barnum*, tells an interesting story of Indian chiefs calling on the Great White Father in 1864.[44] President Abraham Lincoln held a parley with White Bull (Sioux), the nephew of Sitting Bull; two Kiowas, Yellow Bear and Yellow Buffalo; and four Cheyennes, War Bonnet, Black Kettle, Lean Bear, and Hand-in-the-Water. Barnum bribed the interpreter in charge of the delegation to bring the Indians to New York, where he took them through his museum, then displayed them on the stage to an audience daily. But it cost him: the Indians demanded trinkets, and one wanted an ancient mail breastplate that had cost several hundred dollars. Barnum, making money on the Indians, was forced to let him have it "to fight the Utes." This, then, was probably the coat of mail found in November, 1864, on the Kiowa killed at Adobe Walls.

At this fight, Carson's men found a spring-wagon and an ambulance in possession of the Kiowas. The ambulance probably belonged to Chief Dohasan. Robert M. Peck, who in 1859 was a soldier under Major John Sedgwick, then in command of troops along the Arkansas, told the following story of an ambulance given to Dohasan:

> That was before the Kiowa war broke out in 1859. To'hau sen was always friendly to the whites, and tried to keep the Kiowas peaceable. A small part of them, his immediate following, kept out of that war. These were mostly the old warriors, but the younger men, who constituted a majority of the tribe, went on the warpath after Lieutenant George D. Bayard, of our regiment killed one of

[43] *Ibid.*, 943.
[44] 206–207.

the Kiowa chiefs, called Pawnee, near Peacock's ranch, on Walnut Creek.

That summer (1859) we had been camping along the Arkansas River, moving camp occasionally up or down the river, trying to keep Satank and his turbulent followers from beginning another outbreak. Old To'hau sen used frequently to come to our camp. Lieutenant McIntyre wanted to get rid of this old ambulance, which he had on his hands and which in some of its parts was nearly worn out. After inducing Major Sedgwick to have it condemned as unfit for service, Lieutenant McIntyre had his blacksmith fix it up a little and presented it to the old chief. McIntyre fitted a couple of sets of old harness to a pair of To'hau sen's ponies and had some of the soldiers to break the animals to work in the ambulance. But when To'hau sen tried to drive the team, he could not learn to handle the lines. He took the reins off the harness and had a couple of Indian boys ride the horses, and they generally went at a gallop. The old chief seemed very proud of the ambulance.[45]

This was probably the first time the Plains Indians took to wheels; Dohasan must have cut quite a figure with his riders and his horses and buggy galloping across the prairies!

LITTLE ARKANSAS TREATY, 1865

The United States military forces gave attention to the outrages in Kansas and Colorado, but Texas had to protect itself, since it was Confederate. This confirmed the Indians' belief that the Texans and the Americans were two distinct and hostile nations. It is quite possible that this notion of the Indians was useful to the Union soldiers and sponsored by them. The frontier line in Texas receded one hundred miles. In Kansas a war against the Indians did not mature; the soldiers were too busy trying to catch Quantrell and Shelby, Confederate raiders. In September conditions were bad. A number of persons had been killed, and thou-

[45] Grinnell, *Beyond the Old Frontier*, 154–56. Peck's story of the ambulance is also given by Grinnell in "Bent's Old Fort and its Builders," *The Kansas Historical Quarterly*, Vol. XV, 43.

sands of horses, mules, and cattle had been stolen. Communications between Missouri and Colorado were disrupted. Coaches crossing the Plains had to have escorts, and immigrants were forced to seek safety in numbers. The government could not spare troops to send to the border. Governor John Evans of Colorado raised forces of volunteers against the Indians, and it was believed that all of the Plains Indians were hostile.[46]

Early in the fall of 1865, a commission was sent out to meet with the Kiowas, Comanches, and Kiowa-Apaches. The members met at the mouth of the Little Arkansas on August 15, near present Wichita, Kansas. The Indians talked with the commissioners and promised to meet again in October. Colonel Jesse H. Leavenworth, son of General Henry Leavenworth, was the moving figure in the new peace policy.[47] For some time he had tried to secure a peace. He believed that if he could get General G. M. Dodge at Fort Leavenworth to delay marching against the Indians, he could reach a settlement peacefully. Upon receiving Leavenworth's letters to this effect in Washington, General Henry W. Halleck instructed Dodge to desist. But Dodge wrote back such a convincing letter that the Secretary of War was convinced and told Dodge, on April 29, 1865, to go ahead, regardless of Leavenworth.

Leavenworth then experienced the Indians' outrages—his mules were stolen and he just missed getting killed. Meanwhile, Dodge decided to see whether Leavenworth's peace policy might do any good. The Civil War had ended, and the Indians were told that they would have to make peace with the United States. But the Indians were still unfriendly and bitter over the Sand Creek Massacre of 1864. Among themselves, they were divided on the feasibility of a real war against the whites.

Five tribes met with the United States commissioners in October,

[46] John Evans (1814–97) was appointed territorial governor of Colorado on March 26, 1862. See the *Dictionary of American Biography*, VI, 204–205.

[47] Jesse H. Leavenworth graduated from West Point in 1830, served in the Fourth and Second Infantries until 1836, then resigned to engage in civil engineering. In 1862 the Secretary of War commissioned him to organize a regiment of cavalry in Colorado, known as "Rocky Mountain Rangers," which did valiant service in guarding the Western frontiers.

1865, at the mouth of the Little Arkansas. Treaties were made with the Cheyennes and Arapahoes on October 14, with the Kiowa-Apaches on October 17, and with the Kiowas and Comanches on October 18. At this time the Kiowa-Apaches were officially placed with the Cheyennes. The Kiowas and Comanches agreed to give up their claims in Colorado, Kansas, and New Mexico, and to remove south of the Arkansas to reservation lands (in Oklahoma, north of the Red River). They also surrendered five white captives. Doha-san, though outspoken against the white man, signed the peace, along with Guipago ("Lone Wolf"), Set-dayá-ite ("Many Bears"), Satanta ("White Bear"), Tené-angópte ("Kicking Bird"), and Set-imkia ("Stumbling Bear"). For the Kiowa-Apaches, Set-tadol ("Lean Bear") signed, and there were eight signers among the Comanches.[48]

Dohasan made protests against being confined on a reservation; nevertheless, the treaty was completed. The Indians agreed not to disturb the passage over the Santa Fe Trail. Present at the signing were Kit Carson, William Bent, Agent Jesse H. Leavenworth, and two interpreters, William Shirley and Jesse Chisholm.

Apprehension was still felt in 1866, and some persons believed than an Indian war was in the making. Indian hostility increased as the railroad engine puffed its way across Kansas, and as the buffalo hunters chased the game and killed the animals wantonly. General Winfield Scott Hancock held a council with the Kiowas on April 24 at Fort Dodge, with Agent Leavenworth present, and Kicking Bird and Stumbling Bear representing the peaceful elements of the Kiowas. On May 1 a similar conference was held with Satanta of the Kiowas. The Kiowas promised peace and arranged to give up their captives. They insisted they did not know that a peace had been made with Texas.

Because the Cheyennes refused to listen to peace talks, General Hancock set his troops in motion to crush them. General William Tecumseh Sherman visited Hancock and reviewed the situation. A war against the Indians of the Plains would be deplored; perhaps more attempts at effective treaties would be worth while.

[48] Mooney, "Calendar History," 180–81.

Dohasan, who led his tribe and allies for over thirty years, died in 1866. Without his sage guidance, the Kiowas split into factions, each trying to outrival the other. He was succeeded by Guipago ("Lone Wolf"), but his power was shared by such others as Satanta and Kicking Bird. Although Kicking Bird favored the peace policy, Lone Wolf and Satanta scorned it. Kiowa raids began as of old.

Satanta took a war party to Texas in August, 1866. He brought back to Fort Larned five captives to sell to Colonel Leavenworth. These were Mrs. Box, whose husband, James Box, had been killed, and her four children. Leavenworth refused to buy them and scolded Satanta for his treaty violation. Satanta took them to Fort Dodge and sold them for even more than he had asked; the post commander pitied the Box family.[49]

TREATY OF MEDICINE LODGE, 1867

The Department of the Interior obtained an appropriation for a peace commission to treat with the southern Plains Indians. On July 20, 1867, President Andrew Johnson approved an act to establish peace with certain hostile tribes. The purposes were to prevent attacks on emigrants, frontier homes, and railroad construction; to abolish Indian wars by removing their causes; and to encourage farming and stock-raising among the nomadic Indians. Thomas Murphy was sent west to make arrangements with the Kiowas, Comanches, Kiowa-Apaches, Cheyennes, and Arapahoes.

Nathaniel Taylor, commissioner of Indian affairs, was appointed chairman of the peace committee, which included Senator John B. Henderson, William S. Harney, Alfred H. Terry, C. C. Augur, J. B. Sanborn, and S. F. Tappan.

Two ambulances and thirty baggage wagons loaded with provisions and presents moved across the Plains to Medicine Lodge Creek. Three companies of United States Cavalry and a battery of

---

[49] *Ibid.*, 181; Nye, *Carbine and Lance*, 53–56. Satanta observed that white women brought better prices than horses. Louise Babb, sister of T. A. ("Dot") Babb, was ransomed from the Comanches for $333. See T. A. ("Dot") Babb, *In the Bosom of the Comanches.*

Gatling guns accompanied the wagon train, which was joined by newspaper and magazine reporters, including Henry M. Stanley, of later African and English fame.

Medicine Lodge, Kansas, was the site of the peace treaty made on October 21, 1867. The Kiowas, Comanches, Kiowa-Apaches, Cheyennes, and Arapahoes—five thousand Indians—met for the peace. Major Joel Elliott commanded a squadron of the Seventh Cavalry to protect the peace commissioners. Satanta became angered when Elliott's soldiers hunted buffalo and killed the animals for sport. Several officers were placed under arrest, and the Indians felt better.

The Indians had their "talks." Philip McCusker was the main interpreter. Since he spoke only Comanche, the peace provisions may not have been clear to all the Indians. Mrs. Margaret Adams, who accompanied the commission as an interpreter for the Arapaho Indians, was strikingly dressed in crimson skirt, black coat, and small hat with a large ostrich feather. This garb caught the eye of the Indians and they said, "She must be the daughter of a great chief." (She was the niece of one—her mother was Snake Woman, sister of Chief Left Hand of the Arapahoes. Margaret Poisal, daughter of John Poisal [or Poindal] was the widow of Thomas Fitzpatrick, who died in 1854. Sometime before 1856 she married Lucius J. Wilmot. Little is known of her. In 1865 she served at a treaty council as an interpreter for the Arapahoes, perhaps at the Little Arkansas Treaty. Perhaps later she married again to become Mrs. Adams. Her daughter Virginia [Jenny] Fitzpatrick was with her at the council. Alfred A. Taylor [son of the Commissioner of Indian Affairs], who was a young teen-ager present at the council, said that Virginia was a "sprightly, pretty girl of French-Arapahoe descent" and although "not over fifteen" [actually thirteen and a half] served as one of the interpreters. She was the daughter of Mrs. Adams "by her first husband, Major Thomas Fitzpatrick, who was the first government Agent of the Arapahoe, Cheyenne, Comanche and Kiowa Tribes.")

Thousands of splendidly dressed and painted Indians rode before the assembled commission with its army escort. Ten Bears, Comanche chief, welcomed the commissioners thus:

> My heart is filled with joy when I see you here, as the brooks fill with water when the snows meet in the spring; and I feel glad as the ponies do when the fresh grass starts in the beginning of the year.

Ten Bears also expressed the Indians' grievances:

> There has been trouble on the line between us, and my young men have danced the war dance. But it was not begun by us. It was you who sent out the first soldier and we who sent out the second . . . . The blue-dressed soldiers and the Utes came from out of the night when it was dark and still, and for campfires they lit our lodges . . . .

> So it was in Texas. They made sorrow come in our camps and we went out like the buffalo bulls when the cows are attacked. When we found them we killed them, and their scalps hang in our lodges. The Comanches are not weak and blind, like the pups of a dog when seven sleeps old. They are strong and far-sighted like grown horses. We took their road and we went out on it. The white women cried and our women laughed.[50]

The Indians agreed to things that they had expressly said they did not want, probably without understanding the full meaning of the agreements. The Medicine Lodge Treaty did little to settle the Indians; warfare broke out on the Plains shortly after the treaty was signed, but the railroads were allowed to go through.

General Sherman later said that the Union Pacific Railroad had reached the Rocky Mountains at Cheyenne and that the Kansas Pacific had built to about Fort Wallace; a part of the plan had been to organize two great reservations into regular territorial governments, with General Harney temporarily assigned to that

[50] Ernest Wallace and E. Adamson Hoebel, *The Comanches*, 282–84. Quoted from Recorded Copy of the Proceedings of the Indian Peace Commission, MS, Office of Indian Affairs, I, 104. National Archives, Washington, D. C. See also Grinnell, *The Fighting Cheyennes*, 269–75.

of the Sioux in the north, and General W. B. Hazen to that of the Kiowas, Kiowa-Apaches, Comanches, Cheyennes, and Arapahoes in the south. But this failed. Sherman noted: "Still the Indian Peace Commission of 1867–'68 did prepare the way for the great Pacific Railroads, which, for better or worse, have settled the fate of the buffalo and Indian forever."[51]

The Kiowas and Comanches signed a joint treaty on October 21, 1867. They agreed to live on a reservation on the lands leased from the Choctaws and Chickasaws, between the Canadian and Red rivers, west of the ninety-eighth meridian. Wolf's Sleeve (Mah-Vip-Pah) and Poor Bear (Kou-Zhon-Ta-Co) of the Kiowa-Apaches agreed to confederate with the Kiowas and Comanches and live on the same reservation. Signing for the Kiowas were Satank and Satanta, and for the Comanches, Ten Bears (Parra-Wah-Say-Men) and Painted Lips (Te-Pe-Navon).

The northern boundary of the reservation began at a point where the ninety-eighth meridian crosses the Washita, extended up the Washita to a point thirty miles west of Fort Cobb, and ran thence due west to the North Fork of Red River. The boundary on the east was the ninety-eighth meridian, the western limit of the Chickasaw and Choctaw nations.

The Cheyennes and Arapahoes were given a reservation to the north, but on August 10, 1869, by executive order, President Grant changed its location. The new reservation was limited on the east by the ninety-eighth meridian and the Cimarron River, on the north by the Cherokee Outlet, on the west by the one-hundredth meridian, and on the south by the line of the Kiowa-Comanche Reservation. The southeastern part of the area, south of the Canadian and east of ninety-eight degrees and forty minutes west longitude, was assigned to the Wichitas, Caddoes, Delawares, and other Indians by executive order in 1872.

The Kiowas, Kiowa-Apaches, and Comanches were regarded officially as confederated tribes. They agreed to reside on their reservation and subject themselves to supervision, civil and military.

If the treaty seemed harsh, it was the only practicable solution.

[51] *Memoirs of General William T. Sherman*, II, 434–36.

Texas was driving the Comanches northward; frontier settlements from the Mississippi were pushing west, taking advantage of the Homestead Law of 1862. In addition to those following the Santa Fe Trail route, there were thousands of emigrants crossing the Plains by various roads to California, Colorado, and Oregon. The Mormons had settled Utah and more were coming. Many were gold seekers; others were seeking homes in an attempt to disprove the theory of the Great American Desert. To avoid extermination by chronic warfare, the Indians had to have a restricted area of their very own. William Bent had said earlier that they would have to become agricultural and pastoral unless a "desperate war of starvation and extinction" was to be allowed.[52]

Colonel Leavenworth, as agent for the Kiowas and Comanches, hoped to civilize them and convert them to agriculture from their nomadic hunting life. As usual, the Kiowas maintained their independence; nor did they or their women take to even limited horticulture. In 1868 the Kiowas congregated about the agency at Eureka Valley near Fort Cobb. Their main interest was in food and presents. They became sullen and threatening when no provisions had been made for food. Then they stole food and horses from the Wichitas and Caddoes near by. Leavenworth first called on Fort Arbuckle for help, then changed his mind and decided he did not need the soldiers. After a Comanche raid on the Wichita agency, in which the Indians robbed the agent's and trader's store and fired the buildings, the settlers fled and so did Colonel Leavenworth. A military post had to be located near the agency. Medicine Bluff was explored under Major General Benjamin F. Grierson and selected for the site.[53]

In August, 1868, the Kiowas and Comanches went to Fort Larned, Kansas, to receive their first annuities. Meanwhile, the Comanches camped at Eureka Valley while the Kiowas and Yamparika Comanches moved northward hunting buffalo.

[52] Mooney, "Calendar History," 181–83, citing William Bent, Report to Commissioner of Indian Affairs, Oct. 5, 1859. See also Carl Coke Rister, *Border Command, General Phil Sheridan in the West*, 45–70.

[53] Nye, *Carbine and Lance*, 65.

211

OUTBREAK OF 1868; WAR OF 1868–69

Numerous Indian attacks characterized the Outbreak of 1868. Acting Agent S. T. Walkley and Philip McCusker, interpreter, reported many depredations, all in north Texas. In January, 1868, twenty-five persons were killed, nine scalped, and fourteen children captured. Afterward the children were frozen to death in captivity. In February seven persons were killed, fifty horses and mules were taken, and five children were captured. Two of the children were later surrendered to Agent Leavenworth; the remaining three were taken to Kansas. The Indians became very bold, and pursuit of them was fruitless.[54]

Satanta's band, along with the Kotsoteka and Nokoni Comanches, raided Texas. The Indians returned to the site of Eureka Valley on June 10, 1868, after an attack in Montgomery County, bringing back the scalp of a young white man and three captive children named McElroy, along with stolen horses. On July 14 another party returned from a raid on the Brazos with four scalps. On September 1 the Comanches and Wichitas, led by Tosawi's son-in-law, invaded Spanish Fort, Texas. Thirteen Indians ravished, killed, and scalped one woman and killed three or four of her children. At one time they took along two white women for nefarious designs, then "threw them away." They related their exploits to S. T. Walkley, who had become acting agent after Leavenworth fled.

There were many attacks on wagon trains. Led by Satanta, a party attacked a train on Sand Creek, Colorado, on October 14. They ran off cattle, captured Mrs. Clara Blinn and her child, and killed her husband. (The woman and child were later killed by the Indians in Custer's attack on Black Kettle's camp.) Sheridan said that the Indians raided in the summer and when winter came they retreated to their remote northern homes to "glory in the scalps

---

[54] Lieutenant General P. H. Sheridan, *Record of Engagements with Hostile Indians within the Military Division of the Missouri from 1868 to 1882*, 16. From June, 1862, to 1868 no less than eight hundred persons were murdered in the Division of the Missouri.

taken and in the horrible debasement of the unfortunate women whom they held as prisoners."[55]

Other raids continued. Even after receiving annuities at Fort Larned, depredations went on. The hue and cry over the Cheyenne and Arapaho raids in Kansas finally brought about the War of 1868. General Sherman denied charges that he sought to exterminate the Indians. He said that the army did not want to fight the Indians or exterminate them. That was for the Indians themselves to determine.[56] Major General Philip H. Sheridan was put in charge of chastising the Indians.

The Kiowas near Fort Larned were instructed to gather at Fort Cobb with their new agent, General W. B. Hazen, loaned from the army to the Indian department. There they would be fed and removed from the hostile tribes. Hazen was under constant intimidation by the Indians. When he warned them that they would be punished by the army, they laughed, saying that they had heard that before and nothing had ever happened.[57]

General Hazen had to have military help from Fort Arbuckle. Some Kiowas and Comanches met the troops and ordered them back, but Major Meredith Helm Kidd's squadron of Tenth Cavalry pushed on to Fort Cobb. The Arapahoes and Cheyennes hoped to make a peace with General Hazen, but he told them that they would have to negotiate with General Sheridan. In November, Satanta returned from a raid near Fort Griffin, Texas. By the middle of November all of the principal Kiowa chiefs, Lone Wolf, Satank, and Eagle-Heart, were camped near Fort Cobb. Kicking Bird was near by and known to be friendly. Woman's Heart and Big Bow had joined the Cheyennes and Arapahoes. On November

[55] *Ibid.*, 16. From March 2, 1868, to February 9, 1869, officially reported in the Division of the Missouri, there were 353 officers, soldiers, and citizens killed, wounded, or captured by Indians. Indians reported killed were 319; wounded, 289; and captured, 53. (*Ibid.*, 17.)

[56] Rister, *Border Command*, 67.

[57] Nye, *Carbine and Lance*, 73. George Hunt, son-in-law of Millie Durgan, gave much pertinent information to Colonel Nye in 1935. He was the nephew of I-see-o, Indian scout, and was the uncle of Adolph Goombi, who related to me the capture of his grandmother, Millie Durgan. (Author's conversations at Anadarko with Adolph Goombi, July 17, 1957.)

26 rations were issued to the Indians, but they grumbled because they wanted more. Specifically, they hoped to get arms and ammunition.

SHERIDAN'S CAMPAIGN

In November, 1868, General Philip Sheridan's plans took shape.[58] Sheridan was in charge of the district embracing Missouri, Kansas, Indian Territory, and New Mexico.[59] When he went on active duty in this area in March, 1868, he reviewed the situation and held talks with the Indians and others. He found much discontent over the Medicine Lodge Treaty; it obviously had not settled the difficulties. He said: "The principal mischief-makers were the Cheyennes. Next in deviltry were the Kiowas, and then the Arapahoes and Comanches." All of them could put on the warpath "about 6,000 warriors," and "subjugation would not be easy."[60]

> The Plains [in 1868] were covered with vast herds of buffalo— the number has been estimated at 3,000,000 head—and with such means of subsistence as this everywhere at hand, the 6,000 hostiles were wholly unhampered by any problem of food supply. The savages were rich too according to Indian standards, many a lodge owning from twenty to a hundred ponies; and consciousness of wealth and power, aided by former temporizing, had made them not only confident but defiant.

Sheridan determined to protect the people of the overland routes and of the settlements first, and then

> . . . when winter came, to fall upon the savages relentlessly, for in that season their ponies would be thin, and weak from lack of food,

[58] For Sheridan's campaign, see his *Personal Memoirs*, II, 281–347; General George A. Custer, *My Life on the Plains*, ed. by Milo Milton Quaife; Rister, *Border Command*, 71–213; and Nye, *Carbine and Lance*, 76–123.

[59] Gen. P. H. Sheridan, *Personal Memoirs*, II, 282.

[60] *Ibid.*, II, 283, 285, 290–91, 295.

and in the cold and snow, without strong ponies to transport their villages and plunder, their movements would be so much impeded that the troops could overtake them.[61]

Arrangements for a campaign were made. "Buffalo Bill" (William Cody) helped Sheridan by carrying dispatches. A three-pronged invasion against the Indians was planned: from Fort Bascom, New Mexico, eastward; from Fort Lyon, Colorado, southeastward; and a large thrust southward from Fort Larned, Kansas.[62]

BATTLE OF THE WASHITA

General George A. Custer's Seventh Cavalry was ready and waiting for the Kansas Volunteers. It was decided that Custer, marching south from Fort Larned, should meet the Kansas troops at the junction of Wolf and Beaver creeks, where a supply base was located. When Sheridan arrived there, a blizzard blew up. The Indians could not move about in such weather. (It should be mentioned that, in good weather, the troops were no match for the Indians, who could fly swiftly to their haunts on the Staked Plain, where they could find water holes, and the heavily laden troops burdened by supply wagons would always lose them.)

Sheridan ordered the Seventh Cavalry to march against the hostile Cheyennes on November 23. Along with Osage guides, they also had California Joe (Moses E. Milner), Romeo, Jack Fitzpatrick, Jimmy Morrison, and others. Custer mentioned that Neva, a Blackfoot, one of his guides, was a son-in-law of Kit Carson.[63] Custer left his supply train at the Canadian and hastened on

[61] *Ibid.*, II, 297.

[62] *Ibid.*, II, 300–301, 307, 313–24.

[63] Custer, *Life on the Plains*, 492–93. California Joe's language was expressive. An excellent guide, he was a friend of Sheridan's, having known him on the north Plains. Later, in writing to Custer from San Francisco, he described Chinatown thus: it "smelt like a kiowa camp in August with plenty buffalo meat around." (*Ibid.*, 607.) See also Keim, *Sheridan's Troopers*, 101–52; and Gen. P. H. Sheridan, *Personal Memoirs*, II, 313–21.

through the biting blizzard; it was hard going to catch the Cheyennes and the Kiowas, who were thought to be with them.[64]

The village was located and attacked early in the morning while its people were asleep. The fighting lasted for hours; many Indians were killed, including Chief Black Kettle, and the women and children were captured. With some fresh Kiowa warriors coming up from below the Cheyenne village, Custer decided to withdraw. He had about seven hundred captive Indian horses shot, and he burned the village with all its property. The sudden attack on the village had resulted in the Indians' killing of three white prisoners. One Indian woman killed a captive boy before she was shot. Two white captives, Mrs. Clara Blinn and her two-year old son, were killed in the Kiowa camp as the Indians took flight. In all, 103 Cheyennes were killed, and 53 prisoners were taken. Custer hastily moved his forces back to his supply train, and then the whole force proceeded to Camp Supply. From here, they moved down to Fort Cobb.

On December 7, Sheridan set out with a force to retrace Custer's march. They went to the Wichita Mountains and over to the Washita. There they viewed the battle site, found the mutilated bodies of Major Joel Elliot and his men, who had been cut off in the battle, and of the white prisoners, and buried them.[65]

The Kiowas and Comanches had moved downstream before the Washita battle. Warned by Big Bow and Woman's Heart, they then fled west of the Wichita Mountains. There the fleeing Cheyennes and Arapahoes joined them. Eagle Bear and Satanta moved to Rainy Mountain Creek. Lone Wolf returned, and the Kiowas camped along the Washita near Fort Cobb. Hazen had received instructions from General Sherman to keep the friendly Indians near by and away from the hostiles. On December 16, Hazen sent word to the officers in the field that the Indians camped near him were friendly. But his couriers were captured by the Kiowas and

---

[64] Mooney, "Cheyenne" in Hodge, *Handbook*, I, 250–57; Grinnell, "Black Kettle," in Hodge, *Handbook*, I, 152–53; and George W. Manypenny, *Our Indian Wards*, 217–42.

[65] Gen. P. H. Sheridan, *Personal Memoirs*, II, 330–31; Custer, *Life on the Plains*, 305–52.

held as hostages. It was uncertain what the Kiowas were going to do.[66]

On December 17 the Kiowas under Lone Wolf and Satanta met General Custer and Colonel J. Schuyler Crosby and sought to show their friendship. They proceeded under a white flag, and one delivered General Hazen's letter. The chiefs promised to come in and give themselves up. Custer refused to shake hands with them. From evidences of raids found in the camp after the Battle of the Washita and from the death of the white prisoners found at the Kiowa camp, they were suspect. Custer bitterly resented the Department of the Interior's trying to shield the Indians while the War Department was seeking to punish them. Sheridan insisted that they accompany the troops to the Fort Cobb agency. It was difficult to talk to them without an interpreter. Satanta told Walking Bird, who was supposed to know English, to talk with the officers, but all he could master was "heap son-a-bitch," having heard the soldiers use such endearing terms on their horses. This did not help the situation.[67]

Satanta and Lone Wolf were held as hostages, and Tsa'-l-aute, Satanta's son, was instructed to have the Kiowas come in. The other Kiowa chiefs had gradually slipped off, and only two were left. The Kiowa camps were frightened by the detention of Satanta

---

[66] Keim, *Sheridan's Troopers*, 185. Keim said: "The principal bands . . . and in the order of their importance, are those of Satanta, Lone Wolf, Timbered Mountain, Kicking Bird, and Stumbling Bear. Big Bow, with his band, during the recent troubles, went over to the Cheyennes, influenced by jealousy of his rivals and hostility to the government."

Hazen said that most of the Kiowas were not hostile. Drawing rations at Fort Cobb were Lone Wolf, Satank, Timbered Mountain, Black Eagle, Sytimore, Fish-a-more, Little Heart, Wolf Captain, and Ermope, according to Philip McCusker. All the headmen were there except Big Bow and Dohasan, who had about thirty lodges with them and were encamped near the Cheyennes and Arapahoes and were present in the battle. These Kiowas never came to Fort Cobb but moved south with the Cheyennes. See the editorial in regard to the Kiowas at the Battle of the Washita and *Some Corrections of 'Life on the Plains,'* in *Chronicles of Oklahoma*, Vol. III, No. 4 (December, 1925), 295–318, with excerpts from General W. B. Hazen, *Some Corrections of 'Life on the Plains.'*

[67] Nye, *Carbine and Lance*, 95. See also Gen. P. H. Sheridan, *Personal Memoirs*, 333–34; Custer, *Life on the Plains*, 441–67; and Keim, *Sheridan's Troopers*, 157–59.

and Lone Wolf, and even those camped near Fort Cobb were preparing to run away. Most of them fled to Elk Creek, twenty miles away. After days of negotiations, Custer finally told Tsa'-l-aute that he would hang Satanta and Lone Wolf if the Kiowas did not come in by sundown of the next day. Custer said that Satanta lost his lordly demeanor, and was visibly frightened. Lone Wolf gave the instructions to Tsa'-l-aute, and he hastened off. The Kiowas came in, after having gone some fifty miles in their flight. Satanta and Lone Wolf were kept in confinement. Things quieted down.[68]

Medicine Bluffs to the south was considered a better place than Fort Cobb. After a final exploration there was undertaken by Colonel Grierson, Sheridan decided to abandon Fort Cobb and move to the new site. Thus was Fort Sill finally located near Medicine Creek and the Wichita Mountains.[69]

Meanwhile, war against the hostiles had gone on in the west. Major A. W. Evans left Fort Bascom, New Mexico, on November 17, 1868. He marched down the Canadian, through snow and sleet, toward Antelope Hills and on to the camp of the Nokoni Comanches near the site of the old Wichita village. Horseback, the Comanche chief who was friendly to the whites, was away, and Arrowpoint, a war chief, was in command. The Indians charged the soldiers, and the Battle of Soldier Spring took place. Chief Arrowpoint was wounded, and later died, and the Indians fled. Some Kiowas from Woman's Heart's village at Sheep Mountain took part in the battle. The soldiers lost one man. This was more of

[68] Keim, *Sheridan's Troopers*, 164. All the Kiowa bands were in, save that of Kicking Bird, off on a raid in Texas. Custer said all were in except Woman's Heart's band. (Custer, *Life on the Plains*, 466.) Nye said that the Kiowas "state today that the message delivered by Satanta's son contained no reference to the fact that the two chiefs were threatened with hanging. They were told that if they arrived at Fort Cobb by sundown they all would be given large quantities of free rations. They state that if they had known that Satanta and Lone Wolf would be hanged, they would not have come in at all." (Nye, *Carbine and Lance*, 96.)

[69] Gen. P. H. Sheridan, *Personal Memoirs*, II, 338–39; Keim, *Sheridan's Troopers*, 231–51. Sheridan said: "A permanent military post ought to be established well down on the Kiowa and Comanche reservation to keep an eye on these tribes in the future." (Gen. P. H. Sheridan, *Personal Memoirs*, 338–39.) Fort Sill was established on January 7, 1869. (Custer, *Life on the Plains*, 467.)

a skirmish than a battle, but it indicated the importance of Sheridan's plan of forcing subjection upon the Indians from several directions. The Nokoni Comanche village was burned, destroying all the Indians' property and their winter food supply.[70]

On December 30 at Fort Cobb, clothing, food, and tobacco were given as annuities. In January the Indians remained about Camp Wichita, later Fort Sill. Hunting was good; the area abounded in wildlife. In February, Satanta and Lone Wolf, now proclaiming their love of peace and readiness to follow the white man's road, were released. Sheridan held a conference with fifty or more Indian chiefs, with Gunsadalte (or Baa-o, "Cat") as interpreter, wearing a major general's uniform given to Stumbling Bear, his cousin, at Medicine Lodge by General Hancock. He wore only the coat (the trousers were missing) and a cavalry saber. Sheridan insisted that any future crimes of murder or raiding would be punished and that they were to live in peace.

All promised, including Black Eagle, Kicking Bird, Stiff Neck, Lone Bear, Stumbling Bear, Timber Mountain, and others who had not been present at former interviews. They were exceedingly friendly and happy and asked about gifts. Sheridan told them that General Hazen would see to that in a day or two. The Indians respected Sheridan; he was firm and convincing.[71]

The Cheyennes and Arapahoes had been desultory about getting in for peace talks. Custer had moved against the Cheyennes on January 21, 1869, with a few soldiers, Little Robe of the Cheyennes, Yellow Robe of the Arapahoes, Mahwissa, sister of Black Kettle, and another captive Cheyenne woman. A young man looking for his lost sister also accompanied them. Little Robe and Mahwissa fled to the Cheyennes, but Little Raven succeeded in influencing the Arapahoes to come in and make peace. This party was not successful, save for getting in the Arapahoes.

Custer was then sent with troops to round up the rest of the

---

[70] Nye, *Carbine and Lance*, 106–107. Sheridan said that Evans killed twenty-five warriors in the Red River campaign. (Gen. P. H. Sheridan, *Personal Memoirs*, II, 338.)

[71] Keim, *Sheridan's Troopers*, 275–76; Nye, *Carbine and Lance*, 120–21.

Cheyennes. They were anxious to rescue some white prisoners among them and conclude a peace. Custer wanted to avoid a battle which might result in their killing the white prisoners. This was a dangerous but successful feat performed by Custer, resulting in the saving of the lives of two young women, Mrs. Morgan and Miss White. Mrs. Morgan met her brother who had accompanied Custer. It forced the Cheyennes to submit to the military. Mahwissa, already with the Cheyennes, and Mo-nah-se-ta, the Cheyenne woman with Custer's party helped to bring about the success of the mission. The danger came when Custer held some of the chiefs as hostages until the white prisoners were brought in. This submission of the Cheyennes was the end of Sheridan's winter campaign. Sheridan left on February 23, 1869, for the north. Most of the Indians were settled on the reservations. Some had been punished; some had settled because of fright.[72]

[72] Custer, *Life on the Plains*, 529–609.

CHAPTER SIX

❖ PEACE AND WARS

ULYSSES S. GRANT was inaugurated as President on March 4, 1869. He promptly turned the Indian affairs over to the Quakers or Society of Friends. Lawrie Tatum, new Indian agent for the Kiowas, Kiowa-Apaches, and Comanches, stated that President Grant met with the Friends and took great interest in their advice. Grant had said:

> Gentlemen, your advice is good, I accept it. Now give me the names of some Friends for Indian agents and I will appoint them. If you can make Quakers out of the Indians it will take the fight out of them. Let us have peace.[1]

Thus was inaugurated the peace policy of Grant.

Although they were pacific and altogether unacquainted with the Indians of the Plains, the Quakers were fearless of their own lives and honest and sincere in their efforts to convert the Indians to Christianity. The war was over for the time being, and the peace policy had much to recommend it. General Sherman of the army was instructed to give full support, and army officers remained in

[1] Lawrie Tatum, *Our Red Brothers and the Peace of President Ulysses S. Grant,* xvii-xviii.

charge temporarily. General Hazen was superintendent of tribes in Indian Territory. Colonel A. G. Boone was the agent for the Kiowas, Comanches, Wichitas, and other tribes at Camp Wichita. Colonel B. H. Grierson was the commander at the new post of Fort Sill, which had been named by General Sheridan in honor of Brigadier General Joshua W. Sill, killed in the Civil War at the Battle of Stone River on December 31, 1862.

The Kiowas and Comanches did not grasp the peace policy. The treaty stipulations were diametrically opposed to their culture, traditions, and social practices. The agents were tolerated, albeit at times intimidated and threatened. They were harassed but not personally harmed. Rather, the Indians viewed with amazement and scorn the beliefs of "Washington."

Lawrie Tatum arrived in Indian Territory to relieve General Hazen.[2] The agency property was turned over to him on July 1, 1869. He let contracts for several stone buildings to be erected. Then he went to Chicago to purchase a steam engine, materials for a sawmill, and millstones for grinding corn. Tatum, hoping to bring the "wild blanket Indians" to farming, speedily began this work, but the Kiowas and Comanches were only interested in eating up the green watermelons.[3]

A council was held with the Indians in the middle of July, 1869. Some of the chiefs expressed satisfaction at having the commissioners with them. Tatum said:

> Satanta, a Kiowa chief, made two speeches, which were said to be characteristic of the man, who is a daring and restless man. He said that "he took hold of that part of the white man's road that was represented by the breech-loading gun, but did not like the ration of

[2] *Ibid.*, 25, 27.

[3] Nye, *Carbine and Lance*, 132. Old Files at Fort Sill, cited by Nye. The agency doctor treated them for cases of "Devil inside my belly." Charley Ross, a Comanche, said that his father died of this complaint. Watermelons were not new to the Kiowas and Comanches; they had eaten them many times when visiting the Wichitas and Wacos on Red River. Vestal and Schultes, *The Economic Botany of the Kiowa Indians*, cite this as a new reservation food, ignorantly eaten "green." However, this sickness came not from ignorance but from greed and theft.

THE MESCAL TIPI
on the Kiowa Reservation, Oklahoma
(Gunavi is in the right foreground)
From a photograph by James Mooney, 1892

A REAR VIEW OF A MODEL OF THE TAI-ME
medicine god of the Kiowas

KIOWA AND APACHE INDIANS GAMBLING UNDER A BRUSH ARBOR
about 1900, in the Lawton-Anadarko, Oklahoma, area

KIOWAS DIVIDING THE MEAT AT THE BEEF ISSUE
Photograph by James Mooney, 1892

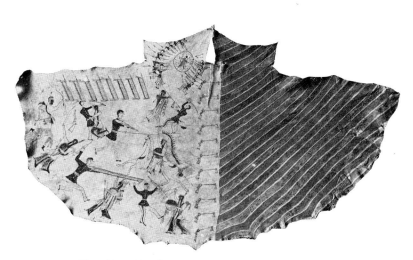

THE DO-GÍÄ-GÚAT, OR TIPI OF BATTLE PICTURES

DOHASAN (THE YOUNGER) AND HIS WIFE ANKIMA
(Note his war shirt, decorated with ermine and Navaho scalps)
Photograph by James Mooney, about 1893

ANKO
Photograph by F. A. Rinehart, 1898

Ápiatan, or Wooden Lance
was the Kiowas' chief delegate to Washington
when he was photographed there by
the Bureau of American Ethnology in 1894

corn; it hurt his teeth." He also said, "The good Indian, he that listens to the white man, got nothing. The independent Indian was the only one that was rewarded." They wanted arms and ammunition.[4]

The commissioners told them that they would get no arms or ammunition, but that they would be protected if they settled on the reservation. If they left the reservation, then it was war. The buffalo came through the reservation twice a year, and this would provide for them.

Thus was Tatum apprised of the character of his charges. He was also told that if "Washington" did not want the young men to raid in Texas, then it should move Texas far away; also, the Indians felt that they were not getting a liberal supply of provisions.

> They told me a number of times that the only way they could get a large supply of annuity goods was to go out onto the warpath, kill some people, steal a good many horses, get the soldiers to chase them awhile, without permitting them to do much harm, and then the government would give them a large amount of blankets, calico, muslin, etc., to get them to quit.[5]

As the Indians got over their fear of Sheridan's campaign, they began to leave the reservation for raids. Big Bow and his band had never come in to the agency; many joined with the Kwahadi Comanches, who were still living in Texas. Mohway, however, was convinced that it was futile to hold out against the white man.[6] Colonel Grierson of Fort Sill, busy with the building program there, believed that it was just a question of time before the Indians would settle down, since the buffalo was fast disappearing.

In May the Indians left for a buffalo hunt; then they planned to hold their annual Sun Dance. Grierson intended to prevent the Sun Dance, but his soldiers were kept busy with quelling the frequent raids into Texas and trying to recover stolen animals. On May 28, Tabananica and his Comanches raided Tatum's agency,

[4] Tatum, *Red Brothers*, 29.
[5] *Ibid.*, 30.
[6] *Ibid.*, 74–75.

taking off twenty horses and mules. Following the Sun Dance, the Kiowas rushed off on raids to keep their pledges to the sun god. On June 12 the raid of White Horse relieved Fort Sill of some seventy mules. A new enclosure had to be built to keep stock in. Big Tree, a little later, tried to steal all the stock, but his plan was ruined by an Indian firing a premature shot. The Indians moved off quickly, killing a woodcutter on their way. The party wounded Levi Lucans, an employee of the quartermaster, and a Mexican was killed near the agency corral. White Horse attacked a party of Texans driving cattle and killed one man.[7]

A herd of over four thousand Texas cattle was transferred from the military department to Tatum to be used as a commissary for the Indians. The herd had to be kept sixty or seventy miles east of the agency. Tatum held a conference with the Kiowas, with Colonel Grierson present. He warned the Indians that they would not be given rations until the government stock was brought back. Two Quakers from the Cheyenne agency at Darlington visited Tatum and reproved him for having a military guard.[8]

Kicking Bird, who had lost face in the tribe by his peace policy, led a raiding party of one hundred warriors into Texas along the Red River, thereby regaining the loyalty and plaudits of his people. Some left the main party and robbed a mail coach at Rock Station, near the site of Jermyn, Jack County. They were followed by a force of troops from Fort Richardson under Captain Curwen B. McClellan. A fight ensued on July 12 near the site of Seymour, Texas, but the Indians outnumbered the troops two to one. Three soldiers were killed and twelve were wounded. In the evening the Indians retreated, and the soldiers were reinforced by twenty cowboys. They returned to Fort Richardson the next morning. Kicking Bird, "face resumed," determined to fight the whites no more but to try to bring his people to peace. It was an uphill struggle, and one in which he lost much of his power.[9]

[7] *Ibid.*, 33–34; Nye, *Carbine and Lance*, 139–41, related to Nye by George Hunt from information obtained from Big Tree before he died in 1927.

[8] Tatum, *Red Brothers*, 36, 40–41.

[9] Nye, *Carbine and Lance*, 145.

The numbers of the Indians in 1870 were given by William Nicholson when he visited the Kiowa and Comanche Agency. The Kiowas numbered 1,896; the Kiowa-Apaches, 300; the Comanches, 2,742; and the Kwahadi Comanches, 1,000—a total of 5,938 on the reservation.[10]

During Nicholson's visit, Lone Wolf complained of the withholding of ammunition and the nonarrival of annuity goods and clothing. Satanta grumbled that he could not get ammunition, and he wanted the Superintendent of the Indian Agencies, Enoch Hoag, again to tell the Great Father to move Texas farther off and he would not raid there any more.[11]

Satank, one of the Kiowa Koitsenko soldiers, lost his favorite son in a raid in Texas in the summer of 1870, and harbored a bitter hostility toward the whites. At one time he challenged Tatum to a duel to the death over the right to a stolen mule that he was riding.[12]

White Horse returned from Texas with Mrs. Gottlieb Koozer and her children, after killing her husband. Martin B. Kilgore was another captive. Tatum promptly refused rations until the white captives were delivered up. A council was held on August 7, and Tatum reproved the Indians for their bad conduct. Colonel Grierson told them that they would have to give up the warpath. Lone Wolf insisted that as many Kiowas as Texans had been lost, and that all should be forgotten. Satanta, with his usual oratory, said that he preferred the red man's road. The situation grew tense. The Indians flexed their bows and made arrows ready. Some put cartridges into their guns. Tatum continued to lay down the law— they would get no ammunition and only their usual rations, but the white prisoners must be given up. Lone Wolf stepped over to Tatum and put his hand inside Tatum's vest to see if there was any "scare," but he found none. The Indians told Grierson and

[10] William Nicholson, "A Tour of Indian Agencies in Kansas and the Indian Territory in 1870," *The Kansas Historical Quarterly*, Vol. III, No. 3 (August, 1934), 289–326; Vol. III, No. 4 (November, 1934), 343–84.

[11] *Ibid.*, 353–54.

[12] Tatum, *Red Brothers*, 48–49.

Tatum that they would not raid the agency or post area that summer. The whites continued to insist on their giving up the captives. Finally a compromise was reached. The Koozers were ransomed for one hundred dollars apiece, and rations were issued the Indians. Still they got no ammunition, and some angrily threw their rations on the ground and demanded double rations of sugar and coffee. Shortly after this, Isa-hab-it of the Comanches brought in Martin B. Kilgore. Tatum said that he would give one hundred dollars for him. Isa-ha-bit wanted more; then he saw soldiers approaching and quickly decided that one hundred dollars would do. Tatum realized that it would take the military to bring the Indians to good behavior. From then on, even though the Quakers disapproved, he used a military guard.[13]

The settlers of Texas were bitter over the constant raiding on their lands. Much of this was just below Red River, and they justly suspected the reservation Kiowas and Comanches. They even suspected the agency of giving the Indians arms, for they had good carbines and repeating rifles. This was unjustified; Tatum was not guilty of such conduct. George Washington, a Caddo Indian, sold them some guns, but most were taken in their raids or were bought in illicit trade. Colonel Grierson sought to patrol the area, but small war parties could easily evade the soldiers. Not all of the raiding was Indian—some desperadoes operated in this area and threw the blame on the Indians by disguising themselves in Indian clothing and hair wigs.

During the winter of 1870–71, the Indians remained quiet. Occasional raids into Texas increased during the spring. On January 4, 1871, Mama'nte and Quitan took some Kiowa warriors to Young County, Texas, near Flat Top Mountain on the Butterfield Trail. They killed and scalped four Negroes who were hauling supplies to Fort Griffin. One of these was Britt Johnson, who had ransomed the captives taken at Newcastle in 1864. Soldiers from Fort Richardson under Lieutenant William A. Borthwick buried the bodies, then pursued and overtook the Indians. Lieutenant Borthwick was wounded and had to fall back. The Indians returned to the

[13] *Ibid.*, 45, 46–50.

reservation, after throwing away the kinky-haired scalps as useless.[14] Near Salt Prairie, a danger spot, a white man was later scalped alive; other horse raids and attacks were made near Fort Richardson. Fourteen white people were killed in the spring of 1871.

THE WAGON TRAIN MASSACRE

In 1871 there occurred a Kiowa outrage that focused the attention of the nation upon the problem of the reservations. This was the Warren Wagon Train Massacre in Texas. Texas' protests over the lack of federal help on the border finally brought a visit of inspection by General William Tecumseh Sherman. He went to New Orleans, by boat to the Gulf, then to San Antonio, and then north to inspect the border forts. He was accompanied by Colonel John E. Tourtelotte, Colonel James C. McCoy, and Major General Randolph B. Marcy. His party rode in an ambulance accompanied by fifteen cavalrymen. Sherman was not inclined to believe all the stories that he had heard. True, the country was not as thickly populated in the north and west as it had been before the Civil War, but this might be due to the effects of the war as well as to fears of Indian depredations. Marcy was again traveling over the road he had laid out before the war; it had become the Butterfield Trail, then was abandoned just before the Civil War.

On May 17, 1871, Sherman's party reached Fort Belknap, where a few soldiers were still stationed. The next day they set out for Fort Richardson. Shortly after noon on May 18 they crossed Salt Creek Prairie, going toward Cox Mountain. This was an area of constant Indian raids. They saw no Indians anywhere, but Indians peeping over the mountain saw them. Over one hundred Kiowas and Kiowa-Apaches, and at least one Comanche, hidden in the rocky terrain of a small hill, watched the military group go by. Many of them were ready to attack; they had been waiting all night and most of the day. But they allowed the troops to pass.

[14] Nye, *Carbine and Lance*, 158–59. As told to Nye by George Hunt, whose information came from Quitan.

The Kiowas were led by Mama'nte, a chief who became a powerful medicine man and took a new name, Dohate ("Owl Prophet"). His strong medicine made him a war chief. He seems to have gathered up the power that once was Dohasan's and towered over the other chiefs. He was of fine figure, tall and straight—a man of authority, wisdom, and great influence. In fact, he led most of the raids in the 1870's.

The Indians had left some of their horses under the guard of boys the evening before and had spent the night on the hill awaiting Dohate's commands. Dohate made his medicine and told them that two parties would travel by. The first was not to be attacked; the second was theirs to attack. It would be successful. Thus, Dohate's prophecy saved General Sherman from an almost certain death.

A guard of honor under Captain Robert Carter was sent out to meet General Sherman. Carter and his soldiers were to give Sherman a salute with a cannon, offer him fresh mules, and tender the use of Brevet Major General Ranald S. Mackenzie's quarters. (Commissions dropped in rank after the Civil War. Mackenzie was now Colonel Mackenzie of the Fourth Cavalry.) Sherman greeted them but declined the mules and the quarters, saying that he would pitch his own tents and that Carter's party should follow on at leisure since their horses looked tired. He pushed on to Fort Richardson so quickly that the soldiers did not get to fire the salute.[15]

At Fort Richardson, Sherman listened to a citizens' committee which sought relief from Indian outrages. The delegation of citizens told a bitter story of murders, raids, and thefts committed by the Fort Sill Indians and displayed a number of "scalps, some of them female, which had been recovered from bands known to be the Ki-o-was and Comanches from the reservation, and petitioned him for assistance in recovering their stolen stock and punishing these savages."[16] Sherman did not believe them; he had not seen

[15] Captain Robert Goldthwaite Carter, *Massacre of Salt Creek Prairie and the Cow-Boy's Verdict*, 31; and Carter, *On the Border with Mackenzie*.

[16] Carter, *Massacre*, 32.

any trouble and felt that the danger was overrated. Shortly he was to change his mind.

During the night a wounded man, Thomas Brazeal, came to the fort and was treated. Before daylight Sherman visited Brazeal in the hospital and heard his story. Brazeal said that he and four others had escaped from an Indian attack on Salt Prairie which had occurred a few hours after Sherman had passed.

A wagon train of corn, owned by Warren and Duposes, government contractors, which was hauling supplies from the railroad at Weatherford to Fort Griffin, was attacked by over one hundred Indians at about three o'clock in the afternoon. There were ten wagons in charge of Nathan S. Long, with ten teamsters and a night watchman—twelve men in all. As the Indians rushed down the mountain at a blast from Satanta's bugle, the teamsters made a circle of their wagons, with the mules facing the center. The Indians were upon them before the last wagon could be turned in. Long and four teamsters were killed or wounded in the first charge. When the second charge came, the seven remaining white men left the wagons and ran for the woods, the Indians pursuing. Two of the seven teamsters were killed and some were wounded. The Indians, not knowing how many were in the wagons, turned back to plunder and kill. Meanwhile, the five remaining teamsters reached the woods. Brazeal believed all the others had been killed and that he was the only one who had escaped.[17]

The Indian account of the story gives more details and also tells what happened after the five men fled.[18] Yellow Wolf led the charge, and Big Tree made the first coup. Yellow Wolf made the second coup, followed by two Kiowa-Apaches. Ord-lee, a Comanche, ran to engage the teamsters in a hand-to-hand fight but was suddenly shot dead. Now the Indians became wary. They began circling the wagons. They had Spencer carbines, breech-loading rifles, and pistols, mostly obtained from Caddo George Washington.

Storm clouds began to pass across the sun, but the firing and the

17 *Ibid.*, 32–33.
18 Nye, *Carbine and Lance*, 165–69.

fury went on. Tson-to-goodle ("Light-Haired Young Man"), a Kiowa-Apache, was wounded in the knee and fell off his horse. Two men rushed in and saved him. The shrill cries of two women, Yo-koite and another whose name was not remembered, on the hill spurred the warriors on. The Indians then followed seven fleeing men to the timber, killing two of them; then they rushed back to the wagons. They saw three dead men. The leaders cautioned the young men to wait. Hau-tau ("Gun-Shot") ran to the wagons to secure a coup. White Horse and Set-Maunte said, "It's too dangerous," and sought to keep him back. But Hau-tau rushed on to count coup, touched a wagon, and claimed it. The wagon sheet was lifted a bit, and a wounded teamster inside thrust a gun in the Indian's face, shot, and wounded him. White Horse and Set-Maunte dragged Hau-tau off. Then, as Yellow Wolf said, the Indians were enraged and "tore up everything."[19] The Indians buried Ord-lee on the hill and fled with their wounded and with the captured mules. They rode fast, for the storm had descended upon them and everything was flooded.

General Sherman, after hearing of the attack from Brazeal, sent dispatches to Fort Sill and Fort Griffin. He ordered Major General Ranald S. Mackenzie to the site to investigate. If Brazeal's account was true, Mackenzie was to follow the Indians and report to Sherman at Fort Sill.[20]

Mackenzie found the dead before dark on May 19. It was raining, and the remains of the fight made a ghastly picture. Everywhere grain, bloated bodies, broken harness, arrows, and ashes lay strewn about. The skulls had been crushed, bodies mutilated, and one which had been fastened by a chain to the wagon pole was charred, lying over ashes face down with its tongue cut off. All but one had been scalped. Mackenzie buried the bodies in a common grave marked by stones.[21] Then he rushed on to catch the Kiowas, but their trail had been obliterated by the rain. Four of the Indians,

---

[19] *Ibid.*, 168.

[20] Carter, *Massacre*, 33.

[21] *Ibid.*, 34; Nye, *Carbine and Lance*, 169. The grave was a mile west of Monument School in a field owned by James Barnett.

Quitan and Tamasi (a Mexican captive) and two others, had stopped to kill some buffalo which they found crossing the Big Wichita River. They had killed some and were butchering when Lieutenant Peter M. Boehm and twenty-five men from Fort Richardson surprised them. In the ensuing fight, Tamasi was killed and one of the soldiers was wounded. The Indians fled and swam the river, concealing themselves among the buffalo herd. The main body of the Indians had raced ahead, but Quitan and the others managed to join them. They crossed Red River and returned to their village. Hau-tau died after a few days. Part of his face and head had been shot off, and the blowflies, scourge of the Plains for man and beast, had got in the wound.[22] The Indians had lost three warriors, killed seven whites, and brought home forty-one mules and some plunder. Dohate had promised them success. They had it.

Sherman arrived at Fort Sill on May 23. He had learned something about raids; he had barely escaped being attacked. At Fort Sill he was the guest of Colonel Grierson, with whom he visited Agent Tatum and related the details of the massacre. Tatum did not know definitely of any Indians being away but suspected that Satanta and some others were. They were to come in shortly for their rations, and he said that he would find out whether or not they were responsible for the attack.[23]

Tatum had realized for some time that the Kiowas wanted war. At a conference at the Wichita Agency with the peaceful Indians on April 24, 1871, they had smoked the peace pipe but were still averse to giving up their raiding proclivities.[24] Tatum said:

> Before issuing their rations I asked the chiefs to come into my office, and told them of the tragedy in Texas, and wished to know if they could tell by what Indians it was committed? Satanta said:

[22] Nye, *Carbine and Lance*, 170. Quitan to George Hunt, informant for Nye.

[23] Tatum, *Red Brothers*, 116. Sherman also inquired after Millie Durgan on behalf of her grandmother, Mrs. Elizabeth Clifton, but was told that the child had died. When Millie's adopted mother took her to Fort Sill, she stained the child's face dark so that she looked like other little Indian girls. The agent and soldiers saw her but did not realize that she was a white child.

[24] *Ibid.*, 107–109.

"Yes, I led in that raid. I have repeatedly asked for arms and ammunition, which have not been furnished. I have made many other requests which have not been granted. You do not listen to my talk. The white people are preparing to build a railroad through our country, which will not be permitted. Some years ago they took us by the hair and pulled us here close to Texas where we have to fight them. More recently I was arrested by soldiers and kept in confinement several days. But that is played out now. There is never to be any more Kiowas arrested. I want you to remember that." He said that because of these grievances, he led about a hundred warriors to Texas to teach them to fight, with Satank, Eagle Heart, Big Bow, Big Tree and Fast Bear, and fell upon the mule train, killing seven and losing three. It was not necessary, he said, to say any more about it. They had no intention of raiding "around here this summer" but expected to raid in Texas. "If any other Indian claims the honor of leading that party he will be lying to you. I led it myself."[25]

To this the other chiefs assented, lauding Satanta. Tatum, now convinced that they were guilty, told the men to issue rations to the Indians, and he set out for Colonel Grierson's quarters to request him to arrest "Satanta, Eagle Heart, Big Tree, Big Bow and Fast Bear."[26] Meanwhile Satanta, eager to see the Washington "Big Chief," Sherman, came to Colonel Grierson's quarters where the soldiers detained him as Tatum left. Grierson called the Indians to meet with him and Sherman. Preparations were made for defense. The General was determined to arrest the leaders.

Satanta was already on the front porch at Colonel Grierson's when Kicking Bird and Stumbling Bear arrived; Horace Jones, interpreter, and a number of officers were there also. Sherman paced up and down. Kicking Bird was sent to bring in the others. By the porch steps were two soldiers with bayonets. When the Indians gathered, Sherman questioned them through Horace Jones about the destruction of the wagon train. Satanta again took credit for the deed, thumping his chest. Sherman told them that Satanta, Satank, and Big Tree would be sent to Texas for trial and that

[25] *Ibid.*, 116–17.
[26] *Ibid.*, 117.

forty-one good mules would have to be turned in. The Indians, hot-tempered, grasped their weapons. As they did so, the shutters of the windows swung open at Sherman's command, and soldiers covered the Indians with guns. Satanta yelled: "Don't shoot!" Kicking Bird then pled with Sherman for the prisoners, saying he would not let them go. Kicking Bird said to Sherman: "You and I are going to die right here." This was evidently not interpreted properly, for Sherman tried to quiet Kicking Bird by saying that he and Stumbling Bear were not to blame and would not be harmed.[27]

Big Tree was brought in, and soldiers took their stations near the porch. Eagle Heart had fled when the soldiers pointed their guns. Other Indians appeared, bringing weapons. Kicking Bird motioned to Lone Wolf to come up on the porch. He got off his horse, put two Spencer repeating carbines on the ground with his bow and arrows, tied his horse, picked up his weapons, and came up on the porch, keeping his carbine ready and handing one gun to Stumbling Bear. Sherman continued to talk with Kicking Bird. Stumbling Bear was getting ready to shoot Sherman as he paced toward him. Two Indian women whooped for Stumbling Bear to give him courage. Then a soldier grabbed Stumbling Bear, Grierson grabbed Lone Wolf, a scuffle took place, and they tripped and fell on the floor. Kicking Bird dropped on top of them, and several slipped off the porch and landed on the ground. Lone Wolf jumped the fence and fled with some other Indians. In the skirmish several were killed and wounded. A large group swept out of the post on horseback.[28] For a while, everything was in confusion. Gradually, order was restored. The soldiers held their guns ready to shoot. Sherman was quiet and undisturbed. The three chiefs were held.

The Indians then got the idea that if the mules were delivered the chiefs would be released; Kicking Bird asked the chiefs to contribute the mules, and told Sherman that they agreed to the terms. The Indians left and joined their families, who had become fright-

---

[27] *Ibid.*, 118–19; Nye, *Carbine and Lance*, 179.
[28] Carter, *Massacre*, 37–38. Lone Wolf, Big Bow, Fast Bear, and Eagle Heart fled. They were equally guilty but were never arrested.

ened and were fleeing. The culprits were then put in irons and the
tense situation was over. Sherman was the hero of the post that
evening when word of the affair went around.[29]

Shortly afterward, General Sherman returned to the East, leaving word for Colonel Mackenzie to take the prisoners to Texas.
Colonel Mackenzie arrived on June 4, after leaving the scene of
the massacre on May 19. Preparations were made to take the three
chiefs to Jacksboro for trial.

On June 8, in handcuffs and leg irons, Satanta and Big Tree
were put in one wagon, and Satank, who had tried to commit suicide but had been held by Big Tree, was forcibly put in another
wagon. Satank began to chant his death song and told Caddo
George Washington, who rode near him, to apprise his tribe of his
death. He also told a Tonkawa scout that he might have his scalp.
As the wagons moved off, he continued singing his Koitsenko song.
As they neared Cache Creek, suddenly he freed his hands of the
irons and with a knife that had been concealed in his breechcloth
fell upon one guard. The soldier flung himself out of the wagon,
dropping his carbine. Satank grabbed it to shoot but the cartridge
jammed; then Corporal John Charlton, Sergeant Varily, and other
soldiers shot him. He died in the road near the site of the present
railroad station at Fort Sill. The Tonkawa scout was anxious to
have his scalp, but it was not allowed. Satank's body was buried at
Fort Sill. Thus ended the life of one of the most formidable warriors of the Kiowas.[30]

The command moved on. The guards, at night, fearing that the
Kiowas might follow and attempt a rescue of the chiefs, pegged
the prisoners at each hand and foot, binding them securely with
rawhide. On June 15 they rode into Fort Richardson. Satanta,
celebrated chief of the Kiowas, was now a prisoner. Carter said:

> He was over six feet in his moccasins, and mounted on a small
> pony, he seemed to be even taller than he really was. He was stark

[29] Tatum, *Red Brothers,* 118–19.

[30] *Ibid.*; Carter, *Massacre,* 41. Carter said that the Tonkawa Indian scalped him.
(Carter, *On the Border with Mackenzie,* 90.)

naked . . . except for a breech clout and a pair of bead embroidered moccasins.

His saddle blanket had slipped to his loins.

His coarse jet black hair, now thickly powdered with dust, hung tangled about his neck except a single braided scalplock with but one long eagle feather to adorn it. His immense shoulders, broad back, deep chest, powerful hips and thighs, contrasted singularly with the slight forms of the Ton-ka-ways . . . . The muscles stood out on his gigantic frame like knots of whip cord, and his form proud and erect in the saddle, his perfectly immobile face and motionless body, gave him the appearance of polished mahogany . . . . Every feature of his proud face bespoke . . . disdain . . . . His feet were lashed with a rawhide lariat under his pony's belly . . . .

Big Tree . . . was much lighter in color, smaller in stature, and much inferior in his general appearance. His features were quite regular, and his nose more acquiline. There was something in his face, however, that betokened the crafty sneak, and he lacked nobility of manner and expression.

He watched and listened to the band playing music, "but not Sa-tan-ta . . . . Big Tree had a single feather to ornament his scalplock, and, like Sa-tan-ta, he also was naked."[31]

On July 6 the two chiefs were removed from the post guardhouse to the county courthouse in Jacksboro for trial, the first Indians to be tried for murder by a jury in a civil process. They were tried before Judge Charles Soward of the Thirteenth, later the Forty-third, Judicial District. The town of "Jack" was swarming with men. Horace Jones, Fort Sill interpreter, was present. The district attorney was S. W. T. Lanham, later to become governor of Texas.[32] Frank Ball was one of the counsel to defend the Indians. "Every man was armed to the teeth." As the trial proceeded, the chiefs grunted approval as Ball urged that they be allowed to

[31] Carter, *Massacre*, 43–44.

[32] His nephew wrote of the massacre and trial in a historical novel. See Edwin Lanham, *The Wind Blew West*.

fly away as "free and unhampered" as the eagle. The district attorney painted a picture of a cold-blooded massacre. The brows of
the jury "grew black," and one could see the verdict plainly written on them. The Indians were sentenced to be hanged. They were
held at Fort Richardson until October or November, and then
sent to Huntsville.

On the way to the penitentiary, Satanta and Big Tree were observed by another passenger. Bud Matthews, later known as Judge
John A. Matthews, traveled on the same stagecoach for a part of
the way. Matthews sat on the box with the driver for a while, but
the driver was drunk and drove under a *bois d'arc* tree, a limb of
which knocked off Matthews' hat. He got inside the coach with the
chiefs and almost smothered in tobacco smoke—the Indians kept
their pipes going constantly.[33]

Governor E. J. Davis commuted the death sentences to terms of
life imprisonment. A year later, in September, 1872, Captain R. G.
Carter escorted them from Dallas to the Indian commissioners at
Atoka, Indian Territory, then on to St. Louis, where they met
members of their tribe, and back to Texas.[34] In 1873 they would
be returned to their tribe.

After the prisoners left Fort Sill in 1871, the Kiowas quieted
down. Kicking Bird brought in the stolen mules and was warned
to get his Indians east of the reservation line, else they might be
attacked by Mackenzie, who had determined on a campaign to the
west, especially against the Comanches. He believed that the Kiowas should be dismounted, disarmed, and kept on the reservation.
Some depredations continued. On September 19, Captain J. B.
Vander Wiele, patrolling the Red River from a camp on Otter
Creek, was attacked. A wagoner, Foster Larkin, of the Tenth Cavalry was killed. On September 22 two cattlemen were killed northeast of Fort Sill. They were scalped and one lost an ear, a common
mutilation ascribed to the Kiowas. The guilty Kiowas were Koyan-te, Mo-hain, and Kee-tau-te.[35] The Comanches escaped to the

[33] Matthews, *Interwoven*, 85.
[34] Carter, *Massacre*, 45–48.
[35] Nye, *Carbine and Lance*, 193.

Staked Plain. Mackenzie followed but was forced to give up the campaign as he was not prepared for the blizzard weather.

In 1871–72 the Kiowas stayed on the reservation, hoping for the release of the imprisoned chiefs in Texas, but the Comanches kept up their raids. Finally, the Kiowas got restless and bored with inactivity. On April 20, 1872, Big Bow, with White Horse of the Comanches, attacked a government wagon train at Howard Wells, a stopping point on the San Antonio–El Paso road, and killed seventeen Mexican teamsters. The train had no military escort. Captain N. Cooney and two troops of the Ninth Cavalry from Fort Concho, on patrol, found the charred remains of the massacre. They trailed the Indians and fought them, but it was a victory for the Kiowas and the soldiers had to withdraw. An officer and an enlisted man were killed. White Horse was shot in the arm, and Tau-ankia, son of Lone Wolf, was shot in the knee.

Some Kiowa boys joined in a Comanche raid. On their way back, L. H. Luckett's party of surveyors fought them near Round Timbers, twenty-five miles from Fort Belknap. Information of the death of the two young Kiowas was brought back to their tribe. White Horse learned that his brother had been killed in Texas and organized a war party for revenge. They left the reservation in June and went to the Brazos near the site of old Camp Cooper. On June 9 they attacked the Abel Lee home, killed Lee and one child, wounded and scalped Mrs. Lee, and took the three remaining children captive. Soldiers tracked them, but they fled too quickly to be caught. They returned to the Kiowa reservation and held a scalp dance that lasted for several nights.

On June 4, An-pay-kau-te, oldest son of Satank, and some others killed a cowboy, Frank Lee, near Fort Sill. They scalped him and took an ear. Tatum became much upset over these raids; he felt that the Indians would have to be stopped by the military. Meanwhile, the Comanches under Tenawerka raided Fort Sill on June 15 and ran off fifty-four horses and mules.[36]

In August, 1872, another council was held, with some Cheyennes, Arapahoes, Caddoes, Wichitas, and Delawares in attend-

[36] *Ibid.*, 196–97, 198–200. Tenawerka to Nye.

ance. All the Kiowas save Big Bow came in. White Horse inquired for "Bald Head" (Tatum). Horace Jones replied that he had gone to Fort Sill; his wife was sick. White Horse then said he was looking for him "to kill him." They boasted of their raids and killings and were admonished by the Indians of the civilized nations. When Cyrus Beede, representing Superintendent Enoch Hoag, asked for the return of the captives and the government stock, Lone Wolf said that they would not comply until their chiefs were returned. Kicking Bird, as usual, tried to help out and promised to use his influence to return the Lee children. Cyrus Beede sent a report to Enoch Hoag which indicated that the Indians were showing a friendly attitude; he even recommended that arms be sold them. On reading this, Sheridan endorsed the letter, saying: "The writer of this within communication is a little too simple for this earth."[37]

It was believed that if the Kiowas could be sent to Washington, they would develop some appreciation of the power and the threats of the government. A delegation of Kiowa Indians was selected to make the trip. Special commissioners, Captain Henry Alvord and Professor Edward Parrish, were to escort them on the tour. The Indians were averse to it until their chiefs should be released, but they were promised that Satanta and Big Tree would be brought from Texas to see them. Colonel Grierson, fearful of a breakout, insisted that the meeting should be not at Fort Sill but elsewhere. The prisoners, escorted by Captain R. G. Carter and some soldiers from Fort Richardson, met the Indian delegation at the Everette House in St. Louis. The prisoners were then returned to Texas, and the others went on to Washington with commissioner Alvord.[38] The Kiowa delegation included Lone Wolf, Stumbling Bear, Sun Boy, Fast Bear, Woman's Heart, Red Otter, Wolf-Lying-Down, and young Dohasan. In Washington the Commissioner of Indian Affairs promised them that he would release Satanta and Big Tree, if they would stop raiding. (This he had no right to promise.)

[37] *Ibid.*, 203. Report of Commissioner of Indian Affairs (1872), 99, cited by Nye.
[38] Carter, *On the Border with Mackenzie*, 335–68. Professor Parrish died at Fort Sill before the trip began. (Nye, *Carbine and Lance*, 159.)

After the delegation returned, Ten Bears, lonely, ill, and deserted, died.[39]

Mackenzie, on September 29, 1872, destroyed the lodges of a Kwahadi Comanche village at McClellan Creek and the North Fork of Red River. Twenty-three Indians were killed, and over one hundred women and children were taken prisoners. Four of Mackenzie's men were killed, and several were wounded. Shortly thereafter, Parry-o-coom (Bull Bear) and his people came in to Fort Sill. Four captive children were given up, and four Comanche women were returned to their own tribe, although one woman died. Parry-o-coom cried when he had to give up Presleano, a small Mexican boy. The Comanches also delivered the stock stolen by Tenawerka. Kicking Bird rounded up from the Kiowas seventeen stolen mules and returned them.

THE PAROLE AND RELEASE OF THE CHIEFS

During the winter of 1872–73 the Kiowas and Comanches camped on the reservation. The Kiowa group under Kicking Bird camped on Two Hatchet Creek; the hostile Kiowas under Lone Wolf camped north of Mount Scott. Thomas Battey now joined the Kiowa Agency as a teacher; Tatum resigned and was succeeded by James Haworth.

Thomas Battey and Lawrie Tatum were both remarkable men. Battey first taught the Caddoes and then felt that he was called by God to go to the Kiowas. He had a deep friendship with Kicking Bird and was respectfully treated by all the elders of the tribe, even though some, like Lone Wolf, were definitely hostile to the white man's way. Repeatedly the Indians counseled and said: "His talk is good." He never feared for his own life, although there were plots to hold him as a hostage, and several times he and the agent, Tatum, realized that his life was in danger.

Tatum was appreciated for his sincerity, uprightness, and lack of fear. He was harassed and intimidated, but he was staunch and straight-forward. One time a Kiowa felt his heart, to see if there

[39] Battey, *Life and Adventures*, 90–92.

was any "scare." Above all, these Indians knew courage when they saw it. Had both Battey and Tatum stayed with the Kiowas longer, the Indians' path might have been an easier one. Factions within the Kiowa bands led to much difficulty. The recalcitrants, Satanta, Lone Wolf, Big Bow, all hated the reservation system. Kicking Bird and Stumbling Bear, foreseeing the future, tried to bring about cohesion and acceptance of the white way. Battey was called "Tho-mis-y," and Tatum, "Bald Head," after the manner of the Indians in using nicknames. (Jim Bridger, for example, was called "Big Throat" from the capacious goiter that thickened his throat.) Battey and Tatum each wore out under the undue strain of their jobs. Tatum gave up his job largely because of the Friends' criticism of his policies; Battey finally had to leave because of illness. Neither ever ran off from the demands or dangers of their positions.

Spring came. The government had not returned the prisoners, and it began to be doubtful if it would. The Modoc Indian War in California inflamed the nation. The federal government did, however, order the Comanche prisoners, women and children, released. On June 10 they arrived from Fort Concho at Fort Sill under the charge of Captain Robert McClermont. There was great excitement and joy for the Comanches. But the Kiowas could not understand why a war in California kept them from getting back their chiefs. Thomas Battey now wrote a letter to the Indian Commissioner stating that the Kiowas had faithfully lived up to their agreement and that the chiefs should be returned.[40] A letter of Ed. P. Smith, commissioner of Indian affairs, of June 26, 1873, to James M. Haworth, Indian agent, advised that the Secretary of the Interior was engaged in steps leading to the release of the prisoners and that the final decision was with the Governor of Texas. The latter was expected to "visit Washington in a few days," and they would urge him to give the Kiowa chiefs their liberty. (President Grant had to do the urging, finally.)

Battey counseled patience for the Kiowas, and Kicking Bird upheld him. But there were some ominous aspects. Other tribes wanted the Kiowas to join them in raiding. Meanwhile, they

[40] *Ibid.*, 161.

camped on Sweetwater Creek and prepared for their Sun Dance. The whole Kiowa tribe joined in, and about five hundred Comanches visited, along with some Cheyennes and Arapahoes. About three thousand Indians were encamped together. Battey visited the Sun Dance ceremonies and met with the chiefs.[41]

Lieutenant Colonel John W. Davidson was the new post commander. He did not get on well with James Haworth, the Indian agent. Davidson feared that war might break out. The Indian Commissioner seemed to have forgotten his promises to the Kiowas, and they were again raiding in Texas. Davidson said that the Indian reservation was a "City of Refuge" for the marauders, and the Texans agreed with him.

On August 19, 1873, Satanta and Big Tree left the Huntsville, Texas, prison, in charge of Lieutenant Hoffman. They were brought to Fort Sill on September 4, and lodged in the new guardhouse.[42] The Texas frontier was bitter over this transfer. Newspapers flayed Governor Edmund J. Davis (Republican governor during the period of Reconstruction) and accused him of playing politics with Washington. Governor Davis was present at Fort Sill on October 3, and a council was held on October 6. Commissioner of Indian Affairs E. P. Smith of Washington, D. C., and Superintendent Enoch Hoag of the Plains tribes came for the council. Every precautionary measure was taken at the post to prevent an outbreak. A tent was put up for the council. The prisoners sat on a bench, and the Indians sat on the grass. Governor Davis was the chief speaker. He outlined the terms of the release. The Indians had to settle on farms; a government official was to be in each camp to check on them; rations were to be given to individuals,

[41] *Ibid.*, 173–84.

[42] The guardhouse at Fort Sill, Oklahoma, is today a museum. The cells of Satanta, Big Tree, and the Apache Geronimo are to be seen. Weapons, artifacts, clothing, painted skins, and pictures of Kiowas and Comanches are displayed, and many are of great interest.

Also exhibited are paintings on skins—one by Silver Horn, loaned by Mrs. Winifred Laurence of Lawton, Oklahoma (the Laurence family operated the original Red Store which carried on trade with the Indians) ; a Kiowa beaded buckskin bag, made by Chief Ar-co's wife in 1889; beaded leggings of the wife of Big Tree (1884) ; and Dohasan's spear, which the chief gave to his grandson, Charles Buffalo.

not distributed by chiefs, every three days instead of all at once; the Indians were to give up arms and horses; and they were to become farmers and civilized Indians. The chiefs would be held until these terms were met; otherwise the Texans would have to resort to open war.

Haworth talked to the Indians and made it clear that these were not his terms, but the Texas Governor's terms. Then various Indians spoke: Lone Wolf, Kicking Bird, Horseback of the Comanches, and Pacer of the Kiowa-Apaches. All insisted that they would keep the peace, if the prisoners were released. Kicking Bird said:

> We have met and the sun shines on us all. We have met to make a permanent peace . . . . My friends from Washington and from Texas have given us a good talk, you want us to live like the white man. If with the talks you will give us the chiefs you have we will do as you want and take the white man's road.
>
> The Kiowas long ago quit raiding in Texas . . . I have been trying for a long time to keep peace between my people and the whites, but they are like boys they sometimes do right and sometimes they do not. By delivering up the chiefs, it will do more towards making peace between us and Texas than anything else . . . . There are many here on the reservation who know of our efforts to restrain our tribe.[43]

Satanta's old father hounded the Governor to give up his son. The conditions set forth were almost impossible to meet. The Indians got excited, drew their bows, and a "deadly kind" of excitement "shaded the countenance and gleamed in the eye." Kicking Bird said that his "heart was a stone" and that the government had deceived them; that nothing was left "but war" and that "we had rather die than live." The agent, aware of the danger, reasoned with the Governor, and plans were made for another meeting.

The Kiowas held a secret meeting that night and planned to take the prisoners by force. They attended the next meeting (October 8) with loaded carbines, revolvers, and strung bows; their

[43] Speech made by Kicking Bird in the Council at Fort Sill, November 4 [October 6], 1873. MS, Indian Affairs Papers, Archives, Texas State Library, Austin.

warriors and horses were ready, and even some women were mounted. Governor Davis changed his propositions, insisted that they stop raiding and the prisoners would be returned. Then the prisoners were released, and a joyous occasion it was, with all the chiefs embracing the Governor and the authorities. The Indians promised to bring in the outlaw groups who were raiding in Texas, although they knew not where they were. (They did try later but with no success.) The chiefs were "on parole."[44]

Britton Davis, son of Governor Davis, told an interesting story of his father's visit to the Kiowas to return Satanta and Big Tree. An aged Kiowa chief was so grateful that he gave Davis a treasured possession—a beautiful robe made of six skins of the gray wolf (lobo), lined with red flannel. It had human scalps set about a foot apart along two sides and on one end of the robe. The chief apologized for the incomplete end. Seeing the expression on Davis' face, the chief assured him that the scalps were all Mexican and Indian, "no squaws or whites."

Davis then insisted that he could not deprive the chief of the scalps—prowess of his warrior days. If the chief would keep the scalps, he would be pleased to accept the robe as a token of peace between the Kiowas and the people of Texas. It was so arranged and all parties were satisfied.[45]

The Comanches had difficulty meeting the terms laid down. They were to put up five hostages until they brought in the five outlaws demanded by Governor Davis. They were to have no rations. Several Comanches went with Chief Cheevers (Comanche) to Double Mountain in Texas but did not find the raiding bands. Then the government reversed itself and went ahead with the rations. Meanwhile, Battey urged the Kiowas to move in close to the agency. White Wolf, a Comanche, although hostile, received Battey into his lodge with hospitality. Battey then went on his way to find Kicking Bird to get him to bring the Kiowas in, which he agreed to do.

After his release from prison, Satanta resigned his chieftain-

[44] Battey, *Life and Adventures*, 199–205; Mooney, "Calendar History," 199–206.
[45] Davis, *The Truth about Geronimo*, 121–22.

ship by giving his red medicine or arrow lance to Áto-t'ain ("White Cowbird").

In the fall of 1873, the Kiowas were raiding again. Governor Davis wrote Fort Sill that Indian depredations into Texas had not stopped. It was known at the post that raids were being made. One party of Kiowas and Comanches went to the West Fork of the Nueces River, left their horses there, and made a charge into Mexico below Eagle Pass. There were 14 Mexicans killed at Olmos, 150 horses and mules captured, and 2 Mexican boys taken prisoner. The Indians continued to raid along the border. Lieutenant Charles L. Hudson, scouting with 41 men near Fort Clark, found the Indian pony headquarters. He received word of the raiders from Fort Clark and hastened after them. A fight broke out in which 9 Indians were killed and 1 trooper was wounded. The soldiers recaptured 50 horses. Several prominent Kiowas were killed. In the Indian flight Tau-ankia was left behind, and his cousin Guitan turned back to help him. Both were killed, as was Isa-tai's uncle. News of their deaths reached the Kiowas on January 13, 1874, and the whole tribe went into mourning. Lone Wolf cut off his long hair, burned his property, became completely hostile, and swore revenge. Thomas Battey was then in the Kiowa camp and described their grief and lamentations. Although Lone Wolf did not know it, Captain Hudson, who had shot his son, was already dead of an accidental gunshot wound. Lone Wolf vowed to kill a white man for the death of his son.

OUTBREAK OF 1874

The buffalo was fast disappearing; its extermination was actually planned by the military authorities and condoned by the government. Settlers were coming nearer and nearer, with thousands crossing the Plains and riding the railroads. They killed the buffalo and used their hides for leather. The destruction of the buffalo was a senseless waste of a noble animal, but it served its purpose: Indian subjugation, which had not been effected by either peace or war.

Thirty Kiowas and Comanches were slain during the winter of 1873–74. The Indians sought revenge, and seemed to be planning a general war. A surveyor was killed near Anadarko, and soldiers at Fort Sill were fired on. Lone Wolf organized a war party to go to Texas to secure the bodies of Tau-ankia and Guitan. The party was in charge of Mamay-day-te. They wanted revenge for their dead and thereby prestige. The Texans were warned and expected them. Major William Bankhead and two companies of the Fourth Cavalry went out from Fort Clark. They came upon the Lone Wolf party, which had to bury the recovered bodies hurriedly before they fled to the Staked Plains. Major Bankhead followed for some 240 miles, coming upon the main El Paso road, 28 miles above Fort Concho (San Angelo). Here the Indians had attacked a company of the Ninth Cavalry, killed a trooper, and stolen horses before they fled. They returned to the reservation and camped near the Wichita Mountains just in time to get ready for the Sun Dance.

There now arose a Comanche prophet, Isa-tai (Rear End of a Wolf). He sought to lead the Indians back to their old ways and kill off the whites. The Comanches had never had a Sun Dance, but Isa-tai planned to gather them all in for one. He commanded them to attend. The Cheyennes and Arapahoes also attended in large numbers. The subject was war and how to attack. Some planned to attack the Tonkawas, who had aided the whites as scouts.[46] Cohaya, a Comanche, told Colonel Nye: "The Tonkawas are bad. They eat people. They think human game tastes better than deer or buffalo."[47] Finally it was decided to lead a raid against the buffalo hunters who were then operating out of old Adobe Walls.

BATTLE OF ADOBE WALLS

Isa-tai and Quanah led the raid. Quanah Parker, a war chief, son of Peta Nocona and Cynthia Ann Parker, rose to fame in the Battle of Adobe Walls, June 27, 1874. The chief of the Kwahadis, Parry-o-coom (Bull Bear), was ill of pneumonia, and Quanah took

[46] Mooney, "Calendar History," 201.
[47] Nye, *Carbine and Lance*, 151.

his place and won war honors. Parry-o-coom died while the battle was in progress. Accompanying the Comanches were some Kiowas and Kiowa-Apaches, including Satanta, Bird Bow, Lone Wolf, White Horse, White Skull, and Howling Wolf.

Some Cheyennes and Arapahoes also joined the war party.[48] While the Cheyennes were holding a medicine lodge made by Crazy Mule on the head of the Washita River, the Comanches visited them, gave a feast to the Cheyenne chiefs and chiefs of the soldier bands, and solicited their help. The Cheyennes smoked the pipe and joined.

The great war party, after three days of marching and gathering recruits, stopped five miles from Adobe Walls and prepared the war medicine. The morning of the fight, they formed in line. Isa-tai stood on a hill to the right of their line. He was naked save for a cap of sage stems. Just as daylight appeared, he called on the warriors to charge.

The hunters barricaded themselves in their buildings and fought off the charges of the Indians. Three Indians were killed early in the battle—Stone Calf's son and Horse Chief of the Cheyennes, and one Comanche. Hard fighting continued into the afternoon, when they drew off. Six Cheyennes were killed. In addition to the two above, they were Stone Teeth, Coyote, Spots on the Feathers, and Walking on the Ground. A total of fifteen Indians died in the fight. Among the Comanches killed were Tsa-yot-see (brother of Esa Rosa), Co-bay, Esa-que, and Tasa-va-te. And a Mexican named Sai-yan died.[49] One Cheyenne named Hippy angrily seized the bridle of Isa-tai and started to quirt him, but another Cheyenne stopped him. Isa-tai was disgraced.

The Indians, after long, hard fighting, were forced to retire. One Indian was knocked off his horse by a mile-long shot.[50] Troops under Lieutenant Frank D. Baldwin rescued the survivors at Adobe Walls. General Nelson A. Miles said that at Adobe Walls

[48] Grinnell, *The Fighting Cheyennes*, 323–24.

[49] Nye, *Carbine and Lance*, 191.

[50] Billy Dixon shot him with his buffalo gun. The distance was actually seven-eighths of a mile. See Olive K. Dixon, *Life of "Billy" Dixon*, 180–81.

the heads of the dead Indians were placed on the gateposts and that the troops who arrived several days after the siege "saw this scene."[51]

Isa-tai lost face, but he explained that his medicine had been ruined by the violations of a taboo. A skunk was killed by an Indian on the way to battle, and that had ruined the "medicine."

Adobe Walls was not the last fight of the Indians with the buffalo hunters in the Texas Panhandle. In 1877 there were Comanche fights with more buffalo hunters. John R. Cook relates that he and other hunters aided some of the troops sent out to gather in the last remnants of the Indians for the reservations. In 1878 buffalo-hunting was over in the Panhandle.[52] The Battle of Adobe Walls almost extinguished it in 1874.

The Kiowas held a Sun Dance from June 3 to 7, but their gaiety was marred over the death of Tau-ankia and Guitan. Most of the tribe had followed Kicking Bird back to the reservation.[53] Lone Wolf was eager to avenge the death of his son and Guitan and tried to recruit a raiding party. Finally, Mama'nte (Dohate) agreed to lead the raid. Then began the dances and beating of raw-hides. Great excitement prevailed, and Dohate made his medicine, "owl medicine," and promised success. The war party crossed Red River, met some buffalo, and stopped to hunt and feast. They entered Texas north of the present site of Quanah, cached their equipment, and painted themselves for battle. There were about fifty warriors; included were Tahbone-mah (later called I-see-o), Trau-tonkee, Lone Wolf, Red Otter, Pago-to-goodle, Mamay-day-te, Komalty, Dohasan, Qui-tan, Sanke-doty, and many others. They crossed the Big Wichita River and came on a herd of cattle. They killed some, roasted and ate them, then set off again. Near the site of Seymour, Mama'nte again made medicine and announced a favorable future. All now readied themselves for battle.

On July 16 they rode across Salt Prairie between Flat Top Mountain and Cox Mountain. This was where the Wagon Train

---

[51] General Nelson A. Miles, *Personal Recollections*, 159–60, 163.

[52] John R. Cook, *The Border and the Buffalo*, ed. by Milo Milton Quaife.

[53] Mooney, "Calendar History," 338.

Massacre had occurred. Revisiting the scene of the crime, they rode up the mountains to see the grave of the Comanche Ord-lee, who had been buried there. Then they saw four cowboys and chased them but found that their own horses' hoofs were bleeding on the rocks and they stopped. They shot several calves and shod their horses in the raw hides of the calves. Then they rode off and waited. At the place where the calves were killed they saw men approaching wearing white hats. These were the Texas Rangers, part of an escort of Major John B. Jones, commanding the Texas Frontier Battalion. The Rangers were looking for Comanches who had killed a cowboy at Oliver Loving's ranch.

A fight ensued. This was later known as the Lost Valley Fight. Jones kept his men together but sought to gain the woods by charging through the Indians, which was done. William A. Glass was severely hurt. The men dismounted and took cover behind a shallow ridge. Glass cried for assistance, and three men ran out and carried him in. Soon the Indians disappeared, knowing that the men would have to get to a water hole sooner or later. When Mel Porter and David Bailey went to get water for the wounded, twenty-five Indians charged. Bailey was surrounded and killed. The Indians then left. After dark Major Jones and his men (Glass had died) went to the Loving Ranch on foot, using what horses were left to carry the wounded.

The Indian version of the fight held more details. Tahbone-mah thrust one ranger off his horse, but the firing was so thick that he could not count coup. Dohasan thrust the other ranger, Bailey, from his horse with a spear, and Mamay-day-te made the first coup. Lone Wolf chopped off the victim's head with a brass hatchet-pipe and disemboweled him with a butcher knife. Others then made coup, and Lone Wolf made a speech of thankfulness to complete his revenge for his son's spirit. Then Lone Wolf made a gift of his name to Mamay-day-te.[54]

[54] Nye, *Carbine and Lance*, 256–57. Tahbone-mah later became the army scout I-see-o. He enlisted in 1892 and served for years. He was an uncle of George Hunt, one of Colonel Nye's chief informants. Mel Porter, thrust from his horse, dived into the creek, then swam underwater and was almost shot by his comrades as he returned.

END OF THE PEACE POLICY

There were Indian attacks in many places in 1874. The Cheyennes and Arapahoes were on the warpath. On July 3 they burned a wagon train under command of Patrick Hennessey at the site of the present town of Hennessey, Oklahoma. The Cheyenne Agency at Darlington had to call for military help. There were a number of depredations near Fort Sill. Colonel Davidson ordered that no Indians could come into the post unless accompanied by the interpreter, Horace Jones. This had its humorous side. On the night the order was issued, while strolling back to the post from the trader's store, Jones, in his cups, was stopped by a confused guard because he did not have an *Indian* with him.

News of atrocities near Fort Sill reached General Sherman, and he submitted a plan to the President for absolute control over the Indians. On July 26 orders were received by the post commander and the agent at Fort Sill that the Indian management was to be turned over to the army. The peaceful Indians were to be enrolled; the hostiles, punished.

On August 19 a white man was killed at Signal Mountain by some Kiowas and Cheyennes. After receiving rations on August 20, Kahtaison and some of Satanta's band killed two white men on Cache Creek, then boasted of it to Philip McCusker. They killed two cowboys near Fort Sill and went north to the Wichita agency at Anadarko, where all of the enrolled Kiowas save Kicking Bird's band were gathered. They were told by agent Haworth to return to Fort Sill, but they refused.

On August 22 there occurred the Anadarko Battle. It was ration day for the Wichitas, Caddoes, and Delawares, but the Kiowas and Comanches helped themselves to the others' rations. As a column from Fort Sill appeared, they mounted their ponies and painted themselves for a fight. Colonel Davidson rode to the agency and told some men to send for Red Food, a Comanche. He arrived and was ordered to surrender as a prisoner of war. He finally did so. They went to the camp to collect arms, and Red Food would not give up his arms; they had never been taken before. The Kiowas sneered at Red Food, and a skirmish broke out. The Indians charged Lawson's company, previously sent to the sawmill. The fight lasted just a few minutes. No one was hurt then, but as Lawson cleared the area, the Indians rushed off and shot a Negro boy. It was difficult to tell the friendly Indians from the hostiles, but it was known that the Kiowas under Woman's Heart, Poor Buffalo, Satanta, and Big Tree had fired on the soldiers. Many moved down the river, and four civilians were killed later. The Indians then looted Shirley's store, tied ribbons to their ponies, and dragged bolts of cloth around. In the evening things quieted down. Davidson had the agency defended, and civilians helped guard.

The next morning more skirmishes took place. The Kiowas fled upstream after firing the grass and trying to burn the agency buildings. The hostiles were now known. The fight at Anadarko scattered the Indians, but, fearing reprisals, they began to come in to Fort Sill seeking protection from the army. By the end of September about half of the Kiowas, Comanches, and Kiowa-Apaches were settled. There were 585 Kiowas, 479 Comanches, and 306 Kiowa-Apaches on the reservation. The remainder sought safety in Texas.[55]

WAR AGAIN: THE HOSTILES IN THE SEVENTIES

General Sherman's campaign was to bring in troops from four directions. Colonel Nelson A. Miles from Camp Supply was to move south; Major William R. Price, east from Fort Union, New Mexico; Colonel Ranald Mackenzie from Fort Concho, Texas, north; and Colonel Davidson, west from Fort Sill. Lieutenant Colonel G. P. Buell was also to operate between Davidson and Mackenzie. But the summer of 1874 was so hot that the campaign was put off until fall.

Lone Wolf, Mama'nte and some Comanches camped in the Palo Duro Canyon. On September 9, Captain Wyllys Lyman's wagon train was attacked by Kiowas while hauling goods from Camp

[55] *Ibid.*, 269–72; Mooney, "Calendar History," 205.

Supply to Colonel Miles. The soldiers fought off the Indians, who retired to the ridges near by and kept up a fire. In the evening they circled the wagon train, then at dark they left. The soldiers threw up breastworks. In the morning the fight began again and continued all day. The soldiers suffered from thirst. At midnight Scout William F. Schmalsle volunteered to go to Camp Supply for help.[56] A small party of the soldiers and a white Kiowa captive, Tehan, set out for a water hole. Tehan deserted his captors, rejoined the Kiowas, and told them that the soldiers were suffering for water.

On the third day of the fighting, Botalye rode through the soldiers' lines—a dangerous feat. As he came back, unhurt, the Indians tried to stop him. But he would not listen. Four times he rode through the lines, bullets hitting his saddle, robe, and even cutting off the feathers in his hair. Each time he threw himself on the side of his horse. This was amazing. Satanta said:

> I could not have done it myself. No one ever came back from four charges. Usually once or twice is enough. I'm glad you came out alive.

Botalye was then given a new name by Poor Buffalo, chief of the band. It was Eadle-tau-hain ("He-Wouldn't-Listen to Them").[57]

On September 14 help finally reached the wagon train from Camp Supply, as a result of Schmalsle's message. The wagons then moved out to find Major Price, who was still wandering over the prairie.

With the army after them, the Indians now began to rush back to the reservation. Mama'nte and Lone Wolf stayed in Texas, moving to the Staked Plain. Woman's Heart, Satanta, and Big Tree went to the Cheyenne Agency at Darlington. There they were placed under arrest and sent to Fort Sill. Satanta was returned to the Texas prison on September 17. Little Chief, in resisting arrest, was killed by Davidson's forces. Davidson skirted the edge of the Staked Plain, and after traveling some five hundred miles, returned to Fort Sill in October.

[56] Miles, *Personal Recollections*, 172–73.
[57] Nye, *Carbine and Lance*, 218.

Colonel Mackenzie reached Palo Duro Canyon on September 27. He moved up the canyon and found the hostile Kiowas and Comanches and some Cheyennes. A fight broke out and the Indians fled. It was a complete rout. Their villages and property were destroyed. Some fourteen hundred Indian ponies were captured. Some Kiowas fled to Yellow House Canyon. The Cheyennes and Comanches scattered in all directions. Mackenzie withdrew without following them farther.

The war was continued into October. On October 9, in what is now Greer County, Oklahoma, Lieutenant Colonel G. P. Buell's army fought a band of Kiowas. Major W. R. Price and the Eighth Cavalry fought some hostile Indians in what is now Hemphill County, Texas. Captain Adna R. Chaffee, with a part of Colonel Miles's troops, surprised an Indian camp north of the Washita River, and as the Indians fled, burned out their camp.

The Comanches under Tabananica, Red Food, and others surrendered to Major G. W. Schofield and the Tenth Cavalry, giving up over two thousand horses and mules. They came in to Fort Sill as prisoners of war. Colonel Miles and Major Price consolidated their forces to hunt the Indians who had fled to the Staked Plain. On November 6 one hundred hostiles fought Lieutenant H. J. Farnsworth. On the eighth Lieutenant Frank Baldwin overtook them and charged them with his infantry in uncovered wagons. This was one time when the infantry moved fast—in wagons. The Indians were defeated, and two white girls, Julia and Adelaide German, seven and nine years of age, were recovered.[58]

In December, 1874, the Indian war was over. It had been the most successful campaign in the Indian country of the south Plains. The Indians continued to straggle in to Fort Sill and to

[58] Mooney, "Calendar History," 213–14. The four German sisters were all later retrieved; their ages were fifteen, thirteen, nine, and seven. Four of their family had been killed in Kansas by the Cheyennes on September 13, 1874. (Nye, *Carbine and Lance*, 290–91.) Colonel Miles was appointed guardian of the girls. Ten thousand dollars were taken from the Indian annuities and set aside for them. As each reached majority, she received her fourth of the money. All were later happily married. (Miles, *Personal Recollections*, 159–60, 174–75.)

Fort Darlington. There were no more treaties. The leaders of the revolt were put in cells and locked up in an unfinished icehouse. Women and children were put in camps off Cache Creek. Many horses were killed; then it was found that they could be sold at auction. At about $4.00 per head, the sale brought in $22,000. With no horses and no buffalo, there remained the reservation to live on. And that was all; there would not be any more Golden Age.

Kicking Bird helped the authorities to settle his people in January, 1875. Colonel Davidson promised Big Bow that he would not be punished, if he brought his people in. He did so. Then Big Bow was sent out to get Lone Wolf. On February 26, Mama'nte, Lone Wolf, Red Otter, Dohasan, and Poor Buffalo came in. With them came 68 warriors, 180 women and children, and 475 horses and mules.

The war against the Kiowas was over, but it continued against the Comanches and Cheyennes. During the winter and spring of 1875, Colonel Nelson A. Miles continued the campaign against the Cheyennes. As a result the Cheyennes broke down and surrendered under their principal chief, Stone Calf. The Arapahoes had remained friendly. Among the prisoners sent to Florida were thirty-three Cheyennes and two Arapahoes. In a skirmish on April 6, Black Horse was killed while being put in irons, and some Cheyennes fled. Some were later killed by the army.[59]

It was decided to send all the prisoners to Florida. Kicking Bird was now recognized as the principal chief of the Kiowas, and he had the task of selecting the prisoners. The hostile chiefs, White Horse, Mama'nte, Woman's Heart, and Lone Wolf, and some lesser tribesmen, even Mexican captives, were sent to Florida— seventy in all. Lieutenant R. H. Pratt, later famous for his Carlisle Indian School in Pennsylvania, was in charge of the prisoners.[60]

Kicking Bird, whose Indian name was Tené-angópte, served his tribe faithfully, but he had many enemies. He even believed that the agent had cast him aside—"thrown him away"—but final-

[59] Mooney, "Calendar History," 211–13.
[60] *Ibid.*, 214–16.

ly Battey reasoned with him, and he continued his efforts to save and settle his people.[61] Kicking Bird died on May 4, 1875, after becoming sick from a cup of coffee. Many believed that he was poisoned, but the Indians said that Mama'nte or Dohate "hexed" him.[62] But Dohate denied the charge, saying that if he had used his power to kill Kicking Bird it would have killed him (Dohate), too. Dohate died on the trip to Fort Marion, Florida.

The Kwahadi Comanches in Texas were the last to come to the reservation. In April, 1875, Dr. J. J. Sturms and Sergeant John B. Charlton carried to them Mackenzie's offer to come in peaceably. (Mackenzie was the commanding officer at Fort Sill.) On June 2, Quanah led the Kwahadis into Fort Sill.[63]

Thus ended the independence of the savages. Other raids and defections from the reservation occurred, but the way was clear for the future. In 1878, Sun Boy's band of Kiowas, while hunting buffalo under a reservation escort, was attacked by the Texas Rangers. On June 29 a band of Comanches made the last raid into Texas and fought the Texas Rangers at Mustang Springs on the North Concho River. It was to be a long, hard "civilized road," but the only one open.[64]

[61] Tatum, Red Brothers, 197-99; Battey, Life and Adventures, 304-07.

[62] Battey, Life and Adventures, 317; Tatum, Red Brothers, 197; Mooney, "Calendar History," 217.

[63] Carter, On the Border with Mackenzie, 473–524. See also Captain Robert Goldthwaite Carter, The Old Sergeant's Story.

[64] Mooney, "Calendar History," 343–44; Nye, Carbine and Lance, 303–308.

CHAPTER SEVEN

❖ THE LAST COUNT

In the summer of 1875, Colonel Ranald Mackenzie decided to purchase sheep and goats for the Indians with the money from the sale of their horses. Twenty-two thousand dollars worth of New Mexican sheep and goats were bought. Many died on the way to Fort Sill. The stock were fattened over the winter and spring and then turned over to the Indians. But it was soon discovered that they were not pastoral Indians; they preferred buffalo meat or beef to lamb and mutton. It had been hoped that the wool would be used for weaving. However, the Kiowas did not know how to weave a blanket, and none cared to learn. The stock were run by the dogs and shot at with bows and arrows by little Indian boys. Wolves and coyotes finished off the rest.

Cattle given the Indians were appreciated, but all were eaten up and none saved for breeding. With the buffalo practically exterminated, the Indians were often hungry. Temporary relief was afforded by army rations. Colonel Mackenzie wrote to General Sherman on August 31, 1875, that the Indian department was not feeding the Indians, "and unless these Indians are fed and the obligations of the Indian Department to them fulfilled, we may expect certainly a stampede of the Kiowas and Comanches from their reservation."[1]

Homes were built for ten leading chiefs in 1876 to wean them from the tipi and brush arbor. They became show places, and the chiefs were proud of them, but they did not live in them. In 1877 an epidemic of measles gave much trouble. In 1878 the Florida prisoners were returned to the reservation. Tribes and communities began to break up into small family groups. Herds of Texas cattle went across Indian land to the northern markets, and the cattle drivers, to keep the Indians from helping themselves, gave beeves to the chiefs. Some of the Indians began to build up herds of cattle. This was more suitable to their inclinations than farming, but the Indian agent still tried to teach them to farm. They said that they did not want their women working in the fields. When the agent explained that the warriors were to do the plowing, the Indians found that unthinkable.

In 1879 the Kiowa and Comanche Agency was consolidated with that of the Wichitas, Caddoes, and others and moved to Anadarko. Lone Wolf died in 1879 and was succeeded as principal chief by Mamay-day-te, who had taken the name of Lone Wolf, given to him in the Lost Valley fight of July, 1874. Asatoyeh of the Comanches died in 1878, as did Satanta who committed suicide at Huntsville, Texas. Proud and defiant to the last, Satanta, the "Orator of the Plains," jumped from the prison hospital to the ground and ended his life.

An Indian Police was organized on October 1, 1878, with Sankedoty as captain. He had two lieutenants, four sergeants, and twenty-two privates in the group. The officers received ten dollars per month and the privates, five dollars. Cattlemen caused some difficulty on the Indian lands. Those caught trespassing with their cattle on the grasslands were fined. But it was impossible to keep out the cattle. In 1885, Agent P. B. Hunt finally sought better arrangements and leased the grazing lands for the Indians. In Febru-

[1] Nye, *Carbine and Lance*, 319. Mackenzie to Sherman, August 31, 1875, File 4608, Adjutant General's Office, National Archives, Washington, D. C.

ary, 1885, a delegation of Indians, accompanied by the interpreter Horace Jones, went to Washington to secure official approval of their renting their lands. The Indians were allowed to make their own arrangements. While on the trip, the Indians, including Saddey-taker ("Dog Eater"),[2] Quanah, and others, were entertained in St. Louis by William Quinette, the post trader at Fort Sill.

The Indians and the cattlemen had their difficulties. Jim Williams helped drive steers up from Texas to Anadarko for the Box K outfit of Dick Steel in 1884 to furnish food for the Kiowas and Comanches. He said: "There were about 6,000 of both tribes, both Kiowas and Comanches, and everyone had a pack of dogs but few papooses." The distribution of the animals was interesting. The agent told them to put one hundred steers in the corral. They did, and

> . . . the agent had his warriors brave at the corral gate on their ponies with their shooting irons. They were bare-backed on their horses and them just as poor as they could be . . . . When they came out of that pen the wild riding and high shooting would come off. Sometimes they would kill their steer in just a short while, and again they might empty their sixshooter into a steer and not have him down—maybe kill him two miles from camp . . . .
>
> The old buck wouldn't turn his hand at anything, the old squaws did the work—what little there was to do. And when they cleaned up a carcass there was nothing left but a pile of grass.[3]

Williams said that when the Indians got their money from their Burnett and Waggoner grass lease, they had a big gambling spree. They gambled all night and all day until the money got into a few hands. They played monte, which was a new game to the cowboys. When an Indian lost, "he was satisfied," and there was no scrapping or complaining. He "would go to his tipi," and "you didn't see him

---

[2] Saddey-Taker is given as "Gaddo-taker" in the Stephenson Album, Barker History Center of the University of Texas Library. His picture is in the Old Stone Guardhouse at Fort Sill.

[3] J. E. (Jim) Williams, *Fifty-eight Years in the Panhandle of Texas*, 18–20.

anymore." Williams said that the Indians would not work, and "they don't know how to do anything." He noted that "the government is still feeding them and that is as it should be."[4]

Williams said that he accompanied Matt Byrd up to the Arkansas River with a herd of cattle. Cheyennes and Arapahoes thought that they should be given beef. Their interpreter was an old Indian fighter.

> He came and stayed with us one night. The next morning we let the cattle off the ground and hadn't gone far until fifteen Indians came up . . . and demanded that we give them each a wohaws, and they proceded to cut a bunch out. We boys would turn them back into the herd. After a while the old interpreter heard the commotion and ran up on top of the hill. Those Indians saw him and when they discovered that he had caught them they didn't bother us any more but just skulked off . . . . That man was Amos Chapman and he was one of the survivors of the Buffalo Wallow Indian fight and he lost one of his legs in that fight . . . . He had turned Indian as he had a squaw or two and some of as good land and cattle as there was in Oklahoma.[5]

While working for the Hart Ranch, Williams was sent to Greer County to winter a bunch of saddle- and cow-horses in camp about eighteen miles east of Mangum, Oklahoma, with food enough for the winter in a tent. He said:

> But they didn't know these Indians. When they visited me a few times while I was away from camp they ate me out in less than a month. There was always some of them laying around camp and what could you do about it in a tent? They could go through everything we had.

He had to take a boy sick with asthma back to the main camp. Then he was by himself and was

[4] *Ibid.*, 21.
[5] *Ibid.*, 59.

. . . a little afraid of those Indians. They would come around and if you were at home they would spread out all over your tent and all around it and just sit and watch every move you made and make signs at each other and grunt a little.

Later, Williams noticed cow and horse tracks crossing a fence. He rushed to the main camp to get Mr. Whitten and two cowboys.

We trailed them over onto Elk Creek and there they were red-handed. They had just killed all of them and hanged them up in the elm trees in their camp. There lay the hides on the ground. Mr. Whitten began cursing them when they denied and said they had bought them. Mr. Whitten could talk Indian just about as well as the Indians could. Then he took one of the hides and turned it over and showed them the brand and they could not deny it . . . . Whitten cut out five of their best looking horses they had and we drove them back with us. Next day about twenty of them came over wanting their horses . . . . Whitten told them "When you bring back those wohaws (cattle) I will give you your horses."[6]

Whitten told Williams that was the only way that the government would pay him for his cattle. Whitten's voice often "changed on him." The Indians called him "Old Two Time Talk and they were certainly afraid of him."[7]

Conditions were changing, and the Indians began to show a patient resignation. There were times, though, when they were displeased with their rations and sought by magic to forecast the return of the buffalo, but there was not much hope. In 1882 there was an epidemic of whooping cough and measles. In 1883 the first church was built for them, and in 1887 the Methodists began working with them.[8]

After the close of the Indian war in 1875, a detachment of Indian scouts was used at Fort Sill. In 1892 the government formed sev-

[6] *Ibid.*, 63–64.
[7] *Ibid.*, 64.
[8] Mooney, "Calendar History," 219.

eral Indian troops of cavalry. Troop L was organized at Fort Sill and was commanded by Lieutenant Hugh L. Scott. It consisted mostly of Kiowas. Quanah of the Comanches did not believe that the Indians should join, because the missionaries were teaching them not to be warriors. I-see-o was appointed first sergeant. Under his real name of Tahbone-mah, he was aged forty-two, but under his new name of I-see-o, he was aged twenty-nine. The Kiowas made good soldiers. It was a means of gaining prestige, and their discipline was good. For some it was a means of encouragement as their old customs and ideas were undergoing change. One of the duties of Troop L was to furnish turkey and deer for General Miles's holiday dinners. Troop L lived north of the trader's store with their families in canvas tipis. They spent much of their time playing monte and other games. In 1897 the War Department disbanded all Indian troops.

The Kiowas, Kiowa-Apaches, and Comanches were crushed in spirit. It was difficult for them to accept the new conditions. The old chiefs were dead or dying. Their horses and their weapons had been taken from them. Their vanished sovereignty was voiced with regret by the ancients. But the old men no longer opposed schools; they wanted their children taught the new ways. The buffalo had now totally disappeared—a calamity so awful that it was difficult to comprehend. Millions of the great beasts had been wiped out—a phenomenon unparalleled in the course of natural history. Disease, too, played its part in the improverishment of the Indians. Pneumonia and tuberculosis, heightened by exposure and lack of the white man's sanitation and cleanliness (absolutely necessary for use of the white man's type of clothing and for life inside of houses), were always present. Measles, whooping cough, and fevers cut down their numbers, and at times malnutrition and starvation confronted them. In 1879, with the complete failure of their annual hunt, the Indians had to kill and eat their few ponies to keep from starving. In 1881 there was dissatisfaction over their rations. Their threatening attitude alarmed the whites and the near-by Wichitas, whose farms suffered. Troops were sent from Fort Sill to ward off trouble; the Indians were fed by the army and the unrest was quieted. Conditions improved some with the first money payments of the cattlemen who leased their grasslands. But some were afraid to take the money, fearing that they were giving up their lands.

In 1881, Datekan (son of Woman's Heart), a medicine man, began to preach and to foretell the return of the buffalo.[9] He renamed himself Pa-tepte ("Buffalo Bull Returns") and invited all the tribes to join him in ceremonies, copying the ritual of the Sun Dance, to bring back the buffalo. Near Mountain View a medicine lodge was constructed. Fourteen assistants helped the medicine man. Great numbers of people gathered, but not all were devout; in fact, some were rather skeptical of his powers. According to Pa-tepte, the buffalo were supposed to issue from a hole, covered by a flat rock, inside the lodge. Songs were sung, medicine was made, and the grandmother gods were invoked to bring up a buffalo. But days of attendance failed to achieve results. Even skin cut from arms and legs of the devotees was useless. For ten days and nights the prophet carried on his prayers, but there was no buffalo. Finally, he explained that his medicine had been ruined by the lack of faith of the Indians. He lost face as a prophet and died within a year.

Another prophet, Botalye, then tested his powers. His was a more difficult job: to bring the sun down from the sky. Many gifts were received, and hopeful devotees hovered about. The medicine was made but he had no success.

Missionary work abong the Kiowas and Comanches began in 1883. The Reverend J. B. Wicks, an Episcopalian who had been conducting services among the associated tribes for two years, built a church at the agency, supported largely by the Wichita and affiliated tribes. The Methodists, under J. J. Methvin, in 1887 began to work among the Indians. The Mennonites established themselves at Post Oak Creek; the Baptists, at Rainy Mountain; and the Catholics, at Anadarko. Later, in the nineties, the Dutch Reformed Church built a mission just north of Medicine Bluff at

[9] *Ibid.*, 219; Nye, *Carbine and Lance*, 337–39; Marriott, *The Ten Grandmothers*, 142–54.

Fort Sill. The minister, Reverend Frank Wright, was a Choctaw. Although Christian teachings seemed to confuse the Indians, the civilizing value of the work was great. Many became devout Christians and surpassed in behavior the white people of the frontier. Understanding the new language was one of the chief difficulties of the Indians. When the ministers raised their voices and shouted, the Indians would get frightened and rush out, saying that the minister was "mad at them."[10]

The ministers wanted to change social conditions as well as to promote Christianity. When the Indians accepted Christianity they found that there were certain other conditions to be met before they could join the church; they had to give up their multiple wives. After living comfortably together for years, families had to be broken up. The white man's ways were difficult ways, and living did not get any easier. The Kiowas were made to feel disgraced by having two or more wives. The government was not particularly concerned for it realized that in time, as the old folks died, the old customs would die also. But the ministers were insistent. Sometimes a wife would voluntarily leave her husband to a younger sister and go off to live with her children or relatives, thereby reducing the family to a monogamous union, which made its members acceptable to the church.[11]

The Comanches were less concerned with and less given to religion, being more individualistic than other Plains Indians. Quanah Parker was asked by President Theodore Roosevelt why he did not give up his eight wives and keep only one. His reply reflected his sense of humor. He said, "You tell them which one I keep."

In the spring of 1887, Pá-ingya or P'oinkia, a medicine man, revived the doctrine of the return of the buffalo and the good old days. The whites and the unbelieving Indians would be destroyed by fire and whirlwinds. Great excitement stirred the Kiowas. Pá-ingya claimed the ability to raise the dead and to kill his enemies

---

[10] Mooney, "Calendar History," 219; Nye, *Carbine and Lance*, 341–42.
[11] Marriott, *The Ten Grandmothers*, 216–21.

with a glance. At the western end of the reservation, on Elk Creek, he set up headquarters and developed a following. The Indians were to make a sacred fire by the old methods of friction, and to discard white clothing, manners, and food. They must also be blessed by the prophet. They were told to take their children out of school, thus saving them from destruction. Many did so. This was a mistake and led to Pá-ingya's downfall. Big Tree, who had become a good Baptist, Gotebo, and others scoffed at the pretensions of the prophet.[12] Again the whites were apprehensive, and troops from Fort Sill were sent to Anadarko. Joshua Given (he took the name of Given from Dr. Given, a surgeon at the post who had helped him), son of Satank, an educated missionary, begged to visit Pá-ingya and save his people from the troops. He was allowed to visit Elk Creek while the agent held the troops at the agency.

Joshua Given informed Pá-ingya of the danger of the situation and proposed a test of supernatural powers. Let the soldiers shoot the prophet; if he arose on the third day, he would be acclaimed the true Messiah to be accepted by all, Indians and whites alike. But Pá-ingya was not ready for such a test. He agreed to dismiss the soldiers, and he sent the children back to school. He would await a more favorable time for a meeting. The excitement was over, and Pá-ingya's influence disappeared.[13]

In 1887–88, E. E. White, special Indian agent and inspector, served temporarily as agent for the Kiowa Indians. During his tenure White was called to Washington to represent the Indian office in an appeal which the deposed agent at Anadarko had made for reinstatement. During his absence of two months the agency beef and flour contractors failed, and when he got back on February 1, 1888, he said, "Many of the Indians were actually starving."[14]

A Kiowa delegation met him and then held a council, agreeing that it was useless to write letters, because: "The only way to at-

[12] Mooney, "Calendar History," 220.
[13] *Ibid.*, 220; Nye, *Carbine and Lance*, 342–45.
[14] E. E. White, *Service on the Indian Reservations*, 310–12.

tract the notice of Washington was to kill somebody."[15] Who should it be? "Cat" (Baa-o or Gunsa-dalte) argued the question:

> Here are Tom Woodard, Bill Shirley, Fred Schlegel, Jim Carson, Joe Becker, George Madera, Jack Nestell, Major Campbell, George Rose and Dr. Graves—all been here long time. Maybe so Washington forgot all about them—all same as forgot about Injun. Injun kill one of them, maybe so Washington never hear about that. Injun kill all of 'em, maybe so Washington not much care—No ask what's the matter. Heap o' trouble, too, to kill lots o' white men like that. White man heap big fool. Maybe so git mad and heap shoot and kill it some Injuns. Cat no like it, that. But Washington see Agent, just little bit ago. Maybe so Washington no forget about Agent. Indian kill Agent, maybe so Washington hear about that purty quick and send it wire paper and say, "What's the matter now? Injun hungry? All right, I send it something to eat purty quick." That's the best way. Kill Agent. That not much hard work, and Washington come quick to ask it what's the matter.[16]

Cat's argument prevailed, and it was agreed that he and "Komalta, Polant, and Little Robe" should go to the agent's office early the next morning and ask every two or three hours through the day about the beef and flour. By the middle of the afternoon, if they did not get a satisfactory answer, White said that he learned he was to be stabbed to death with knives.

The Indians appeared at the agency about eight o'clock, seated themselves on the floor around the stove, made a lot of cigarettes, took a comfortable smoke, and asked the agent if he had heard anything of the beef and flour. He said "no" and they received the answer "like wooden men." Then at nine o'clock an Indian arrived with news that the contractors' men had camped with a herd of beef cattle twelve miles down the river the night before and would be at the agency in two hours. White said, "This news produced a perfect jubilee. Cat shook hands with me with many demonstra-

[15] *Ibid.*, 314.
[16] *Ibid.*, 314–15.

tions of joy and affection," not knowing that some of the Kiowas had divulged the plot.

> Notwithstanding I was to be the victim, I could not find it in my heart to condemn Cat . . . . Polant and Komalta were two of the most turbulent Indians on the Reservation, and . . . Little Robe was [not] very much better; but Cat was really a good Indian, and I am sure he thought a great deal of me and was only going to sacrifice me that his famishing women and children might live. In their situation, and with their experiences in previous emergencies, they believed that was the only "letter" they could "write" to Washington that would bring prompt and adequate relief to their starving families . . . . I did not believe any white people on earth would have borne their neglect half as long or half as patiently as they did.[17]

Some statistics of the agency are interesting. White said there were 1,151 Kiowas and 325 Kiowa-Apaches at the agency in 1888. With the Comanches and Wichitas, the total was 4,182 Indians.[18] The agent was paid $2,000 per year; the clerk and physician, $1,200 each; and twenty-seven employees, from $120 to $720. There were three superintendents of schools, two at the agency and one at Fort Sill, each paid $1,000. There were twenty-seven school employees, paid $150 to $720. The traders had to be licensed by the Indian office in Washington. White served for eleven months before he was replaced by a permanent agent, Major W. D. Myers.

The last Sun Dance or K'ado was held in 1887. In 1889 a Sun Dance was planned, but it was prevented by troops from Fort Sill.

The loss of their Sun Dance was a crushing blow to the Kiowas. Their culture was all gone—no horse, no buffalo, no Sun Dance. This undermined their faith and destroyed their religion. They were broken in spirit. Actually, the Sun Dance was harmless; behind it were their beliefs in good medicine for the health and future of the tribe. It brought them together in a religious and social way. The ritual and dances were stimulating, preserved their

[17] *Ibid.*, 317.
[18] *Ibid.*, 317ff.

religious history, and gave them emotional outlets. It should not have been discarded because it was pagan and non-Christian. Elsewhere the Indians were encouraged to keep up their religion and their dances. They still do today, even though they are varnished over with Christian ideology. The K'ado was for the Kiowas a source of individual and tribal strength and a means of preserving native beliefs. When the Kiowas lost their Sun Dance, they lost their religion, save for individual attempts at "medicine" or praying to the grandmother bundles.[19]

The Ghost Dance religion with a native messiah intrigued the Kiowas in 1890.[20] It followed the ideas of Datekan and of Pá-ingya. The prophecies were begun by Wovoka, or John Wilson, a Paiute Indian, and diffused over the northern Plains and thence south. The earth was to be renewed, and the animals, especially the buffalo, were to be brought back. Dead relatives were to be resurrected, and the golden age, before the white man and his destructive ways appeared, was to return. There were to be no white men—only Indians living happily as heretofore, free from death, misery, and disease. The magic of the Ghost Dance would carry them into the renewed old land. It seemed harmless enough, at first, but the increasing idea of the destruction of the white man gave apprehension to the settlers, even though with its concept of the messiah, the new religion was based on Christianity. Dances brought to the participants visions (looking directly at the sun helped) and trances. Herein, they foresaw the future.

The Ghost Dance came to the Kiowas in the fall of 1890, by way of Sitting Bull, an Arapaho, a dedicated believer; and the Kiowas received it heart and soul.[21] Fearing trouble, the commander at Fort Sill called on Lieutenant Hugh L. Scott, in whom the Indians had great confidence, to watch the actions of the Kiowas and keep the post informed. Scott, with the help of I-see-o, kept a close watch but was of the opinion that the dances were

---

[19] Mooney, "Calendar History," 220–21.

[20] *Ibid.*, 221. See also James Mooney, "The Ghost Dance Religion and the Sioux Outbreak of 1890," B.A.E., *Fourteenth Annual Report*, Pt. 2 (1896), 641–1,100.

[21] Mooney, "Calendar History," 221–22.

harmless and that the prophecies would soon be discredited; as it turned out, this was true and no military control was necessary. However, military interference in the north resulted in battle and death, as, for example, in the pitiful massacre of the Sioux at Wounded Knee.

The dance itself consisted of dancers forming a large circle, hands clasped, moving about to chants and songs with the individuals finally succumbing to hypnotic trances. This was part of the old "vision quest." Sitting Bull received many gifts. Some thought him an imposter, but he was sincere. Ápiatan was particularly impressed, having lost a son with whom he wished to communicate. He was sent by the Kiowas, who made up a purse for his journey, to seek out the prophet Wovoka, and to report back to the Kiowas. He undertook the long journey and finally reached Wovoka. He found an old man lying on a bed in his lodge and covered with a blanket. The messiah was not much of a proselyter. There were no crucifixion marks on his hands, as Ápiatan had been led to believe. The messiah could not help him get in touch with his dead child. Ápiatan was thoroughly disillusioned and lost faith. He returned to denounce the religion, and the Kiowas gave it up.

On January 9, 1891, three Kiowa boys ran away from the government school at Anadarko following harsh punishment by a teacher, Mr. Wherrit. While they were crossing thirty miles to the Kiowa camps on Stinking Creek, a sudden blizzard blew up and froze them to death. Tremendous excitement gripped the Kiowas, and threats of punishment were made against the teacher, who fled the country. Again Lieutenant Hugh L. Scott with I-see-o helped to quiet the tension, and a military force was not needed. The burial of the children drew tears from all the mourners and portrayed the deep emotion of the Kiowas.

A further calamity came in the spring of 1892 with a measles epidemic. It wrought havoc among the children and resulted in the death of 220 persons, almost all children. It was the worst tragedy in years for the Kiowas and the Kiowa-Apaches. Every family lost a loved one, and thousands of dollars in property were consigned to the burials for destruction, in keeping with their old beliefs.[22]

Another threatened outbreak of the Kiowas occurred over the death of Polant ("Creeping Snake"). Polant was preparing for a Peyote festival, then rapidly diffusing as a religious ceremony and as a curative ritual among the Kiowas, Comanches, and Kiowa-Apaches. He needed a steer for the feast and sent some young men to get one from a cattle ranch near present Warren, Oklahoma. The cowboys refused to give them one. The next day, Polant went himself. He had cut out several steers and started off when he was stopped by one of the cowboys. Polant was quarrelsome and threatened to draw his gun. As he did so, he was shot and killed. Some of the Kiowas heard about it and went to claim the body for burial. This called for revenge, according to tradition, and a war was feared. Lieutenant H. L. Scott made a forced march with troops to see Big Bow and held a talk with the leading chiefs. It was pointed out that Polant had left the reservation, that he was on others' property when he was shot, and that he was to blame. Finally, the chiefs agreed to settle the matter legally. Even though they would have preferred to see the cowboy hanged, he was legally acquitted. However, the owner of the ranch gave the Indians several beeves, and satisfaction was made, following the old indemnity sanctions of the tribe which had so often settled difficulties in the past.[23]

In 1892 a commission visited the reservation to negotiate the distribution of individual allotments (the Jerome Agreement) and the sale of the remainder of the reservation. The Indians vigorously opposed it, and determined to protest it. In March, 1894, a delegation went to Washington and opposed the measure. Delegates were Ápiatan, Apache John or Gonk'on ("Stays-in-Tipi"), and Piana'vonit, a Comanche, along with Captain Scott and Andres Martinez (Andele), the Mexican captive who had been raised with the Kiowas and who served as interpreter.

Still, progress was made by the Kiowas on the reservation,

[22] *Ibid.*, 223.
[23] Nye, *Carbine and Lance*, 352.

despite many hardships. The leasing of their grasslands brought in an annual rental of nearly $100,000. This money was put into the building of homes and in buying stock, improved breeds of cattle and horses. Small farms were operated, if not to full production at least for subsistence value, and the schools were successful in educating the children.

Some took to Christianity, and many found help in its practical aspects. Others developed the Peyote cult into the Native American church. There was some opposition to this, but James Mooney believed that it was helpful for the Kiowas.[24] The Peyote ritual was patterned upon Christian teachings, but it involved the chewing of the peyote buttons and blossoms (called "mescal"), which brought about sleep and colored dreams. Although it was not classed as a drug, many believed it to be dangerous because it resulted in stupefaction, trances, and sometimes death.

[24] Slotkin, *The Peyote Religion*, 28ff., 41–47, 137. Mooney helped the Indians to develop the Peyote cult and incurred the wrath of those opposed to it. So bitter was the opposition to Peyote that Mooney was not allowed to visit the Indians in his last days. See also Weston La Barre, *The Peyote Cult*, Yale University *Publications in Anthropology, No. 19* (1938). The Kiowas, Comanches, and Caddoes helped to diffuse the cult among the Plains Indians. The Kiowas and Comanches had used it as "medicine" for a long time but not in cult form.

CHAPTER EIGHT

❖ TODAY-ACCULTURATION

THE bloodthirst and barbarism of the southern Plains have disappeared. Gone, too, is the mastery, but the feeling of superiority and the independence of the Kiowas remains.

The tails of the fabric of white man's civilization have been caught, but full grasp still eludes them. The work of the schools has been monumental; perhaps a belief in the efficacy of education for the future is the Indians' real religion, as indeed it may be ours. Upon this, the interested Indians pin their faith. The long history of politics, confusion, and reversal of policy in dealing with the Indians has left its mark. Still there are signs that the Indian can become an active citizen and make a future for himself.[1]

[1] For a discussion of present conditions among the Indians, with emphasis upon legislation, termination of federal trust policies, land sales, education, health, and relocation, see Walter M. Daniels (comp.), *American Indians. The Reference Shelf*, Vol. XXIX, No. 4 (1957). There are 400,000 Indians in the nation, 61,000 of whom cannot speak English. Nearly as many cannot read or write in any language. Some 26,000 of their children do not attend school. The death rate in communicable and preventable disease is much higher than for the white population. The picture is still essentially one of povery and frustration.

In regard to present attempts at relocation: "Some 6,200 of the established 245,000 Indians on reservations had been resettled by late 1954." (*Ibid.*, 159.) (Relocation has not been too successful, according to conversations with officials and

Acculturation, the borrowing of a new culture pattern, is at best a difficult process. But it was especially so for the Kiowas, who had to move from the Stone Age to the highly complex and increasingly mechanized Euro-American culture.

Speaking sociologically, there was some accommodation, but acculturation would take a long time. There was acquiescence to authority on the surface, but the "heart" of the Indians was not in acquiring new ways of life. Some made the jump in one generation —they realized that the golden past was irrevocably gone. Others drew off and lived in a dream world, never accepting the new ways of life, drawing out the days, living only for the reality and release of death. Those who understood urged their children into school— they realized that changes must be made.

Changes meant for the Indian learning to make garments of cloth, exchanging skins for canvas to use in making the tipi, using a gun rather than bow and arrow for limited hunting, and wearing shoes and hats and suits. Coats were uncomfortable but vests were much like the old hunting shirts. Blankets were still tied about waists, and moccasins were more comfortable than shoes. The men continued to wear their hair in braids, painted their faces, and wore their ornaments.

New food habits had to be learned. Flour and cornmeal were easy to use but were unappreciated. Satanta, when confined to the reservation, said that corn "hurt his teeth." Meat was the preferred food, wohaw (beef) replacing buffalo. The use of coffee and sugar was learned before reservation days, and these were liked better than other new foods.

Preferred jobs went to the whites, and the Indians, even those few who were eager to work, did not get pleasant jobs. Hauling, work in livery stables, agricultural and road work were the usual positions open to them. They were often criticized for sullenness

Kiowa Indians, and information gathered by the author at the Kiowa Indian Agency, Anadarko, Oklahoma, July 17, 1957.)

More organization and help is needed in health programs. The Kiowas had had no provision for Salk polio shots in the summer of 1957.

See also John Collier, *The Indians of the Americas.*

and nonprogressive habits and for being dirty in clothing and in housekeeping. But washing fabrics and keeping a house clean were utterly foreign to them, and had to be learned.

The old native habits of smoking tobacco, drinking and using stimulants without moderation, and gambling were increased with leisure of the reservation. The whites could not understand the Indian's gift-giving and beggaring of his resources. They tried to teach him their own acquisitive habits, which were at variance with the old tribal solidarity in giving and sharing. The Indian considered the white man selfish, and too hard-working to enjoy himself.

Some Indians saw the changing order and the way ahead. Chief Running Bird of the Kiowas summed it up thus:

> I am getting old now, and I am getting up in years, and all I wish at the present time is for my children to grow up industrious and work, because they cannot get honor in war as I used to get it. They can get honor only by working hard. I cannot teach my children the way my father taught me, that the way to get honor is to go to war; but I can teach my children that the way to get honor is to go to work, and be good men and women.[2]

The policies and goals set for the Indians were confusing and changed with each administration. Subdued by force in the early days of the reservation, around 1875, the Indian lost or never developed ambition. When the hostiles were forced in from the Staked Plain, they were crowded into the horse corrals at Fort Sill and meat was thrown from wagons over the fence to them; as Gotebo said, they were fed like they "were lions." Early attempts at education took the children away from their families "as young as possible" and educated them as white children were educated— an unrealistic training, after which they returned as strangers to their own people. Educators and missionaries deplored these children's "return to the blanket," but social discrimination and lack of opportunities for employment nullified the results of their long period of education.

[2] Francis E. Leupp, *In Red Man's Land*, 87.

White ways shocked the Indians. The long training for civilized life was a grind. Life did not get simpler by adopting white culture —it became more complex, and new decisions had to be made.

There were a few patterns that suggested the honors of the old life. Agent P. B. Hunt organized the Indian Police, provisions for which were enacted by Congress in May, 1878, designed to check crime on the reservation and to take the place of the old military societies. The headmen did not like this at first; they objected to having young men boss them. The chiefs were then given the right to arrest anyone committing a crime on the reservation. This gave the chiefs a semblance of their old authority and helped rebuild lost ego. The police force did a commendable job, aided by the chiefs.

There was constant pressure to open the Indian reservation to white settlement. On October 6, 1892, the Jerome Agreement was made at Fort Sill between the Kiowas, Comanches, Kiowa-Apaches, and the United States. By this agreement each Indian, young or old, got 160 acres of land of his own selection. It was said that in earlier allotments some Indians had laced up puppies in cradleboards and registered them, so the government was careful to check all claims.

The allotments were to be held in trust for twenty-five years, then were to be given to the owner as fee-simple titles. The period of trust could be extended if the government found it necessary. The government agreed to pay the Indians $2,000,000 in installments of $500,000 each. The money was to draw 5 per cent interest in the United States Treasury. Congress had to approve the pact. The Indians were in much disagreement over this and claimed that they were misled. General Hugh L. Scott and the cattlemen who leased Indian land helped the Indians to oppose it. A delegation led by Ápiatan went to Washington in the spring of 1894 to protest. But eventually, on June 6, 1900, Congress approved the Jerome Agreement.

As the Indians selected their land, it was recorded and the title was issued as a trust patent; 2,759 tribal members got 443,338 acres of land. The unalloted land was then sold by lottery to the public. It was an orderly procedure, not a "run."

Almost overnight, the reservation was gone, and the Indians formed an island in a sea of whites. People were building everywhere. The last of pasture or reserve lands, 480,000 acres, were opened on September 19, 1906, and sold under sealed bids sent to the Secretary of the Interior.

The Indians became individual landowners, taking them farther along the path of acculturation. But owning land did not make "white men" out of the Indians. Many leased their lands to whites for small sums and barely lived on the returns. Some were exceedingly poor.

In time, there were indications of progress. But as they learned, their numbers lessened. It was thought that they were a vanishing race. Then, after the 1920's, the Indian showed a remarkable increase. In 1940 there were 450,000 Indians in the United States. About one-third of them live among the general population, but two-thirds still live on reserved land. They are the least known of our minority groups. In 1924 all Indians were declared to be citizens of the United States. Many were citizens before 1924. They are not a solid or uniform group. In culture, language, and history they were and are diverse, hence quite distinct from other minority groups. Poverty and discrimination are still problems.

The Indian has had some able help from interested organizations, especially the American Association on Indian Affairs and the Indian Rights Association. Suggestions for help have stressed the importance of a broad educational program, larger appropriations and better schools, better governmental employees and agents, better food, and better health clinics.

In 1929, during President Herbert Hoover's administration, the Office of Indian Affairs was under the head of men interested in Indian welfare. Charles J. Rhoads was commissioner and Henry Scattergood, assistant commissioner. In addition, a Director of Education, Dr. W. Carson Ryan, was appointed. A number of reforms were made.

In 1933, President Franklin D. Roosevelt appointed John Collier as commissioner of Indian affairs. Collier had worked long and sympathetically for Indian rights and was the executive secretary of the American Indian Defense Association. Secretary of the Interior Harold Ickes, in whose department the Office of Indian Affairs was located, was especially sympathetic. Many reforms were brought about.

In 1934, Congress passed the Indian Reorganization Act which made possible many constructive changes in Indian policies. Indians could borrow money for business purposes, and organize for self-government, and incorporate if they voted to do so. Tribes had to vote in secret ballot on the law in order to accept it. For the first time, they could make up their own minds—a stimulating and unusual experience. But many did not accept it. The Oklahoma Indians were not included in this act, but later legislation gave them similar rights. Thus "home rule" became a part of Indian life. They could keep their own ethnic and social traditions and language and still learn to become normal Americans.

New schools stress family and community life. Indians are not forced to take medical treatment, but they are beginning to see the advantages of it. Actually, the children teach their elders in these matters. Even if they fear the hospitals and turn to the old medicine men, they want the better things for their children. Clinics are particularly helpful.

Freedom in regard to "religion, conscience and culture" was established in 1934. Redeveloping old arts and crafts has been stimulating and profitable. Pottery has become a best seller for many Indians, and other crafts help to woo the "tourist dollar"— weaving, basketry, jewelry, production of wool yarn and other salable things.

Interest in better farming and cattle-raising are being developed, and loans that have started co-operative enterprises and helped individuals have been important. A special act for Oklahoma Indians set aside two million dollars for loans. A promising beginning is underway and may form a lasting pattern for the future. Indians' lands are of greater worth and value with care and conservation.

275

The Relocation Act was designed to help the Indians move out of enclaves and into the major stream of American life. It has not been a great success, but it does offer opportunity. It could be important if an Indian family can learn to live alone or with a few neighbors of their own kind as friends. Usually the Indian gets lonely for his old home and returns to his own folks.

Indians are still subject to many regulations that differ from state to state. The United States Supreme Court ruled that Indians can be both citizens and wards of the government, and that being wards of the government and possessing citizenship does not affect the right of the Indian to tribal or other property. Those whose property is held in trust by the government and those still having treaties are government wards, even though they pay all taxes save those on reservation lands.

Indian management is improving, and democratic processes are being learned. Initiative and responsibility are desired objectives. Indian leadership is needed badly. The help and co-operation of the American public is also needed. Both whites and Indians must give up discrimination for any real and lasting progress.

The Kiowa-Comanche-Apache Intertribal Business Committee has twelve members who make recommendations to the Indian office. This committee, which has five Kiowa members, is influential in matters relating to the tribes. Its constitution provides for monthly meetings at Anadarko, and its members are elected every four years. Prominent Kiowas who have served on this committee are Robert Goombi, Louis Toyebo, Guy Queotone, Gus Bosin, Frank Kauahquo, Jasper Saunkeah, and Scott Tonemah.

About one-half of the Kiowas are full-blooded members of the tribe. Before 1900 about one-fourth of the tribe was of mixed blood, descendants of captives taken by the Kiowas—Mexicans, Mexican Indians, other captive Indians, and some Texas whites. Today the mixed-blood Kiowas include Indians of other tribes found in Oklahoma. In 1951, Muriel Wright gave the numbers of the Kiowas in Oklahoma as 2,800, and said that there were approximately 400 Kiowa-Apaches.[3]

[3] *A Guide to the Indian Tribes of Oklahoma*, 169, 178. Some of the Kiowas state

In 1907, Oklahoma became a state. Among its growing population the Indians settled into a "minority problem." There are Kiowa and other Indian claims against the government today for violation of the terms of the Medicine Lodge Treaty of 1867. Under the provisions of that treaty the reservations were guaranteed to them until 1898. The Kiowas are also suing for the return of the Black Hills.

The Kiowas are generally a rural people. One large settlement is near Carnegie in Caddo County, Oklahoma. Their homes are modern and well cared for. Many have gained wealth from the discovery of oil. Most of the Kiowas are Christians. In church membership, the Methodists and Baptists predominate. The Kiowas take part in the American Indian Exposition held at Anadarko. Some of the Kiowas have served as directors of the exposition and have helped present various tribal dances and historical pageants.

Many of the Kiowa-Apaches live in the vicinity of Fort Cobb in Caddo County. Some of the Arizona Apaches still live in Oklahoma after having been brought to Fort Sill from Florida. Those who did not want to go to the Mescalero Reservation in New Mexico were given land at Apache and near Fort Sill. (These Indians are not to be confused with the Kiowa-Apaches.)

The Kiowa-Apaches have two members on the Kiowa-Comanche-Apache Intertribal Business Committee. Among those who have served on the committee are Tennyson Berry and Alfred Chalpeah. Tennyson Berry has helped to direct the historical pageant at the annual American Indian Exposition at Anadarko.

Of interest in reviving Indian art are several well-known Kiowa artists. These include Stephen Mopope, Monroe Tsatoke, James Auchiah, Jack Hokeah, and Spencer Asah. Other artists who have received recognition are Lois Smokey, Woody Big Bear, Blackbear Bosin, and Al Momoday.

The Kiowas are a resigned people uncertain of the future—not necessarily bitter—rather than a forceful and dynamic minority.

that the Kiowa-Apaches had a larger admixture of Mexican blood than did the Kiowas.

They are apathetic, fearing the new, unused to using political freedom and organization, inured to futility, when they could be using the voting franchise as a lever for lifting the weight of their problems. The Kiowas have served admirably in America's wars and need to serve in its peace. They need a forceful organization, something comparable to the tribal unity of the Navahos—if not by tribal control at least by political entity. Many of them are averse to the sale of individual land, and rightly so. The United States government, during the Eisenhower administration, sought to make them citizens in their own right. The Kiowas are intelligent and deserve a future. They are still a proud people, perhaps too sensitive and too clannish for their own good, but they are ambitious. They need to master the professions and the techniques of modern life to be able to experience the satisfactions that come in a highly competitive society. They need to be encouraged to use their citizenship to advantage and to discard the discrimination that has robbed them of self-respect.

The Indian has been a much greater problem than the Negro or other minorities. The Indian had a free and dynamic way of life and lost it, and the losing was bitter. The Negro never had that, and yet has made a remarkable advance by constant, nay militant, erosion of civil rights barriers. There are many ways to help the Indian to a better and more fruitful life. Education is the real need, the talisman that will open the door to opportunity, the *manito*, the "medicine" for the future.

❖ ARCHAEOLOGY
OF THE PLAINS

*N*AMED from the Folsom points found at Folsom, New Mexico, the Folsom hunters were the first people, archaeologically speaking, of the Plains. Possible descendants of the Folsom folk were the people of the Old Signal Butte culture of the Archaic period. The Archaic people (before 500 A.D.), including those of the Plains, used the spear and spear thrower, had no pottery, and lived a hunting, fishing, and gathering life with no knowledge of horticulture. The population was small and settlements were few. The Folsom point was a spear point with a shallow groove in the middle.

The Old Signal Butte culture was found in western Nebraska. Villages were marked by many small pot-shaped storage pits or caches, some lined with rock slabs, and shallow fire pits. No dwellings were found, which indicates seasonal occupancy.

In the Intermediate period (around 500 to 1300 A.D.) Indians from the east penetrated the Plains, moving along and up the river valleys. They had pottery and agriculture, and some built semisubterranean houses. A Hopewell-like group of Indians existed sometime during this period, with affiliations eastward. The Sterns Creek culture of eastern Nebraska, the Mira Creek culture of central and west-central Nebraska, and the Kansas Hopewell culture of northeastern Kansas existed in this period.

The late Prehistoric period (around 1300 to 1600 A.D.) was characterized by an intensive settlement of sedentary horticultural groups of Indians in fairly large villages. They farmed, used pottery, and hunted with the bow and arrow. The Upper Republican culture of Nebraska and Kansas falls within this period.

Villages were composed of earthen lodges, rectangular or circular and partly underground. The small gardens lay along the river bottoms in rich silt and leaf mold and near moisture. The subsistence of the people was mainly corn, squash, and beans (the ubiquitous triad of planting people in America), supplemented by meat, fish, and fruits of all kinds—seeds, berries, and nuts. The dog was the only domesticated animal and probably accompanied the first Mongoloid tourist from Asia across the Bering Strait and into the Americas.

Large rounded pots were used in cooking. Some vessels had smooth surfaces. Some had incised and decorated rims. Fragments of coiled basketry have been found. Wooden digging sticks and bison shoulder-blade hoes were used. Wooden tools were probably used for grinding corn. The main hunting weapon was the wooden bow and flint arrow. Fishhooks and pipes of stone or fired clay are also found. Bone pendants, bone gorgets, beads, and shells were used as ornaments. Bracelets were made from antlers. One bracelet showed the eye-in-hand design associated with the southern death cult. Copper-covered wooden ear ornaments were found; they may have been obtained from the middle Mississippi cultures, mostly Southeastern, which were contemporary. Obsidian was obtained from Yellowstone Park, and conch shells from the Gulf of Mexico indicated much trading. On the whole, close affiliations with the Southeast culture area (probably Caddoan) are shown.

The Nebraska culture of the same period in eastern Nebraska and northeastern Kansas had villages of partly underground houses along the river. They were rectangular pits covered by roofs of poles and earth supported by large central posts. Covered passageways or ladders through the roof openings allowed entrance. Some houses were as large as forty feet long and thirty feet wide.

Pots, bowls, and bottles were found in profusion, many of them in a reddish brown color. Some were smooth or polished, and some were decorated with incised geometric designs. Some of the rims were of scalloped piecrust character. Some had modeled decorative additions to handles or lugs. Again one sees affiliations with the middle Mississippi area and the Southeast (probably Caddoan) cultures.

The bow and arrow was the most important hunting weapon. Numerous shell and bone ornaments were found. Some shell pendants were decorated with incisions suggesting birds and fish. Well sculptured effigy heads made of pottery or stone are similar to types found in the middle Mississippi area. Skeletal remains were probably kept in special temple houses and eventually buried in mounds or hillocks, strongly suggestive of the Southeast.

The Early Historic period (1600 to 1800 A.D.) is shown by the Dismal River culture of western Nebraska. Villages were located on terraces in the river valleys. Some had circular earth-covered lodges. The tipi may have been used. Shallow refuse pits with round bottoms and bell-shaped roasting pits were found. The villagers possessed corn, squash, and gourds but were primarily hunters of bison, elk, deer, antelope, beaver, land turtles, and other animals. They sometimes ate dogs. Their pottery was buff to black in color. Most of the vessels were small or medium-sized jars with conoid bottoms.

The main hunting weapon was the bow and arrow. Pipes of clay and of stone were found. Ornaments were few. The Dismal River culture was contemporaneous in part with the Upper Republican and Nebraska cultures. It shows some white trade materials and may have descended from the Sterns Creek culture.

The Early Historic period lasted about two hundred years— longer in the Plains than in most other areas because settlement by the white men lagged as the frontier line met the Plains. The horse preceded the white man onto the Plains, coming up from the Spanish settlements of the south. The horse caused the Indians to become nomadic buffalo hunters, although some of the Indians stuck to their river valleys and continued to care for their cornfields; others—the atypical Plains group—both farmed and hunted with the horse.

Displaced Indians from the east crowded onto the Plains in the Historic period and became a part of the "horse culture." Around 1700 to 1800 A.D. the typical Plains culture pattern emerged, and many old cultural associations were lost or transformed. The old hunting tradition was never completely lost even by the horticulturists. Some continued to live much as they had in the Late Prehistoric period (these were the edge-of-the-Plains or river valleys or "Marginal Plains" people).

The nomadic hunters could sweep the Plains from Canada to the Gulf of Mexico and Old Mexico on swift horses better than any land vehicle could do. Their bows and arrows were superior to the early muzzle-loading gun of the white man and were not surpassed until the repeating gun appeared. The "horse Indian culture" was a radically different life from that of sedentary plant cultivation. The hunters became aggressive, warlike, and much more efficient killers of both beast and man. This led to competition, conflict, and war; there arose, in fact, an antisocial setup against those not counted in their own confederacies. This emphasis on war, predation, and ferocity extended in time to the white man, when he ceased to be a trader and became a settler, and bore within the Historic Plains culture the seeds of its own decay, for in part it was retrogressive. The "horse Indian culture" food supply—primarily the vast herds of bison—was as efficient and as nourishing as farming, especially considering the limitations of horticulture on the Plains—subject to periods of drought and abandonment.

The Plains farmers—old and modern—suffered from the weather, especially drought and dust storms, throughout the history of the Plains; this undoubtedly caused movement out of some devastated and denuded areas. The Plains water supply seems always to have run in five-year cycles from drought to drought. Then, as now, when rainfall increased, the land became again suitable for farming. This cycle of drought is substantiated by tree-ring studies. At present the water table of the Great Plains shows constant and progressive lowering.[1]

Where do the Kiowas fit into the archaeologic picture? Not until the Historic period are they known. They probably moved out from the mountains of Montana and the Yellowstone area along with their Athapascan friends, the Kiowa-Apaches, about 1700. Their affiliation with the Sarsis (also Athapascan like the Kiowa-Apaches) may have been of ancient character. There was a western prong of Athapascans that pushed into the Columbia River region and occupied an area from Oregon to northern California— the Kwalhioqua-Hoopans.[2] From the mountains the Kiowas moved east to the Plains. For some time they occupied the Black Hills and then moved south.

Just when the Kiowas joined with the Kiowa-Apaches is not known. The Athapascan-speaking peoples moved south from central Canada, probably in many waves—some to the mountains and some to the Pacific Northwest, some to the Plains, and some, like the Navahos (late-comers to the south), moving down into the Great Basin area and between the mountains. The Kiowa-Apaches have historically always been attached to the Kiowas.

Mooney derives the Kiowas from the Yellowstone Park area of Montana and Wyoming.[3] Kroeber suggests that they may have moved north into the mountains from the south before the historic period, largely on linguistic evidence; he associates the Kiowa-

[1] See Paul S. Martin, George I. Quimby, and Donald Collier, *Indians before Columbus*, 319–36, for a detailed account of the archaeology of the Plains. See also Wedel, *An Introduction to Kansas Archeology; Archeological Remains in Central Kansas*; and "Cultural Sequence in the Central Great Plains," *loc. cit.*

See William Duncan Strong, "From History to Prehistory in the Northern Great Plains," *Essays in Historical Anthropology of North America*, Smithsonian Miscellaneous Collections, Vol. C (1940); and H. M. Wormington, *Ancient Man in North America*, Denver Museum of Natural History, *Popular Series No. 4.*

[2] John P. Harrington, "Southern Peripheral Athapaskawan Origins," *Essays in Historical Anthropology of North America*, Smithsonian Miscellaneous Collections, Vol. C (1940), 508–32.

[3] "Calendar History," 245–53.

Apaches also with a southern origin, but adds that the early history of the Kiowas is impossible to trace in detail.[4]

Harrington, from a study of Tanoan and Kiowa languages, derives the Kiowas from the south.[5] This is contradicted by Whorf and Trager[6] on linguistic grounds and by Vestal and Schultes[7] on ethnobotanical evidence. Vestal and Schultes state that if there were a close language relationship, it could mean a northern Tanoan origin (splitting off from the Kiowas and moving south), as well as a southern origin (splitting off from the Tanoans and moving north) for the Kiowas.

The linguistic evidence of Athapascan origins in the Canadian region of all Apache peoples would seem to place the Kiowa-Apaches there perhaps until just before historic time. They have no southern affiliations with any other Apaches. The Sarsis and other Athapascan tribes moved toward the west from central Canada, some going southward far down into Oregon and California. The Sarsis intermarried with the Kiowas in the Historic period. They continued to live in Canada. Somewhere in the Rocky Mountains the Kiowa-Apaches took up with the Kiowas.

The Tanoans of New Mexico, if closely related linguistically to the Kiowas, may have had a northern origin and may have moved south long before the Kiowas did. Perhaps they were the dissident members of the tribe who moved away after a hunting quarrel, as told in the legends of the Kiowas. In the same way, the Navaho Apaches were late-comers to the south, being preceded by many nations of Apaches into the Southwest, on the edges of the Plains (the Prairie Apaches or Padoucas, so-called, up to 1750), and into Texas and northern Mexico. Undoubtedly, the Lipan Apaches and the Jumano Apaches in Texas were aboriginal, for they were de-

[4] A. L. Kroeber, *Cultural and Natural Areas of Native North America*, University of California *Publications in American Archeology and Ethnology*, Vol. XXXVIII (1939), 33, 48, 79–80, 86. See also Wedel, *An Introduction to Kansas Archeology*, 68–69, 78–79; and "Culture Sequence in the Central Great Plains," *loc. cit.*

[5] Harrington, "Athapaskawan Origins," *loc. cit.*, 510.

[6] Whorf and Trager, "The Relationship of Uto-Aztecan And Tanoan," *loc. cit.*, 609–10.

[7] Vestal and Schultes, *The Economic Botany of the Kiowa Indians*, 83–84.

scribed in early Spanish writings. Harrington also mentions that linguistically there is a wide gap between the Lipans and the Canadian Athapascans. The part hunting, part corn-raising culture of the old Apaches may have come from associations with the south and southeast, perhaps with the Wichita and Caddo tribes, and possibly with the Tonkawas who also had some horticulture, all of whom were aboriginal in the area of present Texas and Oklahoma.

The Plains culture was definitely historical, and its members were of diverse origins. There were so many different languages that the sign language evolved for communication. All of the tribes of the Plains culture area were entirely peripheral before the acquisition of the horse. The horse is the basis of the Plains culture, and without the horse it would never have existed. In the sixteenth century the people were centered in the prairies and not on the Plains. The prairie tribes show affiliations with the Northeast and with the Southeast. Other origins included tribes from Canada and the Rocky Mountains. Presumably, until there is clearer evidence, the Kiowas and Kiowa-Apaches came to the Plains from the northern Rocky Mountains.

❖ BIBLIOGRAPHY

PRIMARY SOURCES

Abert, Lieutenant J. W. *Guadal P'a, the Journal of Lieutenant J. W. Abert, from Bent's Fort to St. Louis in 1845.* Ed. by H. Bailey Carroll. Canyon, Texas. 1941.

Babb, T. A. ("Dot"). *In the Bosom of the Comanches.* Dallas, 1912.

Battey, Thomas C. *The Life and Adventures of a Quaker among the Indians.* Boston, 1876.

Bell, John R. *The Journal of Captain John R. Bell, Official Journalist for the Stephen H. Long Expedition to the Rocky Mountains, 1820.* [Vol. VI of Harlin M. Fuller and LeRoy R. Hafen (eds.), *The Far West and the Rockies Historical Series, 1820–1875.*] Glendale, 1957.

Bent, George. "Forty Years with the Cheyennes." Ed. by George Hyde. *The Frontier, a Magazine of the West,* Vol. IV, Nos. 4–9 (October, 1905–March, 1906).

Bolton, Herbert Eugene. *Athanase De Mézières and the Louisiana-Texas Frontier, 1768–1780.* 2 vols. Cleveland, 1914.

Carson, Colonel Christopher. "Nov. 25, 1864. Engagement with Indians at Adobe Fort." In U. S. War Dept., *The War of the Rebellion* (q.v.), Ser. 1, Vol. XLI, Serial No. 83. Washington, 1902.

Carter, Captain Robert Goldthwaite. *Massacre of Salt Creek Prairie and the Cow-Boy's Verdict.* Washington, 1919.

———. *The Old Sergeant's Story*. New York, 1926.

———. *On the Border with Mackenzie*. Washington, 1935.

———. *Tragedies of Cañon Blanco*. Washington, 1919.

Catlin, George. *North American Indians*. 2 vols. Edinburgh, 1926.

Chivington, Colonel John, Maj. Scott J. Anthony, *et al*. "Nov. 29, 1864. Engagement with Indians on Sand Creek, Colo. Ter.," *The War of the Rebellion (q.v.)*. Ser. 1, Vol. XLI, Serial No. 83. Washington, 1902.

Chronicles of Oklahoma. Editorial and Letters from "Some Corrections of 'Life on the Plains,' " by General W. B. Hazen (St. Paul, 1874), in *Chronicles of Oklahoma*, Vol. III, No. 4 (1925).

Clark, Captain William P. *The Indian Sign Language*. Philadelphia, 1885.

Cody, Colonel W. F. *An Autobiography of Buffalo Bill*. New York, 1920.

Collot, Victor. *A Journey in North America*. 2 vols. Firenze, 1924.

Cook, John R. *The Border and the Buffalo*. Edited by Milo Milton Quaife. Chicago, 1938.

Custer, General George A. *My Life on the Plains*. Edited by Milo Milton Quaife. Chicago, 1952.

De Smet, Rev. Pierre-Jean, S. J. *Life, Letters and Travels of Father Pierre-Jean De Smet, S. J. 1801–1873*. Ed. by H. M. Chittenden and A. T. Richardson. 4 vols. New York, 1905.

Dixon, Olive K. *Life of "Billy" Dixon*. Dallas, 1927.

Dodge, Colonel Henry. "Journal of a March of a Detachment of Dragoons, under the Command of Colonel Dodge, during the Summer of 1835." United States, 24 Cong., 1 sess., *House Doc. No. 181*. War Department (U.S. 289). Washington, 1836.

———. Letters to the Secretary of War, accompanied by Lieutenant T. B. Wheeloch's official report, "Journal of Colonel Dodge's Expedition from Fort Gibson to the Pawnee Pict Village [1834]." United States, *American State Papers*, Military Affairs *(q.v.)*, V (1934).

———. "Report on the Expedition under Colonel Henry Dodge to the Rocky Mountains in 1835." United States, 24 Cong., 1 sess., *Sen. Doc. No. 654* (1836). Also in United States, *American State Papers*, Military Affairs *(q.v.)*, VI (1935).

Dodge, Colonel Richard Irving. *Our Wild Indians*. Hartford, 1882.

Evans, Hugh. ". . . Journal of Colonel Henry Dodge's Expedition to the Rocky Mountains," ed. by Fred S. Perrine, *The Mississippi Valley Historical Review*, Vol. XIV (1927).

────. "The Journal of Hugh Evans Covering the First and Second Campaigns of the United States Dragoon Regiment in 1834 and 1835," ed. by Fred S. Perrine and Grant Foreman, *Chronicles of Oklahoma,* Vol. III, No. 3 (1925).

Fowler, Jacob. *The Journal of Jacob Fowler.* Ed. by Elliott Coues. New York, 1898.

Gainesville *Register,* August 22, 1932. "Woman Believed Dead 65 Years Returns to Scene of Childhood near Graham." Newspaper clipping about Millie Durgan in "Indian Captives Scrapbook." MS. Archives, University of Texas Library.

Gass, Patrick. *A Journal of the Voyages and Travels of a Corps of Discovery under the Command of Capt. Lewis and Capt. Clark.* Pittsburgh, 1807.

Gregg, Josiah. *Commerce of the Prairies, 1831–1839.* [Vols. XIX and XX in Thwaites, *Early Western Travels (q.v.).*] Cleveland, 1905.

────. *Diary and Letters of Josiah Gregg.* Ed. by Maurice Garland Fulton. 2 vols. Norman, 1941, 1944.

Hildreth, James. *Dragoon Campaigns to the Rocky Mountains.* New York, 1836.

"Indian Treaties and Councils Affecting Kansas," The Kansas State Historical Society, *Collections,* Vol. XVI (1923–25).

Irving, Washington. *A Tour on the Prairies.* [Vol. VII of The Works of Washington Irving.] New York, n.d.

James, Edwin (ed.). *Account of an Expedition from Pittsburgh to the Rocky Mountains . . . under the Command of Maj. S. H. Long.* 3 vols. London, 1823.

Kappler, Charles J. (ed.). *Indian Affairs: Laws and Treaties.* 3 vols. Washington, 1903, 1913.

Keim, DeB. Randolph. *Sheridan's Troopers on the Borders.* Philadelphia, 1885.

Kendall, George Wilkins. *Narrative of the Texan Santa Fe Expedition.* 2 vols. Facsimile of original edition, 1844. Austin, 1935.

Kneale, Albert H. *Indian Agent.* Caldwell, Idaho, 1950.

Larpenteur, Charles. *Forty Years a Fur Trader on the Upper Missouri.* Ed. by Elliott Coues. 2 vols. New York, 1898.

Le Page du Pratz, Antoine M. *The History of Louisiana.* 2 vols. London, 1763.

Lewis, Meriwether, and William Clark. *History of the Expedition under the Command of Lewis and Clark.* Ed. by Elliott Coues. 4 vols. New York, 1893.

———. *Travels in the Interior Parts of America.* Reprinted from Thomas Jefferson, *Message from the President of the United States, Communicating Discoveries Made in Exploring the Missouri, Red River and Washita, by Captains Lewis and Clark, Doctor Sibley and Mr. [William] Dunbar . . . 1805.* [Vol. VI in *A Collection of Modern and Contemporary Voyages and Travels.*] London, 1807.

Lowe, Percival G. *Five Years a Dragoon, '49 to '54, and other Adventures on the Great Plains.* Kansas City, Missouri, 1906.

Mallery, Garrick. *Picture-Writing of the American Indians.* Bureau of American Ethnology, *Tenth Annual Report.* Washington, 1893.

Manypenny, George W. *Our Indian Wards.* Cincinnati, 1880.

Marcy, Randolph B. *Border Reminiscenses.* New York, 1872.

———. *Thirty Years of Army Life on the Border.* New York, 1866.

Margry, Pierre. *Découvertes et établissements des Français dans l'Ouest et dans le sud de l'Amérique Septentrionale (1614–1754). Mémoires et documents originaux.* 6 vols. Paris, 1888.

Marriott, Alice. *Greener Fields.* New York, 1953.

———. *The Ten Grandmothers.* Norman, 1945.

Matthews, Sallie Reynolds. *Interwoven.* El Paso, 1958.

Methvin, Rev. J. J. *Andele, or the Mexican Kiowa Captive.* Anadarko, Oklahoma, 1927.

Miles, General Nelson A. *Personal Recollections and Observations.* New York, 1896.

Nye, Wilbur Sturtevant. *Bad Medicine and Good: Tales of the Kiowas.* Norman, 1962.

———. *Carbine and Lance: the Story of Old Fort Sill.* Norman, 1942.

Parker, W. B. *Notes Taken during the Expedition Commanded by Capt. R. B. Marcy, U. S. A., through Unexplored Texas, in the Summer and Fall of 1854.* Philadelphia, 1856.

Parsons, Elsie Clews. *Kiowa Tales.* New York, 1929.

Perrin du Lac, M. [François Marie]. *Travels through the Two Louisianas, and among the Savage Nations of the Missouri.* [Vol. VI of *A Collection of Modern and Contemporary Voyages and Travels.*] London, 1807.

———. *Voyage dans les deux Louisianes et chez les nations sauvages du Missouri . . . en 1801, 1802 et 1803.* Lyon, 1805.

Pettis, George H. *Personal Narratives of the Battle of the Rebellion,* No. 5. Providence, 1878.

Pike, James, *Scout and Ranger.* Reprinted from edition of 1865. Princeton, 1932.

Pike, Zebulon Montgomery. *The Expeditions of Zebulon Montgomery Pike.* Ed. by Elliott Coues. 3 vols. Reprinted from edition of 1810. New York, 1895.

Price, G. F. *Across the Continent with the Fifth Cavalry.* New York, 1883.

Remington, Frederic. *Frederic Remington's Own West.* Ed. by Harold McCracken. New York, 1960.

————. "Horses of the Plains," *The Century Magazine,* Vol. XXXVII, No. 3 (1889).

Seger, John H. *Early Days among the Cheyenne and Arapahoe Indians.* Ed. by Stanley Vestal. Norman, 1934.

Shawanoe Baptist Mission House. *The Annual Register of Indian Affairs within the Indian (or Western) Territory, No. 3.* Indian Territory, 1837.

Sheridan, General P. H. *Personal Memoirs.* 2 vols. New York, 1888.

————. *Record of Engagements with Hostile Indians within the Military Division of the Missouri from 1868 to 1882.* Chicago, 1882.

Sherman, General William T. *Memoirs of General William T. Sherman.* 2 vols. New York, 1875.

————. *The Sherman Letters.* Ed. by Rachel Sherman Thorndike. New York, 1894.

Sibley, John. "Historical Sketches of the Several Indian Tribes in Louisiana, south of the Arkansas river, and between the Mississippi and river Grande [1805]," in United States, *American State Papers,* Indian Affairs, IV (1832).

Strong, Captain Henry M. *My Frontier Days and Indian Fights on the Plains of Texas.* Waco, 1926.

Stuart, Lieutenant J. E. B. "The Kiowa and Comanche Campaign of 1860 as Recorded in the Personal Diary of Lt. J. E. B. Stuart." Ed. by W. Stitt Robinson. *The Kansas Historical Quarterly,* Vol. XXIII (1957).

Tabeau, Pierre-Antoine. *Tabeau's Narrative of Loisel's Expedition to the Upper Missouri.* Ed. by Annie Heloise Abel; trans. by Rose Abel Wright. Norman, 1939.

Tatum, Lawrie. *Our Red Brothers and the Peace Policy of President Ulysses S. Grant*. Philadelphia, 1899.

Taylor, Alfred A. "Medicine Lodge Peace Council," *Chronicles of Oklahoma*, Vol. II, No. 2 (1924).

Texas Indian Papers. MSS. Archives and State Library, Austin, Texas. See also Winfrey, Dorman.

Thoburn, Joseph B. "Horace P. Jones, Scout and Interpreter," *Chronicles of Oklahoma*, Vol. II, No. 4 (1924).

Thomas, Alfred Barnaby. "An Eighteenth Century Comanche Document," *American Anthropologist*, Vol. XXXI, No. 2 (1929).

Thomas, Alfred Barnaby (trans. and ed.). *Teodoro de Croix and the Northern Frontier of New Spain, 1776–1783*. Norman, 1941.

Tibbles, Thomas Henry. *Buckskin and Blanket Days*. New York, 1957.

Tixier, Victor. *Tixier's Travels on the Osage Prairies*. Ed. by John Francis McDermott, trans. by Albert J. Salvan. Norman, 1940.

Thwaites, Reuben Gold (ed.). *Early Western Travels, 1748–1846*. 32 vols. Cleveland, 1904–1907.

Trudeau, Jean Baptiste. "Journal of Jean Baptiste Trudeau among the Arikara Indians in 1795," trans. by Mrs. H. T. Beauregard, Missouri Historical Society *Collections*, Vol. IV (1912–13).

———. "Trudeau's Description of the Upper Missouri," ed. by Annie Heloise Abel. *The Mississippi Valley Historical Review*, Vol. VIII, Nos. 1 and 2 (1921).

United States. *American State Papers*. Documents Legislative and Executive of the Congress of the United States.

———, ———. Military Affairs, Vol. V (1934); Vol. V, No. 613 (1935) [Report of the Secretary of War, November 30, 1835]; Vol. VI (1935) ["Report on the Expedition under Colonel Henry Dodge to the Rocky Mountains in 1835"].

———, Bureau of Indian Affairs. Annual reports of the Commissioner of Indian Affairs. Reports to the Secretary of War; reports to the Secretary of the Interior. In United States Congress, Senate, and House of Representatives documents, beginning in 1839. Earlier reports of Indian agents in reports of the Secretary of War.

——— Congress, House of Representatives. 24 Cong., 1 sess., *House Exec. Doc. No. 2*, Vol. II, No. 2 (1835). [Annual Report of the Secretary of War, November 30, 1835.]

────, ────. 35 Cong., 2 sess. *House Exec. Doc. No. 2*, Vol. II, Pt. 2 (1858–59). [Report of the Secretary of War.]

────, ────. 38 Cong., 2 sess., *House Exec. Doc. No. 1*, Vol. V (1864–65. [Report of the Secretary of the Interior, including Annual Report of the Commissioner of Indian Affairs.]

────, Senate. 35 Cong., 2 sess. *Sen. Doc. No. 1*, Vol. II, Pt. 2 (1858–59). ["Earl Van Dorn reporting fight against Comanches."]

────, ────. 36 Cong., 1 sess. *Sen. Exec. Doc. No. 2.* Vol. I, Pt. 1 (1859–60. [Report of the Secretary of the Interior.]

────, ────. 36 Cong., 2 sess. *Sen. Exec. Doc. No. 1*, Vol. II, Pt. 2 (1860–61). [Report of the Secretary of the Interior.]

────, ────. 37 Cong., 2 sess. *Sen. Exec. Doc. No. 1*, Vol. I, Pt. 1 (1861–62). [Report of the Secretary of the Interior.]

────, Office of Indian Affairs. Records in National Archives Building, Washington, D.C. MSS. Files of Indian Territory Miscellaneous, Central Superintendency, Upper Arkansas Superintendency, Treaties, Talks, and Councils, Wichita Agency, and others.

────, ────. Letters sent and letters received, 1838–61. MSS. Photostats in Archives, University of Texas Library. Originals in National Archives Building, Washington, D.C.

────, War Department. Records in National Archives Building, Washington, D.C.

────, ────. *The War of the Rebellion. A Compilation of the Official Records of the Union and Confederate Armies.* 130 vols. Washington, 1880–1901.

Vestal, Stanley. *New Sources of Indian History, 1850–1891.* Norman, 1934.

White, E. E. *Service on the Indian Reservations, Being the Experiences of a Special Indian Agent.* Little Rock, 1893.

Williams, J. E. (Jim). *Fifty-eight Years in the Panhandle of Texas.* Austin, 1944.

Williams, R. H. *With the Border Ruffians, Memories of the Far West, 1852–1868.* New York, 1907.

Winfrey, Dorman (ed.). *Texas Indian Papers.* 4 vols. [Vol. IV, James Day and Dorman Winfrey (eds.).] Austin, 1959–61.

Winship, George Parker, *The Coronado Expedition, 1540–1542.* Bureau of American Ethnology, *Fourteenth Annual Report*, Pt. 1. Washington, 1896.

SECONDARY SOURCES

Baker, D. W. C. (ed.). *A Texas Scrap Book.* [Contains article on "Texas Indians" from *Texas Almanac, 1869.*] Austin, 1935.

Bancroft, Hubert Howe. *History of the North Mexican States and Texas.* 2 vols. San Francisco, 1886.

Benedict, Ruth Fulton. *The Concept of the Guardian Spirit in North America.* American Anthropological Association, *Memoir 29.* Menasha, Wisconsin, 1924.

————. "Configurations of Culture in North America," *American Anthropologist,* Vol. XXXIV (1932).

————. *Patterns of Culture.* New York, 1934.

Biggers, Don H. *Shackelford County Sketches.* Albany, Texas, 1908.

Billon, Frederic L. *Annals of St. Louis in Its Early Days under the French and Spanish Dominations.* St. Louis, 1886.

Brininstool, E. A. *Fighting Indian Warriors, True Tales of the Wild Frontiers.* Harrisburg, 1953.

Brown, John Henry. *The Indian Wars and Pioneers of Texas.* Austin, n.d.

Chittenden, Hiram Martin. *American Fur Trade of the Far West.* 3 vols. New York, 1902.

Collier, John. *The Indians of the Americas.* New York, 1947.

Corwin, Hugh D. *Comanche and Kiowa Captives in Oklahoma and Texas.* Guthrie, 1959.

Crouch, Carrie J. *Young County History and Biography.* Dallas, 1937.

Cullum, George W. *Biographical Register of the Officers and Graduates of the U. S. Military Academy.* 2 vols. New York, 1868.

Daniels, Walter M. (comp.). *American Indians.* [*The Reference Shelf,* Vol. XXIX, No. 4.] New York, 1957.

Davis, Britton. *The Truth about Geronimo.* New Haven, 1929.

Debo, Angie. *And Still the Waters Run.* Princeton, 1940.

Devereux, George. *Reality and Dream, Psychotherapy of a Plains Indian.* New York, 1951.

Dictionary of American Biography. Ed. by Allen Johnson. New York, 1928–58.

Douglas, Frederic H., and Rene D'Harnoncourt. *Indian Art of the United States.* New York, 1941.

Driver, Harold E. *Indians of North America.* Chicago, 1961.

Eggan, Fred (ed.). *Social Anthropology of North American Tribes.* Chicago, 1937. Revised edition, 1955.

Embry, Carlos B. *America's Concentration Camps, the Facts about Our Indian Reservations Today.* New York, 1956.

Emmitt, Robert. *The Last War Trail: The Utes and the Settlement of Colorado.* Norman, 1954.

Ewers, John C. *The Blackfeet: Raiders on the Northwestern Plains.* Norman, 1958.

———. *The Horse in Blackfoot Indian Culture.* Bureau of American Ethnology, *Bulletin 159.* Washington, 1955.

———. *Plains Indian Painting.* Palo Alto, California, 1939.

Forbes, Jack D. *Apache, Navaho, and Spaniard.* Norman, 1960.

Foreman, Grant (ed.). *Adventure on Red River: Report on the Exploration of the Headwaters of the Red River by Captain Randolph B. Marcy and Captain G. B. McClellan.* Norman, 1937.

———. *Marcy and the Gold Seekers: The Journal of Captain R. B. Marcy.* Norman, 1939.

Gates, R. Ruggles. "Blood Groupings and Racial Classification," *American Journal of Physical Anthropology,* Vol. XXIV, No. 1 (1938).

Gilmore, Melvin Randolph. *Prairie Smoke.* New York, 1927.

———. "Uses of Plants by the Indians of the Missouri River Region." Bureau of American Ethnology, *Thirty third Annual Report.* Washington, 1919.

Goldfrank, Esther S. *Changing Configurations in the Social Organization of a Blackfoot Tribe during the Reserve Period.* American Ethnological Society, *Monograph No. 8.* New York, 1945.

———. "Historic Change and Social Character, a Study of the Teton Dakota," *American Anthropologist,* Vol. XLV, No. 1 (1943).

Goldstein, Marcus S. "Anthropometry of the Comanches," *American Journal of Physical Anthropology,* Vol. XIX (1934–35).

Grinnell, George Bird. "Bent's Old Fort and Its Builders," *The Kansas State Historical Quarterly,* Vol. XV (1919–22).

———. *Beyond the Old Frontier: Adventures of Indian Fighters, Hunters, and Fur-Traders.* New York, 1913.

———. "Black Kettle," in Hodge, *Handbook (q.v.),* I.

———. *The Cheyenne Indians.* 2 vols. New Haven, 1923.

———. *The Fighting Cheyennes.* New York, 1915; Norman, 1956.

———. "Who Were the Padouca?" *American Anthropologist,* Vol. XXII, No. 3 (1920).

Hafen, LeRoy R., and W. J. Ghent. *Broken Hand, the Life Story of Thomas Fitzpatrick.* Denver, 1931.

Haines, Francis. "The Northward Spread of Horses among the Plains Indians," *American Anthropologist,* Vol. XL, No. 3 (1938).

———. "Where Did the Plains Indians Get Their Horses?" *American Anthropologist,* Vol. XL, No. 3 (1938).

Hamersly, Thomas H. S. *Complete Regular Army Register of the United States.* Washington, 1880.

Harrington, John P. "On Phonetic and Lexic Resemblances between Kiowan and Tanoan," *American Anthropologist,* Vol. XII (1910).

———. "Southern Peripheral Athapaskawan Origins," *Essays in Historical Anthropology of North America.* Smithsonian Miscellaneous Collections, Vol. C (1940).

———. *Vocabulary of the Kiowa Language.* Bureau of American Ethnology, *Bulletin 84.* Washington, 1928.

Heitman, Francis B. *Historical Register and Dictionary of the United States Army, 1789–1903.* 2 vols. Washington, 1903.

Hodge, Frederick Webb (ed.) *Handbook of American Indians North of Mexico.* Bureau of American Ethnology, *Bulletin 30.* 2 vols. Washington, 1907, 1912.

Hoebel, E. Adamson. *The Cheyennes, Indians of the Great Plains.* New York, 1960.

Hoijer, Harry. "The Southern Athapascan Languages," *American Anthropologist,* Vol. XL, No. 1 (1938).

Hollon, W. Eugene. *Beyond the Cross Timbers: The Travels of Randolph B. Marcy, 1812–1887.* Norman, 1955.

Hrdlicka, Ales. *Tuberculosis among Certain Indian Tribes of the United States.* Bureau of American Ethnology, *Bulletin 42.* Washington, 1909.

Hunt, George. "Millie Durgan," *Chronicles of Oklahoma,* Vol. XV, No. 4 (1937).

Hyde, George E. *Indians of the High Plains.* Norman, 1959.

———. *Pawnee Indians.* Denver, 1951.

———. *Spotted Tail's Folk: a History of the Brulé Sioux.* Norman, 1961.

Irving, Washington. *The Adventures of Captain Bonneville.* [Vol. XI of *The Works of Washington Irving.*] New York, n.d.

Jablow, Joseph. *The Cheyenne in Plains Indian Trade Relations, 1795–1840.* American Ethnological Society, *Monograph No. 19.* New York, 1950.

Jenness, Diamond. *The Indians of Canada.* National Museum of Canada, Anthropological Series, *Bulletin 65.* Fifth edition. Ottawa, 1960.

Keleher, William A. *Maxwell Land Grant.* Santa Fe, 1942.

Koch, Lena Clare. "The Federal Indian Policy in Texas, 1845–1860," *The Southwestern Historical Quarterly,* Vol. XXVIII, Nos. 3 and 4 (1925); Vol. XXIX, Nos. 1 and 2 (1925).

Kroeber, A. L. *Cultural and Natural Areas of Native North America.* University of California *Publications in American Archeology and Ethnology,* Vol. XXXVIII. Berkeley, 1939.

La Barre, Weston. *The Peyote Cult.* Yale University *Publications in Anthropology, No. 19* (1938).

La Farge, Oliver. *As Long as the Grass Shall Grow.* New York, 1940.

———. *A Pictorial History of the American Indian.* New York, 1957.

Lanham, Edwin. *The Wind Blew West.* New York, 1935.

Lavender, David. *Bent's Fort.* New York, 1954.

Leupp, Francis E. *In Red Man's Land.* New York, 1914.

Lewis, Oscar. *The Effect of White Contact upon Blackfoot Culture.* American Ethnological Society, *Monograph No. 6.* New York, 1942.

———. "Manly-Hearted Women among the North Piegan," *American Anthropologist,* Vol. XLIII (1941).

Linton, Ralph (ed.). *Acculturation in Seven American Indian Tribes.* New York, 1940.

Lowie, Robert H. *Indians of the Plains.* American Museum of Natural History, *Anthropological Handbook, No. 1.* New York, 1954.

———. "A Note on Kiowa Kinship Terms and Usage," *American Anthropologist,* Vol. XXV, No. 2 (1923).

———. "Societies of the Kiowa," American Museum of Natural History, *Anthropological Papers,* Vol. XI, Pt. 11. New York, 1916.

McAllister, J. Gilbert. "Kiowa-Apache Social Organization," in Eggan, *Social Anthropology of North American Tribes (q.v.).* Chicago, 1937. Revised edition, 1955.

———. "Kiowa-Apache Tales," in Mody C. Boatright (ed.), *The Sky Is My Tipi.* The Texas Folklore Society, *Publications,* XXII (1949).

McConnell, Joseph Carroll. *The West Texas Frontier.* 2 vols. Jacksboro, Texas, 1933.

MacGregor, Gordon. *Warriors without Weapons, a Study of the Society and Personality Development of the Pine Ridge Sioux.* Chicago, 1946.

McKenzie, Parker, and John P. Harrington. *Popular Account of the Kiowa Indian Language. Monographs* of the School of American Research. Albuquerque, 1948.

McReynolds, Edwin C. *Oklahoma: a History of the Sooner State.* Norman, 1954.

Martin, Paul S., George I. Quimby, and Donald Collier. *Indians before Columbus.* Chicago, 1947.

Mayhall, Mildred P. "The Indians of Texas: The Atákapa, the Karankawa, the Tonkawa." MS. Ph.D. dissertation, University of Texas, 1939.

———. "Indian Relations in Texas, 1820–1835." MS. In possession of author, Austin, Texas.

———. "The Taovaya Villages." MS. In possession of author, Austin, Texas.

Mishkin, Bernard. *Rank and Warfare among the Plains Indians.* American Ethnological Society, *Monograph No. 3.* New York, 1940.

Mooney, James. "Arapaho," in Hodge, *Handbook (q.v.),* I.

———. "Calendar History of the Kiowa Indians," Bureau of American Ethnology, *Seventeenth Annual Report,* Part 1. Washington, 1898.

———. "Cheyenne," in Hodge, *Handbook (q.v.),* I.

———. "The Cheyenne Indians," American Anthropological Association, *Memoirs,* Vol. I, No. 6. Lancaster, Pennsylvania, 1905–1907.

———. "The Ghost Dance Religion and the Sioux Outbreak of 1890," Bureau of American Ethnology, *Fourteenth Annual Report,* Pt. 2. Washington, 1896.

———. "Kiowa," in Hodge, *Handbook (q.v.),* I.

———. "Kiowa-Apache," in Hodge, *Handbook (q.v.),* I.

———. "Staitan," in Hodge, *Handbook (q.v.),* II.

Nasatir, Abraham P. "Jacques d'Eglise on the Upper Missouri, 1791–1795," *The Mississippi Valley Historical Review,* Vol. XIV (June, 1927–Mar., 1928).

Neighbors, Kenneth Franklin. "Robert S. Neighbors in Texas, 1836–1859." 2 vols. MS. Ph.D. dissertation, University of Texas.

Nicholson, William. "A Tour of Indian Agencies in Kansas and the Indian Territory in 1870," *The Kansas Historical Quarterly,* Vol. III, No. 3 (August, 1934); Vol. III, No. 4 (November, 1934).

Noel, Virginia Pink. "The United States Indian Reservations in Texas, 1854–1859." MS. M.A. thesis, University of Texas, 1927.

Phillips, Paul Chrisler, and J. W. Smurr. *The Fur Trade.* 2 vols. Norman, 1961.

Pichardo, Father José Antonio. *Pichardo's Treatise on the Limits of Louisiana and Texas.* Ed. by Charles Wilson Hackett. 4 vols. Austin, 1931, 1934, 1941, 1946. [Vols. I and II contain excerpts from Perrin Du Lac, *Voyage (q.v.).*]

Powell, J. W. "Indian Linguistic Families North of Mexico." Bureau of American Ethnology, *Seventh Annual Report.* Washington, 1891.

Provinse, John R. "The Underlying Sanctions of Plains Indian Culture," in Eggan, *Social Anthropology of North American Tribes (q.v.).* Chicago, 1955.

Richardson, Jane. *Law and Status among the Kiowa Indians.* American Ethnological Society, *Monograph No. 1.* New York, 1940.

Richardson, Rupert Norval. *The Comanche Barrier to South Plains Settlement.* Glendale, 1933.

———. *Texas, the Lone Star State.* New York, 1943.

Rister, Carl Coke. *Border Captives.* Norman, 1940.

———. *Border Command, General Phil Sheridan in the West.* Norman, 1944.

———. *Fort Griffin on the Texas Frontier.* Norman, 1956.

———. "The Significance of the Jacksboro Indian Affair of 1871," *The Southwestern Historical Quarterly,* Vol. XXIX, No. 3 (1926).

Roe, Frank Gilbert. *The Indian and the Horse.* Norman, 1955.

Sandoz, Mari. *The Buffalo Hunters.* New York, 1954.

———. *Cheyenne Autumn.* New York, 1955.

———. *Love Song to the Plains.* New York, 1961.

Sauer, Carl O. *Aboriginal Population of Northwestern Mexico. Ibero-Americana: No. 10.* Berkeley, 1935.

———. *The Distribution of Aboriginal Tribes and Languages in Northwestern Mexico. Ibero-Americana: No. 5.* Berkeley, 1934.

Sayles, E. B. *An Archeological Survey of Texas. Medallion Papers,* XVII. Gila Pueblo, Arizona, 1953.

Schmitt, Martin F., and Dee Brown. *Fighting Indians of the West.* New York, 1948.

Schoolcraft, Henry R. *Information Respecting the History, Conditions* and Prospects of the Indian Tribes of the United States. 5 vols. Philadelphia, 1853–1856.

Schultes, Richard Evans. "Peyote and the American Indian," *Nature Magazine*, Vol. XXX, No. 3 (1937).

Scott, Hugh Lenox. "Notes on the Kado, or Sun Dance of the Kiowa," *American Anthropologist*, Vol. XIII, No. 3 (July–September, 1911).

Skinner, Frances. "The Trial and Release of Satanta and Big Tree: State-Federal Regulations during the Reconstruction Era." MS. M.A. thesis, University of Texas, 1937.

Slotkin, J. S. *The Peyote Religion, a Study in Indian-White Relations.* Glencoe, Illinois, 1956.

Sonnichsen, C. L. *The Mescalero Apaches.* Norman, 1958.

Spier, Leslie. "Notes on the Kiowa Sun Dance," in Clark Wissler (ed.), *Sun Dance of the Plains Indians.* American Museum of Natural History, *Anthropological Papers*, Vol. XVI, Pt. 6. New York, 1921.

———. "The Sun Dance of the Plains Indians: Its Development and Diffusion," in Clark Wissler (ed.), *Sun Dance of the Plains Indians.* American Museum of Natural History, *Anthropological Papers*, Vol. XVI, Pt. 7. New York, 1921.

Strong, William Duncan. "From History to Prehistory in the Northern Great Plains," *Essays in Historical Anthropology of North America,* Smithsonian Miscellaneous Collections, Vol. C. Washington, 1940.

Swanton, John R. *The Indian Tribes of North America.* Bureau of American Ethnology, *Bulletin 145.* Washington, 1952.

Thomas, Alfred Barnaby. *Forgotten Frontiers: A Study of the Spanish Indian Policy of Don Juan Bautista de Anza, Governor of New Mexico, 1777–1787.* Norman, 1932.

———. "San Carlos—A Comanche Pueblo on the Arkansas River, 1787," *The Colorado Magazine*, Vol. VI, No. 3 (1929).

Turner, Katherine E. *Red Men Calling on the Great White Father.* Norman, 1951.

Underhill, Ruth Murray. *Red Man's America.* Chicago, 1953.

Unrau, William E. "The Story of Fort Larned," *The Kansas Historical Quarterly*, Vol. XXIII (1957).

Verrill, A. Hyatt. *The American Indian.* New York, 1943.

———. *The Real Americans.* New York, 1954.

Vestal, Paul A., and Richard Evans Schultes. *The Economic Botany of the Kiowa Indians as It Relates to the History of the Tribe.* Cambridge, 1939.

Vestal, Stanley. *The Old Santa Fe Trail.* Boston, 1939.

——. *Warpath and Council Fire.* New York, 1948.

Vigness, David M. "Indian Raids on the Lower Rio Grande, 1836–1837," *The Southwestern Historical Quarterly,* Vol. LIX, No. 1 (1955).

Voegelin, C. F., and E. W. Voegelin. "Map of North American Indian Languages," American Ethnological Society, *Publication No. 20.* New York, 1944.

Wallace, Ernest, and E. Adamson Hoebel. *The Comanches, Lords of the South Plains.* Norman, 1952.

Wallace, Irving. *The Fabulous Showman, the Life and Times of P. T. Barnum.* New York, 1959.

Webb, Walter Prescott. *The Great Plains.* New York, 1931.

——. *The Texas Rangers.* Cambridge, 1935.

Wedel, Waldo R. *Archaeological Remains in Central Kansas and Their Possible Bearing on the Location of Quivira.* Smithsonian Miscellaneous Collections, Vol. CI, No. 7. Washington, 1942.

——. *Culture Sequence in the Central Great Plains,* Smithsonian Miscellaneous Collections, Vol. C. Washington, 1940.

——. *Environment and Native Subsistence Economies in the Central Great Plains.* Smithsonian Miscellaneous Collections, Vol. CI, No. 3. Washington, 1941.

——. *An Introduction to Kansas Archeology.* Bureau of American Ethnology, *Bulletin 174.* Washington, 1959.

Wellman, Paul I. *The Indian Wars of the West.* New York, 1954.

Wharton, Clarence. *Satanta, the Great Chief of the Kiowas and His People.* Dallas, 1935.

Whorf, B. L., and G. L. Trager. "The Relationship of Uto-Aztecan and Tanoan," *American Anthropologist,* Vol. XXXIX, No. 4, Pt. 1, (1937).

Wilbarger, Josiah W. *Indian Depredations in Texas.* Austin, 1889.

Wissler, Clark. *The American Indian.* Second edition. New York, 1922.

——. "The Influence of the Horse in the Development of Plains Culture," *American Anthropologist,* Vol. XVI, No. 1 (1914).

——. *North American Indians of the Plains.* New York, 1927.

Wormington, H. M. *Ancient Man in North America.* Denver Museum of Natural History, *Popular Series No. 4.* Denver, 1957.

Wright, Muriel. *A Guide to the Indian Tribes of Oklahoma.* Norman, 1951.

———. "A History of Fort Cobb," *Chronicles of Oklahoma,* Vol. XXXIV, No. 1 (1956).

❖ INDEX

302

THE KIOWAS

has been designed for legibility and ease in handling. The text has been set on the Linotype in eleven-point Old Style No. 7 with two points of spacing between the lines. In its evolution from the original Scotch letter form, Old Style No. 7 has become one of the most popular Linotype book faces.

THE UNIVERSITY OF OKLAHOMA PRESS

Norman

The Kiowas

By Mildred P. Mayhall

Today highly respected citizens of the United States, the Kiowa Indians were once, along with the fighting Cheyennes, the most feared and hated of the Plains Indian tribes. Here, told in full for the first time, is the story of their evolution from mountain dwellers to Plains nomads and, finally, after the Indian wars of the 1870's, to settlement on a reservation in Oklahoma.

The acquisition of the white man's horse was basic to Plains culture, and the Kiowas were drawn ever south from their native Yellowstone region by the lure of horses and captives to be found in Texas and Old Mexico. Fierce and unrelenting in warfare against both red men and white, as early as 1790 they assumed a dominant position on the Southern Plains. By 1840 they, along with their allies—the Comanches, Southern Cheyennes, and Arapahoes —placed themselves athwart the Santa Fe Trail on the Arkansas River and harassed traders, trappers, the military, and peaceful Indian tribes.

In the wars of the 1860's and 1870's, when the United States Army fought for control over the Plains Indians, the Kiowas were a formidable foe. The army did not completely conquer them until their commissary, the buffalo, was destroyed and the Indians were unhorsed. In defeat

(Continued on back flap)